MW00987943

AREA 187
ALMOST HELL

by

Eric R. Lowther

LIBRARY OF THE LIVING DEAD PRESS

Area 187: Almost Hell

A Library of the Living Dead book
Published by arrangement with the author

ISBN - 1461159490
ISBN - 978-1461159490

This book is a work of fiction. People, places, events, and situations are the product of the author's imagination. Any resemblance to actual persons, living or dead, or historical events, is purely coincidental.

Copyright © 2011 Eric R. Lowther and Library of the Living Dead Press. All Rights Reserved.

Cover art by Laura Conkle
Put-Together by Dan Galli
Edited by Felicia A. Tiller
Layout by Owen CLB

No part of this book may be reproduced, stored in a retrieval system, or transmitted by any means without the written permission of the author and publisher.

Dedicated to the Memory of
Marion Joseph Lowther Sr.

They say there are no heroes left in this world.
Only now do I understand just how true that sentiment is.

Prologue
The Buffer Zone

Maury glanced around at the four severe-looking men surrounding him. "You guys do this a lot, Lieutenant Colson?" Maury asked. He grimaced at his own voice, so loud in the small chamber.

"As little as possible," the big man with the lieutenant's insignia answered. "First time inside?" The young technician was sweating bullets, his breath noisy bursts through his nostrils.

"Yes sir," Maury said.

It'd been easier in the first years after Area 187 had been created, when Homeland Security and the Feds ran it all. That was before Homeland decided it was more cost-effective to farm out the maintenance tasks of the facilities and perimeters to private contractors. At least they'd listened to reason and had been convinced against privatizing the security forces.

Colson pulled a clipboard off the wall and scanned a few documents. "You've completed your perimeter training. Where's your checklist?" he asked, his eyes narrowing. Maury's grew wide for a moment before he patted a few pockets and came out with a folded piece of paper.

"I have it here, sir. Sorry." Colson snatched it from his fingers and looked it over.

"You sure you have everything?" he asked as he looked over the list. "I don't want to do this again 'cause you forgot pliers."

"The company has toolkits for each job. We're required to carry two when there's only one technician going out," Maury said.

_____

He looked at the other three men but they had already pulled their form-fitting hoods over their faces, making them unreadable.

"Okay then, let's review. No noise. Once we walk out you're a church mouse and keep your tool noise to a minimum. You work quietly and you work quickly. The time allowed for a sensor relay replacement and diagnostic for this sector is 38 minutes, minus travel. It will take us 12 minutes to reach the work site and 12 minutes back. I want to be back in this room in less than one hour, got it?"

Maury nodded, the full realization of the work ahead settling as comfortably as a rusty hacksaw. He was going into Area 187. This wasn't in the technical college's brochure. "What if we... what if *they* come around?"

"Contact isn't your job," Colson said with a hint of menace. "Focus on your job; we'll worry about everything else. The faster you do it, the less we'll have to worry about it. Just shut up, move when we move and you'll do just fine."

Maury nodded again and took a shuddering breath. Colson looked at him dubiously then slid his own hood into place. Sempertech was a union shop, the easy work of maintaining the facility buildings and equipment snatched up by seniority. That left the dangerous work of maintaining the sensor networks and physical defenses to men with the lowest seniority, consequently the men with the least experience not only in their jobs but in working within the Area's buffer zone.

"Communications check," Colson announced. Each man put a hand to the small control unit strapped to their tactical harness as the control room cycled through a series of tones. Each tone carried its own meaning, such as "stop", "go", "right", "left", "contact" and a host of other commands and information.

Maury looked around slowly as the unfamiliar tones sounded in his own earpiece. Anyone going into the Area received extensive training and the signal tones were a big part of it. That was another problem with being forced to use the lowest seniority; just when you had a tech that had really absorbed the system he bid out to a better job.

_____

"Test back-up voice," Colson said into the small microphone on his collar. Maury jerked as Colson's voice bit into his ear. Colson grimaced at him then reached down to Maury's radio and turned the volume down. "Voice is a last resort, kid."

"Yes, sir." He was trembling now, a fact that hadn't escaped Colson.

"Look, kid, I haven't lost a tech yet. You'll be fine. It's just another job." Colson spun Maury roughly and started tugging on his straps and equipment. After several adjustments, he spun him back. "Your straps were loose. Loose makes noise - and handles. Lock and load, gentlemen."

Maury had expected to hear the crack and snap of metal as the men charged their weapons. Instead the metallic sounds were softer than two dimes clinking together, the well-oiled, composite materials deadening most of the noise.

"Control," Colson said into the air, "ready for odor neutralization."

"Standby for odor neutralization," a woman's voice said into the room. Colson looked pointedly at Maury's head and nodded. Maury, confused, touched the top of his head then realized he was the only man in the room without his hood on. He pulled it out of his back pocket quickly and struggled it down over his ears, rolling it until the Kevlar-laced material completely covered his head and neck. Just as the young technician adjusted the hood for his eyes and mouth, small jets in the ceiling spewed a fine, powdery mist down onto them. Maury hacked and wheezed for several moments, eyes and nose running into the itchy, reinforced fabric of his hood.

"Guess I should have reminded you to hold your breath, huh?" Colson said, smiling. "You'll be okay in a second." The other men chuckled lowly as Maury tried to wipe the tears from his eyes.

"What the hell's in that stuff?" Maury asked, punctuating the question with a sneeze.

"Can't pronounce it, I just know it works. Your scent will be deadened for about an hour, as long as you don't start sweating like a whore in church," Colson advised.

"What happens if I do?" Maury asked when his breath

finally coming back.

"The more you sweat, the harder you breathe and the more likely we are to make contact. And what's the first rule of Area 187?" he asked.

"Don't make contact," Maury said robotically. That rule had been drilled into him every day for the last two weeks during his training.

"Well, at least you made it to class *that* day," Colson said. "Control, final sit-rep?" he asked into his mike.

"All quiet on the southern front, Lieutenant. We haven't had a sensor hit all night. Current time is 01:45, current temperature is 48 degrees. Skies are clear and the moon is full. Satellite reports show no major activity in your area of operation, video surveillance negative. Sensor report for grid location 36 at 30 and 2 is still a blank page. We're hoping you can fix that for us. Video surveillance unaffected, we should have visual on you for the duration. We are ready and waiting for your mark."

Colson took a quick glance at his team, his gaze lingering for a moment longer on Maury. "Don't fuck this up." He waited for Maury's uncertain nod then brought up his HK and flicked off the safety. "Mark." A moment later the large door before them slid soundlessly into the wall, giving Maury his first look at the mile-and-a-half buffer zone behind the wall that separated Area 187 from the rest of the world.

Arc sodium lights turned the night to day as far out as he could see. The zone had been deforested as much as was possible, the monthly chemical drops ensuring nothing green could sprout to provide concealment. Vast networks of pressure plates, sensors, video cameras and other electronic monitoring systems had been deployed in the zone over the years. More than three thousand men had lost their lives in the 18 months it had taken in the initial push to establish the monitoring network and fortification lines that walled the plague off from the rest of humanity. Even today the zone could be counted on to kill at least a dozen or so a year, by official numbers, from work groups like this one tasked with maintaining it.

They moved at a fast walk over the gray-green stubble. Running reduced the ability to fight and think to near zero, and considering their enemy couldn't move faster than a walk themselves it was practically unnecessary in all but a swarm situation or to get to a better firing position. Union rules forbid Maury from going into the Area armed, though few technicians ventured out without at least a personal firearm. Maury had decided not to arm himself though. He had no experience and worried that he would be found with the weapon and disciplined; best to leave the guns to the soldiers. He kept his eyes locked squarely on Colson's thick neck ahead of him as the group made their way smoothly and silently across the day-lit sparseness.

They made the steel pole at just over the ten minute mark. A high-pitched tone sounded through their ear pieces as Colson brought the group to a halt. Using hand signals, he positioned his men at the compass points around the base of the pole and took the northern point himself, facing into the great unknown of Area 187. Without looking behind him, Colson tripped the "go" tone to Maury's earpiece. The technician hesitated for a moment, swallowed hard then threw his climbing belt around the pole.

Maury scaled the tower, his childhood fear of heights falling to the onslaught of adrenalin. He'd been a high school kid in Palisades, California when the outbreak hit, making jokes about redneck zombies roaming the hills of West Virginia eating their cousins instead of having sex with them. Now, he hung twenty-five feet over that very ground suspended by only a strip of ballistic nylon.

Maury rolled up his hood, pulled the cover off the sensor relay module and turned on the small penlight attached to the band around his head. He poked around the masses of thin wires with a rubber-coated screwdriver then moved his face closer to peer at a particular clump of wires bound with electrical tape; the thick, red power wire had a charred spot just beyond the tape causing a short to the sensor relay and denying it reports from its clusters for a half-mile around. Someone had thrown this non-regulation repair together, obviously some time ago by the faded appearance of the

_____

tape.

He prodded a bit more and found the long-ago tech had wired the sensor relay directly into the main power line that fed the powerful light a few feet above him. The amperage coming through the pole's electrical service had been far too strong for the delicate wire, causing it to burn like a candle wick. Further probing showed the reason for the jury-rigged repair; a crispy, blackened spot on the relay's motherboard where the live wire should have been soldered. He pulled his radio and stared at the multi-colored buttons. Each was assigned a tone. Pressing two or more at the same time produced a combined tone, further widening the menu of commands and responses. The problem was remembering them all. Maury pulled the hard plastic card from his coveralls and read through the options, trying to find the proper code for a scrub. He found it and pushed the orange, red and black buttons together. The result was an uncomfortable tone of medium pitch, like three dogs barking in unison. Almost immediately he heard another tone. A quick check of the card and watching for which colors lit up on his radio found he was being asked for a status report.

How the hell could he explain that the last guy that shimmied up this pole had thrown a band aid on a major sensor relay and a new wiring harness and motherboard was needed to make it all better? What combination of buttons was that? Maury scanned the card again and found the code for "repair beyond tool/part capability" and punched it in. He was rewarded with a thin, piercing tone. You didn't need special training to know that wasn't good regardless of the circumstances. Moments later, Colson's whispered voice came over his earpiece.

"What the fuck is the problem up there?" Colson hissed through the radio.

"The last guy up here fixed a problem with chewing gum and it's failed. I need parts I don't have to fix it right," he responded softly. There was a long pause, then Colson's voice again.

"Can you fix it *wrong* until we can get another detail out here in the morning? That sensor you're playing with is blinding Control for half a square mile."

_____

Maury poked around the box, considering his options. "I'll need to bring down the pole to do it. All the electrical in a given sector junctions off from the main pole; it's just our luck that's the one I'm hanging off of right now. Every pressure plate, infra-red sensor, camera and light array for this sector will be down while I re-link the power supply to the relay. Why the hell did they schedule this at night?"

"Just fucking do it," Colson interrupted. "Control, do you copy?"

"Copy, lieutenant," a soft feminine voice answered in their ears. "Technician, please advise."

"Shut down main power to…" he looked around the pole for a moment before he found the brass identification tag. "…unit 127 at 36 and 30, all services will be affected."

"Estimated time to complete repair?" Control asked.

"Just as quickly as I can get it done, ma'am," Maury replied.

"Power to unit 127 at 36 and 30 will be shut down in ten seconds, mark. Detail, we will attempt to keep visual for the duration of the lights-out from other surveillance points in neighboring sectors. Use extreme caution; we will have limited monitoring capacity until the unit is powered up. Resume radio silence. Control out."

Maury froze when the small hum from the large torch above him faded away along with its light. They still had some illumination from other poles spaced fifty yards to either side, just enough to make out the tree line ahead. That light did little to help Maury at this height. He pulled another flashlight from his belt and hung it from his harness, pointing the light into the control box to add to his penlight's feeble illumination. Maury pulled a tool roll from his belt, hung it from a hook on the pole, selected a pair of pliers and started his work.

Colson could sense the tension from his men. They'd been in worse spots, but that hadn't been for a few years now. *So far, so good*, he thought. He kept his eyes moving over the line of trees ahead that marked the true start of Area 187, watching and listening for any motion or sound. Those things out there weren't smart;

their intellect was lower than that of most animals. But they could tell when something changed, when something moved or stopped moving - or when light that had been there suddenly wasn't. If there were any of them within sight of the zone that had been looking this way when the light was powered down the sudden change in the environment could give them cause to investigate. Colson cocked his head towards the wood line, his ear a better early warning than his eyes in the now-gloom of their little part of the buffer zone.

Maury snipped several wires then put a screwdriver to the brackets that held the offending gadgetry in place. While his conscious mind was on its assigned task his subconscious couldn't help but have great fun mulling over the myriad dangers of his current predicament. He paused to wipe away the sweat threatening his eyes with his free hand as his subconscious treated him to a vision of dozens of moaning zombies swarming around the base of his pole, glazed eyes staring up at him. He'd never seen one of them personally, but he'd seen enough television reports from the early days before the news blackout went into effect for his mind to come up with vivid images to lend authenticity to the thought. He fought to keep his hands from shaking and stay focused on the job while the belly of his mind toyed with the idea of jagged, broken teeth tearing into his flesh.

"I can't believe they expect me to work like this," he mumbled. Colson's head swiveled up to him just then, catching his attention. Maury's cheeks reddened at his Area faux pas and he turned back to his work just as a low buzzing sound caught his ear. He tapped on his ear piece, thinking that the speaker was malfunctioning or picking up interference. That's when he saw the dull yellow and black spots coming from behind an inspection plate. In moments a small cloud of hornets filled the air around him, registering their distaste for his intrusions. He swatted at them and nearly lost his grip as several of the winged warriors landed on his exposed hands and cheeks, burying their venom deep in his skin.

Pain shot through him as he struggled to keep his body against the pole. He reached for his transmitter and frantically punched the buttons as the hornets continued their assault, not caring what combination of tones he made. The men reacted instantly to the cacophony in their ears. Three of them shifted to a pyramid formation around the base of the pole while Colson fell back and turned his eyes skyward to the whimpering technician. Maury's whimpers turned to hoarse screams as his tools and flashlight fell from his lofty perch, pelting the men below as his cries rang through their ears from his microphone.

"Control! Control! The operation's a scrub!" Colson said into his mike. "The kid's freaking out - get an extraction team ready."

A sudden tone, high and piercing, drowned out his words. Any soldier in the buffer knew that tone: Contact had been made. Colson turned to his former point and watched over one of his men's shoulders as several distinct forms shambled from the dark trees. "Control," Colson said into the air, his voice still low and modulated, "Contact confirmed. Get that extraction team out here."

"Fall back," the woman's voice came to the team.

"Negative, Control. We still have a man up the pole." Colson looked up at Maury. He'd stopped his frantic movements but continued moaning and wailing, a beacon in the dark for the dead. "Maury!" Colson said. "Report! Damn it kid!"

"Technician's communications have been terminated," the voice said. "Fall back."

Colson turned back and saw the six figures had become a dozen, their moans adding to Maury's pained bleating as they stumbled and limped towards his men. The moaning would bring more of them, the dire, maddening sound a precursor to swarming. Anything dead within a mile would come to investigate like farmhands to a dinner bell. They were closing now, the leaders of the pack now less than ten yards away. "Control, power up the light!" Colson said. He could feel his men tense, the muzzles of their silenced weapons already drawing beads on their targets.

"Negative. Tech disabled it. Combat team ready to deploy in two minutes, lieutenant. Get your team out of there. Do not fire; repeat, do not fire. Fall back."

Colson cursed under his breath, glanced once more up the pole then trained his weapon on the growing horde ahead of them.

"You heard Gladys, boys, fall back. Port arms, go to batons." The men reacted immediately to his order and let their small submachine guns rest against their chests as they pulled back from the pole. Almost as one they deployed their thick steel batons, the polished, blackened and heavily-oiled steel strong enough to crack a skull or shatter vertebrae with a single strike. The crowd had reached the pole now. A few of them turned their heads to look up at Maury's dangling body, his own soft moaning crowding them around the pole.

"Control, we've got a tail," Colson said as a half dozen of them continued plodding after them, the slow-speed chase almost comical. "Scratch the team, that'll just work them up more. We need a diversion, get these guys to stop thinking about us long enough to get back inside." Colson sighed out loud, his finger itching to touch off a burst from his weapon into the advancing zombies. "Control, drop the bait on my mark," he said as put his baton away and raised his machine gun.

Maury managed to open his swollen eyes to slits. He'd been horribly allergic to most stinging insects throughout his childhood. It had been so long since he'd been stung he didn't even carry an epinephrine pen anymore. With the volume of stings he'd acquired though, the little spring-loaded syringe would have been like pissing on a forest fire. The venom had swelled more than his eyes. His throat had constricted to a wheezing moan and his fingers had swollen to the size of sausages. He felt his weight supported solely by the safety belt, his hands useless now for holding onto the pole. He was dangling, helpless, with a chorus of moans pulsing up to him.

Maury's mind was too far gone from the pain to register panic, but not far enough to ignore the predicament. All he had to do was stay calm and hold out until they came back to get him. Just stay calm, keep himself from swinging on his lifeline and wait for someone to get him down. If it wasn't for the ringing in his ears, he may have heard the hiss of the silenced report from Colson's weapon, a soft sound that would have carried easily in the deathly stillness of the buffer zone. The next sound he heard was the bullet smashing through his skull, the guarantee he wouldn't rise again. The last thing Maury heard just after the shot was a small explosion like a pistol being fired next to his head as Control detonated the tiny charge rigged into the safety latch of his belt. Maury was dead before he hit the ground, the ghouls falling upon the fresh meat like slow-motion sharks.

"Hit the e—lights," Colson said as he lowered his weapon and pulled out a thick pair of black-lens goggles. "Put your blinders on, boys." The men in his fire team copied their leader and pulled on their own goggles just as several brilliant shafts of light bathed the buffer zone from the powerful halogen searchlights that ran the length of the battlement some half-mile behind them. The light pierced the decaying eyes of the zombies, stopping them in their tracks and forcing them to turn away. Their heads turned from Colson's fire team, they now saw their brethren feasting on the body of the dead technician behind them. Almost as one they crept back the way they'd come, the scent of fresh blood from the human carrion drawing them to join the rest.

Eric R. Lowther

Chapter 1
Josephine

"Welcome to the Morning Show, Professor Dowling," Josephine Terrell said to her guest, her plastic smile fixed to her face.

"A pleasure as always, Ms. Terrell," the aging scholar said, returning her smile with a reserved grin.

"So tell me, Professor, you believe there's no truth to the rumors of survivors in Area 187?" Josephine asked.

"You mean currently?" he asked, stroking his close-cropped, graying beard subconsciously. "There are always exceptions to the rule, of course. But on any kind of measurable scale I would have to answer 'no'. Homeland Security sweeps the entire area regularly with heat sensing equipment that can spot a rabbit from 500 feet up. And while Area 187 does boast populations of fauna that have learned to deal with their new predators, no trace of human survivors has been found."

"What about the grave robbers? Shouldn't those same sweeps catch them as well?" Josephine asked. She leaned forward slightly in the time-honored pose of television journalist interest. The studio lights seemed more intense than usual this morning, adding to her headache.

"Grave robbers are a different matter entirely. These are outlaws, Ms. Terrell. Outlaws don't *want* to be found. I could only assume if there were survivors in Area 187, they would have a decidedly different outlook on being discovered," the Professor said.

"So you don't believe the theory that the government doesn't *want* survivors found?" Josephine asked.

"That is nothing more than conspiracy theorists bored with the grassy knoll, Ms. Terrell," Dowling answered. The smile on his face bordered on the patronizing. "This isn't China. This is America. America doesn't sacrifice its people for the sake of quiet in this country. If it did, those in your profession would seize it like the latest pop-tart scandal."

Josephine could sense her subject drawing away from her. She should have expected that from her line of questioning. This was supposed to be a piece about new advances in the science of the undead, not an exposé into Area 187 policy and rumor. She took a deep, modulated breath and hoped the cameras wouldn't notice while she mentally shifted gears. "Have any new developments come through on the scientific front concerning necrotic infection?" Dowling smiled at her slightly, sensing her shift back to the advertised reason for the interview.

"There are scores of scientists and researchers working on it, of course. You must understand; little is known about the virus. Unlike cancer, necrotic infection in this form has been around less than a decade. A cure is nothing more than a science-fiction pipe dream since the brain is damaged beyond repair from lack of blood and oxygen shortly after the virus takes control. Even if the effects could be reversed, the mind would never revive and the cells of the body would be changed too drastically to ever declare a victim 'cured'. The best tactic is the one most heavily researched and tested; the vaccine. Those that have been infected are lost, Ms. Terrell. The key now is to develop a vaccine that will ensure the virus never spreads. Such a vaccine is years away, if it comes about at all."

"I understand there have been limited trials of a type of poisoned bait dropped in the area. What are they dropping and what are they hoping it will do?" Josephine asked. Dowling's mouth hung open for a moment before he cleared his throat then sipped at the steaming cup on the table beside him.

"I wasn't aware of such testing, but I can tell you that an

article in a recent medical digest spoke of developing an anti-virus. To my knowledge, such a program is only in the theoretical stage," Dowling said.

"How would such an anti-virus work?" Josephine asked. Dowling paused again for another sip.

"I have no involvement in those or any other such programs. I wouldn't want to step on the toes of my colleagues in the research profession by speaking out of turn. As for any sort of *tainted bait,* the undead will consume any sort of fresh meat they find. Studies have shown the virus feeds on the raw proteins found in fresh meat and blood, absorbing it through the stomach lining. The body of an undead doesn't pump blood. This is also why a previously dead body can't be reanimated. The virus relies on the living circulatory system to spread throughout the body to a degree where it then causes what we call 'death'."

"If that's the case, Professor, then how does the virus benefit from consuming protein in the first place? With no circulatory system, how do virus centers in other parts of the body not in contact with the stomach receive these proteins?" Josephine asked. Like the beginning of a sequel, she was covering old information now, information that most everyone knew about the virus and the dead. But just like those sequels, some audiences often needed reminding of what they already knew.

"The virus operates like cancer in a way. Over the course of time, the virus metastasizes to form literal chains of cells that eventually create a network throughout the infected body. Proteins from the stomach are transferred along this network, feeding it. If such an anti-virus program exists, theoretically, the anti-virus would travel along this network in the same manner as other proteins," Dowling answered. Josephine could tell he was as bored with the question as she, but Mr. and Mrs. America had to have something to go with the bacon and eggs.

"What about waste products? How does the body of an undead eliminate them without what we would call a working digestive system?" Josephine asked. Dowling frowned at her. They were moving away from his reason for being on the program;

plugging his new book. He sighed softly and answered her anyway.

"Undead are like dogs and will eat so long as there is food to be had, even after their stomachs rupture. Some waste may be excreted from the bowels, though this is only due to movement and gravity since they no longer have autonomic control over such muscle groups necessary to work the lower digestive tract. Specimens have been found with bloated midsections where so much had been consumed that the stomach tears, introducing the overflow into the reanimate's body cavity. Still others have been found with food clogging their esophagi all the way up to their mouths. Though really, Ms. Terrell, I find it hard to believe your viewers see this as a proper breakfast topic," Dowling said, smiling.

That was it. Josephine could feel the Professor shutting down on her, his folded arms blocking her from any real discourse.

"Have there been any other breakthroughs or advances in the field?" she asked. Generic questions and his book would be the only way to fill up the segment now.

"There has been some discussion about protein inhibitors or the introduction of necrotic bacteria into the Area. As we have already discussed, the infected are not completely dead as in the sense of Hollywood cinema. The protein it takes in is the sole fuel for the body and the virus, creating a circle of life within an infected body. It must consume protein to survive and its only reason for survival is to consume protein. The infected body becomes nothing more than a machine with only one function. Again theoretically, if protein inhibitors in sufficient quantities could be introduced they could in effect starve an undead body."

"And what happens when an infected body is denied protein?" Josephine asked.

"Eventually, it will die. However, that death will come at an exceptionally slow rate. Research has shown that an infected body denied protein from outside sources will absorb it from the body itself. Muscles, organs and other tissues that contain protein are absorbed into the body to provide the virus with fuel. This occurs at a very slow rate, and it has been proven that the virus can be rather selective about what tissues of the body it consumes first when no new proteins are introduced. Organs it no longer has use for such as the heart, liver and other circulatory and waste processing organs are usually the first consumed. The virus in a sense 'knows' it needs to keep the body mobile to seek out protein so it leaves the major muscle groups and skin as its last resort, providing just enough energy to keep the body mobile for as long as possible which slows overall decomposition. While protein inhibitors may work, the challenge would be in introducing enough of them into a body, and even then it would be far from an instant solution since the virus can cannibalize from its own host for a long period of time."

"Is there any truth to the rumor that these...*infected* prefer human flesh to other meat?" Josephine asked. She had ventured fully into the common script now with every question asked and answered by talking heads and academics thousands of times.

"I don't believe it to be a preference based on the meat itself. I have always contended since the first experiments into your question that human meat is not necessarily preferred by an infected body. Rather, it is far easier to catch and consume. We are not particularly fast when compared to practically every other animal on the planet and we lack the thick hides and natural weapons of these lesser animals. The sight of an infected person shambling towards us would fill many of us with such fear that we freeze to the spot or hide in irrational or easily-discovered places.

Humans have occupied the top spot on the food chain for thousands of years. In that time we have lost many of the traits of other mammals. We are incredibly loud and depend on our sight far too much to make fleet prey. The virus uses all the senses of the human body equally, much in the same manner as a blind man unconsciously develops his hearing and sense of smell to compensate for the loss of the primary sense. In a flight-or-fight situation, the human animal breathes noisily, steps heavily and often vocalizes. These sound cues, along with scent in some cases, can attract many infected at one time leading to the classic 'swarm' attacks made so famous in cinema and in footage from the early days in the containment of Area 187."

"I see. In your new book, *The Blind Dead*," Josephine held

up a copy of the thick book for the camera, its cover filled with silhouettes better suited to a video rental package than an academic text, "you discuss the effectiveness of the various methods used in Area 187's buffer zone to keep the infected from massing against the physical barriers. Why do they shy away from bright light and stay out of daylight? Do they fear light?" She couldn't help feeling like one of the middle-aged models that displayed the fine wares on the *Price is Right*.

"To say they fear anything is a dangerous oversimplification. They don't have the capacity to experience emotions of any sort or kind. Their aversion to strong light is a direct result of the physical damage and deterioration that occurs to their eyes over the course of time and the fact that their eyes don't dilate like they did in life. They produce no tears to cleanse the eyes and don't blink involuntarily as we do. The blemishes that develop act much as a chip in a pair of sunglasses or a crack in a windshield, reflecting the light wildly within the eye and causing a sort of sensory overload to occur." Dowling smiled as he hyped his book.

"So bright lights cause pain?" she asked.

"Not according to our research. Their nervous systems in regards to physical sensation are for all practical concerns dead. Instead, my research indicates intense light can overwhelm them to the point that the other senses are ignored and they will shy away from it involuntarily. However, light will not dissuade them from hunting. The need to consume is their one goal. Short bursts of intense light can stun them in a fashion for a moment or two, but if their other senses tell them that prey is near they will continue to seek it."

Josephine put on her fake smile again. "Is it true the buffer zone can now be seen from space?" A little trivia always goes over well with Mr. and Mrs. America's morning cup.

"Only at night," he said, still smiling. "The buffer zone is a mile deep into Area 187 in most places. Considering the massive size it only stands to reason that a mile-thick ring lit up at night and low-light weather conditions by the brightest and most intense artificial light yet developed could be seen from orbit. By keeping industrial and other sudden, noticeable sounds away from the buffer zone on our side and keeping the area bathed in natural and artificial light on theirs we have had almost no incidences of swarming against the walls and barriers of Area 187. If there's nothing to attract them to enter the light they typically won't. The human eye is very delicate, Ms. Terrell. As such it is often the first sense to suffer when a body reanimates. The other senses of the human body have more physical protection and are typically made from stronger stuff and thus are the last to succumb to time and deterioration."

"You say 'their side'. How long will we have to wait before reclaiming Area 187? How do we combat it and reclaim the land?"

"We don't. Our current policy of containment has worked flawlessly. So long as we as a people and our government continue the practice and bide our time, we will win."

"So how long before Area 187 can be reclaimed?" Josephine repeated.

"Of course, research is limited into how long an infected body can survive without consuming fresh proteins. Obviously, we know that the average human body contains enough protein for an infected body to survive for at least ten years if the body remains at rest and expends no energy. Laboratory tests have shown that an infected body denied food for several months has the ability to enter a hibernation-type state to conserve energy. We don't know how long this state can last in the field, but there are published reports showing some test subjects have been in this state nearly since they were captured for study and are still functioning. We also know that sound and smell can reactivate them, as it were. The best estimation at this time would be another eight to ten years before an attempt to send forces into Area 187 could have any relative expectation of safety and overall success."

"Thank you, Professor Dowling," Josephine said. She turned to the camera and smiled. "Coming up, what you can do to fight illiteracy. And later, Chef Marty will take to the kitchen and show us the wonder of fruit pies."

A voice counted down from three somewhere behind the lights and declared they were 'out'. The hot studio lights dimmed significantly, instantly easing the pounding in Josephine's head. Technicians came out of the wings and relieved her and Dowling of their tiny pin microphones and scuttled away as the pair rose.

"Thank you for your time, Professor. Very enlightening."

Dowling scowled at her and moved a step closer to her. "Stick to the script next time, or find yourself another expert. The last thing we need is for some news bimbo to spread rumors."

Josephine glared at him for a moment then softened her features. "We both know you have a lot more to do with Area 187 than commentary, Professor. It will all come out in the end." Dowling continued his scowl for a moment then turned and marched off the set. Josephine sighed and rubbed her temples as she tried to make for her dressing room but her assistant, a perky little blonde intern that went by the name of Cassie and dotted her "i" with a tiny heart, fell in step beside her.

"Great interview, Jo'. He seemed a little standoffish, but you were great!" Cassie said, far too enthusiastically for someone this early in the morning without a camera on them.

For the last two weeks Josephine had been up far too late for the five a.m. calls to the set. Morning network news magazines were great for steady work but left little time for real investigative journalism. Real stories didn't get up at five and sit at Starbucks waiting for you to come and find them, especially the story she was chasing now.

"You've got a meeting with the wardrobe department at eleven to go over your clothes for the broadcast week in Italy next month. God, I can't wait to go there!" Cassie said as the two threaded their way between the cameras and lights at the back of the set. "Then you have a lunch at twelve-thirty with-"

"Cancel it all," Josephine said as she stopped at the craft table and poured herself a tall espresso.

"Cancel? Jo', I've already rescheduled your lunch with the Mayor twice now. He may not give you another shot."

"Are you his assistant or mine?" Josephine shot back with more force than she'd intended. "I said cancel it. In fact, I want you to clear my calendar for the next few days. I'm taking some time off."

"Does Bill know?" Cassie asked.

"Yes, Cassie, Bill knows. Julie will be here while I'm gone."

"Great. That means I'll be stuck doing research for everybody else until you come back. I don't think Ms. Sommers likes me," Cassie said, an unaccustomed frown on her smooth face.

"Ms. Sommers doesn't like any woman younger and blonder than her," Josephine said.

Josephine finally made it to her dressing room, slid out of her jacket and melted into the overstuffed loveseat beside her dressing table. Cassie had left a large bundle of newspapers and files for her, the stack topped off by a black CD case marked "Canadian show you wanted" on a sticky note in her cute, high school-like script.

Josephine pulled her laptop out and slid the disc in, making sure her earphones were on. Though Canadian-made, possessing something like this would be enough to get her hauled off for questioning by Homeland at worst and a severe talking-to from the network at best. With all the censorship about Area 187 in the U.S. media the only way to get any real stories was to rely on foreign reporters compiling and broadcasting their reports from their home soil. Only Britain had agreed to enforce the U.S. government's censorship requests while other nations dependent upon U.S. support and aid had been forced into accepting the terms to continue receiving their boons. Surprisingly, Canada had rejected the U.S. request for compliance. They didn't rely on U.S. aid, and the simple nature of their shared border guaranteed that mutual defense wouldn't be compromised by Canada forcing their gruff, overbearing southern neighbor to face their own problems.

She adjusted the computer screen and settled even deeper into her seat as the screen lit up with the graphic for *O, Canada*, a news magazine similar to her own American show. She'd met the host, Josh Mason, a few years ago at a journalism convention. Their shared interest in Area 187 had made them close contacts since, sharing whatever information each gained. She knew he'd be upset when he discovered she'd neglected to fill him in on what she was working on now, but the less anyone knew the better.

"Welcome to *O Canada*, I'm Josh Mason," the good-looking, brightly-smiling man said as the show's theme music faded. "Americans take one day out of the year to mourn their losses and remember the victims of the tragedy of Area 187. We here in Canada grieve and remember with them. But there are many in the States that grieve and remember the events that led to the containment of the world's greatest threat every day of the year." He turned on his stool, his cameras switching flawlessly to catch a different, softer angle of his face.

"Each year at this time, *O Canada* has presented you with an hour of commercial-free time with survivors of Area 187, those brave and lucky people able to overcome insurmountable odds to escape the undead and return to the world of the living from the state of West Virginia and large parts of Pennsylvania and Virginia that became the land of the dead. Those stories have scared us, enlightened us and, in one particular case where a man escaped a horde of the dead on a unicycle, have made us laugh," Mason said.

The image changed to stock footage of the early days of the plague, images Josephine was all too familiar with. Mason's voice-over played atop the mute scenes of military equipment rolling through burning towns, swarms of shambling zombies subjected to blinding spotlights and barrages of gunfire and file footage of the temporary hospitals and shelters complete with fields of bodies covered by plastic sheets. "These images of death and struggle are well-known to practically every television viewer alive since the plague was born. We've all seen them; pictures of the horror of war against an adversary already dead and the devastation of what is known as the Appalachian Region." The screen faded to black for a moment before another piece of video rolled, one Josephine was intensely familiar with.

"Of course, many of us have seen this footage as well. It was taken by a documentary film crew more than two years ago from the top of the infamous concrete and steel wall that runs around much of Area 187." The trembling video starts by panning across a portion of the buffer zone until several figures can be seen. The camera zooms in to see a group of perhaps half a dozen creatures running for the wall. Shots and shouts can be heard in the background, the reactions and speed of the bodies running towards the wall clearly demonstrating each was very much alive. Moments later, the tree line behind them comes alive with hundreds more bodies, their lurching motions evident and their moans carrying across the wasted buffer zone to the sound man's equipment.

"Tonight we have the story of a group of survivors that not only escaped Area 187, but did so five years *after* the land was officially declared void of human life," Mason said as the video froze on a tight shot of the battered, bloodied survivors staring up at the camera from the ground below. Josephine pulled out a note pad and poised her pen as the screen returned to the studio. Mason sat in a chair in the middle of a barren soundstage flanked by two chairs to either side of him, the only light to be had shining down on his own seat. His subjects remained visible in silhouette around him, their features invisible in the cast-off light. No studio audience cheered Mason in from the video clips, no flowers, carpet or heavily-laden bookshelves cheered the atmosphere of the room.

"We've spent a great deal of time discussing the tears and fears of Area 187. Tonight, I'd like to present you with a story of courage, of survival, of the human spirit at its best. With me tonight are four of the survivors that appear in the video you just saw. The video that has come to be called the 'PBS Tapes', so named because it was a public television crew that captured it. This is the first time so many of them have come together on one stage to talk about their experiences and their ultimate escape from Area 187. They have requested we keep them in shadow and disguise their voices for the sake of their privacy and to comply with their own nation's laws. To my Canadian viewers I can assure you, they are the genuine article. To any Americans that may see this, I can assure you they are highly-paid actors telling stories for our amusement and nothing more." Mason said with a wry grin. "Ladies and gentlemen, welcome." Mason nodded to each. They mumbled their replies, a few of them nodding their darkened heads in his direction.

Mason started off having each tell their story up to the point where they met the others in the group. One of the women talked about hiding in her root cellar for almost three years, living off the larder she'd stocked and rainwater that would leak through the foundation before she finally emerged. She was half-mad from the isolation and fear when she met another of the evening's guests, a man that had been in the federal penitentiary in Elkton. His story of survival in Area 187 was just as violent as his life before the plague, when he was a thug that drifted between Charleston's and Huntington's booming illicit drug trades. He'd been left for dead in the bowels of the prison and had managed to stay alive by constantly moving, afraid that either the dead would devour him or the living would find him.

Those two drifted together for a time before they encountered the rest, that "rest" being the other two on the stage that night as well as a few others. The small group had holed up in Tyler County High School, a sprawling campus designed to hold every high-school aged youth in the county and had managed to survive there since nearly the beginning by barricading themselves into the central buildings of the campus and laying low. By the time the group had become fully joined they all had many of the same stories to tell. Almost all of them had been ignored in some cases and fired upon in others by the military helicopters and planes that would pass over from time to time. Those of the group that had ventured to the edge of the Area reported being shot at by snipers on the wall. One even talked about break-dancing on the edge of the buffer zone to prove he wasn't a zombie and still bore the scar from the .50 bullet that had grazed his calf. It was apparent that no one had had any interest in rescuing them from the Area. It wasn't until they started meeting grave robbers that they discovered some of the dark truths about Area 187 and the government's handling of it; truths that kept even the grave robbers from helping them escape back to the world.

Some grave robbers were free with their words. Others would offer nothing more than an update on where the greatest concentrations of the dead seemed to be in the local area. Some would even trade, providing fresh ammunition, medicine and batteries in exchange for information on where to find certain addresses or spoils. Some of the more unsavory characters would also trade, but their price for sundries from the world of the living was typically to be paid in flesh. One of the panel admitted she was still in therapy, not because of the horrors of the dead she experienced but from some of her dealings with the living inside Area 187, grave robbers and other survivors that reveled in the anarchy of that blasted land inflicting their will and amusement on any they came across.

Mason listened intently and rarely spoke, letting the recollections of the survivors meander where they would, from how they collected enough water to survive to the sometimes-necessary evil of cannibalism. After more than a half hour Mason took advantage of a lull. "Now, who can tell me more about John Heath?" he asked. The panel fell silent at the mention of the man's name, their shadowed heads turning towards one another. Mason waited a few seconds before he gave the signal for his camera to zoom in on him.

"No story about these survivors would be complete without mentioning John Heath, the man credited with leading them from that hell on earth. Great efforts were made to contact Mr. Heath, to invite him here tonight to talk about his own unique experiences. Unfortunately we couldn't locate Mr. Heath and as such will have to rely on his fellows to fill in his portion of the tale." Mason looked to either side, waiting for one of the survivors to speak up. He waited several precious seconds of live airtime before he settled back in his chair, his legs crossed and chin supported by a cupped hand, the picture of the bored psychologist. "No one has any recollections to share on Mr. Heath's behalf?"

"John Heath wasn't one of our *fellows*," one man's shadow said, his voice made all the more eerie by the modulation used to disguise it.

"He saved our asses, yours included," a woman's voice across from him retorted.

"He killed my daughter!" the shadow returned, the bitterness ripping through Josephine's ears. She cringed at the otherworldly sound of it but stayed rapt to the screen.

"She was bitten, Ra..." she began, stopping only when she realized she was about to use the man's name. "She was bitten," she repeated slowly.

"Easy for you to say...he saved your noisy little bastard," the man started again. The panel erupted into violent arm waving and shouting, the buzzing din making their voices blend together like a thousand locusts. Mason stood and put a hand out to each side, calling for calm.

"Please, everyone, I realize the intensity of all this but I must insist that each be allowed to speak." The panel calmed and seated themselves, their low murmurs still buzzing. Mason turned back to his camera to address his audience. "We know very little about John Heath after he entered the Area. Although his status as hero or horror has been the topic of dispute by Area experts, the media and, apparently, even those he is credited with saving little is really known about this shadowy figure of Area lore. His previous military record as well as his debriefing upon his return has been sealed by the Department of Homeland Security and the United States Air Force citing national security interests. According to U.S. officials those records will remain sealed until 75 years after Area 187 is declared free of the undead plague. Since your own government and even Mr. Heath won't help us understand the events surrounding Area 187, the undead and the ultimate failure of the United States government to protect its people, perhaps each of you can bring a piece to his puzzle so that we may see the whole man." Mason sat down and adjusted his jacket. "Now, who would like to start?"

"You want to know about John Heath? Huh?" the first man said. "Well, let me tell you a little something. We were just zombie food to him. He just charged in and said we were going for the wall. That bastard led hundreds of those things right to our door. We didn't have a choice but to go with him. My daughter was sick, too sick to travel. He didn't care. We were just a diversion to keep the dead off his back. Thanks to that my daughter's dead-"

"You know that's not true!" the woman's voice shot back, interrupting his tirade.

"Isn't it? Do you see my daughter sitting here?" he asked.

"Funny, I don't see your kid. Where's he tonight? Is he doing his homework, maybe playing video games? I kept my daughter alive for five years in there. Five Goddamn years! And then that bastard comes along and manages to kill her inside of a week! He's still drawing breath and my little girl was left behind to feed the fucking zombies! Maybe you gave him a few little favors back at the school before we headed for the wall, huh? Is that why he saved your kid but left mine to rot?"

"You fucking bastard!" the woman said, her shadow coming up out of her chair. One pump-clad foot made it into Mason's spotlight before the shadow-man seated next to her got up and pulled her back to her chair. "You've had your say! Now it's my turn!" she said from her chair. She was leaning as far out of it as she could without rising from it, her panel-mate's arm across her chest to keep her on her side of the stage.

"Oh, I'm not through with that bastard-"

Mason held up a hand and called for order. "Please, you've had time to express your thoughts. Now let's hear another view." Mason looked at the woman to his right and nodded. "The floor is yours." The woman adjusted her posture to a more proper sitting form though still balanced on the edge of her seat.

"It was nothing like he said. Heath was with us for almost a week before the swarm hit. And it wasn't him that led the dead to us." She paused for a moment while the arm across her chest withdrew, the hand coming to a comforting rest on her shoulder. "Heath came to us, gave us a duffel bag full of medicine and stuff he'd scrounged up in exchange for a safe place to rest for a few days. We had a pretty safe place. A few grave robbers made us a regular stop for the same reason. He said he was going for the wall and didn't need the stuff anymore."

"Didn't you think Heath was just another grave robber?" Mason asked.

"Oh, no, it was easy to tell a grave robber from a caretaker," she said, using the phrase coined to separate those left behind in the Area after the wall went up from the grave robbers. "Though a few people in our group called Heath a grave digger, especially after they saw what he could do to them."

"Don't glorify that fucking-" Mason shot the man him a look that the camera quickly shied from and the voice died off. Mason was nothing if not the master of his program.

"It's not glory, it's just what it was," the woman said in response.

"Grave robbers, diggers and caretakers-" Mason interrupted. "Can you clarify these labels for the benefit of our less knowledgeable viewers?"

"Well, everyone knows what grave robbers are," she said. "Caretaker was what some of the robbers started calling us, I guess to keep it in the whole graveyard theme. The ones left behind to look after the graveyard, the survivors that were just stuck there. Grave robbers were afraid to take us out of there, either because we would slow them down or because of what we all knew was happening at the wall."

"You put John Heath in the category of a 'grave digger'. Tell me more about that."

"*I* didn't say he was a digger, but some did. A grave digger was a survivor. The difference was in how we lived. Caretakers found places to hide, to carve out some kind of life, waiting to live or die. Diggers went out looking for the dead, to kill as many of them as they could. Most of them were completely insane, just survivors that had gone around the bend. Then there were the reapers..." she said, her voice trailing off.

"Reapers?" Mason asked. The man beside her leaned forward as she leaned back, her head in her hands.

"Reapers were what the robbers started calling survivors that preyed on anyone they could. They were thugs that looked for people like us to steal our supplies, our safe places and...lots of other things," he said, his darkened arm bracing the woman's shoulders. "I don't know why robbers even started using those names, or how they stuck, but they did. After awhile we started using those labels, too."

"So you thought Heath was a grave digger?"

"At first some of us thought he was a robber," she said softly.

"Heath was big, a lot bigger than any of us, but he looked just as drawn and drained as us, maybe more. But you could tell from his gear, from his clothes that he hadn't been staying in one place and that he'd seen plenty of action. Most of the diggers we saw were just nuts, babbling about cleansing the Area. Heath was the exact opposite, really quiet and calm; maybe too calm. We didn't know much about him, about why he was in the Area until we got out and the media got hold of him. Anyway, we gave him one of the classrooms and he stayed in there for two days before he came out. When he told us he was going there were more than a few of us that were willing to go with him and take our chances."

"Why would you have been so ready to follow him after past experiences at the wall?" Mason asked.

"I don't know," she said after a long pause. "He was confident, resolute. He said he was going and that was that. It'd been a long time since any of us were so sure, so confident of anything. It was like a beacon, something to cling to."

"Did he offer to take any of you with him, to protect you?"

"No. But he didn't tell us we couldn't follow him, either. When I asked him if my son and I could go with him, he said it was 'a free tomb' and if we wanted to follow it was up to us, and that he would take no responsibility if we did."

"But he *did* end up taking responsibility for you, at least of a fashion didn't he?" The man to Mason's left guffawed at his comment and shook his head.

"You could ask my daughter that question," the voice came back in again. Mason ignored it and continued staring at the woman.

"It was...complicated. At that point, my son and I were the only ones that had really decided to try our luck. The rest entertained it but ultimately thought it was suicide since they'd tried before. We were getting ready to leave that last night when the swarm started to form. A robber, maybe a reaper, we never knew which, had made it as far as the school's parking lot before he died from a bite he must have picked up trying to reach us. We had a party out collecting supplies most of the day and the guy reanimated in time to see our group enter the school. All it took was for it to start moaning. The dead knew we were somewhere around the area, they looked for us all the time. But we'd always been pretty smart in covering our tracks, taking roundabout ways when we went out to forage. Guess it couldn't last forever."

"Did you see this so-called body? Huh?" the angry man shouted across the stage. "I was in that party and I didn't see anyone out in the lot. Heath picked up a tail when he was coming into us. That fucker knew they were back there and he figured he'd lose them by putting them onto us."

"Ray..." she started, then checked herself. "We've been through this a hundred times. We had a lookout, just like always. The lookout saw the guy fall in the parking lot just as you and the rest were coming back. He was afraid to signal you in case it would have heard him," she said. "Heath was already in the process of heading out when the dead showed up. It was a huge swarm, the biggest I've ever seen, and I was in Morgantown when the bombers came. There must have been every zombie for fifty miles around in that mess."

"Yeah, now tell him what your fucking boyfriend did then," the shadow across from her said. "Tell him how the great John Heath got us out of there. Tell him how he sacrificed my daughter to save his ass!"

"She was bitten," she said, stressing each word through clenched teeth. "I'm sorry it happened, everyone is. I liked your daughter. She was a great kid. Maybe if you would've listened and pulled back with the rest of us..."

"Those doors would have held if we would have worked together!" he screamed. "Steel doors, wire mesh in the windows! If we would have worked together we could have braced them. But the rest of you just walked away, sneaking out the back with that coward. We pledged we'd be there for each other, that we'd protect each other, die together if we had to."

"That's the problem - we didn't have to. She didn't have to," she added, "if you would have pulled her back with the rest of us."

"Heath shot her in the fucking head!" he growled. "Right in front of me!"

"Why did he do that?" Mason asked, his tone even, non-threatening.

"She was in front of a set of double doors, we had them chained together. There were just so many of them, pushing against the doors. The doors opened up a little against the chains, enough that one of them got hold of her arm and pulled it through the opening. She screamed, we saw blood. They had hold of her arm and she was bit. John shot her because no one else could," she said, her voice choked with tears.

"If he was a hero, such a tough *Rambo* mother-fucker, why didn't he go to her? He could've got her in time, amputated her arm, something, *anything*! He didn't even try!"

"Neither did you! You ran! You fucking *ran*, not *to* her but *away* from her!" The woman took a shuddering breath, her fists balled on the chair's armrests. "Do you think she would've wanted to reanimate? What if John hadn't shot her? Would you have wanted to hear your daughter's screams while they ate her alive? He did what you couldn't do for her. What none of us could've done for her."

"So Heath *did* shoot your daughter, but only after she was bitten?" Mason asked the man. There was a long pause before the dark head nodded.

"It was like a feeding frenzy. Those things smelled her blood and they surged, broke through the door. There were dozens of them, tearing her apart..." he said, his voice stopping abruptly in a choke.

"Mr. Mason?" a woman sitting beside the sobbing man spoke up. "It's all true to some degree, what they've both been saying. But Heath didn't kill her until she was bitten, and it would've been suicide for any of us to go after her no matter how badly we wanted to. Nobody planned for it to happen that way, it just did. I'd give anything to have her here, we all would. But she's not. The zombies concentrated on her, gave us the time we needed to get out. After that we just followed Heath. We didn't know what else to do. He was the only one with a plan, no matter how suicidal it was. He didn't lead us, but we followed anyway."

"Thank you," Mason said, relief evident at a calm voice in the storm. "What happened from there?"

"We walked all night, moving around a few smaller swarms that were following the moans from the rest back at the school. It was probably two or three hours until we were far enough away not to hear them anymore. It was the ones we couldn't skirt that showed us what Heath was capable of. Only a few of us had guns, and even those weren't reliable. Most of the bullets we had were old, stuff we'd found over the years. Heath had the only gun with a silencer and he gave that to one of us that didn't make it to the wall," she said. "He had this big piece of steel, like a crowbar. Any of them that we couldn't go around or run from, he just walked up to and bashed them." Her arm chopped through the air for emphasis. "I watched him wade into a group of them, must have been twenty or so, to get to her son," she said, nodding to the woman across the stage. "He'd fallen when we were moving around one of the swarms. None of us noticed till we were pretty far away from him. Heath turned and went back into the swarm, mowed them down one by one...chop, chop, chop..." Her voice rose, her arm motions more violent as she punctuated her words. "It was that last one, though..." she stopped at that as if just realizing how her silhouette must look.

"What 'last one'?" Mason asked.

"This zombie, we came through a thicket and Heath practically walked right into it. It opened its mouth and just... stopped. They just stared at each other, Heath and the zombie, for a long time. Then it just turned and walked away."

"It didn't try to attack him? It didn't moan?" Mason asked.

"No, nothing," she said. "After we'd made it out, when we were sitting in a holding cell under quarantine, I asked him about it. All he said was, 'it takes one to know one'. I think that was the most words I'd ever heard him say at one time since he showed up."

There were no further outbursts after that, just a retelling of how the group had made it to the buffer zone two nights later, their numbers reduced to eight and with a long trail of the dead shambling after them.

Josephine turned off the video and packed her laptop away. She knew much of the survivors' story and had even interviewed two of the panel members herself shortly after they were released from quarantine, including *O Canada's* outspoken shadow Mildred Harris, mother of the child Heath had saved. As to John Heath, she knew little more than what Mason had managed to get out of his guests. Mildred had, of course, spoken highly of him, just as other survivors and some third-hand sources had pegged him as an unstable grave digger. Josephine had tried off and on to locate him since his return to the world but had come up empty. She didn't take it as a slight to her investigative journalist abilities, though. Every newspaper, network and cable outlet in the country had tried at one time or another to find the elusive Mr. Heath. To her knowledge, none had been successful.

When the survivors had first appeared, PBS had been able to air their footage. That permission had been taken as a green light for the rest of the media to start producing their own Area 187 stories and interviews. Homeland cracked down quickly though, explaining that the PBS footage had been properly cleared for airing. But even though most of the interviews, stories and productions the various media outlets had gathered during that time were quashed didn't mean they would go unread or unseen. Leaks both engineered and accidental occurred across the board. Foreign news outlets and web media services were more than happy to show what the U.S. media couldn't, fanning the fires of conspiracy theorists and Area critics worldwide.

The "PBS Survivors" became the unwitting poster children for all sorts of Area causes in the process, their lives proof that the United States was engaged in a massive cover-up of Area 187 and the zombie plague. Homeland and the military quickly chalked the survivors up to a fluke. They pointed to the fact that the survivors had hidden themselves away, and even claimed they hadn't wanted to be found in the first place. They answered the charges of firing on survivors in the rare instances they were encountered by claiming the flight crews thought them to be zombies, grave robbers or even terrorists. They had even gone so far as to allow a Congressional review of security tapes and records from the buffer zone during the periods the individual survivors claimed they'd attempted to make contact with the outside world.

Of course, they found nothing. No evidence existed that the survivors had even tried to contact the outside world before they showed up at the wall under the watchful eyes of the documentary crew's cameras. But in the end, all Homeland had to do was sit back and wait for the media to burn itself out like it always did. With no fresh information or further survivors coming to the fore, the stories went from hard-edged, factual reporting to wild speculation, eventually returning Area 187 to page six news and foreign tabloid fodder just as it had done when it first began.

The network big-wigs had shot down Josephine's current investigative endeavor, an exposé into the grave robber culture, for the same reasons. These men would risk death not only from the undead in Area 187 but from their own government, somehow slipping past the Area's defenses to retrieve items of value to bring back to the world. Usually, they were contracted for specific things like family heirlooms and other personal items left behind at the creation of Area 187. Sometimes they would be sent after works of art from museums for sale to foreign interests, though most grave robbers passed on those contracts. Everything left behind in an established institution would have been extensively cataloged during the days before the pull-out. To have a work of art that everyone in the industry and Homeland Security knew to be in Area 187 would bring the immediate arrest of all suspects involved. Any person found guilty of entering Area 187 without sanction would receive the death penalty carried out within 48 hours of the passing of the sentence. No appeals, no halting calls from the governor. Everything having to do with the Area was squarely within the jurisdiction of Homeland Security, every infraction swiftly punished through its own federal laws.

But Josephine wasn't one to let little things like death by firing squad or even the network's lack of support stop her from a story. Unbeknownst to the network's upper echelons she'd continued her story in secret, gaining valuable contacts and even speaking with a few genuine grave robbers. She'd found that for every one that had been brought to trial there were a dozen more killed while entering or leaving the Area or hunted down and eliminated by shadow operatives in their homes and on the streets. The official reasoning seemed sound enough to justify the harsh punishments; if a grave robber became infected or brought out infected tissue the virus could spread beyond Area 187.

It was bad enough that the military and the government had to publicly admit the source of the virus to stem world-wide panic; the last thing they needed was for it to spread beyond the confines of the Area. Additionally, the virus' suitability as a terrorist weapon gave them further power to institute their zero-tolerance policies, allowing prosecution not as trespassers but as traitors and compromisers of national security under both federal law and various anti-terrorism acts. Media outlets and special interest groups had filed dozens of public information lawsuits over the years concerning Area 187. Each had been summarily dismissed in the interests of national security. Families of those infected had lost out as well with the passing of laws specifically barring action against the federal, state and local governments involved in the creation of Area 187, citing that its creation had been a tragic necessity and not the result of negligence or intent.

Time had colored the facts behind the creation of Area 187 as well. National and world attention had focused laser-like on the sleepy Appalachian state and pieces of the surrounding states in the first few months after the spread and lethality of the virus had been officially accepted as a hopeless condition. But just as with the Oklahoma City and World Trade Center tragedies of the past, the public eventually lost interest. Even the continued attentions of former residents, conspiracy theorists and others that had been touched directly by the virus had not been enough to keep Area 187 on the front pages and lead stories for more than the first year. The drama of the walking dead hadn't been enough to distract the American public for long. By the end of the that first year most Americans had gladly turned their attentions back to their *American Idol* favorites, their sports teams and their efforts to make the earth a greener place while the most contagious plague the world had ever known raged behind a three-foot thick wall less than 70 miles from the nation's capitol.

America had had enough. They wanted to forget about the virus and Area 187. They were happy to mark the government holiday in its honor. They could even wait out the twenty-plus year period the government claimed it would take before moving in to cleanse and reclaim Area 187 for the living. But even zombies weren't enough to merit more than the distraction they had already provided. As long as they weren't slouching down Main Street or eating their pets, the people were content to let the government handle it, let it fall away from their daily lives.

Josephine wasn't one of those. She'd lost her grandparents in the first month of the plague, their stubborn natures keeping them on the farm where Josephine had grown up until the amassing hordes had overrun them. She could blame the military for the plague, but she knew the authorities had tried to force their evacuation. Like many of the proud old-timers though, they refused at the ends of their shotguns and chose to weather the storm. Some had done it out of sheer pride. Others believed the police and the army would be able to control the spread before it reached their remote homes and land. A few went to their deaths thinking the whole thing a government-sponsored hoax, a way to trick them into giving up their land for whatever obscene purpose Washington had in mind.

She'd pleaded with her grandparents in that last phone call, had tried to make her grandfather see reason. The call ended abruptly with her grandfather telling her that a few people had come up on the porch and he had to "take care of them". The next day communications with the whole state were shut down; land lines, cell phones, even internet connectivity was cut, blocked or otherwise jammed. The only method of communication was from satellite link-ups reserved solely for military communications and short reports from journalists embedded with the troops.

Josephine's position at the time with a syndicated news magazine had given her no special access to even this method, though she'd been able to see an unedited report from Morgantown and her alma mater, West Virginia University. The whole city had been overrun, the booming population of co-eds feeding the already-growing army of the dead. The last thing she saw on the report were the fighter jets and Apache helicopters roaring in overhead, their eventual mission the same as with any of the few heavily-populated areas of the state; level any building more than two stories tall.

Josephine climbed out of the loveseat, changed into street clothes and pulled her long red hair back into a severe ponytail. She was playing a dangerous game with this story, and not just with her career. Her boss and news director, Bill Hartman, knew she was continuing her investigation. At first he'd towed the line laid down by the penthouse offices. Not only could Josephine face criminal charges for consorting with grave robbers, Homeland could subject the network to stiff fines and even the loss of their broadcast licenses for allowing her to work her story. But even though Josephine knew the risks, she'd gone too far into the robber subculture to turn back now. She'd been perfectly willing to complete her work and slip quietly off into Canada where the story could be broadcast and she could file for amnesty with the Canadian government, safe in the knowledge that no matter what the U.S. government charged her with, Canada would never deport her since she would face the death penalty. But that was before another disc ended up on her dressing table nearly two weeks ago.

The case carried no cute sticky note, the DVD inside bore no label or even a manufacturer's mark. But the video etched into it had not only changed the entire scope and direction of her story, it had been enough for Bill Hartman to defy their superiors and covertly support her work all the way to the end. The story wasn't hers anymore, and it wasn't Hartman's or even the network's. It had become much more than that. But she would have to do far more than conduct a few interviews and smile for the cameras to do justice to it; she would have to live it.

She checked her watch, then grabbed her coat just as her cell phone went off. She scanned the number and hurriedly answered.

"Hello, Jo!" a man's heavy Danish accent said.

"Any news for me, George?"

"Your hunch may have paid off. The software says there's a 60% chance the woman is who you thought she was," George said, choosing his words carefully. You never knew who could be listening.

"You're sure?" she asked, trying to contain her excitement.

"The computer seems confident."

"Thanks, George. I owe you one."

"You just remember that when you make it to my little corner of the world, eh?" George said with a laugh.

"I will, George, and thanks again. You don't know how much." She closed the phone and nibbled at the antenna for a moment in thought. This changed everything. Checking her purse, she pulled out two DVD cases and flipped one open. Satisfied, she tucked that one back and placed the other under the loveseat's cushion, checking to make sure the edges of the case couldn't be felt through it. It wouldn't do for anyone to find it just yet, especially for her. Someone had risked their life to get the message to her, and even more lives depended on how she acted from this moment on.

The drive into Pittsburgh had been long but thankfully uneventful. Bill had already established her cover, sending her on "special assignment". Julie Sommers, her chipper yet venomously perky replacement had called, of course, spending an hour pumping her for information and telling Josephine she would keep her chair warm in her absence. Josephine despised the girl and didn't trust her farther than she could throw her, but the advertising sweeps period was almost upon them, and without Josephine to keep her loyal fans tuned-in, Bill needed something to keep them watching her show.

Much to Julie's chagrin, Josephine was considered a rising star at the network, a hard-nosed reporter that knew how to work a story or a guest while still retaining a classic, low-maintenance sort of beauty; the kind of woman that would make a serious contender for the big anchor spots. Julie relied far too much on her youthful beauty, perfect body and her father's political connections to be considered any sort of serious competition for Josephine. Those qualities had made her more than acceptable to step in on Josephine's current morning show, but Julie had made it known from the start that she wanted more. It had grated against her every nerve that the best she'd been offered so far was the spot as Josephine's understudy and fluff story correspondent.

When she wasn't sitting in for Josephine's numerous special assignments and rare vacations, Julie was relegated to covering the dreaded "human interest" pieces. She'd recently put Bill Hartman on notice that she was tired of playing second banana to Josephine, that she was just one more dog show or craft fair away from unsheathing her claws. But Bill, the network and even the viewers knew that while Julie Sommers was the kind of woman that female viewers wished they looked like and male viewers wished they had in their hot tubs, Josephine Terrell was the kind of woman female viewers wished they were and male viewers wished they'd married. Julie chaffed at that, acutely aware of how the rest of the world saw them in comparison. Even more chaffing than that to Julie was that Josephine herself didn't seem to notice, and if she did she didn't seem to care.

Josephine parked her car uptown, donned a pair of dark glasses to try and conceal her often-recognized face, and hailed a cab to take her through downtown then deeper into the city. She had the cab let her off at the head of a dark and oddly quiet side street, preferring to walk the last few blocks rather than let the driver know exactly where she was headed. The neighborhood had a dangerous reputation, but she'd frequented this part of town for the last several weeks now and had little fear of its regular denizens. It was a well-known yet seldom mentioned fact that this part of town was home turf to some of the most capable, and most dangerous, grave robbers ever to strut through Area 187. The police didn't come here unless they absolutely had to; neither did the gangs or other criminal elements. As a rule, grave robbers liked things calm and quiet, as much for their safety as for their comfort, and they weren't above taking out the trash to keep it that way. Men that routinely faced the full might of Homeland Security just to enter a land full of the walking dead tended to make poor marks for muggers and street toughs.

Josephine made it to the end of the block and passed through the now-familiar chipped and faded door of Wally's Café, a round-the-clock diner with more cockroaches than spoons. As rough and grimy as it was, it was still the best place to find a grave robber looking for work. She'd discovered it months ago when she'd first gotten the idea for her story, and it had taken that long before she'd been able to gain the confidence of the clientele to even talk to her. Josephine sat down at the counter while an old, grizzled woman brought coffee in a chipped mug then walked back into the kitchen without a word. There were three other people in the diner, all seated at the same table at the opposite end of the room. The man she knew only as "Bub", a rough-looking, 30ish man with a crew cut and a scar on his unshaven chin glanced at her over his shoulder then left the table to take the stool beside her.

"Well if it isn't Josephine," Bub said. His leering eyes made her less than comfortable, but his reputation as a highly successful grave robber was without question in their community. "I didn't expect to see you back here again. You ain't still serious about this, are you?"

"Why? Are you getting cold feet on me?"

"Me? Nah. Walkin' in the Area is like walkin' in the park." Bub was still smiling, his eyes on her chest.

"Bub, I'm up here." Bub's smile widened as he finally looked up at her face then leaned in close.

"Okay then, if you've got the money, I've got the time." Josephine reached into her pocket and came out with a small key, the kind used to secure bus station lockers. She held it up where he could see it but snatched it into her fist just as he reached for it. "Hey, now, what's the deal?" Bub asked, pulling away from her slightly.

"The deal's changed." She picked up her coffee and selected a relatively clean spot for her lips to take a sip. Bub leaned back, his leer still in place.

"Lady, I don't care who the hell you think you are. If you're playing me I'll skull-fuck you." Josephine suppressed the shiver his tone and proximity sent through her as she set her cup down and swiveled her stool towards him. Her right hand was in her lap, her fingers curled around the grip of a big-bore revolver.

"Easy, Bub. The deal's changed for the better, at least where you're concerned. I'm not going into the Area, with you or anyone else. What I need right now is information. Whoever can give it to me gets the fifty grand behind this key." Bub shook his head, a low, oily laugh leaking from his lips.

"You think that gun means anything to me? Lady, I get worse threats going out for cigarettes. I took a big chance even talking to you in the first place."

"And now you'll have even less risk. You give me the right address, I give you the money. You don't even have to leave town to get it."

"Information, huh? What kind of information?" Bub asked.

"I need to find John Heath."

"Heath? What the hell do you want with him? That guy hasn't set foot in the Area for years."

"So you're saying you *don't* want to pick up an easy fifty grand?" Josephine asked.

"I didn't say that, exactly."

"Look, I've got things to do. We both know you know where to find him. If you're afraid of him just tell me. If you can't, I'll bet one of your buddies over there can."

"Afraid of John Heath? Lady, I ain't afraid of any man, living or dead. He's nothing but a shell-shocked grave digger. What's he gonna' know about the Area that I can't tell you?"

"And what's it matter to you? What, you up for an on-camera interview?" she asked.

"Yeah, right, and ten minutes after your story comes out I've got MIB coming down on me."

———————

"See? You *are* afraid of something after all. If I'm not going in to see it for myself, I need someone that *isn't* afraid to talk about what they know. All the other survivors are played out. He's the only one nobody's gotten to yet. Now, are you going to tell me where I can find him or do I have to start the auction?" she asked, holding up the key again. Bub stared at the key for a minute.

"So what's my guarantee that there's money behind that key and not Homeland?"

"Don't be stupid. Each of us has enough on the other to get Homeland excited. If there's no money, you'll turn me in. Considering I'm a hotshot TV star, I'm too visible, too easily noticed if I just disappear. They wouldn't be able to do much more than arrest me, question me and release me. My career would be over, but at least I'd still be alive," she said, returning his slick smile. "If you give me bogus information though, I'll turn *you* in. You, *Bub*, you don't exist as it is. You're just one bullet away from an unmarked grave to end your unmarked life. You give me Heath, I give you a shitload of money and neither one of us ever has to see the other again." Josephine pulled out her notepad and pen and laid them on the battered Formica counter. They stared at each other a moment before Bub finally shrugged his shoulders and picked up the pen.

After a few hours at City Hall, Josephine made her way to the address Bub had given her. She'd been in bars, clubs and taverns across the country but never one quite like this. Bub had told her the place would be hard to find and he'd been right. No signs marked the entrance, no name had been emblazoned in neon over the steel door set into the crumbling brick wall in the middle of the non-descript, trash-strewn alley that reminded her of the underground and after-hours clubs of her college days. She'd just raised her hand to knock when a small slit opened at eye level in the door. She said the words Bub had scrawled on her pad and stood back as the heavy door swung noiselessly inward, admitting her into the club. The doorman was nowhere to be seen.

After Wally's, Josephine wasn't sure just what to expect

———————

from this nameless den. Her mind had pictured the place like an alcohol-soaked Wally's; stained floors, rum-soaked patrons and tattooed, bearded rough-necks watching ugly, naked women gyrate on the battered tables. Instead, she found a very clean though dimly lit room, the kind of place you'd find behind the door of the neighborhood corner bar. The first thing that got her attention was the sound. Or, more notably, the utter lack of it. There were perhaps ten men sitting at the bar not counting the elderly, painfully-thin man behind it. A television over the bar mutely replayed that afternoon's Pirate's game. The patrons' attentions were seemingly fixed to the screen, but that didn't stop the hairs on the back of her neck from rising, the same hairs that usually told her she was being watched.

Josephine shrugged off the feeling and walked towards the bar, her footfalls like thunder in the silence of the place. Josephine leaned against the bar and tried to get the bartender's attention with her eyes. When that didn't work she waved him over, breaking his gaze at the baseball game and bringing him and his taciturn scowl to her.

"You don't belong here, miss." His tone was soft but firm, audible at any volume.

"I'm looking for John Heath." She tried to speak as quietly as possible, but by the slight twitches and furtive peripheral glances she received from the men at the bar she knew they could hear her as if she'd whispered in their ears.

"Goodbye, miss."

"A friend told me I could find John Heath here." She pulled a folded fifty from her purse and slid it across the bar to him. The old man didn't even look down.

"I'm being polite, miss. This place ain't for you and there ain't no Heath here." The bartender cocked his head slightly, like a dog hearing a high-flying jet. He sighed, palmed the bill off the bar and hooked a thumb over his shoulder. "Back booth." Josephine left the bar and moved towards the back of the room. Now that her eyes were adjusting to the gloom she could see a large man seated at the last booth. She approached the table, stopping just before it.

"John Heath?" She'd tried to use her best, professional voice but her attempt at whispering made it quiver slightly. The bald-shaven, powerfully-built man at the booth barely looked up at her from under his heavy eyelids as he absently peeled the label from his lager. Josephine stood awkwardly at the booth for several moments before the headstrong nature her grandfather had gifted her with reminded her that timid journalists never got their stories. She slid into the booth across from him uninvited and waited for him to acknowledge her. When he did finally look at her, she almost wished he hadn't. While his eyes were a bright blue she could see dark voids passing across them like storm clouds blotting out the light of the moon.

"What do you want?" His voice was a deep, rolling baritone more felt than heard. The timbre mixed with the dead stare of his eyes made a cold chill run down her spine. She cleared her throat softly, ignoring the thundering sound in her ears.

"I'm looking for John Heath."

"Why?"

"Are you John Heath?"

"I'm not interested in an interview." He turned his attentions back to the slowly disintegrating label on his beer bottle, giving Josephine a welcome respite from his stare.

"I don't want to interview you, Mr. Heath."

"Then what *do* you want?" he said as another piece of the damp label fell to the Plexiglas-covered table.

"I need to get into Area 187." Heath's eyes flicked up at her for a moment before falling back to his bottle.

"Why don't you just step outside and put a bullet in your head now, save all the time and trouble," he said, the trace of a smile on his lips.

"Look, I'll get right to the point-"

"Don't bother. Nothing there for me, and there sure as hell isn't anything there for you. If you want something from in there, find yourself a good grave robber."

"I already found a good grave robber; that's how I found you. I don't need a *good* one, Mr. Heath. I need the *best* one."

His smile was gone now. "Guess you're fucked since I'm not a grave robber. Go back to the prick that gave you me. If he's stupid enough to give you that, he's just stupid enough to get you killed, too."

"Mr. Heath, you know who I am. Knowing that, I don't think I need to tell you that I know all about *you*, too. I know what happened, why you went AWOL and why you lived in there for almost five years."

"So you know how Google works. Your mother must be so proud," he interrupted.

"My parents died while I was still a child. I was raised by my grandparents, and I lost them during the first few weeks of the plague." John held up his thumb and forefinger for a moment and rubbed them together in the universally-accepted gesture of playing the world's smallest violin.

"Lots of people lost lots of people back then, Ms. Terrell. I don't think your granddaddy wants to look down or up at you and watch you go the same way he did."

"I need someone that will take me in there and get me back out again. You're the only one that's ever been able to bring survivors out and lived to tell about it."

"I don't tell about it."

"No, but a lot of others do. The rest of the PBS Survivors still speak highly of you; most of them, anyway."

"You mean the ones that are still alive? I don't do the reunion shows. But I read the papers enough to know that three of the eight are dead now. Unknown causes. I got a lot more press than they did, but I know after a few more years pass the powers that be will feel it's enough of a dead issue. Sooner or later they'll come for me, too. It'll be sooner if I do stupid shit like talking to the morning news's principal set of tits and ass."

"You don't have to be an asshole," she said, her professional composure dropping at his assessment of her professional standing just enough to redden her face.

"Yeah, and you don't have to be stupid."

"Please, just hear me out. If you still feel that way when I'm done I'll never darken your doorstep again."

"Do you really think you're the only one wanting me to go in there for one reason or another? I fought my ass off to get out of there and all of you just want me to go back in." Josephine held up her hand and repeated his violin gesture. It was becoming obvious that John Heath was not the kind of man that responded to polite discourse.

"You were in there because you *wanted* to be. And the bitter, jaded anti-hero bullshit may make you feel like a tough guy but if that's really how you are you wouldn't have bothered bringing back survivors that didn't exist. You'd have just left them there and got out alone, slipped back into society."

"Honey, you don't know shit. I'm no hero. I'd decided I'd had enough and they just followed me. I didn't ask them to come along."

"Yes, but you didn't stop them, either. One of the survivors, Mildred, even told me the story about her son, how you went back to get him."

"Mildred was a stupid bitch, too. I told her to keep hold of the kid and she didn't. I didn't see the sense in the kid getting munched just because his mom was an idiot."

"Back here, we call that *giving a shit*."

"Yeah, and back here a 'zombie' is a drink," he returned. "And I didn't go back after the kid because he was special or had cracked my cold black heart or even because he offered me a Coke. I went back for him because Mildred had stopped in her tracks and was screaming. The rest of the group stopped like the good little sheep they were and the women started screaming and crying along with her. I went back for the kid so they'd get their asses moving and the women would stop wailing. There were no heroics to it, no selfless act of bravery. It was a calculated act for the good of the majority, not the saving of the minority from their own bullshit hysterics. It was survival. No more, no less." He lifted the naked bottle to his lips and emptied it. "Still think you know everything?" He pulled a short, rough-twisted cheroot from his coat and lit it. Josephine held her breath as the acrid smoke eased across the space between them.

"No matter your reasons, you're still the only one that's ever been able to do it. You know that place better than anyone."

"I'm forgetting a little bit each day."

"All the more reason why we need to get in there now."

"Honey, have you been in this conversation at all? I'm not going in there. Not for your story and sure as hell not for you."

"I thought you were going to hear me out."

"*You* said that, I didn't."

"The story is only part of it," she said, pointedly ignoring his last words. Josephine reached into her bag and pulled out a small, portable DVD player. She popped the open lid, slid the disc from her purse into it and plugged in a pair of ear buds. "Watch this and tell me what you think."

"No."

Josephine exhaled slowly, counting off ten in her mind. She looked around the room. None of the other patrons seemed to be paying attention. "Do you trust these people?"

"More than I trust you."

"I'm serious. What I'm about to show you could get both of us in a lot of trouble."

"Then why do it?"

"Because there's someone on here that I think we both know." She slid the player across the table to him and waited for him to put in the ear pieces. "Please."

John stared at her for a moment, a thin plume of smoke rising up into the still air between them. Josephine sighed again and pulled the notepad from her purse. She scribbled a few words on it and slid it over to him. He glanced at it then shook his head. "It's a hoax. No grave robber's stupid enough to bring something like that out. There's nothing in it except a death sentence, especially if he gave it to a TV reporter."

"Maybe whoever brought it out valued life more than money."

"Robbers police themselves. Bringing something like this - a *real* something like this - out into the world would have the rest of

51

them coming down on him almost as much as the government. The last thing guys like that want is a big task force to round them all up after a publicity stunt like this."

"Yes, but you're not a grave robber, remember? You already have a history, and it would only take a little prodding for people to remember your name and what you did before. You'd be too well known..." she paused a moment and tried to reign in her slowly-climbing volume. "Look. Just watch it. If you still think it's a hoax - "

"Yeah, I know, you're gone." John shook his head and reluctantly slid the ear pieces in place.

Josephine watched as he turned the volume control down to practically nothing. Bub and her other sources had told her about how grave robbers and military men that still had call to enter the place learned to hone their senses. Area 187 was dead in more than just the figurative sense. No living inhabitants meant no unnatural sounds, and enough time had passed that industrial and human-related odors had fallen off to nothing in most areas.

Moving quickly and quietly was imperative for the successful grave robber since no sounds existed in Area 187 to cover their movements or even their words. Even the very human odors of sweat, blood and viscera via open wounds could attract undead attention from a hundred yards away if the wind was right. For humans to survive for any length of time inside, they had to train themselves and their senses to work in the same fashion as the zombies did. Most robbers carried this proclivity with them outside the walls as well, hence their gathering places tended to be exceptionally silent. She had no doubt the men in the bar knew she was coming before the door ever opened.

Josephine waited until the light from the player hit his face then went to the bar to fetch drinks. By the time she got back to the table she knew what part of the video message Heath had reached. The man's eyes had turned to peering slits, like someone trying to see an image on a screen through heavy static. Suddenly, Heath snatched her wrist in a painful grip as she set his drink down beside him, his eyes still on the screen.

"What kind of bullshit game are you playing?" he said, his

tone low, menacing. Her shivers returned in a continuous wave, his viselike grip closing tighter around her wrist as each second of the message played. She gasped loudly at the pain, freezing his continuing pressure but not abating it. He got up quickly and pulled her to her feet, the player still going in his free hand. She made an unintelligible squawk as he practically threw her through a door beside the booth then followed after her.

"Christ!" she screamed as he shut the door behind them. She rubbed at her aching wrist and got up from the floor. They were in a small office, presumably where the bar did its books. "What the hell was that for?"

Heath pulled the disc out of the player and dropped the machine to the floor. "I don't know what kind of bullshit you're trying to pull here," he growled as he went to the television cart in the corner and slid the disc into the DVD player. Josephine sidled slowly towards the door, touched the knob, found it immobile. "The door doesn't open until I say it opens. The room's soundproof. You've got as long as this thing plays to come up with a real good reason why I should let you leave on your legs and not in buckets."

"The message is real," she said softly, almost pleadingly. He punched the play button on the remote and stepped back a few feet from the television. Its screen was far larger and with better resolution than the tiny device could muster, and for this he had to be sure. The screen filled with static for a few moments before a very haggard-looking man with a rough gray beard and a torn jacket popped onto the screen. His eyes were sunken into their sockets, the dark bags under them standing out proudly against his slightly yellowed skin.

"I am Dr. Alan Richards," the image said. Several people could be seen milling about in the background. "The date of this recording is February 26th, 2014. I implore whoever sees this message to contact the authorities and report our location. We are a group of 38 survivors trapped in what you call Area 187 since rescue operations ceased in 2007. We are safe for the time being. I have been told by mercenaries that messages like this are tantamount to the death penalty for anyone that holds them. But our situation is dire, and I fear we can't hold out much longer. Please deliver this to Homeland Security. We just want to-"

Heath paused the recording just then, his attention on a woman that had entered the background while the doctor pleaded for help. "It can't be..." he muttered.

"It could be," Josephine said. He continued to squint and stare at the woman on the screen, cocking his head to different angles subconsciously in the vain and technologically impossible effort to see her face from a different angle.

"How did you know she...how did you know this woman resembled Eileen?"

"When you first came back my network did its fair share of research. We knew about Eileen, why you stayed." John wheeled away from the screen then, his blue eyes nothing but storm clouds now.

"Bullshit!" he roared. "This is bullshit!"

"Mr. Heath – John. What if it's not? Look, I isolated her image and had it run through the same Homeland software the airports use to compare photos of known terrorists against their video surveillance footage. The image quality is grainy, but it still returned a 67% chance of a match against the photos of your wife I found on one of the Area websites."

"Those airline reports are only right about half the time," Heath murmured.

"Which means there's still better than a 30% chance that she is Eileen Heath; you stayed in there on a lot less hope than that." Heath stared at her for a moment then turned back to the screen. He touched the play button, his eyes locked on the woman in the background rather than the old man in the fore.

"...come home," the doctor continued. "We have moved several times over the years. When we first banded together, there were more than one hundred of us. Disease, accidents and the dead have whittled us away to almost nothing, and I fear the next time they overrun us will be our last. To the government, I ask only that you bring us home. We will swear on any book and sign any contract to release you from all harm and liabilities and we will melt away into the landscape never to be heard from again. And since you are our last hope for survival, we will also give you the same hope. One among us was bitten and infected, and though sickened to near-death, survived to make a full recovery. Such a person may be the key to producing a vaccine against the virus. If you come to our aid, they have agreed to cooperate fully in the search for a vaccine. All we ask in return is that you don't let us die this way. We are located..." A final burst of static clouded the screen and the player shut off.

"What the fuck?" Heath said as he advanced on the television. He swung around to Josephine again and stared at her, the plastic housing of the remote protesting weakly in his grip. "Is that *it*? Is that all there is?"

Josephine folded her arms across her chest to keep him from seeing her shaking hands. She knew he'd be upset, but she hadn't known how forceful and brutish he would be. Now behind a locked door in a forgotten part of Pittsburgh she realized her plans had not necessarily been completely thought through.

"No. There's more," she managed to say. The stress had turned her voice husky and tears shined behind her eyes, threatening to spill out without warning. Still, timid journalists never got the story. She had to stand her ground now. If she didn't, not only would she lose her story but those people trapped in the undead gulag of Area 187 would lose any chance of coming home.

"So where the fuck is it?" John asked.

"We have to come to an agreement first." Josephine's voice lacked the bravado she'd so desperately hoped for but there was no helping that. This would either work or it wouldn't. Heath advanced on her, the broken remote's pieces tumbling to the floor as he neared. She took a step back defensively and slid her hand into the pocket of her coat. The revolver came out, shaking and level with his stomach. "I don't want to shoot you."

Heath stopped in his tracks while a long smile slowly spread across his face. "You don't have the guts and I don't have the patience." His thick hand shot out and torqued the weapon violently, turning her already-aching wrist a few degrees past its most comfortable angle to turn the muzzle skyward. He pulled her into him, grabbed her chin in his rough, calloused hand and painfully jerked her face up to look into his. "I'm only gonna' ask you one more time. Where?"

"Tough guy," she said through gritted teeth. "Famed zombie killer and feared woman-beater."

"There's one thing that place teaches you - young, old, man, woman, child; everything's against you, and I won't lose a bit of sleep if you make me crush your fucking throat."

"If I tell you where they are, you'll go without me. You need me to tell you where to go, and I need you to get me there and get us back. Neither of us is going there if you keep up this schoolyard bully crap."

"You willing to die with that little nugget of information lodged in your brain?" he asked.

"Yeah, you willing to go back out there again with no idea where to look? Knowing every day you stumble around is one less day she has to live?"

"Let's get something straight right now. I could give a rat's ass about *they*. Fuck 'em. If that woman is Eileen, I'm going to yank her out of there."

"And if I don't come back with you, my bosses know exactly where I'm going, and who I'm going with. If you want any chance of going in there, getting her and coming back to the world you're going to need me and all my pretty cameras to tell your story, make you too hot to touch. Otherwise Eileen will have a very short homecoming before Homeland comes to cart both your asses away for *debriefing*. Now let me go and we can discuss this like adults."

John stared at her for long moments before he released her and stepped away. He wasn't stupid enough to leave the gun in her hands. "I'm listening." He shoved the revolver behind his belt buckle.

Josephine rubbed her wrist and put a few more feet between them before she felt her heart rate fall back to something approaching a normal rhythm. "This is how it's going to work. You're going to get us into Area 187. Once we're well inside, I'll give you the location. Then it's up to you to get us there and get us out. Just remember, if I don't make it the authorities will be alerted to our actions. My bosses will play it off like they didn't know I was going and will absolve themselves of any residual suspicion by turning over my conveniently-found notes to them; notes that spell out exactly what I was doing and who I was doing it with. At that point, no amount of press coverage would save you from a shoot-on-site manhunt." Josephine resisted the urge to smile at her own cleverness. Once she'd gotten past the physical threats, dealing with Heath wasn't any more difficult than dealing with the network at contract time.

"And what if I say go fuck yourself? Or better yet, what if I report your ass to the feds to buy *my* ass back from them, then go on my own little manhunt for your digital geek buddy? I'll bet he remembers where the Doc said they were. He probably watched that thing a hundred times, probably made his own copy," John said.

"And do you think I'm stupid enough to use somebody in this country? You're blowing smoke, and every minute we waste here is another minute off the clock for those people to live. For Eileen to live," she said, stressing the last sentence. "My network will pay very well for a story like this, one that blows away Area 187 and their suppression of survivors still trapped in there. You and Eileen will need some seed money, something to help you buy your lives back."

"Your bosses know you're doing this?"

"My *boss* knows, no one else. It won't matter though. Once the real story comes out we'll all be too hot to touch, by the government or anyone else."

John passed a hand over his smooth-shaven head and chuckled to himself. "You think you got this all planned out, don't you? Have you got a plan for just how your ass is going to survive? This ain't some high school field trip you're talking about. You think you can handle it?"

"Yes."

"You think you're capable of dropping the hammer on a five

year old little dead fucker? You think you can smash a man's skull? If you can't, you'll find yourself the Area's most famous walking corpse."

"I know I'm capable of defending myself if that's what you mean."

Heath's shoulders slumped for a moment, his smile gone. "You're talking about suicide. You don't know what you're trying to get into."

"But *you* do. That's why I need you. That's why Eileen needs you."

"Pretty slim chance that it's her."

"Mr. Heath, even if that woman *isn't* Eileen, isn't that woman's life and the lives of everyone else in there worth saving? If you don't help me you're dooming every single one of them to a fate worse than death."

"What's it been? Two weeks since that message was *supposedly* recorded? Probably means they were just days from being overrun anyway. They're probably dead already. And what was he talking about, somebody that survived a bite? That's bullshit on a stick, honey. I've seen a hundred people bit and every one of them turned; turned or got torn apart so there wasn't enough left of them to come back."

"There are exceptions to every rule. If there was one disease or virus out there that every single person was vulnerable to we would all be dead from it a long time ago. Even the black plague had people that were resistant. If he's telling the truth, someone with a true biological immunity would be invaluable. And besides, what if they're *not* already dead? They're obviously secure and their light source wasn't flickering. Wherever they are, they have some source of power."

"Not possible. The military scans all the time. If they found an operational power source, it wouldn't be operational for long. They don't like loose ends. Besides, even if they aren't lying about someone with immunity, who's to say Homeland doesn't already have someone like that? It's probably just a lie, something to sweeten their stance to get Homeland to get them out."

"Both are possible... considering where they are."

"Well, I don't have that little bit o'information, now do I?"

"I'll trust you when I know we're in this together, if not in the same goal at least in the same direction."

Heath went to the door, slid a key in the knob and opened it. "You can't trust me, I can't trust you. See ya'." He went to the television and pulled out the DVD. "I'm keeping this. Call it a little insurance policy in case I get any late night visitors. Your fingerprints are all over this as much as mine."

Josephine stood slack-jawed for a moment before she was able to move towards the door. She stopped a few paces from it and looked up at him.

"You're really going to let them die, huh? You're going to let *her* die?"

"I don't even know it's her."

"Does it really matter if it's not?" Josephine asked. "Would it be so bad to save *anyone* from that place?"

"I'm not a Boy Scout, Ms. Terrell, and the money end's no good if you're not alive to spend it."

"Is that what you're doing now? Living? You say you're not a grave robber, but you own half this place."

"Who told you that?"

"The city of Pittsburgh did. Real estate transactions and liquor licenses are matters of public record, once you know the right city to place the name to. Journalist, remember?"

"What of it?"

"You sit in here with a bunch of grave robbers but you say you aren't one. Do you go anywhere? Do anything? Anything at all?" She stepped into him and craned her neck to lock her eyes with his. "You don't. I know you don't. You have an apartment upstairs, right? I'll bet you it's just a little SRO job, isn't it? Hotplate, maybe a little TV with a lot of dust on it, real lone wolf-type shit, huh? You never left Area 187. You're still there, aren't you? I bet you look for her over and over again, every time you close your eyes."

Heath stared at her for a moment until the smile slid back on his face, this one more dangerous than sarcastic. "You think you can guilt me into this? You think your psycho-babble will reach into my soul and give it a little tweak? You could at least work up a tear or two for this little drama. You ain't the first to come to me with a load of horseshit. Been no less than a dozen people wanting me to go back to find this relative or that wife or this son 'cause they just *know* they're still alive. A dream they had or some ten dollar psychic told them that Uncle Bud was still alive and just waiting for someone to come save him from the zombies. At least those people had some real emotional investment in it."

"You're playing with their lives."

"You're playing with *my* life."

"You don't *have* a life," she said matter-of-factly. "Your life is still in there, and no amount of macho bluster bullshit you pump out is going to change that." She stepped back from him then and regarded him coolly. "If that thirty percent chance turns into one hundred I'll be sure to give her your regards. I'll leave it up to you to explain why you couldn't be bothered to give them in person." Heath took in the set of her jaw and bright, defiant eyes. She held out her hand and nodded at his belt. "I'm going to need that, with or without you."

John pulled the gun out and held it up for inspection. "You know how to use this thing?"

"My grandfather taught me. He gave it to me when I went away to college. Nothing says 'no' like a .357."

"Smart man. Too bad his granddaughter didn't pick up some of those smarts." He handed over her weapon and swung the door open for her. "I'll think about it." Josephine hid her smile as she took the gun and slid it back in her coat pocket.

"I'm staying at the Radisson out by the airport. You're not my last stop. Don't think too long."

"And you should think longer. You mention this to anyone else - *anyone* else - and not only am I no longer thinking about it, I'm sending this off to Homeland," he said, holding up the disc. "From this moment on, anyone else you tell becomes a liability and a body. The feds are real particular about the Area and they wouldn't think twice about bringing you and anybody else that knows about this in for questioning. There are a lot of grave robbers out there that could use you as a get-out-of-jail-free card." He opened the door wider. "Goodbye, Ms. Terrell." Josephine glared at him for a moment before charging out the door, her footfalls like thunder in the silence of the bar. John swung the door shut, locked it and stared at the shiny disc in his hand. He turned to the television, slid the disc in and turned it on.

Josephine's eyes fluttered open, the smell of fresh coffee rousing her from sleep. She smiled for a moment before she remembered that she'd been alone in the hotel room. She fought her instincts to rip the blankets off and jump into the dark and obviously occupied room and instead slid her hand under her pillow. "You shouldn't keep it there," a voice said from the darkness. It took a few moments for her to place it. She sat up slowly and flicked on the lamp. Heath sat at the room's desk, and her gun was lying on its dark cherry top beside a large cup of strong-smelling coffee.

"How the hell did you get in here?" she asked.

"Me and Criss Angel are like this," he said, holding up two crossed fingers. Josephine looked at the clock beside the bed.

"Where did you find Starbucks at four in the morning?"

"I hear they're opening one in the Area next month. Maybe shitty coffee will take care of them for us," he said, raising a large non-descript Styrofoam cup that had obviously come from a gas station. "Enjoy it while you can." Josephine reached out and took the cup. It was still hot enough to enjoy but lacked the normal scalding properties.

"Do you often break into hotel rooms to deliver coffee?"

"I don't make a habit of it."

She sipped her drink then made a face. "Nothing in it, huh?"

"There's coffee in it."

She shook her head and smiled despite herself. "I don't do booty calls."

"I'm in. I need to know where we're going. Now." Josephine sighed, plucked her jeans from the floor and struggled into them under the blankets.

"Modesty's a trait best left back in the world. We're going to be in very close confines for the next few weeks."

"Well we're not there yet, are we?" she said as she pulled the blankets away and stood to button her pants. "And as far as giving you that much information, well call me an untrusting bitch but I can't do that yet."

"You're an untrusting bitch, but that doesn't change the fact that I need to know."

She snatched a fresh t-shirt and a bra from an open bag and walked to the bathroom to change from her nightshirt. "The North Gate is closest," she called through the open bathroom door as she slipped into her clothes.

"Two things. First, closest isn't always best. We're not trying to get choice parking here. Second, nice tits."

Josephine stopped at that and looked through the bathroom door at the full-length mirror placed just outside it to see him smirking from his seat across the room. She stomped back and sat down on the edge of the bed.

"Very funny."

"It's my curse to be naturally witty and charming. We leave in three days."

"Three days? Why are we waiting?" Josephine asked.

"We won't be *waiting*, we'll be *working*. You're not ready. You won't be ready in three days, but that's the minimum mission prep we can afford. You've got a hell of a lot to learn in a very short time. I hope for both our sakes you're a quick study."

"'Mission'?" she asked.

"I'll make this simple. I don't want to fuck you and I don't want to be your friend. We do this as professionals; establish the goal, formulate the plan and carry it out with Russian efficiency. No personal bullshit, no baggage - from either of us. We focus on the mission and nothing else."

Josephine took a drink then set her cup on the nightstand. "And if I refuse to tell you before we get inside?" she asked.

Heath picked up her gun and held its barrel to the ceiling.

He pulled a long, silver cylinder from his coat and screwed it into the barrel.

"This barrel wasn't milled for this, but it'll work for a round or two. You're a liability to me if you go and a liability if you don't. You made the offer, I've accepted. If we're not in this together, *we're* not in this. That's a very dangerous situation for me. If we go inside, you can very likely get me killed without even trying. If you go in there without me and Homeland found out I knew they'll have reason to haul me in. If that happens I'm as good as dead. I was in this the minute I watched the damn thing. I'd have better chances killing you than I would if you go there without me and get caught. Going in there with you is higher on my preference scale... slightly higher."

"So I tell you where they are and go in there with you, or you're going to shoot me. Is that it?"

"No, I'll *kill* you. I can shoot you without killing you. For a word jockey you're not very precise, are you?" Heath asked. Josephine looked into his eyes. They were as hard and cold as they'd been at the bar. She picked up her coffee and briefly entertained the notion of throwing it in his face to scald him while she screamed for help.

"What if I tell you I changed my mind; that I don't want to go? What if I gave you their location? What happens then?"

"The same thing, just you'd say something different before you died. You'd know I was going, that would still make you a liability. Besides, we know you're just blowing smoke. You want to go in there just as much as I don't, so why don't we drop the dramatics? You wouldn't pass up this story for love or money. Get your things. You can tell me where they are on the way."

"On the way to where?"

"To the bat cave, of course," he said as he removed the silencer and pocketed both it and the gun. "Hurry up. We have to make a stop first."

Josephine stood and extended her hand. "This is getting to be a habit," she said, her fingers wiggling expectantly.

"You'll get it back when I'm reasonably certain you won't shoot me in the back or yourself in the foot. Until then, it's safer where it is." He stood and came out from behind the desk, grabbing her long duffel-style bag as he headed for the door. "We'll take your car."

"How do you know I even have a car?" she asked his back as he went to the door.

"Tight jeans. I can see your keys bulging in your pants pocket. Most people that fly put their keys in a checked bag, one less thing to deal with at security," he said without looking back.

Josephine stood mute for a moment, her hand going unconsciously to her pocket before grabbing her two remaining bags and hurrying to catch up with him.

Heath directed her through the city in a dizzying array of left and right turns to the point she wasn't sure they were even still in Pittsburgh. Finally he had her pull up to a corner. "Come on," Heath said as he got out of the car. She didn't realize where Heath's convoluted tour of the city had taken them until she followed him through Wally's door.

"What are we doing here?" Josephine asked. Heath didn't reply as they stepped inside the diner. Josephine looked out of habit towards the table where Bub and his friends always sat and was surprised to find them there at that hour. Heath strode across the scuffed linoleum towards them. "What the hell?" Josephine mumbled.

Bub and company looked up as Heath came near, hands moving into their coats as their asses left their seats. Heath suddenly took a long step forward and dropped his shoulder into Bub's chest as the man tried to get to his feet. The force of the blow lifted Bub off the floor and into the man to his left, dropping them both to the ground in a mix of flailing arms and legs. Heath grabbed the edge of their abandoned table and spun in a half-circle. The heavy, solid wood tabletop went from horizontal to vertical in the blink of an eye to slam into the last man's chest. He went down hard, his pistol flying from his hand. Josephine ducked reflexively as the pistol spun past her head to clatter against the far wall of the diner. By the time she looked up again Heath had separated Bub from his friend.

"This isn't your fight," Heath said to the unknown man. The robber drew back his fist and opened his bloodied mouth in soundless rage, not knowing it would be his last act. Heath brought his right arm around, the meat of his palm slamming into the base of his skull while his fingers wrapped around the back of the man's head. The blow went from strike to shove in that moment as Heath continued the motion, driving his head into the counter. Heath stood for a moment, staring at Bub as the grave robber got to his feet.

"You broke the code," Heath said to Bub.

"You're not a robber, you stupid fuck. The code doesn't apply to you," Bub said. Without taking his eyes off Bub, Heath suddenly whipped his victim's head up off the counter. The sick, wet snapping sound from his neck evoked a sick, wet choking sound from Josephine's throat. She swallowed her bile and leaned against the doorframe for support, her head turning away from the slack body as it slid to the floor.

"No, I'm a digger, remember?" Heath said. Bub's hand shot under his coat but not fast enough to draw his blade before Heath was on him, his large hand wrapping over Bub's smaller one. Bub struggled against Heath's iron grip, but it was no use. Heath guided Bub's handful of sharpened steel until the needle-sharp tip of the blade brought a dribble of blood rolling down its length from the soft flesh between his jaw and Adam's apple.

"Heath...stop..." Josephine said from the door.

"Stop?" Heath repeated without looking at her. Bub's eyes were wide and his breathing shallow. He wanted to cough, to swallow the blood from his dislodged tooth suffered in Heath's first attack but feared any motion of his head or throat would impale him on his own blade, held in his own hand. "This piece of shit here is a card-carrying, bona fide real-life mother-fucking grave robber. That means he lives by a code. Part of that code is that you don't sell out. Right, Bub?" Blood and spittle gurgled in Bub's throat as he fought the need to swallow, even to breathe. "Well, you know what they say...live by the code..." Bub's eyes went wide as he felt Heath's muscles tense. He opened his mouth to scream, inadvertently giving Heath a perfect view of the blade as it slid up into his mouth, piercing the soft pallet and sinking another six inches into the bottom of his brainpan. No scream came from his ruined mouth as Heath released the hilt of Bub's blade to let his body fall to the floor.

"Heath...the police...we're going to get arrested. We have to get out of here - now!" she said, her voice bordering on hysteria.

"Not just yet; one more thing to clean up." Heath walked past her to the man groaning on the floor beneath the upturned table.

"No! He didn't tell me anything! Let's get the hell out of here!" Josephine said.

"Guilt by association. That's how Homeland does it, you know," Heath said. He kicked the table off the prone man and hauled him to his feet by his throat. The grave robber was as limp as a rag doll, the blood from his shattered nose rolling down his face and onto Heath's hand at his throat, mixing with Bub's own crimson stains. "If you're going to play in the Area, you need to know the rules. You cast your lot with someone and your fates are tied together for the duration. These two could've stopped your friend Bub. They knew the rules. They didn't stop him. They share his fate."

"He didn't do anything. Put him down and let's get the hell out of here," Josephine said softly. Before she could blink Heath brought his free hand up, driving the heel of his palm into the helpless man's nose. The cartilage broke cleanly, the force of the strike sinking it deep into the robber's frontal lobe. Josephine gasped and took a step back from him, her eyes wider than even Bub's had been at the moment of his death.

Heath let the last body join the other two on the floor. "Sorry for the mess, Wally," he called out towards the kitchen. He produced a tightly-rolled bundle of cash from his coat, tossed it towards the counter then walked past her and out the door. Josephine stood trembling in the doorway a moment more before her senses returned, and those senses told her that a room with three freshly-murdered grave robbers was the last place she wanted to be found.

Chapter II
Jasper's House

He directed her around the city, through the airport sprawl and out into the Pennsylvania countryside. They didn't speak save for the repeating of the GPS coordinates she'd promised. He hadn't written them down and instead used their drive time to memorize them, repeating them over and over until the car reverberated with them. Josephine concentrated on driving, letting the complicated, poorly-maintained two-lanes they were driving occupy her thoughts. Anything was better than remembering Bub's sightless eyes as his blade sank into his head or the sound Heath's first victim's neck made snapping under his hand. They drove like that for more than an hour with her rearview mirror adjusted for his eyes and not hers, his directions crossing them back and forth across the deep-rural lanes before finally pulling off onto a steep dirt track winding down a long hill to end at a large, rough-looking barn with an equally rough-looking farmhouse tucked behind it. Heath got out, opened the barn door and waved the car inside it.

"Funny, this looks nothing like the Bat Cave," Josephine said as she got out and took her bags from the back seat. She knew from various experts and even the few grave robbers foolish enough to talk to her that many of them had rather elaborate hide-outs concealed in and around the city. Abandoned warehouses, run-down homes in the worst parts of town and, of course, dilapidated farms topped the A-list of clandestine real estate. Heath picked up her duffel and nodded at the wall behind her.

"See that pitchfork?" he asked.

She looked over her shoulder and could just make out the rusty implement in the gray light of dawn through the open barn door. "Yes. What about it?"

"It's a switch. Pull on it and the elevator will lower us into the lair." Josephine looked back and forth between Heath and the tool several times before she left her eyes on him.

"You're shitting me," she said. Heath shrugged and put a hand on the car's hood as if bracing himself. She looked back at the pitchfork and let her bags slide to the floor before walking over and placing a tentative hand on the smooth wooden handle. She tugged on it then stumbled back against the car, the lack of expected resistance throwing her off balance. She stood and waited for a moment, the pitchfork still in her hand, praying that the ground would either start its gentle descent or simply open and swallow her before she had to look at the bastard again. After a moment he walked around the car and stopped beside her. Josephine refused to look at him. If she did and he was smiling she knew where she would put the pitchfork. "You think you're really funny, don't you?" she asked, her eyes fixed on the ground.

"No. I think you're romanticizing," he said. She turned her head as if slapped and locked eyes with him. He wore a grim expression, not the smirk she'd expected to see.

"Romanticizing?" she repeated indignantly. "You are so fucking full of yourself."

"Maybe so. But you need to get it through your head before we go any further - there are no heroes, super or otherwise. There's no rocket boots, no amazing powers and no secret underground lair filled with fantastic weaponry and a tidy butler. You ain't Lois and I'm sure as hell not Clark. We're strolling into a landscape where a sprained ankle or an infected cut can kill you just as easily as a swarm of those pus bags can. The only thing that'll kill you faster is trying to be a hero. You understand all that?"

Her stare turned to a glare as she tossed the pitchfork against the wall. "Yeah, I understand."

"Then say it."

"What?" she asked.

"Say it; *there are no heroes.*" His voice had turned to ice across her nerves and her hands trembled slightly from a mixture of fear and something else...something that could easily become hate. He waited a moment then stepped near enough to her that she could smell the grave robbers' blood on his hands and feel his breath on her cheek, his whispered voice raging through her ears. "Say it."

"There are no heroes," she said softly, her tone seething with each word, "but there's no shortage of assholes, either." He smiled at that, the act completely devoid of any semblance of humor.

"Love me, hate me - doesn't matter. You keep me alive and I'll keep you alive. And if we make it back from this kamikaze bullshit I won't even expect so much as a Christmas card." He extended his hand towards the door, ushering her out of the barn with a wave.

"Santa is like heroes, Heath," Josephine said as he closed the barn door. "He doesn't exist either."

They walked around the side of the barn and up a narrow track of packed, foot-worn dirt to the bottom of the porch steps. "This is Jasper's place. He's a friend of mine, someone we can trust. Probably the closest thing to a hero we'll come across," Heath said.

"You mean he won't threaten to kill me?" Josephine asked, her tone cold. "Or maybe he's only killed two people before breakfast, not three?"

"I didn't say that. Jasper's not above killing those that need it, but if he *does* threaten you he'll probably be a lot more polite about it."

"So what exactly are we doing here? Aren't we putting your friend in jeopardy?"

"Jasper? He's no stranger to jeopardy. In fact, I think he'd be offended if we didn't come here."

"Is he going with us?"

"No, Jasper's retired. But if I had to take someone in there with me, if I had the choice that is, he'd be the only one I'd consider. He's got the best maps of the whole Area, most of them he made himself. Besides, we don't have time to gather the proper equipment and supplies without attracting a lot of suspicion. He'll have everything we'll need." They reached the house, went up the creaking steps and crossed the wide porch. They stood there for several moments, staring at the weather beaten door without knocking or speaking.

"Aren't you going to knock?" she asked.

"Salesmen knock. He knew we were coming and knows we're here. Patience, Ms. Terrell, is a virtue. Inside, it's an absolute necessity. The dead run on their own clocks and they have all the time in the world. You need to get on their schedule 'cause they sure as hell aren't going to get on yours." They waited the better part of three more minutes before the door silently opened. An old man, as old as her grandfather would've been today, stood in the doorway. Several wisps of unkempt silver hair stuck out of his liver-spotted scalp over a pair of brown, dull eyes. He was perhaps as tall as she and seemed solidly built under his work-softened jeans and worn flannel shirt. He gave a cursory nod to Heath then took a long, unnerving stare across Josephine.

"Well, come on in then," the old man finally said, a smile brightening his face. "I got breakfast on." He stuck out his hand and took one of Josephine's bags then shook her empty hand with his. "Jasper Conley."

"Josephine Terrell," she responded, shaking his hand. His skin was rough, calloused, and dotted with age but his grip was what she would've expected of a far younger man.

"Shoot, I know who you are Ms. Terrell. I ain't so far out in the sticks that I don't get the news. Now come on in and make yourselves at home."

Josephine smiled as Heath ushered her inside. Jasper's accent was the same as her grandfather's had been, the same she'd worked through three different voice coaches to rid herself of; West Virginia born and bred. It was the first comforting thing she'd heard since coming to Pennsylvania.

Jasper led them down a long hallway into the large, practical kitchen. Josephine felt like she'd stepped into a time machine. Though it was physically different from her grandparent's home it *felt* nearly identical, right down to the lithograph of an old man praying over his loaf hanging on the wall above the table. The smells of coffee, bacon and eggs filled the air as he waved for them to sit while he tended the stove.

"Hope all this trouble isn't for us," Heath said to the old man's back as he worked a huge iron skillet.

"No trouble, John," Jasper said over his shoulder. "My grandma would come on up outta' her plot if she knew I wasn't showing proper manners to guests." Josephine caught Heath smiling at that, though he put the expression away when he realized she was watching him. Jasper turned and came to the table to dump a skillet-full of bacon onto a serving plate. "'Sides, I don't get much in the way of company these days." He put the skillet back on the stove and took a towel-covered plate out of the oven.

"Biscuits, Jasper?" Heath asked.

"My grandma's own honey biscuits," Jasper beamed. He set them beside another serving plate filled with scrambled eggs as Josephine got up and took the old percolator from the stove. Jasper looked down at the bloody runnels on Heath's hands and frowned. "Now I just *know* you don't intend to sit at *my* table like that." There was a smile on his face that wasn't repeated in his eyes. Heath shrugged, sighed then went to the sink to wash the robbers' blood from his hands. Josephine almost smirked at the men's exchange, so like how her grandfather would have treated her had she come to the table with creek mud on her elbows and brambles in her hair. She poured the steaming coffee for each then took her seat while Jasper sat opposite her. "Thank ya' dear," Jasper said to her with a nod. Josephine picked up her cup, the light smell of chicory furthering her nostalgia.

"We're supposed to be getting ready to go in there, Jasper. A spread like this may make us reconsider," Heath said as he sat back down, his clean hands contrasting the dark pink stains on his cuffs. Josephine averted her eyes, more than happy to leave them on the country breakfast spread before her instead.

"You know I don't take to that way of thinkin', John," Jasper said around a mouthful of eggs. He turned to Josephine and wagged his fork at her. "See, lot of these pups, they get too worked up 'bout what's inside and what's *not* inside. They get all moody and quiet, tryin' to be like 'em. I say you need to remember why you wanna' come back, so before you go you need to do whatever the hell it is that makes you happy."

"I couldn't agree more," Josephine said. She smiled at Jasper, the perfect counterpoint to Heath's frown. Heath put a few pieces of bacon and a spoonful of eggs onto his plate along with two of Jasper's grandma's biscuits and still managed to frown while he ate. "So how do you two know each other?" she asked Jasper, elated she had someone to talk to that wasn't Heath.

"Oh, we go back a few years," Jasper said. She gave Heath a quick look and found he was chewing quickly, likely in preparation to stop the old man's talk.

"She doesn't need to know all that, Jasper."

"You know somethin', boy?" Jasper said, his fork wagging in Heath's direction now, "you gonna' have to learn to trust a few people now and again. Ya just gonna' eat yourself up inside if you don't. It'll turn you into one a' those dried up diggers that sit around that bar of yours if you ain't careful. That's okay though. It'll be nice to work with a clean slate, an' such a pretty one to boot," Jasper said with a wink towards Josephine.

"I don't follow you," Josephine said, confused.

"See, while Johnny here goes over all my maps and charts and does all his other little preparations and invocations, I'm going to give you some education." Jasper went back to finishing his bacon and digging into his eggs.

"Education?" Josephine asked, her food forgotten.

"You've never been inside," Heath said as he finished his meal. "There's a lot that needs to be done and there's even more you need to know. Jasper has been kind enough to volunteer his services as your personal tutor of all things Area 187."

"My tutor?"

"Now, don't take offense Ms. Terrell. I'm sure you're just as smart as a whip, but Johnny's right. It's a bit different in there, and being that you've never been there's a lot of little things you'll need to know. Except for Johnny here, I'm likely the best one to tell you about it."

"Off the record," Heath said pointedly, "Jasper was one of the first grave robbers... and still the best."

"A grave robber?" she asked. The man had to be edging seventy.

"Retired now," Jasper said, "did my last run just a couple months ago. And I don't know if I was the *best* of 'em but I always came back, and never empty-handed. That's more than I can say for a lot of 'em."

Heath got up from the table and took his plate to the sink. "I need to get started." Heath turned on his heel and left the room.

"So how *did* you meet Mr. Sunshine?" Josephine asked after Heath was gone.

"John and I happened to pick the same little building in the same little town one night. After some gun-barrel negotiations we figured it was big enough for the both of us. We discovered we was heading the same way when the sun came up so we traveled together for a few days. I found what I came for and told him to look me up if he ever came back to the world."

"What were you looking for?"

"There's ones out there that'll go in after anything if you pay 'em enough. A lot of those eventually burn out or get real greedy and sloppy. If the Area don't get 'em they end up getting tapped going in or coming out. Then there's a lot of us that specialized. Some got a reputation for getting things out of really secure places... museums, banks, that sort of thing. Me? I never took those jobs. Too dangerous, and the people that sent you in there like as not would have a bullet waiting for you when you came out. I went after the important things. Photo albums, family heirlooms, shoot, I once went in there to get a teddy bear."

"A teddy bear?" she asked, a smile breaking across her face.

"Yup, little brown one, missing one eye. Answered to the name 'Mr. Winky'," Jasper said with one eye closed by way of example. "A couple with a little tot sent me after it. They'd managed to get out of Charleston all right but Mr. Winky got left behind. That little one a' theirs just wouldn't sleep at night, cryin' for her bear.

Not even the psychologists could make her stop. Found ole' Winky right there in their old driveway. He wasn't in the best of shape after layin' out there for better than two years o' course, but you should a seen her face when I brought that crusty little bear back to her."

"People *paid* you to go after stuff like that?"

"Yup, almost every time."

"Almost?" she repeated. "Somebody stiffed you on your fee?"

Jasper sighed softly. "You got to know what's important enough to you to make you want to go in there. Some, it's money. Some idiots do it 'cause they want the adventure, got a nephew like that, all that extreme sport crap. Most of those don't last too long. Tell everybody else whatever the hell you want, but you can't lie to yourself on why you're goin' in there. Now, John tells me there's some good people that don't need to be there, and one of 'em could be Eileen. Not to mention the one that got bit and didn't turn. He *knows* why he's goin' back there. Why are you insistin' on it?"

"I want to help those people, and if they didn't make up having someone that's immune it could help a lot of others. If I can get their story..."

"Their story? Or *your* story? Let's suppose you weren't a big TV reporter. Let's suppose you were a doctor, or a secretary. Would you still be goin' in there?" He held up a hand when she opened her mouth to speak. "Now don't answer me. I don't need to know why; it's enough for me to know you're goin'. But before you get on the other side, you need to answer that question for yourself." Jasper stood up and stretched again then cleared away their dishes while Josephine sat staring into her cup.

"Why were you a grave robber? What was your reason?" Josephine asked as Jasper scraped her unfinished breakfast into a large, well-gnawed dog bowl on the counter.

"I never really thought of it as robbin' graves, Jo. You don't take nothin' from a graveyard. Last thing you need's one a them ghosts coming with it."

"My granddad used to say the same thing. I wouldn't have thought you to be the superstitious sort though, Jasper."

"Funny thing about superstitions...they had to start somewhere, and inside each one you usually find at least a little bit of truth." He walked back to the table, set the bowl down and pulled his work-stained coat off his chair-back. "I never took anything from the dead, Jo. What's theirs is theirs, and it ain't for me to take. People paid me to bring their memories back. Great grandma's wedding dress sittin' in a hope chest, old photo albums nobody ever got around to putting into a computer, that sort of thing."

"Seems like a noble reason. I wouldn't have thought there'd be much money in it though."

"Like I said, to some people there's more valuable things than money. There's a lot of young people, and not so young people that came out of those hills to seek their fortunes in the better states and big cities," Jasper said, the disdain obvious on his face, "but their family, their roots, those were still back in the hills an' hollers. Funny thing, growing up, growing old. You tend to find the things you ran from as a young 'un you run *to* when you're gettin' near the end. Lots of people with lots of money had their start in there, Josephine. And though you can't go home again, if you're lucky enough to find someone nuts enough you can bring a little bit of home back to you. Now come on. I'll bet Jake's hungry. We can walk and talk awhile."

"Your dog?" she asked as she stood and pulled her own coat around her.

"Ain't mine, near as I can tell. He just followed me out of the Area one trip and never left the farm after. Smart animal, that Jake." He waved her to the kitchen door in an after-you gesture, then followed her out into the brisk morning air.

By the time the sun went down, Josephine's face hurt from smiling and her brain hurt from overload. She'd spent the entire day with Jasper, going about the farm doing chores and with generous breaks of hot coffee in the cool spring air seated in hand-hewn rocking chairs on the porch. Jake had turned out to be a ¾ wolf/ German Shepherd mix. Josephine had naturally been fearful but Jake had warmed to her almost instantly, trotting about the farm at her heels. The day reminded her of days spent with her grandfather, though then it had been her blue-tick hound Baby trotting at her feet and grandpa's stories of family long past. Jasper's stories, while as colorful and full of hidden lessons as her grandfather's had been, were of much darker fare.

They made their way to the porch again as the last rays of the sun colored the western horizon. Josephine closed her eyes for a moment, reveling in the comfortable rocking and creaking. Even before the appearance of Heath and the rest of the "PBS Survivors," many had suspected there were more than a few people still trapped in Area 187. Aside from the obvious and seemingly one-time anomaly though, how could survivors continue on in that shattered landscape inhabited by insatiable, undying predators? Homeland used satellite imagery, aerial photos and even heat scans to show that *homo sapiens* simply didn't exist there. Naysayers were labeled as conspiracy theorists at best and kooks at worst, with Homeland and the military dismissing the first-hand accounts of the few real survivors that had made it out as little more than fantasies concocted for fame and personal gain.

Men like Jasper knew differently though. Grave robbers ran into survivors all the time, sometimes in groups though more often separately or in pairs. They took great pains to hide the fact they were only passing through, for many reasons. It was difficult enough to enter and leave the Area undetected. The more people involved, moving around, running and giving off heat signatures, the more likely they would become target practice for the continual "military exercises" that destroyed as much of the Area as the zombies and unchecked industrial works had done. Going in and out meant death if you were caught and most grave robbers had no intention of bringing back survivors that would end up splashed across the evening news leading to a very large, very lethal and highly-publicized crackdown on their profession. As an added bonus, the offending grave robber would often end up splashed across some dark alley.

Homeland claimed the dangers inherent in the Area made it an issue of national security from the beginning, and not just in controlling the spread of the virus. They warned Mr. and Mrs. America of terrorist plots to breach the Area, releasing the undead hordes to ravage the rest of the western hemisphere. They even claimed a victory by making a public spectacle of a small cell they claimed planned to bring a live reanimate out of the Area to create a "plague bomb" in Times Square on New Year's Eve. The deadliness and incurable nature of the virus gave them carte blanche to defend Area 187 by whatever means necessary, both inside and out. Josephine had always believed there were survivors still scavenging a life in the Area. Voicing those beliefs, though, was a different matter. She and Bill Hartman, her boss, were taking huge risks with this story. But if she and Heath managed to bring back even a few of them it would show that the PBS Survivors hadn't been a fluke. It would be the biggest story in a hundred years, blowing the lid off the government's conspiracy. The ensuing public outcry would virtually guarantee that Homeland would be forced to enter the Area well ahead of their comfortable decades-long schedule to rescue the rest and begin the reclamation.

Jasper had laced his nuggets of advice and gobs of information with a few of his own theories as well. He could easily agree that the government would have a huge black eye if the two of them managed to come back with survivors in tow so long after the Area had been declared devoid of human life, and in so doing reawaken America's outrage with its own government for giving up so easily on its own soil and its own people behind the wall. He also believed Homeland and the military were still looking for records, computers, equipment and anything else involved with the creation of the virus. While no one in the government or the military was foolish enough to think the stories they created about the virus being a "mistake" were believed, no one had been able to produce enough credible evidence to prove that the virus was not the by-product of their research but rather the end design. If tangible proof could be found and released to the public not only would all involved be completely discredited and ousted from public service, but the ban on lawsuits would be challenged and overturned on the basis that the government was well-aware of the Pandora's box they'd created and what it could do. The resulting wave of litigation would crush state and federal governments and would practically evaporate mega-insurance companies and many corporations overnight.

"So you still want to go in there?" Jasper asked as they watched the sun set over the far pasture.

"It's not a question of want. Your friend says he'll kill me if I don't."

"Oh, I don't think he'd do it. He's a better man than that."

"The man's threatened to kill me – twice - with my own gun! I watched him kill three men with his bare hands this morning!"

"I'm sure he had his reasons."

"What the hell reason could validate that?"

"John tells me you lost your grandparents," Jasper said, changing the subject. He waited for her nod then continued. "You know they're dead, right? You accept that they're gone. Probably took you a long time to accept that bad truth, didn't it? And I bet it hurt real bad then and still don't feel too good now, does it?"

"No."

"You weren't in the state when it all happened, were you?"

"No. I'd already graduated college and was working in New York."

"John was right smack in the Area, and right where his wife was last known to be. To top it off, he was a soldier, trained to go into bad places and get out all the good people. 'Cept he missed one... his own wife. Trained most of his life to go into those bad places after those good people, and when it came down to it he couldn't save the best person he knew. That affects a man, Jo, affects him all the way to the bone."

"So that gives him the right to be an ass to everybody he meets? He didn't have to stay in there."

"If you'd have been there when it happened, been close

enough to your grandparents when they made their stand, would you have left without knowing? Not guessing, not using your head, but *knowing* they weren't still alive in there?" Jasper asked. Josephine was quiet for long moments before she looked at Jasper, eyes rimmed with a tinge of red.

"No, I wouldn't have left them. Not without knowing." Jasper gave her a warm smile.

"Of course not. John didn't either, at least not till he searched everywhere he thought to look. For five years he survived in there, Jo'. He looked for her for *five years* and found nothin'. Then you come along with proof that she may still be in there, alive after all this time." Jasper took a slug of coffee and started rocking his chair. "I don't claim to know how he feels or what he's thinkin', but after seeing that I'll bet he's thinkin'; what if I'd have checked out one more building, one more hospital, went one more day," Jasper said, his voice trailing off. They fell quiet for long moments, enjoying the last of the sunlit breeze while the sky went from pink to red in the west. Heath had been gloriously absent the entire day and she'd made it a point not to discuss him until now. Getting Jasper's story had been a different matter though, and not just by virtue of her professional curiosity.

Jasper had been one of the original survivors of the first outbreaks, defending his farm until troops had come along and forcibly removed him. She saw in him everything she'd loved about her grandfather, and it helped in no small amount that he seemed the polar opposite of John Heath. "You know when you all was lookin' for John, right after he came out?" Jasper asked. Josephine stared at him for a moment and sipped her coffee.

"I remember. He dropped off the radar for several days after he came out of quarantine. Everybody was looking for him." She sipped again then leaned back into her chair's own gentle, creaking motion. "He was here, wasn't he?"

"Yup. Said the reporters was worse than a swarm. At least those he knew how to handle. If you two make it out, your own prospects can only look up. You'll have one heck of a story and maybe you can help some people besides. Maybe more than just the ones you're looking for if you get enough people worked up to make the government do somethin'."

"That's the idea. But it's not like Heath won't get anything out of this. If that's Eileen in there-"

"Yup," Jasper interrupted, "*if* that woman is Eileen, he'll be on top of the world and probably want to kiss your hand besides. But if she *ain't* Eileen," Jasper fell silent for a few moments and pulled his pipe from his coat. "He's a strong man, Jo, but every man has their limit. When you look down off that cliff, you got two choices; step back into the world or step off into nothing. He was already at that cliff and he decided to step back when he brought those others out. I ain't so sure that he'll step back again this time. He's already left a whole lot of himself in that place. If he doesn't find her this time..."

"You think if it's not Eileen he'll...do something...to himself?"

"I don't think nothin' of that sort. That wouldn't be his way. He's agreed to get you in there and back again, and he tends to stick to what he says. But if she ain't her, what's left of his soul is gonna' stay behind." He struck a kitchen match off his thumb and touched the flame to his bowl. It wasn't the same tobacco her grandfather had used, but it was close. Josephine shivered though the air didn't warrant it. Just because sociopaths were sick didn't excuse the violence they caused.

"Jasper, you didn't see him this morning. When he killed those three, I was there, Jasper. He *enjoyed* it."

"Jo', I gotta' tell you, if Bub would've rolled on me I'd like as not done the same. I might not have done it so public, mind you, but the code's the code."

"Yeah, but I bet you wouldn't have been smiling when you did it, quipping like some action movie gorilla." She suddenly wanted a cigarette to go with the coffee though it'd been more than four years since she'd craved one.

"Now Jo..." Jasper began as the front door swung open. Heath walked out onto the porch, a mug of coffee in one hand and a small device in the other. He leaned against the porch rail near them, his attention on the softly glowing screen in his palm.

"You say this thing's good for ten seconds before they triangulate you?" Heath asked Jasper without looking up from the GPS device.

"Yup," Jasper said, his eyes still on Josephine. "Don't know how it works, just know it does. Got it from a friend of a friend down Quantico way. If you're within a half mile of a tower you only got about five seconds if it's live." Heath nodded absently. It was a common practice for Homeland to power up cell towers at random or in areas they suspected survivors to be hiding. If anyone powered up a cell phone or other wireless device they could often get a "ping" on the location when the device logged on. He turned it off and slid it into his pocket.

"You learn anything today?" Heath asked Josephine.

"Yes, I think so. It's just really hard to comprehend how screwed up it all is, how everyone is willing to just let people linger and die in there."

"Pretty simple concepts to it all. It makes perfect sense from Homeland's point of view."

"It makes *sense*?" Josephine repeated, incredulously.

"If a zombie comes out, in whole or in part, the chances of another outbreak go through the roof. If a grave robber goes in there and gets infected and manages to make it out before he turns, the same thing happens. If terrorists get hold of a specimen then all kinds of things go wrong."

"That's bullshit. They could go through there and mop up."

"They could," Heath agreed, "but I'm sure Jasper's shared his theories. You would have a whole lot of soldiers exposing themselves to infection, and a whole lot of people that could find things they weren't supposed to find. Add to that, they tell us we're dealing with a virus. If the thing mutates you could have survivors coming out as carriers. The time to go through and wipe the whole place clean would have been in the beginning, but nobody in Washington wanted to sign off on it. So contain it and let a future administration deal with it. Makes perfect sense to me."

"You're the last person I'd have thought would have empathy for Homeland," she said.

"I didn't say I supported the logic, only that I recognize it. You're thinking with your heart again, Ms. Terrell," Heath said. "The plague spread too fast. By the time they figured out the containment plan they'd lost almost the whole state. By the time they put it into motion it had already spread into neighboring states. We're lucky we're all not shuffling down main street USA right now. For the record, no, I don't agree with their policies regarding survivors. There's a dozen ways to find people and get them out of there, but all those ways require Homeland to admit they've been lying. They're not about to do that, especially since most of the architects of the containment and the cover-up have long since left public office. No politician in there now is going to go down for the sins of the fathers. And none of it has anything to do with us. Now, did he teach you anything useful or did you two just talk politics all day?"

"It was a very enlightening day." Josephine pulled her knees up against her chest to ward off the coming chill of evening and wrapped both hands around her mug.

"Good. Tomorrow we're going to get a little more practical. I need to see what you can do before we get in there," Heath said.

"Practical?" she asked. Heath didn't answer her and instead looked to Jasper.

"Did you set everything up?" Heath asked him.

"Done and done, John. You've got the green light," Jasper said.

"Okay. I'll leave you the account numbers. Once we're inside you can transfer the money," Heath said.

"Money?" Josephine asked.

"One guy who knows what he's doing sneaking into the Area is one thing. You don't get *two* people into the Area and across the zone without crossing a few palms."

"What about coming out?" she asked.

"We're on our own," Heath said as an electronic chirping sound started up. Josephine pulled out her cell phone but Heath snatched it from her before she could flip it open. "Christ. Fucking amateur," he mumbled as he flipped the phone over and pulled off the battery.

"What the hell do you think you're doing?" Josephine asked as she shot up out of her chair.

"You have GPS on this thing? Have you made any calls since we got here?" Heath asked her.

"It has maps," she said, Heath's dark look to her even more grim in the failing light.

"Any calls?" he asked her again.

"No," she said.

"Good." He handed the phone and battery to Jasper. "Lock that thing up."

"You can't do that! I have to let my boss know--"

"No one knows anything from this point on. If Homeland gets even a hint that we're in there, especially to find survivors, they'll throw everything they can at us. If they do I guarantee you the first thing they'll do is pull bank and cell records to track where we went in. Now, are you sure you haven't used this for *anything* since we got here?"

"No, I haven't used it," she said. Heath stared at her a moment then turned and marched into the house. Josephine turned to Jasper. The old man hadn't moved from his seat and wasn't even looking at her. "Do you see what I mean? He's fucking *impossible*! This paranoid bullshit-"

"He's right, Jo. John and I might differ on philosophy, but you can't argue with facts. What you two are doin' ain't gonna' win you friends in high places, and if they finger you before you have smilin' survivors to put up for your cameras they'll use everything short of a mushroom cloud to make sure you stay in there. You need to remember Jo, it ain't paranoia if everyone really *is* out to get ya'."

The rest of the evening went by without incident. John had given her a few maps to go over with Jasper while he disappeared into the basement for the night. Jasper took her mile-by-mile along the routes Heath had traced, explaining his key and giving her first-hand accounts of the areas he'd been through. Josephine listened intently, jotting notes about specific areas to avoid.

The survivors had holed up in a practically unknown fallout

shelter designed for members of Congress to use in the event of a catastrophe. The pre-plague states were a perfect location for such emergency shelters, reachable by relatively short overland routes and comparatively instant air routes from D.C. Each new administration since the start of the Cold War had commissioned their own shelters, eventually creating a network of self-sufficient, underground complexes designed to keep several hundred people supplied for months, even years.

Homeland had tried to destroy the shelters early in the containment effort to try and keep survivors from going to ground. The newer shelters were designed to be operated either remotely or on-site in the event they were compromised or needed to be administrated from the outside. These computer-controlled clubhouses of the powerful were easy enough to either deactivate or secure against outside entry with a few keystrokes. Older sites had largely been ignored, mostly because closing them up required someone to physically go there and bar them. While these older sites held nowhere near the technology, equipment and capabilities of their newer cousins, any one of them would be Eden to an Area survivor lucky enough to stumble into one.

Jasper told her how he'd found such a site once. It was obvious survivors had found it and used it for a time, though by the time he came across it the place had been overrun. Like many of Jasper's stories, this led to other stories warning of the dangers of going underground; into basements, parking garages or the lower levels of buildings. These areas were darker than tombs and could easily be filled with dead that had wandered in and stayed, spending their un-lives bumping around in the dark waiting for prey to come to them. Still, he told her such places could also be treasure troves of supplies for the ill-prepared or needy grave robber as long as extreme care was used in searching them. Josephine filed the nugget of knowledge into her over-stuffed mental Area folder and continued watching his finger trace first their primary route, then both secondary routes Heath had marked on the maps until finally her eyes turned red and bleary and Jasper ordered her to bed.

The room he'd given her was decorated in typical farm

fashion and showed a definite lack of a woman's touch. Her bags sat on the bed, evidence that Heath had done more during the day than skulk about and plan their foray. She put the heavy duffel and suitcase on the floor, unzipped her flight bag and dug around for a moment, smiling when her fingers wrapped around her personal cell phone. Her days as a roving reporter had taught her to always have more than one way to communicate at hand, and while the network-provided phone Heath had taken from her was equipped with GPS she knew her own phone wasn't. She opened her door and scanned the hall, half expecting Heath to be standing there waiting for her. Satisfied she was alone she locked the door behind her, fell onto the bed and punched up her boss's number.

"Hello?" a groggy voice answered.

"Bill? It's Josephine, I can't talk long."

"It's after midnight..."

"I know, sorry. Just checking in, first chance I've had."

"Where the hell are you? You're not *inside* already, are you?" Bill asked, his voice much more lively now.

"Not yet. We're going in the day after tomorrow."

"Okay. Call me before you go."

"I don't know if I'll have the chance. Heath's a frickin' fanatic with his cloak and dagger bullshit. He's threatened to kill me twice already and confiscated my work phone."

"I wondered what was going on when I tried to call you earlier. Look, I'm having second thoughts about this. This is turning extremely dangerous for you, for me and for the network. Maybe we should kill the story."

"Don't you dare do this to me, Bill! This is the story of a lifetime. Besides, I'm in too deep now. If I try to back out I'm pretty sure you'll never find my body," she said as she kicked off her shoes. The line went silent for a few moments before Bill sighed softly.

"Okay, Josephine. God, I hope you know what you're doing. There's a hell of a lot riding on this, and you know if something goes wrong the network will throw us both under the bus," Bill said, tension evident in his tone.

"I know, Bill. It'll be okay, I promise. In a few weeks' time we'll be popping champagne corks and working on our Pulitzer acceptance speeches."

"I'll settle for both of us being alive by then."

"Goodnight, Bill. I'll check in with you again if I can. If not, it could be a long time before you hear from me. Don't worry about me, I'm a big girl. You just remind Julie that I'm only on a *temporary* assignment. I don't want her getting too comfy in my chair until I'm ready to leave it."

"Yeah, I'll tell her that," Bill said with a laugh. "Night, Jo." Josephine snapped the phone closed and shoved it back inside her bag before kicking it to the floor as well. She had to admit, it felt good to disobey Heath. She wasn't foolish enough to completely discount his warnings, but she wasn't paranoid enough to let them rule her the way they ruled him either. She undressed and slipped beneath the thick, hand-made quilt, letting her giddy school-girl joy at having gotten away with disobeying the teacher lull her to sleep.

Josephine woke at 3 a.m. out of habit. The life of a morning news program star made sleeping in past five nearly impossible. Taking Heath's warning about their day being physically active to heart, she opened her heavy duffel and put on a set of clothes she planned to wear on their suicide mission, all in basic black; broken-in, high-laced military jump boots, carefully-bloused BDU pants and a long-sleeved, ribbed cotton shirt. She pulled her long hair into a tight ponytail and spiraled a nylon cord around it to keep stray hairs from sneaking out. Her gun belt came next, the low-slung holster noticeably empty. Heath hadn't returned her gun yet. She checked her speed-loader pouches, then made sure each bullet loop on the wide leather belt grinned copper at her before slinging it around her waist and securing the leg tie at the base of the holster around her lower thigh. A long, heavy leather coat topped the ensemble, its pockets loaded with small sewing and first aid kits, extra ammunition and a collapsible steel police baton. Confident she was ready for anything Heath could throw at her she grabbed a few DVDs from Mason's Canadian show she'd promised Jasper he could watch, left her room and made her way to the kitchen.

She found the kitchen empty and scrounged around to put together a pot of coffee in the percolator on the stove. When she turned back to the table she jumped a bit at the sight of Jasper seated there and looking over the maps they'd covered the night before. She hadn't heard the man come in, even with the utter silence of the house and his heavy work boots. He looked up at her small gasp and smiled sheepishly.

"Sorry, Jo, didn't mean to scare you. I guess old habits die hard."

"You mean you really can't teach an old wolf new tricks?" she asked. Jasper smiled at that then sat back in his chair and looked at her, whistling his approval.

"Girl, count yourself lucky I ain't twenty years younger."

"Hey, count yourself lucky I'm not twenty years older," she said through a smile. "Are you always up this early?"

"Usually. Another one a' them old wolf habits I guess." He fingered through the stack of discs she'd left on the table for him and nodded at a few before setting them down again. "Now what would you like for breakfast before going off on your little adventure?"

"Oh no," Josephine said as she crossed the room to the refrigerator, "you've done so much already. The least I can do is make breakfast."

"Well, never let it be said I ever got between a woman and a stove." They smiled at each other while she busied herself with breakfast and he continued staring at the map. By the time she finished stirring the pancake batter Heath had joined Jasper at the table as silently as the old man had done.

"Did you take enough time out from your domestic duties to study the maps?" Heath asked her without looking away from the table. Josephine wondered how hard she would have to swing her spatula to break Heath's nose before she turned back to the stove to flip the hotcakes.

"Yeah. I even found the time to fill your pipe and fetch your slippers."

"Buck Owens... ain't never gonna' be another one like him," Jasper said. Both he and Josephine laughed at that. Heath just shook his head.

"Am I the only one that's taking this seriously?" Heath asked the room. Jasper and Josephine turned from their respective tasks and stared at him. "It's been better than two years for me, and you've never been. I'm willing to bet the worst predicament you've been in was a frat boy trying to spike your gutter beer at a kegger," Heath said, staring pointedly at Josephine.

"No, I've had worse than that. Like this one time, where this whacked-out Area digger threatened to kill me twice in less than 24 hours," Josephine said, then turned to hide her rapidly-heating face.

"He'd have done us both a favor. Better to die out here with a bullet in your guts than in there with them *eating* your guts."

"Well I for one ain't goin' in there, and I always appreciate a woman's touch in the kitchen," Jasper said, his voice both soothing to Josephine and a veiled warning to Heath. "You just leave her be, John. She ain't hurtin' nothin'."

Heath locked eyes with him for a moment before getting up from the table and walking out of the room. "Meet me out back when you two are done," Heath called out from the hall before disappearing through the cellar door. The disgust in his voice was clear. Josephine brought the pancakes to the table while Jasper took down plates for them. They sat together, though they didn't eat together, Jasper shoveling forkfuls into his mouth while Josephine merely stared at hers.

"Jake will likely appreciate eatin' so good two days in a row," Jasper said. Josephine looked up at him, her eyes wet with threatened tears.

"If I told you I'd changed my mind, that I didn't want to go, would you defend my choice?" Josephine asked. "I don't think I can do this. Not with him. I don't feel safe with him. It's like he's just waiting for the opportunity to dump me off, even kill me."

Jasper put down his fork and reached across the table to chap the back of her hand with his weathered palm.

"Jo, honey, don't you see what's happening to him?"

"To *him*?"

"Yeah, that's what I said. Can't you see he's scared, too?"

"Him? Scared? That's bullshit on a stick."

"No, no it ain't. He's not sure if he's up to this and he ain't sure he can handle what he finds in there. Now he's got to worry about you on top of it all. He talks a good game, but he ain't gonna' leave you in there to die and he ain't gonna kill you. All his life he's tried to save people, and he's scared he ain't up to it no more. Now you can believe that or not as you will, but it don't change the fact of it. And the last thing either of you need is tears. Maybe John's too hard on all this, and himself. Maybe I'm too soft on it now, a part of me knowin' I won't be goin' back there again. But you're that middle ground, and he's gonna need you as the anvil, and you're gonna need him as the hammer. You understand?"

Josephine stared at him for a moment then gave him a small, thin smile. "So, do you have *all* the answers?" she asked, pulling away from him to wipe her eyes with her napkin.

"Nope. And I'd never tell you I did. But I know what I know, and I got no defense for it." The smile in Jasper's eyes matched the one on his face, causing her smile to broaden and whiten. "Now finish up. I'm sure John's got a lot to do with you today."

They found Heath out in the back pasture, sitting on an old picnic table Jasper used as a rest for sighting his guns. Josephine paused for a moment and hitched her breath as she caught sight of several figures further downrange shrouded in that cold, clinging morning fog peculiar to western Pennsylvania. She quickly dropped to one knee and feigned retying her boot as an explanation for her pause. The last thing she wanted was for Heath to think a few of Jasper's wooden targets had spooked her. "So glad you could come," Heath said to them when they got to the table. Josephine looked down and found the table laden with all sorts of gear, including her magnum.

"I've been looking for that," she said, nodding at the gun but almost afraid to pick it up without Heath's say-so. She shook her head, throwing the thought away almost as soon as she'd processed it and picked up the gun. "Can I keep it this time?"

"If you're good, but the belt, coat and the hair have to go."

Josephine stared at him for a long, puzzled moment before she spoke. "What the hell are you talking about? I had this rig and holster custom-fitted. And what the hell's wrong with my coat and my hair?"

"Holster your weapon," Heath said. Josephine stared again but slowly complied. As soon as she had, Heath began moving towards her slowly, stumbling but with the obvious purpose of invading her space. He said nothing, only continued towards her. She took a step backwards but not before he got within arms' length of her. With Jasper looking on, Heath took up a handful of the long coat and started pulling her towards him while she struggled to move away. She panicked, pivoted and made to run. Her legs came out from under her as they tried to move forward but her coat kept her torso in place. She collapsed in a heap, Heath falling to the ground beside her. He kept his movements slow and deliberate, getting to his knees just as she scrambled to her feet. She tried to break away again but Heath's fingers had found the low-hip holster on her leg, bringing her to ground again. She screamed as he crawled up her torso, his hand gripping her ponytail, pinning her head to the ground. He stopped then, their noses almost touching, his eyes locked on hers.

"Zombies only have three things going for them; hands, teeth and stamina. If you let them use any one of them on you, you're as good as dead. Loose and long means handles, and I'd advise against screaming regardless of the situation. All that'll do is bring more while you've still got the first one hanging off you." He got up and extended his hand. She stared at it for a moment, her chest rising and falling heavily as the adrenaline finished its course through her before finally taking it and getting to her feet.

"You could have just said that," Josephine said, brushing off her coat and suppressing the chill that was creeping up her spine. Heath's expression had been utterly blank during his demonstration, completely devoid of life or meaning. For a moment, just a split second, some small part of her mind thought he was truly undead.

"I hear, and I forget. I see, and I remember. I do, and I understand," Heath said over his shoulder from his place back at the table. Josephine took her ponytail in hand and looked down at it like an old friend.

"Do I really have to cut it? Can't I just tuck it under my coat or something?"

Heath cut her off with a look and picked up a two-foot long tool that looked like a straightened crowbar. "This will be your best friend," Heath said as he handed the tool to her.

"What the hell is it?" Josephine asked as she hefted the octagonal black steel bar in front of her. The end of the tool was bent only slightly and shaped like a very large screwdriver. The back end had been fitted with a neoprene grip long enough to easily accommodate both her hands. The steel behind the grip had been milled into a sharp, clean point.

"Here in the world it's a hardened-steel pry bar. Mechanics use them to lever engines around. Inside, it's equal parts weapon, tool and all around good buddy. If we do this thing right, it'll be the only weapon you'll need." He reached down and picked up another from the table. This one was even duller in appearance than hers and showed signs of extreme use across its length. Heath hefted it for a moment, staring at it intently as he bounced it softly in his hand.

"Named mine Bonnie. Me and Bonnie, we were inseparable," Jasper said, smiling. Josephine mimicked Heath, the dull weight alien in her hand. She put it back on the table and reached into her coat.

"That thing's too heavy for me. I'll stick with mine," she said, flinging her hand to extend the sectioned steel baton for emphasis.

"Those police models are designed as non-deadly blunt force. They're hollow, too weak to trust. Carry it as a back-up if you want, never can be too careful I guess. This," he said, holding up his weapon, "is one single piece of solid steel. It doesn't break, it doesn't bend. It can open doors and makes a quick lock on a set of double doors." He put the tool down on the table then produced a ballistic nylon belt and holster rig from one of the duffels on the table. "Try this on."

Josephine removed her own custom belt and strapped the military rig around her waist, cinching it tightly. The holster was deep enough to accommodate her revolver with the silencer installed and rode very high on her hip, eliminating the need for a tie-down across her thigh. She screwed the silencer into the muzzle of her revolver and holstered it, the high position letting the weight of the heavy-framed weapon hang from her center instead of her leg. She could immediately see the value, especially if they were forced to run, but she wasn't about to let Heath know that. "Feels okay, I guess."

"I'm so glad," Heath said as he pulled two exceptionally short rifles from the bag. "The pistol will be your back-up weapon. With any luck, you'll never need to pull it. This will be your primary firearm." Heath handed one of the rifles to her. "You and your grandpa shoot rifles much?" Josephine examined the wood stock and short barrel a moment before walking up to the table and pulling a long, curved magazine from the bag. She slipped it into the port in front of the trigger, charged the weapon and pulled up downrange then tapped off three rounds at one of the man-shaped silhouettes some 20 yards away, letting the morning sun shine through two punctures through its head and one through its chest.

"Yeah, we shot a few times. They wouldn't let me in the turkey shoots anymore by the time I was a junior in high school."

"Two out of three ain't bad. Just remember if it's not in the head, it's not dead. At least we shouldn't need to drill on firearms, saves a lot of time."

"Damn fine shooting, Jo," Jasper said.

"Thanks, Jasper. It's nice to know I haven't lost my touch."

"Uh, if you two are done we have a lot of ground to cover," Heath said. "As far as clothes, you have a pretty decent handle on that. Pack only one extra set, along with two pair each of socks and underwear."

"You're going to tell me how much underwear to bring?"

"Everything you take not counting your weapons has to fit in one of these," he said, holding up a small rucksack. "We're not going into a desert. The evacuation happened so fast there's still plenty of businesses and private homes we can use to resupply if necessary, even now. It's not something I want to do, but travelling speed is our highest priority and I'd rather lose an hour every few days by stopping to resupply than I would lose six hours in that time because we're moving slower due to weight." Josephine cast a glance at Jasper and he gave her another of his slight nods.

The rest of the morning went much the same way. Where Jasper had used stories to convey his Area expertise, Heath simply told her what she would wear, what she would do, how she would move, even how she would breathe. Jasper had spoken of specific instances, using his individual experiences to impress his lessons. Heath tended towards more clinical explanations and pointedly avoided talking directly about his own experiences. Jasper stayed close, interjecting here and there when he felt he had something to add. Josephine knew he did so as much to teach her as he did to keep her mind from wandering from Heath's running, drill instructor-styled monologues.

By noon they were both dressed as they would be for the next few weeks. Her long leather coat sat in a heap on one of the porch rockers, replaced with a plain belt-length, thick-leathered black coat. A matching pair of leather chaps expertly cut to allow freedom of movement covered her fatigue pants, making her lower body as bite-proof as it could be while still allowing her to move. The smooth leather would also make it difficult for leathery hands as well as briars and brush to gain purchase. A pair of extremely thin neoprene gloves lined with cotton and interwoven with Kevlar material topped off the ensemble, providing warmth and wicking as well as bite and injury protection. Heath didn't use head protection. Anything that would properly protect the head couldn't help but cover the ears, and he wasn't willing to sacrifice his longest-ranging sense to the protection of the Kevlar hoods and caps favored by Homeland and the military.

"Do you feel like a real, live grave robber yet?" Jasper asked her.

"I feel like I'm wearing a whole cow."

"Eh, just the best parts of a few of 'em," Jasper said. Jake had joined them during the morning and now sat at Jasper's feet, the old man scratching absently at the dog's ears. Heath had moved them from the field to the barn and had left her and Jasper outside. "Feeling better about all this?"

"I don't know if *better* is the word I'd go with," she said.

"Well, he ain't threatened to kill you in awhile, that's got to count for something," Jasper said with no trace of humor in his voice. Josephine couldn't help but give him a tired smile as the loft door high above them opened.

"The object is to get into this building as quietly as possible. You have 30 seconds until you're spotted. If you make it inside, you'll need to barricade and search the area for threats. Once you're sure you've found and neutralized any threat on the ground floor, call out the word "clear" to end the exercise. And no guns. Understood?" Heath said from the open loft doorway.

"You're kidding, right?" Josephine called up. Heath didn't answer, only closed the door. She looked at Jasper, exasperated. "He *is* kidding, right?"

"'Fraid not, Jo. You better get to it." Jasper took several steps back and folded his arms. "I can't help you from here. You need to learn this. Trust me. Just...be careful, Jo." Jasper pulled out a stop watch and pressed the plunger. Josephine stared at Jasper for a moment before taking out her blunt weapon and moving to the large doors.

The double doors were secured by a thick padlock. She examined it for a moment, thought for another then slid the tapered end of the tool between the hasp and the old weathered wood. Old nails squeaked as she levered the heavy hasp away from the wood. She left the lock dangling from the other door and slipped between them into the cool dark of the barn.

"Easy enough," she mumbled to herself. She slipped a small LED flashlight from her pocket and found the stack of tools leaning just where Heath had used them to embarrass her the day before. She gripped the offending pitchfork and pulled it towards the door, causing several of the implements she'd dislodged during that lesson to clatter against each other on their way to the floor. She winced at the crashing metal then slid first the pitchfork handle then a garden hoe through the steel rings attached to the door, effectively barring it from the inside then put her back to the door to find her car wasn't there. Adrenaline poured into her muscles now. Heath was in here somewhere, ready to jump out to scare the piss out of her.

The barn was far from sealed against the weather. Chinks and cracks in the aging structure let light into the wide space at a far greater level than she would've thought. She dropped her stance and started along the wall opposite the implements, keeping it at her back as she moved towards the corner. A shuffling noise came to her just as she passed the corner and slid along the wall towards the back of the barn; feet dragging through loose bits of hay across the wood-plank floor. Heath was going all out for this one.

"Alright, you bastard - the gloves are off!" she said in a harsh whisper. If he was going to try to belittle and embarrass her again he had another thing coming. She gripped her weapon in both hands before her and took a few steps away from the wall. The shuffling grew louder as the shape of a man materialized out of the gloom from the opposite corner of the room. He moved slowly, feet dragging across the scrabble of hay and dust, a low and guttural moan wafting from his lips. "Heath, if I have to hit you, believe me, I'm *really* going to hit you." Still he kept coming, one arm stretched out before him, fingers opening and closing as if trying to reach for her from across the room.

Josephine held her ground, her weapon shaking in her grip despite her bravado. "Damn it Heath, this isn't funny. I'm gonna' brain you if you don't knock this shit off."

More shuffling sounds came to her from somewhere deeper in the shadows followed by the sound of what could only have been a coffee can filled with hoarded screws and bolts hitting the wood floor. She traded glances from the advancing threat and the sounds coming from deeper in. It had to be more than just Heath. She hoped if Jasper was in on this he'd back off before she was forced to swing at him in the dark. "Heath, stop. I see you and I hear Jasper back there. At least him I don't want to hurt." The figure ahead of her continued its slow advance, its moan louder now. "That's it! I fucking warned you!"

Josephine took several steps towards him, her weapon bouncing ahead of her, its weight now reassuring in her hands. She reared the club back over her right shoulder and held it there, giving Heath one last chance to stop. At that moment he passed in front of a slat of light streaming from a crack near the ceiling. His flesh was gray, dry and stretched across his face. His eyes weren't the blue she'd noticed at their first meeting. These eyes were green, or at least they had been. A thick miasma covered them, dulling their color. Deep maroon stains decorated his face and stained his cheeks around a mouth of blackened gums and chipped, sharp teeth. Josephine took a step back as a slight, cloying smell she could only liken to old road kill wafted towards her.

"Holy shit!" Josephine's reflexes took over, her weapon singing through the air before she realized her muscles had acted without her. She heard the crunch of bone and felt the force of the blow reverberate up her arms as the man stumbled to the side. He teetered for a moment before he fell in a crumpled, motionless heap on the dusty floor. Josephine screamed again then looked up at the loft. "Heath! You fucking bastard! What the fuck are you doing?" The last word had barely left her mouth before the thick, dusty air came alive with moans and shuffling. Josephine cast wildly about the room, every nerve on fire, every shadow a potential threat. She wanted to run for the door but her feet wouldn't cooperate. The shadows had indeed come alive around her. She managed to turn a slow circle, her mind finally channeling her adrenaline into more useful action and clearing of all thoughts save for the immediate danger and the steel in her hands.

"Heath," she called out, "after I kill every last one of these things, I'm going to kill *you*." Her voice was calm now, a surprise even to her. She'd already killed one, and they were slow. If she both kept and used her head she could get through this, if only for the pleasure of caving Heath's skull with his precious weapon of choice after. "High ground..." she mumbled. Her car would have made the perfect platform, most likely the reason it had been removed. A stack of wooden pallets about three feet high sat against the wall to her right, another of the dead shambling into the space between.

This time her feet responded. Jasper's voice was heavy in her head now. Move fast but don't run. Stay aware of the immediate area but stay focused enough to deal with the closest threat. And above all, keep moving until you have the position of advantage. She heeded the directives, letting her eyes focus on the dead woman moaning and reaching with ripped fingernails ahead while her ears cataloged the sounds of the others around her, giving her a mental picture of where they were coming from and where they were going. She swung at the female zombie without stopping, using her momentum to add even more power to her swing. What was likely a very attractive woman in life flew to the side from the force of her attack, the zombie's jaw snapping audibly as she hit the floor.

Josephine gauged the distance and leaped for the top of the stack of pallets, barking her shin but gaining the top without stopping. She tested her leg gingerly. The leather chaps kept her from cutting her leg open but they did little against bruising. Her mind raced as she tried to count the remaining creatures. There were two of them coming from what was likely an old tack room across the way. Another, likely the one she heard before she'd killed the first, had come out into the open and was moving slowly but surely across the floor towards her position. The woman she'd struck was already getting back on her feet. The blow Josephine had administered had struck far too low, ripping the dried flesh and muscle of her cheek to leave her jaw hanging down from the right side of her face without fracturing the skull. If her hands didn't get too close, Josephine could save her for last since she'd already inadvertently destroyed that zombie's most dangerous weapon.

There were four of them she could see. The female reached her position first, her floral-print dress ragged and stained with old blood and dirt. Her right eye had been torn from the socket, the ganglion crusted to her cheek. Josephine discounted her and her hanging jaw for the moment and focused on the next closest. He'd been short and obese in life, making him even slower in death as he forced his deteriorating muscles to shift his bulk from one foot to the other. Still he was relatively whole and much closer than the last two, both of which looked to be of average height and build. The female grabbed hold of the slats near Josephine's feet and pulled with single-minded strength, bringing Josephine completely out of strategy mode and into action as the pallet shifted and slid forward. Josephine crouched out of reflex and lashed out with her club, breaking the fingers first on the zombie's right then left hands. The zombie stumbled back a few paces and looked down at her mangled digits, seeming almost to comprehend the damage before continuing to paw mindlessly against the rough wood. Josephine brought her weapon up in both hands and let it fall, the heavy steel burying itself across the top of the female's skull. The born-in fissure gave way easily, gray matter squeezing up around Josephine's weapon like spring mud between a child's toes.

Josephine tugged her weapon free and turned to her left just as the fat zombie came near. He didn't bother with her perch as the female had done and instead went straight for her ankles. His pudgy fingers found the toe of her boot just as she realized the last two zombies were moving at her far more quickly than the others had. Fresh equals fast, Heath had told her. She tugged her boot away from the fat zombie and swung down at his balding pate with the same motion, but the sudden shift of her weight against the pallet caused it to move rapidly backwards to its position before the female had pulled it out of place. Josephine pitched forward as her precarious dais slammed against the barn wall, the jolt meshed with her toppling, carry her off the pallets to land face-first on the floor between the fat ghoul and the remaining pair.

Josephine scrambled to her feet, the taste of blood in her mouth where she'd bitten the inside of her cheek. She squawked in her pain and rage and spun on the rotund beast, sinking the back end of her weapon and its honed steel point into his eye. The eyeball popped and split like a hard-boiled egg as she plunged the weapon deep into the ocular socket, her thrust carrying it through his brain until more than three inches of the point protruded from the back of the zombie's shattered skull. He went instantly rigid then fell back against the stack of pallets, his bulk taking her weapon with him.

She looked over her shoulder at the last two. They were close now, so close she could smell their fetid stench. She reached down and tried to rip her weapon free of the fat zombie's skull but it was no use; she didn't have the strength to shift his massive bulk so his head would loll back and release its bind on her weapon. One of them moaned from behind her. Josephine spun and tried to step back but only managed to tangle her feet in the re-killed one's stubby legs. She crashed to the floor again, this time on her back. She screamed in frustration and fear and rolled away just as both of her attackers leaned down to snare her. Now it was the undeads' turn to be unbalanced. She got to her feet before the zombies could straighten themselves, slid her baton from her pocket, flicked it to its full length then brought it down in a windmill motion. The steel cracked the closest zombie's skull as easily as Heath's heavier, clumsier weapon had done to the female, sending it to the floor atop the fat one. The last stood completely and turned to her, his odd gait giving him pause as he tried to negotiate his feet around the bodies of his fellows to get to her.

Josephine used his pause to her advantage, putting another step between them. She raised the baton and brought it down with all the power her arm could muster. The zombie stumbled back a step, but that was all. The skin on his forehead had peeled from the force of the strike but his head was otherwise whole. He moaned and reached for her, arms scissoring closed on empty air as she backpedaled against the rough wall behind her. She held her baton up and found it had bent at a severe angle, enough that its striking power was all but lost. "Fuck..." she mumbled. She looked up to see the zombie nearly on her, his fingers close enough she could see the grit and dried blood under his cracked nails. Just then a soft, metallic whisper hissed through the air. The bullet entered the right side of the zombie's skull, its exit out the left side leaving a ragged hole several times the bullet's diameter to paint the nearby corner with dried viscera.

"Clear," Heath said. Jasper repeated the word from the loft above and came to the edge to look down at her.

Josephine stood silently for several moments, trembling, staring at the corpse at her feet. She turned her head to find Heath standing across the barn near the door, the silenced muzzle of his rifle trailing a wisp of smoke into the air. She turned her body square to his, her eyes filled to burning with hatred, fear and adrenaline so they shone slick and glossy in the scattered bits and streams of errant, dust-mote light. She looked down at the revolver at her hip, her mind only mildly shocked she'd forgotten it was there in the sudden onslaught of the dead. She drew it slowly and aimed it at Heath with her trembling hand.

"Jo! Don't do it, girl!" Jasper called down to her. "Put the gun down!"

"You're no better than he is!" she said, her voice verging on tears.

"I had to know you could keep your head," Heath said quietly. His voice was calm and even, the voice of a man that had looked down more than one barrel in his lifetime.

"You fuck!" Josephine screamed, the tears coming unbidden. She was shaking uncontrollably now, the revolver wobbling dangerously. "I could have been killed! Worse - one of those bastards could have bitten me!"

"Jo, we had to know you wouldn't freeze up, that you could handle yourself. It wouldn't have been the same if we'd told you. Heath and me, we had you under watch the whole time," Jasper said. Josephine swung her arm up to the loft, her sights shaking on Jasper's face.

"Damn you both!"

"Ms. Terrell-" Heath began.

"My name is *Josephine*! Do you get that? Josephine!" she screamed as she swung the gun back to Heath. "We're supposed to be in this together and you won't even call me by my name! You never intended for me to go with you. You were hoping these things would kill me, weren't you? Take a load off your conscience, right? Well, they didn't!"

"You're right. They didn't," Heath said. "I had to know you're willing to drop the hammer."

"Yeah, drop the hammer." Without realizing it her finger tightened on the trigger. "You know what? I learned something from this little attempt on my fucking life. I learned I *can* drop the hammer." The sound of the revolver's hammer falling on the empty cylinder rang like a thunderclap in the still, emotion-charged air. Jasper gasped as Josephine looked dumbly at her weapon. "You knew it wasn't loaded, didn't you?" she said, her face going blank. If the weapon had been loaded and at this close range, Heath would've been a dead man.

"Didn't you?" Heath asked. "Didn't you check your weapons before you came in here?" There was no superior smirk on his face. "Don't take anything for granted." He turned towards the door, removed the tools she'd placed and opened it. Daylight burst into the barn, illuminating the bloodless charnel house she'd made. "For what it's worth, you did well," he said, surveying the permanently dead bodies that littered the barn. "Get that temper under control, keep your mouth shut and we just may make it through this, *Josephine*."

Julie Sommers looked around Josephine's dressing room, a room much larger and far better appointed than her own. A room that by all rights should be hers, not given to a hick like Jo. She stopped to look at the diploma from West Virginia University Jo so proudly displayed on her wall above her beat-up loveseat. Looking around like a schoolgirl set to mischief she stepped up onto the cushions, fingered the dime-store frame with a giggle then put it just slightly askew.

What the hell did the network see in the flame-haired hillbilly? Julie had graduated with honors from UCLA, with not only her stunning good looks but her family's Beverly Hills money and sizeable political clout besides to launch her in her broadcast career. But it seemed no matter how blonde and perky she was or how many strings her father pulled, the best she could rate was weekend girl on the morning magazine show or, the most degrading, filling in for Jo when she took vacations or went on assignment. The only reason she'd been admitted to Jo's private sanctum today was to keep her out of the way while they repainted her own tiny hovel of a dressing room.

Julie sat down at Jo's make-up counter and examined the products. Off-the-rack mall brands winked back at her, the whole collection with barely the street value of the blush Julie wore to hang around the house. She sneered at the cosmetics then looked around the room at the piles of papers, files and books in haphazard stacks. Jo had only one intern beneath her, and even that one she only used minimally. Jo read all the books touted by her guests herself and did most of her own research. All Julie would need would be a few interns, the bullpen of writers and a teleprompter. They were a network, after all. That meant a division of duties between the beautiful people and the drones. It was the way broadcast worked. Jo had a few years on Julie, and soon the hillbilly flower's own barely-passable television looks would falter to the point the network wouldn't keep her on, leaving Julie to swoop in and take her rightful place. And if Julie kept screwing Hartman it could happen even sooner. She grimaced at the thought. They were supposed to meet tonight at the hotel, and Bill's perversions and lack of prowess made the task that much less enjoyable.

At least the show had gone well this morning, further proof she could do the job as well - and look better doing it – as Josephine. Julie turned to the mirror and checked her make-up and hair. Daddy was flying in for lunch with her this afternoon, and it wouldn't do for him to see his princess at less than her best.

"Shit!" she said suddenly as she spied her empty left earlobe in the mirror. The earrings were a birthday present her father had sent last month and likely cost more than Josephine's entire wardrobe. If she showed up without them today he'd be furious. She looked around the floor in a panic to no avail. She glanced at Josephine's crooked diploma on the wall then went to the battered loveseat beneath it and looked across its back and cushions; still nothing. She growled in frustration then flung one of the cushions to the floor. A glint of light winked at her from the thin layer of pocket flotsam and jetsam beneath the cushion.

"Yes!" she said, plucking the earring from the mass. That's when she saw the unmarked disc in its clear plastic case. She snatched it up and turned it over in her hands a few times, looking for labels or marks. "What do we have here?" Julie asked the unmarked disc, "And why are you hiding like that?" A dozen thoughts ran through her head. Why would Josephine hide a disc? Was it a story she was working on, or perhaps a little home-grown video of her and her favorite cousins? Julie smiled wide and slid the disc into her bag before practically running from the room. If there was a story she could steal or dirt she could dig up on sweet little Josephine, maybe she wouldn't have to fuck Bill tonight after all.

Josephine stared down into her coffee mug, the bright late afternoon sunlight on the porch and the warmth of the cup doing nothing to shake the chill from her bones. Jasper sat with her, his pipe smoldering in his teeth. Heath had disappeared after he'd left the barn and hadn't been seen since. "It's a bit of a shock the first time you see one comin' at you," Jasper said.

Josephine looked up at him, her expression blank. "I don't know if I want to talk to you right now," she said, the bitterness dripping from her tongue. "God damn it, I trusted you."

Jasper nodded at her slowly. He puffed on his pipe a few times then pulled it away from his mouth to look down into the bowl. "Jo, I wouldn't have let anything happen to you. But you had to prove to John, to yourself, that you could handle it. Hell, it was probably for the best you didn't even think about that magnum on your belt till the end. If you'd have drawn and tried to shoot one of 'em it may have sent you into a panic when it didn't go off. I've seen more than a few all full of bluster and hardware until they got up close and personal. I already knew you were strong, but it takes a different kind of strength to get by in there. I'll understand if you hate me now, guess you've got a right to. But we had to know. *You* had to know."

Josephine returned her stare into her cup. "I would've killed him, you know? If there'd been even one bullet in that gun..." Josephine trailed off, her voice soft but resolute. "Did he *want* me to kill him?"

"Nope. He set up the barn to make sure you could survive." Jake loped up onto the porch just then, padded to Josephine's chair and sat before it, his head resting on her knees. Josephine smiled despite herself and scratched half-heartedly at the animal's ears.

"I expected him to come after me, thought he just might use that rifle on me after that."

"There's more than just zombies and industrial hazards. There's living, breathing people in there too, some what don't want to be found and some that'll kill you in a heartbeat for your food and weapons and...whatever else you may have," Jasper said, the last coming uncomfortably off his tongue. "You may find you have to kill something other than a zombie. I know men that think nothin' of dropping a dozen dead like they was makin' breakfast, but when it comes to the living they get squeamish. 'Course, if the worst happens and John gets, well, infected, he's gonna' be counting on your gun being loaded. You understand me?"

Josephine looked up at him again and nodded slowly. "I've never been so scared and so angry in my life as I was in that barn." Her trembling had finally subsided now, her mind clearing from the events of the day.

"Hmm. Probably good you got that out of your system now, huh?"

"I get it Jasper. I guess in a way I understand, but it would have been the same had I known what was in there."

"Life comes at ya pretty fast, Jo. There ain't a place in the world where that's truer than in the Area. Always expect trouble, always plan for the worst while you're hopin for the best, and always keep your powder dry," Jasper said, a smile creeping onto his face.

"Jasper, I have to ask; where the hell did those things come from?" Jasper looked down into his pipe as if it held the mysteries of the universe.

"That ain't something I can divulge, Jo. Let's just say there's those out there that can get you anything you want if they trust you enough, and the price is high enough, and leave it at that." Jasper stood then, his arm dropping behind him to massage the small of his back. "Well, time's a wastin. It'll be a crime, but we need to do somethin' about all that pretty hair of yours."

"Yeah, that." Josephine reached behind her back and hauled her ponytail over her shoulder. "I made it through this morning all right with it." Jasper gave her a stern glance and put his hands on his hips.

"I don't like it any more than you do, and I'll cry every snip, but it's got to be done. You can grow your hair back, but your neck don't come back so easy."

"*You're* going to cut my hair? What would you know about cutting hair?" Josephine asked, her ponytail held defensively in both hands. Jake whined at the sudden loss of scratching and padded away off the porch.

"I was a barber for near fifteen years."

"A barber," Josephine repeated.

"Yup, in the Army."

"An Army barber, cutting this?" she asked, shaking her ponytail at him. "I have a television career to think about, you know?"

"Don't you worry Jo, I was the best there was, even had some of the officers' wives coming to me," Jasper said with pride. "I'll even donate your hair to one a them wigs-for-kids charities. I'm sure there's some little Irish girl out there that would be grateful," he said with a wink. Josephine looked down at her hair then got up with a sigh.

"All right, let's do it then."

"That's a girl." Jasper opened the door for her. "Now, you want a flat-top? I'll bet a high-and-tight would really show off those pretty ears of yours."

Heath rubbed his eyes and got up from Jasper's well-worn basement reloading bench. Sleep hadn't come easy the night before. He'd had to resort to relaxation techniques, forcing rest just to get a few precious hours of sleep. Even those had been filled with nothing but Eileen. He kept seeing her face as the woman in the video, his dreams colored in the same grainy, grayish hue. Unlike the video image, the woman who against all odds could be Eileen stared directly at the camera that was his mind's eye. It wasn't the pleading, pained look as he'd envisioned so many times before though. Her eyes weren't blaming him for not finding her as the worst of his nights had shown him, though his conscious mind knew her too well to think she'd ever blame her fate on him.

John Heath, famed zombie killer and Area 187 survivor had once been known as *Captain* John Heath, commander of one of the Air Force's premiere combat search and rescue teams. It would have been expected for him to charge off into the great undead unknown in search of his beloved bride. Eileen knew this as well as she knew her own name, knew without doubt or hesitation that her search-and-rescue husband would come looking for her with enough air cavalry and guns blazing to mow down the Persian hordes. That's exactly why she'd demanded he not do that very thing.

The last time they'd spoken was over a satellite link a few days after the outbreak had become a full-blown national emergency. She'd told him she was in her well-protected, stocked medical research facility though refused to let him charge to her rescue. There were thousands and thousands of others lost, stranded and fighting for their lives that didn't have such luxuries as she and the rest of her group. Eileen and the rest of the research staff were as safe as they could be. She told Heath that his job was to help those others, the ones with no food or medicine, the ones that were in imminent danger and that rescuing groups like hers was a job for a Huey pilot and an accessible rooftop, both of which they had already. But even as he'd said the words, promising he wouldn't damn the works and sally forth to her, Heath knew it was a promise he wouldn't keep. And as field commander for all Air Force extraction missions for the state, it was far too easy for Heath to personally slate his team for her extraction. But in the end Capt. Heath hadn't been able to bring the full might of the nation's fire-breathing dragons and knights-errant to her aid, had he? His commander, Colonel Lightner, knew Eileen was in the Area and pulled rank to change John's extraction assignments even as his team was boarding their helicopters, issuing counter orders to send Heath and his men into the fray to collect refugees and survivors far from Eileen's last known location to keep "emotional involvement" from interfering with the rescue sorties. And, in keeping with the erroneous phrase "military intelligence," Lightner's orders had created the exact opposite effect. Heath had designed not just his own team's plans but *all* of the extraction plans and strategies. He sent his team on their amended orders, hopped the large transport chopper slated for Eileen's extraction and left his captain's bars and a hastily-written resignation of his commission behind on the pad.

Eileen had been working for a private research firm with an array of government contracts out of a rurally-built, semi-clandestine facility a few miles northeast of Beckley. As soon as the outbreak became known the facility had gone on lockdown to await extraction not only of its high-value personnel but of its high-value data as well. As Eileen had assured him, the place was fortified, well-stocked and maintained a sizeable armed security staff. The only thing it couldn't protect against was fate. Ten minutes before the chopper reached the facility, Heath received word that the building had suffered severe damage from an exploded chemical tank and fire was raging inside and out, creating a plume of thick, dark smoke the rescue team could see miles before Heath and crew arrived at the facility. What the update hadn't said was the exploding chemical tanks had also breached an exterior wall, allowing masses of the dead to pour into the building in search of prey even as the facility burned around the building's staff. The rescuers found what was left of them on the roof, anxiously awaiting their impending rescue while the building burned out beneath them.

The chopper hadn't even touched the rooftop before Heath was out of it. The downdraft from the propeller had kept the worst of the smoke away, allowing him to check each face as they boarded. There had been more than a dozen of them, singed and dirty. Some of them were wounded. One was unconscious and another was dead of smoke inhalation. None of them had been Eileen. He'd called out over the whine of the rotor even as the flames encroached on the roof, the smoke thick enough at that point to ignore the downdraft. One of the evacuees knew Eileen and told Heath Eileen had sent the rest ahead while she gathered medical supplies for the injured with the promise she'd catch up to them. She never did. The survivors had finally had to bar the access door to the roof when the dead coming in from the outside had found their escape route. At that, Heath had grabbed his gear, ordered the pilot to return to Pittsburgh and charged off towards the roof access door. He wouldn't be seen again until his return to the world five years later. In deference to his previously-sterling record, Lightner had buried his resignation and had listed him as "missing in action" instead of the more appropriate moniker "absent without leave" or even "desertion". When Heath had come back alive, the military could do little else than publicly acknowledge him as a hero for bringing out survivors and grant him an honorable discharge.

Heath had run into more grave robbers than just Jasper in his time inside the Area, and when he'd finally decided to leave he knew Homeland would rather have shot him and his ragged band as soon as they came into view of the Area's Northgate facility. Northgate was not only Area 187's northern control facility and monitoring station, it housed the command center for all Area 187 operations from its north-central vantage point conveniently located some 30 miles south of Pittsburgh near Washington, Pennsylvania. Heath and the survivors that had followed him hadn't been given the chance to try and cut a deal with Northgate. By the time they'd fought their way from the southwest to get to Northgate they'd amassed a veritable horde of shamblers hot on their tail. No one in the group had to be asked if they'd prefer their death come from well-aimed .50 sniper bullets or from the hands and teeth of the hungry dead so they made straight for the wall. Had it not been for a documentary film crew on the wall at Northgate that fateful night, John Heath had no doubts it would have been done in just that way. It'd been obvious to everyone watching that his party was very much alive as they ran across the barren expanse of the buffer zone towards the wall, far too obvious for the snipers and soldiers on the wall to claim the party was just the leading edge of the approaching mass. From that night on, the resulting footage of the thousand-strong zombie horde that came in the survivors' wake had become *the* stock footage in any news report concerning survivors and the dead.

But the film crew had accomplished more than simply adding indelible images to the collective psyche, more even than reminding the world of the contained, festering cancer behind the walls and lights. It bought Heath at least a few more years before he, too, could become a mysterious and unexplained corpse. He held no illusions that the government had forgotten him, especially with the recent and unexplained deaths of two of the survivors that had come out of the Area with him, and he knew well he was considered the ace of spades in the slim deck of Area 187 playing cards. To this day, Homeland still feared what he may or may not have found as he searched for Eileen. Not of the dead or the existence of more survivors though, at least not as their first thought. Capt. John Heath was smart, well-trained and highly skilled in his life's work. Having a man like that searching the ruins of every hospital, research facility and military-related site in the Area for his scientist-wife meant he could just as easily have stumbled upon information that hadn't been sanitized during the last-ditch pullout of the state. But papers, memos, formulae, even blame had mattered little to John in his time inside. He'd kept one thought and one thought alone to guide him; *find Eileen.*

When they'd asked if he'd learned anything about the virus during his official debriefing, he'd told them just that.

The clear truth of Heath's apathy mattered little to the paranoia of the powers-that-be, and he'd learned enough to know they suspected he knew far more than he was telling, that he knew enough to permanently silence him. Luckily, Col. Lightner had become General Lightner while Heath had been inside. By ignoring his hastily-scrawled field resignation of his commission, Lightner had been able to keep Heath's officer's status alive, using it to pull Heath away from the standard Homeland debriefing procedures and into the military's purview. That act had likely saved Heath's life.

Of course Heath *had* learned a few things. How could he not? The fact was, he hadn't really cared. Names and dates wouldn't bring Eileen back, and pointing fingers now would only earn him a swift death and a shallow grave. The day he'd made it back alive Heath washed his hands of it all; the Area, Homeland, the conspiracies. He didn't do interviews or talk to the media. He ignored invitations to speak at horror conventions about his experiences, didn't own a computer or cell phone and did everything in his power to remain invisible. Even for all that, he knew they were still watching him though, waiting for him to slip and give them the opportunity or the reason to eliminate him that wouldn't garner public suspicion and media attention. But Josephine had been inarguably right about one thing; if Eileen were alive, if he could bring her and the rest home, the resulting firestorm of media attention would make their names secondary to the irrefutable proof that the government not only knew a sizeable number of survivors remained trapped in Area 187 but had been actively keeping their existence from the world.

Heath mentally chided himself and returned to his preparations. Even if the woman in the video was Eileen it'd been more than a month since the message had been recorded. He knew better than most that the safety of any place in the Area was subject to rapid change. Any number of things could have happened to the survivors since. Granted, they were in as safe a place as they could be given their environment. But the facility they occupied was old and without even nominal upkeep it could have its own hazards; collapsed retaining walls, clogged ventilation shafts, even flooding from underground springs. They had as much to fear from the collapse of their bubble as they did from the roaming hordes outside it.

All of that was of secondary importance, though. If he couldn't manage to get Josephine and himself there alive the rest would be nothing more than an academic exercise. He knew he'd been hard on Josephine from the first moment she'd walked into the bar. At first he'd been so to protect his own interests. He hadn't lied to her when he'd told her that he'd had several requests to go back. Half the time they were either CIA or FBI trying to trick him into incriminating himself or undercover reporters going for a story. That's what he'd thought Josephine was until she played the message. When she'd convinced him she wouldn't budge about going he had to remain hard on her to protect *her* interests, namely staying alive long enough to tell the tale. She turned out to be a lot tougher than he'd first thought, and even though he ultimately had to step in to keep her from getting killed he still regarded her barn performance as a success. There weren't many people that could walk into a dark, dead-infested room unawares and manage to kill four zombies in hand-to-hand combat.

He sat back down and finished loading their rifle magazines then those for his pistol. He'd picked a Desert Eagle in .357 from Jasper's personal armory so they would be using the same ammunition for their side arms. He would have preferred a lighter caliber for a secondary weapon, something less hefty than the bulky magnum. But Josephine was comfortable with her revolver and he didn't have time for her to get used to something different. He'd already loaded their packs save for her additional clothes and had left just enough room in her ruck for the job to keep the pack weight hovering at 25 pounds. Not a lot of weight, but enough that they would feel the effects at the end of the day. Water was always an issue in the Area, though. Many of the natural sources had been polluted by runoff from crumbling industries and unmonitored flooding. Heath had decided they'd start and end with canteens designed to minimize sloshing noises and outfitted with a chamber to hold water purification tablets. The water they found on the way might taste like chemical shit from the tabs, but it would be enough to keep them hydrated while eliminating a great deal of excess weight from having to carry large amounts of potable water with them.

Heath finally stood and hefted a pack in each hand. Josephine seemed to be in good physical shape, and though he expected her to bitch for the first few days, their provisions shouldn't be overly taxing. He threw a pack on each shoulder, turned out the lights and stood in the dark basement, taking a moment to close his eyes and let Eileen's face come to him. Not the face in the video, not the one that haunted his dreams but the face that had looked up at him when they stood at the altar, hands clasped and their lives ahead of them. He traced the underside of the slim, white-gold band on his left hand with the tip of his thumb, the spot worn thinner than the rest of the circle from years of the practice. If Eileen was there, he knew this would be her last chance. If she wasn't, it would be his.

"Angela, I need to see Bill. Now," Julie told the plump, gray-haired receptionist. The woman looked up from her desk and pushed her glasses back on her nose, a look of mild amusement on her face.

"That simply isn't possible, Ms. Sommers. Mr. Hartman is in a meeting and can't be disturbed." She tapped a few keys on her keyboard and checked the screen. "I can set an appointment for you, say, tomorrow at four?"

"Dust off your résumé Angela. You're going to need it," Julie said as she walked past her desk towards the wide double doors that separated Bill's office from the waiting room.

"Ms. Sommers!" the receptionist called after Julie but the words bounced off the doors as they closed behind her. Julie pulled a paper sack from her bag as she crossed the office and dropped it on Bill's desk, effectively stopping his conversation with the evening news show's producer.

"Julie! What the hell?" Bill asked as he rocketed up from his chair. "I'm in the middle of something here."

"We need to talk, right now." Bill looked down at the bag on his desk then upended its contents; a tube of hand lotion and a jar of petroleum jelly.

"What's all this for? What's going on here?" Bill asked. Tom, the news director, looked at both of them and got up.

"Looks like you're busy, Bill. We'll talk later," Tom said.

"No, we have to -" Bill began before he was abruptly cut off.

"The lotion's for you to use tonight since I won't be there,"

Julie interrupted, "and the Vaseline's for you to use when everybody from the president of the network to Homeland Security comes after a piece of your ass. Still too busy to talk to me?"

Bill stared at her for a moment, at the gleam in her eyes and the set of her jaw. "Yeah, Tom, let me take care of this. Can you wait for me outside?" Bill said without taking his eyes off Julie.

"Yeah, sure thing Bill."

Julie waited until Tom left the office before she walked around Bill's desk, pushing him out of the way to take his thick, high-backed leather chair.

"Ooh, this is nice," Julie said as she made herself comfortable. "And here I thought you were just in this job for the side benefits."

"Julie, you want to tell me what the fuck you're doing?"

"It's not what *I'm* doing, Bill, but what the hillbilly slut's doing and what you know about it."

Bill's expression darkened as he leaned on the desk towards her. "What the hell are you talking about?"

"Don't play games with me, Bill. Your darling Josephine came into possession of a dangerous little home movie, didn't she?"

"I don't know what you're talking about," Bill said even as tiny beads of sweat broke out on his upper lip.

"Oh, I think you *do* know, Bill. I think you know all about it. And you're going to tell me everything, or another little home movie I know of goes to your wife while my father shows Homeland yours and Josephine's little secret. You remember my father don't you? *Senator* Sommers?"

"Julie, what did you tell your father?" Bill asked through clenched teeth.

"Oh, nothing. At least, not yet. I just told him that I was doing an investigative piece and if anything of interest came from it I'd be sure to let him know. He's expecting my call later this evening, and if I don't call for *whatever* reason, he'll be sure to come looking for me," Julie purred, warning him. "One can never be too careful, you know?"

"You don't know what you're playing with, Julie. Peoples' lives are at stake here."

"You're right; there are a lot of lives at stake, most notably yours and Josephine's," Julie said as she pulled out a tiny voice recorder and placed it on the desk. "Here's how it's going to work. Tomorrow you'll replace Steve with me as the lead anchor on the evening news. Oh, and you're going to fire that bitch of a receptionist, too."

"What? I can't do that! Julie, please..."

"Don't beg. It's pathetic in bed or out. I watched the video, Bill. I know it's only a couple of months old. I checked with the travel department and there's no itinerary for Josephine's sudden *assignment,* and there's no expense account in the system for her. Wherever she's going, she's going there without the network's sponsorship, at least not publicly anyway. The video, a sudden stealth assignment, no paper trails. It's the kind of thing that makes a girl wonder just what's going on. That's where you come in."

"You're nuts! You have no idea what you're getting involved in. Look, I'll get you a raise, a better dressing room. You've been complaining about your dressing room for the last six months. You can even have Josephine's room. Hell, you can have her job. Just stop right here, and we'll pretend this conversation never happened."

"I don't want the top spot on a 6 a.m. coffee show, I want *the* top spot, period. And you're going to give it to me. I get what I want, and nobody finds out that you two are working with contraband. If I don't, everybody loses, except for me of course. If nothing else I walk away with Josephine's job anyway. You won't be able to stop that because you'll be in a deep, dark hole somewhere, won't you? You and Josephine both. Now, you're going to sit down and we're going to have a little chat all about what you and Josephine have been hiding about Area 187 and what you're doing with the information. Think of it as posterity."

"And if I refuse?"

"Your wife gets the little video I made the night you needed my *discipline*. My father gets the video from those poor, poor people that don't exist along with a statement from me detailing where I found it, who had it and who knew about it. Do you think they'll send you to prison after they torture every last bit of information out of you, or do you think they'll just shoot both of you in the head and drop you in an unmarked grave?"

"You fucking whore!" Bill said, taking a step towards her.

"Careful, Bill. Daddy's still waiting for my call." She flipped on the recorder and settled back in his chair. "Now, Mr. Hartman, why don't you sit down and make yourself comfortable? I so enjoy a good interview."

It was full night by the time Heath woke from his nap. He dressed in the dark, his hands sliding buckles and adjusting straps with practiced ease. It felt oddly natural, being wrapped in protective leathers again. What he'd worn in the Area had been scavenged, battered and often ill-fitting; the cast-offs of a dead land. This time he had nothing but the best of gear and garb compliments of Jasper's extensive collection of both. He left the room and went down the stairs without a sound, his feet and mind already in the Area ahead of him. He stopped a few steps from the bottom when he heard a man's voice say his name and looked into the living room. Jasper and Josephine were sitting on the couch with their backs to him, watching one of Josephine's DVD's. When Heath had gotten out of the Area he'd wanted nothing more to do with it. He didn't watch other countries' news specials, didn't read the articles and books and didn't bother with the remembrance ceremonies held every year. Jasper on the other hand was an Area aficionado. When he wasn't in the Area he was studying it from every angle and source he could find. Satellite maps, books both fiction and non, and especially foreign television programs filled much of his idle time.

Though Heath had never actually watched one of the programs he knew Josh Mason's reputation. The Canadian television journalist had haunted him since the day he was released from quarantine, even going so far as to come to Pittsburgh to look for Heath more than once over the years. Mason's programs on Area 187 were contraband in the U.S., but America's Hat ate up anything having to do with zombies and survivors of Area 187.

Many Canucks had come to consider Area 187 their best answer to the constant jokes and jabs many Americans made against their northern neighbors. Canadians might say "eh" after every question and they might have more moose than soldiers, but at least their government wasn't letting hordes of zombies hold a large chunk of its sovereign land hostage and damning its citizens that were still lost to horrific lives and deaths in the necrotic wilderness.

"I haven't seen this one," Jasper said. "Where'd you get it?"

"Mason and I are good friends. He sends me DVD's on the sly of all his Area shows. This one has a lot on it about Heath, or at least a lot of opinions of him."

"Good or bad?" Jasper asked.

"This show was taped about six months after Heath came back," Josephine said, ignoring Jasper's question. "It's old news."

"If I ain't heard it yet, it's news to me." The show's theme music faded and Josh Mason's face filled the screen.

"Tonight, we have our own expert on Area 187," Mason's recorded visage said. "Not some professor, and certainly not anyone from America's wistfully-named Department of Homeland Security, though for the record they have declined our repeated invitations to come on the program. We have with us tonight a *real* expert, an actual 'grave robber' as they've come to be called. We've altered his voice and appearance for obvious reasons, but I can assure you he is the genuine article."

The camera angle changed to show Mason sitting across a low coffee table from a man in a heavy wig, obviously fake beard and large dark glasses. "Thank you for being with us tonight, Mr. Smith, is it?"

"That's the name," "Smith" said, his voice quaking with the show's tinny, metallic voice modulation they used for Americans that came on Mason's Area programs.

"Mr. Smith, I'd like to start off with the name that's been on everyone's lips for the last few months. I'm speaking of course about John Heath, hero of the PBS Survivors." Smith grunted then chuckled, his head shaking slowly back and forth.

"Heath's nothing but a digger that just got lucky," Smith

said, still chuckling. "If they were smart, Homeland would've put a bullet in his brain right there at the wall."

"Why do you say that?"

"Look, the guy was in there for, what, five years? He's nuts. You'd have to be after that. Scrabbling around, eating what you can scavenge, killing zombies. I've been doing this a long time, and believe me I know diggers when I see them."

"'Diggers'?" Mason asked.

"Yeah, diggers; survivors that snapped. They just roam around killing zombies and anything else that gets in their way. They're like mad dogs, ya know, just killing because they can. Some think they're getting revenge on the pus-bags, some think they're doing God's will, all that bullshit. They're nuts, and they're dangerous. You can't let people like that back into the civilized world, man." Smith lit a cigarette and stuck it between his fake moustache and beard.

"And you think John Heath is a digger? As far as the American government is concerned he's been successfully repatriated into normal life."

"What the hell do they know? They don't know shit. Ask any farmer what they do to a dog that gets a taste of blood on the hoof. You have to put 'em down 'cause they never lose the taste. Letting a digger loose in the world is like putting a kid in a candy store and locking the door."

"You feel he's a danger to the public? As far as I know he hasn't done anything to warrant that kind of thinking."

"Well, that's as far as *you* know," Smith said through a thick exhale of smoke. "See, I live in the same town he does. I know the dude, seen him with my own eyes lots of times. I know what he's done since he's been out, even if you or the cops don't."

"Really?" Mason asked, leaning towards his subject. "Enlighten us, please."

"Well, first off, those PBS Survivor assholes as you guys call them? I have it on real good word that those people were nothing but his little doomsday cult. Just fuckin' away the days and slaughtering zombies at night. I know robbers that stayed in their little compound, see? The women in there'd fuck you for a bottle of water, and a pack of cigarettes would get you a god-damned orgy," Smith said with an odd glee.

"That's bullshit, by the way," Jasper said, leaning over to Josephine like they were in a live audience.

"Well, Heath never came out to deny that story or any of the rest about him, good or bad." Josephine turned her attentions back to the screen.

"I find that a little hard to believe," Mason said to Smith.

"Do you? Then why the fuck am I here, huh? Have you ever been in the Area, huh? Have you ever been face to face with a hundred of those damn things comin' after you? I'm here to tell you that I have, and I'll take the word of a fellow robber over your stuffed shirt or the little feel-good stories from some of those so-called survivors. The only reason they came out in the first place was they got overrun, lost their good thing. What the hell reason do I have to lie to you? It doesn't make a bit of difference to me. I mean, I can just get the hell up out of here right now if you don't believe what I'm tellin' you."

"Please, Mr. Smith," Mason said, trying to calm the situation, "for the sake of argument let's suppose that what you're telling me is true, or at least the truth as you know it. What other tales of John Heath have you heard from your comrades?"

"Well, this one guy I know told me he ran into Heath once, on the inside. Saw him just goin' to town on a big swarm of pus-bags, just clubbin' their asses. Said the dude was just laughing and singing while he did it."

"What song was he singing?" Mason asked.

"I don't know, the dude didn't say. But what the hell does it matter what he was singin? The dude was crushing skulls and *singin'* while he did it. Zombies or not, that just ain't normal," Smith said, shaking his head. "Then this other guy I know ran into him in a house they both picked to hole up in for the night. He told me that Heath just sat there all night, mumbling prayers and talkin' to God about sending all his children's souls back to Him where they belonged. He said he finally had to leave 'cause he was afraid

Heath's talking would bring the zombies into the house with them. Like I said, man... once a digger, always a digger."

"You alluded that Mr. Heath is involved in things that, as you said, even the police don't know about. What do you know about his activities since he's been back?"

Smith again shook his head and chuckled. "I can't really tell you what the guy's into, call it 'professional courtesy'."

"Have you ever actually met John Heath?"

"Not on the inside, but I've run into him a few times. The dude just has this real weird look in his eyes, man, like he's still lookin' for zombies or something. The old 'Nam vets had a name for that kind of look; they called it the 'thousand yard stare'. That's what the dude looks like, man, just a whacked-out vet lookin' for a target."

Heath shook his head and stomped down the remaining steps. Josephine fumbled with the remote control while Jasper got to his feet. "Didn't hear you come down, John. I must be getting' old," Jasper said.

"That's because your ears were full of shit," Heath said, nodding to the frozen image on the screen.

"My apologies, John. Guess that was pretty disrespectful of us to be watchin' that, huh?" Jasper said, scratching his chin.

"Jasper, I could really care less," Heath said.

Though his mouth said the words, Josephine could see the storm clouds racing through his eyes again. "Maybe that's your problem, Heath," Josephine said. "You know, a lot of people think of you just like this guy does. You've had countless opportunities to come out and shut guys like that down and do a lot of good for the people left behind."

Heath stared at her, his gaze narrowing. "Yeah, guess it's all my fucking fault, huh? Well you know what? Maybe if you people with your fucking stories and your cameras would have just let it go, maybe we could have all lived normal lives when we got out. We could've been just a footnote in history, just a question on the Area version of *Trivial Pursuit*. Do the names Gonzalez and Host ring a bell for you?"

"Yes, two of the people that came out with you," she said.

"Correction, they *were* two of the people. Here's a newsflash for you, honey. Your buddy Mason there? He tracked them down, got them to do an on-camera interview, got them to do it without hiding their identities. He convinced them he could get their story out there, that it would help make people demand Homeland bust out everybody on the other side. He made them think they would be the saviors of every poor bastard that was still wading through zombie shit. Both of them turned up dead less than a week later, on separate coasts but both with the same cause of death - 'unexplained'. Why do you think Mason is so adamant now about hiding anybody he has on that claims they've been in the Area?"

"How the hell would you know that?" Josephine asked. "How would you have even known they were even on Mason's show?"

"Because Gonzalez came to Pittsburgh and found me two days after they taped the show. Her cousin was a desk jockey at the Pentagon and got wind of her impending demise. He warned her and she came to me," Heath said.

Josephine stared at him, her jaw working silently for a moment before she gathered her thoughts. "So...what did you do?"

Heath returned her stare but his lips remained tightly together. "What's it matter? She's dead now." Heath picked up his ruck from the hallway floor and started to move towards the basement.

Josephine exchanged glances with Jasper; the old man shrugged his shoulders slightly, his bewildered look telling her this was a story he didn't know the ending to, either.

"Heath!" Josephine called to him. "I have to know," she said, stepping from the living room into the hallway. He stopped at the basement door, his hand on the knob, his back to her.

"Why?" he asked without looking back. "It doesn't change anything and it doesn't affect what we're doing."

"Because all I know about you is what I've seen from the survivors, from guys like that Smith, from what I've seen with my own eyes. I need to trust you, and I don't quite know how I can pull that off," Josephine said, her voice quivering slightly. "Tell me you're different than that. Tell me what I've seen so far is bullshit. Tell me that you wouldn't have carried out your threats to me. Hell, tell me you didn't enjoy killing Bub or even tell me you did, whichever is the truth." Her voice rose in volume as she went on, her eyes slowly filling with unshed tears.

"Jo..." Jasper said softly as he placed a comforting hand on her shoulder. "This ain't helping..."

"'Ain't helping'?" she said, mocking Jasper's accent perfectly without taking her eyes off Heath's back. "For Christ's sake, Heath, you fucking locked me in a fucking barn with a bunch of fucking zombies! I need to know that you won't leave me for zombie food. I need to know that you're in this regardless of whether or not Eileen Heath is there. You've treated me like shit from the first minute and now I'm going into fucking zombie Disneyland right behind you!" The stress of the last two days welled up from her guts now to spray Heath's back there in the hallway. "I need you to trust me with some kind of truth. Give me something I can hold in my hands that's true and from your own goddamned mouth; good, bad or ugly. I need to know you can feel something, trust me with something – anything - before I can even think about fooling myself that I can trust you with my life."

Heath stayed where he was, motionless in the emotion-charged air. Finally he turned his head to look at her over his shoulder. "I gave her a gun."

Josephine stood staring at him, unblinking as the tears streamed down her cheeks and her body trembled in her rage. "You gave her a gun? That's *it*? That's what you did? The woman was afraid for her life. She came to you for help, and all you did was to give her a *gun*?"

"Survival's a bitch. As far as I was concerned, she was bit and just waiting to turn. If you can't put them down yourself you have only two ways to go; you walk away or stay there and let them bring a swarm down on you."

"You weren't inside! She wasn't bitten, you weren't inside and she wasn't dead! Jesus, Heath, I might be leaving home to go into the Area, but for you it's just the opposite, isn't it? She came to you for help in Pittsburgh; living, breathing fucking *Pittsburgh*, not in Area 187."

"Survival's the same, inside or out. If she would've needed directions to Wal Mart, a hot meal, a loan, I would've been more than happy to help. But they'd already bit her, she was already infected, and the rest of the horde could hear her moaning and was coming for her. You wanted the truth and I gave it to you. I've got work to do, and you still need to get that fucking hair hacked off. I hope you enjoyed this little outburst 'cause we're done with this shit as of now. If you can't keep your emotions in check it'll be a very short fucking trip, for both of us," he said as he disappeared through the door.

"At least I have some," Josephine said, her bitterness bouncing off the closing door.

After an hour's worth of cooling-off, Heath came upstairs and found them sitting in the living room going over one of Jasper's maps.

"Well, how's this?" Josephine asked as she stood and struck a pose. She was dressed in her full Area regalia topped off by her freshly-sheared locks. Jasper had gone with a very short yet oddly-stylish pixie cut that hadn't left a hair on her head longer than an inch. Heath threw her pack onto the couch.

"I would've gone with the high-and-tight," Heath said.

Josephine sat down on the couch, opened her pack and looked inside. "Heath, there's hardly enough room in here for my clothes. And where am I supposed to put my camera?"

"What camera?"

"The camera I'll be using to get footage inside Area 187 and to get interviews with the survivors." She pulled out a digital video camera about twice the size of her open hand.

"You should be able to cram that in there," Heath said.

"Not when it's in this," Josephine said, holding up a plastic case that was a good bit larger than the camera. "Jasper gave it to me. It's lead-lined, in case they run an EMP where we are," she said, referring to Jasper's warning about the military's recently-developed ability to use electro-magnetic pulses in the Area. There was still plenty of equipment that was capable of broadcasting a signal left behind in Area 187 to someone who knew what they were doing. The pulses were a way to fry any equipment that had been powered up that regular monitoring may have missed.

"Guess you'll have to leave it behind. Everything else in that bag goes. No exceptions." She glared at him for a moment then took to examining the pack more closely. Heath turned to Jasper, nodded and headed for the kitchen. Jasper walked off behind him, leaving Josephine to stew over her luggage issues.

"Everything set with your friend?" Heath asked as he sat down at the kitchen table. Jasper went to a cupboard and brought a bottle of Lynchburg's best to the table along with two highball glasses.

"Yup," Jasper said as he poured each of them a few fingers and sat down. "Ready and waitin'. Everything set with you?"

"As set as it can be," Heath said, picking up his glass. "You know, we're probably not going to make it."

"If that's what you think'll happen then that's what'll happen," Jasper shrugged, picking up his own glass. "Still, it'd be a shame if it's your negative ass that gets her killed."

"She's a big girl. She knows the risks," Heath said. "And it's not negativity, its realism."

"Call it what you like, it means the same thing."

"Either way, I left the papers in the basement. As of today you're the proud half-owner of the bar and you've got power of attorney for my financials. If I'm not back in three months, clean it out, close it out and buy yourself something nice."

"Not much left after buying those targets, but I should still be able to supersize at the finest drive-throughs in town." The two old friends laughed at that then fell silent as Josephine came into the room, her pack cinched tightly on her shoulders.

"Okay, I think I have this figured out - oh, sorry. I'm not intruding on some macho male bonding time, am I?" she asked through a sarcastic smile.

"Not intruding at all, Jo. In fact, I think we need another glass." Jasper got up from the table, fetched another glass, and poured for her. "Have a drink with us. It'll be the last one you get for awhile," he said, handing her the glass. She took it and stepped over to the table to join them. "I think a toast is in order."

"We're celebrating now?" Heath asked. "A little premature, don't you think?"

Jasper cleared his throat, ignoring Heath. "May you have the hindsight to know where you started, the foresight to know where you're going, and the courage to take that long and winding path full circle," Jasper intoned. Heath raised an eyebrow at the same time he raised his glass to clink against Jasper's and Josephine's.

"At least it wasn't a prayer," Heath said.

"Ain't nothin' wrong with prayin', John. If you're smart, you'll send up a few while you're in there," Jasper said.

"You think there's still a God? That's cute," Heath said after he downed his whiskey.

"Has to be," Jasper said, "I'm still alive, ain't I?"

"I think that has more to do with stubborn nature than divine intervention," Heath said as he walked out of the room.

"Well, I'll say a few for you both regardless," Jasper said to Josephine.

"Thanks, Jasper." She tossed down her drink with a wince and a cough then hugged the old man tight. "Thank you for everything. I don't think I'd be able to do this if it wasn't for you," she said in his ear.

He patted her back then returned her hug. "Don't thank me for that now. Thank me when you get back."

Chpater III
One Foot in the Grave

They rode in silence from Pittsburgh to just outside Washington in Jasper's old Grand Cherokee, their goodbyes and good wishes expressed before they'd left the farm. The old grave robber drove down a utility company right-of-way for nearly another mile before silently depositing them in the moonlit woods at only a shade over a mile from the wall that separated the living from the dead. They moved quickly and silently away from the drop-off spot, careful of every branch and twig.

Jasper had warned of the roving patrols that prowled a half-mile strip around the outside of the wall, a tour of duty performed mostly by members of the Pennsylvania National Guard. Grave robbers regarded them as little more than bored security guards as the guardsmen rarely stopped their humvees while patrolling the border, and foot patrols were virtually unheard of anymore. The comparatively loud engines and searing spotlights sweeping the edge of the woods announced the Guardsmens' presence for a quarter-mile around, making it easy for Heath and Josephine to avoid them as they made their way to the edge of the woods at the brink of the barren earth between the wall and the world.

They stayed just inside the line of cover afforded by the trees while Heath checked his watch. Josephine could see him clearly in the branch-dappled light from the full moon. His face bore no expression as he stared first at his watch and then at the glow of the lights on the wall ahead of them. Josephine closed her eyes for a moment and willed her hands to stop trembling. By the time she opened them again Heath was staring at her. He waved towards the wall, got up from their hiding place and stepped clear of the brush. Josephine got to her feet and stayed a few feet behind him, just as she'd been instructed. From that moment on she was to stay behind him the whole way. It was up to her to keep up with him. He wasn't going to look back until he was on the other side of the field of light, past the buffer zone and again standing inside Area 187.

Jasper had told Josephine that *getting into* Area 187 could be as deadly as *being* in Area 187, though he'd assured both of them that his contacts would give the pair at least a fighting chance to get across the buffer zone. What they did from there was up to them. A lot of would-be grave robbers ended up watering the buffer zone with their blood from a bullet through their hearts. The snipers manning the wall gave no quarter and asked no questions. If something moved in the buffer zone that wasn't supposed to be there, they shot it through the heart. Grave robbers didn't carry identification as a rule, and the .50 caliber rifles used by the snipers tended to make an unidentifiable mess of any noggin they passed through. Dropping the target with a heart shot not only made identifying the grave robber easier, it made it easier on the team assigned to retrieve the body. Leaving a fresh corpse in the buffer would only attract the dead and give them a reason to brave the eye-searing light. If the target moved after the heart shot, the snipers then knew to shoot for the head.

Heath started across the clear-cut swath towards the wall. Josephine kept her eyes on him, stepping where he stepped and keeping enough interval not to run into him if he slowed yet not so far back that she would fall behind if he sped up. Heath did neither, his steps little more than a fast, controlled walk through the field of stunted grass and faded range markers left over from the early days of the wall when snipers watched both sides with equal determination, a practice that was abandoned once the guardsmen started their continual patrols. When they finally closed within a few dozen yards of the wall Heath veered to the right, changing their approach to an angle rather than their original head-on course, then stopped inside the shadow of the wall and dropped to one knee. Josephine repeated the gesture behind him, watching as he paused, slipped his pack from his shoulders then rolled his body to the left, disappearing as if the ground had swallowed him whole. Josephine moved to his previous position and repeated his motions, holding onto her pack by the straps ahead of her to follow it down through the narrow slit in the ground.

She landed roughly beside Heath inside the pitch-black rain cistern, thankful that the last few days had been dry ones. The cisterns were designed to protect the wall's foundation by keeping heavy rains or snow run-off from collecting along the base of either side of the wall, holding it in the tank they now occupied to await drainage by a pump truck. The wall's designers had believed the system of tanks to be more secure than running miles and miles of traditional sewer tunnels beneath it. Jasper or one of his cronies had discovered the broken security grating covering the cistern on the living side of the wall years ago and had been exploiting it ever since, even fabricating a new grate that appeared to all but the closest of inspections to be permanently set into the ground.

Keeping the buffer zone itself from flooding had required more conventional means, though. Drain beds had been engineered throughout the zone at its creation to keep pools of standing water from developing. Those drain beds allowed water to seep first into strategically-placed cisterns within the zone, which then passed into the spider web network of 3x3 pipes that ran through areas that were prone to flooding or near natural underground springs. Those pipes brought the water to tanks like the one they now occupied to be safely emptied by private contractors outside the wall. The system had been designed with no openings on the zone side large enough for even an infant to fit through, and even though the zone was kept free of vegetation and trees that could cause materials to clog such a system under normal conditions, those openings had still been covered with thick wire mesh as an additional precaution. As they were designed, nothing was getting out of Area 187 through those tunnels. But with a little aftermarket engineering and ingenuity, they made a perfect way in.

Jasper's road into the Area was a far more sophisticated

affair than a simple breach of one of the narrow pipes with a crude tunnel to the surface. He and others like him had mapped out the entire drain network in this part of the zone and had made their point of exit not into the buffer zone and its lights, cameras and snipers' scopes but rather 20 yards past the zone's field of light, into Area 187 itself. If used from late spring through early fall, a good grave robber familiar with the system and the Area didn't need outside help to slip in and out of the drain network undetected, even though the opening was within sight of the buffer. Jasper's tunnel emptied into a copse of willow trees, their wispy though thick fronds hiding anyone coming into or out of the tunnel opening from being seen in the buffer's light or by its cameras and rifle scopes. But during nature's own defoliation program, commonly known as fall and winter, anyone coming into or out of the tunnel ran a good chance of being spotted by the buffer's sharp eyes or the even sharper motion-sensing cameras and heat sensors. If the pair could follow a list of lefts and rights traversing almost two miles of the twisting, turning pitch-black drain network on their hands and knees with their packs dragging behind them, and do it in the next 45 minutes, Jasper had assured them they would find not the revealing light of the buffer zone waiting for them at the end of the line but the dark of Area 187.

Jasper's reassurances seemed far away to Josephine as she crept along behind Heath with only the soft glow of his penlight to guide them, and though she'd never been a victim of claustrophobia she could easily sympathize with its sufferers. She found she could only keep her eyes open for a few feet at a time before she had to close them for a few seconds to ward off tunnel vision. Since neither Jasper nor Heath had shared the obviously complicated schematic of the drain system with her and Heath wasn't referring to any kind of paper or chart as he threaded them through, she could only assume he'd memorized the route.

They went on for what seemed to her an eternity to the point she wasn't sure if she would remember how to stand upright again. Her wrists and knees hurt and her shoulders warned she hadn't heard the last of them, either. To her credit she hadn't made a sound the entire way, even when she'd cracked her head on the tunnel a few thousand turns ago. She was so lost in thought she almost ran into Heath's trailing backpack. He'd finally come to a stop ahead of her, his penlight tracing the surface of the solid, dead-end cap ahead. He shifted to a sitting position and slowly ran his hands around the edges of the seal until a single finger disappeared from view. A thin band of light appeared as he leaned into the cap, finally dislodging it from the end of the pipe and spilling him unceremoniously into the smuggler's roughly dug tunnel beyond.

Josephine crawled out behind him and stepped down onto a pallet placed there to keep anyone emerging from the drainage system from sinking into the dirt floor of the tunnel. A soft glow lit the tunnel from its opposite end, evidence that the lights of the buffer zone were still shining on their escape route. Josephine kept her eyes towards the light and stood slowly, her hair just brushing the tunnel's earthen roof as she massaged her lower back.

Heath was several yards ahead of her at the end of the upward-sloped tunnel, his pack shouldered and facing the light from the tunnel's end. Josephine checked her watch. They were at the 44 minute mark. She put on her own pack and took up her position behind Heath as he gripped the wire mesh previous robbers had installed to keep from having a nasty surprise waiting for them in their own tunnel. He flicked the latches off the frame and pushed gingerly on the mesh. It popped up a few inches, ready to swing out of the way when, and if, the lights above went out. Josephine stretched her legs and made ready to sprint after him. If the lights ever went out in the buffer zone, she knew they wouldn't be out for long.

Grace Clemont walked across the Northgate control room to the bank of monitors that dominated one wall. There'd been no activity anywhere since the unfortunate death of one of Sempertech's technicians a few weeks before, making it just another quiet night on the wall. At least that one had been at Southgate; not her post and not on her watch. She took a sip of her piping-hot

131

coffee then took a moment to admire her ring, a ring that had once belonged to her mother.

Her father had been a simple man, a Green County miner that hadn't been able to afford a proper wedding ring when he married her mother. He'd saved a few dollars a week, stashing it away in the webbing of his hard hat for almost 25 years until one Saturday afternoon when he took young Grace away in secret to the only jewelry store in town to help him pick it out. It was to be the first and last piece of jewelry her father bought for her mother before he died in a mine collapse early in 2003. Her mother, ever the practical sort, rarely wore the ring for fear it would become damaged during her daily chores and her job at the laundry. She kept it in her hope chest, wearing it only for special occasions. When her father died, Grace's mother told her the ring would be hers when she finally went to join him. Grace enlisted in the Army out of high school and was serving her first tour in Iraq when the outbreak happened. By the time she was able to get back to the states the perimeter of the Area had already been established, locking both her mother and her inheritance away in those dead lands.

Grace checked her watch and went to one of the monitoring consoles, setting her coffee down so she could lean on her arm towards the screens. "All quiet, Corporal Javens?" she asked the young man at the console. Although Homeland Security was responsible for the operation of Area 187, many of its soldiers, guards and monitoring personnel were loaned from the various branches of the military, with the natural enmity between the agents of Homeland and the regular military personnel in full effect.

"Yes, Lieutenant," the corporal replied, his eyes locked on his video screens. Javens knew better than to look up at her. His job was to watch the screens and monitoring devices assigned to his station, no matter what happened around him, until properly relieved. A four-star general could walk into the control center and not a single soldier monitoring the buffer zone would stand at attention.

"Good." She stared intently at his screens then at her watch. "Corporal, pan camera three out to the inside perimeter, magnify by four."

"Yes, Lieutenant," Javens responded then confirmed, "Panning camera three out to the perimeter, magnifying by four." Without looking away from his screens he spun a roller-ball controller in the center of the console to pan the camera then reached out to his right for the zoom control, spilling her abandoned coffee onto the console in the process. Sparks flew from a few of the more delicate controls while the hot liquid rolled across the station, scalding the corporal's legs on its way to the floor. He winced and gasped at the searing heat, yet to his credit never looked away.

"Shit!" Grace said. Under normal circumstances and in a normal place every eye in the room would have been on them. But a buffer zone control room was far from a normal place. Not an eye in the room settled on them.

"We've lost connection with the pressure plate sensors, sector six, locations A through G," Javens said nervously, his hands moving across the console to switch the delicate sensor networks to another workstation to compensate.

"I have pressure plate sensors A through G on my con'," a woman at another station called out.

"You have my apologies, Corporal. That was stupid of me. I'm certified on your station, why don't you take five and go clean yourself up. Send me your cleaning bill, too," Grace said.

"Thank you, Lt. Clemont. Leaving station from proper relief in three... two... one... mark."

"Mark," Clemont repeated, her eyes fixed on the screens as the corporal slid out of the chair and she slid in. She checked the adjustments he'd made to the pressure plate sensors and dialed them back from the other work station to hers, now blinded by the short circuit on the console.

"Lost pressure plate sensor readings for A through G," the voice called out.

"Copy pressure plate sensors A through G. I'm pulling them back for a systems check," Clemont said. The systems check would take 30 seconds and required the main power to the affected sectors to come down to minimum levels so the computer could run its diagnostics. These tests were usually run on sunlit days when the dimming of a sector's lights wouldn't be felt, but standard procedure required the tests after an incident such as this regardless of daylight conditions. Grace's hands flew over the controls as she set up the diagnostics. She knew she'd catch hell from her CO in the morning for the sheer stupidity of the accident, and she wasn't going to make Javens suffer for it. Accidents did happen though, and she hoped nothing else would be discovered to make it seem more than that.

"Engaging E-lights, sector six, concentrating A through G," the other voice called out.

"Copy E-Lights on sector six," Grace returned. She powered down the lights for the sector and engaged the diagnostic. The E-lights came from spotlights mounted at intervals along the wall that could be aimed anywhere in their sector. The lights were powerful, but their intensity petered out a full ten yards from the wood line that marked the true start of Area 187. In 30 seconds the computer would complete its diagnostics, make its amendments then power up the lights and sensors in the sector. Grace hoped those 30 seconds would be enough to repay an old debt.

The light above them slowly dimmed until only moonlight remained. Heath wasted no time. He swung the grating away and went up, rolling to the side as Josephine rushed out behind him and ran at a crouch away from the buffer zone. Heath swung the grating shut, making the sure the latch held before he moved out, easily overtaking Josephine and back into his place. He led her to a thicket of briars a few dozen yards away and came to a stop, crouching behind the winter-slept blackberry thicket to face the buffer zone. A few seconds later the whine of the lights coming back to their full brightness greeted them, the silence of the dead land around them making the electric hum the dominant sound. To Josephine, no sound could compete with the drumming of her heart in her ears. She looked around nervously, expecting rotting hands to reach for her at any moment. Heath waited until the discs of the E-lights went out before he turned away from the thicket and moved them fully into Area 187.

He took them along a thin swath of moonlit forest, perhaps a park that had overgrown since the dead took over. Jasper had recommended such tactics to Josephine, so long as she could keep her own feet quiet. Anything that tried to come at them from the woods, especially in the dry of early spring, would announce their presence while they picked their way around deadfall and their feet crunched on dried leaves and twigs. Josephine's ears heard such rustling and at one point a soft, trailing moan from deeper in the thicket. Thoughts of what had made the sounds allowed her to keep up with Heath so well she had to consciously drop back several times to keep from stepping on his heels, her subconscious knowing that to lose sight of him now could mean her very painful end and quite possibly her resurrection.

They continued on through the night at a brisk pace due south. After a few miles, Heath began to slide to the east to drop them into a bowl-shaped valley with a house much like Jasper's place in its center. He stopped them at the base of the porch steps, un-slung his rifle and used hand signals to send her around one side of the house while he took off around the other. He didn't wait to see if Josephine had anything to say about the assignment.

Josephine hefted her rifle and stared at her corner of the house, gathering her wits before she moved off in a slow, deliberate walk. She walked an arm's length away from the wall; far enough where something couldn't reach out from behind an open door or broken window yet close enough she could put her back to it if necessary, just as Jasper had told her. She kept her head moving and her eyes scanning as she went, her foot just missing a weathered, chap-less and upended skull near the corner of the house. Stopping at the corner, Josephine leaned out slowly, keeping as much of her body hidden as she could to check the next angle from a distance. Something lay on the ground ahead, about halfway down that side of the house. She looked behind her again before tucking the short rifle against her shoulder and moving around the corner to make a slow approach to the body. Jasper had told her "tranced" zombies, those that were still active but had gone catatonic to conserve energy, could sometimes be found just lying about in the open. Even if its eyes had completely given out or it'd lost muscle control, it could simply lay like a necrotic land mine waiting for an unsuspecting foot to come too near.

Josephine came within a few feet of the body and stopped. She didn't dare risk a light but could tell enough from the moon to see it was indeed a body with its shredded, flannelled back to her. She gave it a wide berth while still keeping her silenced muzzle on its head and came around to the other side. She couldn't see eyes in its skull but could tell the body had lain for some time in the weather, its gray paper skin stretched thin across the facial bones. Josephine held her rifle in her left hand and drew her club. She landed a single, decisive blow to the skull, the sound of the dried bone cracking overly loud in her ears. When the thing didn't move she held the weapon up for inspection; nothing. Whatever it had once been, live or undead, it had lain long enough for the brain and eyes to rot away. She breathed a sigh and turned to see Heath standing a few feet away, his own arc of the house completed in the time it took her to deal with the body. She couldn't see his features very well in the low light, but she was sure he was frowning at her. He made a quick follow-me motion and headed off back the way he'd come.

Jasper had set up the place as a safe house for times when he had to wait for an opportune time to cross back into the world of the living or when he was forced to enter the Area at night like they had done. The small windows were securely boarded, the doors braced with 4x4 railroad ties set at an angle from the floor to each of the doors. The stair treads and risers had provided the wood that covered the windows, not only protecting them from entry but ensuring that the upstairs would remain free of the dead. Heath found the ladder right where Jasper had told him it would be. He set the ladder up in the naked stair box and motioned her up it, followed then pulled it up behind them to the second floor. After securing the ladder they felt their way down the narrow, pitch-black hallway, Heath counting doors with his hand until they came to the third on the left. He tried the knob and the door swung open without a sound. With rifle leveled, he took in the room with precision sweeps, floor to ceiling. If you found a good hiding place, you may not have been the first one to find it. Safe houses such as these made excellent bases for grave robbers and survivors alike, and it wasn't uncommon to find a caretaker squatter playing house where you intended to lay your head.

After checking the closet Heath looked at her and emphatically pointed to the floor before leaving the room, his gesture virtually pinning Josephine to the spot to await his return. Josephine kept her rifle at port arms across her chest and stood in the inky blackness of the room, its only window covered by a thin mattress that had been placed over it as much to keep light from escaping as it was to dampen noise. Heath came back a few minutes later and eased the door closed behind him, setting another of the railroad ties against it to secure it as the doors on the first floor had been.

"So far, so good. We'll be safe here until we head out at dawn." His voice was quiet but still conveyed an edge. "We're high enough off the ground and Jasper's got the window already covered so our voices shouldn't carry. Still, the quieter, the better."

"Right," Josephine said, hoping her volume and tone matched his. She pulled her canteen, suddenly aware of how thirsty she was and spun the top.

"Don't waste that." He opened the closet door and came back with a small battery-powered lantern, a bag of beef jerky with a faded label and two plastic bottles of water. "Jasper keeps extra supplies here, stuff he's managed to scavenge. He's invited us to continue to partake of his hospitality." He handed her a bottle, turned the lantern to its lowest setting and set it on the floor before sliding off his pack to sit cross-legged beside it. Josephine did likewise with her pack but then lay down on the wooden floor, the boards easing the tension in her lower back and shoulders.

"Those packs are heavier than they look," she said between sips of water.

"A heavy pack means you won't go hungry." He popped a

piece of the jerky in his mouth and offered her the bag. She took a piece and chewed on it while she worked her shoulders against the floor as he pulled a laminated map out of his pack and opened it between them. "We're here," he said, putting his finger on a spot just past the Washington line. "We want to get here." He slid his finger across the map to a point almost 100 miles south by southwest. "If we can maintain our speed, allowing for breaks and night we'll be there in four days."

Josephine frowned. They would have to cover better than twenty miles a day, a grueling pace in even the best conditions. Though Josephine had practically committed the map to memory it looked somehow different here on the floor of an abandoned farmhouse in Area 187 than it had in Jasper's well-lit, honey-smelling kitchen.

The route would have them head just east of their present location, to the edge of a wide patch of forest. From there they would move south, the forest giving them some measure of cover from the geo-synch satellite miles above them should its camera lens turn in their direction. They would follow the wood line across the state border into West Virginia, near the little town of Jere until they neared the site of an old chemical plant that the forest had reclaimed. Heath would decide from there whether they would skirt the plant by going deeper into the woods to the east or belting west around the plant to continue their southerly direction. Veering west would make for easier and faster traveling but would leave them with no natural cover. East would make the going slower but would keep them in the woods.

"Do you think the chemical plant is dangerous enough to lose time going around?" she asked, her own finger tracing their route to that point.

"I was near there about five years ago. A couple of the tanks had ruptured, probably from the lack of temperature control or off-gassing. The tank labels were too faded to read from a distance, don't know what was in them. I still don't want to know. Some of that stuff was raw gasses that wouldn't have been treated with their common scents. I'd rather not be walking around there and pitch over dead from inhaling something I couldn't smell or taste. Besides, you never know when one could pop or just have a slow leak. The last thing you want to do is walk into a pocket of methane or formaldehyde." He took a slug of water and put the cap back on the bottle. "The biggest problem we'll have tomorrow night will be finding shelter. The area is pretty rural and a lot of the houses down that way were compromised on my last trip through. We may have to use the stars as a blanket if we don't come across something better."

Josephine rubbed her arms as if chilled. The thought of sleeping outside in Area 187 was less than warming. "Anything is better than sleeping outside, isn't it?"

"That depends on what the second choice is. Pick the wrong place and you could end up being someone's dinner guest. A lot of what had been in that region were family farms. That means big families that would have tried to stick it out to the end. And *that* usually means a far higher probability of contact."

Josephine nodded absently. The experts she'd spoken with had agreed on one score. If a zombie didn't have a reason to leave an area, it usually didn't. Especially if the terrain worked against it or it had lucked into finding prey in the past. Once a zombie thought there was prey to be had they could stay there for years, alternating between searching and hibernation on their own unknown clock. Jasper's own stories agreed, with tales of finding zombies he had seen the year before still in their same spot or very nearby a year later.

Flatlands and urban areas could be a different matter. If a zombie saw prey and started after it they could continue on in the same direction for days or even weeks after what they pursued was lost to their sight. This single-minded drive was a typical cause of the swarms so feared by Area guards and survivors alike as well as causing migrations of large groups from one place to another. Zombies had no speech capability save for their moaning and wailing, something they did only when they thought prey was nearby. While not capable of group tactics, the sight of one zombie walking and moaning, reaching at the air was taken as a sign by others that it had found prey. Others within eyesight or earshot would join the first until they became a literal parade of rotting flesh.

"Better get some rest; we need to make the woods by dawn and that means going a few miles while it's still dark." Heath stretched out and flicked off the light. "We can both sleep tonight. From here on out unless we stumble into another place as safe as this we'll sleep in shifts."

"Maybe you'll sleep tonight. I doubt that'll be so easy for me."

"Figure out a way. I don't want you slowing us down because you didn't get your beauty sleep."

Josephine awoke with a start but lay still, Jasper's warning to never jump out of bed running through her mind. You never knew what could be near you, and it was always best to take stock before making your morning noises. The temperature must have dropped through the night and the cold, hard wooden floor had stiffened her muscles to the point of rigor. She groaned softly and rolled to her side, her shoulders grumbling along with her lips.

"Breakfast?" Heath asked from the dark beside her. She could smell the mix of plastic bag and dried meat waving under her nose and her stomach growled from hunger as much as disgust.

"Got any of grandma's honey biscuits?" Josephine asked as she managed to lever herself to a sitting position. She stretched her arms over her head and groaned.

"I told you, you should have gotten used to Area cuisine before we got here."

Josephine ignored the bag and rolled to her feet to stretch her legs then checked her watch; three-thirty. Her internal clock was spot on.

"Man, I must have really passed out last night," she said.

"At least you didn't snore." He rolled the bag back down, took it and the lantern to the larder then returned with a bundle of thin nylon rope. He threw it around his body, cinching it bandolier-style across his chest before sliding into his coat and zipping it to keep the rope from becoming a handle for dead fingers. "You can never have enough rope." They left the room and made their way down and outside.

So far, the weather reports he'd pulled were accurate. There wasn't a cloud in the sky with none forecasted until early the next afternoon. "Nice day for a hike," she said.

"Bad day for a hike," he replied as he regarded the clear sky, the lack of cloud cover meaning Homeland would be clicking many a picture in the daylight hours. "Stay close and stay quiet." They moved out towards the east. It was Josephine's job to keep an eye to their rear while they moved and she needed no additional prodding. She was now locked into the most dangerous place on Earth, with limited provisions and ammunition, moving through a landscape where dead things wanted to eat you and living things would kill you for your boots. Add to that she was completely dependent on a man that was a sociopath at best and a shell-shocked Area vet at worst and her reasons for astute observation were clear.

Heath led them across rolling fields full of dead weeds and rusting farm machinery at a much faster pace than the night before, the lack of ground cover and the clear skies giving them haste. Over the last seven years the forest had grown considerably, reclaiming land that man had once taken to build their towns and farms. At their present speed Josephine was more concerned with what may be on the ground in front of them than what may be coming at them from behind. She knew from survivor accounts that "crawlers" could be found anywhere. Similar to the tranced, crawlers were zombies that had lost the use of their legs or had suffered collapses in their nervous systems or spinal cords. The darkened fields of shin-high weeds they traversed could be home to any number of them. They could also be home to ankle-twisting chuck holes, rocks or even rusty, tetanus-laced bits of metal from decaying tools or even weapons that had been abandoned in the sleeping grasses. She stayed close to Heath with only cursory looks behind them, preferring to concentrate on putting her feet where his had just been and praying they would make the woods before dawn, if for nothing else than to slow their pace so her breathing and her heart wouldn't be so loud in her ears.

They covered the four miles to the woods in a little more than an hour just as the sun was starting to rise. The going was considerably slower once they made the woods and turned due south, more a normal walking pace now that they had trees and undergrowth to contend with. They continued picking their way with only a few moments' pause here and there to listen to the woods and scent the air until the noon hour came near.

Lunch consisted of a protein bar and a few sips of water taken on the top of a relatively clear hillock. Josephine munched on the mostly-tasteless bar, surveying the area while Heath climbed a few feet up a large, naked oak to scout their way ahead. She soaked up the sun through the comparatively thinner cover of the oak's bare branches as they rested there, the sun warming her face more of a boon than the engineered snack she chewed on. Heath came down the tree and peeled the wrapper from his own lunch, his eyes remaining southward. A few birds chirped from deeper in the forest, the first sounds save for their own they'd heard all day.

"Birds. That's a good sign, isn't it?" Josephine asked.

"Yeah." Most of the animal kingdom eschewed the dead. Whether it was their scent or something on a more primal level, animals typically avoided them. The same couldn't be said for the zombies though. The dead would eat anything they could find, human or animal. Studies had shown the large herds of deer that had been tagged and tracked by colleges and the state DNR had suffered over the years of undead occupation but hadn't been completely eliminated. The use of signal jamming and EM pulses had made the tracking tags virtually useless now, but satellite and other aerial observations had borne out that, though the zombies had had a definitive impact on the wildlife population, they hadn't completely destroyed it. The animal world had adapted to the conditions, cataloguing this new menace at the top of their list of predators and moving on with their lives just as the humans that survived the Area had done. If you heard or saw sensitive wildlife in an area there was a high likelihood you wouldn't see the dead or be near any industrial hazards.

"That, or there's some around that are hibernating. Animals aren't infallible." Heath finished his lunch then folded the wrapper over several times, making it as small as he could before sliding it in his pocket. Josephine did the same with hers then leaned against the tree, keeping her eyes the way they'd just come.

"How far do you think we've gone?" Josephine asked, feeling that "are we there yet" wasn't the appropriate question for this trip.

"About 16 miles. We're making good time. If we can keep up the pace we'll be a few miles into West Virginia by nightfall, near your old stomping grounds." Josephine knew they'd be close to Morgantown through the first day or so of their walk. One of the few true "college towns" the state could boast, it'd been alive with tens of thousands of students and the various support industries they bring. The town had been practically leveled from the air even before anyone had thought about creating Area 187 as a preemptive measure. But even with carpet bombing, military analysts held that the city would have remained thick with the undead. The airstrikes and falling buildings would have destroyed some, but the singular-target nature presented by the typical zombie meant that head shots and the resultant confirmed kills couldn't be guaranteed by such generic methods. By design, it would likely be as close to any real pre-virus population center as they would get. But even as far away as they were, they were still close enough to warrant caution. As the zombie walked, so to speak, their present location was still well within range considering time and migration.

"Have you been there? To Morgantown, I mean?" Josephine asked as they started down the hill.

"Once," Heath said over his shoulder as he resumed the pole position. They made it to the bottom of the hill and back into the cover of the trees before Josephine's curiosity got the better of her.

"What was it like? How bad was it?"

"As bad as you would think. Time to shut up now." His pace quickened to take advantage of a particularly clear deer track.

Josephine stared a laser beam through the back of his head and matched his speed from a few feet behind. It was time to get back to work, but that didn't mean he had to be a dick about it. Besides, she could still hear the birds.

She could still hear them after another two miles when Heath suddenly crouched in mid-step, his fist raised in the silent signal for her to do the same. She followed the command instantly and dropped beside him, facing the way they'd come. Even though the birds still sang and the sun still dappled through the weave of skeletal branches above Josephine could feel a palpable chill running down her spine. Heath slid his rifle from his shoulder and put it across his knee, his eyes still staring off into the south. Josephine clutched her rifle in sweaty palms, burning to look to the south but resolute in keeping to her post. Seconds passed like hours as she tried to slow her breathing. Heath's had fallen to the point she couldn't hear it anymore, the sound swallowed up by the silence of the forest. After an eternity she heard the unmistakable sound of rotors chopping the air coming from the east. She watched as the outline of the small gunship passed less than 100 feet over the treetops. They stayed motionless for several minutes after the noise had faded away to the west before Heath tapped her shoulder twice and started moving again.

By late afternoon, Josephine's pack felt like it was full of bricks when their track had taken an uphill turn shortly after their encounter with the helicopter. The first few miles had been a gentle slope upwards but the last four or so had been a continuing pattern of steep, briar-choked rises, each leading to a choppy plateau of old-growth forest. The appearance of the chopper had slowed them even more so than the tangled undergrowth warranted. Sound meant food in Area 187, and any sudden or foreign noises had the capability to attract the dead. It was possible the low-flying helicopter could have left a trail of them heading aimlessly west, looking for the source of the sound. They paused often across the few flat areas they crested, listening and watching. The steep hills they climbed would be next to impossible for a zombie to navigate, but that didn't mean there weren't other ways to reach the flats than the one they'd used, or that one hadn't tumbled down from one of the flats above. That was the thing about West Virginia; no matter how many hills you climbed, there always seemed to be another in your path.

The sun was low in the west when they stopped again. Josephine's entire body ached now from the uphill climbs and their slowed progression. Heath left her under a tree to rest while he braved the open to scout a rare downhill slope they were approaching. He came back a few minutes later, his rifle in hand. "Decision time," he said as he scanned the woods around them.

"What are the options?" Her headache continued to assault her, making her own words thunder in her ears while dimming his. Heath stared at her face for a moment and grimaced, obviously aware of her exhaustion.

"You just answered it. My fault; you weren't ready for this. It's one thing to be fit enough to take the stairs instead of the elevator at lunch. It's another for all this, huh?" She'd expected snide comments about her endurance, not his tired half-smile. "There's a house down there. The question would have been; do we use the last hour or so of daylight for a few more miles and take a chance on finding shelter farther down the road or do we hole up in there for the night?"

"I can make it," she said. Heath looked at her again, his smile fading back to a blank face.

"You have to know your limitations, especially when they can get both of us killed. I'll sacrifice a few miles tonight to keep us fresh for tomorrow. Come on, it's just down the hill." She tried for an indignant look but knew he was right as she got to her feet and trudged off behind him towards the house.

They found the front door of the plain, two-story house relatively intact, though it displayed dozens of thin scratches and missing slivers all along its surface giving mute testament that the house had once been besieged. They repeated their search pattern as they had done on Jasper's safe house. This time she could see footprints in the soft dirt around the house as well as a generous amount of bones, both human and animal, scattered around the yard. Many of the windows on the first floor had been broken out, some from outside and some apparently from within. Josephine stepped over a nearly-intact human rib cage and met Heath at the back porch. This door had long since succumbed, its fractured frame and torn hinges the obvious victim of a determined swarm attack. It lay on the floor just inside the kitchen, like an open drawbridge beckoning them to enter.

Heath stepped onto the small porch and peered through a window frame of jagged glass before stepping into the doorway, his pistol in one hand and a powerful flashlight in the other, letting the pair lead him wrist-over-wrist into the darkened house. He stepped inside and swung his head forward, her signal to follow. Josephine left her rifle on her shoulder and drew her revolver and flashlight, moving up and taking his left flank as they advanced into the kitchen. The table was full of an odd assortment of yellowing cardboard boxes, some empty and some with Ball jars of varying contents. Those that had been opened contained nothing more than black and gray masses, their previous contents lost to years of decomposition. Four bowls sat in a neat stack on the table beside a rusty crowbar stained with old blood and a clump of dark hair stuck to its claw.

They moved from the kitchen to sweep the rest of the house. It was obvious the place had seen more than its share of sorrow. Someone, likely a family, had made a stand here. Josephine hoped it wasn't their last stand, that the unknown occupants had been evacuated in the beginning when the government had at least pretended it cared more about its people than its secrets. That hope was shattered when they moved up the creaking stairs to the second floor. They found nothing in the first room they came to. Clothes and toys had been scattered across the floor, the mattresses from the beds held against the room's windows by slings made from hastily-torn bed sheets nailed into the walls. Josephine toed a small, open backpack on the floor and winced inward at the contents; a small red flashlight with Spiderman on it, two cans of Pepsi, a few pairs of socks and underwear, and a picture of a laughing boy hugging a yearling beagle pup. It was exactly the kind of provisions a young boy would prepare for his monthly run-away scenario. The fact it was still here brought the chill back to her spine.

Heath tried the knob on the next door and found it locked though the door and its frame displayed deep, numerous gouges along its length. He slid his flashlight into his jacket, nodded at Josephine to put her light on the door then put his bar into the jamb. After a moment of slow, continuous pressure the door creaked open. He pushed it open the rest of the way and exchanged his bar for the flashlight before leading Josephine inside. The room was occupied by four skeletons of varying sizes. Heath used far more caution in this room, moving more slowly and examining the two closets with far greater care. Josephine occupied herself with the rest of the room, taking in the skeletons and their positions as her reporter's mind strived to understand the tableau of death. A variety of weapons both makeshift and by design were scattered around the floor. A tiny skeleton, a girl by its tattered and rotting dress, was on the floor beside the bed. Another adult-sized skeleton slumped in a corner, a bra peeking out from a half-buttoned, faded flannel shirt her only clue to its sex. A larger skeleton clad only in rotting denim and boots lay on the bed, the sheets below it stained a dark rusty hue. Each of these had a hole large enough to push a pencil through punched into the front plate of their skulls, and each had been bound at the ankles and wrists.

The last was unbound and sized between the ones on the bed and corner and lay face-up across the bed-skeleton's leg bones. It was dressed in jeans and a tattered pair of tennis shoes hanging from its bones. A faded, rat-gnawed t-shirt displaying the amazing web-slinger doing his thing across the cityscape of Manhattan brought an involuntarily gasp as Josephine brought up her flashlight hand to place her wrist against her hot eyes for a moment. Heath spun on his heel, his muzzle and beam of light falling on her back. He reached out, tapped her shoulder and pointed down, yet again pinning her alone in a room while he went to check the rest of the floor.

Josephine stepped over a discarded machete to the side of the bed. Instead of the precise, single hole displayed in each of the others, the miniature Spider-Man's skull was missing a huge chunk from the top. Josephine had seen enough in the hunting camps of her youth to know an exit wound when she saw one. She flicked the light against the nearest wall, knowing she would find a years-old blood stain there. A huge revolver, practically as long as the small skeleton's forearm, lay at the foot of the bed near its bony hand. "Rest of the floor is clear," Heath whispered to her from the doorway, causing her to jump slightly. "I was hoping we would find something useful in here since the door was still locked. Unless you want to stay in here, there's another room down the hall with an intact door." Josephine turned slowly from the bed and walked across the room to follow Heath down the rapidly-darkening hall, her steps far heavier than even her exhaustion could account.

Heath led them into what had once served as a sewing room and closed the door behind them then moved the sewing machine to the floor and put its table against the door. It wasn't much, but it was the only quiet way of forming a barricade available to them. Josephine dropped her pack and slumped into a chair while Heath rummaged around a pile of fabric, eventually selecting several dark blue and black pieces to cover the room's only window.

"I'll take first watch," Heath said, taking off his pack. "It's going to be colder than last night. Throw some fabric down to keep the cold off your back and use your reflective blanket." He tossed a few neatly-folded bundles of moth-chewed fabric on the floor for them then sat on the floor across from her chair, his attentions on rummaging in his pack.

"He killed them, you know," she said absently.

"Who killed who?" Heath asked as he pulled a gray and black MRE pouch from his bag.

"The boy, in the bedroom. He killed them."

"Yeah, looks that way." Heath opened the pouch and poured some water from his canteen into it. "I saw an old well pump out in the yard. We need to see if it's still working in the morning. Try the chicken soup, it's almost edible."

Josephine leaned into her chair, her back protesting at being stretched but needing it all the same. "The other bodies in there, they were tied up. That kid couldn't have been more than ten. He tied them up and shot them, then shot himself. But the door was still locked; they never got in. He killed himself and the damn things never got in."

"Like as not the rest of his family got bit when the things finally got into the house. He tied them up before they turned then put them and himself out of their collective misery when they found where he was hiding. Kid must have been a tough little bastard," Heath said, tipping the pouch to his lips to drink his soup.

Josephine stared at him for a long moment before she straightened up in her chair, her head braced in her hands. "How much of this do I have to see before I can just turn it off like you do?"

Heath stopped drinking his dinner and looked at her. "That little scene back there played out in hundreds, hell, maybe even thousands of places just like this one. There's no flesh left on the bones. Their last stand happened pretty early on, probably within the first few weeks. I'm more worried about the bones *outside*. There are different generations of kills out there. We're not the first to come through this way, and it looks like a few others may not have been lucky enough to get out again."

"You didn't answer my question."

Heath sighed and looked down into his soup pouch. "Bad things happen to good people. Have your breakdown when you're back in the world," Heath said in a tone neither angry nor patronizing.

Josephine slid to the floor, using the chair as a backrest. She opened her own pack and pulled her camera case from it in search of her rations underneath.

"The chicken soup is good tonight, you say?"

"Soup of the day." Heath upended his pouch to drain the last drops of broth, then folded the package into the tiniest mass possible before sliding it under a nearby cabinet.

"Why do you do that?" she asked as she poured some water into her soup pouch and shook it up.

"Pass without a trace, leave nothing for anyone to find; at

least, not easily. Anything that shows up in the Area that post-dates it can give clues to Homeland about where survivors and grave robbers frequent. Believe me, that's the last thing you want to do. If they can establish a pattern they'll come for you."

"They *hunt* survivors?"

"Sure. Well, not so much anymore. There's no money left in it. Homeland stopped giving out the bonuses for plain old survivors years ago, and nobody wants to spend the big money on carpet bombing anymore. What do you think that gunship was doing this morning, looking for zombies? That's the official line, anyway, but they'd much rather peg a robber. Those little gunships are Homeland choppers, not regular military. Those crews get bonuses for confirmed grave robber kills."

"It just doesn't make sense to me. They'd engender more good will by saving survivors than by silencing them."

"You'd think that, huh? Maybe on the political side, you'd be right. But when you mix the corporate and military complexes into it the picture gets a bit muddy. There are a dozen reasons why any survivor that comes out of here is a danger to them, and not just in the court of public opinion."

"I know all that. It just seems so damn *un-American*," Josephine said.

Heath looked at her for a moment then spun the top back on his canteen. "Are you good at what you do?"

Josephine stared at him for a moment, not sure if she should be offended. "Yes. I like to think so," she said finally.

"Well, you're going to have to make everyone on the outside at least *think* you are. If there are any of them left to bring back, your story is the only thing that's going to buy back their lives and ours. They get us before the rest of the world gets your story and all involved simply disappear." He lay back then, draping the silvery heat-retaining blanket over his legs and chest.

Josephine tipped her soup and had it gone in a matter of seconds. She hadn't realized how hungry she was. But there was something else gnawing at her.

"Heath? How exactly are we going to do that? I mean, how

are we going to get all those people out without *disappearing*?"

Heath turned his head to her, the last light of day almost extinguished by his makeshift curtain over the window. "I thought *you* were taking care of that."

It may have been the failing light, but she could have sworn the bastard was smiling.

Chapter IV

Julie

Julie got up from the news desk, dropping her sound gear from her ear as she went. Bill had put the regular news anchor, Steve Simmons, on special assignment doing a piece on the Korean War. It was a passion of the old and respected newscaster, one he was more than happy to work on in deference to reading a teleprompter, especially when it was covered within his multi-year, multi-million dollar contract.

"Ms. Sommers?" a stagehand called out. "Bill wanted to see you in his office after the show."

"What does *he* want?" she asked without bothering to look at the young man.

"I wouldn't know, ma'am," the hand returned, as equally bored with the conversation as she. Julie continued walking, making her way off the set and past the production rooms to the offices beyond. Two large men in dark suits and glasses were posted outside Bill's door. Julie recognized them easily.

"Good evening, Ms. Sommers," one of them said as he opened the door for her. "They're expecting you." Julie stopped and eyed her father's bodyguards suspiciously before she slipped through the door.

Bill was seated behind his desk, his tie loosened past office-casual under his ashen face and sunken eyes. It was obvious to Julie that he hadn't slept nearly as well as she had last night. Julie's father stood with his back to her, looking out at the city at night from Bill's executive view. Another man, similar to the guards outside but without the glasses sat in one of Bill's guest chairs.

"Daddy, what are you doing here?" Julie asked as she stopped at the desk. She looked down at Bill. The powerful television executive looked even worse up close. Senator Alan Sommers turned from the window and focused his steel gray eyes on his daughter. After a moment he smiled warmly and spread his arms.

"I don't get a hug?" the Senator asked. Julie returned his smile and came around the desk to hug her father and pecked his cheek.

"I thought you were back home. What's going on?" Julie asked.

"I was worried, what with this secret story you mentioned, and when I saw the promo spot this morning saying you'd be the lead anchor on the evening news tonight I thought we should celebrate. Mr. Hartman has been gracious enough to entertain me until you were available. Isn't that right?"

Bill looked up for a moment before turning his eyes back to the desk.

"What a great surprise!" Julie said. "Just let me get my coat."

"Now Julie, we don't want to be rude. Mr. Hartman was just about to tell me all about this special story you've been working on." Bill didn't acknowledge him. "Unless of course *you* want to tell me about it?"

Julie stared at her Daddy and gnawed on her bottom lip. "Julie dear, don't do that. Those collagen injections aren't refundable, you know."

She stopped immediately like a chastised child. "We'll talk about it over dinner, Daddy. I'm sure Bill has a lot of work to do." Her mind was already racing to concoct a story worthy of the Senator's attentions as she took his hand to lead him out of the room.

"Sit down, Julie," Sommers said, the tone of his voice assuring her he would brook no argument. Julie looked at him with her best pout but complied, sitting in the second guest chair beside the other man. She hadn't told her father anything specific about Josephine's Area 187 message, and she certainly hadn't told him she had Bill's taped, lie-strewn confession about sending Josephine out to do a piece on grave robbers.

"You know how much I love to hear about your work. After financing almost ten years of degrees, I think you owe me at least that much."

Julie thought back, trying to remember if there were any words she may have used when she last spoke to her father to trigger this type of reaction. She remembered saying something to the effect that the assignment could be a "little dangerous". She regretted that now. Julie was the Senator's only child, a West Coast socialite and the apple of her father's eye. Senator Sommers was always ready to charge into the fray at the slightest indication that his daughter may be in trouble.

"It's nothing Daddy, really," Julie said as smoothly as she could. "I'm working on a piece about..." She paused for a moment, sparing a look at Bill. She had no idea what had transpired before she'd come into the room but it was obvious from her father's pressing that Bill hadn't told him. She only hoped that what she came out with didn't fly completely in the face of anything Bill may have made up. "It's about grave robbers, Daddy," she said finally. "You know, finding one, interviewing them in silhouette, real *Deep Throat* stuff."

"Julie! I'm shocked at you!" her father said. "You have no idea what type of criminals you're talking about! I chair the committee on Area 187, you know." He looked down at Bill. "I see now why you didn't want to divulge the nature of her assignment. You two could both be in a lot of trouble for that kind of story. I can't believe you'd be involved in something so irresponsible. Do you realize what you could do to my reelection campaign next year, being involved with something like this?" He came around the desk where he could see both Bill's and Julie's faces. "I want you two to promise me you'll drop this nonsense right now. Have you actually made contact with any of those *animals*?"

"No, Daddy. Not yet, anyway."

"Good. At least I don't have to assign Williams here to you." The man seated next to Josephine smiled at her and went back to picking at his fingernails.

"You were going to put a guard on me?" Josephine asked.

"Of course. You said the work was dangerous. As long as you drop this criminal act you've been contemplating I won't have to."

Bill looked up from his desk, his eyes tired yet piercing into Julie's. "I knew it was a bad idea from the start, Senator Sommers," Bill said. "But let's be realistic. If I would have told her no, she would've just pulled the influence card - *your* card - and slapped it in my face. I really didn't have a choice."

Sommers looked down at him and smiled. "Mr. Hartman, I must say your candor is as refreshing as it is disturbing. Are you saying I would use my position unduly?"

"I'm saying neither of us is stupid and we've both been around the block enough to know that we can drop the bullshit pretense. But while we're being candid, I'd suggest you go ahead and place that guard with her. She's lying. I personally know she has a meeting set up with a robber out of Youngstown for tomorrow night. He was supposed to call tomorrow with the time and place, and he knows who she is." Bill was sitting upright in his chair now. Not just upright, but subtly shifting his body to a 'power posture' like he did during any negotiation; straight yet loose.

Julie nearly came out of her chair. Bill hadn't spilled the real story into her voice recorder last night after all. The executive had played a hunch that a woman like Julie would never consider that even the likes of Josephine would run off into Area 187 personally. Instead she'd recorded that Bill had agreed to let her go into deep cover to find grave robbers that had met the survivors displayed on the disc. Bill was still the only one that knew Josephine's true intentions. The story he'd fed Julie would still be enough to damn him, but they'd probably let him live. If Homeland knew he'd authorized Josephine's foray into the Area he knew he'd never be seen again.

"That's a lie! Daddy, he's lying!"

Sommers looked at Bill.

"I don't have a reason to lie, Senator, and considering your position and your place on the Area committee I have every reason to tell you the truth. I just ask that you grant the network, and me, grace on this one. Besides, I wouldn't want anything to happen to Julie. She's the new anchor, after all. Considering the type of characters she's been talking up, a guard may not be such a bad idea, especially if we're to call off the story. They may think she was trying to set them up," Bill said.

"Daddy, he's lying!" Julie repeated. Sommers looked at his daughter and frowned.

"You have a valid point, Mr. Hartman," the Senator said without taking his eyes off his daughter. "Williams, from this point until further notice you will not let my daughter out of your sight. Mr. Hartman, I trust you will make the necessary arrangements to accommodate Mr. Williams while my daughter is here?"

"Of course, Senator. It'll be my privilege," Bill said with a thin smile directed at Julie. "I wouldn't want anything to happen to my star."

"Daddy, this isn't necessary. I'll be fine. I'm a big girl, you know," she said, her pout back on her face. It had worked well throughout her life but tonight her father totally discounted it.

"Williams will keep you out of trouble and keep you safe, Julie, at least for a week or two until I'm certain there won't be repercussions from your association with that type. He comes highly recommended."

"And, he's in the room," Williams said. "Don't worry Senator. I'll take good care of her."

"And you will let me know if any of this grave robber nonsense comes around," Sommers said, his tone a warning to his daughter as much as instruction to the hired gun beside her.

"You're the boss, Senator."

"This is so unfair! You're ruining my social life! How am I supposed to go out with this ape hanging around? Mother will just die if I show up in the society section with this rent-a-cop hanging around!" Williams shot up an eyebrow at being compared to a mall guard even as a bemused smile crossed his face.

"Young lady!" Sommers said suddenly. "May I remind you that you can be locked up indefinitely for even associating with that type of trash? And how would it have looked? *My* daughter, consorting with grave robbers? Williams and I will be watching you very closely until I'm sure this nonsense has long passed. That is my final word."

Julie shot a death-beam look at Bill. The man deflected it with his slick smile. "Now, go and get your coat. I have a car waiting downstairs. We'll go out for a nice celebratory dinner and put this behind us for the night." He turned to Bill and extended his hand. "Mr. Hartman, you have my apologies if I came on a bit too strong earlier."

Bill stood and shook Sommers' hand with the perfect grip, pressure and precisely-measured pumping gesture. "No apologies necessary, Senator. I have a daughter myself, and I'm sure had our positions been reversed I would have done the same."

"Oh, and one more thing," Sommers directed towards Bill as he started out of the office, "I'll be in town for a few days. You have that long to recall Ms. Terrell. Her sudden absence in light of what you've been working on makes her suspect. I'll want to speak to her, as I'm sure officials from Homeland Security will, about her involvement in all this."

"Senator, Josephine isn't involved. It was all Julie's story," Bill said, his smirk making Julie fume. "She's on an unrelated assignment."

"Well then, it shouldn't be a problem to produce her, should it? I can make sure the investigation is a quiet one, and I can see to it your network keeps its licenses and you can keep your freedom. But first I have to know that Area 187 is secure from irresponsible journalism." With that the Senator left the office, leaving Bill with Julie's hate-filled eyes and trembling, balled fists. Williams looked on, obviously bored with the proceedings.

"You bastard!" she growled at Hartman. Bill kept his smile and opened his desk drawer for the paper bag she'd left with him yesterday. He rummaged around in it and came out with the jar of petroleum jelly.

"Here," Bill said, offering her the jar. "Looks like you may need this more than me."

Heath had awakened Josephine at midnight for her watch and had fallen almost immediately to sleep after, his soft breathing just a few feet away the only sound save for the wind creaking the old house. She checked her watch; almost three a.m. Heath had told her to wake him at four-thirty so they would be out of the house and on their way before first light. She stood and moved out of the room as quietly as she could, though she had no doubt that Heath knew she was moving. Josephine hadn't slept well. One nightmare had led to another to the point she was relieved when her turn for watch came due. She'd dreamed about the barn and its myriad alternate endings, none of them comforting or victorious for her dream-self. She'd dreamed about Heath's demonstration against her coat and hair in the field, except this time he was truly dead. Now in her waking, in this dead house in this dead land, her thoughts had turned to the man himself.

Josephine wasn't being dramatic when she'd told Heath she was having a hard time trusting him. It wasn't that she believed the popular mythos surrounding him, of course. She'd interviewed some of the survivors herself, even if it was off the record. She couldn't believe the women of the group were running a charnel whorehouse like Smith had claimed on Mason's show, and she knew from them Heath had only been in their compound for a few days, making Smith's death-cult remarks completely unfounded. But there were still a lot of disturbing tales about Heath, things he'd neither denied nor confirmed in the eyes of the shadow public that followed the stories. Since its inception, Area 187 had spawned its own underground media machine. And if you knew how to tap into it, you could learn far more about it than the U.S. government would like. The problem was that there was no oversight, no fact-checking. Like an undead *Wikipedia*, rumor was as good as truth in Area lore and often made for better storytelling. The trick was to separate the fact from the fiction. But even if all the truths were lies and all the lies true, she knew he was still her best bet to get her inside and back again.

She traced the wall with her hand as she walked to the window at the end of the hall. The moon was already slipping away to the west, taking its soft light with it. Shadows moved along the ground as the steady breeze whistled through the branches, contorting their distorted shadows like bony fingers caressing the earthly remains scattered about the yard. By the time she broke away from the hypnotic picture, she'd made the mental commitment to put away her notions of Heath, all the stories, all the drama, and focus on the man in the here and now, accept him at face value. *He* wasn't her story. She didn't have to like Heath, though some level of personal faith in the man would've been a comfort. Even discounting everything she knew or thought she knew before she met him, what she'd seen since hadn't been exactly faith-inspiring, either.

She moved back the way she'd come, passing the sewing room door and coming to the large, ghost-infested bedroom. She stood in the doorway for a long time, her gloom-adjusted eyes studying each skeleton before moving on to the other bedroom, the open backpack looking especially forlorn in light of seeing its owner's fate. She reached inside and felt for the photo she'd seen earlier, found it and slid it in her pocket without looking at it again. A glint of the last light of the moon reflected dully off something attached to the pack; a small luggage tag attached to the pack by a ball-chain similar to those used to hold military dog tags. She pulled the tag off the pack and walked slowly to the window, the fading moonlight revealing the pack had belonged to Andy Fitzpatrick of 18 Miller's Lane. She held the tag in her hand for a moment, the image of the dog-hugging, happy and very alive boy warring with the thought of his remains and what the last few moments of his life must have been like. She pocketed the tag and made her way out into the hall just as the sound of shuffling footsteps wafted up the stairs from below.

"So how does this work, anyway?" Julie asked Williams as they walked into her penthouse apartment. "Do you just sit on the couch all night, smoking cigarettes and cleaning your gun?"

"Yeah, something like that, except for the cigarette and gun parts," he said as he followed her into the posh, sunken living room. Julie dropped her coat and bag into a chair on her way to the mahogany bar that dominated a corner of the room. She poured a drink without offering him one and downed half of it before facing him.

"Look, let's make this really easy for both of us. I'm going to set you up at a hotel for as long as Daddy wants you to stick with me and provide you with a healthy little per diem on the side. Think of it as a paid vacation. In return, you get the hell out of here and leave me alone."

"No offense Ms. Sommers, but your father is my employer, not you. I accepted the assignment and I always follow through."

"My father will be back on a plane to LA as soon as Hartman produces the hillbilly princess. He'll never know the difference."

"I'm pretty sure he will, and I *know* I will." He could guess she was referring to Josephine Terrell from the meeting they'd had earlier that evening. Julie let out an exasperated sigh and slammed her drink down, sloshing the top-shelf vodka across the bar's pricey veneer.

"Look, whatever the hell your name is - "

"Howard Williams," he said, interrupting her.

"I didn't *ask* what it is," she said venomously as she crossed the ridiculously expensive white carpet between them. "I could just call the cops and tell them to make you leave. Or, I could make a different call and have five guys here in ten minutes. Big, strong, *real* men," she said as she flipped his tie up into his face. "Men that would snap every little bone in your body just to see me smile, *Howie*," she said, punctuating each word with the poke of a lacquered fingernail.

Williams looked down and smiled at her while he straightened his tie. "Ms. Sommers, I'm a professional. This is my job."

"Not anymore," she turned around and went back to the bar to freshen her drink. "You have until I finish this to get out of my apartment. If you're still here, I'll make one of those calls." She smiled, swirling the ice in her drink. "And when they're done with you, the next call I'll make is to Daddy to tell him you forced yourself on me. After that it wouldn't surprise me if he had you dropped into the Area, naked and covered in bacon grease."

Williams walked to the bar to stand directly in front of her. She let out a squawk as he took the drink from her, downed it in one long gulp then put the empty glass back in her hand. "Call the cops and I tell them about the story you were working on. I'll bet you the *Post* will move faster than your Daddy will. I'll also show them this," he said, holding up a Homeland Security agent's ID. "One of the advantages of working for your father." He leaned in close to her then, locking her eyes with his. "And if you call your buddies, that little plastic smile of yours will be the last thing they ever see. Like it or not, I'm your personal Velcro until such time as your daddy stops signing the checks. Now, we can make this easy on each other or we can make it difficult. Either way, I'm still going to be paid."

"Who the hell do you think you are?" she said, pushing him away from her. "Don't you *ever* get that close to me again! I should just call my father right now."

Williams pulled out his phone and offered it to her. "He's speed dial number two, right behind Mom."

Julie growled and stamped her foot. She stood trembling with rage for a moment before she closed her eyes and took a long, slow breath. It was time to try a different tactic.

"Look, Mr. Williams," she tried, stressing the more polite address, "I'm not in any danger. Honest. It's a waste of your time and mine for you to be here."

"Your father doesn't seem to think so. It's not really the point either way."

Julie looked at him for a moment and put on her warmest smile as she moved near him again. "My father has always been overprotective - of me and of his position. I don't recognize you. How long have you worked for him?"

"A week."

Julie thought for a moment. A week wasn't enough time for

a mercenary like Williams to develop any sort of loyalty, if he was even capable of it at all.

"Well, just so you know, he does this all the time. He thinks I'm in trouble and he comes rushing to my aid. Or rather, he pays someone to come rushing to my aid," Julie said, moving closer still.

"If he does it, you must give him reason to. Again, that's really not the issue. I'm under contract."

Julie replaced her smile with her patented, man-scrambling pout. "I wish you would reconsider my offer. I'm not in any danger at all. It's all just a big misunderstanding."

"Is it now? Let's pretend that has any bearing on my contract. How is this all just a big misunderstanding?" In truth, he really didn't care. A job was a job, and the cushy world of executive security and its high pay and health plans was a far cry from his previous freelance work. But if he was going to be her shadow for a week or more it would help their protector/protected relationship if she saw him as someone she could let into her confidence. If it was a damning enough secret it may even be enough for him to hold over her to make this assignment smoother and easier on both of them.

"You already know why Daddy thinks I'm in trouble. I mean, you were in the room."

"Consorting with grave robbers is pretty dangerous, Ms. Sommers - especially for someone in the media. For both you *and* them."

"That's just it. Look, I can clear this whole thing up for you. That way you can see I'm not in any danger and you can take me up on my vacation offer without worry." She went back to the bar and disposed of the glass he'd drunk from and poured herself another in a fresh glass. "It's kind of embarrassing, really. I told Daddy a little fib is all. I told him I was working on that story and I really wasn't. I wanted him to think I was a real journalist, make him see that even though I'm his daughter I wasn't his little girl anymore. Josephine Terrell was the one that was working on the grave robber story, not me. Pretty petty of me, huh? That asshole Bill has had it in for me, especially when he got the call yesterday that the network wanted me to take the top spot. That's why he went along with the story, trying to get me in trouble with Daddy. Didn't you see how he was looking at me and talking to me?" It was a thin story, but she hoped this one was like the rest of her father's staff; just intelligent enough to be a danger to themselves but not enough to be so for her.

Just then the intercom buzzed. Julie made a move towards the door but Williams beat her to it. "That's *my* door, you know."

"I'm doing my job, Ms. Terrell. No one gets near you unless I know who they are," Williams said as he picked up the intercom handset. "Besides, it's probably just my bag."

Julie fumed behind his back while he discoursed with the doorman, her fuming turning to rage as she heard him give a list of instructions to the doorman and then to building security about his status and stay with her.

The concierge was at the door with his bag by the time he hung up. Williams opened the door, took the bag and slid the young man a five dollar bill. He looked at the bill as if insulted then turned and walked stiffly back to the elevator. Williams watched him go down the hall, scanning it and waiting for the doors to close on the miffed man before coming back into the apartment. "Christ, even the help is snooty here," Williams said under his breath as he dropped his large flight bag on the couch.

"Did you hear a word I said? I'm not in any danger and it's utterly useless to have you here."

"To you, maybe. But unless you want to call your Daddy now and cop to the story you just gave me I'm here till he cuts the check. It's not up to me to figure out the truth of things. That's for types like you to figure out and political types like your father to hide," Williams said as he loosened his tie. "Now, do you have a guest room or am I bunking on the couch?"

This is ridiculous. I'm going to bed," Julie said, disgusted.

"Make sure we have at least 15 minutes in the morning to go over your itinerary."

Julie tromped off, her only response to stick her hand behind her and extend her middle finger before slamming her bedroom door. Apparently, he was on his own for his sleeping arrangements.

Howard listened intently, the soft click of the lock on her bedroom door coming to him through several walls as easily as her murmured insults about his parentage did. He shook his head and sat down on the over-stuffed leather couch, his hands laced behind his head to stretch his muscles. As long as he could ignore her shit, this was going to be easy money. He pulled his Colt Delta from his belt and laid it on the coffee table. He still couldn't get used to seeing the shortened length of the silencer-less barrel, but that didn't mean he missed it.

He glanced over at her discarded coat and bag. She'd dropped the bag on its side, allowing several of its items to spill out on the seat cushion. He sat for a moment, still listening to her sounds. He could hear a shower running and doubted Julie would make another appearance that night. Even though he was a lowly hired gun he doubted she'd emerge from her lair without extensive make-up and costuming, a process that would take an hour and likely more even if she did come back to lambast him further. He got up and went to the chair, poking at the few items that had rolled out. Several loose lipsticks and other obvious cosmetic containers had tried to escape in her rough handling of the bag.

The handle of a compact umbrella poked out of it, as did a plastic jewel case. Williams doubted there was data on the disc, especially with the bejeweled, designer USB drive that had escaped onto the cushion along with the lipsticks. He cast a guilty glance down the hall at her closed door before he carefully slid the case from the bag. He opened the case but could find no label or markings as to the DVD's contents. With a shrug and a last look down the hall he located the entertainment center's remote and popped the DVD into her state-of-the-art theatre, turned the sound down low and stepped in close to the screen.

Josephine froze, her ears straining to verify the shuffling sounds from below. She waited, her breath held tight until she heard it again. It was the sound of a heavy step followed by the dragging of the other foot; step-drag, step-drag. She listened to it repeat several times, first hard and grating across the kitchen floor then softer once the feet progressed into the living room. She slipped down the hall, remembering the loose, creaking board halfway down as she made her way to the sewing room. Heath was already up and moving towards the door by the time she got there, his silent weapon balanced and at the ready on his shoulder. She held up her hand, one finger extended to show how many targets she thought prowled the floor below then let him past her and into the hall. He advanced towards the steps and disappeared into the doorway of Andy's room, the closest concealment to the top of the stairs. Josephine moved a few feet ahead towards the stairs and crouched, her magnum at the ready to cover him in case there was more than one target.

They could still hear the shuffling, muffled steps below, the stairwell providing the perfect conduit for the sound. After several more seconds it stopped. Josephine held her breath, her revolver braced over her knee. She let the breath go, almost happy that the feet below creaked now on the stairs. At least they wouldn't have to keep their positions for hours while the thing bumbled around the ground floor. Josephine lowered her crouch even more. If there were more of them around, she didn't want this one to see her and start moaning. She counted the steps as it came up them. After the fifth riser the oblong shape of its head appeared to her in the darkness over the top step. Josephine remained as still as possible as each step brought more and more of its body into view. The zombie would have to take at least two steps after reaching the top before Heath's doorway would be in range. That's why she had to stifle her gasp when Heath suddenly swung into the hallway, one hand sinking his club into the zombie's forehead while the other reached out to grab the tattered jacket to keep the body from falling down the stairs. He raised and dropped the club a second time, the sound of the skull crushing even louder than the strike itself then quietly guided the body to the floor. Josephine wanted to rush forward but checked herself. Heath had the situation well in hand. If there were more of them he still may need her playing God behind him.

Heath used his foot to roll the dead zombie against the wall and kept his position a few feet from the top step, weapon loose yet ready in his hand. They remained that way for several minutes, both straining to hear the slightest noise from below. Finally Heath moved back towards her, his eyes still locked on the stairs until he reached her position then nodded towards the sewing room. She stood slowly, praying her knees wouldn't pop on the way up as she joined him.

"Time to go." He quickly folded his blanket and put his pack in order.

"We've still got better than an hour till dawn," Josephine said, though it didn't stop her from dropping to one knee to make the same preparations.

"You see one you'll see more." Heath cinched his pack, his club still in hand. "There must be flat ground to the west. I think we're in a pocket of them, probably why there are so many bones outside."

"We'll be tripping all over ourselves without a light in the woods," Josephine said as she climbed into her own pack, her soreness from the previous day forgotten. Glass suddenly crunching underfoot from somewhere downstairs brought both their heads up.

"Like I said, time to go. We need to get our asses outside. Stay close." Heath slipped out the door and down the hall with Josephine close on his heels. He paused at the top of the steps and listened for a moment.

Josephine winced as another crash of breaking glass filled the still air followed by a wet, dripping sound. Whatever it was, it was in the kitchen. Heath didn't wait any longer, his steps carrying him swiftly, silently down the stairs and into the living room. Josephine struggled to both keep up and be silent but settled for keeping up and keeping her feet from tangling on the dark stairs.

Heath charged ahead silently, his feet rolling heel-to-toe along the thin living room carpet towards the kitchen. She paused in the doorway and drew up her revolver and flashlight; the first trained to Heath's right towards the shattered door jamb and the last switched off but ready to come to life. They found an obese male standing in the middle of the kitchen, his back to them. Heath wasted no time covering the distance across the floor, his weapon a blur as it swung down on the top of the zombie's skull.

The zombie dropped to his knees then fell forward onto his corpulence, grinding the shards of the jar of green beans he'd knocked off the table into his chest. Heath gripped his weapon and ripped it free of the zombie's crushed skull just as another one appeared in the outside doorway. This one was the opposite of the first, shorter and far thinner than the whale of a man on the floor. It reached out towards Heath and opened his mouth even as Heath raised his weapon and started towards him.

Josephine knew even as her finger tightened on the silenced revolver's trigger that Heath's attack would arrive too late to stop the creature's vocalizing. Her gun hissed and jumped in her hand as she touched off the trigger, silencing the zombie's summoning moan on its blackened tongue. Heath changed his grip on his weapon in mid-stride, plunging the sharpened spike end into the dead zombie's chest, using it to bring the corpse quietly to the floor. He didn't bother looking at Josephine as he pulled his weapon free and stepped out onto the porch, his head swiveling slowly across the pre-dawn darkness outside.

After a few moments he stepped down from the porch, moving off across the yard and turning south at the shelter of the wood line with Josephine trailing a few yards behind. Heath kept them moving through the pre-dawn. Their night visitors had put Josephine's senses on edge to the point she could hardly trust her eyes. She thought she could see movement everywhere in the trees around them and heard moans carried on every breeze that passed. She attributed it to the utter darkness around them in the hours between moonset and sunrise and the difficulty the lack of light added to their path. To attribute it to anything else would only make it worse in her mind.

By the time they picked a precarious trail up the first rough hillside out of the valley the sun was starting to peek out from the east. Heath stopped them at the top of the rise while he used the day's new light to look ahead on their path while Josephine looked behind. She kneeled down beneath the shaggy cover of a rough pine and munched on a protein bar, her eyes moving slowly but steadily down the hill they'd come up. She expanded her gaze down into the valley, tracing the tree line back towards Andy Fitzpatrick's tomb. She could just make out the small house in the distance, the first rays of the sun reflecting dully off its weather-beaten shingles. She squinted towards the house then blinked several times before putting down her breakfast and pulling out the compact binoculars Heath had packed in her ruck.

She held them up to her eyes and spun the focus wheel a few turns. Even at this distance she could make out the four zombies that were moving around the house. Her breath caught for a moment but she controlled the sound admirably. The dead were too far away to be an issue for them, and the fact they were still haunting the house meant they didn't know in which direction she and Heath had escaped. She swept the ground they'd covered with the glasses all the way to the base of the hill and found nothing alive or dead following their path.

"How many?" Heath asked as he dropped to one knee beside her, still facing in the opposite direction. At least she thought she'd kept her reaction in check.

"Four, maybe more. They're just hanging around the house. Nothing's following us."

"Probably heard the scuffle. Those things don't think, but I can tell you they do have some kind of mental capacity. They can recognize when something's very different if they've been in the same environment for awhile. If they go past a door that's been closed since they first saw it and then one day find it open, they notice. Those guys have probably been through that house hundreds of times over the years, and the corpses we left behind could easily be considered a new addition," Heath said around his own breakfast.

"How's it look ahead?"

"Going to be slow going for the next few miles. We're going to have to move deeper into the woods in about a mile or so. We're coming up on the industrial park and Derry's Corner, a little piss-ant town we'll need to bump around."

"That's going to cost us some time, isn't it?"

"I allotted for it when I planned the route." Heath finished his breakfast and followed his wrapper-folding ritual.

Josephine turned to look at his stubbly profile. "If it's that small, is it more worth the extra time and walking than to just go through it?"

"Do you know how I survived in here? I did it by not taking stupid chances. We're no good to anyone, especially ourselves, if we're dead."

"But you had to have gone through a lot of cities and towns."

"Only when I had to, and only to places I thought I might find something. I didn't do it to save a few steps or a few minutes."

They moved quickly across the comparatively barren hilltop, the sun's light not only lighting their path but warming Josephine's courage. She fought through several chills as they went while the memories of the night before categorized and deposited themselves in her mind. She had no idea why she'd pulled the trigger on the zombie even as Heath was moving towards it. It must have been the right thing to do, she reasoned, else he would have surely taken her to task for it. Her chills and dark thoughts were a hazy memory by the time they hit the next rough, briar-choked hillside and crested it, her body's protests easily running roughshod over her mental woes in the face of the mid-morning sun.

Heath stopped them at the edge of the hilltop. Below them at the end of a near-vertical and sparsely-covered slope lay a huge, fifteen-acre-square skeleton made of dull aluminum and cheap glue-pressed wood, the thin metal roofs poking out of the overgrown field grass and shrubs like bones protruding from a shallow, rain-washed grave. Far to their left at the edge of the trailer park they could just make out a ribbon of cracked, broken asphalt that marked what once would have been a road. It was the closest they'd been to one yet. Heath left her to watch both fore and aft while he pulled out his map and the small electronic device he'd had back on Jasper's porch. Josephine wasn't overly worried about the way they'd come. They were on the top of a hill that had taken them more than a half hour to scrabble up, often having to use both hands to grip the thin trees and roots jutting from it to pull themselves to the top. If there was a zombie that could traverse that hill she didn't want to meet it. Instead she fixed her eyes to the overgrown mobile home community below.

Josephine had seen many such communities over the course of her younger years. The axle-bearing manufactured homes maintained a prized spot in rural lore, and with good reason. Communities like this were a common sight throughout this and many other southern states, giving people who may otherwise never be able to afford a traditional house the chance to own a home. She knew quite a few people growing up that had taken as great a pride in their "trailers" as others did with their traditional homes. She pulled her glasses and started scanning the area below, watching for any sway of the brown, winter-dead grasses against the gentle breeze that could indicate something moving between the trailers.

"This wasn't on Jasper's maps. How the hell did he miss a big fucking trailer park like this? There have to be 150 units down there."

"175, actually," Josephine corrected after a quick mental count. Heath rolled his eyes at her as he switched off the device. He'd checked their true GPS coordinates against where he thought they were on the map and found they were almost identical.

"Maybe he never hit this exact spot," Josephine said, her tone almost defensive. "Even putting both of you together, there has to be places neither one of you ever saw. It's a big state."

"Yeah, but now we have a new problem." Heath put away the map and looked down over the park.

"Other than the obvious, what are you talking about?" she asked after a few moments of fruitless observation.

"We've got flat, open field to the east and a cloudless sky, at least till later this afternoon if I read it right," he said, nodding in that direction.

She looked to the west and saw the edge of a cloud system that was still miles from them. She knew the implications. Until those clouds reached them, any time they spent in the open and without cover would be time they could be picked up by aerial recon'. They could try to move very slowly across the expanse, mimicking a typical zombie's gait. That may fool cameras on high but it would make them sitting and slow-moving ducks should they be spotted by the dead.

"Okay. But there's a little bit of sparse cover on the other side of the trailer park," she said, nodding towards the flat ground dotted with rough-looking scrub pines and clumps of locust trees.

"Look again."

Josephine turned her head and looked at the ground below. At first it looked like the perfect way. The cover may be minimal, but the flat ground and seeming lack of obstacles meant they could cover the distance fairly quickly.

"It looks okay to me. It's flat and..." Her voice trailed off as she looked more closely at the ground. Several of the spots glistened in the sun from patches of standing water. She refocused her eyes to take in the whole expanse of the ground to the west and found brackish water twinkling back at her. The whole plot all the way to the rough hillside to the west was nothing more than marshland. "Total mud pit, isn't it?" she said, a bit crestfallen.

"Yeah. Noisy as hell to cross and a real health hazard. We're still pretty far from Derry's Corner. I'm willing to bet that's a septic bed for the whole park. No telling what kind of bacteria and other nastiness we'd soak ourselves in even if we did make it across."

"So what are our options?"

"Take the field and pray they're not watching this part of the Area right now, double back and try to go completely around this bowl or go straight up the middle," Heath said, motioning to the trailer park. "It'll take us hours to do either of the first two and the last is going to put us struggling through dry and noisy chest-high weeds and briars through a prime hotel."

"Hotel?"

"They're in there. It's just too perfect a place. The sun probably keeps them inside those cans during the day but it would only take one to see us. The road is the only flat ground around here, and I don't see any carcasses out in the mire. If they didn't evacuate the park before the shit really hit the fan, there's no telling how many of them could be in there. Fuck," he said, the disgust thick in his voice.

Josephine knew the reason for that. He'd counted on the delay in their time to belt around Derry's Corner but he hadn't counted on this. Putting the two together should they decide to double back and go completely around the valley would add another full day onto their trip, a day that according to the weather forecasts would be overcast and rob them of precious daylight when they needed it most. Add to that the moon would be entering its new phase after tomorrow night. With the extra day added they would spend their last night before their planned arrival at the survivor's shelter with virtually no natural light to be had. She could tell by Heath's stare and the set of his jaw that he was mulling over the same conditions.

"Maybe it's empty," Josephine said.

Heath rolled his eyes at her again then patted the top of her head. "Optimism. That's just darling of you."

"So what do we do then?" she asked as she brushed his hand away from one of the only more-or-less human gestures he'd given her. This new development had given Josephine a sudden urgency. She had no desire to spend a night in the Area without so much as moonlight. If they found themselves outdoors on that last night... she shuddered inwardly at the thought.

Heath sighed, unzipped his coat then pulled the coil of rope from around his chest. "Stay close and keep your eyes alive behind us. Test your steps, make sure you're not tripping on a discarded bicycle or something lost in the grass and brambles. From the base of the hill to the entry drive into the park will be thick, we'll probably find the same if we make it to the other side. It'll get a little easier if the road that runs between the rows of trailers is paved. And, for God's sake if you have to fire make sure you hit every single time. Every one of those trailers down there could have a propane tank on it. If you pop one of those and it's still solid we're in for a world of shit."

He tied the rope off around the base of a stout tree and let the length trail down the hill. They might be able to make it down without the rope, but the dirt looked dangerously loose for the extreme vertical nature of the slope. Not only would such a descent be noisy, it had a good chance of turning an ankle or causing a complete tumble to the ground.

Heath put on his gloves, grabbed the rope and practically flew down the hill, the short rappelling distance practically a blink for a man trained to do so from a hovering helicopter. He dropped the last few feet to the ground and crouched with his rifle held at his shoulder, covering her and stabilizing the loose end of the rope under his boot while she made her much slower and more careful descent to join him. He spared a moment to look at her then nodded his head. She returned his nod, swallowed back the fear-produced bile that threatened to creep up her throat then followed him into the trailer park.

Williams had found the guest bedroom on his own and was showered and dressed well before Julie made her entrance into the kitchen. Just as he'd suspected, her hair and make-up were perfect. He didn't think she really needed it, though. She may have the personality of a barracuda but he couldn't deny she was stunningly beautiful. "I made coffee. Hope you don't mind," he said over his shoulder from his seat at the table.

"I mind everything about you, Mr. Williams," Julie said, though it didn't stop her from pouring a cup. She tasted it and winced. "Perhaps you hadn't noticed, but that's not some Maxwell House swill there," she nodded to the paper bag of her custom roast. "You don't just slop a handful into the coffee maker. I'll appreciate it if you keep your hands off of anything and everything in this apartment. I may have to put up with you, but I don't have to feed you as well."

"Of course. My apologies. I didn't realize you kept your bed against the wall. I guess we know which side you get up on." Julie sneered at him then dumped her cup. He returned her look with a broad smile as she got a fresh cup and a tea bag from the cupboard over the sink. Williams took a moment to look at her while her back was turned.

She wore a black skirt that clung to her perfectly-formed legs, the hem well above her knees, and a mauve blouse. When she turned he saw it was as low-cut as he thought it would be. It was far more cleavage than he would have expected from a nightly news anchor, but then again he'd grown up watching Dan Rather.

She stared at him for a moment, her sneer turning to a snarl. "How dare you look at me like that!"

"It's my job to know what you're wearing and what you look like at any given time, in case I need to pick you out of a crowd or I have to give a description to the police."

"It's too early in the morning for that much bullshit at one time, Howie," she said, reverting to the childish titling.

Williams checked his watch. It was going on eleven a.m. Then again, she was working nights now. She turned back to the sink and poured hot tap water over the teabag in the cup.

"What's your itinerary for today?" Williams asked as he produced a pen and notepad from inside his coat.

"Boy, you're really playing this thing to the hilt, aren't you?" She shook her head as she dunked her teabag then threw it into the sink. "I told you, I'm not in any danger. There's no big bad grave robber lurking in the closet to jump out and get me."

"Are you sure about that?" Williams asked, almost too innocently.

Julie turned and regarded him coldly, like a judge from the bench. "And what's that supposed to mean?"

"Messing with anything having to do with Area 187 is a quick ticket to some very bad things, Ms. Sommers. Even if you didn't meet with grave robbers yourself, you've been in close contact with those that have or may have. Like Ms. Terrell, for example."

"Josephine? We just work for the same network, so don't try to lump me in with that little backwoods bitch. I don't have anything to do with her stories."

Williams noticed how her voice and mannerisms changed

when she talked about Josephine Terrell. He filed that little nugget away. It was always good to know people had buttons that could be pushed when needed.

"No? You knew enough to know she was working on it. As far as Homeland and some of the seedier elements of the Area culture are concerned you have culpability. If some grave robber out there even thinks you can identify him, you very well could be in danger."

Julie stared at him for a long moment. Even when she'd told him the truth about having absolutely nothing to do with Josephine's story it didn't serve her. If that bastard Bill would have kept his mouth shut she wouldn't have been saddled with Williams in the first place.

"The only thing you need to know about my itinerary is that we're going to go to the office so Bill can tell you and my father that he was lying when he said I had any involvement in Josephine's work so he'll take you off me."

"Absolutely no involvement?" Williams asked. The DVD he'd found in her bag would have gotten any normal, unknown person first class accommodations at a Homeland detention facility just for possessing it. Whether Julie wanted to admit it or not, she was definitely involved.

"None whatsoever. Call the garage and have my car brought around," she ordered as she poured her untouched tea down the drain and made for the door.

"I'm your personal security advisor, Ms. Sommers, not your valet," Williams said, citing the official title on his job description. "Call them yourself."

Chapter V
Canned Dead

If Josephine had thought her senses were on high alert before, it was nothing compared to what they were now. She almost wished Heath would leave information out sometimes, just go with the generic "shut up and stay close". The sounds of the dead weeds moving across her leathers sounded like a pair of corduroys rubbing together, the briars and brambles like the loud zipper on her grandfather's old suitcase. Finally, they reached the driveway into the park. Josephine was never so glad to see cracked and broken asphalt in her life. The trip through the heart of the park would be harrowing enough. At least she didn't have to be as cautious about where she put her feet. If the pavement ran all the way to the other side of the park and no zombies sat sunning themselves outside the trailers they might just make it.

Heath kneeled in the last few feet of tall grass before the pavement to survey the park entrance. The lawns had overgrown, of course, as had the shrubbery planted along the drive and walkways. There were plenty of spots where the pavement had cracked over the years to let the weeds take hold, but those were at least far shorter and sparser than what they'd passed through already. Aside from the few long vines that had managed to grow across the lane between the rows of trailers, their way was fairly clear. There were a few cars parked here and there along the road as well. Those would have to be skirted carefully in case their owners had died in them and were forever locked in their vehicles thanks to the too-complicated seatbelt and door latches.

They moved through the last of the weeds and onto the pavement. Heath kept his rifle at his shoulder but pointed down and ahead, letting his head stay forward on their path and his peripheral vision on the trailers and cars to their sides. They were walking into the perfect ambush site, and if the dead discovered they were here they would be quickly surrounded. They'd made it as far as the second trailer in the row when Heath stopped suddenly, his head angled slightly towards the row of trailers to his left. Josephine almost asked what he'd heard but remembered where she was and clamped her lips together tightly. A light, quick sound like a shoe scuffing on cement came to her and now she was straining her head in the perceived direction of the sound. Josephine caught a quick flicker of movement out of the corner of her eye near the trailer at the head of the lane behind them. She brought the muzzle of her rifle up quickly and placed the sights where she'd thought she'd seen the movement, but there was nothing there now. After a moment it was Heath's turn to raise his rifle and pivot at the waist towards another trailer further up the way.

The crack of a rifle suddenly split the air, followed immediately by Heath spinning in a stumbling half-circle before crashing to the ground a few feet away. Josephine whipped her rifle this way and that, trying to get the shooter in her sights as she moved towards Heath.

"Heath!" she said in a loud stage whisper. Several tinny, echoing moans joined her words as they rolled out of the aluminum and wood tombs around them. Unless the zombies had learned to use guns, she and Heath had two very large and very immediate problems.

"Heath!" she repeated again as the moans were joined by others. Within moments the whole park was alive with the droning of the dead. Rotting heads appeared in the windows around them and rotting bodies started coming from open doors and from around the trailers nearest them. Heath groaned and got to his knees, one hand retrieving his dropped rifle while the other wiped blood from a gash that had opened on his forehead.

"Go!" Heath said as their sniper's rifle cracked again. A chunk of the thin asphalt strip that had once served as a driving lane through this section of the park flew away just a few inches from his knee as the bullet missed its intended target. Josephine grabbed Heath by the strap of his pack and hauled him to his feet with strength borne of panic.

"You're not leaving me alone out here!" The two broke into a stumbling run down the lane. Dozens of the dead were converging on them now, coming from all directions. Heath shifted his course slightly and ran them towards a large, heavily modified pick-up truck. Even with its age-flattened tires, its oversized rims still made it stand taller than its factory contemporaries.

"Get up there!" Heath shouted as they reached the back bumper. He turned and started firing into the massing dead, picking off the closest few with several well-placed and metronome-timed shots while Josephine scrambled onto the open tailgate.

"What about the shooter? We'll be sitting ducks up here!"

"Have you checked out the alternative?" Heath said without stopping his measured slaughter of the approaching dead.

Josephine moved further up the bed of the truck towards the cab, the height giving her a first-hand look at the kind of swarming she'd only seen from archive footage taken during the Area's original outbreak. The rational part of her mind told her there couldn't be more than forty coming at them now, but the close sardine can-like confines of the unit-thick park made them seem like so many more. But even that consolation was quickly driven away as rationality amended its take on her current situation; more of them were still coming, arriving from other parts of the park to swell the numbers to truly pants-shitting proportions.

Heath stopped firing and rolled into the truck bed, swapping his empty magazine for a full one as he got to his knees and charged the weapon.

"This would be a real good time to *start fucking shooting*

them," Heath said to her as he spun her to face the opposite side of the truck. Josephine gasped at the growing collection of rotting bodies moving like a slow, unstoppable wave towards her side of the truck. Time seemed to stop for her and the very comforting memory of the first time her grandfather had ever allowed her to fire his British .303 rifle back on the farm what seemed like a lifetime ago hit her conscious mind. At his insisting, Josephine raised her weapon, sighted, held her breath then released it as she pulled the trigger again, and again, and again.

Julie had refused to let Williams into her car, so he'd hopped a cab and followed her. Julie was visibly upset with the fact that even with separate transportation they ended up sharing the same elevator to the offices. The temporary receptionist outside Bill's office waved them through, her attentions fully fixed on trying to answer the seven different ringing lines on the unfamiliar phone before her. Both Howard and Julie were surprised to find not just Bill Hartman in his office but Senator Sommers and his own security advisors as well. One of them had Bill's shirt front in his fist, holding him down against his chair while the Senator stood to the other side.

"Julie..." Bill croaked, his tie constricting his neck. The senator looked up and frowned at his daughter.

"Julie, wait outside please," he said, his tone telling her he wasn't asking.

"What's going on here?"

"Mr. Williams," the elder Sommers interrupted her, "please escort my daughter to the waiting room and make sure she doesn't come back until I call for her." Williams nodded hesitantly but did as his employer instructed and guided the young woman by the arm out the door into the waiting room.

"Get your filthy hands off of me!" Julie screamed, her shrill voice turning every head in the office. Williams looked around quickly but didn't let go. Instead, he half-drug her into an empty conference room just off to the side of Bill's office. He shut the door softly behind them then put his ear to the wall the room shared with the executive's private office.

"What the fuck do you think you're doing?" She shoved him, but he didn't move from the wall.

"What the fuck do you think *you're* doing?" Williams asked, softer but with more venom than she, his head swiveling towards her. "If you want to know what they're saying in there you need to shut the hell up for a minute." He turned his head back to the wall, his right ear less than an inch from it.

"Right, like you can hear them through the wall. I happen to know Bill's office is soundproofed."

"Do you want to know what's going on in there?" Williams asked her through clenched teeth.

"I... yes..." she said, a bit taken aback by his tone and the look in his eyes.

"Then shut the fuck up." Julie fell silent and stood a few feet away from him. The conference room was well-insulated as well, to keep regular office noises from interrupting the meetings held there. A full minute passed before Julie went to the wall and put her own ear to it. She kept it there for only a few moments, long enough for her to feel like a fool.

"This is ridiculous," she mumbled. Williams shot her a warning look strong enough to make her take a step back. She waited several more moments before she stepped in close again, her curiosity egging her on.

"Can you hear them?" Julie couldn't see how Williams could hear anything. She'd faked enough orgasms in that room to know that anyone outside it couldn't hear anything. Bill had liked her loud.

"I could if you'd shut up for a minute," Williams said, concentration evident on his face. Julie let another minute pass before she sighed. Williams looked at her and moved away from the wall. "Your boss couldn't produce Terrell and your old man got impatient. He wouldn't tell him where she was so they've roughed him up pretty good. We'd better get back out in the waiting room. I couldn't make out everything, but I do know he just spilled the fact that you have a certain DVD in your possession. I'll bet your daddy will want to have a word with you."

Just then the door to the conference room opened. One of her father's guards looked in then waved for them to follow while he wiped a thin rivulet of blood from his knuckles with a handkerchief. Julie and Howard walked out of the conference room and into Bill's office, the guard right behind them.

"Bill?" Julie said. Bill was lying over his desk and raised his head upon hearing his name. His face was covered with blood, his nose bent rather noticeably to one side. His right eye was swelled almost shut and one of his teeth was lying in a pool of bloody spittle on the desk. He groaned once then slumped again.

"Julie, Princess, it has come to my attention that unbeknownst to your network, Mr. Hartman and this Josephine Terrell have been involved in a plot to send her into Area 187. They've even roped John Heath into it. They should have listened to me from the start on that one. I always knew we hadn't heard the last of him," Sommers said.

Williams held his hand up to his face and coughed softly into his fist at the mention of John Heath. His uncle had always told Howie that though he might one day *make* a poker player, with all his tells he'd never *be* one.

"Daddy! What did you do to Bill?"

"Princess, you have to understand that what they've been doing is very, very wrong," Sommers said, addressing her in the same voice he'd used when he had to explain that her puppy had been run over when she was five. "He wouldn't tell me the truth, so for the sake of national security we had to *make* him tell us. You understand, don't you?"

Julie nodded her head numbly, her eyes still fixed on Bill's battered body. Williams kept himself loose and his eyes scanning all the players in the room. He'd taken this job to get away from the Area, to go legit as they say. He would've smiled at the irony of it all if the act wouldn't have caused concern to the Senator.

"Julie, Mr. Hartman claims you have a disc, one that supposedly has a recording from Area survivors on it. Do you?"

Julie nodded again, slowly. "Do you have it with you?" She nodded again and reached into her bag. She felt around for a moment then looked down into her bag with a panicked expression.

"I had it in here yesterday..." she stammered. Then, suddenly, "Daddy! Please! I didn't know all of this would happen! I didn't do anything wrong! I just found it in Josephine's dressing room," she said, real tears rolling down her face this time.

Williams watched her out of the corner of his eye. He didn't think she had any real concern for Hartman, nor likely for anyone but herself for that matter. But it was obvious that seeing the man bloodied and beaten to within an inch of his life had deeply unsettled her.

"I didn't know she was going to actually go!"

Senator Sommers walked across the office and gently took his daughter in his arms. "It's all right, Princess. Hush now," he said, holding her against his chest where her tears left deep black mascara scars across his silk tie. "I know you didn't have anything to do with this. I know you're innocent. But we need that disc. Do you understand?" Julie pulled her head away from her father's chest but stayed in his warm embrace.

"But I don't have it. It was in my bag last night. Oh, Daddy, you know I'd give it to you if I had it."

"Senator Sommers?" Williams said. The Senator shot him a dagger stare but nodded for him to continue.

"Forgive my intrusion, but I saw a plastic case, like a CD case, on the chair where she put her bag down last night. If it was in her bag it's probably what you're looking for." Sommers smiled at him and pushed his daughter far enough away so he could look down at her face.

"See there, Princess? It's all right. It's probably just sitting in your apartment. But I do need it as soon as possible."

"Sir, if you don't mind me saying she seems pretty shaken up. I'd be glad to take her home, get her settled in and bring the disc back," Williams said.

Sommers thought for a moment then nodded. "Good idea, Williams. I'll need to stay here until the Homeland agents arrive to take Mr. Hartman into custody." Sommers released his daughter and smiled at her while he dabbed at her tears with his handkerchief. "See, Princess? It's going to be all right. Mr. Williams here will take you home and make sure everything's safe for you so you can rest. Now go with him and I'll call you later for dinner. I've already seen to it that they have a replacement for your show tonight."

Julie nodded at him, her bottom lip trembling. "Daddy, if I would've known what they were doing, what they were *really* doing, you know I would've told you, don't you?"

"Yes, Princess. I know you would have." Sommers turned to Williams. "Get her home and get the disc. Don't view it and don't tell anyone you have it. Take Mitcham with you," he said, nodding to the larger of his two goons in the room. The big man walked over to join Williams and Julie.

"Really, Mr. Sommers, I don't need the help. I wouldn't want to waste Mitcham's time-"

"That disc is a matter of national security, Mr. Williams. I'll feel better with both of you responsible for its safekeeping until I have it in my own hands," Sommers said, his voice returning to its tone of absolute authority.

"Yes, sir." At a nod from the Senator the gorilla-like Mitcham ushered Williams and Julie from the office.

Time stopped for Josephine. The rifle's weight felt good in her hands as she pulled the trigger. The top of a skull blew away, spewing dried grayish matter into the mass of decayed flesh behind it as the dirge continued around them. She pretended she couldn't hear the low, guttural sound even as her belly clenched from it. She was glad their invisible sniper had stopped adding his attacks to the mix but at the same time would've welcomed another rifle to add to their fire. She sighted another one dressed in a blood-stained cook's apron and pulled the trigger again. She moved to another target, sighted and fired, then another and another. Soon she was twisting at the waist, concentrating on each shot even as the moaning seemed to grow in volume and density. The sound was coming from all around her now, louder and growing ever higher in pitch. She didn't realize she'd been adding her own screams to the maddening cacophony until she pulled the trigger on an empty chamber.

"Fuck! Get it together or so help me I'll leave your ass here!" Heath called over the moaning. Josephine struggled with her rifle, finally freeing the empty magazine and fumbling only once before slamming a fresh one home. She whipped the charge handle and pointed the barrel down at the edge of the truck. Several of them had already massed on the side and were now trying to pull themselves up into the bed. Heath pivoted at the waist and dropped three across the tail end of the box, creating an effective though sadly temporary blockade to those behind them.

"There's too many!" Josephine screamed as she started firing into the crowd that had gathered close enough to touch the truck. Heath's rifle ran dry again as Josephine's firing became more erratic, inaccurate. A cloud of gray-green flesh hung over the knot of undead as her bullets tore through chests, arms and heads. Worse, she seemed to be missing as many times as she hit, the press of bodies taking away even the momentary advantage of a chest shot pushing a zombie back or even taking it off its feet. Heath slung his rifle across his chest then drew his own pistol with his right hand and reached behind him to pull her revolver from her holster with his left. He had a good ten seconds before the press on his side would be able to navigate the moat of corpses he'd made to reach his side of the truck. He used those precious seconds to swing both handguns around to the front of the truck to dispatch the four zombies that had managed to crawl up onto the truck's long hood before he grabbed Josephine by her belt and hauled her bodily up onto the cab's roof. She continued to fire into the crowd of dead flesh along the passenger side of the cab until her rifle ran dry again.

"Fucking run!" Heath yelled as he picked off two more closest to the edge of the hood. Josephine threw her rifle over her shoulder, jumped down onto the hood and then to the ground. There were more of them crowding around the sides of the bed now, their dead brains failing to comprehend their prey's escape plans until both Heath and Josephine's feet were back on the pavement and carrying them towards the far end of the park. The horde of zombies thinned considerably as they ran. Josephine's tears of rage and terror dried in the wind, the release from near-certain death enough to snap her mind back to its proper, if terrified, working state.

She pulled her rifle off her shoulder, removed the spent magazine and managed to slap a fresh one home while she ran. More of them were coming out of the dilapidated trailers now, their moans adding to the long parade they'd gained that snaked back to the other end of the park. She slung her rifle back over her shoulder and pushed herself to keep pace with Heath as they charged down the lane towards the opposite side of the park. Speed was their ally now, and there was no sense in wasting bullets trying to hit a moving target with a moving rifle. Their only hope now was that the bulk of the trailer court's infestation had been attracted to the firefight, leaving their way to the bottom of the tall hill at the other end of the lane unguarded. That hill had appeared to be just as sheer as the one they'd come down, and though it would be a tough climb she was sure that once they got a few yards from the base the steepness would all but stop even the most determined of the dead. At least, she hoped.

The three of them rode back to Julie's building in her car, the silence in the small space thick enough to taste. Williams constantly checked the rearview mirror as he drove, watching Julie's face. She still looked shocked, but the emotion had done something else; it had softened her features. She actually looked like a scared little girl now, not just playing the part. Williams swung her BMW into the underground lot and the trio rode the elevator up to her apartment.

"It was over by that chair," Williams said to Mitcham. "You grab it and I'll make sure she gets settled in." The large man didn't say a word and let his nod be his reply. Williams guided her down the hall and opened her bedroom door for her. "You going to be okay?"

"Yes, yes, I'll be fine. I'm not an invalid," she said, though her tone lacked the cold authority she normally strived for with the hired help.

"Good. Get some rest. With any luck, this will be the last time you see me."

"At least something good came out of today," she said, the intended insult coming out flat off her tongue.

"Ms. Sommers, have you watched the DVD?" Williams asked suddenly. Julie stared at him blankly, her mouth hanging open for several moments before she spoke.

"Yes. Why?" she asked, the oddity of his blunt question bringing an answer from her she might not otherwise have given.

"Just curious. Were there zombies on it? Any gory stuff?"

"No. What are you, some kind of creep or something?" she asked, her face twisting more into her old self for a moment.

"No, just wondered, that's all. I'll let your father know you're safe and sound." He shut the door behind her and went back into the living room. Mitcham was standing by the chair watching him as he came down the hall.

"There's nothin' here." His deep voice was laced with a thick Bronx accent.

"You sure?" Williams said, suddenly concerned.

"I got eyes, don't I?" Williams ignored his answer and leaned down to look under the chair himself.

"Damn it, I know I saw a CD case right here last night - oh, wait, here it is," he said. He pulled his now-silenced Colt from his shoulder rig as he stood back up, placed the muzzle against the surprised man's forehead and pulled the trigger in one fluid motion. The back of the man's head exploded in a shower of gore that painted the wall behind him in shades of red and gray. His mountainous body kept its feet a moment longer before it fell to the floor like a chopped oak, his blood gushing out onto the formerly pristine white carpet.

"Ugh. That's going to stain," Williams said to himself as he looked down at the body. He rifled the dead man's pockets, taking his cash, identification and Glock, then lifted one of the couch cushions. The DVD was right where he had left it. He picked it up and looked at it for a moment. "I should've known the minute I laid eyes on you that you'd be nothing but trouble," he said to it. Howard holstered his weapon and put the dead man's pistol at the small of his back under his coat.

The corpse defiled the carpet with its rapidly-cooling blood. "Thanks, I didn't get a chance to stop at the ATM today." He flipped through the large wad of bills he'd taken from the body then slipped it into his pocket. Howard figured he had an hour, perhaps 90 minutes at best before Sommers would be trying to call.

Williams stuck his hand into the side pocket of his flight bag and came up with a cheap, pre-paid and virtually untraceable cell phone, the type you could buy in any grocery store check-out line and dialed. It rang three times before the phone on the other end picked up. "Uncle Jasper," Howard said then listened for a moment. "Yeah, it's me. I have a situation here..."

Heath and Josephine rounded a bend in the road and suddenly found themselves up against a blockade made from several cars, trucks and even 5th wheel campers that had been rammed together with thick stands of West Virginia's real state flower, multiflora rose, clogging the way past to the sides of the makeshift barricade. Junk and debris had been added on top of these, creating an impromptu wall of twisted, rusting steel and garbage more than fifteen feet tall at its lowest point. Apparently the last living people to grace this place had either made a stand or had attempted to slow pursuing undead while they escaped up the steep hill on the other side of the barrier. Heath and Josephine would never know if the tactic had served those long-ago survivors, but it practically doomed them today. The road behind was choked with a mass of moaning, reaching zombies and the way up onto the next hill, a hill that would be impassable to the walking corpses, was blocked. They exchanged looks as Heath shrugged and tossed her revolver back to her. "There's one bullet left in it. If we get overrun, it's up to you how you use it."

Heath reloaded his rifle and started a controlled fire into the creeping horde. Every hiss of the rifle dropped another at the head of the snake, serving to slow the progress of those behind as they stumbled over the bodies of their fellows. Josephine followed his lead for several rounds, her mind suddenly calm and her hand equally steady. She thought they would have enough ammunition to drop every zombie in this crowd. But she knew that the zombies here were just the immediate threat. Anything dead within a mile would have heard the collective moan rise up, the claxon call of the dead carried on the wind.

"Get on the cars!" Heath said between shots. He stepped near her, putting him more towards the center of the gaining masses and increased his rate of fire to cover her while she climbed.

With agility she didn't know she possessed, Josephine made it to the top of the closest car, a late 70's Buick from what she could tell. As soon as she was on her feet she returned Heath's favor and started firing at the horde, her elevated position not only giving her a better sight picture but letting her see the true extent of the press of the undead coming at them.

Heath took a few more shots before he stepped onto the door frame of the other car, an ancient land-barge Ford LTD. He spared a moment to look inside, hoping he could pass through the vehicle to the other side. Transmissions, engines and all sorts of junk had been stuffed in both the front and back seats making the throughway impossible. He knew without asking that the car Josephine stood on would be the same way. Both of them had just enough room on their respective roofs to stand. The collected debris stacked high above the cars made further progress almost impossible under fire. Still, it was their only hope. He knew he had ten rounds left in his current magazine with only two more full ones in his pack. He pulled his pistol. There was no way he could miss at this range and he'd rather run out of pistol ammo than rifle so early into the mission.

"Climb!" he called over to her. "Get to the top and start shooting or find us a hole through this thing!"

"You can't keep them back with only one gun!" Heath took precious seconds to toss his rifle to her. She caught it awkwardly, nearly pitching from her Detroit steel tightrope as she snagged it from the air. "What the hell are you doing?"

"They're too close for both of us to stop shooting. They'll be crawling over each other as soon as they hit the cars, and if a bunch of them and their weight grabs hold of all this junk it could be enough to pull it and us down. One shoots, one climbs. Find a hole or get to the top and start firing down on them!"

Josephine immediately understood his train of thought. If she could reach the top and find solid footing she would be a one-woman ghoul-slaying army, able to concentrate on nothing but shooting, allowing him the time he would need to climb up after her. She secured both rifles across her shoulders, turned into the pile of sharp, rusted and precarious detritus and put Heath's imminent danger out of her mind as her hands and feet went to their work.

The problem wasn't the height of the pile but rather in the climbing. Sharp pieces of scrap metal, car parts and furniture reduced to bare steel and wood frames jutted out from the wall, making safe hand and foot holds virtually impossible. Still, it was their only way out. Josephine moved a few feet up the metal mountain, grabbing the frame of what once must have been a large recliner and tried to ignore the little bits of the metal and wood cutting through her leathers to bite the soft skin beneath as she hauled herself up and over the chair's skeleton. She paused for just a moment to see how Heath fared then wished she hadn't. The horde was much closer now that there was only one gun firing. The motley crew of the dead had also been able to expand their flanks now that they didn't have the confines of row upon row of trailers to force them into a tight column, allowing even more of them to spread out before Heath and force him to cover a much wider field of fire. Josephine made a snap decision, turned her body just enough to get one of the rifles off her shoulders and sighted on one of the zombies that had unknowingly managed to move itself into a flanking position just below her and to Heath's left. She squeezed the trigger and a large chunk of the dead man's scalp tore away as the rest of the body dropped like a stone.

"Don't stop! Get the fuck up there!" Heath yelled up at her.

"You're welcome!" Josephine yelled over the moaning. She'd no sooner re-slung when she felt a pair of strong hands grab her around the shoulders. She screamed as she tried to both compensate her balance and fight against the pull from within the stack of debris but it was no use. She screamed for Heath as she was pulled head-first through the frame's empty seat and into the depths of the pile itself. Her next scream was cut short by a lightning bolt of pain at her temple.

Heath looked up just in time to see Josephine get pulled inside the pile. From his angle he couldn't even see the exact spot where she'd been pulled through. Regardless of what had happened to her, he couldn't help her until he helped himself. He holstered his pistol just as the first of the many hands got within reach of him. With his hands free Heath turned into the stack and scrambled in earnest for the top. He made it only another foot to the vertical before his climbing caused a section of the pile to shift, the loud screech of metal on metal drowning out the horde's collective moan. As if in slow motion, Heath and hundreds upon hundreds of pounds of the junk wall slid from the cars. As one chunk of cast-off garbage, engine parts and old furniture fell victim to gravity's pull another section gave way. Heath found himself falling along with it, turning his head just in time to see the dead reach up, their arms open and ready to embrace him.

Chapter VI
Rude Awakenings

Julie awoke to find herself strapped to an unfamiliar bed in an equally unfamiliar room. She choked against the gag in her mouth, her gorge suddenly rising. She was going to throw up, but if she did so with the gag she'd drown on her own vomit. She turned her head to the only light in the room, a lamp beside the bed. Williams was sitting on the edge of the bed by the lamp, a large plastic bucket in his hands.

"If I don't take off the gag so you can spew, you'll choke to death. Neither one of us wants that to happen. So, I'll make you a deal; I take off the gag so you can do what you have to do if you don't start screaming your head off when you're done. Deal? Blink once for yes, twice for eat shit and die," Williams said.

Julie wanted so badly to blink twice and almost did. Her rising bile won out though and she blinked once.

"See? You can be agreeable after all." He placed the bucket and pulled the gag from her mouth. Julie erupted violently, spilling her stomach and gasping between rounds until all she had left was a series of dry heaves laced with threats against his manhood and random cursing. When she was finally empty she turned her head away from the bucket, exhausted and feeling sick all over.

"You... what do you..." she said between gulps of air. She turned back towards the bucket and coughed several times. Williams took the bucket away when she was done then gently lifted her head and put another pillow under it.

"Here, take a little sip," he said, holding a small glass of water up to her lips. "Just a little for now. It'll help settle your stomach. Sorry I had to go with the chloroform, but the corner druggist was fresh out of nitrous." She took a sip of water. She tried to take more but he pulled the glass away before she could. "You can have more later."

Julie lay quiet for several moments while her insides churned and her rage built. She turned her head to him, eyes glistening and opened her lips in a snarl. "You fucking bastard!" she screamed at him, her voice hoarse from purging and the after-effects of the chloroform he'd used to knock her out.

"Careful, there," he said, holding her gag up, "it goes back in just as easily." She glared at him, her mouth open but her scream held on her tongue. "Remember our deal."

"Where am I? What the hell do you think you're doing to me?" Her voice was elevated to just below a scream.

"Calm down. I don't want to hurt you, but if you force me to I will. How you come out of this is completely up to you from this point on."

"Come out of what? Why are you doing this to me?" She struggled through a wave of nausea and lay spent and groaning when it was done. "It's about money, isn't it?" she asked weakly. "You'd better let me go. My father will have the FBI, the CIA, Homeland and the whole fucking Marine Corps looking for me by now."

"Yeah, it's a warm feeling to know so many people are thinking about you." Williams set the bucket on the floor and turned to better face her, his leg brushing up against hers. She bucked away from him as if he were on fire, her chest heaving against the bonds that secured her to the bed.

"If you so much as *think* about touching me I'll see to it they cut off your balls when they find me!"

"Well *someone* thinks rather highly of themselves," he said, his smile nearly driving her over the edge. "Okay, I'm going to give you the short version of all this, so listen up. Nothing's going to happen to you, I just needed to make sure you were in a nice, safe and secure area to keep you out of trouble just like my job description says."

"What trouble? Untie me right now and I might even ask them to let you live."

"I'm afraid I can't do that. Now, you can shut up and listen or I can put the gag back in for a few hours to give you time to think about changing that attitude of yours. Like I said, how it goes from here on is up to you."

Julie worked her mouth open and closed a few times until she finally closed it and glared at him.

"There, isn't that better? Now we can discuss this like adults," he said then sighed as if he were trying to talk to a small child. "You're involved in this whether you wanted to be or not. The minute you watched that DVD you were involved. The bullshit you pulled with it to get the anchor job and to try and impress your daddy only served to sink you deeper."

"Deeper into what? I have nothing to do with any of this. *You're* the one that's in too deep, Howie. When my father finds me he's going to hold you down while I cut your balls off, and then I'll let him kill you with his bare hands." Her lips were smiling and eyes were glinting.

"You should really check into some anger management," he said as he got up, leaned over her and shoved the gag back in. She struggled and screamed anew, stopping only when he started towards the door. She stopped as quickly as she'd started, her screams turning to a garbled, almost whimpering sound. He stopped and walked back to her bedside. "Ready to listen?" he asked. She grudgingly nodded her head and he removed the gag once more.

"All right. Tell me what the hell you want from me," she said, her tone exhausted.

"The only thing I want from you is to stay the hell out of the way while this little drama you helped create gets resolved. You're doing a fine job of it right now. Keep up the good work. Other than that, there's not much else you really need to know. This set-up is only temporary. If you can keep your mouth shut and do what you're told then I'll move you into a room tomorrow morning where you don't have to be tied up. I'll keep you there for a few days and then the door will open and you'll be free to go."

"You're insane. You won't get away with this! My father - "

"Your father is part of the problem, little girl. If you only knew the half of it," he said.

"Wait a minute - you're one of those Area nut-jobs, aren't you? So what are you, huh? A reporter? Maybe even a fucking grave robber?" she asked, spitting out the last words. He just looked down at her and shook his head slowly.

"No. At least I wasn't anymore. I may have to go back to it though. You kinda' fucked up my grand reentry into the world of gainful employment."

"Me? You kidnap me, drug me, tie me to a fucking bed and then claim that somehow it's *my* fault?" she said. "I'm really going to enjoy watching my father put a bullet in you."

"Make up your mind. Is he going to kill me with his bare hands or shoot me?"

"Both, you fucking bastard. But, if you let me go right now I promise I'll ask him to pick just one," she said. He leaned down close enough to smell the remnants of the bile on her breath.

"There's a big change coming to your little world, Julie. If you value your life, I suggest that when you do get out of here you find some nice little place to hole up. The name Sommers may get just a little stained in the very near future."

Julie tried to spit in his face but the after-effects of the chloroform and the gag had left her mouth as dry as the Gobi. He chuckled at her frustration and went to the door. "I'll bring some dinner in a little while. If you can promise to be good, I may even feed it to you."

"You're going to die, Howie. As soon as my father finds me, you know you're going to die, don't you?" she asked, her voice as sweet as she could make it.

"Yeah, but you better hope he doesn't find you and me in the same place at the same time. If he does, we'll be walking the path to hell together."

"Hell hath no fury," Jasper said absently as Julie's muffled threats, screams and curses filtered down to them through the ceiling. He was sitting on the couch, one of his maps spread out on the cushions.

"That's one way of putting it, Unc'," Williams said, falling into his childhood address for his mother's brother. "And that one has plenty of it to go around," he said, sitting down on the floor in front of the couch where he could see the map.

"Girl's been at it for hours now."

"You told me to leave the gag off, said it was the proper thing to do."

"That was 'fore I knew she was part sailor and part banshee," Jasper said with a wink. "Ah well, we reap what we sow. Let her go at it. She'll get tired eventually." They shared a quick chuckle and went back to studying the map.

It was a complete accident that uncle and nephew had fallen into the same line of work. Howard Williams had been a Green Beret stationed in the Middle East when the outbreak happened. By the time he was rotated back to the States, the military had pulled out of the Area and had turned over the construction and security of the buffer zone to Homeland. An admitted adrenalin junkie, he fell into grave robbing shortly after leaving the Army as much for the lucrative possibilities as for the excitement.

Uncle Jasper had tried to talk him into going straight as soon as he found out. Jasper tried for months to convince him it was no life for a young man of his experience. He tried to talk him into going back to college or taking a job with one of the six-figure private security companies still protecting Americans and their interests in the Middle East, reasoning that even that job was far less dangerous than making a living in the Area. Eventually, Jasper stopped trying to convince him against being a grave robber and accepted him into the secretive cabal of their work. But that didn't mean he had to like it.

"Ya know Howie, if you'd have listened to me-"

"If I'd listened to you, you wouldn't know your buddy Heath was in deep shit right now," Williams said to the only man on the planet he accepted calling him "Howie". "So what do we do now?"

Jasper rubbed his eyes then sat up straight on the couch, wincing as his back popped from spending too much time bent over his maps. "We gotta get a message to him, let him know that they're onto him. The only saving grace in this is that you've got the damned disc. The one Jo brought here had the coordinates edited off it. If Homeland had the location of the survivors they'd already be dead. You'll want to hide that thing downstairs. Been gettin' a lot of calls, Homeland's crackin' down. They're roundin' up robbers."

"How safe are we here?" Jasper chuckled at him softly.

"Safe is a relative term, Howie. Ain't none of us truly safe. I don't know any of 'em that know I'm here, but I'm not sure we can take that chance for too long. Especially when we got Senator Sommers's daughter strapped to a bed upstairs."

"You told me to bring her here, Unc'."

"Yeah, I know. There wasn't much else we could do about it at the time, and it's probably the safest place for us and for her at the moment. I've never met the man, but I just don't trust the good Senator. I look in his eyes and I feel like the devil's lookin' back at me."

"Right now she's insurance. Sommers can't come at us with guns blazing if he thinks he'll catch his little girl in the crossfire, devil or no."

Jasper stood up and lit his pipe. "Don't be too sure 'bout that, Howie. It's an election year comin' up, and sympathy for a dead daughter cut down by evil-doers would mean as many votes for him as crackin' the ring of said evil-doers."

"You think he'd do that?"

"It might not be his plan A, but it'd make one hell of a contingency." Williams looked closely at the map. Jasper had made a mark about five miles long according to the key.

"That where you think they'd be about now?"

"Yup, if they're on schedule," Jasper said. Williams traced the line from the North Gate down to Jasper's mark.

"They weren't planning on moving very fast for traveling so light."

"Heath's idea. He could've got there a lot quicker, but he didn't want to burn Jo out."

"No offense, but I never did like that guy," Williams said.

"John? Why not?"

"I don't really know. I mean, I'm not stupid enough to believe a lot of the bullshit out there. Anybody that's been on the inside knows that," Williams said, his voice stopping oddly.

"So what is it you don't like about him then?"

"I saw him in Pittsburgh once. It was his eyes, Unc'. I think that's what did it. It was like there was nothing left in him. If I'd have been on the inside I'd have thought I was looking at a digger."

Jasper sucked on his pipe thoughtfully and looked down at his nephew. With Howie on the floor and him standing, Jasper couldn't help think about the times when they were both twenty-five years younger and in Jasper's house; his *real* house, the one Homeland had dragged him from. The one the dead owned now. Howie had spent a lot of summers at that house in his youth. Back then they talked about things like Jasper's '53 Ford and their plans for spending a whole week at the county fair. "Times they do a change," Jasper said softly, shaking his head.

"What?"

"Nothin Howie. Just thinkin'." Jasper's mind slowly came back to the present. "John's good people, Howie. He's got his problems just like anybody else, and he's doin' a good thing here."

"Why him though? He isn't a grave robber, is he?"

"Nope, he ain't a robber. He ain't lookin' for somethin', Howie, he's lookin' for some*one*. Same thing he was lookin' for all those years."

"He thinks his wife is with those caretakers?" Williams asked.

Anyone that knew anything about the Area's own John Heath knew why he'd stayed. PBS had played up that angle in their documentary in an attempt to turn the story into more than just a survival epic. Foreign media and the 'net had carried it on in one form or another, with some expanding upon it and others believing it a convenient and heart-warming cover for Heath's real

Homeland-sponsored mission; to find and destroy evidence about the creation of the virus.

"Yup. A woman that looks an awful lot like her shows up in the background on that message," Williams thought back to the video and tried to picture some of the faces behind the doctor.

"So that's how Terrell got the legendary John Heath to saddle up and ride into the death lands again. Very John Wayne; very stupid."

"No help for that now," Jasper said. "You just take good care of your little princess up there. I don't want to see anybody get hurt out of this."

Williams looked up at him, confused. "What are you talking about? I thought we were just going to let her go after we got word to Heath and we figured out where we were going."

"I know where *I'm* goin, Howie. You may want to rethink what you're doin' with the girl. You may need a bargaining chip once this all comes down. If I were you, I'd hold onto her until this is over. It may be the only thing that keeps the dogs off ya."

Williams got to his feet, the memories of times past receding for both of them now that he could look his uncle in the eyes.

"You're going, aren't you?" It was more a statement than a question.

"You know of another way to get a message in there?"

"Unc', be reasonable. They have three days and better than twenty years on you. How the hell do you think you're going to catch up to them? You aren't exactly a spring chicken, you know. That's why you said you retired in the first place; too many close calls, getting too slow. Do you even remember that conversation?"

"I'm too old to go chasin' after money, Howie. But I'll never be too old to help a friend."

"I'm going with you, Unc'. I can't let you go in there alone."

"No, you're not. You got responsibilities here with that girl. Besides, I've been runnin' the Area since before there was an Area. I'll be just fine," Jasper said. Williams opened his mouth to speak but Jasper silenced him with a look. "And that's my final word on it." He kept looking at his nephew until the younger man nodded.

"I don't like it, Unc'. It's bad enough in there, worse when they'll have every bird they can scramble scouring the Area for them."

"Which is exactly why I got to get goin'. Help yourself to the kitchen but clean up after," Jasper said as he started for the basement. "You know how I hate to come home to a dirty kitchen."

The first thing Heath was consciously aware of was the intense weight and pressure across his legs and a sense of utter claustrophobia. His last few moments of consciousness came rushing back to him; holding off the zombies, Josephine climbing the wall of junk and being suddenly and inexplicably sucked inside it, his own attempt at climbing and the horrific results, the crowd of the dead waiting hungrily for him at the end. He stayed in the same tightly tucked fetal position he'd put himself into when he realized the wall of garbage was falling down on him and did a mental check of his body. He realized he could feel all the parts he'd been born with, especially the ones that were cramped and injured. Most importantly, he was still breathing, still thinking, still alive, though by the soft, disjointed moans and shuffling feet he heard from all around the outside of his rusty prison he wasn't sure that was the most advantageous status to have in his current situation.

He opened his eyes and found he could see his surroundings just as well as he could when they were closed. His sense of smell was working fine enough to tell him he wasn't the only one that had suffered in the collapse. There were other bodies mixed in with the wreckage around him. The burning questions would be how many, were any of them still active and, if so, how close where their mouths to him in the blackness of their shared confines. He lay still and quiet for several more minutes with his eyes closed, allowing his more useful senses to paint a mental picture of his immediate area.

The first thing he would have to overcome would be getting his legs free from the crushing weight that had landed on his hips, pinning his already tucked, leverage-deprived legs to the ground.

After that, he would need to extricate himself from the debris while trying to keep the undead both outside the pile and those he may unintentionally free that had been trapped along with him from tearing him to shreds. There was no telling where his rifle had gone in the collapse, but his pistol still dug into his side where it lay in its holster under his body and he could still feel the weight of the pry bar laying against his opposite hip.

Still being armed was a big check in the "pro" column, but so far it was the only hash mark on a page practically black with "con" marks. A mini-gun wouldn't do him any good if he couldn't get free of the twisted pile of wreckage around, and on, him. There was other debris on him as well, but from the lack of punishing weight on his torso and head he had to assume the rest of him was in some sort of accidental pocket. He added another check to the "pro" column in recognition of blind luck then took a deep breath. There would be no waiting them out. He could already feel the tell-tale numbing of reduced blood flow in his lower extremities, and the dead outside could remain there for hours, days, weeks, even months. If he was going to act, it had to be now while he still felt more or less whole. He started pushing and pulling his legs, testing the extent of their capture. He could move them barely an inch in any direction and even then his thighs remained pinned. But even that slight movement had caused enough noise to reverberate through the metal around him to gain notice. The pitch and volume of the moans around him increased, and in seconds he could both hear and feel the horde outside pawing at the end of the pile towards his feet.

Heath kept swinging his calves and feet, but only those parts, back and forth as much as his confines would allow. The sound of his legs moving drew the dead outside to that end, egged them on to get through the pile to find the meat moving within. Heath would've felt more comfortable using bait not connected to his body, but like anyone alive in Area 187 he made do with what he had. It took several minutes, but he was finally able to feel a lessening of the weight that had kept his lower body against the ground. Dim light had started to filter through the junk as had the tireless dead hands that kept pulling the mountain of debris away from him a piece at a time. The moans had grown to a fever pitch now, a sure sign that they'd removed enough junk to let the smell of his blood from what had to be dozens of tiny injuries he'd suffered from the falling wall to waft up to them. Like sharks, the smell of viscera would soon infect the dead with nothing less than a frenzied, single-minded desire to feed. If he managed to get free of the pile, and if his abused legs would function well enough to allow him to stand, he would be faced with an unknown number of blood-crazed zombies with nothing but a pistol and a crowbar for defense.

A wide shaft of dingy light suddenly poured in just below his knees followed by a rotting arm with a human mouth-sized chunk missing from the muscle just above the wrist. Judging by the color and appearance of it, its owner was likely one of the first generation of the dead, one that had been infected and succumbed in the early days of the outbreak. Heath tried to move his legs again and they flew out and away from him, their constant small motions enough to both attract the dead as well as keep his blood pumping and the limbs limber. Heath braced his hands on the ground at his chest and gave a heave, pushing his upper body down where his legs had been. He drew his now freed pistol with one hand and gave the other to the searching, undead hand. With a triumphant moan the zombie outside the pile pulled with whatever strength remained in its body, dragging Heath's upper body free of the pile and allowing him a crucial moment to steady himself on his feet before the rest of the dead that had climbed onto the pile could register his presence. The zombie locked eyes with Heath and opened its mouth as it lunged toward him. Heath jammed the muzzle of the big automatic pistol into the monster's mouth. Blackened, broken teeth broke free from its rotting gums as it reflexively bit at the blued steel. The back of the zombie's head ripped open, the heavy slug tearing a huge chunk from the back of the zombie's head and transferring its energy to what remained to send the body tumbling down the pile and into a group of its fellows that had started to make their ascent.

"Thanks for the hand," Heath said to the tumbling, rotting

corpse, "but I think I can take it from here."

He turned in a circle, placing a bullet in the head of any zombie with the misfortune to be within his personal comfort zone. Four more bodies rolled and tumbled down the sides of the pile while two remained virtually where they fell, their bodies trapped by the same pile that only moments before had trapped him. Those were only a drop in the bucket considering the size of the rest of the horde, but removing the immediate threat they imposed gave Heath the opportunity to completely free himself from the tangled mass and find more stable footing on wide piece of steel that was likely once a hood from one of the cars now completely buried beneath him. Even though he now had the high ground, Heath knew he was still not in the best of situations. The digging zombies had likely undermined the pile, and there was a high probability that as the entirety of the horde became motivated to climb up after him the whole thing could come crashing down, burying him yet again in rust and garbage.

There were two rounds left in his pistol and only one spare magazine remaining, and though his pack and its multiple magazines of rifle ammo had survived the avalanche along with him, Josephine had his rifle. He looked back towards where the wall of garbage had once stood. It would be a lot easier to get through the barricade now that he'd torn down a goodly section of it, but the way still wasn't clear enough for him to do it quickly. By the time he would pick his way over the junk where he now perched, those on the ground would easily fill the gap. If he was going to escape through the remnants of the trailer park's defensive wall, he would have to thin out the herd.

Chapter VII
The Last Hero

"We'll find them, Alan. I've got the best and the brightest from Homeland down looking for them," General Franklin Haig told the senator. They'd been college fraternity buddies, and when Sommers ended up chairing the Area committee it only took a few strings to get his old friend the comparatively cushy post as military attaché to Homeland.

"God damn it Frank, I don't want to hear you're *going* to find them, I want to hear they're *found*!" Sommers pounded the table in frustration. "We're talking about my daughter here! Besides, do you have any idea how this will make me look if it gets out to the press? Any press? Not only that a God damned grave robber managed to get close to me but that I in turn hired the bastard to guard my daughter *from* grave robbers? I want Williams' head on a platter beside my eggs in the morning; period. Then I want you to find these God damned survivors and I want you to shove a dozen missiles into their little nest. Is all of that clear, *General*?" he said, his inflection on Haig's rank telling the officer he may not have it for much longer.

"Alan, calm down. You know better than I do that the Area is Homeland's show, not the military's. It'll take some time to get everything organized, but we'll get them and bring your daughter back safe and sound."

"Yes, Frank, you will," Sommers stopped at the knock on the door of the Homeland conference room they'd taken over.

"Yes?" Haig called out. A nondescript man in an equally

nondescript dark suit stepped half inside the door.

"General, we got a hit on Josephine Terrell's cell phone. It was last used three days ago to call Hartman's cell."

"Where was she then?" Sommers asked.

"A few miles outside Pittsburgh. We're scrambling hostage rescue and three tactical teams and my regional men are on their way now to get the location under observation."

"Good work, Agent Ross. Call Kempler, have him lean on Hartman. I want to know exactly what was said in that call. Keep me posted at every step," Haig told him. Ross nodded and went to close the door.

"Keep you posted?" Sommers repeated. "Get a helicopter, General. I want to see Williams die with my own eyes."

"Alan," Haig said quietly, "we don't even know if they're there yet. Let's wait-"

"Get a helicopter."

Haig stared at the Senator's cold eyes for a moment before he turned to Ross. "You heard the Senator."

Jasper cinched his pistol belt and hoisted his small pack over his shoulders. It had felt good to retire, natural almost. He knew it had been time to get out of the business then, his age and declining health becoming something more than a hindrance on his jaunts into the Area. Still, it felt just as natural to be back in his faded jeans and well-broken pungi boots. His thick leather jacket bore marks from every trip into the dead lands like the destination labels decorating a weary world traveler's steamer trunk. Each mark had a story to tell; teeth indentations along the left forearm from a near life-ending foray into Charleston, rough scars in the tough leather spaced as human fingertips down the right breast from a run-in near Cox's Mills, even a bullet hole through the upper left shoulder, compliments of a digger he'd happened upon one night near Parkersburg. That had been one of his last runs, and the first one to prove to him that grave robbing was a young man's game.

Jasper's arms were much the same as Heath carried. The

same rifle was slung over his shoulder and his own steel tool hung in a special sheath down the length of his left thigh. He'd chosen a far more practical though lower-power sidearm than Heath and Josephine had done, but his trusty .22 caliber was small, quiet and had never misfired yet. He pulled his battered leather bushman's hat from its customary peg on the wall and turned to go but found his nephew standing at the bottom of the stairs.

"Unc', come on, I can't let you go in there alone."

"Boy, we've had this talk already, and you know I hate repeating myself." Jasper adjusted his hat.

"It's bad enough without all this on the inside, and there's no telling what you're going to find when you do get in there. If Homeland has already found them…"

"I got friends, Howie; if Homeland had found 'em, I'd have known by now. You just take care of the girl and know when the gettin's good. You're already too far in this and my sister, Lord rest her, would never forgive me if I drug you in all the way. This ain't your fight, Howie. You take care of your part of things and I'll take care of mine."

"This isn't your fight, either. You did enough to help Heath and this Josephine chick go in there to get themselves killed. I admire your loyalty to your friends, Unc', but some fights aren't yours no matter who's fighting them." Jasper looked at his nephew and shook his head slowly.

"Howie, you don't understand, and I don't expect you to."

"Then *make* me understand," Williams said.

Jasper eased himself down onto a high stool in front of his reloading bench and pulled his pipe from his coat pocket.

"It was my last run into the Area. I ran into some trouble I barely got out of and I was out of time, luck and wind. They took me in for a couple days, those survivors. Let me rest and resupplied me. If it wasn't for them I wouldn't be sittin' here right now," Jasper said. He lit his pipe and continued. "They coulda just let me die out there - hell, they coulda added me to the stock pot if they'd wanted to. But when I came to I was warm and dry and not a bullet had been taken. First face I saw was one Eileen Heath."

_____

"John Heath's wife? You can't be serious?"

"Dead serious," Jasper interrupted. "I recognized her right off the bat from a picture John carried with him. Still carries it as far as I know. I told her all about John lookin' for her, how he'd stayed behind to try to find her all those years. I offered to take her with me. But, she wouldn't go."

"Why the hell not?" Williams asked. He'd encountered plenty of survivors, caretakers, as the grave robbers had taken to calling them, over the years and he'd never had one that didn't want him to take them out with him.

"Well she wouldn't go unless she could take everyone, and I knew there was no way I could lead that many back to the world alone. Hell, even if I could I knew they'd be good as dead if we just showed up at the wall one day unannounced, wantin' to go for a cheeseburger on the outside. A man's got to know his limitations, especially an old man."

"So what did you do?"

"Well, she made me promise I wouldn't tell Heath where she was. After she found out he'd been on the inside for five years lookin' for her and had managed to escape and take some with him she didn't want him to come chargin' back in after her. He'd made it, she didn't. She didn't want him to risk his neck again. So, we compromised."

Williams stared at him for a long moment before he shook his head and smiled ruefully. "The message," he said under his breath.

"Yup," Jasper said, his head surrounded in pipe smoke. "We made a deal. If they made a message I'd smuggle it out, make sure it'd get to somebody what could help them get out; all of 'em. Together. Problem was I didn't know anybody else good enough and damned fool enough to go and do it 'cept for John. When I got back, I did my research, asked around. I knew Jo' - that's Josephine - was workin' an Area story. I checked her background and her work. I knew she'd be perfect to get the word out an' she wouldn't let a thing like certain death or Homeland get in the way."

"So how did Heath get involved in all this?" Williams asked.

_____

"Simple enough. I'm the one that worked the camera to record their message. Eileen didn't know that I'd managed to get her face into the camera angle for most of it."

"And you knew that Josephine would do her homework on the faces, put two and two together..." Williams said, his voice trailing off. He shook his head again then laughed out loud. "That's Uncle Jasper, always doing things the hard way. Why the hell didn't you just tell Heath yourself and save all the cloak and dagger stuff? I'm sure Eileen wouldn't have bitched too much if the end result was their rescue."

"I made a promise, Howie, an' a man ain't nothin' if he's not good for his word. In the end that's all you really got to hang your hat on." Jasper stood, tapped his pipe out on the heel of his boot and slid it back in his coat. "John ain't goin' to like me much when he finds out how it all happened, but that can't be helped. So ya see Howie, this *is* my fight. I got the two a' them into this."

"Unc', I..." Williams's words were cut off by a muffled explosion from upstairs. Jasper plucked a shotgun from the rack beside him and tossed it to Williams then both flew up the stairs. Dancing beams of laser light cut through the smoky haze in the hall as men shouted from the front door and the living room.

"Get the girl out of here!" Jasper hissed at his nephew. "Go on, git!" he said, shoving the younger man down the hall.

The smoke was thick enough to cover his passage down the hall and into the kitchen, but just to make sure the invaders weren't concentrating on Williams, Jasper tucked himself into the basement door jamb and fired down the hall. The soldiers' shouting and stomping provided enough noise to mask the report of Jasper's silenced rifle and two of them near the door went down with bullets in their brains before the rest realized they were under attack. They made up for the lacking quickly though as those near the hall took defensive positions and crouches to bathe the hallway with automatic gunfire.

Williams made the bottom of the back stairs just as another crew of soldiers burst in through the kitchen door. He pivoted on the bottom step and fired into the chest of the team's point man, his Kevlar no match for the .12 gauge slug fired less than a foot from his chest. His body flew backwards into the next behind him, giving them enough pause to carry Williams up the stairs and onto the second floor before they dared come into the kitchen. He tried to put the blasts of gunfire he heard from downstairs out of his mind while he raced for Julie's room. His uncle was a proud and stubborn man and an excellent shot to boot. He could take care of himself. Williams reached her door and barreled through it, finding her just as he'd left her though far more animated.

"I told you they'd find me!" she screamed triumphantly. "I'm up here! Kill this bastard!" Williams ran up to her bedside and stared at her sharp, enraged eyes and did the only thing he could do; he hit her, hard across the temple. She stopped screaming, the jolt practically short-circuiting her. He could hear heavy boots coming up the back stairs now. His only way down was either through the window or down the front stairs, and that would mean stepping out into a hallway filled with shooters. He flattened himself against the wall beside the open door and closed his eyes for a moment, letting his other senses reach out into the hall.

Unless things had changed from his entry days there would be three or so spaced out down the hall with the rest waiting on the stairs to rush the floor. The point man was coming closer, his heavy breathing coming easily through the open door. Williams ran his fingers along the wall, feeling for the seam in the old wallboards. Finding it, he spun and put the muzzle of the shotgun against the wall between the studs and pulled the trigger. The heavy slug tore through the first wall to lodge in the wall opposite him in the hall, the point man's head disintegrating in its path. The invader had reached the edge of the door just as Williams had fired, close enough for him to pull the body into the room as the hall erupted with the chattering of small arms fire.

Williams moved quickly, arming himself with the corpse's weapons, equipment belt and vest while the fire in the hall was called down. Gun smoke hung thick in the air and was starting to seep into the room as he pulled two small canisters off the body's belt then popped off their tops and lobbed them blindly down the hall. The first hit the floor and rolled a few feet towards the advancing men while the second got more air, soaring through the cordite-choked air directly into the press of soldiers positioned on the stairs.

"Grenade!" The word echoed down the hall and stairwell, the sounds of tramping feet and cursing washed out by the punishing explosions from the two "flash-bang" grenades, munitions that weren't designed to cause severe damage but rather to shock and stun the enemy with a blinding phosphor explosion and an eardrum-shattering sonic boom. The light from the explosion had barely faded before Williams swung out into the hall, his borrowed automatic chattering away happily in his hands. He'd caught the two remaining lead men crouched in the hall, their arms wrapped around their heads to protect their eyes and ears. Williams gunned them down where they cowered against the walls then turned his attentions to the end of the hall. He could only see one soldier, and that one was slumped with his legs trailing down the stairs. Another explosion rocked the house, this one from something far more incendiary that sent smoke, flame and human debris shooting up the back stairwell.

"Howie, get your ass down here!" he heard Jasper call from downstairs. Williams didn't bother to ask questions. He ran back to the room and pulled Julie out of bed. The noise of the battle in the hall had roused her from her shock but she was oddly subdued now. Williams looked back at the practically headless body on the floor by the door then back at her.

"Him or me," Williams said as he swung her around to drape her down his back. He slung her bound wrists around his neck from behind to keep her in place then reloaded his weapon.

"You... you blew his head off..." Julie mumbled in his ear. Williams stepped over the pool of blood from the soldier's shattered head and glanced down the hall before heading for the main stairs with Julie bouncing against his back at every step.

"Jasper!" Williams called out. He found the old man kneeling at the front door, his rifle pointing out into the night. "You get the ones in the kitchen?" he asked.

"Yeah. Gonna' need some remodelin' back there, though." There were still three incendiary grenades in a commandeered web belt rig at his feet. "They ain't in the house anymore but that's not going to last for long. We need to get outta here before they have the whole county blocked off."

"How do we do that?" Williams asked. Julie was sobbing in his ear now, mumbling about wanting to go home.

"If we can get to the jeep we got a shot. They won't do anything too foolish once they see we got her with us but we'll have to move fast. You ready?" Jasper asked.

"Yeah. Where's the jeep?" Williams asked.

"Out back. Like as not they'll have a guard on it if they haven't disabled it already."

"So how do you propose we get to it?" Williams asked. Jasper smiled at him, stood and put his sidearm to Julie's head.

"We walk right on up and get right on in," Jasper said, smiling. They went down the hall and through the shattered kitchen. The grenades had compromised the wall, letting them pass into the backyard without using the door. As soon as they hit the grass the night around them lit up like the buffer zone as agents and soldiers trained powerful spotlights on them from humvees parked fifty feet away.

"Release the girl or we will fire," a megaphone voice from behind the powerful lights warned. Jasper thumbed the hammer back on his revolver and pushed the slim barrel into Julie's ear, an act he knew wouldn't be lost on the rifle scopes trained on them. He and Williams started turning this way and that, keeping their movements random to keep the snipers from drawing a bead on either of them without risking a hit on Julie while they covered the distance to Jasper's jeep. They were in luck; they hadn't booted the four-by-four's tires.

"Move away from the vehicle and surrender!" the voice came again, this time more animated. "We *will* fire!"

Williams reached down and pulled the radio from his stolen equipment belt and keyed it. He knew they would've gone to another channel as soon as it was obvious he and Jasper had access to their communications but also knew some radio jockey out there somewhere would be monitoring all their channels.

"We have the senator's daughter. If even one shot is fired, at us, at the car, we'll kill her. We're leaving the party, gentlemen. If we get out of here safe and sound we'll drop her off somewhere without a scratch on her. If she dies now it's on your hands," Williams said into the radio. They kept moving towards the jeep, the radio squawking at them just as they reached it.

"Hold your position and prepare to turn over the girl. Do not, I repeat, do not attempt to enter the vehicle." It was the same voice they'd heard over the megaphone.

"We're not going to attempt to enter - we *are* entering the vehicle." Jasper opened the back and front driver's side doors.

"We *will* fire!" the radio warned again.

"Then she *will* die!" Williams answered in the same tone. They made one final turn, depositing Williams and Julie into the backseat in the same motion that landed Jasper behind the wheel. They slammed the doors shut and Jasper started the jeep.

"Gee, I think that went well," Williams said as he spread Julie out on the seat. She was awake and staring at him, her eyes wide with fear.

"Please God...don't kill me," she whispered.

"Be good and I won't have to," Williams said, then to Jasper, "They're not going to let us just drive out of here."

Jasper dropped the transmission into gear and rammed the accelerator to the floor. The old V-8 came alive, its tires churning the ground as it leaped first forward and then spun around to race directly towards the lights.

"There's an old loggin' road just past the driveway. If we can get to that we got a chance," Jasper said as he aimed the nose of the jeep straight for the lights.

"Unc! What the hell are you doing? They're going to open fire!"

"Not while we got the Senator's pride and joy aboard," Jasper said over the roar of the engine. "Well, at least I hope not." The men behind the lights did in fact open fire, their bullets seeking to pierce the radiator or get a lucky hit on a tire. Williams laid his body atop Julie's as the Jeep reached the lights, destroying one of them as the heavy steel cow-catcher bars bolted to the front of the 4x4's frame broke their line. With the bright lights behind them Jasper could see a few more of the humvees parked behind the line. Men were scrambling to them now, pausing only to fire off a round or two at the fleeing vehicle. Jasper bobbed and weaved them through the rough yard to keep the snipers from getting a fix on him through his driver's side window until he reached the head of the logging road. A helicopter suddenly appeared overhead, its bright searchlight tracing the Jeep's path as best it could.

Jasper bounced the jeep onto the road and roared down into the woods. He knew the logging road like the back of his hand, its every twist, dip and turn. He hoped the soldiers hadn't taken the time to map it, that they had been over-confident in their ability to take them in his own home. If it wasn't for the pain in his side and the blood that coated him under his clothes they would've been wrong. Jasper had taken out twelve Homeland agents and soldiers counting the ones from the blasted kitchen. He'd always said that if he ever went down he'd make sure to take as many of them as he could to hell with him, though he'd always thought it'd be zombies making the trip.

"What now?" Williams looked out the back window and saw the lights from the humvees bouncing along the trail behind them. "We're going to have to find somewhere to hole up."

"They're on us too tight for holin' up," Jasper said as he guided them down the rutted, log-choked path.

Williams waited a few moments for him to continue. When he didn't he leaned up over the front seat. "Okay... so?"

"You're gonna have to get in there a different way," Jasper said. He cut the wheel to the right, sudden and hard. Williams gripped the back of the front seat just in time to keep from landing bodily on Julie. "She okay back there?"

"Yeah, just really scared. And what do you mean? Get in where?" Williams asked.

"There's only one place you're gonna go where they ain't

gonna chase you, Howie," Jasper said as they bounced over a particularly large root that had been exposed on the path. He'd left the main logging road now and was careening down a much rougher and slimmer track.

"Unc, if it was just me I'd stroll right on in and lay low for awhile, but I can't do that with her," Williams looked behind and saw the lead humvee's headlights go past the turn, but the second had been far enough back to slow and stay on their tail. The light from the helicopter peeked at them through the cover of the bare branches overhead, lighting their way and letting Jasper keep the headlights off to make it harder to pinpoint them from above.

"I know she's been through a lot and not much of it her fault directly," Jasper said. Williams looked at him in disbelief. They were bouncing through the woods at high speed in the dead of night with agents and soldiers chasing them. His uncle spoke as if they were on their way to the grocery store. It was then that Williams was able to pick out the soft, wet wheezing sound accompanying his uncle's breathing.

"Unc'? You okay?"

"Eh? Hold on a sec'," Jasper said. His head was bobbing loosely now with the jolting motion of the Jeep and his breathing was noticeably labored. He reached over on the bench seat and picked up the grenade belt, giving Williams a clear view of his blood-drenched hand.

"Unc'! You're hit! You have a kit on board? We have to get stopped somewhere."

"Too late for that. Now you listen to me, and listen to me good; there's a tractor trail comin' up, leads farther down in the valley. You're gonna follow that all the way down into the holler and back up the other side. That's gonna take you up to the backside of Devon's pasture. Turn west from there and you'll see his old barn. His kid's some multi-millionaire banker or some such and a real amateur pilot, turned part of Hanson's pasture into his own private little airstrip. He's got a helicopter there last I knew. You still remember how to fly one?" Jasper asked, his voice growing weaker by the word.

"Yeah, Unc'. Don't worry; we'll get you out of here."

"No, you won't. I'll be bled out by the time we get up the other side. You're gonna have to go in my place, you and the girl, let Heath know what's happenin' out here. There's a lot more to this, Howie. There's a chance to really help everybody still trapped in there. If you don't go, I'll understand. I can't ask you to do this if you don't want to..." Jasper's wet cough cut off his words, flecking the windshield with frothy pink blood; lung blood.

"Unc'... no..."

"Yes, Howie. Nothin' to do for it now. Hang on..." Jasper cut the wheel again, the tires just barely keeping to the even rougher tractor trail through a stand of old-growth pine. Branches pulled and snapped against the speeding Jeep as it spun and slid towards the valley. They drove about 30 yards down the slope before Jasper slid to a stop. The light from the helicopter barely cut through the thick lacing of pine boughs overhead, giving them a reprieve from the blinding searchlight. "This old girl will get you there," Jasper said, patting the steering wheel, "but I won't." He opened the door and climbed out, stumbling, finally coming to rest against the trunk of a tree to keep from falling over.

"Unc', what're you doing? Get back in here!"

"Go on, get going!" Jasper said, waving him down the hill weakly. "They'll figure out which way we went soon enough." Williams climbed out of the back seat and went to his uncle.

"Unc', don't do this," he said, looking down at the bloody grenades in Jasper's hands.

"Stop wastin' time, Howie. I'll give 'em something to think about while you get up to Devon's place. Now go. I'm dead whether they catch up to us or not, might as well make myself useful."

Williams looked at him with a silent pleading, knowing even as he did it would do no good. When Uncle Jasper said a thing, it was as if his words were made of concrete and steel.

"Just do me one thing, Howie...when you find Eileen, tell her I kept my promise. And when you find John, tell him I'm sorry."

"Sure, I'll tell them," Williams said, then "I love you, Unc'." He backed away towards the open jeep door.

"I love you too, boy. Now go on." Jasper looked back up the hill. The lights from the humvees had stopped at the head of the tractor trail. "They've figured us out. Get going."

Williams stared at him a moment more, grunting in frustration as he got in and continued down the hill.

Jasper watched the Jeep disappear behind the slapping pine boughs then faced uphill. The first of the humvees was coming down, the much wider vehicles having more difficulty navigating the thin track than his old Cherokee had. Jasper coughed again and felt a rivulet of warm blood trickle down his chin. His head was swimming a bit now, the headlights of the lead humvee blurring in his vision. He waited until they were just a few yards away before he stepped out from the shelter of the branches directly into their path. The humvees slid to a stop in the loose dirt of the trail, coming to rest just a few feet away. It was easy to see his condition in their lights.

"Drop your weapons and get to your knees!" a voice called out from the humvee. Jasper could hear the snap-crackle charging of the unit's roof-mounted chain gun and fell first to his knees and then completely prone, face down in their path. Four soldiers got out and approached him, their weapons trained on his still form. They got to his position and formed a ring around him, the commander turning Jasper over with his foot. Jasper stared up at them, smiling a bloody smile.

"Where did they go, old man?" one of the soldiers asked.

"They're goin' to hell, but don't worry none, I promise we saved ya'll a seat," Jasper said as two slim pieces of metal shot away from each of his hands, the accompanying metallic clangs recognizable to any soldier.

"Grenades!" one of them shouted. The men stumbled backwards, the last things they would ever see being an old man's bloody smile and a blinding flash of white. The force of the grenades and their accompanying shrapnel and concussive force peppered the lightly-armored lead humvee, shredding the radiator and front right tire, leaving the rest of their pursuers blocked by the confining branches and rough skin of Jasper's woods.

Eric R. Lowther

Chapter VIII
Out of the Frying Pan

Chapter VIII
Out of the Frying Pan

Josephine shot to a sitting position, a small gasp escaping from her lips. A constant, many-voiced moan echoed around her to the point she wasn't sure if the sound was real or a figment of her abused imagination. Her head throbbed relentlessly, the pain arcing every time she moved her head. She shifted her body, keeping her head as still as she could and felt around in the darkness for a wall. Her hands found rough, irregular dirt and stone behind her and she scooted against it, letting it prop her up while her vision cleared.

She was in some sort of cave or hole only a few feet square and not tall enough for her to stand. A set of roughly-welded bars filled the room's only opening just a few feet ahead of her. Light that was soft but steady accompanied the echoing moan through the bars, bright enough for her to check her body for additional wounds or, far worse, bites. She found plenty of nicks and bruises where the wall of junk had compromised first her leathers and then her flesh, but nothing else. This of course raised the even more uncomfortable question; if a zombie hadn't pulled her into the junk pile, who had?

Whoever it was must know the value of weapons and supplies. She was still, thankfully, dressed, but that was all she had. Her pack, weapons and other supplies had been taken away. That her supplies and weapons were gone yet she was alive and captive made her stomach roll in her gut. In a word, she was screwed. She wondered for a moment what had happened to Heath but quickly shoved the thought away. Her first order of business was survival; nothing more, nothing less. Just as she'd made up her mind to test the bars, a short man limped in front of them, his body cast as a silhouette from the light behind. Josephine froze. She'd screwed up again, another in a long list. She should've stayed exactly as they'd left her, make them think she was still out cold while she examined her options. She stared at the man for several moments before she spoke.

"Why am I here?" she asked, choosing her words and tone carefully. Becoming irate could only hurt her. "Where am I?" The silhouette was silent though she thought she could hear him wheezing on the other side of the bars. "Do you have some water?" she asked, turning the conversation to the humanitarian. "Please, I'm very thirsty..."

"You're purty," the silhouette said. The voice sounded young and was thick with the central West Virginia accent and...something else. Something she couldn't fully describe. Josephine decided if there was ever a time to put her minor in psychology to the test, it was now.

"Thank you," she said as warmly and earnestly as she could muster. She put on her studio smile and cocked her head to the side, the act making her grit her teeth behind her lips from the jab of pain it produced. The boy made a rough, giggling sound and turned his head away from her. "What's your name?" she asked, not wanting the avenue of communication to close.

"Enos," he said, turning back to face her.

"Hi, Enos. I'm Josephine. But you can call me Jo'. That's what all my friends call me."

"I'm yer friend?" he asked, his voice hopeful yet doubtful at the same time.

"Sure. I mean, if you *want* to be."

"Really? I never had too many friends before. Just my brother an' Paw. Oh, yeah, and PawPaw, too."

"Well, I'll be your friend, Enos." The pain was lessening now though her brain still felt foggy. "Enos, can you tell me why I'm locked in here? How long have I been here?"

"Henry brought you inside this mornin'. It's purty close to sundown now I guess. Henry said you'd just run off if he didn't lock you in till you got used to us." Enos turned his head down as if ashamed. "I told him it ain't a nice thing to do to such a purty lady, but since it was to help ya, I guess it was okay."

"Well, couldn't *you* let me out?" Several moments went by without an answer. Josephine cursed inwardly. She'd pushed too fast for that.

"I guess I could..." Enos finally said. He put his face against the bars, his voice low and filled with conspiracy. "But you'd have to go back in there after 'while. If Henry knew I let you out, he'd whip me real hard."

"I don't want to get you into any trouble," Josephine said, hoping to build upon the trust she was engendering in the young man. Enos seemed lost in thought while he turned his head this way and that on his side of the bars, apparently looking to see if he was being watched.

"Aw, it'll be okay, they're watchin' wrestlin'. Be a good hour 'fore either one of 'em would call for me, if they did then even. Just remember now, if you go runnin' off or somethin' they'll both whip me but good." Enos grabbed the padlock on the gate. "I ain't got the key. Henry keeps all the keys, but I think I can open it." Enos produced a long, thin piece of steel and worked it for a few moments inside the lock. The tumblers rasped as if full of rust but the lock popped open after less than a minute under his skilled fingers.

Josephine controlled her urge to blast through the opening bars, to bowl Enos over in her wake and find her way out. She didn't know where she was or where her supplies and weapons were. Add to that there were at least two others besides Enos, and if he were to be believed those others would be very upset that she was out. Then there was the moaning to think about. She waited until he'd opened the bars and swung them away before she crawled out of her dirt cell.

Josephine made it out and stood slowly, her legs trembling under her. She looked down at Enos, finally able to make out his features in the light and had to check her gasp. He was about five feet tall, dressed in a dirty pair of ripped, grease-stained coveralls. He wore no shoes, and now that she was standing beside him the reek of his body odor almost made her gag. But all of that was secondary to the boy's face.

His features were stretched and contorted, his forehead protruding almost to the same length as his nose. Josephine had done some voice-over work for a friend's college documentary, a study of the genetic condition lionitis. She'd cried several times while she tried to record the voiceover atop the footage of those brave yet tortured children and adolescents. Enos' disfigurement was by far more pronounced than any of the documentary subjects had been. It was a wonder the young man was still alive, especially trapped in the Area with no medical care to speak of. After a moment, Josephine realized she was staring.

"Oh, Enos, I'm so sorry. I didn't mean to stare. It's just, my head still hurts a lot and..."

"It's okay, Jo'. I know I'm ugly. You don't have ta be my friend if you don't want to," he said, his face swiveling to stare at his filth-crusted feet.

"No, no Enos! Of course I want to be your friend. I think you're very polite, and very sweet." Josephine took the opportunity to look around them. A few dim light bulbs had been strung from a single, heavily-spliced extension cord that ran down the narrow corridor. Like her cell, the walls here were little more than earthen tunnels that were shored up every few feet by thick pieces of timber. The tunnel dead-ended several yards behind her and ran an almost equal distance ahead before it disappeared around a sharp bend.

"You don't think I'm ugly?"

"Of course I don't think you're ugly," Josephine assured him. "Can I ask you a few questions?"

"What kinda questions?"

"Well, first, I had a friend with me. Do you know where he

is?"

"Henry said the rots got 'im. He said it'd be okay though. Said if the rots didn't end up carryin' it away maybe he'd let me have his pistol next time we go up." Enos suddenly brightened. "I'm a real good shot!"

Josephine fell silent for a moment with her eyes squeezed tightly shut and her fists balled at her sides. She'd lost Heath, her weapons and supplies, her way and now, apparently, even her freedom in the space of what seemed to her only a few moments. Even if she could escape, what would she do? Where would she go?

"Jo'? Gee, I'm sorry 'bout the man. I didn't think that maybe he was your husband or somethin' like that."

"No, Enos, he was a...a friend, I guess." Josephine opened her eyes and wiped a few tears from them. She had a choice to make. It was the same choice that Heath had believed governed all people in all situations; live or die. Circumstance had taken away his choice in the matter, but not hers. She quickly prioritized her questions, falling back on her interview skills to get them in just the right order. She didn't know how much time she had before the others discovered she was loose but she'd made her choice. There was no way in hell she was going back in that hole without a fight. "Enos, where are we, exactly?"

"We're home," he said simply.

Josephine couldn't help but crack a real smile. "I was thinking more in general terms. We're underground, I can see that. I mean, how far are we from where you took me in? From the trailer park?"

"Well, I didn't bring you inside. That was Henry. He thinks yer real purty, too," Enos said, blushing again. "And we ain't really underground, I guess. We're in Hanover Mountain, our mountain. We used to live up on the top, but that was before the rots. Paw and Henry moved us down into the old mine tunnels back before I can even remember."

Josephine remembered the exceptionally tall hill they were trying to get to and realized she must be inside it. At least she had her bearings now. She was close to where Heath had fallen, and she was sure she could at least find her way back to the North Gate once she got free.

"Okay, what about the moaning? Is that coming from outside? Maybe through a ventilation shaft?" Enos smiled broadly at her question.

"Oh, no Jo'," he said, giggling at the way the words sounded together. "Come on! I'll show ya!"

The Jeep's radiator hadn't fared any better than its owner. A plume of steam started from the vehicle's grill as Williams pushed the old truck up the other side of the valley. The chopper had found them again, its searchlight turning the night to day on the cleared hillside leading to the property line Jasper had shared with the Devons'. Williams traded his eyes between the hill they were climbing and the temperature gauge needling into the red on the dashboard. The rough, steep climb wasn't helping the rapidly burning engine. If the old Cherokee died before they reached the promised helicopter he'd be done for.

"What's going on? Let me up!" Julie cried from the backseat.

"Now would be a good time to shut the hell up and enjoy the ride," Williams said without looking over his shoulder.

"Please, just let me go! I'll ask them to go easy on you! Just let me the hell out of here!"

"I liked you better whimpering and pissing yourself." Williams crested the hill. Devoid of all cover in the flat, clear pasture, the helicopter dropped lower, riding less than 50 feet in the air to their right.

"Stop the vehicle and exit with your hands up!" a voice blasted at them over a loudspeaker mounted on the helicopter.

"Do what they say and I'll make sure you're alive in the morning!" Julie said, sitting up in the backseat. "It's over. Let me go!"

Williams ignored both the girl and the helicopter as he rammed the accelerator to the floor. He could see the barn ahead, bathed in light from a few poles. The helicopter was there, just as

Jasper had said it would be. The chopper suddenly ascended and sped ahead of them, the sight of the helicopter on the ground making Williams' plan easy to read. The government helicopter flew to a spot just above the other and hovered there, daring Williams to try and take off.

"It's over!" the stolen radio barked at Williams as he skidded to a stop just a few feet from the chopper. He crawled into the backseat with Julie and loosened her bonds.

"Glad you came to your senses," Julie said as he freed her ankles and knees. Williams stopped then and looked into her eyes.

"No. To be honest, I'm losing them by the minute." Williams cut the rope that bound her upper arms to her torso then held her still-bound hands in his, catching her eyes again. "You're going to go out there and you're going to drop the lines holding the rotor in place. Then you're going to come back here and we're going to get into the chopper together."

Julie looked at him for a moment then actually laughed. "Do you think they're going to let you get away with that? As soon as my feet hit the ground I'll be gone and they'll blast you," Julie said, a bit of her normal, bitter nature coming back with her victor's smile. "Face it, you're done."

Williams returned her smile. "Remember the body back at the farm?" he asked. Her look changed and she shrunk back from him involuntarily. He pulled roughly on her wrists, bringing her face even closer than it had been to his. "I'll bet you do. You're going to do what I say or you're going to look just like him. You're going to release the right line then come around the front of the chopper to release the left, and then you're coming straight back here. If I even think for a minute that you're going to try and duck me I'll put so much lead in your skull it'll rattle when the pall bearers carry you out."

"You're fucking insane."

"Yeah, how 'bout that?" Williams said, still smiling. "Believe me lady, I know the risks, but if we don't get in that chopper together I'll be dead and I can guarantee you I'll take you with me." He kept her wrists in one hand and pulled out the stolen radio with

---

the other. "Chopper jockey, can you hear me?" he said into it. After several seconds Senator Sommers' voice crackled over the small speaker.

"Williams! Let my daughter go!" Senator Sommers' voice crackled over the radio. Williams let his eyebrows rise.

"Senator, I'm impressed you'd come all the way out here yourself."

"Let her go, Williams. It's your only chance."

"Let's pretend like neither one of us is stupid. If I let her go I *lose* my only chance, Sommers. If you watch real close, you'll be able to see your little girl. She's going to drop the rotor lines off this bird for me. My sights are going to be on that pretty blonde head of hers the whole time, and since I don't see any tubes on your bird I'm not worried about missiles. If one shot gets fired from on high at me or at the chopper, I'll blow your daughter's head apart. When she drops the lines she's going to come back to the vehicle and together we're going to get in the whirly-bird here and take off. If I don't see signs of pursuit for ten minutes I'll drop her off somewhere safe for you to pick up and then you can come at me with everything you've got. I don't want to kill her, Senator, but don't doubt that I will. It would be the least I could do since you killed my uncle."

The radio was silent for a few moments until Sommers' voice came through it again. "You're not going to get away with this."

"If you want your daughter to live longer than the next few seconds, I will. Do what I tell you and I promise you she'll live. Don't and I'll pop her right here and now. Okay, Julie, say hi to daddy. If either one of you do anything really stupid it'll be the last chance you have to talk." Williams turned the radio around to Julie's face. "Tell him hello or tell him goodbye. It's your choice."

"Daddy?" Julie said tentatively into the radio.

"Julie! My God, Julie! Are you okay? Has he hurt you?"

"I...I'm okay. He means what he says, Daddy. I watched him kill those soldiers tonight. He'll kill me too if I don't do what he says," she said, her voice quivering slightly.

"It'll be okay, Princess. This will all be over soon. I'm here

---

now; I'll take care of everything," Sommers said as Williams pulled the radio away from Julie.

"All right, Sommers, she's coming out and I'm locked and loaded. If I even think you're going to cross me, well, I hope you have a spare daughter hanging around. We clear?" The radio went silent again and stayed that way. Williams looked at Julie. The tears were flowing freely now and she was shaking.

"Okay, you're on. Let's hope for both our sakes your daddy loves you," he said, pulling up his weapon and pointing it at her.

"My wrists are still tied," she said through her tears.

"You can work the lines just like you are. They're just looped over those hooks in the ground to keep the rotor from turning in the wind." Williams reached across her and popped open her door. "Move, and stay towards the front end of the chopper. If you try to duck around the back you'll be dead." Julie looked down at her feet. Her trembling had spread to the rest of her body now.

"I can't!" she screamed. Williams put the muzzle against her temple.

"Then we're both as good as dead. You're saving your own life here. I meant what I said. If they don't follow for ten minutes I'll let you off and it'll all be over. But for that to happen we have to get in that chopper. Do you understand?" Julie sat for a few more moments trembling like a leaf in the wind before she nodded her head and wiped her eyes.

"Yes," she said softly then slid out the door. The downdraft from the helicopter hovering overhead nearly knocked her off her feet and she stumbled a bit.

"Back it off!" Williams said into the radio. "If she falls I'll kill her before she hits the dirt." There was no response from the radio but the chopper rose another 30 feet higher, turning the downdraft into a breeze. Williams lay down across the backseat then, the machine gun trained on Julie's head as she moved slowly to the first peg. She struggled with the line for a moment and was finally able to release it.

"Pull it off the rotor!" Williams called out to her over the noise from above. Julie looked back over her shoulder for a moment then up to the rotor. She tugged and the noosed line slipped easily off the smooth rotor. She stopped there for a moment, her eyes turned towards the rear of the aircraft. It was her moment of truth. Williams took up the slack on the trigger and held his breath. If she took even one step towards the back of the chopper they'd both die. Finally, she moved around the front of the helicopter and freed the other line. Williams let his breath out and kept her in his sights while she made her way back to the Cherokee.

"Stop right there," Williams said when her body was fully blocking the door opening from view. He slid out of the vehicle and picked her up, draping her around his neck like a stole, the barrel of the submachine gun in his right hand jammed into her neck. His head and back protected by her body and the gun placed so that he couldn't miss if they attempted to knock him down with a shot to his legs, he charged across the fifteen feet distance between the Cherokee and the chopper. The helicopter above responded by dropping back down to just above their chopper, the downdraft punishing them as Williams threw open the thin door and hauled them both inside.

"Back the fuck off!" Williams said into the radio, flipping switches with his free hand. The console lit up under his fingers and the engine started its whine to life, causing Sommers' chopper to drop even lower, its skids just a few feet above his awakening rotor. Williams looked up, annoyed, then grabbed Julie's bound hands. "Hey, Julie, tell daddy what I'm doing right now," he said, holding up her hands. Julie stared at him, tears rolling down her face.

"He's got my hands," Julie said, her voice shaking. Williams set the radio down with the microphone facing them, flipped the catch to keep the channel open then grabbed her left index finger and started bending it back. She screamed as her finger passed the point of a comfortable range of motion. "He's breaking my fingers!" she screamed. "Daddy, help me!" Williams suddenly jammed her finger to the side. Julie let out an even louder shriek and tried to pull her hands away but Williams wouldn't let go.

"Stay tuned to this station, Senator. I've got nine more then I take a knife to her nipples. Back the fuck off; now," Williams said.

There was no response over the radio, but the chopper rising away was the only response he needed. Williams closed the channel and let Julie have her hands back as he finished checking dials and flipping switches. The rotor was singing now, the helicopter ready to take off.

"Williams, I'm going to kill you myself!" Sommers' voice came over. Williams picked up the radio.

"Yeah, she said the same thing. If you want the chance to do that and have your daughter alive when you do it I suggest you set down in the pasture here for ten minutes and I'll radio to tell you where to pick her up."

"We're not setting down, Williams," Sommers said.

"Suit yourself, but you're going to burn a lot of fuel just hanging out." A loud, aggressive whirring suddenly rose up around both choppers. Williams dropped the radio, put on the pilot's headset, handed another pair to Julie then took the controls. The chopper responded instantly, rising only a few feet from the ground before dipping its nose and moving off across the field.

He didn't have to look to know the Apache attack helicopter he'd heard was following him from somewhere above and behind, with enough firepower to level a city block. Though incredibly fast and capable gunships, the Apache fleet along with the Blackhawks had almost been grounded due to their age. But the creation of the Area had breathed new life into the venerable killing machines and the versatile Blackhawk platforms, keeping them in active service in the skies over the dead to keep from diverting the new equipment away from the nation's other wars.

"Your daddy's probably just killed you, you know?" Williams said to Julie through the headset. She didn't answer, just sat in the seat beside him nursing her aching yet unbroken finger.

"I want to see you bleed," Julie said.

"You just may get your chance, but let's not get ahead of ourselves," Williams said. He pulled the chopper up to a hundred feet and turned it south. "I really didn't plan for it to happen this way, you know? I mean, you're a mega-bitch and all but this is pretty excessive even for that. I'm not sure how this is all going to work out, but I *will* drop you somewhere if they give me half a chance."

"I don't care what happens to me, I just want to see you dead." She was still crying but her voice had turned as cold as ice.

"Civilian aircraft, set down or I will be forced to open fire," a calm male voice said in his ear. They'd found the helicopter's usual radio frequency, it seemed.

"Negative, big bird o'death." He kept the chopper on a due-south course. There was no point in fancy maneuvers or in trying to out-fly the Apache. Only the best pilots skippered those gunships, and even if his piloting skills weren't rusty he knew nothing short of a fighter jet would get it off his back. The only weapon he had was Julie. "Back off, give me some room and I'll drop my passenger."

"Negative, civilian aircraft. You have just crossed into controlled airspace. Lethal force has been authorized. Set down or I will open fire," the voice repeated. Williams swore under his breath. He hadn't even realized that at this speed they'd already breached Area 187's no-fly zone.

"Not going to happen, big bird. I'm dead if I do. If you shoot me down, at least me and the Senator's daughter get a pretty fire ball to look at while we go."

"Apache pilot, this is Senator Alan Sommers," the senator's voice broke in with as much emphasis on his title as he could muster. "Do not, I repeat do *not* fire! My daughter's aboard that chopper!"

"Senator, so nice of you to join the party," Williams said. "I'll let you guys hash this thing out. Let me know if I have to kill your daughter, okay?" Williams knew the two pursuing choppers would change frequencies to discuss.

"I guess we get to see just how big your daddy's balls are," he said to Julie. A loud, piercing chime cut through the cabin. Williams scanned the cockpit gauges for a moment before he found the offender. "I hope they figure something out pretty damn quick though. Looks like young Mr. Devon didn't fuel up after his last joyride."

Julie turned to look at him, alarm replacing her look of pain and anger. "Can this get any worse?" she said, not realizing her microphone picked up her soft voice.

"Uh, yeah. They could blow us out of the sky. We have a slight chance of surviving a controlled loss of altitude resulting in the achievement of terminal velocity - you might know that one by its generic name 'crash' - than we do a hellfire missile up our tail rotor," Williams said.

Julie kept staring at him. "Are you taking any of this seriously? We're going to fucking *die*! I don't deserve this! I didn't do anything to you!"

"My therapist says I use humor to deal with stress. She said it comes from watching too much *Muppet Show* when I was a kid," Williams said, his eyes on the falling fuel gauge. "So which one was your favorite?"

"Which *what* was my favorite?"

"Muppet. Which Muppet was your favorite? If we're going to die together the least you can do is tell me who your favorite Muppet was."

"I...you're...you..." she stammered. The fuel alarm sounded again, cutting her off. Julie looked out through the Plexiglas windshield to see a bright light glowing in the distance. "Is that the Area?"

"Yup."

"We're heading right for it," she said.

"Yup." He touched a button on his headset and tightened his grip on the controls.

Eric R. Lowther

Chapter IX
Into the Fire

Heath dropped his knees onto the hood and shoved off from the pile with his free hand, the combined weight of his body and the heavy chunk of smooth steel enough to send the two into a jerky, halting slide down the side of the mountain of junk. A fleeting picture of Wile E Coyote attempting the same trick passed through his mind as he slid, the pile shifting and twisting under the hood as his passing dislodged chunks of it. The ghouls that weren't tangled up in the hill of junk were already starting to come around the sides of the pile to form a hungry, gruesome welcoming committee, their moans bringing others that had wandered away from the barricade while Heath had been buried alive.

Heath waited until he was just a few feet from the bottom of the pile and rapidly-forming mob then reached out and took hold of the top of a car door jutting up from the mass of debris. Had he been moving any faster, the sudden stopping of his and the hood's momentum would have likely dislocated his shoulders, maybe even dislodged the door from the pile. As it was, both his shoulders and the impromptu brake held. He stepped off the hood then picked it up by its steel frame as the swarm started to push itself into the first few feet of junk. The uneven, cluttered footing made the entire vanguard of the horde lurch and struggle to stay upright as they tried to surge towards Heath.

Had it been any group other than bloodthirsty, undead cannibals the sight may have even been considered funny. Heath allowed a few more precious seconds, allowed a few more to stumble their way into the twisted mass of steel, wood and garbage before he gripped the hood like a large riot shield, shoved it out before him and made a precarious charge directly into their midst. The zombies didn't know enough to even try to get out of the way of the human juggernaut. Heath grunted as the first few bodies met his shield. The hood completely blocked his view ahead, so he concentrated on the sounds of junk-trapped ankles snapping, bodies falling into the wreckage ahead and to the sides and the growing chorus of moans while he kept his eyes down to find the best places to put down his churning legs that wouldn't leave him as trapped as the dead that had made it into the pile.

By the time his feet were back on solid ground his advance had turned into a slow walk. He pushed on a few more feet then changed his grip on the slab of Detroit's finest steel to swing it back and forth in wide, vicious semi-circles. More zombies were knocked to the ground as Heath kept moving, seizing every opening his brutal attacks made in the swarm to move towards more open ground. After what seemed like hours but in truth was only a matter of seconds, he'd moved far enough away to be out of arms' reach of the dead. Heath finally dropped the heavy shield and trotted several yards away from the slowly stalking swarm. He ignored the painful protests virtually every part of his body was sending up the chain. His back and shoulders were on fire from using the hood as a battering ram, his legs ached from their long period of rest under the pile into sudden, hard use and his skull thumped dully against the grazing wound from the unknown sniper's bullet. The rest of his parts and pieces babbled on about their numerous cuts, scrapes and wounds from the junk pile, their stinging murmurs running in low, constant harmony with the more pulsing and demanding pains.

Heath pushed all these from his mind as he pulled his heavy pistol, dispatched the two closest zombies, then reloaded. He started walking slowly backwards, taking his time and making each bullet from his last magazine count.

"I have my orders from Secretary Fremont, Senator

Sommers. I'm sorry, Senator, but if the aircraft refuses to land before it reaches the wall I'll be forced to destroy it," the Apache pilot said in the Senator's headset.

"Lieutenant, if you fire on my daughter I will personally guarantee you will spend the rest of your military career scraping bird shit off of runways in Guam!" Sommers screeched.

"I have my orders, Senator," the Apache pilot came back though his voice lacked the surety it had had before. Then another voice came over the airwaves, this one dripping with anger and authority.

"This is Homeland Defense Secretary Harold Fremont. Lieutenant Barris, if the aircraft refuses to land on your next warning you are to destroy it and return to Pittsburgh. Senator Sommers, I am ordering your aircraft to proceed *immediately* to North Gate Control. You have a lot to answer for, Senator," Fremont said.

"Who the hell do you think you are, Fremont? That madman has my daughter!"

"The civilian aircraft has violated the Area 187 no-fly zone. I regret your loss, Senator Sommers, but it is secondary to national security. Had this been handled properly instead of behind my back it may not have come to this. I am ordering your pilot to bring you back here - now. Pilot, do you copy?" Fremont said.

"Affirmative, Secretary Fremont. Changing course for-" Sommers' pilot started.

"Belay that, pilot, if you know what's good for you!" Sommers said as he shot up from the back seat to his own helicopter's pilot. "You don't take orders from him, you take them from me!"

"Secretary Fremont, civilian aircraft is within five miles and closing with the wall. Issuing final warning," the Apache pilot cut in, then more tentatively, "Do I still have orders to fire?"

"Carry out your orders, Lieutenant Barris."

"If you kill my daughter Lieutenant Barris-"

"Carry out your orders, Barris. I'll deal with the Senator," Fremont said, his tone cutting through Sommers' objections. "Knock them down."

"They'll shoot us down if we try to fly over the Area!" Julie stared in shock as the lights from the buffer zone grew brighter ahead of them.

"The fact they haven't yet tells me your Dad may be good for something after all." The low fuel warning had become a constant tone now and Williams struggled through several buttons and switches before he found the one to quiet it. "There, that's better."

"Civilian aircraft, this is your final warning. Set down now or I will open fire," Barris's voice came over the radio.

"Not much of a threat, Big Bird. Tank's almost empty, I'm going to drop either way. Back off and I'll drop on the live side of the wall. Stay on me and you're running a big risk of my charred ass coming down in the buffer. I'm thinking that much excitement might bring out a whole bunch of rubberneckers from the bad part of town. Wanna' risk that?"

The wall had been designed to hold back swarms in the thousands, but such an uprising would only bring publicity and unwanted attention to Homeland's doorstep. Add to that Homeland's failure to keep a simple civilian helicopter shadowed by one of the deadliest killing machines ever to hit the skies from breaching the Area and you had the ingredients for the perfect public relations nightmare.

"My orders don't involve politics, civilian aircraft. Set down now," the pilot warned.

Williams switched off the mike and sighed. "Ever been to Area 187, Julie?"

"Of course not!"

"First time for everything. It's really nice this time of year. The zombies get really frisky in early spring, I guess to make up for the cold weather turning them into deadsicles. We'll be just in time for the opening of the Shakespeare in the Park season. You haven't lived till you've heard Macbeth done completely in moans."

"We can't go in there! Set us down right now!" she ordered, all trace of shock and pain gone from her voice. She grabbed the mirror controls on her side of the cockpit. "Set us down or I'll put us down!"

Williams took his hands off the controls. "Go ahead. Dead is dead," he said as the chopper took its own head and started bucking wildly in the air. Julie screamed as the controls jumped in her hands.

"Fly this damn thing!" she said. Williams took the helm again and straightened out their flight.

"Civilian aircraft, are you in distress?" Barris asked over the radio. Williams flicked his microphone back on.

"Friend, you don't know the half of it. Hey, by the way, which was your favorite Muppet?" Williams asked. His answer came in the form of the Apache's Vulcan cannon chattering at them. The assault helicopter had swung around to the side and had made a pass at the rear of their chopper, strafing the tail just before the rear stabilizing rotor. It was all Williams could do to keep them above the treetops. "Fozzy was mine," Williams said into the microphone as he struggled to keep them airborne. Other alarms went off now and the fuel level had dropped to the point that there was no way to silence its alarm.

"Civilian aircraft, set down now!" Barris said, his voice as animated as the controls under Williams' hands. They could see the wall now, their chopper on a straight but sputtering course for it. The Apache streaked ahead and turned to face them in a hovering position just before the living side of the wall. "Set down now!"

"Going to be a beautiful evening," Williams said, taking a glance out his door's window. They were closing the distance between them and the Apache fast. Williams struggled with the controls, barely managing to keep them at a steady elevation. "Julie, I just want you to know, I've always loved you."

"*What?*" she said, her eyes locked on the wicked-looking bird bathed in light from the buffer zone growing larger in their windshield.

"I don't know... I've always wanted to say that in its proper context. It wasn't as fulfilling as I thought it would be. Might have something to do with the fact you're a raging she-bitch."

"Why the hell aren't you landing this thing?" she said, her screaming adding to the warning buzzers and sirens coming from nearly every one of the helicopter's systems.

"Probably because the controls aren't responding anymore and we're losing altitude. Didn't I mention that?"

"No, you sonofabitch!" Julie screamed. "What the hell are we going to do?"

"Well, if he shoots us down in the next five seconds we'll die in a big, fancy explosion with our parts fusing to our seats. If he doesn't then we'll stay on this course and play chicken with him. Don't worry though, he'll flinch. The Air Force gets really upset with pilots that let someone crash into them while they're standing still. He won't risk picking up a handle like 'Crash' for us," he said, his knuckles white on the controls as he fought in vain to keep them in the air.

Williams counted off the seconds in his head and stopped at five. They were too close to both the wall and the Apache for it to shoot them down now without risking their wreckage impacting and compromising the wall. Williams hoped either the pilot or his commanders recognized that fact as well. The Apache held its position until the last possible moment, finally shooting up into the air to avoid having their helicopter crash into him. "See? I told you he'd blink."

"We just passed over the wall!" Julie said, looking down through the chopper's floor observation windows.

"Hey, how 'bout that?" Williams said, looking down himself. "I've never seen it from this angle before. With a few rosebushes they could really brighten up the place, huh?"

More bullets suddenly ripped through their craft, coming from the snipers on the wall. A few of the high-powered .50 rounds made it into the cockpit, smashing through the rear of the cabin and into the controls situated in the array between their seats. Sparks flew from the console as the last of their fuel vapors gave out, leaving the chopper to drop rapidly to the buffer zone below.

"Welcome to the Area, honey!" Williams said. Julie screamed and gripped the bottom of her seat, hunching her shoulders and lowering her head, inadvertently giving her a perfect view of their impending crash through the floor window.

Senator Sommers charged into the conference room with General Haig in tow and slammed a fist on the table in front of Secretary Fremont. "What the hell are you doing, Fremont? You have no authority to order me anywhere! That maniac has my daughter! He was torturing her for God's sake!"

"Alan," Haig said, putting a cautioning hand on Sommers' arm, "this isn't helping her or you." Haig had been in the chopper with Sommers but had wisely kept silent. He'd be more than happy if Fremont never found out he was there in the first place. His stars were no match for the Secretary of the most powerful collection of government agencies the United States had ever created. Sommers shook off his hand and leaned over the table.

"My daughter could be dead right now because of you, Fremont. And if she's not dead, then she's inside the Area with a lunatic!" Fremont hadn't taken his eyes off the report in his hands from the moment Sommers had barged into the room. When he finally did he laid it down on the table, pulled off his wire-rimmed glasses and leaned back in his chair. Fremont was practically the photo-negative of the Senator. He was a full head shorter than Sommers with a well-receded hairline and the start of a paunch. The sleeves of his expensive shirt were rolled half-way up his hairy arms and his silk tie had been loosened far past what was considered office casual. Fremont produced a non-filtered Camel from his shirt pocket and lit it with a thin Zippo lighter.

"Senator Sommers, sit down," Fremont said. Sommers stood to his full height as suddenly as if he'd been shot.

"E*xcuse* me?" Sommers said.

"Gentlemen?" Fremont said, looking at the two large men in black suits near the door. "If the good Senator from California doesn't sit down in the next three seconds I want you to escort him to a holding cell until he decides to cooperate with this investigation." Sommers' face turned several shades of red as he looked down at the smaller man.

"I can have you busted down to doorman at the embassy in Kenya, Fremont," Sommers said.

"One," Fremont said through a hazy cloud of cigarette smoke.

"If you think for one second that I'll–"

"Two," Fremont continued as if Sommers hadn't spoken. "Senator, if I get to three these agents will carry out their orders; flawlessly, immediately and ruthlessly. Your place as a duly elected representative of the people means nothing to me or to federal laws pertaining to violations of the Area 187 Act. Now sit down and cooperate in this investigation before I have you incarcerated under that Act. And believe me, Senator, I have the authority to do it."

Sommers looked at Haig and could tell from the General's eyes there was nothing his rank could accomplish here. Homeland ran Area 187, not the military. Haig was merely the liaison, facilitating Homeland's requests for men and material when needed and providing air power to defend the no-fly zone.

"Get out of my sight, Haig. You're useless," Sommers said as he angrily pulled out a chair out and sat down.

"Yes General; leave, but don't go too far. You and I need to have a little discussion about *your* involvement, including orders that came down from you for a military operation utilizing several Homeland agents that, somehow, was countersigned by me yet never crossed my desk," Fremont said. Haig didn't respond, merely turned and left the room. Fremont nodded to one of his agents and the man slipped quietly out the door behind Haig.

"You're in a lot of trouble, Senator."

"You have no idea who you're dealing with, Fremont. I can have you relieved of your position with two phone calls. Now you tell me what you're going to do to go after my daughter."

"And I can have you disappear in a tragic helicopter accident with only *one* call, Senator. Area 187 is mine. Nothing happens in, above, or around it that I don't know about. You violated my authority without even so much as the courtesy of a phone call. If you'd have told me what was going on from the start your daughter may be alive today. She'd be in prison for her involvement, but she'd still be alive."

"My daughter wasn't involved with any of this. It was a misunderstanding. She's young and did something stupid."

"I can see where she gets that from," Fremont said. "Josephine Terrell and John Heath have been listed as fugitives from justice, with every badge in the country on high alert for them for all the good it will do. William Hartman and one of your 'personal assistants' are in my custody, and both had a very interesting story to tell. Now settle in, Senator, and start from your beginning. I want to know everything you know about all of this."

"I'm not going to sit here and let you interrogate me like some common criminal. If my daughter survived that crash, every minute we waste here is a minute she's closer to...to..." Sommers said, his voice trailing off.

"To being eaten? Perhaps resurrected?" Fremont said, almost enjoying the words. "I have a team surveying the wreckage, Senator. If she's there, we'll find her. Now, please. From the beginning..."

Josephine hurried off after Enos, afraid she may run into one of the others without the boy with her. She rounded the bend and skidded to a stop in the soft dirt floor. The tunnel opened into a large, round alcove perhaps 30 feet in diameter with at least ten feet from floor to ceiling in most places. Electric lights hung with no real pattern to their placement to cast their light on the most incredible yet ghastly sight she'd ever seen.

The center of the room was filled with at least a dozen contraptions that resembled old-fashioned, non-motorized treadmills. A large steel drum was attached to each unit with thick wires running from them to long rows of car batteries. The moaning of the zombies walking the treadmills blended smoothly with the constant sound of the mills' rollers to produce the droning sound she'd heard back in her cell. Each zombie was blindfolded and secured using chains and restraints in such a way that they couldn't turn their bodies or collapse, and each treadmill had a small cage attached just past its zombies' reach housing rats, moles and other live rodents providing the fuel to keep the zombies walking in the right direction.

"What the hell?" Josephine said softly, not believing her eyes. "How… Enos… what the hell is all this?"

"I built it!" Enos said proudly.

"*You* did this?" Josephine asked.

"Yup!" He ran towards the nearest treadmill, stopped far enough away so the zombie wouldn't be distracted from its bait and waved excitedly for her to join him. She did, but hesitantly and swung wide to come up from behind the zombie dynamo. "Paw said we needed 'lectric, and everybody knows the rots don't stop moving if they think they can get fed. When the bicycle genny' broke, I got to thinkin' and here it is!" he said proudly. "Took a long time to get all the parts together, but like Paw says we ain't got nuthin' but time."

Josephine stared at the undead as they plodded along, blinded and moaning, their steps turning the generators attached to their treadmills to charge the row upon row of batteries that powered Hanover Mountain. While she couldn't deny the logic and thought Enos should be a prodigy at MIT she almost felt sorry for the undead.

"So you bring zombies in here and make them power your generator?" Josephine asked. "Aren't you afraid they'll break free?"

"Naw!" Enos said over the droning. He pointed to a door at the other end of the room. "You just got to look through the hole in the door to make sure they're all there. If you see one of 'em off its machine you just come in and either catch it or kill it. We get near three months out of a rot 'fore it either quits movin' or just dies on its own."

"And you built this?" Josephine asked again.

"Well… Henry and Paw helped me build 'em, and Henry goes and gets more rots when we need 'em but the idea how to build it was all mine."

"What's that big door there?" Josephine asked, happy to

have something to pull her attention away from the zombies.

That's the door to the outside...that's where Henry brought you in from. He keeps it trapped now though, since the rots found the other door so don't get no ideas, now," Enos said.

"What do you mean *trapped*?" Josephine asked.

"In case the rots or the other sinners try to get in here. Happens sometimes. If you don't know how Henry's got it set up, the whole tunnel will just cave in. He don't even let me watch him set the trap on it. Now, see that other hole there a little ways over? That's another tunnel to outside, but its smaller. We stopped usin' it once Paw and Henry built the big one so's they could get bigger stuff inside to us. Rots found it last spring and Henry caved in part of it so's they couldn't get in."

Josephine noted Enos' warning then turned back and watched the hellish hamster wheels for a few moments before a sudden urge to leave the room hit her. "Enos...the noise is giving me a headache. Can we go?" she asked. Enos looked a bit deflated at that but quickly brightened again as he led her to the door.

"Come on, I can show you some other stuff I made," he said, obviously thrilled to have someone with which to share his treasures.

Enos led Josephine through another of the rough tunnels until they came up to a door. He paused there and held a grimy finger to his malformed lips. Josephine nodded, smiled and pantomimed a key-lock gesture on her own. Enos opened the door slowly and poked his head inside for a moment before he slipped in and waved to her to follow.

"Got to be real quiet in here. That hole up there's a vent. You can hear everything upstairs from here if yer too loud."

Josephine nodded and looked around the dimly-lit room. It was rough-hewn like the tunnels and crammed with a haphazard array of tables and shelves. Weapons, tools and all manner of equipment sat in piles and stacks making Josephine feel like she was inside a deranged child's toy box.

"This is my workshop," he said, beaming at her. "Well, I

guess it ain't just mine since Paw and Henry store stuff in here, but I use it the most." He moved away from her and started going through one of the piles while she tried to take a mental inventory of the room.

She saw hers and Heath's rifles atop a stack of long guns, the newest addition and thus the highest in the pile. Her grandfather's revolver sat on a table with its silencer lying beside it. An open case with cleaning rods and oil sat nearby as well.

She moved towards that table slowly, one eye on the gun and one on Enos as he foraged. She could see one of her speed loaders beside her gun. It would take all of two seconds for her to flip open the cylinder and drop the bullets in. Just as she came within reach, Enos turned back to her with a large pair of goggles held triumphantly in his hands.

"I found it," he started to say then stopped as he realized how close she was to the gun. "Jo'...you ain't tryin' nuthin', are ya?" he said, his voice sounding pinched and hurt.

Josephine stopped in her tracks, glad that she hadn't yet raised her hand towards her weapon.

"No, Enos, of course not. I wouldn't want to get you in any trouble. It's just, well, that gun is very special to me. My granddad gave it to me. He was killed when, well, when all this started," she said, holding her hands out to her sides to figuratively encompass his world. "It was the last thing he ever gave me."

Enos cocked his head to the side for a moment, like a dog trying to understand its master's motivations.

"Well, I'm sorry 'bout that," he finally said. "I'm glad my PawPaw's still 'round for us. But Henry's taken a likin' to that gun, and like Hanovers' always says; finders keepers. 'Sides, you won't need it since we're gonna protect you now. But I promise Henry'll take real good care of it. He's always real careful with his guns."

"Paw-Paw? How many Hanovers' are there, Enos?"

"Just me and Henry, I told you 'bout him, he's my brother. Then there's Paw, and PawPaw." Josephine knew the last two referred to Enos' father and grandfather, both common colloquial addresses for this part of the world.

"Enos, what about your mother, maybe a grandmother or sisters? Any cousins?"

"Naw." He walked over to her and put the goggles down on another table. "Paw told me we lost ma and the rest of 'em when the rots first came along. I was too young to remember all that. But PawPaw says you'll do just fine as Ma!" Josephine tried to suppress her shudder. If she'd had any doubts as to the Hanover's plans for her they'd been eliminated.

"They said that?" Josephine asked carefully.

"Sure did. Well, PawPaw said it, but Paw and Henry agreed quick enough. I'm glad we're friends, Jo', 'specially since you're gonna be my Ma. Paw and Henry said they'll share ya, real equal-like. You're pretty lucky to have two husbands as good as they are. PawPaw tells me most women's not lucky enough to get even one good man."

Josephine blanched visibly at his blasé description of her impending conscription into the Hanover clan.

"Enos..." she began as delicately as her churning insides would allow, "I can't stay here. I don't belong here." Enos's face shot up at her suddenly.

"You don't want to be my Ma?" he asked, his voice several notches over the whisper it had been. She could see the tears welling up in his deeply-shadowed eyes to glint in the room's faded light. "I thought you was my friend!"

"Enos, please, I *am* your friend. But if you keep me here, and I don't want to stay, that's just wrong." Josephine needed to keep him quiet and on her side, at least for the present. She switched gears, trying a different tactic. "Enos, have you read the Bible?" Enos nodded with enthusiasm. "Well, it'd be a sin to keep me here like that, Enos, and I'd be sinning if I had two husbands. You wouldn't want me to sin, would you?"

"Shoot, is *that* all?" Enos said, wiping at his eyes. "Don't worry none 'bout that, Jo'. PawPaw already talked to God 'bout it. God said he sent ya to us, on accounta' we been good, decent folk and all. PawPaw says you're doin' the Lord's work, whether you know it or not." Josephine stared at him, not sure what to say while she tried to process it.

"Does your PawPaw talk to God a lot?" Josephine asked, keeping her voice measured and light. Enos was young enough to have known no life other than Area 187. Everything he would've learned up to this point would've been fed to him by his small family unit. Enos believed his grandfather spoke to God personally and on a regular basis and she had no doubt where his loyalties would lie if push came to shove.

"Every day. God even told 'im that He may have made me ugly, but He gave me smarts." Enos tapped his forehead. "Says that's why He had to make my head so big, to hold all the smarts."

"Enos, you have to understand. I can't stay here. There are a lot of people counting on me to get where I'm going."

"That was us, and now you're here. God said so. And if there's one thing us Hanovers won't argue 'bout, it's God's word."

"So, what did you want to show me?" she asked, changing the subject back to Enos' prizes. He picked up the goggles and held them up for her inspection.

"I found these. Paw said they were what soldiers use to let 'em see in the dark. He said they was junk 'cause they needed power that we couldn't make. Paw don't even know it yet but I figured out how to charge these little batteries off the genny. You're the first one to see 'em!"

"Wow. You sure are smart, Enos. What else can you show me?"

"Really?" Enos asked. "You really want to see more of my stuff?"

"Of course. Why wouldn't I? We're friends, aren't we?"

"We sure are!" he said. He turned his back on her to rummage through another pile.

Josephine wasted no time in picking up her revolver and loading it. Enos spun around to face her at the sound of the cylinder being swung back into the revolver's thick frame. "Josephine, you can't be doin' that. Hank said that's a man's gun. He's sure gonna be mad if he finds out you had it." Josephine couldn't bring herself to point the weapon at the boy so she held it with the muzzle pointing to the ceiling.

"Enos, I don't want to hurt you, but I can't stay here. I have to go," she said as she backed towards the pile of rifles.

"Jo', you can't do that!" Enos' voice was loud and whining. "Paw and Henry'll beat me till I can't sit down if they find out I let you out!" He pulled a small derringer from the chest pocket of his coveralls and pointed it at her in his shaking hand. "You got to put that gun down and go back to your room 'fore they find out."

"Enos, that's a prison not a room and I can't do that. I don't think you want to shoot me, and I know I don't want to shoot you. But you need to put that gun away before someone gets hurt," Josephine said, her voice trembling slightly. Standing as she was, she couldn't see the room's opposite door open silently behind her on its well-oiled hinges.

"It's like the boy said," a rough voice said from behind her, "finders keepers." She turned at the waist just in time to see the cattle prod stabbing at her. Pain arced through her body for the second time that day, though this time it was far more intense and lasting. Every nerve in her body screamed as she was jolted again and again, the high voltage coursing through her until she lost the world in a white-hot blaze of pain.

Eric R. Lowther

Chapter X
Hanover Mountain

Josephine awoke at the last remembered moment of her consciousness, still feeling the ghost of strong hands gripping her and pulling her through the mountain of junk, to find she was now in the dark, nearly naked and slumped on the floor against an earthen wall. Her whole body felt numb yet sore, and her fingers trembled as much as her mind did from the after-effects of the electrified cattle prod. She stayed in her position for a few moments and performed a self-inventory. Her tank-styled undershirt and panties were still there, but that was all. The protective leathers and clothes had been removed during the time she'd been unconscious. The sudden realization sickened her, churning her stomach into knots of fear and rage. Her white shirt, bare thighs and the front of her white cotton panties displayed filthy handprints and smudges, mute witnesses to her physical molestation while she lay unconscious, vulnerable. It didn't matter that she didn't feel they'd fully penetrated her. She'd come here to help people like these, had left her comfortable home and successful life to risk it all for them. She'd been betrayed and violated for her efforts, the ghosts of their hands on her still weighing heavily where their grime marred her.

Josephine kept her head in its slumped position but turned her burning eyes towards her surroundings. She was in another earthen chamber like the workshop but almost twice as large. The lighting was dimmer, too, but that may have been a trick of the much higher ceiling. Odd lots of furniture sat in haphazard fashion around the floor. Couches, chairs and recliners in all states of repair

Eric R. Lowther

vied for space with a collection of tables and desks with no order to their placement. Most of the earthen walls had been covered with road signs, posters and cheap velvet art. The whole thing would have reminded her of a frat house basement if not for the threat of her impending nuptials to the Hanover men.

She'd explored with her sight and now it was time for the other senses to have their turn. Smell was obvious and nearly overpowering. The odor of unwashed bodies hung in the room like a palpable cloud, the tomb-like nature of their un-aired, underground lives making the Hanover smell a living presence. But the appearance of the room and the horrid smell were things she expected in a survivor's lair. It was the sound she heard that took her completely by surprise.

Of all the things she expected, television wasn't one of them. When Enos had mentioned his Paw was watching wrestling Josephine had assumed a pre-Area recording. If they had electricity it would only make sense they would have amassed electronic equipment over the years. Depending on how much earth surrounded them, not even EM pulses would've wiped out their delicate circuitry. When the ringing in her ears finally subsided she clearly heard the news break, a break not only about early candidates for next year's elections but voiced by none other than Julie Sommers. That had been enough to make her raise her head, enough to let on she was awake.

"Paw! She's awake! Jo's awake," Enos said. He'd been sitting so quietly only a few feet away that she hadn't noticed him. Josephine turned her head to look at his smiling face and saw the long black cattle prod in his hands. Enos leaned over to her and smiled at her. "Don't worry, Jo'. I ain't gonna' zap ya', they just wanted me to make sure you didn't try to run off again." He winked at her, the gesture almost lost behind his deep-set eyes. "You ain't gonna' try that again, are ya'?" Josephine struggled to her feet, gripping the crumbling dirt wall behind her for support. Her legs were trembling, weak and sore from her last run-in with the prod. It was an experience she didn't want to repeat.

"No, I don't think I could if I tried." Her voice was weak and her throat felt like it was on fire. "Water..."

"Let me ask Paw. Hey, Paw!" Enos shouted over the roaring television. "Can Jo have some water?"

"Shut the hell up!" a man's voice came back, the same voice she'd heard before the prod had dropped her. "It's the last match of the night!"

"Well, I don't see how it'd hurt nothin', anyway," Enos said with a shrug. He reached behind him in the horribly stained, over-stuffed chair and handed her a canteen; her canteen. She opened it and put it to her lips, her eyes never leaving the boy or the prod he held. The water inside tasted fresh and clear, much like the water her grandfather had pumped up from his natural spring. She took several small sips and then a much larger pull, feeling the cold, clean water invigorate her then put it back in his eager hand. Enos took in her dark, fearful expression and cocked his head.

"You look sad, Jo'. This is supposed to be a happy day! The Lord finally brought ya to us!" Enos added a stutter of clapping to punctuate his joy. Josephine knew the look she was giving the boy right now could very well alienate him to her cause completely, but at the moment she just couldn't find the strength of will to change it.

Enos's expression slowly changed to one more matching her own. "It's prob'ly the man, huh? Jo', I bet he didn't feel a thing when they got him. Hank says there's so many of 'em out there he was prob'ly pulled apart so fast he wouldn'ta' had time to feel any pain."

"Yeah, Enos, that must be it."

He was referring to John Heath, the mystery man of Area legend and lore. The man had been an Air Force captain in charge of search and rescue teams when the outbreak first showed itself to be unstoppable by normal military means. The man had forsaken his commission and defied direct orders to enter the war zone to search for his wife, a research scientist at a secretive bio-testing facility near Beckley. He'd stayed for five long years searching for Eileen Heath, stayed until something inside him had said *enough*, and when he did finally decide to leave he hadn't come out alone. A group of survivors had followed him to the massive wall that separated the worlds of the living and the dead. Heath and his people would've been killed before their feet had ever touched Pennsylvania to keep Homeland's dark secrets save for the documentary film crew that happened to be filming on the wall that night. That was a full five years after the Area had been founded and marked the first departure from the iron-fisted information blackout Homeland and the United States government had allowed. There'd been none since.

But Heath had paid the price for proving that survivors still existed. Homeland had maintained the chances of survivors still in the Area so long after their official declaration was virtually zero. He'd proved the conspiracy theorists right, saved seven souls from their living hell, and earned a suspended death sentence for his trouble; a sentence that could be carried out whenever Homeland and its shadowy connections felt like it. But much to Homeland's chagrin John Heath didn't turn into a grave robber, the name given to those thrill seekers and treasure hunters that defied every Area law and authority by slipping in and out for fun and profit. That would've made it far too easy for them to put him to death for violating the zero tolerance laws against illegal entry into the Area. Instead, he carved out the semblance of a normal, quiet life in Pittsburgh, keeping to himself and staying clear of anything having to do with Area 187. Anyone that knew anything about the shadowy world of Area politics knew that all it would take was for Heath to make one mistake, any mistake, and his life would be forfeit to a sudden and untraceable demise.

Homeland and the military powers attached to it both hated and feared him from the moment he'd emerged from the Area. Their hatred came from shattering their long-held and oft-touted claim that no living human remained in the Area, and their fear came from what he may have learned while scouring the countryside for his missing wife. There was only one thing that could've brought John Heath back to Area 187 again, and Josephine had it in the image of a woman that very closely resembled Eileen Heath in the background of the video message that had been anonymously dropped into her eager hands.

Just because Heath had come along with her hadn't meant they'd become best friends. Heath had made it clear from the start that he was only there to find his wife and in his mind both Josephine and the rest of the survivors could rot. They needed each other; she needed him to find the survivors and he needed her to tell the story to the world when they came back to keep them all from being hunted down and killed for violating the dozens of laws and anti-terrorist acts they'd already broken and the dozens more they would break if they'd ever been able to escape. He'd threatened her life several times, had killed men in the middle of downtown Pittsburgh because they'd dared utter his name to her, had made a complete fool of her many times over and had even turned live zombies loose on her to test her mettle long before they'd even entered the Area. He'd been a dangerous, murderous sociopath that clearly had been deeply scarred by his time spent searching for his wife and living among the dead on their terms and in their world for half a decade. And if there was only one thing Josephine could have beside her right now, short of a platoon of Marines, it was John Heath.

"Yeah, that makes me feel a lot better to know he didn't suffer when they tore him apart," Josephine shook her head slowly, the complete and undeniable feeling of being completely lost and alone settling on her shoulders like a yoke. Without Heath, she had nothing left to lose.

"So, is *this* how you treat your new Ma? I thought we were friends, Enos." Josephine turned her hands over and used them to make brackets around her body, drawing his eyes to her injuries and the tell-tale handprints marring her underclothes. Her voice was stronger now for the water, but it was also heavy with outrage. The boy looked at her with genuine hurt as he jumped out of the chair and came within inches of her. She backed a step from reflex and threw her hands across her chest. Josephine's eyes focused on the boy's outstretched hands then pulled her arms away enough to look down her body. None of the handprints she could see were small enough to be Enos's. Josephine was to be his mother, not his wife.

"Oh I *do* want you to be my Ma, and my friend. But you can't be tryin' to run off. You'll make 'em mad if you do. We all have to follow rules. You can't run off, that's your rule," Enos said as if he were telling her she couldn't run in the house. "Paw said that I'm supposed to help you, that you're my responsibility. If you try to run away again or you don't listen right, that'll mean I ain't teachin' you proper and I'll get whipped for sure."

"Does everybody have a rule of their own?" Josephine was getting control of her voice again through a mix of unconscious professional skill and the channeling of her anger. Enos was still as much on her side as he could be. It was obvious he didn't make the rules and had no control over his own fate, much less hers.

"Yup, at least one."

"What's your rule, Enos?" Her strength was coming back to her, her legs trembling less and her horrible emotional cocktail clearing her mind more by the moment. The boy looked down at his filthy brown and black feet at her question.

"I can't talk to nobody outside the mountain no more." Josephine looked down at him.

"What do you mean?"

"Just what I said. Paw took my radio away, said I couldn't talk to nobody outside the mountain no more."

"Enos, do you have a working radio; one that can talk to people outside the Area? And is that real TV I heard?"

"The Area?" Enos asked, confused. He thought for a moment then looked up at her. "You mean outside of Purgatory?"

It was Josephine's turn to look confused until she realized Enos's God-talking PawPaw would have replaced the term with the name 'Purgatory'.

"TV was easy. I figured out how to get those radio waves to come down a pipe up on top the mountain and down here on a wire. That's how I got my radio to work, too. But PawPaw says it's a sin to talk ta people outside Purgatory. He says God told him He made Purgatory on earth to punish the sinners."

"Then why are all of you here? If your PawPaw talks to God

then he's not a sinner, is he?" she asked, hoping to poke holes in the boy's indoctrination.

"God's testin' us. Boy, you sure got a lot to learn, don't you?"

"Yes she does, boy," a man's voice said from deeper in the room. The television volume had been dropped to almost nothing now, letting the voice echo a bit. "Now bring her on out here so we can all have a talk."

Heath fired his last bullet just as the last real light of day was fading into the night, leaving just enough illumination for him to see the finally dead creature crumple to the ground. He'd concentrated his fire on the ones that looked the freshest and fastest but there were still dozens to contend with, and anyone that had spent any time in the Area knew that night was no friend to the living. He holstered the now useless pistol and drew his pry bar as he started to move off to his right. The head of the swarm moved with him, their wide front naturally pulling thinner as the faster of them moved away from the rest. Had they had even an animal's intelligence and cunning they may have realized all they'd accomplished was to give their prey fewer targets to face at once.

He darted in and brought down the first few with several vicious blows before stepping back and continuing his sweep to the right, forcing the swarm to continue its pinwheel in on itself. Several of the slower, weaker ones tripped over their own feet or the feet of others as they tried to change course, buying Heath more time to rush in and repeat the process. He did this three more times, his continuous circling eventually bringing him around again to the junk pile.

His arms had joined his shoulders now in their protests, forcing him to change weapon hands with each attack to keep from completely exhausting one arm or the other. But even with that division of labor his pain and exhaustion were beginning to show. He'd killed another fifteen of them by the time he reached the base of the junk pile but each one had sapped a little more of his flagging strength. Even though he recognized this, there was little he could do about it. There was no way he could stop now. Even if he could get out of sight, they had his scent now. His numerous cuts and scrapes, even the smell of his sweat would be beacons in the night for the zombies, robbing him of even the cover of darkness. He would have to finish this fight or be finished by it.

Heath made another lunge in the almost complete darkness. Like the dead, he was relying on his other senses to make up for the loss of light, swinging his bar blindly into the night towards the closest moan. Had he not been so mind weary, so physically drained, and so intent on hearing his targets, he may have noticed the broken chunk of cinderblock lying on the ground between him and his next foe. His right foot hit the chunk of concrete just as he shifted his weight to it to add more power to his fading strike. He stumbled against the block then suddenly shifted his weight backwards to keep from falling head first into the horde. He realized his mistake a fraction of a second before he felt a lightning bolt of pain shoot up his leg as his ankle twisted under him.

Heath went down hard, falling on his ass as the shambling bodies continued their press. He managed to get to his feet before they were on him, but in those few seconds he'd lost that precious buffer of open space with no way to get it back again. All thought of tactics and hit-and-run attacks left him as he struggled to keep his feet.

He was alone again in Area 187; alone again, wounded again, and with nothing but a chunk of steel between him and a swarm of the dead. Again. Eileen had been little more than a concept to him before as he crisscrossed the Area. That concept alone had been enough to sustain and drive him; keep him searching. He knew now, knew with crystalline certainty that the woman on Josephine's contraband disc was Eileen. She wasn't a concept anymore. She wasn't a fleeting vision in a fitful night of broken sleep anymore. She was real, and she was waiting for him. John Heath took his pry bar into a two-handed grip and smiled into the moaning darkness ahead of him. He even thought about singing a little tune.

Again.

Chapter XI
Purgatory

Food; cannot see it. Hear it. Smell it. Cannot reach. Walk. Speak. Others speak. Speak. Others speak. Feed soon. Close now.

He repeated his call and the other moans joined him, though this time it was a different, softer sound. Had the other voices found their prey? Were their mouths too full to voice the call? He plodded along until an odd prickling came up behind his eyes, eyes that hadn't seen prey for longer than he could remember. He stopped his feet. The prickling meant something. He'd felt it before when he'd searched for other prey, hadn't he? Something was different. Something was missing. The hunting moans had ceased around him as had that other sound; the sound that'd been in his ears. The only sounds he could hear now were the squeaks and jabbers of the prey he'd been following.

He struggled against the unseen force that kept him from changing direction as a new scent came to him. He knew that scent, smelled it before. It was the prey that walked like he did. He struggled harder now. The scent was coming closer. He flailed about with his arms, trying to turn them in the direction of the scent. Something struck his arm, the one closest to the scent. He couldn't lift it anymore so he tried to twist, to send the other arm reaching out towards the prey. If he could only get hold of it he would be fed. His struggles brought his remaining arm around his face and suddenly he could see again, the thing that had been over his eyes now dangling from his grasping fingers.

The prey was there, standing there, waiting for him to feed.

He tried to turn, to face it. He could see very little of its soft flesh under the stiffer not-flesh but could still smell its blood. It was injured. If he could just turn his body, could reach just the smallest bit more he could feed. The prey raised its own arm just then, an arm that ended in something long and black. It hit him with its hard, skinny arm. He no longer felt hunger, no longer felt driven to hunt, to seek prey, to feed.

"Come on. Henry's a bit testy 'bout you, since you had his gun and all," Enos said. Josephine thought better of reminding Enos that it was *her* gun and let herself be led deeper into the room. Three men sat around an old television showing a grainy picture of Thad Nelson, her network's weekend anchor. Why had she heard Julie's voice on the taped promo spot? Spots like that had the lead anchor giving the voice-over. Josephine quickly put the thought out of her mind as the youngest of the three men stood and stared at her. He wore a rough, patchy beard under bloodshot eyes and a faded baseball cap. His skin was rough but pale, what one could expect to see on a man that spent most of his time underground. He was dressed much the same as Enos though he wore a t-shirt that may have once been white under his coveralls. Her .357 hung around his waist and his eyes dared her to mention it.

"You ain't to touch a gun again so long as yer in this house. You understand?" His teeth looked as rotten and black as those sported by many of the zombies outside and the stink of his breath carried across the air to her.

"I already have my rule. I'm not to run away," she said evenly. The look in his eyes was one of pure, unadulterated lust as he leered at her.

"You were right, Henry," another of the men said from his chair. This one was virtually identical to Henry save for being older. "She's real purty."

"Told ya Paw," Henry said, his leer coming to rest on Josephine's breasts. Paw stood and moved closer to her.

"Open your mouth," Paw ordered Josephine.

"What?" she said. Paw's face suddenly contorted in anger and he flung out his hand, catching her across the mouth. Josephine cried out more from surprise than pain but managed to keep her feet.

"Girl, I ain't gonna tell you but this one time; when I tell you to do somethin' you *do* it. You don't question and you don't wait about it. You hear?" Paw growled. "Now I said, open your mouth."

Josephine had no plans to do anything Paw said, something that was becoming painfully clear to everyone in the room. Just as Paw drew back his arm for another blow Josephine felt Enos' hand squeeze hers. She looked down at him and saw he was looking up at her hopefully. She could only imagine what the men would deliver to him if she disobeyed. They'd gambled on the fact she wouldn't want to see Enos disciplined and she cursed them and herself for being right about it. Josephine looked back at Paw and dutifully though violently opened her mouth. Paw stepped up against her and ran a thumb under her upper lip to examine her teeth. She gagged at the tastes on his finger, a conglomeration of everything that should never touch a human tongue. "Them's pro'ly the finest teeth I ever seen." He stepped back from her and regarded her coolly. "That ain't the mouth of someone from Purgatory. You ain't one'a them demons come from the outside, are ya?" Josephine would've laughed had she not been trying to keep her bile down from the tastes assaulting her mouth.

"No," she managed. She wanted to spit but soldiered through and managed to control herself. "I'm here to take some good people out of...of Purgatory and take them back where they belong. That's why I can't stay here. I have to go." Paw snarled at her and raised his hand again. Josephine braced for the blow just as the last Hanover to speak broke his silence.

"Easy, son," the old man's voice cackled. Paw's hand froze where it was though his eyes remained locked on Josephine's. Josephine glanced at the oldest Hanover. He wore no shirt or shoes and was clad only in a pair of old, faded and torn jeans. What few wisps of white hair he had left went this way and that in thin shocks on his pasty scalp. His eyes were faded and rheumy, reminding her again of the undead.

"She's blasphemin', PawPaw!" Henry said from his father's side. Josephine glanced down and saw that both the younger and older Hanovers had become excited at Paw's attack on her. She wished she were anywhere but here, even back in Jasper's barn, unarmed in a darkened room filled with zombies. At least there she'd had a chance. "You said anybody outside Purgatory can't be trusted! You said they could be a demon!"

"The Lord said that, not me, Henry. But He also said it was our duty to make others see the light. This poor girl's been sent to us from God Hisself. Do you know why God created Purgatory here on earth, girl?" PawPaw asked her. Josephine swallowed hard and kept her gaze on Paw's hate-filled eyes.

"God didn't create this. It was a virus, an accident..." Her words were cut short by Paw's fist. This time she went down hard onto the dirt floor.

"Blasphemer!" Paw crowed. Josephine stayed on the floor but turned her head to look up at him. Enos had backed several paces away to hide behind a high-backed recliner, the cattle prod gripped tightly in both hands.

"I *said* be easy, son. And I ain't gonna tell *you* that again!" PawPaw said, mirroring Paw's earlier threat to Josephine. PawPaw leaned as far out of his chair towards her as he could without tumbling to the floor. "I can see you've been taken in like the rest'a the sheep, girl. God works in many ways an' through many men. It was Him what worked through the government, it was Him what told 'em how to make that sickness. He did it that way so's not to tip His hand 'fore the Rapture. It's a comin', girl. The dead walkin' just proves it. Don't matter how it is they get to be walkin'; if God didn't want it to be so then it wouldn't be. The ones what's dead and walkin'? Those are sinners already lost to God's light. The others in Purgatory, they's ones God's givin' a chance to make their lives and hearts right by Him. We Hanovers is God's people, girl. If we wasn't, don't you think we'd be havin' sins of the flesh with ya right now? But we's God's people, girl."

Josephine looked down at the marks their hands had

already made on her helpless body. "If you were 'God's people', you wouldn't have hurt me and locked me up and you would've helped me and my friend instead of kidnapping me and leaving him to die. And you sure as hell wouldn't have been pawing at me like rutting animals!" Josephine said, her voice dropping in volume but increasing in weight.

"God told me to leave that demon outside!" PawPaw said. "I saw your two's comin' in a vision from the Lord just last night. The Lord told me he was too far gone for salvation but you still had a chance at redemption. We Hanovers is God's people, girl, and we're givin' you that chance." PawPaw's expression softened somewhat in the dim light from the television. "Now I'm truly sorry you think you been improperly handled, but I'm sure it was just an accident. My boys's good and God-fearin' and they'd never do what ya claim, even if you were some brazen hussy and not their intended. It wouldn't be proper without the sanctity of marriage in the eyes a God, and they ain't no sinners."

"You're all fucking insane!" Josephine screamed as she spit a glob of blood from her cracked lip at PawPaw. Paw reared back a foot and let it fly into her side. Josephine cried out as she felt her ribs protest from the assault and curled herself into the fetal position as Paw followed the first kick with two more to the same spot. Josephine screamed in agony just as the lights in the room started to flicker.

"Henry, take Enos and go check the batteries," Paw said. Henry knew better than to disobey his father and took only a moment to snatch Enos' hand before half-dragging him towards the door. Enos looked back helplessly at Josephine but let Henry pull him away.

"Now that's enough, son," PawPaw said to his son after his grandsons were gone. "I know what she's sayin' is incitin' the devil but she just don't know no better yet." PawPaw said. "No, girl... we're the only sane ones left in Purgatory. We're here 'cause the Lord needed those lost souls to have a beacon, a bit of His light to shine in the darkness, to lead their souls to salvation and a place at His table. We Hanovers has accepted this role in God's plan." Paw followed his father with a hearty "Amen".

Josephine stayed in her ball, her head tucked under her forearms. She could feel the punch had loosened one of her teeth and her side sent shuddering waves of pain through her body to the point she wasn't sure if she'd be able to stand. She missed her cozy dressing room, her small stage, her strong and overpriced coffee. No story was worth this, *no one* was worth this. With that came the realization that John Heath may have been right after all. There was nothing in Area 187. Not for him, not for her, not for anyone. The only things here were madness and death. And if that was what the Area wanted, then by the Hanovers' God that's what it would get. There in the dirt, with her side on fire from ribs that were surely broken, her own blood on her tongue and the phantom pressure of their hands where they'd touched her she made a vow that she wasn't going to go down without taking the Hanovers with her.

"I'm gonna tell you a secret, girl. Nobody but us Hanovers knows this, but seein's how you're gonna be family it's only right I share it. Many years ago, I lay dyin'. Doctors said I wasn't gonna make it, and I was ready to join our Lord in life everlastin'. But the Lord came to me and He told me He had other plans, I wasn't through servin' Him yet. He laid His hand upon me, and He said a word, and I was healed free from diseases of the body *and* the soul. I still know that word, girl. He left it with me in good keepin'. All I have to do is lay my hand and say that word in His name, and if He wants them to be healed then all sickness leaves 'em and all their pain's washed away in His light." PawPaw said.

Paw closed his eyes reverently and shouted an "Amen" to the darkness over their heads until a sudden thumping sound brought him out of his revere. Something rolled across the floor towards them, something rounded yet not completely round. Paw looked down to see Henry's head roll to a stop at his feet, his son's eyes bulging up at him and his mouth frozen in a silent scream.

"Amen, brother-man! *Amen!*" John Heath said from across the room, the door to the workshop standing open behind him, its light casting his shadow long and thin across the dirt floor. Enos lay on the floor at Heath's feet, conscious but with a huge gash across his spacious forehead and cradling the hand that had likely been fool enough to brandish a derringer at Heath. Josephine lifted her head at the sound of Heath's voice. The first sight she saw was Henry's severed head caked with blood and dirt just inches from her own. She recoiled from it to a sitting position, ignoring the pain from her side to put some distance from Henry's remains. "Henry! My God... you killed Henry..." Paw said, his eyes locked on his son's dead ones. Heath whistled at him and Paw raised his tear-filled eyes and hate filled snarl to Heath's smiling, blood-smeared face.

"I suggest you pay attention to the guy with the gun," Heath said as he trained Josephine's revolver between Paw's eyes.

"You ain't the only one, demon." PawPaw said. He pulled a small-framed .38 revolver from the side of his chair cushion and pointed it at Josephine. "Henry told me the sinners'd killed you. Only a demon could have walked among the dead like that."

"Yeah, whatever," Heath said to PawPaw. "Josephine, come here." Josephine looked up at him. Though he was bruised and smeared with both his and Henry's blood his bald pate and thick body appeared positively angelic to her. Josephine struggled to get to her feet until PawPaw fired a round into the dirt beside her, the un-silenced report freezing her in place.

"You ain't goin' nowhere. The demon's gonna drop that gun or I'm gonna have to kill you, girl," PawPaw said to her, then to Paw, "Go get his gun. He ain't gonna shoot." Paw nodded and took a step towards Heath. Without blinking, Heath sent a bullet streaking across the room just close enough to Paw's left thigh to crease it. The man cried out and grabbed his leg as he fell backwards into his chair.

"Bad idea," Heath said. The lights suddenly dimmed further, casting the room in even deeper shadows. "Next time I kill him," Heath said to PawPaw.

"We all have our sacrifices in service to the Lord, demon. My son's willin' to die for Jesus Christ our Lord and savior just as He was willin' to die for us," PawPaw said. Heath swung the barrel of the revolver down and placed the silenced muzzle against the top of Enos' head. The boy froze when the cold steel pushed against his skull.

"Josephine…?" Enos whispered. She looked at him, could see his eyes widen in his misshapen head in the ever-decreasing light. The blood from his facial wound was pouring freely down his face now, dripping from his chin to feed the hungry dirt below. Josephine tried to feel nothing, to assure herself that Enos's fate was something out of her hands. After a moment, she knew she couldn't. The men were one thing but Enos was innocent, at least as innocent as anyone could be here.

"Heath?" Josephine asked tentatively.

"If you haven't noticed, it's getting a little gloomy in here," Heath said to the room, ignoring Josephine's plea. "See, I got a confession to make, and you being the hand of God and all who better to hear it, right? Well bless me father, but my heart is heavy with hate. I fucking *hate* zombies. I mean I really, really do. So when I found your tunnel and crawled my happy ass up into this little church of yours and saw all those zombies just walking and walking and walking…well, I kind of…*lost control*. After I crushed their rotting fucking skulls my heart was still so filled with that hate that I took it out on your little generation station down there." Heath's stance hadn't changed and there was no smile accompanying his diatribe. That familiar chill ran up Josephine's spine again as the beatific light around him faded.

"You can't do that…" Paw said.

"Did it. My Bad. Now, from what I understand, little Eddie here is the one that made it all work." Heath's face was calm and smooth beneath the three-day growth of beard. There was no emotion, nothing in his face or his eyes to testify to having waded through dozens of the undead after Josephine had been taken, nothing to betray the presence of a drop of rage.

"Enos…" Josephine corrected.

"His name's going to be dead-fucking-Elephant-Boy if I don't start getting some cooperation," Heath said. "Now I'm sure the Pope there might be able to survive for awhile without the headless hillbilly and maybe even that piece of shit that's bleeding all over the fine upholstery. But you can't live very well underground if you're constantly bumping into shit and missing the wrestling matches. So, he shoots you and I blow little Timmy's brains out through his nostrils." Josephine didn't bother to correct him this time. "You're going to lose your piece of ass gramps, that much is a given whether you shoot or we walk. As an added bonus I'll pump this other asshole in the gut a couple times so you can listen to him scream and bleed out for the next few hours. Then you can just waste away here in the fucking dark by yourself. Ten seconds. Pray about it." Less than six seconds passed before the old man dropped his revolver in his lap and sat back in his chair as the lights dimmed even further.

"The Lord wants you to take her away from here, so b'gone, demon," PawPaw said, his voice tired and more frail than even his age could account for.

"Yeah, thought He might tell you that." Heath nodded at Josephine and she managed to climb to a crouch, her hand pressed hard against her side.

"Jo'... you ain't gonna be my Ma?" Enos asked. Josephine got to her unsteady feet. Every inch she stretched to her full height shot pain from her ribs.

"You heard your grandpa, kid. We demons aren't welcome here. Don't worry, you'll do just fine," Heath said without looking down at him. "I'm sure the Rapture will be along any day now and you guys will get sucked right up to the express line for the Pearly Gates. Come on, Jo'... let's get out of here." Josephine looked at Heath then at the two generations of Hanovers seated before her. Paw sat, his body rigid with the pain from his wounded leg, his eyes locked on Heath. PawPaw sat with his chin on his chest, his eyes closed tightly and lips trembling in prayers.

"Tell me something..." she asked Paw, "...do you *really* believe? Do you have faith that your father talks with God... that he can heal with his touch?"

"Paw-Paw's got the faith an' he's got the power!" Paw said, his teeth clenched against the pain. "The two'a you will burn in hell!"

"Let's test your faith... and his power," Josephine said. She reached down and plucked the .38 from PawPaw's lap, turned to face Paw and fired. The bullet punched through Paw's stomach, passing through both his body then the chair back. The Hanover screamed, his hands clutching at his middle. "Testify, brother! Testify!" Josephine said, shouting in her best television-preacher imitation along with the man's howls. Josephine stepped in front of Paw's chair and brought her foot up, throwing him back to a sitting position. She pointed the revolver at his blood-soaked abdomen and fired another round at point-blank range. This time Paw doubled over so violently that he sprawled on the floor at his father's feet.

"You done?" Heath asked as the lights dimmed to almost nothing. Josephine backed away from Paw's groaning, screaming body until she was standing beside Heath, then looked through the open door behind him into Enos' workshop. Henry's headless corpse lay just a few feet inside the door in a patch of red mud. "Anybody pokes their head through this door in the next hour dies," Heath said with a nod over his shoulder. PawPaw had already struggled out of his chair, his hand on his son's stomach. They could hear his low, fervent praying until Heath stepped backwards, the act pushing Josephine through the door. He closed the door behind them and dropped a length of board into the barring brackets. "Your clothes are over there in a pile. I already gathered your pack and the rifles. Get put together and let's blow this popsicle stand."

Josephine stared at him unblinking for just a moment. "You didn't have to be so rough on Enos. He's just a kid..."

"You didn't have to be so rough on the redneck, either. Gut-shooting isn't something you do because the kid at McDonalds didn't get your order right, but we don't have time for that crap now. Get dressed and cowboy up. You can bitch when we get well-clear of the family Geine," Heath said. He put her revolver down on a table beside her and started going through Enos' treasures while she dressed. Josephine dressed quickly then picked up her revolver and paused. Henry's headless body still wore her pistol rig. She looked at Heath and started to say something but thought better of it. From this vantage point she could see the unfortunate Hanover's neck had been cut only a few inches in. The rest of the stump was ragged and uneven, as if the job had been started with a blade but had ended with sheer, brute force. Josephine stepped over the bloody hatchet beside the body, steeled herself, unbuckled the belt from Henry's corpse then rolled it over with her foot. The nylon belt was soaked through and caked with bloody mud. She held it up and regarded it for a moment.

"Here," Heath said, tossing her a can of paint solvent. "Dump some of that on it. It'll cut the blood and the scent until it dries out." Josephine did as he instructed then slung the belt around her waist, not sure if she should feel heartened or sickened that she felt better when the heavy revolver was firmly back on her side.

"How long have I been here?" she asked as she slid into her pack, ignoring her howling ribs and throbbing jaw.

"A day. It's almost dawn." Heath was going through a collection of plastic whipped-topping tubs where the Hanovers had sorted various ammunition they'd scavenged. He held a round up and frowned. "You've still got a couple magazines in your bag. Use those first. There's no telling how old this ammo is but we'll take it anyway." He dumped two of the tubs into two small canvas bags he'd found, dropped one into his pack and handed her the other. Josephine packed away her ammo as the lights dimmed to almost nothing. A white tin box gleamed in the last of the illumination, its red cross standing out blackly against its white background. She snatched that up as well and stuffed it into the main section of her pack. She was relieved to see her camera was still there.

"You've got a lot of explaining to do," she said as she picked up her rifle and chambered it.

"Later." Heath picked up the night vision goggles Enos had been so proud of and strapped them onto his head. Their vision was dim but it would have to be enough. He took off through the door leading back to the necrotic generator, not bothering to see if she'd fallen in behind him. Josephine fell in and followed him down the tunnel, stopping in the food cellar just long enough for Heath to pick up a few items from the larder that sat waiting for him on one of the shelves before they entered the larger dynamo room. The light here wasn't just dim but flickering in and out, the weak strobe effect making the carnage Heath had visited upon both undead and machine look even more surreal. Josephine chose to focus on a tiny red light on the back of Heath's headgear instead of her surroundings as they crossed the chamber.

"This is a dead end!" she said as they passed the way that would lead them back to her cell. If Heath heard he didn't acknowledge as he led her to the smaller hole Enos had told her was caved-in. Heath slowed just enough to be cautious and entered the opening in the wall at a low crouch. With the bulbs overhead finally exhausted she had no choice but to follow.

After a few yards they hit the blockage Enos had claimed was in the tunnel. Heath stopped long enough to pull a few pieces of rotted timber and large rocks from one side of the tunnel, revealing a hole just large enough to wiggle through. They took a moment to put themselves back together on the other side before continuing, the passage now taking a decided downward slope towards a swath of dim light up ahead. Dawn had broken in Area 187.

Julie Sommers stared at her cold, bleeding feet. She'd lost one shoe in the helicopter crash and had abandoned the other when Howard Williams had forced her to run from the wreckage into the Area. Unlike Josephine, Julie had the luxury of remaining awake to relive the hours. Her recollections weren't being colored by nightmares, but they didn't need to be.

Julie may have succeeded in her devil's gambit, but in the end she'd pushed too far. She'd been able to put her boss on the ropes using their illicit affair and the Area video, but her plan had backfired when her father had caught wind that she'd involved herself in Area 187. Senator Allen Sommers, being not only the chair of the Senate committee on Area 187, but also up for reelection, had quickly taken control of his daughter's life the way he'd always done to make sure her activities wouldn't come back to haunt him politically. From there Julie's world had gone into a tailspin. Howard Williams, the hired gun Senator Sommers had brought in to guard his daughter and keep her out of trouble, had turned out to be an ex-grave robber. In a cruel twist of fate, "Howie" had turned out to be a relative of one Jasper Connelly, a retired grave robber and the man that had supplied Josephine and John Heath with the tools they would need and passage into the Area to seek the survivors that had begged for help on that accursed disc.

Everything that had happened after her father had discovered Julie was in possession of the message seemed like it'd played out in fast-forward. Williams kidnapping her as insurance against her father sending guns blazing at them blended with the mad dash under fire from Jasper's house, and though she knew very well they'd come into the Area by way of a helicopter crash, many of the details of that harrowing flight were being blessedly buried by the part of her mind that understood that being hip-deep in zombies was of current and greater importance. But even with that mental buffering there was still a slow, steady stream of images coming through on her memory train. She remembered the attack helicopter that had attempted to stop them and the Homeland chopper that had held her father coming after them. She remembered the crash itself in a series of disjointed flashes and snatches of electronic alarm bells from their damaged craft as Williams buried them well past the Area's mile-wide, deforested buffer zone into the land of the dead itself.

Memories were also filtering in from the aftermath of the crash. The Apache helicopter that had strafed them while they were in the air had been joined by a large, armed transport chopper just as they'd crawled clear of the wreckage. Williams had refused to let her go even then, knowing that between the Apache's night and heat vision scopes and the other's powerful searchlights he wouldn't stand a chance without Julie to serve as his human shield. And so he'd grabbed her and led her off into the woods, her bare feet raked by stones and deadfall.

The helicopters had stayed with them for only a few minutes before they flew off into the night. The noise of their crash followed by the sight and sound of the choppers suspended so close to the ground had roused the dead in the vicinity and no one, not even the daughter of a Senator, was worth the chance of attracting a swarm so close to the buffer zone. With the helicopters gone all it would've taken would've been for just one zombie to catch sight of the pair. Those on the wall had known that Williams wouldn't go back to the buffer and would instead head inland, leading any nearby zombies away from the wall. Of course, they'd been right.

The first undead Julie had ever seen was dressed in a ragged suit. The creature was missing its right arm and possessed a pronounced, limping gait but there proved to be nothing wrong with its mouth. With only his stolen machine gun, pistol and limited ammunition all Williams could do was to pull Julie along and use their superior speed to put distance from their growing tail. They'd alternated between walking and running until finally the moans had died off the wind behind them. It seemed they'd walked for hours after that until they finally stumbled into the house where she now sat, her legs pulled up into her chest and hugging her knees on the dusty bedspread in the master bedroom. She realized early on that screaming and crying would accomplish nothing save to attract more. At first she'd had to bite her lip from unleashing verbal carnage on her captor. But as time wore on she found she'd lost the will even for that. She was tired and hurt, cold and hungry, trapped in a land filled with flesh-eating zombies and the worst threat of all, Howie Williams.

"Okay... the Area will provide," Williams said as he walked into the room to dump an armload of treasures on the bed before sitting down near her feet. Julie recoiled as if he were a zombie himself and hugged her legs even tighter. "We have a little bit of everything; the previous occupants must have got out while the getting was good. I used to love finding houses like this."

"You're a fucking ghoul," Julie said, her voice tired and soft. "You're no better than the zombies." Williams ignored her and held a women's boot beside one of her feet. She tried to recoil further but was already as compact as she could get.

"Might not be an exact fit but close enough for government work." Williams picked a bottle of water from the hoard on the bed and dumped some onto one of the t-shirts he'd found. "Give me your feet. We need to get those cuts cleaned and dressed."

"Fuck you," Julie said. Williams's face darkened for a moment before he sighed, the act returning his good-natured smile.

"Okay. I'm a bastard. I drugged you, kidnapped you and now here we are in Area 187 surrounded by zombies and stuff. I get it. You're upset with me." Julie looked at him, and even in the thin daylight that managed to make its way into the room he could see the fire in her eyes. "But we're here now. I need to get those feet cleaned up and make sure there's no serious damage. Gangrene wouldn't go well with what's left of your fabulous wardrobe."

Julie regarded him for a moment then moved her knees to look down at her body. What had started as a thousand-dollar outfit had become a stained and shredded collection of rags on her body. She looked back at him and sighed softly.

"I meant what I said. I'm going to kill you," Julie said as she extended her feet towards him.

Williams kept his smile and shook his head. "Take a number, line forms at the rear." He held her foot up to the gray light from the window. Julie hissed between clenched teeth as he moved the damp cloth across her foot. There were a few minor cuts and a large blister to take care of but the foot was otherwise in good shape. Williams treated the other one in the same fashion then wrapped each in cloth from the ripped t-shirt. "Doesn't look too serious." He reached into the pile, opened a can of pasta with a faded red label, and stuck a fork into it. "Dinner is served, madam. Would you prefer the white or red this evening?" he asked in a convoluted French accent. Julie looked at the can for a moment before taking it and going after the cold ravioli with gusto. "Perhaps madam would prefer something in a shovel?"

"I hate this shit," Julie said between bites. "I didn't even eat this stuff in college."

"Of course not; no Chef Boyardee or Ramen noodles for the Senator's daughter." Williams said as he watched her devour the too-red sauce and processed pasta. She glared at him while she chewed the last of it then dropped the can off the side of the bed. Williams reached out to catch it but was too late. It hit the floor with a surprising amount of noise, the hollow clang of the fork rattling against the tin can cutting through the quiet room like a tolling bell. Even Julie jumped at the sound.

"Jesus… you want I should just open the window and yell to every pusbag for a mile around that we're here?"

"What's the difference? We're going to die here anyway." Her tone was somewhat cowed this time, though.

"No, we're not. At least, I'm not planning on that outcome."

"You didn't plan on this outcome either."

"Yeah, I know, it looks grim for us. Sure, we don't have adequate weapons or supplies. We aren't dressed for this weather and we're likely going to have to hoof it for days to get where we're going. But at least we have each other," Williams said.

Julie stared at him with a blank expression. "You think this is funny?" she asked. "You do, don't you? As if this isn't bad enough… do you even have a plan to get us out of this?"

"Sure I do," Williams said, "and it's a good plan."

"Do they even let you cut your own meat at the table?"

"Yes, and I almost never cut myself."

Julie folded her arms over her chest and glared at him. "So what's your big plan, Howie?"

"Well, Princess, as I see it the only way is to find Heath and company and catch a ride out of here on their coattails."

Julie leaned up from her pillows to within a few inches of him. "Howie?"

"Yes?"

She reached up and grabbed his face between her hands. "That's the dumbest, most idiotic, most insane excuse for a plan I've ever heard!" she said. She punctuated the last word by clapping her hands together with his face still between them. He jerked back a few inches then rubbed at a cheek. He was still smiling, a fact that obviously infuriated Julie even more.

"I can see you're having some difficulty with my plan. You need to understand just what we're dealing with here before passing judgment."

She reared back and slapped him hard across the mouth. "How dare you talk to me like I'm a child!" Julie said.

Williams was still smiling though admittedly not as broad as he'd been. "At least you're coming out of your shell. Maybe I need to clarify myself. I wasn't talking to you *like* I would to a child...I was talking to you exactly as I *would* a child. Maybe that was wrong of me and I apolo-" another slap, this time to the opposite cheek. "Okay, I get it, you're still upset with me. I'll try to be sensitive to your needs..." Julie brought back her hand again and let it fly. This time it was caught by the wrist less than a half-inch from impact. "That's it, no more MSG for you. The next one's going to cost you, Princess. I need you to grow up and fast," Williams said, his voice suddenly thicker and dark.

"And I need you to eat shit and die," Julie said. She spit in his face then tried to pull her hand away.

Williams responded by yanking hard on her arm and pivoting at the waist, the momentum of his pull dragging her bodily across his lap. "This is going to hurt you more than it is me," he said as she struggled across his lap.

"Let me go or I'll fucking scream!"

"You fucking scream and we'll have a whole lot of company real quick, Princess."

Julie raised her head and looked over her shoulder in time to see his hand poised over her buttocks. "You wouldn't dare..."

"If you're going to act like a child, that's how I'm going to treat you. *We will be zombie chow* if you don't recognize the fact that we're in this together, and that we need to be adults if either one of us is going to get back to the world again. That means no more screaming, no more slapping. I'll listen to what you have to say and you do me the same courtesy. Agreed?"

Julie struggled for a moment until she twisted the wrong way and felt her shoulder scream against his grip. She dropped her head to the mattress and growled into the thick comforter for a moment before looking back at him. "Agreed," she said. Williams let go of her arm and she sat up like a shot, her long blonde hair flipping across his face as she righted herself. "Can I still kill you?"

"When we get on the other side of the wall you can give it your best shot. I'll even give you the first one free."

Secretary Fremont pulled off his glasses and rubbed his eyes. The whole Sommers affair was turning into a huge mess right before his eyes, requiring more clean-up than any Homeland fiasco before it. He'd gone over the Senator's story with him for three hours then poured over the various helicopter crews' after-action reports and debriefings. Lt. Barris, Arnold Geary, the Department pilot that had been in charge of Sommers' bird, and the whole crew of the Huey sent out to recon the crash site beyond the buffer zone had been easy to tidy up. They'd all been piled into the same transport chopper to Washington for further debriefing on a straight course across the Area. Fremont had jotted the word "Letters" on his desk calendar shortly after they'd lifted off to remind him to sign the stack of condolences for the families of those brave civil servants and airmen that would be lost to 'mechanical failure' somewhere over the eastern panhandle of West Virginia. General Haig wouldn't be much of an issue, either, especially when his transfer to the Middle East became effective and he hopped aboard his own chopper to disappear above some unknown tract of desert. But Senator Sommers... now there was a tricky bird. U.S. Senators had a habit of living very long lives. Fremont was also sure Sommers had started covering his tracks and calling in favors even before his helicopter had touched down at Northgate after the botched attempt to free his daughter from Howard Williams. Even the head man had called Fremont that afternoon to remind him that Sommers was a shoo-in for reelection next year and that the party could ill-afford to lose such a key state as California to scandal.

But Fremont wasn't a man to let political whim guide his choices. While he was the top dog for the entire agency, he had taken personal control of Area 187 early on. He saw the Area as the greatest threat going to national security, and even to the world. If the virus managed to get beyond the wall, if terrorists managed to get infected tissue out, there was no telling how the world would fare. Worst of all, if either of those things were to happen on his watch... Still, the matter with Sommers had to be addressed. He didn't think Sommers would be stupid enough to go to the press or let it slip that his daughter had been kidnapped by the man he'd personally selected to be her guardian. Regardless of the danger she may be in, if she was even still alive for that matter, Fremont knew the Senator's pride and public image would never withstand that kind of admission. The most he could do was see to it that Sommers lost his place on the Area committee. Julie Sommers was a lost cause anyway, and from what Hartman had told him about the girl before he was sent to the federal pen he considered it a good riddance. Even the slight knowledge Julie possessed of Terrell and Heath's jaunt to the Area could prove disastrous if she were to let it slip. Judging from what he already knew of Julie Sommers that would've been a certainty. He jotted the word "heart attack" on tomorrow's date on his desk calendar to remind him to take care of Hartman's loose string as his assistant came to the door.

"Secretary Fremont, Senator Sommers is here to see you," the petite brunette said through a crack in the door. Fremont hated intercoms, telephones, radios; any form of electronic communication, really. He'd cut his teeth in the old days of espionage, where the best messenger was always one you could dispose of.

"Send him in," Fremont said without looking up from his calendar; so much to do and so little time in which to do it.

"Has there been any word on Julie?" Sommers asked. Fremont closed the file that had photos of Williams and the girl running for cover from the crash site.

"Senator Sommers, I regret to inform you that your daughter has joined the casualty list of the national tragedy we call Area 187. My crews reported the last time they saw them they were heading into the Area. I can assure you that your daughter is dead now, Senator. Please accept my condolences," Fremont said, his voice sounding bored and tired.

"You son-of-a-bitch! Why aren't you in there looking for her? I refuse to believe my daughter is dead until you show me a body."

"Senator, I doubt there's a body left. The crash and the

search teams I *did* send had the inevitable result of causing a near-swarm. They would've been slow and disoriented from the crash and wouldn't have been properly armed and equipped to deal with that level of contact. And, if there *is* a body left, I doubt you'd like to see it."

"I want action here, Fremont. I want you to find my daughter. Do whatever you have to or so help me I'll-"

"You'll *what*, Senator? Go to the press, perhaps? Let them know you had knowledge of a plot to enter the Area, a plot your own daughter was involved with?"

"I was conducting an *investigation*. I do chair the committee, you know."

"But action and investigation is *not* part of your chair duties, Senator. That's *my* jurisdiction. No one is above the law."

"You just try me, Fremont. I'll have you analyzing satellite photos of China in a cube farm in Quantico. Now what are you going to do about my daughter?"

Fremont looked at him for a moment. The man obviously hadn't slept, just as Fremont hadn't. At least his concern for his daughter seemed genuine. "We've increased our surveillance but a large rain system is settling in, makes it difficult for the satellites but we have teams of helicopters and other aerial platforms. If your daughter does turn up in one of those sweeps I'll do everything in my power to bring her back safely. The Area has killed thousands of others far better prepared and conditioned than your daughter. I just want you to understand that the outlook is very bleak, and the chances of her still being alive are practically zero."

"Is there anything else I can do?" Sommers asked. This time he was softer with a tinge of defeat riding the usually confident pitch of his voice.

"You could tell me anything you left out of your debriefing. You could tell me that you *do* have a copy of this message everyone's talking about, and that you were lying before."

"No. I wish I did."

Without the survivors' location the best Fremont could do was run broad sweeps of the Area, the act akin to searching for a few needles in a state-sized haystack. Fremont deeply wished he'd had Heath taken care of when he first came back to the world, but the media attention had forced him to stay his hand. This time, however, not even Sommers's prattling would keep John Heath from the fate he should've met years ago.

"Pity; now, if you'll excuse me Senator, I have a great deal of work to do. You've made quite the mess for me to clean up."

Chapter XII
Hard Lessons

Heath stopped them at the end of the tunnel and shoved the headgear into his pack. A thick briar bush had grown up over the tunnel opening, obscuring it from the view of the living and making it nothing more than scenery to the dead about forty yards up the hill above the trailer park. "Take a minute, collect yourself but be quiet about it," Heath whispered. "No way they can get up this hill."

Josephine moved beside him and peered through a break in the briar thicket. Several zombies were milling around below in front of the now-deflated junk wall. But it wasn't the walking ones that had her attention; it was the more than three dozen unmoving bodies littering the ground that made walking difficult for the upright ones.

"Yours?" she asked, nodding down the hill.

He looked at her for a moment then went back to loading a pistol magazine with the Hanovers' questionable ammo. "Yeah. More of them kept trickling in, didn't have time to drag the bodies under cover." Heath quietly charged the pistol and put it away. "How you holding up?"

"My side's on fire and I still can't feel the tips of my fingers," Josephine said.

"We've already lost a lot of time as it is but I'm not going to push too hard. If we can get a few miles clear of here and find someplace to hole up we'll break early and get those ribs wrapped. I think we both could use a little rest. Besides, the rain's almost on us. We'll be able to move a lot faster then." Josephine stared at him for a moment then opened her mouth, thought better of it and closed it. Heath cocked his head at her. "What?"

"Nothing. Let's get going." Josephine said. For once, she was the first one up and moving after a break. She'd been beaten, locked up, molested, even electrocuted and wanted nothing more than to just lay down and sleep; real sleep, in a real bed without having to worry about crazed religious fanatics or zombies or even the big bald sociopath. Her side sent waves of pain through her with every step and she was sure her jaw was bruised. She had questions for Heath, questions that'd likely come loud and venomous made all the worse because she knew she wouldn't like the answers, but now was not the time.

It was nearly noon and Julie hadn't said a word since they'd left the house. Williams would've given her credit for that had her eyes and facial expressions not alternated between utter hatred for him and stark fear of the Area as they walked. The man of the house they'd stayed in turned out to have been an avid outdoorsman, and even though there wasn't a firearm or bullet left behind from either the original occupants' flight or from scavengers over the years, there was still a good deal of warm outdoor clothes and camping equipment for both of them. Between the compass, various hiking and hunting trail guides and road maps Williams had found while scavenging the house he'd been able to trace a respectable route to the survivors' coordinates. He'd outfitted them as best and lightly as he could from the remaining gear, but they were still left with only his pistol and the light machine gun he'd taken from the Homeland agents that had burst into Jasper's house after them the night before. At least he'd found the silencer for the machine gun in one of the pouches on the tactical harness he'd stolen along with it, giving him two silenced firearms. He'd armed Julie with the baseball bat he'd found but kept both guns and a crowbar for himself. They were in a truce, but he wasn't sure he could trust her well enough to put a gun in her hand.

The rain that soaked them to the core had also kept the helicopters that had roamed the skies through the night at bay and would play hell with any other earthly or heavenly surveillance. It also served to quiet the woods they covered that morning, letting them make good time despite the condition of Julie's feet. So far, the only sign of the dead they'd found that morning was a lone, distant moan deeper into the woods. Williams hoped the zombie had spotted a wild animal but had shifted their course slightly, just in case. The rain eased up significantly as they broke from the cover of the forest and into the parking lot of a roadside rest area. He stopped them for a few minutes to listen and watch the deserted, half-collapsed pavilion for sounds and movement before leading her to the still-standing end of the structure and out of the rain. Julie sat down heavily on a concrete bench and bowed her head while he sat on the top of a picnic table. "How're you doing?" he asked.

Julie chuckled under her breath before raising her head. "Do you have any idea how fucking stupid that question is?"

"Yeah, guess you're right. If something changes, let me know," he said as he pulled a bag of nearly ten year old trail mix from his pack and chewed on a handful. The mixture of nuts and grains tasted like cardboard but would have to do for now. He offered her the bag and she sneered at it. "Eh, suit yourself," Williams said after another handful. Julie pulled out a bottle of water they'd found in the house and took down several gulps. "Easy there... it may be awhile before we find more potable water."

"Screw you. You got me into this, you find more water," she said, still looking away from him.

"Sure. I'll just be-bop down to the corner bodega and hit up ole' Habib for some Dasani." Williams pulled out his own bottle and took a few sips to wash down the trail mix then put it back in his pack. "We're lucky we found what we did. Bottled water from back in the day is a prized commodity."

"You say that like there's some kind of economy going on," Julie said.

"You'd be surprised. Think of the Area like a prison; there's a bunch of people locked up in here. Over the course of time, they adapt and adjust. They create their own laws and economy based on what's available. For every survivor that lives in a vacuum there are more that band together in small groups. If the group gets too big they usually splinter off. Too large a group attracts attention from dead and alive alike, and most of them are happy to trade with robbers and each other. Hell, I know a few guys that come in here to do nothing but. The survivors and caretakers running around in here find valuable things all the time. The smart ones keep the jewelry and crap like that to trade with robbers for fresh ammo or booze… all kinds of little amenities. I know a guy that got an autographed Mickey Mantle rookie card for a two-dollar box of .22 shells."

"Sounds like you people just prey off them. If any of you had any decency you'd get the people out of here or let Homeland know where to find them so they could be rescued."

"Guess I should have expected that coming from you," Williams said.

"What the hell is that supposed to mean?" Julie asked, her head swiveling around to face him.

"Guys like your daddy-dearest are why there are still people stuck in here. Nobody wants to deal with the fact that the government abandoned these people. Nobody wants to stand up and say, 'look, we fucked up and now we're going in there to get our people out and clean up the mess'. You know why they won't do that? It's because they'd be dead before the words left their mouths. And survivors coming back out? All it would take would be for one to turn up that had real knowledge about the virus and their whole world would've crumbled right before their eyes. The government has a real good idea just who's still behind the walls through Social Security, credit card records and the polls they took during the mass evacuations. Any survivor that just shows up one day on the outside and tries to get their old life back would send up red flags and they'd be carted away for medical examinations and *debriefing*. That's a nice way of saying they'd fucking disappear."

"Bullshit," Julie said. "The government did what they had

to do. All it cost us was West Virginia. Probably the only thing this backwater ever did to really help this country, anyway."

Williams looked at her for a long time before he stood up and let his pack slide onto the table top. "Your Daddy did a nice job of brainwashing you. That or you're just a spoiled little aristocratic bitch all on your own. He and a lot of others like him have damned living, breathing human beings all in the name of politics. You know what? The Northgate is about a day and a half travel that way..." he said, hooking a thumb over his shoulder. "You just run on back there and let them know you're alive in here."

"You won't let me. Without me along you're a dead man," she said.

Williams shook his head and laughed ruefully. "You really don't get it, do you? It doesn't matter who you are, it doesn't matter who your Daddy is or how you got here. Like it or not, you're now considered a carrier. Those guys in the choppers? They'd rather shoot you dead and leave you for the zombies than they would to take you back. That's standard procedure. Face it, honey... you're now an embarrassment. Nobody's going to take the fall for you or the Senator or how it was we ended up in here. Your death would be nothing more than a tear-jerking vote-getter. At worst, your network and Homeland will sacrifice both you and this Josephine chick in the media as a reminder of what happens when people mess with Area 187. If they would leave the esteemed Senator's daughter to rot, just imagine how grave robbers and treasure hunters will be treated." Williams turned and started walking towards the small building that housed the restroom facilities, its glass frontage shattered and jagged, jutting up from the frames like misshapen teeth.

"You're full of shit," she called after him.

He stopped and turned back to her. "Think about something..." he said, his voice far quieter than hers. "...they knew the course we were on. They knew we'd crash into the Area. There was a gunship and a Blackhawk loaded with snipers. Do you really think they couldn't have tagged me right there and then? If you were so god-damn important, why do you suppose they didn't drop a few bad-ass motherfuckers out of that chopper and right onto our heads? We have a whole bunch of guys whose job it is to drop into hostile territory, eliminate their targets and get the hell out," he said. Julie stared at him, hate vying with confusion on her face.

"I don't know what the hell you're talking about," she finally said.

"You're an embarrassment to Homeland, to the military and even to your father. We should never have been able to get as far as we did, and we certainly should never have been able to breach the Area. I'd bet my last dollar that Homeland and even your own father have already disowned you and Terrell, spinning out the story that you were both in on this."

"My father wouldn't let that happen..." she started.

"Keeping Area 187 out of the peoples' hearts and minds is a far higher priority than making Senator Sommers happy. But don't worry. I'm sure your Daddy's people will do some spinning of their own. How's it feel to be the Area's answer to Patty Hurst?" The rain picked up again, drenching him anew and spraying off his lips with every word he spoke. He swung the machine gun off his shoulder and checked the chamber. "Stay here. I'm going to go check out the building."

Julie watched him as he crossed the expanse of dead grass then carefully entered the building through one of the broken ground-to-ceiling windows as if he'd been swallowed through some huge, rotting maw. A sudden feeling of loneliness and fear swept through her as she realized she was completely alone in Area 187. She entertained the briefest notion of running to Northgate. All she had to do was get there, make her identity known and men in shining Kevlar and machine guns would come out and whisk her away to safety.

She'd never been one of *those people*, the kooks and nutballs that made up the core of Area 187 conspiracy theorists. Her father had told her since the beginning that containment of the virus was a necessary evil and that stories of lots of people still trapped within were nothing more than that; stories. Like JFK, the moon landing and even 9/11, the Area had bred a group of fanatics that couldn't believe the government did things in the best interests of its people, and that sometimes it had to sacrifice the few for the many. Julie firmly believed in the separation of society as well, the have-nots relegated to their position through their own sloth, poor education and life choices. To her, if there were survivors of any number in the Area they were there by their own fault. No one, not even Williams, could expect her to have much pity for those that willingly chose to live in the backwaters and sticks of Appalachia *before* the virus, and she wasn't about to throw a pity party for them now that they'd been trapped there. Fuck them. They'd made their beds.

She stood then stumbled as her feet protested carrying even her slight weight and walked to the opposite side of the pavilion. A small speck was moving slowly in the sky, the sound of its rotors coming to her over the pattering of the rain as it grew in her eyes; a helicopter. She threw a quick glance to the building then ran out into the parking lot, waving her arms madly above her head and shouting at the top of her lungs. "Here! I'm here! Get me the fuck out of here!" she screamed like a mantra as she jumped up and down on her punished feet. Williams stuck his head out of the shattered window and swore a blue streak as the chopper neared then came to a hover less than fifty feet above the ground. It swung broadside to them, displaying a single sniper in its open side door, his rifle raised to scope Julie.

"Julie! Run for the woods! Now!" Williams screamed over the roar of the chopper. It just hung there, the sniper watching her through his scope.

"Fuck you, Howie! I'm getting the hell out of here!" she called back without stopping her calisthenics. Williams hunkered down and brought the submachine gun around to the fore. If they'd seen him yet they hadn't given an indication. The bird didn't display any rocket tubes, only the sniper and an unmanned heavy machine gun in the door gunner's nest beside him. This was the moment of truth. He told himself if the chopper came down to pick her up he would let her go. Yes, she was a bitch. But he'd promised if the opportunity came to release her he would. Now it was only a question of how much pull her father had versus how badly Homeland wanted its secrets kept.

Dale Phillips looked through his scope and adjusted the knob on its side. He moved his eye away and looked at the rather striking publicity still of Julie Sommers he'd duct-taped to the chopper's side door then touched a button on his headset. "This is Hawk One to command, have confirmed sighting of female subject."

"Hold your position, Hawk One. Stand by for orders. Be advised weather center reports storm activity increasing in your location," a female voice came back to him even as the rain started driving harder through the open door and the winds began buffeting their previously smooth hover. Secretary Fremont had placed a high priority, and a high cash bonus, to the crew that could find the two that had crashed the Area last night. Phillips knew the target instantly even though his commanders hadn't used her name and knew the political stakes before they'd left the ground. His years as a CIA trigger man had made him a closet political junkie as well, enough to tell him he had the daughter of a multi-term U.S. Senator in his crosshairs.

"Hawk One, this is Eagle Zero," a male voice came over his headset. Phillips stiffened on the inside at hearing the Homeland Secretary's personal radio call sign. "Hawk One, do you have positive visual on both subjects?"

"Negative Eagle Zero, only female subject but confirmed identity. She's actively flagging us and doesn't appear injured. There's a structure about 30 yards away. If the other subject is still with her he may be there," Phillips said, resuming his sight picture of Julie jumping up and down in the parking lot.

"Phillips!" the pilot called out, "Evacuate or eliminate, baby! Weather's tossing my tiny ship and we're drawing a crowd!" he said, pointing to the opposite side of the chopper. The sniper didn't need an explanation for that.

"How many?" he said, wrapping his fingers around his mike to keep from yelling in the Secretary's ear.

"Coming from all points west, spread out across the highway median; at least twenty right now and closing. Somebody needs to make a call soon, I can't hold this position if the weather gets any rougher," the pilot called back. He was struggling to compensate for the wind to keep his ship's position stable as hard cross winds swayed the helicopter several feet to each side. Phillips moved his hand away from his mike.

"Eagle Zero, be advised we have excited the locals. They are converging on the ground position and weather will compromise our platform momentarily. What are your orders?" There was a long pause from the Secretary, the void filled with the whining of the chopper's engine as it was asked to struggle against Mother Nature. The helicopter was swaying violently now, the skill of its pilot the only thing keeping it in the air. Julie had noticed it, too, and had backed several feet away. For the girl's sake Phillips hoped Eagle Zero made his decision soon. The rain wouldn't stop the dead that were steadily advancing across the highway and the noise from their rotors would drown out their warning moan.

"Make a call somebody!" the pilot called back. "I either set down or we head away from the storm in the next ten seconds, and I sure as hell ain't settin' down!"

"Hawk One to Eagle Zero, don't mean to rush you Eagle Zero..." Phillips said.

"Tag her. Avoid the legs. Eagle Zero out," Fremont's voice came over. Phillips shrugged then produced a small plastic case from his pocket, pulled out one of the three bullets and peeled a small adhesive label from the cartridge case. He smoothed the label onto the back of the ID badge clipped to his lapel then chambered the bullet.

Julie staggered back a few steps as the helicopter pitched and swayed above her. What the hell were those idiots doing? She braced herself against a fresh onslaught of cold rain as the already-strong downdraft combined with the resurgence of the wind made her feel like she'd be taken off her feet at any moment. Suddenly she was on the ground, her left shoulder oozing blood through her coat. She lay there panting, the rain pelting her face and washing into her mouth as waves of pain rolled from her shoulder to her brain. She opened her eyes in time to see the helicopter passing overhead and off to the north.

"No!" she screamed over and over to the retreating ship, her fists pounding uselessly on the ground at her sides. "Come back here!" Julie rolled to her right and struggled to stand but only made it as far as her knees. She heard herself scream against the pain and felt hands under her arms, lifting her up.

"Julie... you have to get up now, honey. We have to move," Williams gently said in her ear. He was holding her up now, waiting for her legs to get under her.

"Where did they go? Why the hell didn't they get me?"

"They *did* get you." Williams said. "Right in the shoulder. Feel lucky the wind was up or it would have been your head."

"No..." Julie said, "it was a mistake..."

"You need to stand up. We've got bigger problems. Your Homeland buddies started a party."

Julie willed her legs to solidify under her. She wobbled in his grip, her head clearing as a collective moan wafted to them on the high winds. They could see them now, coming across the far side of the highway at them.

"Oh my God..." Julie whispered. There were perhaps twenty of them coming in a long line across the highway towards their position.

"Can you run?" Williams asked her.

"Just try and keep up!" She spun in a panicked circle, crying out at the throbbing pain. There were more of them coming out of the woods at the end of what had once been a pet exercise area behind the restroom building. "They're everywhere! Where the hell are we supposed to go?"

Williams looked down the stretch of broken, weed-choked pavement to the south. "That way..." he said, pointing. There were a few stragglers coming from that direction as well, though seemingly lower in number than their other options. Williams started to move back to the pavilion to retrieve his pack when Julie took two steps then fell to her knees, screaming.

"It fucking hurts!"

"Yeah, getting shot does that," he said. He stepped back and helped her to her feet. "But it'll hurt a lot more if you don't start putting one foot in front of the other." He pulled her after him to the pavilion as the first of the dead made it to the parking lot to their left. None of them were moving quickly, even for zombies. Williams figured them as first and second generation judging by their exceptionally slow movements and rate of decay. None of those disadvantages would matter though if they managed to get their hands on him and Julie. They would be dead by virtue of sheer numbers alone, devoured in a ghastly pile-on. Williams slung his pack then handed her the bat she'd left on the bench. "If one gets within swinging distance, hit it in the head just as hard as you can," he told her. She gripped the bat weakly and nodded dumbly. The left shoulder of her coat was soaked with blood now. Its loss would make their escape that much slower.

"You're going to make it, Julie," he said. She looked up at him and nodded. Her eyes were pain-filled and rimmed with tears. "No crying in the Area." Williams held the machine gun in his right hand, slipped his left arm around her and together they limped off down the ramp that would lead them to the highway.

"I can't do this," Julie said, her breathing rapid and whistling through her clenched teeth as they got clear of the rest area and made the highway. The largest mass of the dead were behind them now, their shambling bringing the head of the undead parade to the base of the highway on-ramp they'd just taken.

"You have to unless you want to die right here." Williams raised his weapon as they walked and dropped two zombies as they advanced up the highway from the south. The hissing report of the gun startled Julie and she quickened her steps past the two corpses. The road took a steep rise ahead and they struggled up it as Julie's energy ebbed. They reached the top only to find a knot of five zombies coming up the opposite side to meet them. "Remember, the head," Williams said as he pulled his arm away from her waist and loosed his crowbar into his hand. Julie nodded quickly and tried to hold the bat out ahead of her but the effort proved too much for her injured shoulder, the business end of the improvised weapon clinking against the pavement. Williams looked back, registered her difficulty and hurriedly traded weapons with her since the crowbar could be more easily wielded with one hand. She took the crowbar in her right hand as Williams slung his gun, turned and swung for the bleachers.

The zombie, a female, wore a police officer's uniform. Judging from the ragged appearance of the brown-on-black uniform and the creature's taut gray skin it had been around for awhile. The metal bat struck her skull with a dull metallic thud and her eyes went wide before she crumpled to the ground. Three of the remaining four had clustered together, their six hands reaching and clawing at him. Williams took another step to the right, forcing the group to shift with him and away from Julie where she cowered on the other side of the finally-dead police woman.

Williams wound up and let fly again. This time what had once been an elderly man fell, his naked body falling into a heap. The center zombie, a teenage boy frozen in time mindlessly latched onto the end of the bat while the remaining two moved around him towards Williams' flanks. Williams tugged once on the bat before letting go then pulled his pistol. He shot the two on his sides then grabbed the end of the bat with one hand, this time pushing it into the zombie's chest. It came off its feet and landed hard in a sitting position in the middle of the road. Williams brought the bat behind his shoulder with one hand and swung, the blow breaching the dead boy's skull. The rain and wind remained steady and shearing throughout the battle, carrying the unearthly moaning of the dead from behind them. Julie's sudden scream cut through the monotonous drone like a straight razor.

Williams spun to find one of them gripping her by the shoulders, its hand no doubt crushing against the new wound under her scavenged coat as the pair turned in a slow, struggling circle as the larger contingent of the dead neared the top of the ramp. There was now no way Williams could fire or even swing his bat without chancing injury to Julie. He dropped the bat and grabbed the thin, gray neck and hauled backwards. Julie pitched face-first to the road, the zombie keeping his hold as Williams tried to pull him away. Julie's body weight finally overcame the undead's grip as gravity pulled her down on top of the police woman's corpse. As soon as she was free Williams put the muzzle of his pistol against the back of the thing's skull and blew its forehead towards the advancing swarm as they crested the hill now less than ten yards away.

Julie lay atop the corpse, alternating between screaming and cursing. She finally rolled away from the dead cop, jamming her shoulder against the road as she rolled onto her back then looked towards her feet to see the advancing swarm. She screamed again and scrabbled to a sitting position. Williams was saying something to her but she couldn't hear him. All she could hear were the moans of the damned; all she could see was the wall of rotting flesh coming at them. "Leave me alone!" Julie screamed, her voice cracking and hoarse. In an act of sheer terror she threw her crowbar into the mass, her screaming now guttural, unintelligible. She slapped her hand against the dead cop and felt the sting of metal; a pistol still rode in the gun belt. She grabbed it with both hands and ignored the protests from her shoulder as she struggled to defeat the thumb-break holster. She finally, desperately wrenched it free and pointed it at the horde. She started laughing maniacally, pulling the trigger as fast her finger could stroke it. Nothing but dry metallic clicks punctuated her laughter. The dead were within just a few feet as she looked wide-eyed at the gun in her hand.

"Come on!" Williams barked as he hauled her up. Julie was beyond words now, her screams and laughter coming in bursts as tears rolled down her face. He leaned over her shoulder and dropped three zombies at the leading edge of the horde with his pistol then started pulling her backwards down the road. Julie raised her pistol again and started in on the trigger, its clicking barely audible over the moans of their pursuers. Williams suddenly spun her around and braced her against his body. "We've got to get out of their sight." He maneuvered them as if they were contestants in some ghoulish three-legged race through several smaller knots of zombies moving up the road towards the commotion. He only hoped Julie's fear and adrenaline would hold out, keep her on her feet long enough to get them some breathing room. They stumbled along that way for nearly a half-mile before they came upon an exit ramp. There were still a few zombies coming from the wooded area on the other side of the divided highway but they'd left the bulk of the horde behind the last rise in the road. Julie was still laughing and shrieking at odd intervals, the high-pitched keening like a beacon to every pair of dead ears for a half-mile around while she waved the impotent pistol before her.

"Julie... you have to be quiet, okay?" he said in hushed tones.

She swung her head to look at him, her eyes wide and gleaming. Spittle decorated the corners of her open mouth as she brought up a hand to cradle his cheek. "We're going to die!" she said, laughing. "They're going to get us and eat us... get us and eat us..."

Williams turned away from her, shaking his head. He had to get them under cover, had to make sure the few zombies that could still see them couldn't see where they'd gone, and he had to quiet her down before he could do anything else.

"Julie... would you like to play a game?" he asked.

Her eyes lowered a bit as she regarded him. "What game?" she asked, matching his whisper with her exaggerated one.

"It's called the quiet game. You ever play that one?" She nodded as eagerly as her depleted reserves would allow. "Good. Now, the first one to talk loses, okay?"

"Okay," she said, giggling, "but, they're still going to eat us."

Williams shook his head but said nothing. Julie was in shock now, a small, scared child in a big, evil world. He moved them another hundred yards down the road to just past the beginning of the off-ramp. There were still three zombies in view; the farthest approximately seventy-five yards away and the closest just coming across the highway at them, the concrete barriers in the median giving it pause.

The Army had created few better marksmen than Howard

Williams, and he'd always been just cocky enough to know it. The weapon he held was made for spraying bullets in short, controlled bursts, with an accuracy that would be considered fledgling past 30 yards and laughable at the distance his furthest target was from his position. He extended the collapsed metal stock with practiced ease then took careful aim and fired at the furthest target. The ghoul rocked on its heels then fell over in the distance. He fired again, taking the second off his feet as if he'd hit its knees with a board. Williams saved the closest for last, punching a neat hole in the zombie's forehead just as it managed to swing a leg over the concrete barrier. He gauged the distant moans then pulled Julie along down a bank and across the off-ramp, doubling back well-below the highway and moving up the small rural lane.

Julie was good at the quiet game. She hadn't made a peep since they'd left the highway, and he hoped she was still a willing player. Williams had pushed them into various ditches and once behind a six-car pileup, concealing themselves among the rusting hulks against the unseen dead and their moans. After a time it seemed the plan was a success, the moans drifting to the south before finally dying away altogether.

Julie's steps had become slow and faltering by the time they came upon a large concrete building. A faded sign attached to the high chain-link fence proclaimed it had once been "Davis & Son Machine and Welding Co." Julie was barely standing now. If he didn't get her someplace safe and tend to her wound she'd be dead within a few hours, if she wasn't doomed already from infection and blood loss. He hoisted her up over his shoulder and moved around the perimeter until he found a gate secured by a stout, locked chain. The best case scenario was to find the building had once been a safe house but had since been abandoned or its occupants were dead inside from starvation and loss of hope. At worst, it had served as a depository for undead from the first generation, before anyone really knew what they faced or found the strength to destroy those that had once been friends and family. Somewhere in the middle would be the possibility that it was currently inhabited. He'd decided to take his chances when he felt a sudden, sharp pain in the side of his neck. He reached up and swatted there, expecting to find an early-season wasp or bee. Instead a small, red plastic dart fell to the ground. "Shit..." he managed before he felt himself falling.

Dale Phillips peeled the rain-soaked flight coveralls from his body, quickly dried, then dressed in civilian clothes and hustled off into the bowels of the Northgate Command Center. From the ground the building looked like nothing more than a five story office building surrounded by a high chain-and-razor fence with a small airfield attached to its side. The real story to the place was the underground levels. There were as many levels below ground as there were above, each devoted to a different activity. The uppermost was devoted to Sempertech workshops, storerooms and other areas needed to maintain the buffer zone. Next came the Master Control Room, the centralized location responsible for coordinating the various localized control centers throughout the buffer and where data and images from these other regional command centers were collected. The third housed the Deadheads, a unit of the 101st Airborne specially trained for duty in the Area as well as select Homeland agents. The fourth was divided between offices for the military and Homeland Security, where Phillips was heading now. The lowest level was devoted to...well...he didn't really know. In fact he didn't know *anyone* that knew what it was really used for, and he was more addicted to breathing than curiosity to find out.

Phillips got on the elevator, swiped his badge and punched the button marked "S4". He hardly felt the sensation of movement before the elevator doors swished opened onto a tastefully-decorated, empty waiting room. The receptionist, a rail-thin middle-aged woman with her hair in a tightly-wound salt-and-pepper bun barely looked up at him as he neared her desk. "Go in Mr. Phillips, Deputy Secretary Warner will see you now," she said.

Phillips cocked an eyebrow at her and paused at her desk for a moment. He usually reported to Agent Wilkins, a senior agent and part of Fremont's inner circle. This time he was reporting to the Deputy Secretary of Homeland Security. Warner was second only to Eagle Zero.

"Agent Wilkins isn't in?" Phillips asked, looking at Wilkins' brass nameplate on the door ahead of him.

"Agent Wilkins is on assignment."

"Right. Gotcha." He'd met Warner once at a dinner honoring military men that had fallen in Area 187. He normally didn't attend such functions, but since he'd personally killed three of those brave soldiers after they'd stumbled upon information they shouldn't have he thought it only right he honor their memory at the open bar.

Warner hadn't changed since their last meeting. He was a short, portly man with a nose made bulbous from too many years of Scotch and fingers yellowed from the cheap cigars his wife had thought he'd given up after his third heart attack. He lit one of the pungent sticks and used its smoldering end to point Phillips to one of the chairs in front of the desk.

"I don't care... get it done," Warner said into the phone then slammed the receiver down. "You just can't find good help these days, Phillips. Men that just do what the hell you tell them just don't exist anymore, you know? It all started when they stopped keeping score in little league. Everybody's got to be so god-damned special now." Warner chewed the end of his cigar thoughtfully, letting the profundity of his words echo in the room.

"Couldn't have said it better myself, Deputy Secretary," Phillips said.

"Yeah... anyway. You got a positive ID on the girl?"

"Yes sir."

"And you tagged her? Give me the code," Warner said.

Phillips peeled the small label he'd taken from the tracker round's case from his ID badge and handed it across the desk. Warner snatched it then turned to the desk's computer, hunted for a few keys then painstakingly entered the number from the label. A few seconds later a map of Area 187 appeared on the screen with a tiny blip flashing along the southwestern side of the Pennsylvania/

West Virginia border. "And you're sure you didn't kill her with the damn thing, right?"

"She was alive when we bugged out, sir. But like my report said the chopper excited the locals. There was a swarm massing when we left." Warner kept staring at the monitor and zooming in on the flashing point on the screen.

"Well, she's not where you tagged her. If she got herself infected she's made a lot of distance since. Never have trusted those markers, though; just as easy to kill somebody with them as it is with a bullet," Warner said.

"That's a third generation round, sir. It's specifically designed for shallow penetration and has these little barbs to make it difficult to remove without a lot of time and care. The bullet itself is basically made of hardened salt. It almost guarantees non-fatal penetration if put into a major muscle mass so it disintegrates around the tracer." Phillips said. Warner grumbled under his breath and nodded at the CIA agent's reassurance. "So... Deputy Secretary... I believe there's a bonus?"

"Bonus? Hmm... oh, yeah," Warner said. He slid open the top desk drawer, pulled out a silenced automatic pistol then shot Phillips twice in the chest and once immediately between the eyes, the force from the last shot enough to make the chair tip over. Warner returned the gun to the drawer then looked back at the computer screen. "Delores..." he said as he punched a button on the phone, "send in the janitor, please."

Heath and Josephine made it up the hill, passing what must have been the original home of the Hanovers. Time and the dead had not been kind to the dilapidated three-story house. Wide sections of its slated roof had caved in, likely the victim of the heavier snows this elevation could get. All of the windows on the first floor had been broken out as well as many on the second and third. The front door had been ripped from its hinges long ago and lay against the porch steps and clothed skeletal remains were strewn about the yard.

Their trip down the other side of Hanover Mountain was made easier by the same thing that had made it easy for the zombies to assault the house in the first place; a wide dirt road carved into the hillside. Heath didn't like using any sort of road but their wounds and lack of rest gave him doubts that they could move silently in the still winter-dry woods. He'd been good to his word though and hadn't pushed as hard, but that didn't make the walking easier. Josephine knew she wouldn't be able to make it much further, and judging by Heath's heavier and louder steps he was feeling the effects of his own wounds. If they didn't find somewhere safe soon, they would have to risk resting in the open.

They trudged on for almost two more hours before Heath led them to the edge of the town of Derry's Corner. They'd passed a few scattered farmhouses and barns along the way but none seemed suitable to Heath. They would need to rest at the same time and needed someplace that offered at least some measure of security. Most of those structures had been overrun by time, weather, the dead or a combination of all three. Heath didn't like the idea of going near even small towns, but their need for rest was paramount. If they were caught out in the open now, spent as they were, they'd have no hope of surviving. They passed a few small, broken-down houses before Heath found what he was looking for; the Derry's Corner Volunteer Fire Department. The two wide garage doors were down and solid despite the dark maroon stains and fist-sized dimples in their aluminum skins. Heath approached one of them and looked through its grimy window. It had been a common practice in the early days of the virus to lock the dead in large municipal buildings like this one, their stout doors and brick-and-block construction making it impossible for the dead to get out. They made excellent safe havens for the same reason.

There were no fire trucks in the garage. Those would likely be rusting away at the site of the last fire Derry's Corner had ever fought. There was also no indication the building had been used as the community's dumping ground for their dead, either. They moved to the side of the building and tried the main door. Heath smiled when he found it locked. He slid his bar into the jamb and applied steady pressure until the door popped open.

Once inside Heath closed the door, slid the large-diameter barrel-bolt into its place and turned to the cavernous garage. They stood silently for several minutes, watching and listening for any sounds of occupancy. Heath doubted there would be any. It was more likely they were the first to set foot inside since the town's original evacuation. Eventually satisfied of its desertion they moved along the wall, careful to stay away from the garage doors and their telling windows and moved to the back of the building. After completing a circuit and making sure other doors and windows were secure they moved upstairs. They gave every room a thorough inspection before they reached Eden in the form of a small room containing several metal-framed cots, each complete with a thin yet serviceable mattress and bedding.

Josephine sat on a bed in the center of the room. Heath slid out of his pack, took a mattress from another bed and lashed it against the room's only window. Going back to his pack he produced a short, oddly-shaped flashlight. He turned it on then slid a piece of its housing down, turning it into a small fluorescent lamp. He placed it on the floor between their two beds and sat down facing her.

"We should be safe enough here for awhile," he said as he dug in his pack for his medical kit. He pulled off his jacket and shirt and started examining the many cuts and bruises he'd picked up over the course of the last day. Some looked serious, others nothing more than small cuts that looked an angry red even in the dim light.

"Some of those look infected." Josephine said as she looked at him. She could see other wounds across his chest as well, old wounds that had scarred. He was a powerfully-built man made to look even more so as the dark shadows alternated with the soft light shining up at them from the floor. She stood, let her pack slide from her shoulders and pulled out the tin box she'd taken from the Hanovers.

"Thanks, no. I've got it," Heath said as he opened a package of alcohol-impregnated gauze pads and started swabbing at the cuts and wounds and the streaks and smears of what could only have been Henry Hanover's blood.

"Okay tough guy. It'll be fun to watch you get the ones on your back, too," Josephine said in a tone devoid of humor. She took out her flashlight, scanned his back and let out a choked gasp. It wasn't the many small cuts that still seeped blood that made her recoil but a large, blackened wound on the back of his shoulder near the base of his neck. The skin that'd once covered the wound had never grown back, revealing gray-black muscle beneath.

"Jesus, Heath... what the hell is that?" Josephine asked as her fingers reached out involuntarily to touch the mass of dead flesh. Heath leaned forward quickly to keep her fingers from the wound.

"Just an old wound that never healed right. Don't touch it, it's still tender sometimes." Josephine stared at the wound a moment longer before willing her eyes away to the fresher injuries. The collapsing junk pile had been like a thousand rusty scalpels on his skin. If it hadn't been for the heavy leathers he'd insisted they wear Heath would've been sliced to ribbons.

He stopped his work and looked at her for a moment. "Sorry, didn't mean to snap. Not used to having another pair of hands around," he said, handing her a few of the alcohol pads and a pair of rubber surgical gloves.

"Yeah, I noticed already. What's with the gloves?" she asked as she pulled a bottle of alcohol from the kit and a few dry pads then frowned at the empty bottle. Heath held up the pads from his own kit again.

"Evaporation. That shit's been here for years. Put the gloves on. Better safe than sorry for both of us. There's no telling what kind of nastiness was in that junk pile." She pulled the gloves on then took the pads and cleaned the wounds he couldn't reach on his back, careful to avoid touching the gaping, black wound while he finished with those on his chest and abdomen. "Needed a change of clothes anyway," he mumbled to himself as he examined his bloody, savaged shirt.

"A shower couldn't hurt, either," Josephine said. After three days of trekking and fighting neither one of them looked or smelled like a human being should.

"Rain's coming, that'll help." The leathers could be wiped clean, but the clothes beneath them were a lost cause. He stood and stripped out of his chaps, fatigue pants and even his underwear right there in front of her. Modesty was a luxury in the Area.

Josephine turned her head out of respect, but not enough that she couldn't see him in her peripheral vision. It was a shame a man as well-built as Heath had all the personality of a cobra.

Her attempt at being demure hadn't escaped Heath and he chuckled softly as he pulled on a fresh pair of underwear before checking his legs for wounds. "Put the gloves in here," Heath said as he held his shirt out in front of her. Josephine pulled the gloves from her hands by the cuffs and placed them in his shirt. Heath nodded at the latex gloves then rolled his bloody shirt into a ball and deposited it in a steel cabinet the firemen had once used as a closet. "Here, clean up," Heath said as he handed her a small plastic bottle.

Josephine flipped the plastic cap away from the bottle and sniffed it. "What's with the bleach?" she said with a finger under her nose.

"Put some on one of those dry alcohol pads and wipe your hands, cleanliness being next to Godliness and all." When she finished with the bleach Heath took the bottle and put it back in his pack. "Shed the clothes," he said to her as he sat back down on his bed.

"What?"

"I need to see if he broke any of your ribs," he said without looking at her. He had a syringe in his hand and was working up a dose of a thin, clear liquid.

"Oh. What's that?" she asked, nodding at the needle.

"Galaxy antibiotic, cures whatever ails ya'," he said, tapping the syringe to move any air bubbles to the needle then released them. "It's been a full day without treatment, no sense taking a chance on infection. Don't worry, I have a clean needle for you, too, if you need it," Heath wrapped a rubber tube around his bicep, tapped his arm until a vein rose to prominence then injected the antibiotic. Josephine looked away at the moment of the injection and didn't turn back until she heard the tube come off his arm. "A little squeamish, are we?"

"I never could stand needles," Josephine said. She stood up and removed her jacket slowly, her shirt even more so. It had hurt to push her body this far and she was finding that it hurt almost as much to move now that she'd stopped. She touched her side gingerly just below her sports bra and winced. The skin had taken on the sickly blue-purple color of a deep-tissue bruise.

"Turn around and lift your arm as high as you can," Heath instructed. She did so, wincing again when she got her arm level with her shoulder. Heath prodded and poked around the bruised area, evincing a shuddered breath or muffled curse from her each time he did so. "I don't think there's anything broken, but you're going to feel this one for awhile." He reached into her stolen medical kit and pulled out a thick roll of elastic bandages. After a few moments he had her entire lower abdomen wrapped snugly then turned her to face him, his eyes almost level with several of the burns left by Henry's cattle prod. Heath placed his hand just above her right breast and ran a finger over one of the wounds. She shivered unconsciously at his touch as he traced each one of them the same way. "Those will hurt for awhile but you shouldn't have to worry about infection. That high of a voltage burns pretty hot, tends to cauterize the wound. Just keep an eye on them. If they start seeping we'll need to clean them." Heath stood up and pulled the rest of his fresh clothes from his pack, a set identical to those he'd shed. "I'm going to rummage around in the break room we saw," he said, picking up his bar. "You should probably change, too. Might make you feel better."

"I doubt that," Josephine said. She did change her clothes after Heath left the room, and though it made her smell slightly better, it didn't make her feel much better. She looked down at her stained panties and tank top lying on the bed. Without knowing why she snatched them up in a bundle, opened the cupboard Heath had used then shoved them in. She closed the door and walked back to her bed, her eyes still on the cabinet as she sat down. Josephine had had plenty of time to organize her thoughts on their walk to Derry's Corner, the act giving her something to dwell on other than the pain. John Heath had some explaining to do. Heath came back several minutes later with plates and forks. He picked two pint jars out of his pack that he'd taken from the Hanover's larder. "I think this is canned mutton and green beans. I *think*," he said as he divided the two items equally on the plates and handed her one. "It'll be good to eat something solid."

Josephine took her plate and looked down at it. "How long were you in there before you came for me?" Josephine asked, her voice quiet.

Heath shoveled a mouthful of beans, chewed and swallowed before he answered. "A little while."

"How long is a little while?" she pressed, her voice rising. Heath didn't answer and instead put a chunk of lamb in his mouth. He chewed slowly, savoring the first real meat he'd eaten in days. "I asked you a question," Josephine finally said.

Heath finished his mouthful and washed it down from his canteen. "Maybe a few hours," he said then went back to his plate.

Josephine looked down at her plate and then back to him. "This stuff wasn't sitting out the first time I went through the storage room like it was when we left. So, you took time to kill all the zombies they were using, you took time to go through Enos' workshop to dig out all of my stuff and more, and you took time to go through their storeroom to get this food."

Heath nodded at her and went to spear more green beans on his fork.

"If you put those in your mouth before I'm done talking to you I'm going to gut-shoot you, too," she said. The tone of her voice gave Heath no reason to doubt her.

"What is your fucking problem?"

"My *fucking problem*? Well, let's see just what my fucking problems are. In the last few days I've had to fight a swarm of zombies, get pulled through a junk pile and knocked out in the process. I woke up in a little spider-hole kidnapped by rejects from the cast of *House of a Thousand Corpses* to find out that I'm now married to three maniacs *and* I'm somebody's mother. When I tried to escape I was zapped by a God-damned cattle prod until I passed out. When I come to again I'm practically naked and get the shit beat out of me. God knows just what the hell happened to me while I was out. And *then* you come along," she said, ticking off each point with fingers held in the air.

"Bad things happen to good people. It's an imperfect world."

"You knew about Enos and his inventions, about the zombie generator and the goggles."

"Yeah, it was kind of hard to miss the zombies. The goggles were a bonus."

"Heath... the only way you would've known that Enos was responsible for those things is if he'd told you. He wasn't gone with his brother long enough for you to decapitate one and then have a long and meaningful conversation with the other."

"The Nancy Drew shit is getting old and I'm starting to get the idea you think I did something wrong. You know, besides saving your fucking life and keeping you from getting gang raped by a bunch of hillbillies."

"Heath," she said again, "the only way you could have known about Enos was if you'd heard him talking to me. You were fucking there Heath, you were in there somewhere before they found out I wasn't in my hole in the ground and Henry came after me with the fucking cattle prod. Damn it, Heath - you were *there*! Why didn't you get me the hell out of there? Why did you wait so God-damned long? They could've killed me-"

"But they didn't, and you're not there anymore, and you're comparatively safe." Heath said.

Tears started up in Josephine's eyes now. The fear and anger she'd been holding in since waking up inside Hanover Mountain was coming out now as unstoppable as a tidal wave. She stood up suddenly, her plate crashing to the floor and her finger stabbing the air in front of him.

"You could've gotten me out of there! You could've kept me from getting beaten and kicked and fucking *electrocuted* and... and... you fucking bastard!"

Heath stared at her for a long moment, those dark clouds moving across his eyes again. He put his near-empty plate on the bed beside him and stood slowly.

"There's lots of things you don't do in the Area. One of them is waste food," he said, looking at her chipped plate and scattered beans on the floor. His voice was cold and completely devoid of emotion, its whispered volume giving the words a menacing sound. "You don't make noise, like screaming about something that happened a long time ago. You don't get all chummy with somebody keeping you prisoner. And, most important, you don't go charging off into a situation until you know who and where all the players are."

"A 'long time ago'? Heath, we were *just there*..."

"A minute's the same as a year here. The past is the past; the only thing it's good for is education. You focus on each minute as it comes."

"I don't care about all your Area bullshit dogma-" Josephine started.

"And I don't care what you think, and that bullshit dogma is what's kept you alive this long," Heath interrupted. "Now, eat, get some rest and knock off this hormonal bullshit melodrama. You're alive, in one piece, and you haven't been fucked by a hillbilly since high school. That's considered a pretty God-damned-good day's work in this neighborhood."

"That's supposed to make me feel better, that you left me twisting in the wind like that?" Josephine's tears had stopped, though her cheeks glistened with their remnants and her voice had taken on a hard, cold edge.

"I went looking for you. I didn't have to. I could've left you there. Lord knows I'd have made better time with a lot less drama. But I knew it wasn't zombies that had taken you, and women aren't killed in the Area unless it's absolutely necessary... they're worth far too much in barter and entertainment value. By the time I got away from the swarm and found my way into the hill I was exhausted. I passed out for awhile in that tunnel we used to get out of there. When I came to I thought I could hear voices so I dug through the cave-in. The voices turned out to be you and elephant boy chatting it up. I didn't know how many others there were at that time and I was out of ammo."

"*That's* your excuse for not getting me out of there then?" she asked. "And of course you came looking for me... you need me if any of them are going to survive once they get back."

"I needed to know what we were up against. If I'd have crawled out of that tunnel at that moment the little puke would have tagged me with his derringer before I would've been able to stand up. What do you think would've happened then, huh? I would've been food and you would've been fucked. They would've gotten enough meat off me to last them a couple of months if they made a lot of stews, but they'd have had you until your crotch rotted out from under you. I needed time, time to get your gear together and resupply. I knew when I did move I'd have to be right-fucking-quick about it and we'd have to leave fast."

"So you let them beat and torture me as a... a fucking *diversion?*" Josephine was trembling now, enraged at how cavalier he was with her life yet at the same time knowing what he did was perfectly logical; cold, hard, but perfectly logical.

"A necessary one. My coming to find you after hosing dozens of fucking zombies in the trailer park with my God-damn bare hands and you getting pawed and taking a kick to the ribs and a zap or two makes it a real team effort though, huh? And you know what else? You're right. Come to think of it there's no other reporter that would kill for this story, complete with living survivors, is there? All I'd have to do is get them to Jasper's safe-house, slip out alone and call anyone with a camera and a microphone. In fact, I'll bet your buddy from the Great White North would give his right arm for this little exclusive, don't you think?" he asked.

Josephine's expression slowly changed from hatred to wounded at his words. He was right, about all of it. Enos would've seen Heath as a threat to getting the mother he'd always wanted, and ultimately all that the story needed was someone to tell it. There were plenty of people willing to put their reputations and careers on the line with that kind of evidence.

"So you're saying I'm expendable?" she asked.

"I didn't say that. But get it through your fucking head right now; I'm going to continue doing exactly what I feel needs done every step of the way. I won't make a habit of explaining myself and I won't give two shits about your feelings. I told you before, you keep me alive and I'll keep you alive. Well, we're both still alive," he said then sat down and picked up his plate to finish his dinner. Josephine watched him eat until finally she sat down and picked up her own plate. She hadn't realized till now how hungry she was. She gathered up the food from the floor and spared a little water from her canteen to rinse the worst of the grit from it before she ate it. By the time she finished Heath was stretched out on his bed with his jacket over his chest like a blanket.

"Turn out the light when you're done. We're going to move out before dawn, take advantage of the rain and the goggles," he said to the ceiling.

Josephine reached down and switched off the light then stretched out in her bed. Though the mattress was thin and the pillow lumpy she felt like she was lying on a cloud. She left her jacket on the floor, opting to climb under the bed's scratchy wool blanket instead. It was the first time she'd felt anything close to normal since they'd left Jasper's house.

"Heath..." she said into the dark. She waited several moments for him to acknowledge her. When he didn't, she went on. "That *was* mutton, wasn't it?"

"Would it matter if it wasn't?"

"Probably." There was a long pause in the dark before he answered her.

"Then it was mutton. Definitely mutton."

Chapter XIII
Fantasies

Josephine awoke, warm and itchy in her wool cocoon and lay still for several moments, holding her breath and listening to the room. If she strained she could make out Heath's breathing in the cot a few feet from her. His breath came and went regularly but not the slow, measured sound it had when he slept. She pulled the blanket down and tried to see him but all she could make out was a fuzzy silhouette of just slightly less-black than the room around them.

"Here they come again," Heath said.

"Here what comes again?" Josephine asked.

"Choppers; way too many eyes in the air for normal operations."

"You think they saw your pile back in the trailer park?" she asked as she propped herself on an elbow. She regretted it almost instantly from the stiffness in her side and the cold air that rushed under her blanket.

"Diggers leave piles of zombies all the time. They may get an extra fly-over for it, but not like this. Something's up. They may be on to us."

"You think so?"

"If it's not us, then it's *something*. Those little sortie runs don't come cheap and that's an awful lot of birds," Heath said. Josephine checked her watch. She'd slept practically the entire last afternoon and the night away. She was surprised Heath had let her sleep so long but she felt immensely better for the rest.

"I thought you wanted to head out early," she said.

"The choppers have been passing over since about one this morning with no pattern and from all directions. We'd have shown up like we were on fire against all the cold cement out there. I checked and the roof is set up as an emergency helipad, should be enough to hide us from heat scans. The rain sounds like it's picking up and I've heard some thunder. If it picks up we'll move out. They won't keep running this far inside in weather like that."

"But we will," Josephine said, not thrilled with the prospect.

"It's the last thing they'd expect, and the rain will dampen our sounds," Heath said.

"Yeah... and us, too," Josephine said. She flipped the blanket off, stretched, then put her feet down. She hissed as her muscles stretched under the bandage.

"How you feeling?" he asked.

"I've had better days." Josephine stretched her arms above her head as high as she dared then let them fall. "Of all the things to miss, I think I miss coffee the most." A sudden burst of flame startled her before she realized Heath had struck his Zippo to life. The harsh rank of his cheroot drifted as he touched it to the flame. "I didn't think you'd be smoking. Doesn't that fall into the category of 'foreign smell'?"

"We're on the second floor, in a block building and it's raining. If they can smell this, they ain't dead," Heath said, exhaling his point as he picked up her canteen from the floor between them.

"I haven't smoked since college but I'd kill for a cigarette," Josephine said. Heath pulled another cigar from his coat and offered it. "No thanks, I'd be hacking for an hour after."

Heath shrugged, popped the cigar back into his coat then turned on the lantern. He dug in his pack and came out with a small silver tube, snapped it against his leg then dropped it and the contents of a small foil pack into her canteen. He spun the lid back on then shook it several times.

"Here," he said, handing her the canteen after he'd taken the lid back off and had removed the tube. She took it from him and nearly dropped it on the floor. It was hot, and the smell coming from it was suspiciously similar to coffee. She held it under her nose and breathed deeply before she took several sips of the almost too-hot field coffee.

"Oh my God..." she said, taking another and more liberal drink. "I'd fuck you right now if I didn't hate your ass so much."

"Sorry. You're not my type," Heath said.

Josephine had finished almost half the canteen before she realized it. "You better have some of this before I drink it all," she said, offering him the canteen.

"Go ahead. I got my fix, you have yours." Josephine smiled and kept at the coffee, letting it warm her from the inside out. "I have enough for a few more. We'll both need it if we have to spend too much time in that storm," he said.

Josephine felt her heart lift a little. The world couldn't be all that bad if she could have a cup of coffee while surrounded by zombies, madmen and Homeland-delivered death from above. They finished coffee and cigar respectively before they moved out. Heath had decided they'd take the risk and move through Derry's Corner now that the rain covered their noise on the ground and their heads from above. They'd lost too much time already not to take a few calculated risks, especially if the increased flights weren't a coincidence. He'd checked their map position against the GPS device before the helicopters had started their patrols and had found the two more or less in agreement. If they kept a good pace they would reach the survivors' coordinates by the day after tomorrow.

Josephine could feel the rain running down her back before they cleared the first small-town block. The rainclouds had staved off true dawn, leaving a seemingly source-less light in its place. They moved down the center of Derry's Corner's narrow Main Street, the peeling and faded hulks of the houses rolling past their peripheral vision. Most looked intact though there were a few that displayed broken windows and shattered doors. They were still far enough north for snow to be a factor, with more than a few porch and garage roofs showing holes or collapsed altogether. Josephine tried not to let the sadness of it all get to her. Real people had lived here, raised their children here. Every rusting swing set and bicycle reminded her of not just her loss but of everyone's.

They reached an intersection and Heath stopped. He reached back for her and tapped her arm, signaling her to come up beside him. "This isn't right," Heath said.

"You want to narrow that down for me?" she asked.

Heath looked around them slowly, taking in every inch, every detail of the dead street around them. "I've seen a lot of towns, but I've yet to see one that didn't have cars jamming the streets or crashed into buildings. There should be trash all over the place, clothes and bones...it's like the place was scrubbed."

"Maybe they got out faster than a lot of other places," Josephine said, though she couldn't ignore the creeping feeling. There were cars and trucks sitting against curbs and in the driveways, rusting pieces of the American dream complementing the empty, gray houses. But they were all parked in an orderly fashion, the fact they *weren't* out of place giving Heath's feelings a basis. Derry's Corner went from small town to a child's haunted diorama before her eyes.

"Fire," Heath said pointing down the street. There was the faintest glow coming from the next block down to chase away the gray dawn.

"I see it," Josephine said, her wet hands tightening around her rifle in the ice-cold rain. "Do we check it out?" The wind shifted just then, carrying the smell of smoldering flesh.

"Stay close and follow my lead," Heath said. They rounded the corner carefully and came upon a large fountain with a pile of perhaps a dozen bodies trying to burn in it, the heavy rains sizzling and smoking to keep the flames low. Aerial surveillance would have to drop down below the cloud cover and expose themselves to the driving rain and wind to be able to see it. Heath loosed his bar just as a man shot out at them from behind a Dumpster. Heath pushed Josephine further behind him and brought his bar up over his head in time to fend off a blow from the attacker's heavy lead pipe. Heath lashed out with his foot to the inside of the man's thigh and he went down on one knee with a grunt, the femoral nerve kicking and jumping below the skin. From this angle they could see he was more boy than man.

"You're not dead," the young man said as he slowly got to his feet.

"No, we're not," Heath said. The boy took a step back, letting them get a good look at him. He was a gangly youth, no more than seventeen if he was a day. He was dressed in desert camouflage fatigues that had been much-worn and patched and wore a pistol belt around his waist. His faded nametag proclaimed he was a "Miller", and his shoulder said he was a corporal. "Corporal Miller?"

"Yeah... yes..." he said, then, "no... I'm a Miller, but my brother was *Corporal* Miller. Who are you? You don't look like diggers...you ain't robbers are you?" he asked, his hand dropping to his holster. Josephine reacted instantly, putting her rifle sight squarely on the boy's acne-scarred nose.

"Don't do it, soldier," Josephine said. The young Miller didn't draw his weapon. "What's your name; your first name?"

"Robert," he said, his eyes wide from staring down the barrel of her rifle.

"Okay...Robert, I'll lower my rifle if you take your hand off your gun, deal?" she asked. Robert nodded and let his hand fall away from his holster. Josephine lowered her weapon but kept it at the ready. "I'm Josephine, and this is John." She nodded towards Heath and found him looking at her darkly.

"What's with the fire?" Heath asked.

"Have to get rid of the rots somehow, have to wait until a really good storm though so the helicopters can't see," Robert said.

"What're you doing here, Robert?" Heath asked.

"I'm keeping the town safe." Josephine and Heath exchanged quick looks before refocusing on the boy.

"It's a little late for that, isn't it?" Heath asked. Robert's face fell at that. Josephine took a step forward and let her rifle's muzzle point to the street.

"What he means is; *why* are you keeping it safe?" Josephine asked, her tone telling Heath he was a horse's ass. Robert looked at Josephine as if she'd asked him if water was wet.

"From the looters... you know, caretakers and grave robbers and stuff. And the rots, too," he said.

"Rots?" she asked. She'd only ever heard that term for the dead from one other person. "Robert, do you know the Hanovers?"

"Sure. Enos used to come by once in awhile. I've traded with 'em all from time to time," Robert said.

Heath suddenly held up his hand and looked to the sky. "There's a bird still up there somewhere. We need to get out of the open," he said.

"Come on." Robert turned his back on them as if he'd known them his whole life and took off down a side street, eventually leading them to a large, century-old two story home. Though it had the same cracked and fading paint they'd seen across Derry's Corner its overall condition was remarkably different. The commercial-grade, solid steel front door looked completely out of place on the traditional home, as did the tornado shutters over the windows.

Robert ushered them inside then closed the door, flipping the silent, heavily-oiled deadbolt latches before dropping two steel beams across the door itself. With the shutters closed and the door modifications the house was likely as impregnable as the fire station they'd just left. Robert picked up a large emergency flashlight, cranked the dynamo handle on its side then turned it to the lantern setting. The large fluorescent bulb came to life and he set it on a shelf to illuminate the immaculate sitting room. "It ain't much, but its home. Just wipe your feet, please. Mom'll kill me if her new carpet's all stained up."

Heath took a lingering look around as Robert indicated where they should sit. Heath had seen this kind of thing before; people clinging to the life they once had by keeping up their homes as they always did and talking about when their families and friends would come back. It was a coping mechanism for minds that simply couldn't accept the life they knew was gone. He noted a pile of tools leaning in a corner by the front door, ready to be turned into weapons. The gun rack over the much-used though well-cleaned hearth told the history of the Area through its weapons; a muzzle-loader on top, a bolt-action .30-06 with scope and homemade silencer in the middle and a full-dress military AR-15 on the bottom.

"Looks like you've got a good safe place going here, Robert," Heath said, still eyeing the guns.

"Oh, sure. They've tried to get in here before. That's why I took the door off Jack's Hideout... that was Mr. Cavendish's bar... and put it here. I hope he don't mind that I borrowed it," Robert said. He sat down in a chair while Josephine took off her pack and sat down on the couch across from him. Heath remained standing, moving slowly around the room while Josephine fumbled with her pack. They could all hear the passing of a low-flying jet. "I don't know what the army's up to. I know they got their reasons for not bein' able to come in here and all but when they send all that stuff it really riles up the rots."

"The rots in the fountain... did you kill them?" Josephine asked.

"Well, sure..." Robert said, laughing suddenly, "who else is gonna do it? All those danged helicopters got 'em all riled up and comin' outta the woods on the other side of town. Those Hanovers ain't no help with the rots. All they ever wanted to do was make me think their granddad was some kind a god or something, or to trade."

"You said Enos doesn't come around anymore; why not?" Josephine asked.

"Forget she asked that," Heath said to Robert though looking at Josephine. "That's no business of ours," he said, his warning tone not lost on Josephine.

"Shoot, mister, that's okay. 'Bout six months back a few robbers came through, wanting to trade for directions. Enos and his brother, Henry, were here. After we traded and they were walkin' away Henry shot 'em and dressed 'em right there in the street."

"Dressed them?" Josephine asked.

"Yeah, field dressed 'em like they were a couple of bucks right there in the street. Least Henry could'a done was taken 'em into the woods and bury the gut pile. Now, those two didn't do no harm and traded fair and square. Henry had no cause to do that, not when there's plenty of rabbit and squirrel. I told 'im what he did wasn't right and he started comin' after me. I put a round into the street at his feet an' told 'em if they was gonna disrespect the town like that then they'd have to leave. It took me the better part of the day to haul enough water from the creek to clean up the street. They ain't been back since. It's a shame though. Enos was goin' to make it so I could watch TV again."

Josephine suppressed her bile at the thought of their meal from the Hanover's larder and swallowed hard against it. "You're a pretty amazing young man, surviving and scavenging out here all alone," she said.

"Now don't think I've been stealin' or lootin' or nothin' though," Robert said suddenly, defensively. He pulled out a small, battered notepad and flipped the pages at them, not realizing they were too far away to see what was written. "I usually only trade stuff from the hardware store and the other businesses but I put it all down right here, every bit of it." He stopped flipping the pages and leaned towards Josephine, the pad extended in his grubby hand. Josephine accepted the pad and flipped through a few pages. The handwriting was what she'd have expected from a child, a given, since the last time Robert would've seen a classroom would've been more than seven years ago. The neat block letters told a history of sorts of Robert's life, showing what items he'd traded, who he'd traded them to, what he'd received in return and the dates of the transactions.

"Why would you keep records like this?" she asked.

"Geez... I don't want Mr. Henderson to think I robbed his hardware store or Mrs. Harris to think I stole her preserves without thinking to pay her," Robert said. Heath and Josephine exchanged looks.

"I don't get it, Robert..." Josephine started.

"My friends call me Bobby," the young man said with a smile, then, "When they come back I don't want 'em thinkin' I'm a thief. I've been keeping the whole town safe... as best I can, anyway, for when everybody comes back. I write it all down so I can pay everybody back for all the stuff I've had to use or trade of theirs since they left."

"The town didn't look like this when they all left, did it?" Heath asked.

"No sir, it didn't. I've had lots of time to clean it up though. I knew where most of the cars and trucks should be parked. Johnny Filch's dad just got that Mustang a few days before the rots so I made sure it went back into his garage to protect it, but I didn't want to go into nobody's garage or house that I didn't have to so I left the rest in their driveways. I probably should a covered 'em up though, huh?"

"Why didn't you leave with everyone else, Bobby?" Josephine asked.

"My Aunt Sue, she was one of the first the rots got. Mom and Dad are both volunteer firemen and they were on a call so I took her to the cemetery myself to bury her proper. I was only ten then, took me a long time to do it. Guess I took too long, 'cause by the time I got back everybody was gone," Robert said. "I tried to follow 'em, even found the whole lot of them a few miles away at the cross roads. But the soldiers that were loading them into trucks saw me coming down the hill and started shooting at me. I yelled for 'em to stop but they just drove off. So, I came back here. I figure if I keep the town clean and neat and keep the rots out then everybody's sure to come back when it's all over."

"When what's all over?" Josephine asked. Heath rolled his eyes at her.

"The robbers that come through... some of 'em are nice enough folks, told me the rest of the world's doing okay, that the Army says nobody can come until they're sure all the rots are dead and stuff. Well, rots don't last forever, so if I keep everything safe here then everybody's sure to come back."

"So you kill all the rots that come around here yourself?" Heath asked.

"Yes sir!" Robert said, smiling proudly. "I kill every one of 'em that comes into town. I'm the only one to do it till Sheriff Dobbs comes back." His eyes suddenly went wide and he jumped up out of his chair, causing Heath to pause in his slow pacing and lower his hand to his sidearm. If Robert noticed he didn't let on.

"Shoot! Where are my manners? It's just been so long since I've had company. You're probably hungry and thirsty. I'll be right back." Heath opened his mouth to object but the boy was already out of the room.

He walked in front of Josephine and looked down at her. "What the hell do you think you're doing?" he asked, his voice a rough whisper. "You gave that kid our names? What happens if they *are* on to us and they come here? And what's with the twenty questions bullshit, huh?"

Josephine lifted the flap on her pack to show her video camera, positioned so the lens could see out from under the flap at the perfect angle to catch Bobby across from her.

"I came here to get stories from the survivors of Area 187, and if that kid isn't a survivor I don't know who is." Heath opened his mouth in a snarl but Bobby's return cut off his words.

"It ain't much, but like Mom says; nobody should ever leave this house hungry," Robert said. Heath turned to see the boy had a large tray with a pitcher of clear water, stale crackers and several long strips of what his nose told him was jerked venison. "It's all clean. Dad keeps the old well as a back-up, even when they put the town on city water. And don't worry... that's deer." He poured glasses of water and handed them around. Josephine was by no means hungry, especially after hearing about the Hanover's culinary peculiarities. She took a cracker and a small piece of venison for the sake of courtesy but concentrated mostly on the cold, tasteless water.

"Thanks, Robert," Heath said. He downed his water in two long pulls then tucked a piece of the jerky into his pocket. "I hate to be rude, but we need to go. You're doing a fine job here. I'm sure everybody will be very proud of you when they come back."

"You think so?" Robert asked.

"I'm sure of it," Heath said as he turned and started towards the door. Josephine sat for a moment and watched him walk away. She smiled uneasily at Robert then got up and rushed to block Heath's path.

"What the hell are you doing? We can't leave him here like

this!" Josephine said, whispering so the boy wouldn't hear her.

"If you haven't noticed, not only has he survived all this time he's done a pretty damn good job of it. We've got to get moving." Heath made to push her out of his path but she held her ground.

"That kid needs help... he's delusional."

"Around here that's another word for *dangerous*. Let's go."

"That's exactly what they say about you," Josephine said.

"Takes one to know one," Heath said, this time succeeding in pushing her away and getting to the door. "You're a credit to your town and family, Robert. If the world had more people like you in it, it might not be so screwed up," Heath said as he undid the latches and bars from the door.

"Gee... thanks!" Robert said. He came up to the door with them as Heath opened it, practically shoved Josephine onto the porch then followed. The rain had increased in its ferocity and lightning intermittently arced across the sky. Nothing would be flying below the clouds this morning. "You sure you don't wanna stay awhile, wait out the worst of the storm? I sure wish you'd stay awhile."

"Thanks, but we really have to go," Heath said. He moved between Josephine and Robert to shield her while she situated her camera back in its case. If the young man saw it he'd only have more questions Heath didn't want to answer. Josephine slipped into her pack before they moved off the porch and into the driving rain.

"Hey, Josephine!" Robert called out. They both stopped and turned around. "You two... you're from the world, the one where everybody escaped to? You're goin' back there, too, ain't you?" Josephine looked at Heath but he refused to return her gaze. The three of them were silent for a moment before Robert continued. "When you get back, can you tell everybody from town that I'm taking care of the place for 'em, tell 'em I can't wait to see all of 'em again? You seen it for yourself, I've been takin' real good care of the place. You'll tell 'em that, won't you?"

"Count on it, Bobby," Josephine said. She turned then and walked towards the town square, Heath beside her. For the first time that morning she was glad for the cold rain that washed down her face and camouflaged her tears.

Chapter XIV
Realities

Williams awoke with bells in his ears and cotton in his mouth. He lay still and kept his eyes closed, letting his other senses survey his surroundings. The smell of body odor, blood and animal manure hung heavy in the air and in the pile of dirty blankets he'd been tossed onto. His fingers and toes tingled from the too-tight steel handcuffs that bound his wrists and ankles, almost denying him the sensation of a draft from his bare feet. His arms and shoulders were chilled as well, telling him his coat had been removed, as well as his boots. Two men were arguing over the ringing in his ears, the muffled quality giving him the impression they were in a different room.

"I know you're awake..." Julie said from somewhere. Her voice was tired, soft and tinged with pain. "You might as well join the fun, asshole."

Williams opened his eyes, allowing them to adjust to the dim light. She sat on the floor against the wall opposite him, her wrists and ankles bound with a thick chain that connected those bonds to the steel frame from a die machine bolted to the floor. Like him she was shoeless and coatless, shivering in the camisole she'd worn beneath her blouse and sitting on a thin blanket on the cold cement floor.

"Whoever it is must think you're special," Williams said, his voice a rough croak. He nodded at her freshly though less-than-expertly bandaged shoulder as he struggled to a sitting position. His head swam from the activity as the tranquilizer they'd darted him with struggled to keep its hold on his system.

"Yeah, real fucking special. I woke up and found it like this," Julie said. Williams looked around. The only light came from a glass and wire-mesh window set in a door several feet away and from the wide space between the floor and the bottom of the door, illuminating indiscriminate piles of power tools, welding equipment, heavy machinery and other items now useless in the world of the dead. The room's only window to the outside was barely registering sunlight.

"Do you know anything about where we are or who they are?" Williams asked.

"I've only heard two voices," she said. As if on cue the voices stopped. A pair of booted feet broke the bar of light under the door as the jingle and clank of a chain echoed in their prison. Williams went limp and closed his eyes. Julie took the hint and mimicked his actions just as the door swung open.

"Give up the possum act, I know ya'lls awake," their jailor said. Williams opened his eyes and squinted at the light shining into the room around the silhouette in the doorway. "That's better. Have a nice nap?"

"Who are you, where the hell are we, and what's up with darting me, anyway?" Williams asked. Just then another man came up behind the first. The pair walked into the room together and stood between their prisoners.

"I guess we should get acquainted, seeing as how we're going to be real close and all," the second man said. He flicked on a battery-powered lantern and placed it on a hook that hung from the ceiling. "For what it matters, little man, I'm Delmas and this here's Junior." The light showed two men that looked like they were fresh off the set of *Deliverance*. Both were a little to the short side and possessed wiry physiques under their mended jeans and open flannel shirts over stained t-shirts. Delmas sported a rough mullet haircut while Junior was the victim of early male-pattern baldness, the few hairs he possessed sticking out at wild angles from his head. Both were filthy and displayed minor cuts and abrasions on their exposed skin at various stages of healing. Junior smiled down at him while Delmas kneeled in front of Julie and tried in vain to smooth the long hair that trailed down his neck. "Now what would your name be, little lady?" Julie stared past him at Williams, her eyes pleading as the full gravity of her situation took hold. "What are ya lookin' at him for? I asked, what's yer name?"

"Julie..." she said. She was staring at Delmas now, afraid to take her eyes off him. Delmas smiled and put his rough hand on her naked foot. She tried to recoil but he gripped her ankle.

"Don't be impolite, Julie. We could'a left both'a you to die out there. Judgin' by that nasty bullet wound I dressed, you wouldn'ta had much time left anyway. Seems you owe us a debt'a gratitude," Delmas said. He kept hold of her ankle with one hand and slid the other up her leg as far as her pants would allow, stroking her spa-toned calf. Julie started trembling, her arms pulling tight against the chains. "Ooh, that's nice," Junior stared down at the scene, grinning. "Could use a shave, though."

"We can take care'a that," Junior said as he leered over Delmas's shoulder, a straight razor glinting in his hand. Julie caught sight of the weapon and her breath started coming in short, hyperactive bursts.

"No... please..." she said.

"Hmm. I like it when they beg, don't you, Junior?" Delmas said.

"Hey!" Williams called out from behind them. "You guys think you can fill me in on the deal here?" Junior rounded on Williams.

"Shut the fuck up!" Junior said as he brought the razor down through the air, tracing a thin, bloody line from the left edge of Williams's forehead to the eyebrow. He was able to twist his head just enough to keep the blade from falling into his eye and lashed out with his bound feet in the same breath. He caught Junior's left calf with his ankles, sending the man to the floor. Delmas turned from Julie and swung a heavy logger's boot that brought stars to Williams's eyes.

"Boy, you keep that up and we'll kill you slow instead'a quick!" Delmas said. Junior got to his feet and swung a fist downward, breaking the cartilage in Williams' nose and further adding to his personal fireworks display. "Now don't kill 'im yet, Junior, 'less you want to start processin' him tonight while I see to Julie here."

"What're you going to do to us?" Julie asked. Both men leered down at her.

"Well, tonight you're gonna join Junior and me for some good old-fashioned fuckin', then tomorrow mornin' you're goin' to help us get your friend here into the freezer. How does that sound?" Delmas said.

Julie stared between them for a moment. Her face slowly changed from frightened rabbit to something... else. She relaxed her arms and smiled at the men.

"That asshole? He's no friend of mine. That bastard kidnapped me and has been dragging me around for days now," Julie said.

"Is that so?" Delmas asked. He turned to Williams. "Did you kidnap this girl?" Williams looked up at him, eyes crimped from the pain of his broken nose.

"Don't believe a word she says. And, she's ripe with herpes."

"Shit! That's okay, boy... so are we!" Junior said, adding a swift kick to Williams' stomach. Williams doubled over and gasped, the chains keeping him from completely entering the fetal position.

"I think the three of us'll get along just fine," Delmas said to Julie.

"I've got a proposition for you," Julie said, her voice smooth and warm. Williams was forgotten as the two men moved closer and sank to their haunches in front of her. She raised her feet and let her bare toes stroke the growing excitement behind Delmas' jeans. "I've been tied up and beat up enough the last few days by that fucking coward, and I could use a couple of *real* men, men that don't need to tie a woman up to get their kicks. You leave me all tied up like this and I'll fight you every step of the way. But if you untie me, I can guarantee you boys a night to remember," Julie said as she continued her stroking.

Delmas's eyes went glassy and he smiled wide. "So how do we know this ain't a trick?" he asked, his breath hitching in his throat as her toes continued their work.

"Hey! Save some of that for me!" Junior barked as he pushed Delmas. Delmas kept his feet and threw out his left hand to smack against Junior's cheek. Julie giggled at them, drawing on skills she hadn't used since her co-ed days.

"Oh, there's more than enough to go around. And to prove my sincerity I'll take you both on, right here and right now. There's not much I can do to try and escape with both of you fucking me, now is there?"

Williams finally uncoiled and leaned against the wall. "Don't trust her, guys..." Williams said, "you don't know what you're getting into."

"You just shut the fuck up over there. You're interruptin' the lady," Delmas said without looking at Williams. "We'll deal with you in the mornin'."

Julie swung her feet to the other side and started rubbing them on Junior's inner thigh. The results were immediate. Junior folded his razor into its bone-slabbed handle and absently shoved it behind his belt buckle as she worked his leg.

"What do you say, boys?" Julie asked. Her eyes were sparkling now. She let out a soft moan as her tongue gently traced her lips.

"Both of us, huh?" Delmas repeated. "We'll let you out of your leg irons, but the hands stay in the cuffs till I know I can trust you."

Julie pouted at him and stopped rubbing Junior's thigh. "That's hardly fair, but if that's what it takes then so be it," Julie said.

Delmas pulled a large key ring from his belt and fumbled a key into the cuffs around her ankles. He handed the key ring to Junior and stood up, his erection pounding painfully against his fly.

"Get that chain and let's us get into the other room," Delmas said to Junior. Junior took the ring and removed the small padlock that kept the chain looped to its mooring then passed the keys back to Delmas. He clipped the ring to his belt without taking his eyes off Julie.

"Aww..." Julie suddenly pouted up at them as the loose chain chattered against the floor. "I thought maybe we could at least start right here," she said as she climbed to her knees and looked up at the men.

"This ain't no place for that. We got a big ole bed in the other room," Delmas said.

"I want that piece of shit to see this, especially after all the begging for it he's been doing," Julie said. She reached out with her bound hands and slowly tugged down Delmas' zipper then turned slightly and did the same to Junior. The two men exchanged identical smiles before putting their full attentions on Julie.

"That seems fair enough," Junior said.

"I'm telling you guys...don't fall for this. The little slut will say anything..." Williams started.

"Shut the fuck up!" Delmas roared. He turned slightly so that Williams could see Julie on her knees before them, their members jutting, throbbing through their flies. "Just shut the fuck up and watch some *real* men!" Julie turned her head to Williams and spat at him, the globule landing on the tip of his busted nose and rolling down his face to mix with the free-flow of blood over his lips.

"Eat your heart out, Howie," Julie said. She reached out and took Delmas in her hands, sliding them back and forth slowly for a few moments before stopping and moving to Junior.

"Hey!" Delmas growled at her, his manhood bobbing and trembling from the sudden lack of attention.

"Sorry Delmas, but I can't reach both of you with the cuffs on," Julie said, her hands on Junior but her eyes locked with Delmas'. "That's too bad, too, seeing as how you're so much bigger than Junior."

"What?" Junior said, his eyes flying open. "Ain't no way he's bigger!"

"Well, from this angle..." Julie said, giggling like a school girl. Junior tore his eyes from her and looked at Delmas's phallus.

"He ain't bigger than me!" Junior said.

"You heard the lady, Junior," Delmas said as he smiled at Junior. "She'd know, now wouldn't she?"

With their attentions diverted, Julie slid her hands off Junior and snatched the straight razor from behind his belt. He looked down in time to see his razor in one of Julie's hands and his severed penis in the other. Junior's mouth moved but no sound came out as he stumbled backwards and clamped both hands over his gushing stump. Delmas looked down, frozen in horror at Julie's blood-drenched face as she grabbed his member and held the razor against its base. Junior continued stumbling, his breath coming in shallow gasps and expletives until he toppled over a stack of rusted equipment and crashed to the floor.

"Now Julie... ain't no need..." Delmas said quietly, his hands held up to his chest in surrender.

"Toss the keys to the asshole. Try anything else, I'll cut it off."

"Okay now... easy with that thing..." Delmas said. Julie increased the pressure on the razor just enough to make a drop of blood well up under her blade.

"Do it now!" Julie said as Junior started screaming behind them, his flailing sending smaller bits of metal and equipment across the room in a hurricane of noise. Delmas let his right hand drop slowly to his belt then pulled the key ring from it and tossed them at Williams.

"I tried to tell you, but would you listen to me? Oh, no..." Williams said as he picked through the keys, set himself free then painfully got to his feet. He took a folding knife from the sheath on Delmas's belt, clicked the blade into place then went to Junior. He slapped the bloody, reaching hands away then ran the blade hard and deep across the man's throat. By the time Williams had cuffed Delmas' wrists before him, Junior had stopped moving altogether.

"You fucking killed him..." Delmas said. Williams shoved him hard against the wall, the back of his head thumping against the cement.

"It was a mercy killing. Trust me," Williams said as he dropped the keys to Julie. She unlocked her own cuffs and stood up slowly beside him. "Thanks, by the way." Williams said to her.

"I didn't do it for you, you fucking bastard," Julie said softly, her eyes fixed on her bloody, trembling hands. "I... I didn't think there'd be so much... so much blood..." The temptress pout and come-hither stare were gone now, replaced by slack-jawed confusion and disgust.

"That doesn't matter now. For what it's worth, you did good," Williams said. Julie shot him a venomous glare. She was trembling now as she used her shirt front to try and wipe Junior's blood from her face. She let out a small shriek and stumbled against the wall, tearing at her shirt until it came off her back in shreds then used those to scrub roughly at her face and hands. "Easy, Julie. We'll find you some soap and water..."

"Easy?" Julie laughed out the word. "*Easy*?" she screamed as she threw the blood-soaked rag at him. She broke from the wall and hurled herself towards Delmas, murder glinting in her eyes. "I'm gonna' fucking kill you!" she screamed at Delmas. The bound man shrank against the wall as Williams dropped an arm to catch her and shoved her back. She leaned against the wall, panting. The last dregs of her adrenalin were gone now, forcing her to deal with the world. "I just... you..." she looked at her hands then started rubbing them violently against her pants legs.

"You're losing it, girl. Get a grip," Williams said. Julie sank to her haunches and stared at her palms. Most of the blood was gone now but the stains would stay deep in her skin until she could clean them properly. She opened her mouth to speak but heaved instead, dropping to her hands and knees. Williams looked at Delmas. The man's face was a mask of hate and perhaps a tinge of embarrassment for getting tricked. Williams wiped some of the blood away from his own face, careful not to bump his nose in the process and regarded Delmas. "Now; what the fuck is the deal?"

"What the hell you talkin 'bout? There ain't no *deal*, just survivin'!"

"That's not what I meant. First off..." Williams said as he looked down and toed Junior's dismembered member, "...looks like Junior *was* bigger. Second, you're going to have to put *your* winky away if we're going to have a serious conversation," Williams said, nodding at Delmas's own flaccidity. Delmas looked down, suddenly aware of the presentation he was making. He fumbled himself back into his pants and quickly zipped them. "Much better. How many more inbred Jeds here?"

"Ain't nobody, just me and Junior."

"Just you now, hero. Remember that. Out the door, nice and slow," Williams said, pointing with Delmas' knife. They stepped into the next room and found several pieces of mismatched, stained and threadbare furniture arranged in a circle in the middle of what once had been the building's main workshop. The dusty floor showed a few protruding bolts and brackets where machinery had once stood, with the expanse beyond filled with more junk. Two large garage doors sat at the end of the room, their windows spray-painted black. A few mismatched lamps sans shades sat on equally mismatched tables spaced around the room, plugged into thick extension cords that ran here and there across the floor. Several of the cords led to a few rusty chest freezers humming against another wall. The center of the circle of furniture was dominated by two large, wooden crates. As soon as the men entered the room the crates started rocking gently. Williams frowned at them and pushed Delmas further into the room.

"What the hell is in those crates?" Julie asked as she staggered into the room after them then leaned against a couch for support.

"You really don't want to know. Just sit down and relax for a minute, okay?" Williams said to her. Then, to Delmas, "I see lights and batteries and you look like you're pretty well fed. How you manage that?"

"We trade with robbers, like you. We got a few generators, and there's a state road fuel depot a few miles away that's got gallons and gallons of treated fuel sittin' in underground tanks," Delmas said. His eyes were on Julie as she started moving slowly around the couch towards the center of the room.

"Julie!" Williams barked. She turned her head towards him like a deer caught in headlights. "I'm telling you, do *not* go near those." Julie nodded at him quickly but nonetheless turned her eyes back to the crates. Williams shook his head slowly. "Whatever. Anyway... Delmas. You mind telling me how it is you two could truck enough fuel here to keep generators running for years?" Julie had reached one of the crates now and held her hand over the large steel handle that had been bolted to the top. "Julie... honey, please... just leave it be," Williams said, this time softly and gently enough to make her look at him and pause. She nodded and pulled her hand away from the crate. Williams turned back to Delmas and cocked his head to the side, silently repeating his question.

"We got horses," Delmas said with a sigh, defeat ringing in his tone. Williams smiled.

"I thought I smelled livestock before Junior busted my sniffer. And I'll bet a slab-sided building like this does a real nice job of keeping sounds and smells from getting outside, doesn't it?"

The sound of wood hitting cement followed by a sharp gasp pulled both men's eyes back to Julie. She'd pulled the lid off one of the crates and was now staring down into the large box, her hands covering her nose and mouth, her eyes wide. She stumbled back a few steps until her legs struck the couch and she fell into it, still gasping.

"My God..." Julie breathed.

"On the ground, now!" Williams said. He reached out, grabbed Delmas then shoved him downward. Delmas went down hard, craning his neck back to keep his face from bouncing off the floor. "You move, you die," Williams said as he maneuvered around a chair. He pulled the lid back over the crate then stood between it and Julie. Tears were rolling from her eyes to turn the remaining smears of Junior's blood pink as they traveled down her cheeks.

"I just want to go home... I didn't ask for this... I don't deserve this..." she mumbled as she covered her entire face with her hands.

"I'm sorry," Williams said, not knowing what else to say.

"Leave me alone!" Julie said through her hands. "Just fucking leave me *alone*!" Williams went back to Delmas and rolled him over.

"So you're a night runner?" Williams asked. Delmas stared up at him, or more accurately, stared at the knife in Williams' hand.

"Yeah, we've done some runnin'," Delmas said. Night runners were literally the teamsters of Area 187. Some used horses or pack animals, others managed to keep cars, trucks and whatever they could get. Since such rapid transport would be readily seen in the light of day, night runners developed their routes and trails and worked them until they could ride them with their eyes closed. Some served as traders between the few tiny islands of humanity left in the sea of the dead. Others specialized in transporting grave robbers or using their talents to make lightning raids into heavily infested areas in search of heavier, higher-end spoils.

"You any good at it?" Williams asked.

"I'm still alive, ain't I?"

"For the moment. You haul fuel. That means you have a wagon, right?" Williams asked.

"Yeah," Delmas answered. Williams nodded and went back to Julie. She was still sitting on the couch but now her hands were limp beside her as she stared vacantly at the crates. He reached down and pulled her legs up onto the couch. She didn't resist as her torso shifted with her legs, leaving her lying on the couch and staring up at him.

"Get some rest. I'll be back to get you in a little bit," Williams said. Julie didn't answer as she laced her bare arms over her chest and rolled herself into a softly-trembling ball, burying her face in the couch cushions as he worked his fingers several times in frustration. "I know I've really fucked up your life, and I know there's not a damn thing I can say to make it better."

"Take me home," she sobbed into the musty upholstery. Williams extended his hand, meaning to brush the hair from the side of her face but stopped. He sighed softly then went back to Delmas.

"Do you know how to read a map?" Williams asked.

"Of course I know how to read a god-damned map!" Williams had met a few night runners in his travels and had found if they were proud of anything it was their skills in driving and avoiding detection from both the living and the dead. At this time of year they would have the cover of darkness for at least the next eight or nine hours, more if the rains stayed on.

"Good. First you're going to give back all our stuff and show me where you keep the guns. Then we're going to hitch up your team and go for a little ride," Williams said as he hauled Delmas to his feet.

"You're fuckin' nuts! There ain't no moon out tonight, and even if there was the rain's tore up my trails."

"I thought you said you were good," Williams said.

"I'm the best there is, but that don't change nothin'. Besides, I'd rather you kill me right here, right now, than I would for you to do it out there somewhere."

"You get us where we need to go and I promise you'll live."

"Your promise don't mean a damn thing to me. Just kill me and get it over with!"

"You don't like that promise?" Williams asked. His hand lashed out like lightning to leave a gash that matched his own across Delmas' forehead. Delmas cried out and staggered back as he brought his bound hands up against his forehead. "I got another promise for you; if we aren't rolling down the road inside of an hour I'm going to do to you what you did to *them*..." Williams said, motioning to the still-thumping crates, "...and then I'm going to drop you in there with one of them. I need to get where I'm going quick, and I think you can get me there. But I'm not above dropping you in a box and taking your horses if the next words out of your mouth aren't 'sure, I'll get you there'."

Delmas stared at him through his right eye, the left shut tightly against the blood that rolled down his face. "Sure, I'll get you there," he finally said. Williams smiled at him then grabbed him by the hair and shoved him towards a pair of doors at the far corner of the room marked with the word "Garage".

"I think the three of us'll get along just fine," Williams said, echoing Delmas's earlier comment in his best West Virginia accent.

Heath finished his noontime protein bar and sat folding the wrapper absently, his eyes on Josephine. She'd had her camera out since they'd stopped for their break to record stock footage of the Area, adding to what she'd taken as they'd walked through the morning, pausing for a few moments to get long shots of an idled factory and another dilapidated trailer park. She finally closed the lens cover then sat down beside him.

"Get what you needed?" Heath asked. Josephine pulled out her own lunch and opened the wrapper.

"I need filler footage. It can't all be zombies and survivors," Josephine said. She nibbled on the bar as she tried to stretch her side. The damp chill hadn't helped her aches and pains, and the constant rain had further dampened her mood. She was starting to understand how Heath must have felt, how all the survivors trapped in the Area must feel. She was cold, hungry and in constant pain, never knowing if her next moment would be her last. She wasn't sure what bothered her more; that she could feel the minute hardening of her soul with every mile, or that she was coming to understand more about what had made John Heath the man he was than he'd ever willingly tell her.

"Just make sure that thing's powered down when you're not recording. Some of those choppers can detect active equipment." Heath slid the wrapper in his pocket and kept watch while Josephine finished her lunch.

"Are we still looking at tomorrow evening?"

"Yeah," he said.

Josephine stared at him for a moment. Heath didn't have many expressions, but she was learning to read the ones he did have.

"What's wrong? I mean, aside from the obvious."

"The choppers. They were hell-bent on finding something last night. It's daylight, the rain's been slack for nearly three hours now, and we've only seen one bird."

"And that's a problem? Maybe they found what they were looking for, or maybe there's another storm coming," she said.

"Maybe, maybe not," Heath said as he stood up. "Come on. We're going to lose an hour's worth of light by evening with this cloud cover and we still have to contend with Milesburg."

"We're going through a city?" she asked.

"No, but we'll be within a mile of it. We've lost a whole day's worth of travel time. If we're going to make it up we need to cross the Milesburg Bridge, otherwise we'll have to reroute and add another day to our trip. I've seen it once, from the other side of the river. It's packed for miles on either side."

Jasper had warned her about the massive traffic jams in the more populated areas. When the virus hit, people had packed up and started driving in all directions, jamming the interstates and highways seeking escape and help for infected loved ones. Under normal circumstances these transportation arteries would've provided the fastest means of escape. But most of the road networks in the state hadn't been designed to handle the kind of traffic created by such a panicked exodus, quickly becoming parking lots that stretched for miles, especially near cities and interchanges. When infected refugees ultimately turned, the traffic jams became killing fields. Whole families were wiped out in hours, the press of the vehicles making it impossible for people trapped in the center lanes to open their doors and escape.

Josephine tried not to think about the sheer terror those people must have felt. Trapped in their vehicles, they'd have been easy prey as their infected loved ones turned on them to either be devoured or infected themselves. Unable to comprehend door locks and seat belts, many of those undead still inhabited the vehicles they'd died in. If there was a worse way to die, she didn't know what it could be. Josephine stood and looked down at her hand to find she'd folded her wrapper into a tiny parcel without realizing it. She pocketed it and fell in behind Heath as he led them out from under the trees.

Three hours later Heath and Josephine were standing atop a long, hulking fire truck parked across the bulk of the four lane highway. Josephine knew such things had been common near the end, when the government had finally realized they couldn't destroy the dead as fast as they could be produced. Several ambulances, one of them burned to a brooding, charred frame, and a few long-collapsed campaign tents sat scattered on the open side of the highway behind them. Bleached, gnawed bones and the bodies of long-killed zombies littered the ground, the nature of the virus slowing their decomposition even in true death. Years of rain, sun and melting snows had eventually washed away the many blood stains but here and there a few deep maroon splotches remained as symbols of desperate yet futile struggles to survive. Josephine panned the area with her camera, making a slow circle from their raised vantage point to take it all in. Heath stopped her with a hand over the camera just before her turning would have put him in her viewfinder. "They'll know you did this with me," Josephine said.

"The less my face is around the better for everyone." Heath was staring at the roofs of the long rows of vehicles crammed together in the road and on the bridge ahead of them.

"What's with the tents?" Josephine asked, nodding behind them.

"Must've been a checkpoint. Anybody that wanted through here would've been tested. The government claims they didn't purposely create the virus, but within a few days they had a twenty-second blood test that could pick it up within fifteen minutes of infection. The National Guard would've had tanks or APC's blocking the road. Before they would've let a car go through the occupants would've had to submit to the test. If they were clean they'd be sent on their way. If not, the rest of the family would've been told they could go and the military doctors stationed somewhere nearby would see to the infected person. The infected would've been taken to someplace out of sight where they could be disposed of. I'd bet my last bullet there's a huge pile of bones and bodies within a mile of here."

"Horrible," Josephine said.

"Necessary," Heath said.

Josephine stared out at the cars ahead, her skin prickly. She'd lived in New York full-time for years and was used to seeing gridlocked traffic. The difference here was the silence. Mile upon mile of crammed cars and trucks stretched out as far as she could see without the sounding of horns and angry shouts. Josephine shivered then quickly checked her peripheral to see if Heath had noticed. If he had he wasn't showing it.

"'Necessary'? I don't get you. Sometimes it's like you sympathize with what they did."

"What they did was completely logical for the time. If it wasn't for checkpoints like this, and ultimately the pull-out, the virus would've spread further. You've never seen someone turn before, have you?" Heath asked.

"No."

"If you get infected by a wound that puts the virus directly into your bloodstream, like a neck or wrist wound, you could be dead within minutes from loss of blood alone, not to mention the virus itself. As soon as the virus starts replicating it starts killing the body. I've seen reanimation happen as quickly as five minutes and I've seen it take a couple days. There's about ten major cities I can think of within a four hour drive. If even one refugee had been infected, lingered, made it into Philadelphia, D.C., Pittsburgh... with an infection rate like that how long do you think it would've taken for it to take hold? How long before it hit New York or Atlanta or Boston?" Heath asked then stopped suddenly. She could see the conflict behind his eyes; the logic in creating Area 187 versus what that move to save both humanity and political face had cost Eileen, had cost him. "This isn't the time for politics."

"Do you think there are a lot of them in there?" Josephine asked. Her fists had balled at her sides, the nervous gesture the only hint of her dread at what they had to do.

"I don't know, I've never crossed it. I can guarantee they'll be some. If we're lucky they'll be trapped. The problem isn't those, just stay clear of broken or open windows and keep moving. The problem will be if they start moaning. By the time the ripple would hit either end of the bridge we could have one hell of a reception committee waiting for us on the other side."

"So how do we cross the bridge without that happening?"

"The bridge itself is the easy part. It's got a superstructure under it running the entire span. As long as it's still structurally sound we shouldn't have a problem crossing *under* the traffic. The problem is going to be in getting past all of the cars on both sides of it without developing a fan club."

"So how are we going to get through these cars?" she amended.

"Not through; on," Heath said. "We'd never make it if we tried to navigate between them. It's too tight in most places and would leave us vulnerable to one of them seeing us or reaching out a window. If we're lucky, nothing's disturbed the ones in this mess for a long time and they'll be hibernating. Remember; no noise, step where I step and follow my lead."

Josephine frowned. Just because she understood his plan didn't mean she liked it. "Would've been nice if they'd kept the sides of the road clear," Josephine said. The ground to either side of the road closest to them had been filled in with all manner of concrete barriers and heavy equipment to keep traffic from going around the blockade. Cars themselves filled that role as the road neared the bridge from refugees trying to do just what the barriers and equipment closer to their position had prevented.

"Come on," Heath said as he dropped down the ladder on the side of the fire truck. "I'm going to take us right up the center for as long as we can. Keep your hands free, it'll help your balance." Josephine followed him down the ladder then stood behind him, breathing slowly and deeply. "One more thing, one very important thing..." Heath said, his eyes suddenly boring into hers, "...whatever you do, don't look inside the cars unless you absolutely have to. I'm not worried about what's behind us right now. Keep your eyes on where your feet and mine are going."

Josephine kept his stare for a moment then made a show of adjusting her pack so she could forcibly break his gaze. "I'm a big girl, Heath. It's not like I haven't seen plenty of zombies, you know? I can handle whatever's out there."

It was Heath's turn to nod now. "I'm not questioning your bravery, or your stupidity. Just do you and me both a favor and don't look in the fucking cars, okay?" Heath looked ahead at the first few rows and found they were empty. Those long-ago escapees would have been the last few that would've been able to get out of their vehicles with a minimum of hassle, and they were likely either the first killed when the full force of their situation came to them or the last to leave with the retreating military cordon.

Heath stepped up onto the hood of a low-slung Ford coupe and started walking slowly and steadily, avoiding windshields and sunroofs as he went. He wished it were still raining. Though it would have made their path slippery, the constant pattering of the driving rain they'd experienced through the morning would've served to help hide the sounds their footsteps made across the steel roofs and truck beds. Josephine followed close behind, staying to the sides of the hoods where the steel would be stronger and less likely to buckle and creak. She tried following Heath's orders but she found herself peering through windshields more and more with each vehicle they passed over.

The first few rows were simply empty vehicles, their dashboards and interiors faded from years of abuse from the sun. As they passed deeper and deeper into the pile-up though, she started to see what Heath had meant. Many of the vehicles had reddish-brown stains soaked into their upholstery baked dark and crusty by the intense heat of a closed car through seven summers. Smears of dried blood shaped like palms, fingers and in one case the image of a face in profile started to appear on the insides of windshields and side windows. They'd made it about fourteen cars deep before Heath stepped down from a pick-up truck cab and halted them in the bed. He leaned back so they were side-by-side and pointed to the next car in line; a tall, wide SUV with the driver was still in his seat. His body was practically skeletal, his gray flesh stretched over the bones like plastic wrap. His head lay back against the seat's headrest as if he were taking a power nap in a particularly crowded highway rest area. There was no denying it was a zombie; a normal corpse would've turned to bones by now. The only question was if it were truly dead or merely hibernating. Heath held his finger up to his lips needlessly then moved off the bed and gingerly onto the hood of the SUV.

This time Josephine hung back a few steps. She'd felt several of the hoods they'd crossed give a bit as her feet carried her over them. If she and Heath both put their weight on the same hood it would likely buckle, the sudden sound more than enough to wake the dead. Heath passed the hood and made the SUV's roof without rousing the driver. Josephine started again and was also able to pass the driver without his notice. She kept that same following distance, a hood behind Heath, so they didn't occupy the same space at the same time as they continued making their way to the bridge.

The going was painfully slow yet steady. To Josephine it was as if time itself was slowed, each second unable to pass into the next until she properly placed her next step. They encountered other undead as they progressed deeper into the mass of decaying vehicles, the bodies practically mummified by the conditions of their captivity. Josephine had begun to doubt any of them were active anymore. She couldn't see how anything, not even the virus, could keep such a dried husk of a body active for so long. When they reached the tenth car from the bridge though, she learned just how tenacious the necrotic virus could be.

Josephine's heart sank at the sight of the faded yellow school bus a few car lengths ahead. A tractor-trailer sat in the far left-hand lane, meaning the only way they could pass the bus was to follow along either side of it. Heath chose to continue their path up the middle, following the roofs of the three cars to the bus's passenger side for their route. This time she knew she had to follow Heath's advice. If that bus wasn't empty she doubted she'd ever get another night's sleep. She told herself this over and over even when her head swiveled to the bus and she subconsciously quickened her steps, closing the gap between her and Heath to only a few feet.

Josephine couldn't see anything living or dead in the bus from her vantage point. If anything did call the decaying yellow hulk "home" it wasn't sitting up in any of the seats. She prayed if anything were in there it remained on the floor of the bus, out of her sight and nightmares. With her attention on the slowly-passing row of windows she didn't realize that Heath had stopped on the roof of another pick-up truck's cab, surveying the two corpses seated in a dropped-top Jeep Wrangler ahead of them. Josephine ran straight into his back, knocking him into the truck bed below. The jolt made her lose her balance where she stood at the point where the pick-up's windshield met its roof and she fell hard against the side of the bus, the thump of her body and equipment producing a hollow, ringing sound to join Heath's louder, harsher crash into the truck bed.

Josephine scrabbled against the pick-up's windshield until she was finally able to wedge herself between the truck and the bus, her face pressed against its cool metal side. She stayed in that position for several seconds, willing her heart to stop drumming in her ears before pushing herself upright with her hands against the bus, her eyes shut tight in fear of Heath's wordless wrath and in anger towards herself, her face inches from the smoked emergency window set into the bus's hull. She opened her eyes when she heard Heath moving in the truck bed only to find another pair staring at her from the other side of the glass.

A small, torn hand rose up and thumped weakly against the window. It was a soft sound, but loud enough to break their hypnotic exchange. Josephine pushed off from the bus with a Herculean effort, landing in a sprawl across the pick-up's roof. By the time she righted herself to her haunches and looked back, several other desiccated, decaying faces were staring out at her from the bus windows. Josephine sat transfixed by the perversion undeath had played on the innocence of these children, their visages made all the more eerie by their miniature snarls and baked, shriveled features. Then they started to moan.

The sound was soft and thin at first, dampened by their rusty yellow tomb. But as more joined the call it took on a higher, more keening pitch than any she'd ever heard from the dead. Their pounding against the windows increased with the volume and intensity of their moaning until both could be heard clearly through the bus's walls. Something grabbed the front of her jacket and pulled her towards the rear of the truck. Her revolver was in her hand, its silenced muzzle against Heath's chest before her feet touched the bed. She fell against the truck's back window as soon as she registered it was his face hanging over her.

"I'm sorry..." she mumbled through trembling lips.

"Doesn't matter now, gotta go," Heath said. The children's moans were being chorused from other vehicles around them, the first time many of the zombies had stirred in years. "If we're lucky there won't be any of them free this deep into the pile, and if there are those should be pretty damn slow and dried-up by now." Heath turned and started towards the end of the bed then looked back when he didn't hear her footsteps behind him. She was still where he'd left her, her head turned to the small, dead faces peering out from the bus windows. "Come on." He waited only a moment before closing the distance between them and grabbing her again. Her head snapped around as he hauled her off her feet by her leather. "Damn it! I said move it right the fuck now!" he barked then shoved her towards the rear of the truck. Josephine stumbled a few steps before stopping herself just short of tripping over the tailgate and onto the hood of the Jeep behind them. The dead woman in the passenger seat was clawing at the inside of the windshield, her cold, virus-riddled mind knowing only that meat was near. Her driver sat slumped over his steering wheel, unmoving.

Heath slipped past Josephine and onto the Jeep's hood. His steel bar swooped down to crush the un-life from the woman's skull but instead managed to rip the stiff flesh and weather-brittled bone and sinew apart, sending the head into the back seat. Seeing the decapitation jolted Josephine out of her stupor. Her full faculties returned to her, she looked around wildly for only a moment before slipping off the truck and across the Jeep's hood, hot on Heath's heels. Rotted arms and weathered hands clawed against windshields and scratched at the roofs of their tombs through open and broken windows as the pair jumped and ran across the last few cars before making the start of the bridge's concrete abutment. The moaning was a sound more felt than heard now, the nature of the zombies' entombments turning it a low, modulated tone. By the time they'd stepped off the last car and onto an inches-wide steel support on the side of the bridge the moaning had went past them, the call being taken up and passed down along the captives on the bridge.

Heath took hold of a tensed steel cable that ran down

---

the side of the bridge, wrapped his ankles around it and lowered several feet down its length before disappearing under the bridge's concrete platform. After a moment his head poked out and he looked up at her, nodding. With a last look over her shoulder at the flat-tired, rusting caskets, Josephine wrapped herself around the cable then slowly inched her way down to the narrow steel inspection gangway Heath had found under the bridge's deck. The moaning above them was a whisper now, buffered by the several feet of steel and concrete over their heads.

Heath let his pack fall at his feet then sat on the gangway and leaned against a cold steel pylon, his hands on his knees. Josephine sat as well, though several feet from him, and looked out at the river as it rushed from the north to the south. She pulled out her canteen and took several small, slow sips as she tried to keep the faces of the dead children away.

"I'm sorry," she said after what seemed like an hour's silence. "You must think I'm a real piece of work, huh?" she said, chuckling at her own expense. The distant rush of the water below melded with the distant sound of the moaning above. Josephine prepared herself for the verbal lambasting, the string of expletives and threats she knew she deserved.

"The kids are the toughest to get over," Heath finally said. Josephine turned to look at him but all she could see was the left side of his body, the gloom under the bridge hiding his face and easily defeating the weak pre-evening light. "Don't try to forget it; use it."

Josephine reached into her pocket and withdrew the tag she'd taken from Andy Fitzpatrick's Spider Man backpack from the house they'd sheltered in - and had been chased from - on their first full night in Area 187. Andy wouldn't have been much older than the children moaning and pounding their tiny fists against the bus windows when he was forced to barricade himself in his parent's bedroom, forced to kill them before they suffered too much, before they could rise again... forced to kill himself rather than be devoured or recruited by the dead. She put her hand over the pocket that held the boy's picture but didn't take it out. The last

---

thing she needed to see was his smiling face looking back at her. "I fucked up. I could've gotten us both killed."

"Yeah, and you still might," Heath said. "Did you mean to do it? Did you think, 'fuck him, I'm looking wherever the hell I want'?"

"Well, no... for the most part, no."

"It was an accident. I can't blame you for that. We're both still alive and we got where we needed to be. No blood, no foul. Just try not to let it happen again, okay?" Heath stood, stretched then picked up his rifle. "I'm going to look around, make sure nothing's dropped down here over the years. It's getting dark. It'll be a little chilly but we're probably about as safe here as we would be anywhere else. I'd rather have the start of daylight than the end of it when we hit the other side, anyway. If the moaning brought any more to the other side of this pile-up they may thin out if they go a whole night without finding anything."

Josephine continued to stare. She'd been prepared for Heath to go ballistic. She even thought this time she may have deserved it. What she hadn't expected was something akin to understanding. In the excitement, Josephine hadn't noticed how late the day had gotten. Crossing the sea of cars had felt like an eternity, but she hadn't realized it had taken them nearly two hours to traverse the comparatively short distance. She also hadn't realized how utterly, completely exhausted she was.

"Good idea. Are you taking first watch?" she asked.

"Yeah. I'll wake you around midnight. Get something in your belly and get some rest. We're going to have to make some serious miles tomorrow if we're going to reach them by dark."

"Heath?" Josephine asked as he started down the gangway. He stopped and half-turned towards her. They looked at each other for a long moment before she shook her head. "Sorry. Nevermind."

Eric R. Lowther

_____

Chapter XV
Karma

Sommers got in his rental as the private jet's door was pulled shut and the engines whined to life, propelling the small aircraft down the runway and into the failing sun. He pulled the disc from its plastic case and held it to the dome light. It was completely devoid of markings and labels and shined a soft electric-blue in the light. Sommers had connections that even Fremont wasn't aware of, connections within every level of government agency. It'd been a simple matter of counting out the cash to get the disc found during the search of the Connelly house. Those same connections were how Sommers knew the Secretary had authorized more than 200 special observation sorties over the last 24 hours. Fremont was looking for something; something that hadn't been there for the last seven years. Fremont believed enough that Julie and Williams were still alive, and he knew the Secretary's game. He was using them to find Heath and Josephine Terrell and, by extension, the group of survivors. He knew this because, had their positions been swapped, it's exactly what the good Senator from California would've done.

Alan Sommers was a powerful man. And though it had stung him to the core he'd admitted to himself that his power extended only as far as the living side of the wall, and there was nothing he could do for Julie from here. If she were going to survive, he would have to depend on Williams and, ultimately, John Heath to get the job done. That meant he'd not only have to allow but may in fact need to facilitate the one thing he'd tried to bury for the last seven years. The irony was still bitter on his tongue as he dropped the car into gear and started back to the hotel.

Julie opened her eyes and lay still, remembering where she was. She pulled her face from the stinking cushions and rolled over to stare at the still-moving wooden crates. Voices came to her from somewhere else in the building. One had dragged her here to this hell on earth. The other would've gladly kept her there in chains; degrading her, assaulting her. She wasn't supposed to be here, she didn't belong here. Nothing she'd ever done had been bad enough to earn this punishment. She didn't deserve any of this. But she *was* here, wasn't she? The dull, throbbing pain in her shoulder told her that much, reminded her of stark reality. She was beautiful, articulate, educated; practically American royalty. Things like this weren't supposed to happen to her.

Why the hell had they shot her? They should've rushed her back to the real world, where men groveled at her feet and the dead stayed dead. There, she was powerful in her own right, the anchorwoman of one of the most successful news programs on television. She'd clawed her way to the top, and if human waste like her boss, Hartman, had to go down for her to go up then so be it. Julie stood up and her head swam, the loss of blood and the stress of the last few days compounding to send her to the floor in front of one of the crates. She grabbed the handle on the crate and levered against it to her knees. Her hand tensed on the cold metal as her mind flashed to the view she'd had of its contents. It had to have been stress, a trick of the light. No one could blame her for a little mental distress. Her left hand started rubbing subconsciously against her leg again as she relived the damage she'd done to the one called Junior while her right went white at the knuckles around the crate's handle. Without thinking, she slowly lifted the lid and let it down to the floor, her gaze locked inside the crate.

A woman stared up from the floor of the crate, the pallor of undeath not quite powerful enough to completely deny her the beauty that had graced her life. Beneath her high, narrow cheek bones and perfectly-formed chin was a jagged slice that marred the otherwise simple beauty of her long neck. Her bosom hung heavy though perfectly symmetrical below that, leading down to a well-toned stomach and hips. The only things that marred the woman's beauty were the ragged stumps at her shoulders and hips. Julie reached into the crate, her eyes transfixed on the torso's dull and faded ones and touched the woman's stomach. The skin there was taut, cold and utterly lifeless as the limbless zombie struggled to raise her head to sink her teeth into Julie's warm flesh. Julie tore her eyes away from the zombie's and looked at each of the bloodless, terrible wounds. How could anyone have done this to such a beautiful woman? What would drive someone to keep her here, not alive but not dead? A splash of color caught Julie's eye as the undead hips bucked gently, trying to work legs that were no longer there as the zombie's head rose and its jaws bit at the air.

Julie reached down and gently rolled the torso enough to see beneath it. A bright red prophylactic lay there, twisted and spent beneath the still-bucking hips. Julie stared at it, her mind slowly processing the data. The zombie hissed up at her softly then, like air escaping a balloon. Julie shifted her eyes to the gash on the zombie's throat and watched the ragged flesh vibrate as the air she forced through her throat escaped short of her vocal cords.

She let go of the zombie's hips and slowly withdrew her hands, her eyes closed to the depravity before them. Julie tried to picture what the woman had been like when her heart beat and life coursed through her. A woman like that would've had the world at her doorstep. Junior and Delmas; these men were the worst sort of predators, preying on the dead and the living alike. It hadn't been enough for undeath to degrade the nameless woman; they had to come along and remove what last vestiges of dignity her soulless body had left. Zombies were dangerous, deadly. But not one of them had wanted to be infected, not one of them had wanted to rise again to prey on their families, their friends. These men, though... these men made the conscious choice to live as they did, to take what they wanted no matter how depraved or repugnant. They would do whatever they wanted, whenever they wanted, in a land where their tenacity and regard only for themselves made them literally the top of the food chain. But no matter how utterly repulsive, no matter how absolutely vile, she knew they weren't the reason for the tears that were slipping from under her clenched eyelids. Those same qualities that served Junior and Delmas so well in their world... hadn't they also served Julie just as well in hers?

Splinters slipped under her chipped, cracked nails as Julie's fingers dug into the crate. She'd made the conscious choice to destroy dignity and life many times over as well, hadn't she? Snippets of memory came screaming from the secret places and dark boxes of her mind. Every cruel act, every deceitful trick, everything she'd ever done to crush another to allow her to rise came rushing at her naked, defenseless psyche. Nameless high school and collegiate faces spewed out of the darkness at her like screeching bats, retelling the tales of cruelty and viciousness she wreaked upon them in the name of status and popularity. Many of her adult-aged visions came at her too fast to fully recognize but left their pain in a palpable wake as they passed. Hartman came shambling out of her blackness to walk among the raging memories. Blood poured from his eyes and ran down his swollen face as he moaned her name through a mouthful of broken teeth, his hands clawing at her.

Julie screamed in her mind and her eyes flew open, locking with the dead woman's unblinking, milky ones. Sweat covered her face, stinging her eyes and mixing with the tears that still rolled down her cheeks. Julie turned her head to the second crate and watched it bump against the floor before she stood again. She was more successful this time, with only a slight feeling of vertigo as she went back into the room where Junior's body lay.

Julie didn't bother to look at the castrated hillbilly's corpse and walked bare-footed through the huge slick of his blood that had already started to congeal on the cold cement. She grabbed a rusty crowbar from a pile of implements and went back to the open crate, still thumping softly against the floor. She kneeled again at the crate, this time at its head. Julie made the sign of the cross over her breasts then raised the crowbar in both hands and brought it down. The torso stopped moving even before the reverberations of the strike had ceased jarring her wounded shoulder. She reached down and closed the sightless eyes before moving to the other crate and opening it. She looked down only long enough to know this zombie was a short-haired brunette, only long enough to know where in the box to strike. She crossed herself again and closed her eyes before using the crowbar to put this one out of her misery as well.

Julie slid the heavy lid back in place and patted it gently, her Catholic upbringing shoving a whispered prayer to her lips as she moved towards a door in the far wall. She opened the door and found what had once been the small machine shop's office. Three desks had been shoved against the walls along with several cube-wall dividers. Two large beds dominated the room, one on either side, piled high with blankets, quilts and clothes and a bulk-wire spool sat between the beds at their feet, supporting a large flat-screen television. Julie passed the makeshift table and made her way between the beds to a row of tall file cabinets filling the space between their headboards, dreading what she may find but knowing she was going to search anyway.

She opened the first cabinet's drawers to find it full of clothes. She rifled through one and found a pull-over sweatshirt, a fleece jacket and a pair of insulated socks. All the items were far too large for her, but they were moderately clean and would be far warmer than running around in her bra. She put on the shirt, jacket and socks then moved on. The next cabinet in line proved to be a pornography repository stocked with magazines, books, sex toys, condoms and DVDs. The last was full of all sorts and manner of weapons and handguns. She recognized Williams' pistol on top of the pile in the first drawer as well as the gun lying beside it; the one she'd taken from the dead police woman, her own blood still staining the grip. The next drawer down contained a variety of cardboard boxes and plastic cases filled with a mixture of ammunition calibers. The bottom drawer was full of knives and other hand weapons in all shapes, sizes and sharpness.

Julie slid her confiscated weapon into her waistband, put Williams' at the small of her back then went to one of the beds and yanked a pillow from its case. Julie opened the top drawer again, stuffed the guns into the pillow case then added the ammunition. She selected a few knives that had sheaths and added them to the bag as well. Before she closed the drawer though, a familiar shape caught Julie's eye. The movies had told her all she needed to know about this particular weapon. Julie slid the knife into her back pocket then tried to lift the swollen pillow case from the floor. Her shoulder screamed for the effort, causing her to reach out and steady herself against the cabinets until the pain subsided. She stood straight again, her eyes pointing at the men's cabinet of porn. She opened the top drawer and plucked a foil-packed condom from it. Blinking away the last of the pain, Julie grabbed the top of the impromptu bag and dragged it along behind her into the main room.

Julie could hear Williams and Delmas more clearly now, their voices mumbling behind the double doors. She left the arsenal outside the ring of furniture and went back to the still-open crate containing the long-haired, beautiful and now at-peace woman. Julie ripped open the foil packaging with her teeth and slid the greasy, tightly-rolled prophylactic from the package. Using the straight end of the crowbar as a phallus, she unrolled the condom to its full length then slid it off the tool with one hand while the other pulled the knife from her back pocket.

Her thumb flicked the silver button, the click of the shining steel blade swinging out and locking in place almost comforting. Using two fingers she held the mouth of the condom open and carefully maneuvered it around a long, thick strip of muscle hanging from the corpse's right shoulder stump. Julie slid the condom up the muscle until she got to the stump, used the knife to separate it from the body then held up the prophylactic and gently shook it, sending the piece of infected tissue to rest at the bottom. Winding the excess around the contained muscle, Julie tied the trailing end into a knot around the bundle then slid it into her front pocket. She folded the blade, slid it into her back pocket then put the lid into place. Gathering up her sack, she left the crates behind and crossed the room, following the two men's arguing voices into the building's garage.

The smell of horses, molasses and dung immediately filled her nose. She stood just inside the doors, breathing deeply of the smells while the men stopped and stared at her. The odors would've been strong in their own right from being concentrated in the unventilated, concrete-walled room, but together they would be overpowering to the uninitiated. Julie Sommers had had many privileges growing up, but her favorite had been her stable of three Friesians. She'd been an award-winning confidence rider in her youth, and her animals had always placed highly when judged on their own merits. The stables had been more of a home to her than anywhere else through her junior high years, especially when her parents would have their days-long fights. The hustle, bustle and intrigue of high school quickly diminished the urge for competitive riding, but to this day she harbored a secret hatred for the part of her father that had sold her horses without her knowledge or consent when she went off to college.

"Julie, what the hell are you doing? You're supposed to be resting," Williams said. At least he'd recovered his own coat and boots. Delmas stood a few feet in front of him with his hands raised palms-out before the muzzle of the sawed-off shotgun Williams held.

"No rest in the Area, right Howie?" Julie said. "Have you seen *my* stuff?"

"There by the door," Williams said, nodding at the pile to the side of the doorway. Julie dragged the sack into the room and left it near Williams' feet and paused only long enough to collect her boots and coat before going to the two stalls built into the back of the room. Two equine heads swung over the waist-high doors as she neared the stalls. Julie stopped between the two gates and placed a hand on each of the beasts' long faces to rub at the soft hair between their eyes.

"What's in the bag?" Williams called out to her. She didn't answer. "Oh, Julie! Julie, dear! Can you come over here and grace us with your presence?" Williams said in a sing-song voice. Julie continued rubbing the horses for a moment before sighing and coming back to join the men.

"Guns, ammo, a few knives," Julie said, nodding down at the bag. She pulled his pistol from behind her back and handed it to him. "Try to hold onto it this time."

Williams took the weapon and looked down at it like it was an old friend. "Sit down," he said to Delmas. The man eyed him warily but sat on the rear of the makeshift wagon, his still-cuffed hands in his lap. "They have a whole rack of long guns on the wall there," Williams said, holding up the shotgun and nodding to the wall behind Julie. "Let's see what you've found." He set the shotgun down and lifted the pillowcase to deposit its contents on a workbench, whistling at the variety of weapons and ammunition. "Nice work."

"I live for your approval," Julie said as she pulled her pistol. "You need to show me how to use this thing, if it even still works."

Williams put his pistol away and took hers in his hands. He held it up to the light then pushed down on the magazine release with his thumb. The full clip slipped easily from the weapon and into his other hand while he peered down the open action.

"Looks okay in there, and the slide moved pretty easy for a gun that's been exposed to the elements for so long. Beretta makes a good piece, though I wouldn't trust the ammo or the spring in the magazine after sitting around loaded for so long. Guess we should find out though, huh?" Williams slid the magazine into its port, seating it with the palm of his hand. "That's how you load the magazine," he said, holding the bottom of the pistol grip up for her inspection. "This is how you chamber the first round." Williams turned his hand around so Julie could see the wide lever under his thumb. Williams dropped the lever and the slide slid forward with a tight, metal-to-metal click. He frowned at the weapon and turned it over in his hand. "Should've known it would be a little dry but I'm sure Delmas has some oil around here somewhere. Anyway, this is how you shoot a stupid little fucker that just doesn't know what's good for him," he said as his arm extended, pointing the pistol at the back of the wagon. Delmas had stood while Williams had been instructing Julie and had made it a few feet towards the door. Williams pulled the trigger and the weapon responded, the bullet lodging in the side of the wagon just inches from Delams, freezing him in place.

"Whadda' ya' know? It still works," Williams said.

"Well?" Julie asked.

"Well what?" Williams asked.

"You missed," Julie said. She reached up and took the pistol from Williams' hand. "Jesus… do I have to do everything myself?" she said as she pointed the pistol at Delmas.

"Hey! Don't do that!" Delmas said. Julie regarded him coldly down the slide of her weapon.

"I just point it at what I want to die and pull the trigger, right?" Julie asked Williams.

"Uh, yeah, but a head shot isn't as easy as it looks in the movies. So put the gun away. Delmas promises to be a good boy from here on out, don't you Delmas?" Williams asked, an eye on each of them.

"Yeah… sure thing…" Delmas said. He'd looked into many eyes over the years, and he couldn't recall seeing a look as cold as Julie's in any of them, even ones that knew Delmas would be putting their meat in his freezers. Julie motioned him back to the wagon with the end of the gun, putting it away only after Delmas's ass was firmly on the unfinished wood.

"Be careful with that thing, it's what you call *locked and loaded,*" Williams said, nodding at the gun in her waistband. "Flick the little lever on the side to 'S' so it won't go off in your pants, at least. Just remember to flip it back when you need it to go 'bang'." Julie pulled the gun out, engaged the safety and replaced it.

"So what's the plan, Howie?" she asked as Williams sorted through the handguns and ammunition.

"Delmas here is going to hitch the team and take us where we want to go. With any luck we'll get there by tomorrow afternoon," Williams said, his hands deftly separating the ammunition by caliber.

"Tomorrow afternoon?" Delmas repeated. "Ain't no way in hell! I ain't goin' so far that I can't make it back here before dawn! You can threaten me all you want 'cause I'll be dead either way. And if any of those choppers see us in the light of day you'll go up in a big ole fireball right along with me!" Delmas said. "Hey, wait a minute… those choppers that were buzzin' around here… they were lookin' for the two of you, weren't they? Should'a known nothin' as hot as her would've been walkin' around the Area." Julie's cold eyes returned. There *had* been women as hot as she walking around the Area, hadn't there? He'd kept one of them locked in a box in the next room, hadn't he?

"I could tell you, but then I'd have to kill you," Williams said. "But that's really not your concern. This is." Williams pulled the tightly-folded atlas pages he'd taken from their safe house the night before out of his pants pocket and handed them to Delmas. "You're going to get us to that little star on the map, and you're going to do it by tomorrow afternoon." He finished separating the ammo and started checking the various handguns for broken parts and functionality while Delmas read the map.

"No way in hell we're going to get there by then. I got a safe house, an old barn that'll take the horses and the wagon both. It's about halfway there. If we can get there and hole up for the day…" Delmas started.

"Yeah, and get you into a place where you have weapons cached or booby traps? Nope. Straight there. It's up to you how you get back," Williams said without taking his eyes off the small .22 revolver in his hands.

"My horses won't be able to make this long a run all at once," Delmas said, waving the map for emphasis. "They're going to need rest. They won't be any good to me if we drop 'em dead on the trail."

"Wow, sounds like something that is distinctly not my problem," Williams said. He pushed several of the guns off to the side of the bench, the lack of available ammunition making them nothing more than paperweights. That left five with ammunition; three automatics with two magazines a piece and two revolvers. "Take a little food and water with us for the horses, just enough to make do. I don't want to weigh them down more than we have to. It wouldn't be fair to punish them because their master is a cannibal rapist with a raging case of necrophilia," Williams said.

"You do what you can to get by," Delmas said, the smile on his face decidedly lacking in apology.

"Julie, here's another mag that should fit the Beretta," Williams said, holding out the magazine to his side without looking. He waited a moment for her to take it then turned his head to find she was back at the stalls again, the lure of the horses greater than her desire to be anywhere near Delmas. She opened a stall and led the horse out into the room by the halter to get a better look at him. He was no Friesian by any stretch, just your typical sway-backed, fat-assed American Saddle-Bred, but he was by far the most beautiful thing she'd seen since meeting up with Howard Williams.

"I'll get it in a minute," Julie said while she lifted each of the horse's hooves. Delmas and Junior were living cancers to be sure, but at least they seemed to be taking as good care of their animals as the Area would allow. Aside from being a little to the thin side, the animal looked serviceable.

"You know horses?" Williams asked.

"Yeah, I know horses," Julie answered as she finished her inspection. She put that one away and repeated with the other. It was the same dull tan color as the first but had its white sock on the rear right leg instead of the front left. "This one will need a new shoe soon."

"Yeah, Junior was supposed to do that before you cut his dick off," Delmas said. Julie put the last hoof down then ran her hands along the animal's neck. She paused on her second pass as her fingers rubbed over a lump of scar tissue that ran across the front of it, evidence the men had put these beautiful animals through the same horrible, back-alley laryngectomy they'd performed on the zombies back in their makeshift coffins. The meatball surgery wouldn't stop the horses from audibly braying but it would make them unable to make other noises.

"Looks like you'll have to add ferrier to your list of jobs now, huh?" Julie said as she crossed the room back to the workbench. "This mine?" she asked Williams as she held up the loaded magazine.

"Uh, yeah," he said, taking a moment to really look at her.

Her eyes had taken on the same set they'd had when she was tied to the bed back at his Uncle Jasper's house when Williams had first taken her. "Here," Williams said, handing Josephine a can and a clean rag, "it's paint thinner. Smells like shit but it'll get your hands clean."

Julie looked at the can then slid the extra clip into her back pocket. "That's okay. The horses won't like the smell. The blood's bad enough. Speaking of smell, how's your nose?" Williams looked at her with astonishment.

"Why, Miss Sommers... I thought you could care less about my physical state," Williams said in his worst southern drawl.

"I don't. But unlike most of the rest of you, your nose did serve a purpose."

Williams chuckled at her, shaking his head as he secreted the various handguns on his person. "The swelling's going down, should be better in a few hours." He handed her the small revolver he'd inspected. "Put this one where you can get to it easy if you need to, never hurts to have a back-up, though if we're lucky we won't have to fire another shot."

"Now who's naïve?" Julie asked as she pocketed the gun.

"Hey, let me have my delusions, okay?" Williams said. He picked up the shotgun and set it at the head of the wagon just behind the buckboard. The wagon itself was made of a variety of board lengths and sizes strategically placed over the frame of an old pick-up truck. While far from a thing of beauty, it would serve their purpose.

"I'm tellin ya', this is suicide," Delmas said.

"Suicide is doing something that can get you dead because you want to be. Since that's not the goal, this would fall more into the 'reckless disregard for personal safety' category. Words mean things, Delmas. It's never too late to broaden your vocabulary," Williams said as he selected two short-barreled bolt-action rifles, both equipped with home-made silencers, from the rack of long guns.

"Jesus! You're robbin' me blind! And those silencers take forever to make! How the hell am I supposed to defend myself?"

Delmas said as he watched Williams arm himself.

"Well, if a zombie shows up, just ask him to pretty please not eat you. If that doesn't work, run." Williams opened the military surplus ammo crate under the gun rack and selected two boxes of shells from it; one for the shotgun and one for the rifles. The shotgun would be practically worthless unless they found themselves in a swarm, but with all the noise the wagon would make as it trundled along that could become a possibility. It was still a gamble if any of their weapons and ammunition would work properly given time and lack of proper care but it was better than rumbling through the Area completely unarmed.

"You know what? Fuck it! Just kill me 'cause I ain't goin' nowhere!" Delmas said, jumping up from the wagon to face them. "You just kill me right here and right now!"

Williams dropped the ammunition into the wagon and pulled his pistol as he started towards Delmas. Julie was faster though. Delmas raised his laced hands and swung them at her like a club. Julie ducked under them, colliding with him and knocking him back into the wagon. She was beside him before he could get his wind back, the snub barrel of the diminutive revolver jammed into his crotch with her left hand. Delmas looked up at her with hate-filled eyes. "You ain't gonna kill me - you *need* me!"

"Howie, do you know where we're going?" Julie asked without looking away.

"Yeah, I know where we're going," Williams said. He was standing to the side of the wagon now, leaning over it towards them.

"No. I mean, do you know *exactly* where we're going? Can you get us there?" Julie asked. Her voice was cold now, metallic, devoid of any recognizable emotion.

"Yeah...yeah, Julie, but I don't know the little shortcuts and byways..."

"Screw that. You can get us there and that means we don't need this asshole," Julie said.

"Julie, wait a minute."

"Yeah...yeah, Julie...listen to him...wait a minute..." Delmas echoed. Despite the chill the man was sweating profusely. Julie pulled the death-filled condom from her pocket and sank her strong, perfect teeth through the rubber, tearing the knotted end from it. "What the hell are you doing?"

"Julie, what the hell is that? What are you doing?" Williams said.

"This is for me," Julie said as she pulled the trigger. Delmas shrieked and bucked against the wagon's floor as the small bullet tore through his genitals.

"Shit! Julie!" Williams barked as he started around the side of the wagon.

She swung the revolver around and Williams ran into it, jamming it into his throat. "Back the fuck off, Howie!" Julie screamed. Delmas tried to roll away but was stopped by the wagon's side wall. Williams put his hands up and backed away enough to put a few inches between him and her gun. "And I'm not done with you yet, you sick fuck! This is for them!" Julie said as she grabbed Delmas's shoulder and rolled him onto his back. She held the torn condom over his mouth. "Open wide!" Delmas pinched his lips tight while he jammed his bound hands against his crotch as tightly as he could. "I said open it!" Julie screamed as she moved the gun to Delmas's gut and fired another blast. When he opened his mouth to scream Julie squirted the infected flesh from the condom like toothpaste from a tube, the glob of dead muscle choking off Delmas's anguished cry.

"My God! Julie!" Williams said. He advanced again, this time grabbing her by the shoulders. Pain lanced through Julie as Williams gripped her wound but it didn't stop her from dropping the gun and taking Delmas's head in her hands.

"Swallow you bastard! Swallow it!" Julie said as she used her hands to close Delmas's mouth. Delmas gagged several times before he was forced to involuntarily swallow the virus-riddled flesh. Julie finally relented and let Williams drag her away.

"What the hell was that? What did you do?" Williams asked.

Julie got up from the floor, her right hand over her left shoulder, her eyes defiantly locked on his. "We don't need him, and he'd have turned on us in a second. You know where we're going and we can make better time with the horses if they're not pulling the wagon."

"Christ, Julie! What about carrying the guns, the supplies?"

"Travel light and travel fast, right Howie?" Julie said.

Williams looked down at her and then to Delmas. The man had given up on screaming and lay bloody and whimpering in the fetal position. "What the hell did you do to him?" Williams asked again.

"I did to him what he's been doing to everyone he's ever come across - I'm leaving him fucked and dead." Julie stepped to the end of the wagon and leaned down to Delmas, her lips inches from his ear. "Don't worry Delmas...when you turn you'll have some nice, fresh meat waiting for you. Oh, and I lied. Junior was *way* bigger than you. Try not to choke on it."

Josephine shivered inside her metallic-skinned heat blanket. Heath hadn't been kidding when he'd said they would be "chilly" under the bridge. The river made the perfect conduit for the wind; the cold, stiff and constant breeze following it like a child's slot-car track. She didn't even see the point in standing guard in the first place. It was dark as pitch and she doubted even Heath's ears could pick up sounds over the constant noise. There could be twenty zombies there with them and neither of them would know it until cold hands gripped them. She stood and checked her watch for the third time that hour then paced back and forth along the narrow catwalk to invigorate her limbs from first sleeping then sitting on nothing but cold steel. Josephine had been surprised she'd even been able to sleep at all. Had it not been for her dreams she would have thought she'd done nothing but lay shivering until Heath had roused her for her watch.

She'd dreamed of young Andy Fitzsimmons, of how he would have looked in life before the virus, back when a zombie was nothing more than a matinee monster. Though she'd never met the boy in life she could easily picture him riding a bicycle, maybe fishing in a small pond that suspiciously resembled the one on her grandfather's farm. She'd dreamed of the children now long dead yet eternally hungry on the bus above them, saw them laughing and shooting spitballs, heard the bus driver chastise them. But that was when her brain betrayed her, showing her just how horrible little Andy's last few moments of life had been, how a pack of undead ripped through first his home and then his family. The darkest part of her psyche reveled in slowly withering the laughing school children to the dead husks they now were her mind's eye. So much death, so much innocence lost. Josephine had been more than ready to wake up, thinking her dreams would retreat in her waking. Of course, she'd been wrong.

Josephine continued pacing as her thoughts kept rolling through her dreamscape until she almost stumbled over Heath's prone form. Her foot clinked against something hanging from Heath's pack and the man didn't even stir. His reaction, or rather his lack of reaction, to her earlier slip-up was still gnawing at her. He'd gone off on her several times in the few short days she'd known him. Each of those times she'd felt his reactions had been drastic, over-reaching. But when she'd done something so truly bone-headed and inarguably stupid - something that could have gotten both of them killed - he'd hardly batted an eye. Was he getting softer, or had coming back to the Area affected him more deeply than he'd been willing to admit? Josephine didn't know the answer. But if John Heath was anything, he was a man of reason. The reason may be something wholly of his own creation and belief, but he didn't do anything without it.

Area reason, Area logic; Heath did nothing against his perception of those two ideals. He was a machine. At least, he had been until his reaction earlier that evening. *Was* he getting soft, or was he realizing that Josephine simply couldn't develop his same instincts, his same cold approach? Josephine leaned down and felt around her foot, her hand closing on Enos' goggles. Without thought she slipped them from Heath's pack and paused, holding her breath. Heath didn't move under his reflective blanket. Josephine backed away slowly, carefully until she felt a buttress at her back. She slid the headgear on and adjusted the cumbersome goggles against her face before pressing the button on the side of the unit. A soft green glow came up, slowly coalescing into a green-and-black picture of the catwalk under her feet then turned her head back to Heath. He still looked like a lump, but now a definable lump. He was facing away from her, his pack at his feet. With the wind and complete dark, that was likely the only reason she'd been able to get that close to him without his notice. Josephine put her rifle with her pack, checked her revolver, then made sure her steel bar was securely sheathed at her side. If Heath thought her incapable of developing Area reason and logic, he was wrong. But like him, hers would be on her own terms and in her own way.

The trip back up the steel cable was markedly more difficult than the trip down. Her gloves had been designed to protect from cuts and bites, but did little to keep the intense cold emanating from the wrapped steel cable from her fingers. Slowly, hand-over-hand she climbed the cable until she could step onto the bridge. She paused there for several moments, listening to the wind. Moans still carried through the night but now they seemed more like an afterthought, like an old man mumbling while he walked from room to room looking for something. The goggles were by no means perfect but they revealed enough for her to place her feet as she made her way back across the cars the way they'd come. Slowly, steadily, she crossed first a sedan then a station wagon, the rounded bulk of the school bus just a few vehicles away now. Josephine slipped into the bed of the pick-up truck beside the rear-end of the bus and crept across it, putting one foot on the bus's wide rear bumper and the other on the bed wall of the pick-up. She only hoped that after seven years the battery powering the siren on the bus's rear emergency door was as dead as the children inside. She reached out a hand and slowly pushed down on the long, lever handle. It refused to yield at first but finally succumbed after a moment of continuous pressure without a squeak or screech to pop open the door.

Josephine stepped off the truck and slipped into the bus, drawing her silenced revolver with one hand while she closed the door with the other. Her intrusion was noticed almost instantly, the faces of the undead children glowing a ghastly green as they rose up from the vinyl-covered seats and crawled up the narrow aisle. There were at least ten of them, their faces even more drawn and pathetic in the green cast from her goggles. This time Josephine felt no fear as they lumbered towards her on tiny, wobbly legs, their arms outstretched. This time, she felt only pity; pity at the senseless loss of so much life, so much youth, so much innocence. Her eyes saw each as the dried, shriveled faces they were now as her weapon crushed their skulls, and her mind saw each as they had appeared in her dreams; whole, vibrant and alive. As each body fell its image drifted away from her mind and, their innocence restored, away from the wellspring of her dreams.

"Josh! Hey, you've got a call," Harvey Fulcher said over the bustle of crew members wrapping the set. Mason had just finished his show and was chatting off-camera with this tapings' guests.

"Take a message, Harv', I'll call them back," Mason said. Fulcher picked his way through the crowd until he got to the base of the raised platform that served as *O Canada's* stage.

"You'll want to take this call, Josh... in private. It's from the States." Mason checked the look in his long-time assistant's eyes and politely excused himself.

"What's this about, Harv'?" Mason asked as the pair walked towards Mason's office.

"It's Senator Sommers. I had the switchboard transfer the call to your office."

"*The* Senator Sommers?" Mason asked.

"The one and only," Harvey said as they walked into his office. "You want me to... uh...?" Harvey asked, nodding towards the door. Mason looked at him for a moment and smiled.

"No, Harv'. Hang out for awhile, this could be interesting." Mason sat at his desk, punched the glowing button on his phone then switched on the speaker. "Senator! I must say this is quite a surprise. I thought we weren't on speaking terms."

"We're not, especially when you have me on speakerphone,"

Sommers said. Mason exchanged raised eyebrows with his assistant then picked up the handset.

"Sorry, Senator... force of habit. So, to what do I owe this unexpected pleasure?"

"We need to meet. My jet will be in Vancouver at ten tomorrow morning to pick you up. My secretary will call you by eight with details." Mason pulled the phone away and stared at the mouthpiece for a moment before putting it back to his ear.

"I'm sorry, Senator, but we must have a bad connection. I could have sworn you just said..."

"Don't play stupid, Mason. That may work on your countrymen but it doesn't work with me."

"Senator, with all due respect, you aren't in any sort of position to be giving me orders. Now, if you'd like to tell me what this is all about..." Mason said.

"Not over the phone. You'll *want* to meet with me, Mason. It's in your best interests, as well the interests of a mutual friend."

"A 'mutual friend'? Senator, I have a hard time believing you have *any* friends, let alone one we share," Mason said, smiling at Harvey. Harvey returned the smile and perched on the edge of Mason's desk, trying to figure out the other end of the conversation.

"Does the name 'Jo' ring a bell?" Sommers asked.

"I know a lot of men named Joe, Senator Sommers. I'm afraid you'll have to be more specific."

"It's not a man, and I can't say more right now. This line isn't secure," Sommers said. Mason sat for a moment, his mind racing.

"Do you mean Jos..." Mason started.

"Shut up, Mason! Get on that plane tomorrow if you want to help her, and yourself."

"Senator... this is really quite sudden... I can't just pick up and..."

"You can, and you will."

"I can't very well come to the States. You've made sure of that."

"I've taken care of that as well. We *will* see each other tomorrow, Mr. Mason," Sommers said before the line went dead.

"Josh… what the hell was that all about?" Harvey asked.

"I don't know yet, Harvey, but clear my schedule. I don't know what's happened, but whatever it is Josephine Terrell is obviously up to her neck in it. And if it involves both her *and* the esteemed Senator from California, I want to know what it is."

Williams thought back on the events of the day as he bounced along in the saddle and tried to pinpoint exactly where he'd lost control. He was fairly certain it was at the point where Junior's cock had hit the floor. After that, it had all gone downhill. Not only was Julie armed now, she'd proven she was willing and able to kill; a poor predicament for Williams when he considered he was the sole reason she was in Area 187 in the first place. He'd seen the Area break people before, and when they broke they usually didn't come back. It was obvious Julie had opened the crates while he'd been in the garage with Delmas. Williams had known what was in them as soon as he saw them. The practice of keeping "box brides" was not only morally repugnant but incredibly dangerous, but to a lonely man in the Area it was often the only sex available. Williams knew she'd been traumatized by her first sight of the undead sex toy, but he had no idea that a woman like Julie could be moved to such a heinous act by some nameless zombie's plight. But the facts of Delmas' death and resurrection, both by her hand, proved she had. Almost as worrisome was that Julie hadn't let Williams put the undead Delmas down, going so far as to put her hand on the butt of her pistol to back up her words. She'd made sure the man suffered through his last few moments on earth, made sure he not only suffered but knew what would become of him. Then they'd locked Delmas' moaning corpse inside, leaving him there to feast on his dead friend's remains. Julie Sommers was turning out to be full of surprises, and Williams could only hope none of those surprises would be visited on him.

His ass had only been in the saddle for about two hours but it already felt like two days. Williams hadn't been on a horse since his boyhood days with his uncle, and even then the animal hadn't been much more than a pony. It was all he could do to keep himself seated on the beast as he trotted along behind Julie, riding its stable mate. She seemed to be as at home on horseback as she was on her own two feet. They'd even been lucky enough to find what turned out to be one of the dead men's trails, the horses picking up their oft-traveled southerly path of their own accord as soon as their noses were turned in that general direction. Against his better judgment he put his heels into the horse's flanks and spurred it to catch up to Julie just as they reached a natural clearing in the woods. Once beside her he swung the reins, tapping her leg and signaling her to stop.

"What's the matter, you need a break?" Julie asked. He couldn't see her features in the dark but knew if he could he would see a wicked smile.

"If I get off this thing now I won't be able to convince my ass to get back on," Williams said as he fumbled in his saddlebags. "Watch your eyes, I need to use a flashlight." He pulled a small light and checked both map and compass. "We're heading almost due south. It looks like we're going to need to bear a bit westerly in another ten miles or so."

"I don't think that's a good idea. Delmas was right; they won't be able to keep up this pace all the way," Julie said as she patted her mount's neck. They could hear the horses' breathing, and though it wasn't necessarily labored it was certainly heavy. "Maybe we should keep to the trail and see if they'll lead us to that barn he told us about. We can let them rest for a few hours and then keep going. Even with going the extra distance to the south we'd still make better time than we would've on foot."

Williams thought for a moment then cocked his head, listening to the woods. He wasn't sure if it was the wind or a soft, far-distant moan he heard. "Either way it's a gamble. The trail's pretty smooth, but hooves still make a lot more noise than feet. I just don't want to build a tail for a few miles behind us then have it catch up after we stop."

"Well, that won't matter much if we run the horses into the ground halfway there, either. At least with the horses we can outrun any swarm that might come up."

"Yeah, and if that were 100% true there wouldn't be anywhere near the amount of zombies walking around in here. Animals can smell the dead a mile away. Most of the time that's all it takes to send them into a frenzy. You probably couldn't get a horse to go anywhere near a swarm, and if you were unlucky enough to be on one and a swarm would develop around you you'd be more likely to get your neck broke when the horse dumped you than you would be to ride it through," Williams said.

"So what are we supposed to do, ride until the horses fall over then walk the rest of the way?"

"No, that won't work either. If these guys can't get us all the way there in one shot then we'll need rest just as much as they will." Williams sighed and stowed the map, light and compass. "Give 'em their heads, let's see if they lead us to the barn." Julie pulled a bottle of water from her saddlebag and took a pull before offering it to him by bumping it against his hand in the dark. He accepted, sipped then gave it back to her. "So... are you... *okay*?" The only sound to be heard for a long moment was the moan of the breeze as it scraped the bare tree branches together.

"What do you mean?" Julie asked.

"With Delmas and everything... you kind of lost it a little back there, you know?" He regretted bringing it up almost as fast as he'd said it as a black, twisting and invisible wave of tension washed out from her direction.

"I did what I thought I had to do. That's what *you* do, isn't it? Isn't that why I'm here in the first place?"

It was Williams' turn to initiate the pregnant pause. He weighed his words carefully then said, "I'm not saying you weren't justified... all I'm saying is you need to, maybe, channel those emotions a little more... *constructively*."

Julie laughed. "The guy was going to rape me in a Hee Haw three-way. They would've killed and *eaten* you, you stupid prick. They had two women without arms and legs locked in crates like some sort of... of fucking cum-dumpsters! Are you fucking *defending* them?"

"Calm down… and no, that's not what I'm doing. But we can't afford for you to go all ape-shit, either. If you can tell me that you've got it together, that it's out of your system now, great. But if you can't, I need to know now. We were lucky you lost it in a safe place, but if it happens again we may not be so lucky. So I'll ask you again; *are you okay*?" he asked, stressing each word of his question.

"No, Howie…" Julie said after a long pause, "I'm certainly *not* okay. It's not 'out of my system'. I don't think it'll ever be."

"Have I told you that I'm sorry for getting you involved in all this?" Williams asked.

"Yeah, you have. It's your fault I'm here. But you know what, Howie? I don't really care about that anymore. You shouldn't, either."

"I think your father may feel differently."

"Well, I guess we won't find that out unless we get the hell out of here, now will we? And we're not going to do that standing around here. I promise if I feel the need to shoot a man and make him eat zombie meat again, I'll consult you first. Does that make you feel better?" Julie asked as she spurred her horse out of the clearing.

"Yeah. Tons. Thanks," Williams said to empty air as his horse took off after hers without his urging.

Predawn light reflected off the river by the time Josephine made it back under the bridge and slipped the goggles into Heath's pack. As near as she could tell he hadn't moved. Her mission had drained the battery on the goggles to almost nothing and she hoped they wouldn't have need of them later. If not, then she'd gotten away with it. The last thing she wanted to have to do was explain to him what she really couldn't explain to herself. She'd been back less than twenty minutes before Heath stirred.

"Sleep well?" Josephine asked as she sat down beside him.

"Like a baby," Heath said as he sat up and stretched his arms over his head. "Did I miss anything?"

"Nope. Dead all night." Neither of them laughed. Heath

pulled out his canteen and repeated his coffee trick.

"I *so* need this," Julie said. She drank down half of it then handed the canteen back to him.

"Better eat something, too. We've got a long road ahead of us," Heath said as he sipped.

"At least it's not raining," Josephine said as she fumbled with an MRE packet.

"Be better if it was. If those choppers start back up it'll really slow us down. We're too close now to take stupid chances, and the last thing we want to do is lead either the dead or Homeland to the survivors; if they haven't been found already."

They ate in silence then struck camp and made their way to the other side of the bridge. This time they found a ladder leading up to another small inspection platform just below the bridge deck. Heath motioned Josephine to stay on the platform while he continued until he was eye-level with the flattened tires of an eighteen-wheeler. He crept up onto the service deck between the truck's cab and trailer and peered through the back window; empty. The foot pegs built into the side of the trailer used for climbing up to its refrigeration unit allowed him to climb to the high trailer roof, giving him a commanding view of the auto graveyard beyond.

The traffic jam on this side of the bridge stretched for at least a mile. He pulled out his binoculars and scanned the field of steel and glass. As he'd expected, the moaning they'd triggered the day before had indeed swept down the bridge and through the expanse of the vehicles and beyond, attracting others from the surrounding area to crowd around the last rows of cars and trucks. There had to be at least a hundred of them, all shoving and clawing, trying to climb over the cars. A few had succeeded in crawling onto the last row of vehicles, but without their living balance and dexterity they were doomed to slide from their precarious perches, the rest of their unlives to be spent crammed between vehicles parked so closely together that their bodies couldn't even fall completely through to the ground. Heath knew they would never make it through a swarm of that size. The dead would see them coming across the tops of the vehicles almost as soon as they started. Their only chance would be to go around the horde, and unless they chanced climbing down the bank and following along the water's edge they would still run the high probability of being seen no matter what side of the blockage they traveled. He climbed down from the trailer and looked over the side of the bridge, motioning for Josephine to come up.

Josephine suppressed a gasp as she climbed to the roof of the trailer to see the swarm that awaited them. "How many do you think?" Josephine asked as she scanned them through Heath's binoculars.

"Enough."

"What about going down the bank, follow the river?"

"I wouldn't recommend it. The river takes an easterly bend a mile or so down that'll put us off course and do nothing but add more time. Besides, we don't know what we'll be coming up against. If we hit a marina we're going to run the risk of coming up on another swarm."

Any pre-virus location that would've represented transportation had now made the list of least-desirable Area vacation spots. During the panic of evacuation, many refugees had made for marinas and rivers, seeking any sort of watercraft they could find. The late-comers found no boats, only masses of zombies that had followed earlier and more successful survivors. The only thing those doomed survivors had accomplished was to ultimately add their numbers to the ranks of the dead.

"So we're going to have to get past them," Josephine said. She kept the binoculars on the swarm for another moment before she started sweeping them across the end of the silent traffic jam. After a few moments she handed the binoculars back to Heath. "I have a plan."

"You have a plan?"

"I'm not just another pretty face, you know?" Josephine said. "Okay, it may be a little dangerous," she admitted.

"Let's hear it."

"We split up here, you go down the left side and I'll take the right-" Josephine started.

"Split up?" Heath said, frowning.

"Let me finish. When we get close, they'll have to decide one way or the other which side they're going to shift to. The back end of this jam has got to be, what, ten cars wide down there? We stop with about five car-lengths between us and them and give them all the time they need to figure out which way they're going to split up..."

"..leaving the middle at the very least thinned-out," Heath said, finishing her thought. He thought while he looked back at the traffic, visualizing her plan. "We'd have to move fast. How do your ribs feel?"

"Does it matter?" Josephine asked. "We've got a town to the north of us, and this was a pretty big highway interchange. If I remember Jasper's maps, there are a few other small towns in the vicinity. What we're seeing downfield is only be the tip of the iceberg, right?" Heath looked back at her again, this time with a look she hadn't seen since she'd tried to kill him after the barn incident. "The longer we stand here means the more time for however many more to investigate, and if they get much thicker we won't have a shot in hell," she said, then quickly added, "right?"

Heath sighed and started adjusting his pack. "You have a point," he said.

Josephine smiled. If that was as close as his ego would let him come to acknowledging she'd come up with the plan then so be it.

"Anything that could've been awakened in the cars *will* be awake. You're going to have to be on your toes."

"Not a lot of other options, are there?"

"No, I guess not," Heath said. "Okay, once you get in position, watch me and don't worry about how much noise you make. Once we start moving for the center we've made the commitment. Don't stop for anything and don't look back. We'll pick up an instant tail as soon as we hit the pavement so we're going to need to keep moving for at least a mile before we'll have the luxury of looking back. There's no telling how many late-comers we may be walking into, either," he said as Josephine adjusted her own equipment.

"You sure you want to do this?"

"Nope." Josephine's heart was already pounding in her ears as she looked out across the steel and glass wasteland.

"Good. Healthy skepticism. I like that. Just do me a favor... no more side trips, okay?"

She stared at him for a moment longer. He knew. Josephine kept his eyes and nodded. She wasn't about to hang her head like a scolded child and apologize. "Jasper told me I needed to know the real reason why I was coming here, whether anyone else knew it or not. He didn't say I couldn't add reasons along the way."

"Try to keep the additions to a minimum." Josephine nodded. "Okay then..." Heath said through a determined sigh, "... see you on the other side."

They climbed down from the trailer and split up without another word. Heath headed to the far left side while Josephine picked her way down the right. The farther they progressed, the more trapped dead they encountered. It made sense; only the refugees at the ends of the jam would have had much chance of escaping their vehicles. Broken-out windshields and windows became a common sight, the desperation of those long-ago people to get free of their prisons any way they could. Many of the vehicles they passed contained a mixture of both active and inactive zombies as well as bones and empty clothes. Most of the active ones were further trapped by their seatbelts, their hands reaching out through open windows and busted windshields at them. A few even managed to grab their feet and legs as Heath and Josephine passed but those were easy enough to shake off. The virus was powerful in death, but even though it could keep a dead and decaying body active for years it couldn't repair damage. Summer sun turned the parked cars into ovens, baking the moisture and elasticity out of the reanimates while the winter cold brittled their bones in its own time. Their curious ability to enter a hibernation state would be the only reason any of them would still be active now, the resting state preserving the corpses' senses for the time when the brave and foolhardy would come near them again.

The swarm noticed them almost as soon as they split up

from the trailer. At first their plan didn't seem to be working. The mass remained unchanged and in the same large knot of reaching hands and moaning mouths. It wasn't until they were both in their respective final positions that the limited faculties of the dead started pulling them to the sides, splitting the group almost evenly between them to the far sides of the jam. A few zombies to either side were able to crawl onto the lower trunks and truck beds of the last row of vehicles, their bodies pushed up and over by the press of their swarm behind them. Josephine watched these few with her hand on the butt of her revolver. She doubted even those would be able to navigate the last few vehicles to reach her, but the feel of the gun's thick grip made her feel a little more empowered.

The collective moan of the swarm was a drone in his ears by the time Heath reached his spot atop a Ford Expedition and stood looking out over both parts of the swarm. Josephine's plan had worked, at least to some degree. They'd managed to create a fairly clear ten to twelve-foot divide between the two halves of the swarm. The only question that remained would be if they could diagonally navigate towards the center of the last few rows and get through the break before the two halves merged again. Josephine had been right. Without the barriers and the natural confines of the bridge, the four lanes had grown to ten across at this end of the jam. He looked across the field of vehicles and saw Josephine had reached her position and was dividing her time between watching the dead and watching him. Heath waited until her eyes fell on him again then raised a hand to keep her attention fixed. He pointed at another tractor-trailer that sat near the center of the remaining rows then spread his hands and brought them together again in a clap. Josephine nodded, indicating she understood they would pass the truck on their respective sides and would meet somewhere just beyond it for their make-or-break dash to the road. With that, Heath raised a hand with three fingers extended, ticking them into a fist. As soon as the last fell he was moving across the cars towards the back of the truck.

Josephine launched herself from her own perch and made for the same spot. She dodged a pair of withered hands that groped out from a sports car's open sunroof then navigated the top of a panel van near the end of the trailer. She flew off the top of the van and landed hard enough to cave a Cadillac's hood while the zombies on her side of the jam went insane with movement, each trying to move as an individual against the constraints of its group. She crossed the hood of the luxury car and made its trunk, expecting to find Heath there. He wasn't. She hopped to the hood of the compact car jammed against the ICC bumper of the trailer and swung her head around the side of its box.

Heath was another car length from the end of the trailer, his leg hanging down between its tall tires and the Lincoln parked beside it. His hands were braced against the roof of the car to keep the rest of his body from being pulled down by a zombie that had managed to crawl across the last few lengths of the jam but had slipped off into the tight space between the trailer and car. Heath was kicking at the zombie's head with his free leg to little effect, the position of his body keeping him from developing enough force. He looked up from the zombie's gnashing teeth at her.

"Go! Get the hell out of here!" Heath shouted. Josephine shot a quick look over her shoulder and saw the gap was starting to close as the swarm realized the pair were no longer in two different places. She turned back to him, drew her revolver and aimed between the two vehicles. If she missed she would almost certainly hit Heath's leg, and if that happened there'd be no way he could navigate the last of the cars and move fast enough to keep the swarm from catching him. She braced the weapon in both hands and pulled the trigger. The bullet rocketed through the back of the zombie's head, the exit wound tearing open his skull and sending bits of its forehead against Heath's leg and the side of the trailer.

"Fucking *go!*" Heath screamed at her as he shook the stilled hands from his leg and started towards her. Josephine turned and found their gap had reduced to almost nothing. "No choice! Run!" Heath said from behind her when he saw less than a two-foot gap in the closing swarm. They shot off past the last car length and through the gap with Josephine in the lead. Grasping hands clawed at their arms, legs and equipment as they hit the press of the separate masses, their speed and momentum the only things keeping the dozens of hands that brushed them from stopping them. The pair cleared the swarm just as the two halves rejoined into a solid, moaning mass of putrid gray flesh, the confusion delaying their mob pursuit long enough to give Heath and Josephine several yards of clear, unmolested head-start. Josephine glanced over her shoulder at Heath. "Just keep fuckin' running… and don't look back this time!"

Julie had slowed their horses to a walk just as dawn broke behind them, illuminating a large barn with a faded *Mail Pouch* logo painted across its rough boards a few hundred yards ahead. She let her reins go slack and her horse plodded towards it, its course ramrod-straight.

"I think that's the place," Julie said over her shoulder. Williams held a finger to his lips and urged his mount up to ride by her side. They rode in silence until Williams stopped his horse about ten yards from the building.

"Check around the front and work your way back here. Keep your distance from the barn and look for anything out of the ordinary while I check out the inside," Williams said. He didn't wait for her reply before dismounting and moving towards the barn with his machine gun ready, his unaccustomed time in the saddle giving him a bow-legged gait. Julie shrugged, wondering just what would classify as "out of the ordinary" in Area 187, then walked her horse slowly around the barn, her eyes watching for movement and her ears straining for the slightest unnatural sound. When she came back around, Williams was standing in the barn's now open door and waving for her to bring the horses inside. She climbed down, took both animals' reins and walked them into the barn.

Julie led the animals across the bare, rough-planked floor to a pair of stalls fronted by a low trough. Several five-gallon plastic water jugs sat to one side, a pile of old hay and a few moldy sacks of feed to the other. "At least they weren't depriving the horses," Julie muttered as she started removing their tack.

"Is that wise? We may need to get out of here in a hurry."

"They need to rest. Can you rest with fifty pounds worth of gear on your back and a steel bit in your mouth?" Julie asked.

"As a matter of fact, I can."

"Yeah, but them I care about," Julie said without missing a beat.

"I need to check the loft," Williams said. Julie waved him away then picked up a brush and started working on the horses.

Williams found a homemade, hinged ladder leading up to the loft above the stalls, its design meant to allow its bottom half to be pulled up and away from the ground. He pulled a thin rope that ran through steel eyelets bolted along its length to let the bottom half open to touch the ground. If he doubted this was Delmas' barn before, he certainly didn't now. He climbed the ladder and looked around in the dim light coming from chinks in the wooden walls. Two mattresses with a few blankets and sleeping bags had been placed on the floor a few feet apart with a large, suspicious-looking wooden crate between them. Williams went to the crate, cringing as he cautiously lifted the lid to find several cans of vegetables, a few plastic plates and cups, a couple tins of potted meat, a *Hustler* magazine from 1974 and no zombies. Williams breathed a sigh of relief. Delmas and Junior certainly weren't the kind you'd invite for Thanksgiving dinner, but he had to admit they were definitely into their own survival. He replaced the lid then sat down on it to take a much-needed pause. In all honesty, he'd expected either Julie, himself or both to be dead by now. But then, not much over the course of the last few days had gone according to plan or expectation, least of which his "captive". He reminded himself the girl was probably still in shock. Everything that had happened since that night in her apartment was so totally out of the realm of her life experience he could hardly blame her.

Williams went to the edge of the loft and looked down as Julie finished her ministrations and put the horses in their stalls. He waved at her until he caught her attention then motioned her to the ladder. She climbed up and looked around the loft.

"I gotta' tell you, Howie, you keep taking me to all the four-star hotspots and you're going to spoil me," Julie said as she walked past him and sat down on one of the mattresses. Her eyes went to the crate and she froze.

"Just supplies," Williams assured her as he pulled up the bottom end of the ladder and then sat down on the opposite mattress to open the crate. She nodded, tight-lipped and pulled off her coat, placing it on the floor with her two handguns on top of it. Williams watched her carefully for a moment then set about preparing their breakfast.

"Nothing for me, thanks," Julie said as he worked the key to open a tin of meat.

"You need to eat something."

"Maybe before we head out again. Not right now," Julie said as she unlaced her boots.

"You'll want to leave those on," Williams cautioned as he cut a sliver of meat from the tin. He grimaced at the gelatinous goo on the mixed meat but ate it just the same.

"I need to check the cuts," Julie said. Williams nodded as he chewed, surprised he'd forgotten about her punished feet. She finished with her boots then carefully peeled her socks away. The cuts were ugly, but none looked infected or had reopened despite the continued abuse.

"Still hurt?" Williams asked around another mouthful.

Julie looked at him like he was the dumbest creature on the planet. "If I answer that, it'll come with a knee to your groin." She reached down into her coat pocket and came up with a small, flat-glass bottle of cheap whiskey.

"Where did you find that?"

"Beside one of the stalls," Julie said as she spun the top off and tipped it to her mouth.

"Easy there... this is the last place you want to be fucked up," Williams said.

Julie swallowed and made an amusing whiskey-face before offering him the bottle. "The last place? If there's anywhere better to be fucked up, I don't know where it is. I'm willing to chance it." She shook the bottle at him. "You dragged me into this mess,

Howie. The least you can do is to not have me drink alone."

Williams accepted the bottle, took a drink then gasped as the liquid burned its way down his throat. "Christ! You'd think seven years would've helped that a bit." Williams said as he coughed into his shoulder. He handed the bottle back and she took another sip.

"Howie...do you believe in karma?" Julie asked, her sudden change to a grave tone getting his attention.

"What?" Williams asked.

"Karma. You *do* know what karma is, don't you?"

"Yes, I know what karma is." Williams said.

"Do you believe in it?"

"If you mean, do I believe there's some cosmic force that visits good and evil based on what you do then, no, I don't. I've seen too many good people get shit on all their lives while too many assholes just keep getting all the breaks."

"Assholes like me?" Julie asked.

"I really don't see..."

"That wasn't a rhetorical question, Howie," she interrupted.

"Honestly?"

"No, Howie, fucking lie to me."

"Let's just say that money and power can turn anybody into an asshole."

"You're not answering my question," she said.

"What do you want me to tell you? You've already told me you don't give a shit about what I have to say. I fail to see how the opinion of this little peon would really matter to people like you or your father."

"I guess the apple doesn't fall far from the tree in your world, huh?" she asked.

Williams shook his head then closed his eyes and took a deep breath. "Let's not do this, okay?"

"You're right, you know?" she said, ignoring him. "I *am* one of those assholes. So is my father." Julie chuckled as she took another drink. "I get it!" she said loudly, craning her head to the ceiling and flinging her arms out to her sides. "I got the fucking message!"

"Julie!" Williams hissed as he moved onto his knees between the mattresses and put one hand over her mouth while the other took the bottle. "You want to get us killed?" Her eyes smiled at him over his hand before she peeled it away from her mouth. Her lips were smiling, too.

"I get it now. It's not your fault I'm here, Howie. You may have been the vehicle, but you're not the reason."

"You're not making sense. Don't lose it on me now," Williams said.

"I haven't lost anything, Howie. If anything, I've found it." Suddenly, she dropped a hand between them and shoved him backwards. The unexpected attack caught him off-guard, sending him toppling onto his mattress. Julie was on him in a second, straddling him.

"Julie? What the hell..."

"It doesn't have to make sense to you, Howie. It makes sense to me. You don't need to understand it...I do." Julie was smiling at him, her long blonde hair trailing down onto his chest. She leaned down and kissed him deeply while his eyes went wide. He grabbed her forearms and pushed her up gently, breaking their kiss.

"Julie... you're in shock... you need rest."

"Howie... we're in Area 187, surrounded by zombies and the worst examples of humanity. In just two short days I've been drugged, tied up, and in a helicopter crash. My feet have been sliced to ribbons. I've been shot, Howie... fucking *shot*. Then, not only did I fondle two men that wanted to rape me, but I cut one of their dicks off and turned the other into a zombie. I don't need rest, Howie... I need to know that somewhere in all this I'm still a fucking *human being*!" Julie sat up suddenly, her hands going to work on his belt.

"Julie, you don't want to do this..." Williams said, gripping his hands in hers. She leaned down over him again, their noses almost touching.

"Gonzo," she whispered.

Williams' eyes went quizzical. "What?"

"Gonzo was my favorite Muppet," she said. Williams had

never thought he would hear a sentence like that in such a husky, breathless tone. He smiled then slid his hands away from hers, letting them have their will.

"Will you respect me in the morning?" Williams asked.

"That would imply I respect you now," she said, smiling as their lips met again.

Eric R. Lowther

Chapter XVI
Unlikely Alliances

Fremont slid his ID card through the reader. The windowless steel door slid soundlessly into the wall to close behind him just as quickly after he'd crossed the threshold. Six large monitors placed in two rows of three each covered the far wall, filling it from the ceiling almost to the floor. Two of his hand-picked agents sat at a console, sharing the multitude of controls, buttons and still more, smaller screens. Warner got up from the glass-enclosed conference area set up to the right of the room's only door and joined Fremont.

"All right, Walt...what do you have for me?" Fremont asked his oldest friend and conspirator.

"Phillips managed to tag her with the transmitter round, and boy has she been on the move," Warner said, nodding to the screens. "Cline, bring up the map and give me that damn clicker-thingy," Warner said to the back of one of the agent's heads. One of the large screens changed from a satellite weather map to a map of southern Pennsylvania and north-central West Virginia. The old state borders were marked with a dotted line while a bright, white line denoted the border of Area 187. Agent Cline held a small device over his head and Warner snatched it in his meaty fist as he and Fremont walked to the screen. Warner pressed the button and a red dot appeared on the screen at the North Gate. "They crashed here two days ago, 05:00. The next confirmed sighting is here..." Warner said, clicking the button again. Another red dot appeared. "...twenty-five miles to the south, yesterday at 14:00. That's where Phillips tagged her," Warner said.

"Have you taken care of him?" Fremont asked, his eyes on the screen.

"Sure, Harry. You know I don't leave loose ends."

"Are we still receiving a signal?"

"Yeah," Warner said. He clicked again and this time when another red dot appeared there was a line connecting it to the last. "We can see the exact route. She made it another six miles or so after Phillips tagged her and stopped at this location at 16:20. Records say it used to be some kind of machine shop or something. It's probably a safe house now."

"Is she still there?"

"Nope... and that's where it gets tricky. She left here at 22:07..." Warner said, pointing to the flashing red dot on the screen, "...and by 06:14 she was here." Warner clicked and another dot appeared, this time connected to the last by a squiggly, southern-running line. Fremont lifted his head so his bifocals could be brought to bear on the screen.

"Something's wrong with the tracker. How many miles is that?" Fremont asked.

"53 miles," Cline replied without looking up from his console. Fremont lit a cigarette and turned away from the screen.

"You're telling me she walked 53 miles in eight hours?" Fremont asked.

"I didn't say she walked, I just said that's where the thingy says she is now. She must've found a night runner." Warner said.

"No vehicles moving around?" Fremont asked.

"Nothing on the satellite, and you told me to ground the air platforms after the first few sweeps so we wouldn't scare them into going to ground. You want me to get the birds in the air?"

"You can resume operations in the southern sectors, but I want to keep everything north of that grounded. She's moving and in a steady direction. Have we confirmed if Williams is still with her?"

"No, but I doubt she could've made it without some kind of help. I'll bet you ten bucks he's still on her," Warner said.

"Williams knows where Heath is," Fremont said. He checked his watch. Julie Sommers had been at her current location for a little more than an hour now. "I want constant satellite observation, and I want you to let me know the minute they move. I want cell towers within a twenty mile radius of her position powered up and frequency jamming suspended and closely monitored. Roll them on and off as she moves. Get her cell number and start calling it in 30 minute intervals. Maybe we'll get lucky and she's as dumb as she is blonde."

Josh Mason didn't bother standing when Sommers boarded the jet. "Senator! How lovely to see you again," Mason said, raising his drink from his leather-upholstered seat. "Can I get you a drink?"

"A little early for that, isn't it, Mr. Mason?" Sommers asked, taking a seat opposite Mason, a low table between them.

"It seemed like a good idea at the time."

Sommers frowned at him and opened his briefcase. "We don't have time for this."

"Is that why we're meeting on a plane? Are you afraid to even have me set foot on American soil?"

"Shut up and listen before I decide to give this to an American outlet," Sommers said.

Mason sat up a bit then leaned forward over the table. "If that was an option you wouldn't have bothered calling me. But you're right, it's more than time for you to tell me what this *Spy vs. Spy* business is all about."

Sommers grimaced at the journalist's over-exaggerated Canadian pronunciation of the word 'about'.

"Where's Josephine Terrell?" Mason asked.

Sommers looked towards the closed cockpit door then back at Mason. "She's in Area 187 with John Heath."

Mason's jaw literally dropped. "You're joking…"

"They went in a few days ago. Ms. Terrell came across a video message, supposedly smuggled out of the Area, from a group of survivors. She decided to go in and try to rescue them for a story."

"I can't believe that. She would've told me if she were going to do something so incredibly stupid."

"Then it appears you don't know Ms. Terrell as well as you think you do." Sommers pulled a DVD from his briefcase and went to the plane's media center. He turned on the television then slipped the disc into the player.

Mason got up and joined him as the screen filled with the grainy image of a bedraggled, older man. "Is this for real?" Mason whispered as his eyes transfixed on the screen.

"Real enough for Ms. Terrell to risk her career, her life and the safety and security of this country to investigate it."

"Please, Senator, let's not ruin this special day with politics," Mason said as the man that identified himself as Dr. Richards spoke to them.

Sommers let the message go till nearly the end then paused the playback.

"You're trying to set me up for something nasty, aren't you, Senator? No grave robber would ever bring something like this out, much less give it to you."

"I wish I were, Mason. But it's very real."

"So why haven't you just bombed their position? Why even show this to me? What are you getting at?"

"Are you familiar with my daughter, Julie Sommers?"

"If you mean the little pop-tart that handles the weekend edition of Josephine's show, then yes, I know of her."

"She got mixed up in all this, completely by accident. She's in there, too. She was kidnapped and used as insurance by another robber in league with Heath."

"You've got to be joking. What are you trying to pull, Senator? And, I can guarantee you this little conversation is *on* the record-" Mason started.

Sommers suddenly turned on him, grabbing him and shoving him into his chair. Mason's drink flew from his hand, painting his shirt with Scotch before the glass tumbled to the thick carpet. "This is no joke! If I wanted you dead you'd be dead!" Sommers said. "My daughter is in there, and *you're* going to help me get her out."

Mason looked up at the sudden madman's visage. "All right, Senator... let's suppose I believe. Let's suppose the U.S. Senator that actually chairs the Senate Area committee, a man that once called me a 'tumor on the body of modern journalism', is now telling me about an illegal entry into Area 187 by a nationally-known journalist, the infamous John Heath and this particular Senator's daughter, knowing full well that only my death would stop me from reporting it. Let's suppose he has no ulterior motives other than seeing his daughter's safe return. It begs a lot of questions, Senator. Are you prepared to go on record with the answers?"

"It's gone too far to worry about that now," Sommers said. He went to his chair and practically fell into it, his bravado deflating before Mason's eyes. If this was some kind of game, an effort to get Mason to involve himself in Area business, Sommers was certainly playing his part to the hilt. "We can't waste any more time. Ask your questions, Mason."

Mason brushed absently at the alcohol soaking through his shirt then pulled out a notepad.

After almost half an hour of questions and surprisingly frank answers, Mason was ready to bring the anger from the pit of his stomach to the tip of his tongue. As far as he was concerned, Sommers was reaping what he had sown. It seemed the perfect karma that his daughter would fall victim to the same clandestine policies and governmental evil the Senator himself had helped impose. But Mason clenched his teeth and fought the righteous anger back. There was something far greater at stake here than eating the rich, greater than the danger his friend Josephine had placed herself, even greater than the story. This was living, breathing proof of survivors in Area 187 along with a high-ranking Senator ready to back the whole tale. Sommers was an asshole, but under it all he was still a father trying to save his daughter, and he was willing to risk his political career and even his life to do it.

"How much of this does Homeland know?" Mason asked.

"My sources tell me they know about Heath, Terrell and what they're trying to do. And of course, they know about Williams and Julie. As far as I know, they don't have the location of the survivors. If they did they would've killed them already."

"Do you have proof that any of them are still alive?" Mason asked.

"My daughter's alive, Mason."

"But do you have proof-"

"Goddamn it my daughter's alive!" Sommers screamed as he shot up out of his chair.

"Alright..." Mason said, holding his hands up in surrender. "I'm willing to work on that premise... for now. So where do we go from here?"

"We need to make sure that Heath accomplishes his mission," Sommers said, his anger slipping away as he passed a hand over his damp brow and straightened his tie.

"And just how will we do that?"

"You leave that to me. Make up a list of the equipment you'll need to do a live satellite uplink and I'll see that you have it. We're going in there, Mason. I'm going to get my daughter back and you'll have the exclusive on the greatest story in a hundred years."

Chapter XVII
Convergence

Josephine's afternoon runs had taught her she was good for an easy few miles with hardly a sweat. But those runs didn't involve 30 pounds of gear, and this morning's run had a far more powerful motivator than swimsuit season. Heath had resumed his usual lead to set a punishing, steady pace down the sun-cracked pavement. The Area had a way of playing on the senses, turning feet into miles and moments into hours. Her ribs screamed beneath their tight bonds and stars had started winking to life in her vision by the time he'd led them off the highway and into the comparative shelter of the woods that had started filling the gap between the road and river. Only then did he slow their pace as the undergrowth thickened and stopped deep inside a large copse of dense pines. Josephine sank onto the bed of cool needles without bothering to remove her pack.

"We'll rest here for a minute," Heath said, as out of breath as she.

"I feel like we just ran a marathon," Josephine said as she opened her canteen and took several small, slow sips, fighting the urge to upend the thing over her burning face and neck. "How far do you think we are from the bridge?"

Heath wiped sweat from his face with his palm then checked

his watch. "About five miles, give or take."

"And how far back do you think they are?"

"At least three miles, but they won't be stopping to rest. This hook into the woods took us off the straight and narrow course, though. If they're true to form, they'll keep going down the road to the south while we follow the river for another six or seven miles then head west. We'll lose a lot of tree cover and we'll be skirting around a few small towns. The last two miles or so will be pretty deserted. If we can clear the populated areas with a couple of hours to spare before dark, we'll be at their coordinates before sundown," Heath said, joining her on the soft pine carpet but facing the opposite direction.

"Their coordinates? What's that supposed to mean?"

"It's a fallout bunker. The way in will be concealed in another building or disguised. Just because we get to the 'X' on the map doesn't mean we'll be standing in their living room," Heath said.

Josephine looked down and saw his fingers drumming silently on his thigh. She opened her mouth to comment, thought better of it. The man had every right to be a nervous. Josephine tried to imagine what he must be feeling, and how she'd feel if their situations were reversed. She glanced at his face and could almost see the last seven years of his life play out across his eyes and the deep lines around them. Josephine would've sworn those lines hadn't been as deep just the day before.

"Heath?"

"Yeah?"

"I'm sure she's there," Josephine said.

He didn't answer. The wind shifted then, carrying the long-off, droning moan of their pursuers to them. "That was a stupid thing you did back there. We could've both been killed, and that wouldn't have helped anybody," Heath said as he got up. Josephine's mouth formed a blistering retort that was cut short by his smile. "Nice shooting," he added, then started out of the pines.

Josephine followed, her own smile easing her aches and pains.

Williams awoke to a beam of mid-morning sun shining into his eyes through a chink in the wall. Julie was already up, sitting on the crate and gently sliding her feet into her boots. He lifted the blanket away and looked down his body, confirming his nakedness.

"Yes, it really happened. And yes, yours is still attached," Julie said as she laced her boots.

Williams smiled as he slid off the mattress and started dressing. "This... uh... this isn't going to get weird or anything now, is it?" Williams asked as he buckled his belt and pulled his shirt over his head.

"I just rutted like a crazed weasel with the man that kidnapped me and dropped me into zombie-land. God help us both if it gets weirder," Julie said as she stood and put her guns in their places.

Williams sat down on the crate and put on his socks and boots. "Is this the part where I ask if it was as good for you as it was for me?" he asked as he finished with his boots.

She pulled her hair back and wrapped it into a tight package on the back of her head. "No, Howie. That part never actually comes up."

"So you're sure we're... *okay*?" Williams asked.

Julie sighed and dropped her hands to her sides. "Yes, Howie, we're okay," she said, putting on her coat as she headed for the ladder. "And if you can manage to keep your finger out of my ass, it may just happen again."

Williams laughed softly as his face turned red and Julie dropped the ladder to disappear below.

After a brief tutorial on saddling a horse they were off. Williams' backside ached anew as soon as it touched the saddle, bringing yet another smile to his saddle-mate's face. He had no idea just what to make of what had happened, but he shoved it down as soon as they cleared the barn. The Area was far too dangerous a place to let your mind wander, and they were too close and had come too far for him to let that happen. The going would get more difficult now that they weren't relying on their mounts' sense of direction, heading west and away from the paths the horses knew so well. He could already sense the hesitation from his mount and decided Julie would continue to lead them and pointed her west. If they had to run, her superior horsemanship might be the only thing to save them and keep both horses going in the desired direction.

They'd covered better than fifteen miles by the time the noon sun was on their shoulders. Williams had just started to think they would make the survivors well before sundown when their mounts stopped abruptly. An old farmhouse sat ahead of them, directly in their path. The horses pranced, agitated, under them, blowing gusts of fear-laced air through their nostrils.

"Something's spooking them," Julie said as she tried to calm her horse.

"Not a good sign. Let's give the house a wide berth," Williams said. He'd given up trying to calm his horse and spent his energies on staying in the saddle instead. Even that effort was lost when the first moan drifted across the field and his horse reared, dumping him to the ground.

"There!" Julie said, pointing with one hand while trying to work the reins with the other. Williams picked himself up and followed her gesture. Four figures were shambling from around the side of a shed to the left of the farmhouse, their combined moans and scent bringing froth to the horses' lips. Williams' horse moved away from them, doubling back on their path and stopping twenty yards back, its head bobbing up and down in a mute call to its yoke-mate to join it. "You take care of those and I'll get your horse," Julie said. Her horse responded to her direction and tore up chunks of pasture as it made for the other while Williams leveled his weapon at the four approaching ghouls. Even silenced, the report would carry its tinny whisper across the whole meadow. Still, they wouldn't be able to get the horses calmed with the zombies coming after them. Four shots sounded and four kills happened, the bodies crumpling into the high weeds before the last shell casing hit the ground. He looked back and saw Julie had managed to get hold of his horse's reins. He started walking towards her just as several heads rose up from the weed-choked pasture, their moans filling the air.

"Shit! It's a graveyard!" Williams shouted as he ran up and clumsily mounted his skittish horse. Julie looked around, transfixed as many more bodies slowly got to their feet from various parts of the field, their clothing and flesh hanging in tatters from their time spent exposed to the elements. Like as not this group had once been part of a swarm that had followed something to this point and simply stopped where they were. Those that had landed face-down would've been content to lie where they fell, hibernating, lying in wait for new prey. Judging by their accelerated decay they'd been waiting a while now. The group formed a crescent behind their position as they stumbled and limped towards the horses and their riders, blocking them from doubling back on their path.

"Come on! We'll break to the left of the house and worry about picking up our path later!" Williams said. Julie pin-wheeled her mount and gave it its head when it was pointing in the right direction. They'd barely covered thirty yards when more bodies started coming out of the house.

"This is bad, right?" Julie said as she struggled to keep her mount heading towards the emerging zombies.

"Just try to keep us heading that way! If we can keep them running we may be able to break through!" he yelled back over the thunder of terrified hooves. The horses were wide-eyed and foaming now as their riders pressed them into the rapidly-developing swarm ahead.

"Can't you just shoot them?" Julie called out as she fought her horse.

"I'm not John Wayne and you're not Katherine Hepburn! No way in hell to get a head shot from the back of a running horse!" Williams said. With every foot they covered the horses became more unruly. Julie's mount could no longer take the stress and turned broadside to the swarm, its head arcing back the way they'd come, trying to force Julie's reins to pull that way as well.

"This isn't going to work! Slack the reins... let 'em have their heads and get down across the neck!" Julie said. Williams spared a glance at her and repeated her actions, letting the reins go slack in his hand and keeping his profile low in the saddle. The horses instantly recognized their newfound freedom and stopped, heaving and frothing, tossing their heads to all sides as the dead converged from the front and rear.

Suddenly, Julie's horse picked a spot in the growing swarm and barreled towards it. Williams' horse took off after its fellow, its head just inches to the right of the other's flank. Within seconds the animals hit a thin spot in the swarm, their velocity and sheer weight throwing the zombies out of their path like dry reeds or trampling them beneath steel-shod hooves. The animals veered, bounding around the shed and continuing south, the wailing of the dead behind them lost in the staccato bursts of their hoof beats.

Julie let them run out some energy before she started working with her mount, alternating between soothing hands to its neck and more forceful pulls on her reins. As her mount slowed, so did Williams' until he felt he could likewise bring his horse under control. The meadow was more than two miles behind by the time they came to a full stop just inside a lightly wooded area.

"Well, that was a little close," Julie said, her chest heaving almost as violently as her horse's. She slid out of the saddle and moved to the front of her animal, nuzzling its soft nose against her cheek and cooing softly to it. Williams dismounted to face his own horse but couldn't bring himself to imitate Julie's maternal mutterings, mustering only a few slow passes of his hand between his horse's eyes and mumbling about it being a "good horsey".

"You could be a little more appreciative. That horse just saved your life, you know?" Julie said.

"I wouldn't know what to say," Williams said. He cocked his head to the side then pointed northwest. "There's a stream over there. I think we could all use a drink." Julie listened but couldn't hear anything as Williams walked his horse past them. She followed and found the fast-rushing stream about fifty yards from where they'd stopped. He pulled the map and compass from his saddlebag and checked them while the horses rested. "We can cross here and head west. If that swarm manages to keep on us the stream will slow them down. The weaker ones will have a hard time standing up in it, much less walking."

"Okay, but we'll need to take it easy for a little while. That last run took a lot out of them," Julie said as she patted her mount's neck. "Are we still on track to get there tonight?"

"Yeah, I think so," he said, adding, "but we may have to push them towards evening to make it." They mounted the horses and made ready to ford the comparatively shallow though fast-moving water.

"Howie? What are we going to do with the horses when we get there?" Williams looked at her, his expression tight.

"I don't know. Let's see if we get there first. I'll be happy if that's the only thing we have to worry about by then."

"She's been on the move since 09:30, Harry, and moving fast," Warner said. He lit a cheap cigar and added its heavy, blue-tinged haze to Fremont's lighter, wispier cloud. Warner slid a small stack of black-and-white satellite images across the desk then sat back.

"Horses," Fremont commented, his eyes narrowing to take in every grainy detail. "Williams is still with her."

"What makes you sure it's Williams?"

"No night runner would be out on a clear day no matter how she's paying him. Where are they heading?" Fremont asked.

"Pretty much due west. They dipped to the south but came back west again."

"They know where they're going. I want to know, too. I want to know everything there is to know about the Area in a twenty-mile north-south corridor from their current position all the way to the Ohio River. I'll expect a briefing in an hour," Fremont said.

Warner knew a dismissal when he heard one and wasted no time in laboring his bulk out of the office. One of Fremont's men from the observation room passed Warner as he was leaving and the agent was entering.

"Secretary Fremont? You ordered me to keep an eye on Senator Sommers?" the agent said.

"Yes?"

"He's been pretty active, sir, or at least his jet has," the agent said, holding up a manila folder. Fremont waved him fully into the office and the agent handed the folder to him. The Secretary flipped through the folder then lit another cigarette off the dying embers of the last.

"I know he hasn't personally left the greater Pittsburgh area. Find out why his plane has and have it ready for my briefing. One hour," Fremont said.

Josh Mason looked out over a dozen of the largest, angriest-looking men he'd ever seen. "Where did you find this lot?" Mason asked Sommers, careful to keep his voice low.

"I have controlling interest in a private security company. Every one of these men is a hardened veteran of conflicts with the living *and* the dead." One of the men broke away from the group and stalked towards them.

"What the fuck is going on here? Senator or not, you'd better start coming up with some answers! What the hell did you do to us? Cars repossessed, credit cards getting denied, bank accounts frozen-"

"It's good to see you, too, Captain Cartwright," Sommers said through his best politician's smile. "Sit down and I'll explain everything."

"You'll explain it right now or I'll-"

"If you want your lives back, I suggest you sit down and listen!" Sommers said, his voice as hard as any drill sergeant's. Cartwright stood fuming for a moment, his fists balled at his sides then finally went to stand near the back of the room. The mercenary wasn't the type of man to sit when told. Sommers nodded and moved to the podium at the head of the rented hotel meeting room, Mason close behind him.

"Thank you for coming, gentlemen," Sommers said to the room.

"Not like we had much choice," one of the men grumbled.

Several others groused as well, their voices mingling to just shy of an angry mob before Sommers raised a hand and patiently waited for the din to subside.

"I have a mission for you. I regret the need to put your lives on hold, but I need assurance that all of you will be on board," Sommers said.

"Missions are our job, Senator," Cartwright said from the back, his arms folded over his chest. "Talk. You wouldn't be the first politician I've killed."

"Yes, but if you do that then none of you will get anything back, which is exactly what will happen if I don't make a phone call fifteen minutes from now. If you complete the assignment, not only will you get your credit, your accounts and your property back but you'll each be $100,000 richer," Sommers said.

"A hundred grand? Shit, I would've been in for that without the crap," another man said.

"What're you getting at, Sommers?" Cartwright asked.

"Gentlemen, you're going to accompany Mr. Mason and me into Area 187," Sommers said. The room went instantly quiet. Sommers looked around the room, letting his gaze settle on eyes that ran the gamut from bewildered to angry.

"That's Homeland's job," one of them said. "No way in hell I'm going in there, not for your lousy hundred grand."

Sommers leaned over the podium to look at the embroidered name tag on the man's chest at the same time he slipped his hand into his jacket pocket. "Mr. Goodwin, is it? Hmmm. That presents a problem," Sommers said as the room's door swung open and three large, dark-suited men entered, each carrying a silenced submachine gun in their hands. Two of them flanked the door, their weapons leveled at the unarmed men while the third moved to the front of the room beside Sommers. "This is Mr. Smith from the HR department. He's here to administer retirement benefits to anyone that refuses."

"Then who are those two?" Cartwright asked while he nodded at the door. He hadn't changed his posture though his voice carried a razor-sharp edge.

"Those would be *killers*, Capt. Cartwright," Sommers said. He looked back to Goodwin. "Are you still interested in discussing your retirement package, Mr. Goodwin?" The mercenary locked eyes with Smith's dark glasses then slowly shook his head.

"Cut the crap, Sommers. You went through an awful lot of trouble to get us here. What the hell do you want, and what the hell do you think's gonna stop me from putting a bullet in your head at my first opportunity?" Cartwright said.

"Greed, Captain. Simple greed mixed with a tinge of survival," Sommers said as he pulled the DVD from his jacket. "Mr. Mason, if you would please?" Sommers handed Mason the disc and nodded at the large television in the corner. Mason took the disc hesitantly, turned on the combination television/DVD player and slid the disc inside. The men watched the television despite themselves, none more closely than Cartwright. When it was done, Sommers spun his finger in the air at Mason, the universal symbol for "again". Mason restarted it and played the message a second time.

"That can't be real," one of the men said.

"I assure you it is," Sommers said. He nodded to Mr. Smith. "You can leave now. Take the others with you." The man returned the nod and left with the others. "Now, before you get any ideas, all of your names, addresses and the location of your various family members have been collected along with a copy of this message. Your group's detailed plans concerning your illegal, for-profit entry into Area 187 including documents, surveillance schedules and other highly incriminating evidence has been gathered and secreted. If anything happens to me or to Mr. Mason the information will be released directly to the attention of Secretary Fremont of Homeland Security. I don't think I need to tell you that Fremont hates profiteers, other than himself, as well as anyone outside his organization knowing the true identities and locations of survivors inside Area 187, such as those you now have intimate knowledge of."

"I didn't see anything..." Goodwin said as he came up out of his chair.

"Goodwin!" Cartwright growled from the back. Apparently

the man didn't carry the rank of Captain for nothing. "The rest of you, pipe down!" Cartwright said, heading off another wave of growling. He walked around the men to stand beside Sommers. "He's an asshole, but he's right. Homeland won't give a shit, and I'm pretty sure they'll take the Senator's word over ours. And I'm damn sure he's not bluffing." He turned to Sommers. "Okay, Senator, you just fucked us. Now you're going to tell us how we're going to get un-fucked."

"I'm glad you asked, Captain Cartwright," Sommers said.

"Is this the place?" Josephine asked softly as she looked out from behind the cover of the rusting bulldozer.

"Yeah, this is the place," Heath said. The scene before them looked like it could have been lifted directly from a Romero film. The late afternoon sun shined down on a swarm of hundreds surrounding a squat, two-story cement block building in the middle of nowhere, the two-lane blacktop path leading to it long ago overgrown and chunked to pieces. The air was filled with the familiar drone of a horde though far louder and more distinctive than Josephine had ever heard, setting her nerves on edge and her teeth to grinding.

"Why are they here?" Josephine asked.

"There's food in there. Or at least they think there's food." Heath pulled out his binoculars and scanned the throng. There were at least three generations of zombies represented.

"So that's the entrance, then?" Josephine asked.

"Yeah."

"This is bad. Do you think anyone's in there or they're just laying low underground?" Josephine asked.

"I'm willing to bet there's at least one pair of eyes inside the building. They've survived a hell of a long time in the Area. We're not dealing with a bunch of half-naked co-eds from a horror movie here. If they were stupid, they wouldn't be alive."

"So how are we going to get in? Do you think the lookout will let us in?" she asked.

"I'm still working on that. The door on this side is closed. It's bad for us, but good for whoever's inside. That there are so many out here and the door's closed means they can't get in."

"Eileen will recognize you," Josephine said. Heath gave her a blank look then went back to monitoring the zombies. "But can we focus on the 'bad for us' part? It'll be dark soon and I haven't seen a shred of cover for the last few miles…"

"We need a diversion to get them away from the building long enough for us to get in," Heath said.

Josephine stared at the mass of bodies and frowned. "Even if we had one that swarm's so big the leading edge of it would get to us before the back end would get two steps from the building. And what happens if they don't let us in?"

"I'm aware," Heath cut her off. "That swarm's been building for awhile, probably every zombie for ten miles. Somebody screwed up somewhere, got followed or something. You don't get a group this big without something alive in the middle of it." He widened his search with the binoculars, focusing them on a glint of light reflecting off the windshield of a pick-up truck hidden behind a patch of tall, dead weeds outside the clearing to the left of the building. He handed the binoculars to Josephine and climbed the bulldozer's tread, balancing his rifle across the seat. "Keep an eye on them."

"What are you doing?" Josephine asked as he sighted just below the far-off windshield.

"An experiment," Heath said as he touched the trigger. The silenced rifle's metallic pop could barely be heard over the undead chorus as the bullet punched through the truck's grill with a sharp, echoing crack. Josephine watched as a few of the zombies at the back of the horde closest to the truck turned towards it.

"Do it again," Josephine said. Heath shot again, this time putting out one of the headlights. The shattering of glass rang out and several more turned, breaking off into a smaller group and heading towards the sound. "Give it a few this time, a lot of noise in a short burst," Josephine said. Like lemmings, more of the swarm broke off from the building to follow the steps and moans of those closest to the truck. "It's working!"

"Don't count your chickens, there are still enough of them to surround both. The ones closest to the building will probably stay there. The edges will be more willing to move off," Heath said. There were easily a hundred of them forming into a new swarm to investigate the metal and glass sounds. Josephine scanned both swarms, her hopes deflating through the lenses. Even with that many breaking away, there were still at least three hundred more in a giant knot around the entry building.

"Is there anything else out there we can shoot?" Josephine asked.

"Nothing," Heath said as he watched the smaller horde. Josephine started casting about the open ground around the building, looking for anything else they could use as a diversion. That's when she saw several thick pine branches moving at the edge of a patch of woods far to the right of the clearing.

"Heath... we've got more company," Josephine said as she handed him the binoculars and pointed to the pines. Heath climbed down, positioned himself behind the machine's bucket and focused the binoculars on the trees. After a moment he found the bent boughs.

"Whoever it is, they're alive," Heath said.

"What?"

"Zombies don't stand around and watch. Whoever it is, they're doing the same thing we're doing; watching and trying not to be watched." A few moments later the boughs parted again, this time from opposite side of the same tree. "There's more than one."

"Who is it?" Josephine asked.

"Maybe a couple of them got caught outside when the swarm hit, or Homeland's getting ballsy."

"You think that's possible?" Josephine asked.

"That would depend on how many copies of the message you had that still had coordinates, or if they caught up to your boss or the guy that authenticated it for you."

"It wouldn't matter about Bill. He didn't have it," Josephine said.

"There are still other loose ends," Heath said. He pocketed the binoculars then checked his weapon. "Come on. We need to know who's over there."

Williams and Julie had reached the spot more than a half-hour ago, the early evening sun putting a garish red hue on the writhing pile of zombies clawing at the cement-block building. Neither spoke as they watched the literal hell on earth from the line of overgrown pines.

"What the hell was that?" Julie asked after a sudden, soft yet sharp metallic ping. A moment later the distant sound of breaking glass joined it over the droning of the dead. Julie pushed a thick bough down to get a better look.

"Somebody's shooting on the other side of the building," Williams said, looking over her shoulder. He moved around to the other side of the tree, parted the branches and settled his binoculars on the only scrap of cover to be had in the meadow; a rusty, faded-yellow bulldozer. "The shooter's on the move."

"Who is it?"

"I don't know but we'd better get to the horses. Even if we could get through that swarm and inside, I wouldn't want to until we find out who's over there," Williams said. The pair moved quickly through the trees, covering the distance to the old willow where they'd tethered the horses in just a few seconds.

"Are we going to try to find whoever it is?" Julie asked.

"It's too much coincidence that they left cover as soon as I noticed them. They're probably just as aware of us as we are of them." Julie pulled her pistol and started looking around them with just-controlled panic. "Easy… we don't know if it's bad guys or not. It could just be some survivors that got separated." He spared a moment to look at her more closely. She was sweating hard, the hair that ringed her pale face plastered to it in the cool evening air. "You okay?"

"Sorry, Howie… you get a little nervous after you get shot," Julie said as she wiped sweat from her forehead. "I'm fine."

"I can sympathize with that," Williams said as he stepped away from the horses, letting his eyes scan and linger across the thin stretch of woods around them. "Just remember, that piece you've got isn't silenced. If you use it, I can guarantee investigation." Julie looked down at her gun, frowned and then slid it back in her waistband to pull the stolen silenced rifle off Williams' horse. She'd never fired a rifle, but it was better than standing there with an undead siren in her hand.

Heath crouched low, moving silently across the dry leaves and deadfall. Josephine followed, her attention given completely to her feet. She'd learned a lot by watching Heath and imitating the way he walked and where he chose to put his feet, but this was different. If there were living people out there they'd be armed, hardened survivors that could hear a novice coming a mile away. Worse, they could be Homeland's elite Deadheads come to stop them. Either way, the crunch of dry leaves or the snap of a twig would easily give away their position. The still air and the absence of even birdsong would let sounds like that carry a long way off. Heath slipped up behind a thick, rotting tree lying on the ground and put his back to it while Josephine caught up to him.

Heath breathed slowly and deeply through his nose. "Horses." Josephine let out a mental sigh. If Heath was right, the chances of it being Homeland fell to almost nothing. Still, the presence of horses indicated a well-schooled survivor, perhaps even a predatory one. Heath leaned his rifle against the tree then rose up slowly, just enough to get his binoculars above the trunk. After a few moments he slid back down, put his binoculars away and took up his rifle. "Two... a man and woman with horses," Heath said.

"What do we do now?"

"We find out what the fuck they're doing here," Heath said.

"Just like that?" Josephine said, her eyebrows arching.

"I don't know the woman, but I know him." Heath pulled a small, smooth stone painted sky-blue from his pack then heaved it over the deadfall.

"What was that for?"

"I'm allergic to friendly fire," Heath said. Several moments later the stone soared back over the log to land just past his feet. Heath picked it up, brushed it off then put it back in his pack and stood. Josephine stood with him to look over the log at the pair of riders and horses less than twenty yards away. "That's Howard Williams... Jasper's nephew," Heath said, nodding at them.

"Oh my God..." Josephine whispered, her eyes like saucers.

"What?" Heath asked.

"Talk to me," Fremont said as he passed Agent Cline and sat down at the conference table. Warner poured a cup of strong black coffee and put it down in front of him. "Where's Sommers's bird been going?"

"Yesterday evening his plane departed New Castle, Pennsylvania, destination Toronto, Canada and turned right back around to New Castle, landed late this morning."

"Passenger list?" Fremont asked.

"A passenger by the name of 'Alex Smith' boarded in Toronto on a joint Canadian-U.S. waiver."

"Waiver?" Warner asked.

"It means he didn't have to go through security or customs. That's usually only used when transporting high-ranking officials or for those that neither government wants anyone to know about," Cline said.

"And something easy enough for a U.S. Senator to put through," Fremont said. He lit a cigarette and exhaled violently. "I warned that bastard to stay out of my way. I want to know who this Smith character is that is now so very close to my wall."

"Yes, sir!" Cline said, taking the assignment as his dismissal. Warner sat down to Fremont's right and opened a folder.

"She just stopped here, about fifteen minutes ago," Warner said, pointing the end of his unlit cigar to a red star on the map. Fremont glanced at it then took the newest satellite images from the top of the pile in the folder.

"What's there?" Fremont asked as he scanned the photos.

"A swarm." Warner pulled several papers and more pictures from the dossier. "Everything of interest to the river, Harry. I can't see anything there that we haven't used for artillery practice or that just doesn't have any real value," Warner said, shaking his head.

"Something here has value to someone," Fremont said as he flipped through the additional pages then went back to the photos. The last one caused him to pause. "That's a large swarm for nothing being there. Is this where she is now?" Fremont asked.

Warner looked down the bridge of his nose through his bifocals. "It's the vicinity anyway; probably why they stopped. They may be resting before they try to swing around the swarm."

"Why wasn't I notified of a swarm this large before now?"

"Harry, we didn't know about it till just now. You grounded all the flights, remember? We didn't see it till we had the satellite snap it," Warner said defensively.

"I want the focus on this swarm. If there's a change in any way, I want to know about it."

"Sure, Harry, but it's almost dark. We won't be able to see much until morning."

"Then I want pictures from first light. I'll be staying in the executive apartment upstairs. Bring them, my coffee and a pack of cigarettes by 06:30. For now, go help Cline."

"Sure, Harry," Warner said as he got up from the table. "We'll get 'em, Harry... all of 'em."

"What the hell are you doing here?" Heath asked Williams.

"What the hell are *you* doing here?" Josephine asked Julie. "Jesus Christ, Julie! I knew you were desperate for a break you didn't have to get on your knees to get..." Josephine started.

Heath held up a hand between the two women. "Later, girls. The men need to talk now." Both women turned their heads to him, their eyes daggers. "Me first. What are you doing here?" Heath asked Williams.

"We don't have time for long stories Heath, so here's the *Reader's Digest* version. Julie here is Senator Alan Sommers's daughter. Word leaked out about what you two were doing, and by means I'll explain later Julie and I ended up at Uncle Jasper's. We told him that Homeland knew what you two were up to and Uncle Jasper was going to come and warn you," Williams said.

"Old fool," Heath muttered, then, "Where's Jasper?"

"He was killed when Homeland raided the farm, looking for all of us. I promised him we'd find you. I don't know how much they know, but if they found the DVD after we left the farm..." Williams said.

Heath was taking it all in; Homeland, the death of one of his only friends, the new players in the game. "You saw the message?" he asked.

"Yeah... how else would we have known where to look?" Williams asked.

"I thought you said only one copy had the coordinates, that you hid it where no one could find it?" Heath said to Josephine.

For a moment her face looked stricken, but only for a moment. Then it shifted to boiling, red-faced rage as she spun on Julie. "You little fucking whore!" Josephine spat at Julie. Her fist flew out like lightning, catching Julie on the left side of her jaw. The blonde went down hard but to her credit didn't cry out. "What the hell did you do, Julie?" Josephine moved her left foot forward and brought her right up in what surely would have resulted in a kick to the downed girl's head if Heath hadn't caught Josephine around the waist and hauled her off her feet.

"Shut the fuck up!" Heath whispered in her ear.

Williams helped Julie stand then shoved her behind his back to keep the women separated. "Okay, they apparently have some *Oxygen* channel shit to work out," he said as he looked towards the meadow to see if the altercation had attracted attention.

"Jasper's dead?" Heath asked.

"He took a lot of them with him," Williams said, his voice solemn but his eyes glinting. "There's a lot more story than there is daylight. Think we can all concentrate on getting inside first?"

Heath turned his head and locked eyes with Josephine. Her face was contorted with rage, hate and a few tears.

"You think you can do that?" Heath asked Josephine.

"Yeah, I can do that," Josephine said as she stared at Julie. Julie wavered slightly but returned her stare and kept her aching jaw high. "But when this is over…"

"Enough. Whatever it is isn't as important as us getting inside before dark. There's too many of them out there for us to risk a night out in the open," Heath said. He looked back at Williams. He didn't know much about the man, other than he was Jasper's favorite nephew and that he'd been a crack shot Green Beret before becoming a grave robber. That would have to be enough for now.

"We're losing daylight, Heath. Any thoughts?" Williams asked. Heath looked at the horses.

"Yeah, I've got one," Josephine said. "We tie Julie to the bulldozer and whistle, and when they all come after her we just walk through the door."

"Any ideas that don't involve human sacrifice?" Williams asked.

"Yes," Heath said, his eyes still on the horses, then added, "at least, not human."

Julie looked between Heath and the horses. "What are you talking about?" Julie asked warily as she picked up her rifle from where she'd dropped it during Josephine's attack. Her eyes had become heavy now, giving her stare a more menacing look.

"We tie a horse at each of the two farthest points from the building to bait them away from the door. With any luck we can get the people inside to let us in and re-secure the place without the swarm knowing we got past them," Heath said.

"No." Julie said flatly.

Williams turned to her. "Julie… we have to do something. We can't just stand around here. Sooner or later the fringe of the swarm is going to forget why they're there and start wandering around. If they find us…"

"I don't care. I'm not sacrificing them like that. How would you feel if I tied *you* up and used *you* as bait, huh?" Julie asked.

"You have a better idea?" Heath asked the group. Williams looked away, Josephine continued to stare at Julie and Julie kept her defiant eyes on Heath. "This isn't up for a vote, people. We only have two plans on the table; mine and Josephine's." Heath said to Julie, "Who's the bait; you or the horses?"

"Both," Julie said as she grabbed her mount's saddle horn, put a foot in the stirrup and swung gracefully into the saddle leaving the rifle to lay across her leg with its muzzle pointed at Heath's chest, all in one motion. "I'll ride out there, get their attention and lead them away from the building while the rest of you sneak in. I'll be a hell of a lot faster than any zombie or any of you, so once you get the door open I'll come back around. At least the horses will have a fighting chance to get out of here if they're not tethered." Julie blinked away the sweat that was rolling into her eyes, afraid to take her hands off either reins or rifle with Heath standing so close.

"That's insane!" Williams said. "You could barely control it when we broke through a small swarm. Do you really think you're going to be able to do that with *hundreds* of them coming after you? Besides, look at you... you're swaying on your feet and sweating like a whore in church."

"Guess that's my problem, huh?" Julie said.

"Was she bit?" Heath asked, his hand resting on the butt of his pistol.

"No, shot. Some Good Samaritan along the way patched her up, but I'm wondering if it's gotten infected," Williams said.

Heath looked at him. "Time for 20 questions later," he said to Williams, then to Julie, "Look, this hero bullshit will be all fine and good when they make the movie, but it won't work. We're only going to have one shot to get in there before full dark comes on and I'm not willing to waste it. Besides, there are too many of them for one horse going in one direction. As slow as they move it would take half an hour at least to get all of them far enough from the building for us to get in without being spotted," Heath said, adding, "and if you don't find another direction to point that rifle I'm going to take it from you, shove it up Mr. Ed's ass here and pull the trigger."

Julie's jaw dropped slightly but she turned the rifle skyward, balancing the butt on her right thigh. "What about using both horses?" she asked. "We could herd them away from the building. You said yourself there are too many of them. Even if we tie the horses up, the swarm will still cover most of the meadow. But if we keep them moving, keep coaxing them, we can get the attentions of even the ones smashed right up against the building. With so much meat running around, they'd forget all about the building. Right?"

Heath turned to Williams. "She may have a point, especially if we can get some of them to go into the woods. You feel like playing cowboy?"

"Me?" Williams asked, holding up his hands in front of him. "Look, I was lucky enough to get here on that thing. You're talking about some pretty serious horsemanship here. I can't guarantee it wouldn't throw me off right at their feet again."

"Again?" Heath asked.

"Don't ask. All you need to know is I'd be more dangerous to us on a horse than off," Williams said.

"I've never been on a horse, but I've seen what happens to them when zombies are around. Sorry, Julie, but it looks like we're back to plan A," Heath said to her.

Julie opened her mouth to protest but Josephine stopped her by walking between Heath and Julie to the other horse.

"We had this discussion before, Heath," Josephine said as she swung into the unoccupied saddle almost as cleanly as Julie had done. "I'm not just another pretty face."

"What the hell are you talking about?" Heath asked.

"Pocahontas County junior rodeo champion, three years in a row," Josephine said as she reached down and adjusted the stirrups. "It would've been four but I placed second in the state barrel race championship that last year instead," Josephine said.

Heath shook his head. "This ain't a goddamn western..."

Williams caught the determined look from both women and held up a hand. "Tried that one already, Heath. It didn't work then, and I'm pretty sure it won't work now. Besides, it's probably our best chance to get as many of them away from the building as we can."

Heath was still shaking his head, although now the act resembled more resignation than negation. "The only other option is to maim the horses and bait them from the trees," Heath said. He looked up at the two women. "We'll try it, but I swear to Christ if it doesn't work your way, we *will* do it mine."

Chapter XVIII
Eileen

"You know this little plan has a high probability of getting them very dead, right?" Heath asked Williams as they followed the trotting horses back towards the meadow.

"Yup, and they know it, too," Williams said. They stopped a few yards behind the pines where Williams and Julie had spied on the meadow.

"How many?" Heath asked.

"I don't know, better than 300, maybe more."

"Not zombies; how many did Jasper take out?" Heath corrected.

"He was wounded pretty bad, made us leave while he covered our asses. I don't know the final count, but it was at least a dozen," Williams said. "There's something else I need to tell you…"

"It'll have to wait," Heath said as Josephine held her hand over her head. A moment later she dropped it and the two women launched their horses out from cover and into the meadow, screaming and calling to the swarm. The men crouched, watching as the women urged their mounts as close to the dead as the animals would go. "Goddamned fools…" Heath muttered as the horses got within ten yards of the rear of the swarm. The zombies at the fringe had already taken note and were coming towards the women where they held their prancing, nervous mounts. Once the dead on that side of the building started moving towards them in earnest the women parted, moving their skittish horses slowly around the building, their catcalls and shouts adding an odd, vibrant counter to the moaning swarm. Heath pulled up his binoculars and watched first Josephine then Julie.

"Your girl's not doing so well," Heath said. "Her face is red as a beet. You sure she wasn't-"

"No. Her feet got sliced up pretty good in the chopper crash and then she got shot in the shoulder. She could've picked up an infection."

"Chopper crash?" Heath asked, then "Nevermind, later." He turned the binoculars to the building in time to see a piece of a blind move in an upstairs window. "We have the attention of the residents, at least."

"Those two are making enough noise to wake... well, they're pretty loud," Williams said. He pulled out his own binoculars and started scanning the crowd. "It's working." The swarm started reversing their direction, from pressing against the building to moving away from it. Julie and Josephine had made a complete circuit of the building and were starting on their second, moving their skittish animals a little further out and widening their circular path as the zombies started after them. By the time they made their third swing around the building every zombie had noticed them, turning their compact knot into several distinct pockets that stumbled this way and that in trying to reach them. The zombies could hear the women now; no need for silent signals in the face of hundreds of wailing ghouls.

"Julie!" Josephine called out as they neared each other on their fourth pass. "Stay to that side! I need to pull this side to the north. A few more passes and the ones on this side may see the guys!" Josephine said, waving the other woman towards the far side of the building from where the men hid. Julie nodded and swung her horse around in a tight circle to concentrate on pulling that part of the swarm to the north and east. Even Josephine could see from her bouncing perch that Julie was having problems in the saddle. "Don' fall off that thing! If anybody's going to have the pleasure of killing you, it's gonna to be me!"

"Yeah... I'll keep that in mind..." Julie called out, her voice hoarse. She came about near the truck then paused long enough to vomit. Her strength was evaporating at the same rate her fever was growing. It was all she could do to stay horsed. She kept inching away towards the furthest edge of the meadow towards the bulldozer. They knew the two were out there now, and by moving slowly away from the building and in one direction the women could channel them where they wanted to go. Josephine made another partial circuit around the back of the building then rode around the other side, heading towards her.

"They're all out from the back!" Josephine said as she joined Julie. The swarm was coming straight for them now with perhaps thirty yards of flat, open ground separating them. From their higher vantage point they could look over the swarm back to the building.

"The back end is still too close to the door and we're out of pasture," Julie said as she fought her mount.

"We're going to have to get them into the woods," Josephine said as her horse reared. She controlled the beast and got its hooves back to the ground.

"We're just about out of light, too." Julie said. The sun had already started to set behind them, the woods at their back further diminishing the light. "I don't know if the horses will be able to pick their way through the trees without taking off at a full run and dumping us or breaking a leg."

"We don't have any options." The leading edge of the swarm was close enough now that the women could count their rotting, broken teeth and the horses were practically inconsolable in their terror. Josephine spun her horse then put heels to it, launching it behind the back of the dozer and into the woods beyond. Julie repeated the action, taking her horse around the front, past the bucket and into the low brush.

"Sonofabitch..." Williams said softly as the swarm went after the women. "They're trying to lead them into the woods."

"The farther away they can get the back end, the better their chances of swinging back to the door," Heath said.

"It's going to be pitch-dark soon... kind of a dangerous place to be - in the woods, on horseback, and with a few hundred zombies on your tail," Williams said.

"They knew the risks," Heath said. The men moved along the wood line until they could see the back of the building then slipped into the meadow, keeping the building between them and the back of the horde. There were no windows at the rear of the building to get the occupants' attention so they split up and slid around the sides to the front. At least 60 yards separated them from the last rows of zombies even as the front rows hit the woods to follow the horses, tripping and falling in tangles of limbs as their dead arms and legs tried to navigate the rough terrain. Heath stepped out from the front of the building just enough so he could see the window he'd observed earlier then pulled out his blue stone and lobbed it gently up towards the glass.

"I'm not serenading these people..." Williams whispered softly beside him as several slats were pushed down on the window blinds above. The last rays of the sun still lit the second story enough for them to see a head frantically shaking down at them. "Okay, maybe just one song..." Williams said with a nervous look over his shoulder. Heath pointed up at the face in the window then to the door. The blinds closed in response. "They're not going to let us in, are they?" Williams asked.

"I don't blame them. Cover me," Heath said as he pulled his pry bar from its sheath. Williams looked between the bar and the window, wondering which would raise the alarm first.

"Wait a minute... you pop that door and we may not be able to secure it again." Williams said.

"You got a better idea?" Heath asked. Williams looked up at the window then past it to the eave of the flat roof above.

"'Better' may be too strong a word," Williams said as he started around the building with Heath in tow. "Give me a leg up," Williams pointed to the large conduit pipe near the corner that ran down to a point about ten feet up the wall before it entered the building.

Heath saw his plan instantly and laced his fingers together. "You think that'll support you?" Heath asked.

Williams shrugged and put a foot in Heath's proffered hands. "You think we'll get in the door without breaking it down or having to kill someone inside?" Williams asked as he dropped his pack at Heath's feet. Heath returned the shrug then heaved upwards, sending Williams sliding up the rough wall to catch the pipe. Heath supported him until Williams was able to latch his hands securely around the pipe and his feet were braced against the wall. "Go for the door, it might be enough to bring him downstairs. See you inside," Williams said as he climbed up the pipe. Heath waited, inwardly cringing at the soft metallic squeaks from the pipe until Williams made it to the roof.

Williams moved across the roof and crouched low to look over the edge. The second floor window was just two feet below him. If Heath's diversion was enough, and Williams was lucky enough, the high window wouldn't be locked and he could slip in. If not he would have to hang off the eave, break out the window and climb inside, and the shattering glass would surely turn a few heads. Combined with leaving himself completely helpless to gunfire from within, he put that option at the bottom of the list then looked out over the field. Most of the swarm had already stumbled their way into the woods behind the bulldozer though there were still a few dozen that were either too slow or had been bound up by those ahead of them as they tried to make their way through the heavy thickets. If the dead did happen to notice what was happening behind them, though, it would take at least two minutes for the first of them to return to the building. He lay down on his belly with his arms and shoulders hanging down over the eave, making sure to keep his hands well above the top of the window while Heath went to work on the door below. Williams couldn't tell from his angle if the survivor had left the window so he kept watch on Heath, hoping Heath would give him some sort of signal that the survivor had gone down to the first floor to try and keep him from getting in. No one was more surprised than Williams when the window below him suddenly slid up and a rifle barrel poked out.

The un-silenced rifle barked before he could reach for it, but it wasn't pointed at Heath. Williams raised his head to see the front legs come out from under Julie's horse as she broke the tree line on her way back into the field, the horse and rider's forward momentum grinding them across the ground. Josephine broke into the meadow just then and had to cut her horse hard to the right to avoid trampling Julie and her downed mount.

"Take him out!" Heath shouted up to Williams as he put the building to his back and pulled up his rifle. Williams reached up and under the eave, wrapped his hands around the exposed end of a roof beam and swung his body over the edge. A man's voice cursed aloud as Williams kicked the rifle from his hands with one leg and found the bottom of the open window with the other. A moment later he was inside the building, his machine gun sweeping the large, dark, empty room. He didn't want to turn his back on the room's only feature, the stairwell leading down to the ground floor, but there was no time to clear the building now or even to check the stairs for the shooter. He put the safety of his backside in Lady Luck's hands where he usually kept it and turned back towards the window.

He could see Julie and her horse lying out in the meadow, both of them motionless. The shooter must have seen Julie coming out of the woods and had shot the horse out from under her to keep her from making it back to the building. The rifle's sharp report had been enough to gain the zombies' attentions and the two fresh bodies and Josephine's rearing mount had been more than enough to keep it. What had been first the head of the swarm and then the tail became the head again as they slouched and moaned in the deep dusk, turning back into the meadow towards them.

"Williams, get this fucking door open!" Heath called up. Williams looked down the building to see Heath moving into the meadow towards Julie's position, his rifle at his shoulder. Step, shoot, step, shoot; each hiss from his silencer felling whatever zombie had the misfortune of being closest to Julie, but Williams knew that couldn't last long. He left the window and started towards the stairs, ready to shoot anyone living or dead that stood between him and the door.

Josephine struggled to swing her horse's head back towards Julie. The animal was reaching the limits of its physical and psychological endurance. After several precious moments' struggle she managed to turn and race back. "Julie!" Josephine said as she tried to keep her horse's crushing hooves away. Julie's eyes opened slowly, barely registering the danger from Josephine's horse. She lifted her hand weakly then dropped it, the debilitation of the fever mixing with the equestrian crash leaching what little strength she'd had. "Oh no you don't, bitch! Wake up! Get up!"

"Get her or leave her!" Heath called out from behind her. She turned to see him firing into the lead line in the rapidly-reforming swarm, his steps carrying him slowly but steadily towards her. Josephine looked at the approaching zombies then down at Julie. Her eyes were closed but her chest still rose and fell.

"Shit!" Josephine barked. She knew there'd be no way she could control the animal from the ground. She considered trying to lure the zombies away again, but it was too late for that. Some may follow, but the presence of Julie, her horse's body and Heath would give the swarm plenty of slower targets to come after. "What the fuck do I do now?" Josephine called out as her horse suddenly reared up.

"Jump!" Heath ordered as he spun around to face her then fired as soon as she was clear of the saddle. The bullet pierced her horse through the eye, crumpling it instantly to the ground at the same moment Josephine herself touched down. "Is she alive?" Heath asked as he reached them and put his rifle over his shoulder.

"I think so," Josephine said. She let her anger at Heath's killing of the horse feed her, let it flow through her to power the cold part of her mind just as her adrenaline pumped through her muscles.

"Get her to the building, I'll get your gear," Heath said. He pulled a folding knife, leaned down and sliced the belly of Julie's horse open, then went to Josephine's and gutted that one, too. He freed the saddle bags from it while Josephine dragged Julie to her feet and wrapped Julie's good arm across her shoulders.

"Julie… you've got to help me. We have to walk," Josephine said into Julie's ear. Julie's head lolled back and her eyes opened to slits.

"I'm… sorry…" Julie wheezed.

"Save it… move your feet…" Josephine growled. She started moving, dragging Julie along towards the entrance building. Heath threw the saddlebags over his already-overburdened shoulder, pulled his pistol and started walking backwards behind Josephine and Julie.

"Move it! Don't look back!" Heath barked to Josephine. The first of the zombies reached the horses and fell upon them, their hands working into the cuts Heath had made. Within moments dozens of them were clawing at the fresh meat and at each other. The feeding frenzy served to slow their pursuers, with only those zombies on the furthest fringes choosing to follow the living prey as they stumbled towards the building. Heath aimed at one of the shambling silhouettes and fired. The body stumbled back a few steps from the chest impact then continued after them. "Fuck! Out of light and out of time! Tell me that fucking door is open!" Heath said over his shoulder as he holstered his pistol and pulled his bar.

"You go to hell for lying, right?" Josephine asked. Julie's feet were moving but not fast enough to outrun their pursuers. Heath put his back to the zombies and rushed up to take Julie's other arm over his own shoulder. The sudden act and the extreme height difference between Heath's and Josephine's shoulders brought Julie out of her stupor with a scream of pain.

"Oh good, you're awake… now fucking run!" Heath growled in Julie's ear.

"Shit!" Julie screamed as her feet started working. Heath took her arm from his shoulder, letting the women pick up speed as they hobbled at a much faster pace towards the dark splotch of the building ahead.

"Williams! The fucking door!" Heath called out again.

There was no time for careful stepping or even silence. Williams hit the first two steps then hopped the banister rail, hoping the man that had shot Julie's horse would be too preoccupied with keeping Heath out to take a shot at him. The floor rushed up and struck him hard but Williams managed to keep his feet, the thud of his landing spinning the survivor around from the door to face him. He was of average height with close-cropped, dark hair and a wiry, thin frame. He started to raise his large, automatic pistol until he realized he was already looking down the barrel of Williams' machine gun. "Open the door!" Williams barked.

"Fuck you!" the man said. He spun his head back to the door as Heath's fists pounded on it from the outside.

"Williams! Get this fucking door open!" Heath's muffled voice came from the other side.

"I said open the door- I'm not asking," Williams said. The man smiled at him and slid his gun into his holster.

"No," he said, still smiling, "you come open it yourself."

Williams kept the gun trained on the survivor for a long moment until he heard Heath's bar scraping against the steel door frame outside. "He fucks that door up and we're all dead." He stepped away from the door and swept his hand towards it. "It's all yours." Williams looked between the survivor and the door for a moment longer before he swore and ran to it. He kept the man covered with his gun in one hand while he worked at the bar and heavy sliding locks with the other. Williams took his eyes from him for just a moment to find a knee-level bolt and when he looked up again the survivor was gone. He shook his head then threw open the door to find Heath's pistol at level with his nose. Josephine pushed between the two men and dragged Julie into the building, collapsing to the floor with her at the foot of the stairs. Heath came in behind them, the leading rows of the swarm less than ten yards from the door. The men shoved the door closed, throwing its bolts and latches secure just as cold fists started pounding. Williams left Heath breathing heavy and resting with his back against the door while he joined the women on the floor.

"Is she bit?" Williams asked as he pulled out a flashlight and started examining Julie.

"If she was I wouldn't have dragged her ass in here," Josephine said. She slumped against the first few stairs, her breath coming in short, painful bursts as her lungs and ribs pushed against her bruised muscles. After a few breaths she sat up and looked at Heath. "Christ, I'm starting to sound like you now. I've got to get the fuck out of here."

Williams pulled off Julie's coat and inspected her limbs while the pounding of the zombies started coming from all sides, muted to a low, pulsing beat by the thickness of the walls. Even the moaning had been tamed to a point by the unyielding cinderblocks, losing some of its mournful pitch along with its volume.

"I don't think anything's broken but she's got a nice lump on the back of her head," Williams said.

"Couldn't have happened to a nicer whore," Josephine said. Williams shot her a quick, dark look then went back to his ministrations.

"That the bullet wound?" Heath asked when Williams' flashlight beam caught Julie's shoulder.

He nodded. "Homeland chopper; I tried to tell her she was as much a target as any of us but she wouldn't listen. If it wouldn't have been during gale-force winds it would have been a headshot," Williams said as he worked at the bandage.

"You did a piss-poor job of patching her up, then. There's some green in there," Heath said, referring to the soft yet pungent smell of gangrene coming from under the bandages.

"I didn't patch her up. It's a long story," Williams said as he finished exposing her shoulder. Bits of flesh around the wound had already become streaked with brown, black and green.

"Where's the shooter?" Heath asked as his eyes scanned the dark room.

"I don't know. He was right here when I got to the door but I took my eyes off him and he just vanished," Williams said. "Jesus, she's burning up," he added under his breath as he passed a hand over Julie's face.

"No one just vanishes. He probably slipped off down below. What's the situation upstairs?" Heath asked.

"Nothing, just a loft. Not much of a floor plan."

"This building's nothing but a front. All the goodies are underground," Heath said.

"So what do we do now?" Josephine asked as she stood then slumped against the wall. It'd been a long time since she'd been in the saddle, much less for a hard riding like the last hour had been. Her ass hurt as much as her side.

"We find the rabbit hole," Heath said, pulling his flashlight.

"Hold on a minute. Those people aren't going to just let us in, you know? They don't know who we are or what we want. We go ripping open doors and we're liable to get a bad reception." Josephine said. "We've come too far and are too close for stupid risks, right?" she asked, parroting Heath's own words. He looked at her for a moment then sighed.

"Maybe so. You have a better idea?" Heath asked.

"Give them some time to get used to the idea. If they don't get curious enough to send someone up in a little while, *then* we can start throwing open doors. You've waited this long. Let's just let it be a few minutes more, let it be their idea. Okay?"

Heath scanned the bare walls and the steel door for a moment. "Okay," Heath said. He dropped to his knees, dropped his pack and pulled out his medical kit. "We need to see to her before she dies on us," he said as he drew a hypodermic full of the powerful antibiotic. "I don't know if this'll do much at this stage of the game but it's worth a shot." He swabbed Julie's arm and stuck her with the needle.

Williams took the canteen Josephine offered him and offered Julie a sip. She took several, with at least some if it staying down. "Easy, Julie... no more for now," Williams said as he handed the canteen back to Josephine. She tucked it away while Heath set up his small lantern on the floor.

"I'm... sorry, Jo'... sorry..." Julie managed to say between cracked lips. Her eyes closed after the last word and her head lolled back into Williams's lap.

Josephine looked down at her with a mixture of anger, confusion and concern.

"Well, looks like we have a few minutes at least. Maybe we should put it to good use by you telling us these long stories?" Josephine asked, her eyes moving to Williams' face. "Let's start with her," she added, nodding at Julie.

"First off, she's not here because she wanted to be. I sorta kinda maybe kidnapped her a little bit," Williams said.

"A little bit?" Heath repeated without looking at Williams. His eyes were continually scanning the dark room and the small hallway that surely led to the access hole for the complex below. "Maybe you'd better start from the beginning."

Over the next ten minutes, Williams told them about Julie finding the disc and how she'd tried to parlay it into landing the top on-air job at the network. Josephine nearly drew her grandfather's revolver when Williams got to the part where her boss, Bill Hartman, had been beaten then taken away by Senator Sommers' goons. He told them about finding the disc in Julie's possession then kidnapping her when he knew the Senator would kill anyone except his own daughter to get it, and about ending up at Jasper's farm.

When he got to that point, Heath stopped him. "Why the hell did you go to your uncle's? You had to know you were bringing a world of trouble to his doorstep."

"For the same reason *you* went there; where the hell else was there to go?" Williams said. Heath nodded then looked at Josephine. Her eyes were wet and shined softly in the lantern's dim glow. "Heath, Uncle Jasper made me promise to find you, but not just to warn you about Homeland. He wanted me to tell you something else. It may be kind of a private thing, though…" he said, trailing off with a look towards Josephine. She caught his gaze and returned one with an edge made all the harder by her tears for his uncle.

"I can go upstairs," Josephine said as she wiped at her face with the back of her hand and turned to the steps.

"No. Stay. If you want to, that is," Heath said. Josephine

looked at him for a moment then turned back to the room. Williams looked between the two of them before he continued.

"He wanted me to tell you he was sorry for all this," Williams said after a long pause.

"*Jasper* was sorry about this? This didn't have anything to do with Jasper," Josephine said. "None of this was his fault..."

"Actually, it sort of is," Williams interrupted. For a long moment, the only sounds to be heard were the constant wailing and pounding of the dead outside.

"Talk," Heath said.

Williams swallowed hard then continued. "Jasper Connelly was a man of his word. If he made a promise he kept it, regardless of what he had to do or say, or not do or say, to see it was kept." Williams said. He stopped for a moment then shook his head ruefully. "You know, I've been rehearsing this in my head for days now, playing out the scenarios. I gotta' tell you, a few of them didn't turn out so well." He reached into Julie's discarded jacket, found the bottle she'd taken from the barn and took a healthy taste.

"Say what you came here to say," Heath said. Williams offered Heath the bottle and waited until he took it.

"Heath, Jasper knew about the message before you did... even before Josephine did. But he made one of his promises, and you know how Uncle Jasper was with his promises." Williams' voice trailed off just then, and he desperately wished he hadn't surrendered the bottle so quickly.

"My God..." Josephine said, her voice barely a whisper over the swarm outside. Heath simply stood there, staring at Williams. "Jasper was the one that brought the message out, wasn't he, Howard? He was the one that brought it to me..."

"Uncle Jasper got into some trouble on his last run and the people here saved him. Getting their message out was the most they would accept from him in payment."

"But that doesn't make any sense! Why would he do that? He had to know who Eileen was at the very least! Why wouldn't he have brought her out, or at least get Heath?" Josephine asked, her voice rising with each question. Heath didn't move, didn't breath, didn't break Williams' stare.

"Because she refused to leave unless the rest were going, too. Jasper knew there was no way to get them all out, not without getting most or all of them killed. He was too old to be in here himself, much less be responsible for rescuing a bunch of others to boot," Williams said.

"What else?" Heath asked. Both Williams and Josephine turned their heads to him now.

"What do you mean, what else?" Josephine asked. Williams looked away before he spoke again.

"Eileen. Jasper told her about Heath, how he'd looked for her all those years. Eileen didn't want Heath risking his life to come back here again, for any reason... even for her. Not after spending all that time searching for her. She made Uncle Jasper promise he wouldn't tell Heath he'd seen her, that he'd get the message to someone Jasper thought could help them. Jasper kept his promise to Eileen, but he knew if anyone had any chance of rescuing everybody without Homeland carpet-bombing the whole place it would be the great John Heath."

Heath's eyes focused sharply on Williams' at his last remark, narrowing like a cobra's before slowly returning to their normal shape.

"So Jasper got the message to me..." Josephine said. "He knew that I wouldn't just turn the disc over to the authorities, because I'd do anything for a story like that, even bring Heath into it." She looked down at Julie then put a hand over her face. "Christ... I'm no better than she is."

"He was *counting* on you bringing Heath into it," Williams said. "That way he could keep the promise he'd made to Eileen *and* get word to Heath that she was still alive." Williams leaned back against the staircase and started brushing the sweat-plastered hair away from Julie's forehead. "Jasper had a real soft spot for survivors. He hated to leave any of them to rot. He always did what he could for them." He chuckled softly to himself. "You know, it's ironic, really. Jasper always said he wanted to take as many with him as he could when he went. If this thing works, if we all somehow manage to get out of here and Josephine's story breaks, Jasper will have taken them *all* with him."

Suddenly, Heath was moving.

"John! Where are you going?" Josephine asked, her tongue almost tripping over her seldom use of the man's first name.

"Eileen! Eileen Heath!" Heath shouted as he stormed down the short hall. Josephine shot after him, her flashlight beam bobbing against Heath's back as he gained the only other room on the ground floor. "Eileen!" Heath screamed to the room, as if he could bring her into being through nothing more than his will alone.

Josephine bounded into the room behind him. "Heath! Stop! Please..." Josephine said.

Heath dropped to his hands and knees to crawl across the floor, his fists pounding against the cement. "Damn it! Give me my wife! Eileen! Eileen Heath!" Heath continued.

Josephine could do nothing more than stand in one spot and taste her tears as they rolled down her face. "Heath... please... back off... let them open up to us..." Josephine said.

Heath crawled a few feet farther away then stopped abruptly when the slap of his flesh and bone against the cement floor produced an unexpected echo. He pounded on the spot again then jumped to his feet. "Give me my wife or so help me I'll break it open and drag every last one of you out of there and feed you to 'em!" Heath roared as he stomped repeatedly on the spot.

"Heath!" Josephine said as she rushed forward and tried to drag him away. "Heath, please! We're here to help them!" Heath turned on her suddenly, shoving her away.

"You're here for your fucking story! I'm here for my wife!" he said. "You get yours and I'll get mine!" Josephine managed to angle her light up and gasped as it caught the murder in Heath's eyes. He turned back to the floor and drew his pistol. "Open up or I'm blowing the door apart!" Heath screamed at the floor.

Before she realized what she was doing, Josephine had her steel pry bar in her hand and was moving across the floor towards him. She swung low and caught Heath at the top of the calves just below the backs of his knees. The blow took him by surprise, buckling his legs and sending him to his knees. Heath raised his pistol just as Josephine stepped in front of him. She looked down the trembling barrel, her flashlight beam splashing across his heaving chest and reflecting up into his contorted face. "John, look at yourself! Do you want Eileen to see you like this? It's been too long... don't let her first sight of you after everything the two of you have been through be this..." she said.

Heath stared up at her for a moment before he let his arms fall slowly to his sides and his head slump to his chest. "I just want Eileen..." Heath said softly. Josephine took a few steps back then sat down with the seamless trapdoor between them.

"I know," Josephine said. Just then, thin lines of light shined up at them, marking the edges of the concealed door set into the floor.

Heath kneeled there motionless before the trapdoor as it opened just enough for a pistol barrel to poke out.

"Who are you?" a man's voice said from under the door. "How do you know Eileen?"

"Is she here?" Heath asked. Josephine breathed a mental sigh of relief as his face slid back into its usual, unreadable mask.

"I asked you first," the voice said.

"I want to see my wife. Now." Williams walked silently into the room just then, his pistol in hand, and drew a bead on the spot of light coming from the floor. "Is she here?" Heath asked again.

"What's your name... your first name?" the voice asked.

"John." Heath was doing well at keeping his hands at his sides and his fingers from curling into fists, but Josephine could tell by the sound of his voice that seven years of hell was about to be unleashed on the man in the hole.

"We got your message... the one you recorded. Jasper brought it to us," Josephine said. The pistol withdrew and the door closed to almost nothing as soon as Josephine uttered her first word. Apparently the man hadn't realized there was someone in the room with Heath.

"Get away from the door, all of you... against the far wall under the window where I can see you," the man said from under the floor. Heath and Josephine exchanged looks before he got up and motioned Josephine to the wall with him. Williams crouched in his place and slid most of his body back through the doorway. The survivors below weren't taking any chances, and neither was he. Once they were against the wall, the trapdoor swung open and the voice's owner climbed out of the floor to face them. Williams was glad to see it wasn't the same man that'd shot Julie's horse. The survivor kept his revolver leveled at Heath. If he saw Williams hiding in the doorway and out of the thin light coming up from below he didn't show it.

"You're John Heath? The *real* John Heath?" the man asked.

"Where's my wife?" Heath asked.

"I'm Phillip... Phillip Desmond." he said.

"I didn't ask who you were."

Josephine risked a step forward and held out her hands to show they were empty. Desmond had no idea the powder keg he was playing with. Phillip swung the gun towards her.

"Phillip... we're here to help you... all of you. We got your message... Jasper gave it to us," she repeated.

Phillip looked at her for a moment. "Is Jasper with you?" Phillip asked. He looked towards the doorway as if looking for Jasper and finally saw Williams and his weapon.

"Don't do it," Williams said. Phillip froze with his head facing Williams and his revolver still pointed at Josephine.

"Jasper's dead. He died trying to keep Homeland from finding out where you were hiding. That's his nephew, Howard," Heath said.

"Hey," Williams said by way of a greeting, bobbing his barrel to Phillip as if it were waving his hand in a friendly salute. Phillip lowered his gun and let it hang at his side. Williams kept his weapon trained on the survivor until Heath nodded at him.

"We should all get below. We have a lot to talk about," Phillip said.

"I'll go get Julie," Williams said then disappeared into the front room.

"How many of you are there?" Phillip asked.

"Four. Now where the hell is Eileen?" Heath asked. Phillip looked nervously over his shoulder at the open trap door just as Williams came back into the room with Julie in tow.

"Is she bit?" Phillip asked.

"No, she has a bullet wound that's infected," Williams said.

"All right then... I'll go first and you can hand her down to me," Phillip said as he stepped onto the first rung of the ladder leading down into the shelter.

"Phil!" Heath barked as he closed the distance to the hole in two strides. "Where the fuck is Eileen?" Phillip looked up at him and sighed.

"We'll talk when we get inside. I'm a doctor, so is Richards. We need to get your friend patched up before she dies on us," Phillip said.

Heath opened his mouth to speak but stopped when Josephine laid a hand on his arm. "Heath, please... we need to build their trust, and if you snap his head off it'll make it that much more difficult." She left him as Phillip disappeared below the level of the floor so she could help Williams lower Julie down into the shelter. Williams followed after Julie, then Josephine. Heath stood rigid, listening to the pounding fists and moaning corpses outside for a moment before he followed them, closing the trapdoor behind him.

Heath followed the rest down a short hall and into the large chamber at its end. Less than a dozen men and women were there, some sitting at a large table towards the back while others stood or sat in various places around the room. All of them were armed. Heath scanned the room quickly, taking a head and weapon count as he followed the rest to the table. Eileen's face wasn't among them.

"Lay her down," the man Heath recognized from the message as Dr. Richards instructed them. Williams and Phillip hoisted her onto the table as gently as they could while Richards turned on a light over the table. "What happened to her?" Richards asked as he started his cursory examination.

"She was shot... the wound's infected," Phillip said, pointing to her shoulder. Richards looked at the new faces around the table and nodded at them.

"I'm afraid the introductions will have to wait," Richards said as he frowned at Julie's wound. Her head was tossing now as she mumbled "I'm sorry" softly, feverishly and repeatedly. Richards looked up from the table and caught Heath's gaze. "You're John Heath, aren't you?"

"Thought you didn't have time for introductions," Heath said, then "Where's my wife?"

"Phillip... I'll see to this," Richards said, looking at his friend. Phillip nodded his head slowly and walked away from the table. Josephine and Heath followed while Williams remained at Julie's side. "I'm sure you're tired. We have food and water-"

"I'll stay right here, Doc," Williams said. Richards shrugged and went to his work while Phillip led Heath and Josephine to the other side of the room.

"I know you have a lot of questions..." Phillip began.

"No; just one that I'm getting really tired of asking," Heath said. Phillip sat down on a wooden bench against the wall and waved for them to sit as well. Josephine sat on an upturned plastic milk crate. Heath remained standing, looming over Phillip. Phillip sighed and leaned his head back against the wall, his eyes closed.

"I've known Eileen for... well, since before this all started. We were researchers in the same department..." Heath's hands suddenly shot down to grab Phillip by the shirtfront then heaved his body against the wall, his feet dangling uselessly above the floor.

"Fucking *answer me!*" Heath said. Josephine jumped to her feet and grabbed Heath's shoulder as the rest of the room erupted in shouts and the sounds of various firearms cocking, chambering and sliding. Williams looked up from the table, brought his machine gun to his shoulder and fixed it on the largest grouping of survivors in the room. Only a few barrels turned towards him. The rest remained on Heath and Josephine.

"Here I thought we were all getting along so well..." Williams said. He caught Richards out of the corner of his eye. The doctor was still working on his patient though his head shook sadly.

"All of you... calm down!" Richards said without looking up from his scalpel as it deftly trimmed away bits of infected flesh from Julie's wound. The man Williams had encountered upstairs appeared with another survivor from a doorway at the other end of the room, both with weapons raised. Williams immediately reset his sights on the men and thumbed the switch on his weapon to its full-auto setting.

"Heath! Put him down!" Josephine pleaded as she pulled on him with all her strength. She might as well have tried pulling a live oak out of the ground. Heath didn't budge, completely ignoring her and the multitude of muzzles pointing at him from around the room.

"Everyone! Please! Put your guns away!" Phillip called out to the room, his eyes locked with Heath's. "John... there's no easy way to say this... Eileen's gone. She was killed two weeks ago... I'm sorry, John... so sorry..." Phillip said as tears formed in his eyes. Heath kept him locked there for a moment before his fingers seemed to simply lose their grip, leaving Phillip to slide down the wall while Heath stumbled back as if hit by an invisible fist to the gut.

"How?" Heath said. Josephine stood beside him. Her hand was poised over his shoulder ready to give him comfort, but it wouldn't budge. She stood there, horrified, her tears as real as Phillip's as her hand hovered inches from Heath.

"She was out with a hunting party... that's when the swarm outside started, followed them back here... she didn't make it inside... my God, John... I'm so sorry..." Phillip said.

"No..." Heath said softly.

"Yes..." Phillip said. "She's not one of them... she didn't suffer..." Josephine's hand finally came to rest on Heath's arm. Heath shook her off, turning his body to the side and stumbling as if drunk.

"Heath... please... sit down..." Josephine said, not knowing what else to say. Heath stared at her under heavy, half-closed lids. Josephine shuddered at his stare as Jasper's words came back to her on the disposition of Heath's soul.

"Everyone, please..." Phillip said to the crowd again. Everyone except Williams' targets hesitantly put away their weapons. "Craig, Scott... you too." Phillip said.

"Not as long as that one's got a gun pointed at my head!" Craig, the man in the doorway, said. Scott nodded behind him in his usual hanger-on style. Williams slowly lowered his barrel and Craig and Scott lowered their guns as well.

"What happened to her?" Heath asked. His voice was barely above a whisper though it cut through the ears of the room like a rusty razor. "*How* did it happen?" Phillip looked up at him and wiped his eyes on his shirt sleeves.

"The swarm got her..." Phillip said. He paused a moment, waiting to see if his explanation would be enough. He could tell from the look in Heath's eyes that it wasn't. "Eileen, Craig, Scott, Bill and Esther..." Phillip said, nodding towards a tall, lean bald man sitting on a nearby bench beside an overly short black woman, "... they were out hunting and they stumbled into a small group of them over by Ridgeview. That's a little town a few miles south of here. We knew there were a lot of them in the region when we found the place but we had no idea how many. Those drew more. By the time they got back to the Number Two door there were more of them waiting, drawn in from the north and west. They had to fight their way through them to get back inside. Eileen didn't make it. You have no idea how truly sorry I am," Phillip said. Heath stood swaying slightly, his head low.

"That ain't how it happened..." Esther said, shaking her head.

"Esther... don't..." her companion, Bill, said beside her.

"No!" Esther said, jumping up from the bench suddenly. She spun and pointed a finger at Craig. "I'm tired of having to coddle this asshole! Eileen was too good for what happened to her..." Esther said.

Heath turned to Esther and repeated his question. "What happened to Eileen?" Heath asked. Before Esther could respond, Craig was stalking across the room towards them followed closely by Scott. Both still had their weapons in their hands. Williams pulled a bead back on the two men and stepped away from the table.

"You wanna' know what happened to Eileen? She got sloppy, that's what happened to her," Craig said. He was much closer now, but his instinct for self-preservation kept him outside of Heath's reach. "Scott was there, too. She got sloppy, didn't she, Scott?" Craig asked over his shoulder at his partner.

"Yeah... sloppy," Scott agreed. He noticed Williams' weapon pointing at them and started to raise his own but stopped when Williams stopped swinging his muzzle between him and Craig and left it squarely on his chest alone.

"Bullshit. You're the one that got sloppy," Esther said. Craig turned to her, his lips curling into a snarl. Bill stood and put a hand on the knife at his belt and Craig took a step back.

"Don't fuck with me, Bill... I'll shoot your ass right here and make sandwiches," Craig said.

Esther turned back to Heath. "Eileen was a friend, a good friend. She told me a lot about you, said you were one of the good ones. It wasn't till we met Jasper and he told us about how you've been lookin' for her all this time that I really believed her." Esther said. Bill put a hand on her shoulder and tried to pull her back towards him. "No, Bill... if it was me, wouldn't you want to know what *really* happened?" Esther asked. Bill left his hand on her shoulder, but now it was for support.

"Yeah yeah... we've all heard about you. Eileen wouldn't shut up about you. Guess you should have stuck it out with the rest of us in here just a little while longer, huh?" Craig said.

"She's dead 'cause of *your* dumb ass!" Esther barked. "We were making a pass through town for supplies when they spotted us. Phillip was right on one thing; by the time we got to the back door there were more waiting for us. We managed to get through them and get to the door. Bill and me were the first ones inside. Eileen was right behind us and Craig behind her. Craig dropped his pack a few feet before he got inside and wouldn't go back for it. But Craig had been the one that went into the drugstore and Eileen didn't want to lose anything he found in there, so before we knew what was happening she went back for it. By the time I got to the door they already had hold of her. But she didn't scream, John... she didn't scream. Not once," Esther said, as if complimenting the late Eileen Heath.

"It's a hard life. She knew the risk." Craig said with a shrug.

"Yeah, real hard," Esther said. "Now why don't you tell him what was in your pack?" Craig shot her an icy look and tightened his lips and his grip on his gun. "Well, I'll tell him. I'm the one that killed Eileen. I had to, John; they were just tearing her apart. I didn't want her to suffer," Esther said. Her eyes were moist, but years in the Area had hardened her past true tears. Heath nodded slightly but kept staring at her. "After... when she was gone, she dropped Craig's pack. It was full of booze... not medicine or bandages but fuckin' *booze*!" She spun on Craig again and spoke through clenched teeth, "She died for a sack of fucking booze! *Your* booze, Craig! You could have told her not to go back, that it wasn't anything we needed... but you didn't, did you?"

"She didn't ask," Craig said.

"Oh Christ..." Josephine whispered. Heath staggered towards Craig. Craig tried to raise his gun but Heath wrapped a meaty hand around Craig's wrist and dropped his thumb in the space between the weapon's hammer and frame, keeping it from falling on the round. With a twist of Heath's wrist, Craig's gun, an almost perfect twin of Heath's own sidearm, hit the floor while Heath's other hand found the man's throat. Craig dropped to his knees as Heath's fingers cut off both blood and oxygen. Scott made to raise his weapon to Heath's head.

"Don't do it..." Williams warned Scott from across the room. Scott's head swiveled to Williams. The survivor's face carried the expression of a child caught with his hand in the cookie jar as he froze.

"I'm going to feed you to them, piece by fucking piece..." Heath said as Craig's eyes bulged and his face turned shades of blue.

"Leave him be!" Esther shouted in Heath's defense as the room erupted once again, though there were far fewer of them drawing weapons in Craig's behalf. "The bastard deserves it!"

"No! John… stop! You don't know what you're doing!" Phillip scrambled to his feet. He raised his pistol, intending to bring the butt down on the back of Heath's head. Josephine's reflexes were quicker than her thoughts as she pulled her bar and swung it upwards to smash against Phillip's gun. It flew back against the wall as Phillip stumbled back, cradling his hand. Richards grabbed a wad of rags and shoved them over Julie's wound then grabbed Williams' hand and placed it over them.

"Keep pressure on that or she'll bleed to death," Richards said as he left the table. Williams looked down at Julie's bleeding shoulder and back to Scott again. He dropped the machinegun on its sling against his chest and used one hand to stuff the rags against Julie's wound while the other drew his pistol on Scott. Richards shot across the room to stand behind Craig's kneeling, gasping body. "John… you can't do this. You don't understand! Don't make me have to order you shot!"

Josephine drew her revolver in response and held it at the doctor's eye level. "And don't make me shoot you, either, Doctor," Josephine said.

"Listen to me! Craig is vital to our survival, maybe to the survival of the world! You can't kill him!" Richards said.

Heath turned his murderous look on Richards. "He has eight seconds left to live. You've got seven to convince me."

"He's the one I spoke of… the one immune to the virus. He's infected, but he's not dead. Don't you see? He could be the only source for a true vaccine!" Richards said.

Heath looked down at Craig. The man's eyes had turned to slits and his pallor was a dark blue. He relaxed his fingers and Craig collapsed to the floor, gasping and retching. "If you're lying to me…" Heath said.

"No… it's true," Richards said as he dropped to his knees and checked Craig's pupils and throat. Then he reached down and rolled up Craig's left pant leg. A blackened wound the size of an open human mouth peeked up at them. "On the message… this was what I promised; hope. He's our only chance with Homeland to get us all out of here as well as a hope for the world should the virus ever get out."

Josephine slowly lowered her gun and stared at the wound as Craig started coughing and sputtering on the floor. Craig's injury was almost a twin to the one Heath carried on his back.

Heath turned away from them and stumbled towards the hall leading to the surface building. Phillip moved to block Heath's path but Josephine shot the doctor a look and he let Heath pass unmolested. Anyone or anything that tried to introduce itself into Heath's world right now ran the risk of being mowed down by the maelstrom brewing behind his eyes. Josephine watched him go as Richards helped Craig to his feet.

"I'm... I'm going to... kill that fucker..." Craig said, making a point of picking up his magnum as he rose. Richards opened his mouth to speak but Williams' voice cut him off.

"Hey, Doc, she's really bleeding over here!" Williams said. With a warning look to Craig, Richards headed back to the makeshift operating table.

Craig sneered at Josephine then spat a wad of blood-tinged phlegm at her feet. "Your boyfriend's a dead man."

"He dies, you die," Josephine said, her gaze turning coldly on him.

"Hey, if I die so does everybody else here. You just remember that," Craig said. He looked Josephine up and down then looked at Williams over his shoulder before turning back to Josephine. "You guys sure as hell aren't Homeland or military. Just what the hell do you think you're going to accomplish here?" Craig asked. He cleared his throat several times then spit another wad of phlegm on the floor.

"No, we're not. That's why you're all still alive. I'm a reporter..." Josephine started to say. Craig laughed hard at that.

"Hey! Did you hear that, everybody?" Craig shouted hoarsely, turning in a circle to address the room. "She's a fucking *reporter*! Goddamn Walter Kronkite with the sweet ass come to save us all! Oh, praise be to you! I got just one question for you, sweet-tits; just how the hell are you gonna do that, huh? Looks like we just saved *your* asses, don't it? Unless you've got an army and choppers, you're worthless. So, what… you saw the message and just waltzed in here for a bit of man-on-the-street bullshit? Does Homeland even know?" Craig asked.

A large, tattooed bald man sitting nearby turned on his chair and looked at Josephine. "Yeah… if you got the message, why didn't you get it to Homeland? They're the only ones that can help us."

"See? Even a moron like Jeff figured it out," Craig said. Jeff half-stood with his fists balled before he stopped, took a breath and sat back down. "That's right, Jeff. You fuckers *need* me, and I don't need a single one of you. I could walk out of here right now and leave all of you to rot. But I'm a good guy. I've stuck it out here with you. I'm the only way we're getting' out of here." Craig took a step closer to Josephine and smiled. "If you play your cards right, I might even get you out of here, too."

"Once we get out and my story hits the air…" Josephine started.

"You've got to be shitting me! What? You're going to do a fucking *story* on us and that's gonna make it all better?" Craig asked.

"If Homeland knew where all of you were hiding, they'd just bomb this place," Josephine said.

"And lose a guy that's immune to the virus? Honey, I'm our only ticket out of here. But since you didn't get the message to Homeland, I guess we're going to have to come up with something else, huh? Congratulations, you just killed us all, you fucking bitch!" Craig said then walked out of the room.

Phillip came up beside Josephine and watched Craig walk away. "I guess we have a lot to talk about. I'm afraid to say it, but Craig has a point," Phillip said. "Exactly how does your being here help us?"

"You don't understand. Homeland doesn't care about survivors. They'd rather kill all of you than risk stirring up the pot," Josephine said.

"We've already heard that. But we have Craig, for all his… well, he's certainly not my favorite person. But if Homeland would've got the message they would've been curious enough about his immunity to at least investigate if for nothing else than to find out how we had electricity and technology enough to make the disc." Phillip said. Josephine shook her head.

"People have already been killed over this. And Homeland *does* know about you, and us. They're the ones that shot Julie and killed Jasper. If they knew about Craig, he'd be the only one to survive. He's right about another thing; they don't need the rest of you, he'd be the only one they'd want," Josephine said.

"I think everyone needs some time to cool off. Come on, I'll introduce you around and show you the place after I see how Dr. Richards is doing. It looks like you're going to be here for awhile. We can talk more about what you have in mind," Phillip said.

"Being here for awhile isn't the plan," Josephine informed him.

"Unless you've got a way to get everyone through that swarm or the one at the Number Two door, your plans will have to change. It looks like you and your friends are just as trapped as we are."

Chapter XIX
Ellen

It'd taken the better part of an hour for Phillip and Josephine to tell their condensed stories. In that time Josephine had managed to convince Phillip that if Homeland had received the message they'd all be dead, with perhaps the exception of Craig. That done, the two turned to more local and immediate concerns.

"How big is this place?"Josephine asked. Phillip had shown her a few of the smaller chambers in the underground shelter while they'd walked and talked. Most had been converted into dorm-style rooms for the group with others set aside for storage.

"There's the common room, the kitchen, six dorm rooms that hold six or eight each, a few private quarters and a couple of offices. There's a tool room and workshop along with the generators and water tanks by the Number Two door. A lot of us, at least what's left of us, came here from a hospital about fifteen miles south of here," Phillip said as he led her into a large office that had been converted into a meeting room.

Josephine sat down at the large table in the center of the room while Phillip poured two glasses of water. "What do you mean, 'what's left'? I thought there were more than 30 of you here."

"There were, when the message was recorded at least. Eileen and her group weren't the only ones that had been out when the swarm hit. That's how we managed to have a swarm at the main door as well as the second. What you saw out in the common room is just about all that's left of us." Phillip sipped at his water and looked around the room. "This place was like a gift from heaven. By rationing the fuel for the generators we've been able to make it last. We started off with about 10,000 gallons of treated diesel in a storage tank, and after a year we still have better than three-quarters of it left. The water tanks draw from underground springs, so as long as we have power we'll practically never run out of water."

"What about food?" Josephine asked.

"I'd have thought the bastards would've destroyed all their little Senatorial sanctuaries, but apparently they missed this one. Our Congressional benefactors really took care of us, though. I've only seen one other Cold War-era shelter, over near Conroy. But that one had been bombed into a crater. Anyway, we still have a ton of dehydrated foodstuffs and MRE's that came with the place. We try to save those and use them only when we run out of the more conventional supplies. Unfortunately, most of the medical supplies stocked in the infirmary were virtually worthless. The medications hadn't been stocked since the mid-90's and had mostly gone inert by the time we got here, but nothing's perfect, right?" Phillip said with a wry smile.

"I should find Heath and see if he's okay," Josephine said. She'd been thinking about the nearly identical wounds Heath and Craig each bore. It seemed Heath would have another story to tell once he got through his shock.

"About that..." Phillip stopped, unsure how to continue. He spun his water glass in slow circles on the table, his eyes locked on it. "Is he... *stable*?" He asked cautiously.

"The man just learned that the wife he searched five years for out there in the middle of zombie nowhere was killed just a couple of weeks before he found her, and the man that got her killed may be the only hope for a vaccine for the virus. He doesn't have *her*, he can't kill *him* and he's back in the Area," Josephine said then sipped thoughtfully at her water. "Yeah, he's more or less stable."

Phillip cocked an eyebrow and looked at her for a moment before resuming his water glass play. "How long have you been in the Area, Josephine?"

"Please, it's Jo'. And I've only been here a few days. Seems like forever, but just a few days."

Phillip nodded then sighed. "It's like a war zone, Jo', this place. You don't know if you're going to live to the next minute. We got lucky, finding this place, but we weren't always so lucky. Eileen and me, I mean. Like I said, we'd been together since the first zombie walked into our lives. Of course, I knew about John from Eileen long before the outbreak from us having worked together. Then Jasper came along and told us how he'd gone AWOL the day our research center got overrun and burned down. We saw the rescue choppers coming but we were already outside and being chased and couldn't turn back. We didn't know that John was with them. He missed us by half an hour at most." Phillip's glass stopped twirling and he eyed her. "Don't tell him that, please."

"I won't. He doesn't need to hear something like that," Josephine said.

"Anyway, Eileen and I moved around a lot for the first two years. We tried to get out when they were building the first fences, but every time we got close they'd shoot at us or ignore us. We figured out early on that we were all stuck here, whether it was for government reasons or they feared any survivor that hadn't been extracted in the first few days could now possibly carry the virus. I've seen a lot of people get infected. If the damn thing had gone airborne there wouldn't be any of us left alive right now." Phillip stopped and took a breath. "Sorry, bit of a tangent there."

"It's okay." Josephine was a master interviewer, but it didn't take someone with her skills to see that Phillip was maneuvering around something; something he both did and didn't want to say. "There's something else, isn't there?" She tried to prepare herself and vowed that if there were more to the story, she would be the one to tell Heath. He'd had to learn about the death of his wife and of her practical murderer through strange faces and Craig's twisted indifference.

"Eileen and I were... close," Phillip said.

His inflection and the pained expression on his face told Josephine volumes about their closeness. "You were lovers?"

"Once... in the clinical sense," Phillip said. The tension muscles in his neck eased a bit as the words came out. "About five years ago, we found a safe house with a lot of rum in the basement. We drank, we got drunk and we..." Phillip stopped as the muscles tightened again. "Well, it only happened once. We were piss-drunk, and scared, and lonely and... it just happened. It's a war zone here, Jo'... things like that happen in a war zone, don't they?" Phillip asked.

Josephine stared at him for a moment then risked putting a hand over one of his. "Of course they do, Phillip. Even if there was a need to tell Heath, I'm sure he wouldn't like it but he'd eventually understand," she said.

He looked at her then concentrated on her hand on his. "There *is* a need to tell him," Phillip said finally. Just as Josephine was about to question Phillip again, Dr. Richards and Williams walked into the room.

"Is there any more of that water, preferably with some Scotch?" Williams asked as he came to the table and sat down beside Josephine. She removed her hand from Phillip's and passed her glass down to him. Richards went to a cabinet behind the table and came back with a bottle, pouring some into Williams' glass.

"Doc, you are now my god, and I will hold no others before you," Williams said as he downed half the tumbler in one swig.

"Do you need to do that?" Josephine asked.

Richards poured several fingers for himself before sitting down to join them. "We all may need a drink," Richards said as he placed a tiny steel ball in front of her.

"What's this?" Josephine asked as she pushed it with her finger.

"That, my dear Josephine, is a state o' the art tracking device. Christ I was such a damned fool," Williams said, finishing off the rest of his drink, then pouring a bit more.

"Where did it come from?" Josephine asked.

"Julie's shoulder; they weren't trying to kill her, they were tagging her. That's why the sniper didn't aim to kill," Williams said. "Well, ladies and gentlemen it was a nice run, but since Homeland knows right where we are, our own government will be stopping by any time now to give us a two mega-ton parting gift. Goodnight and fuck you for playing!" Williams said in his best television announcer voice.

"Wait…how could they possibly know where we are? There's no way that tracking device works down here," Phillip said.

"The *lack* of signal will tell them just as much as the signal itself," Richards said. "If the signal stops, they'll know she's under some kind of hard cover. If the signal doesn't move soon, they may send someone to investigate." He sounded tired and though he'd washed his hands, the cuffs of his shirt were still stained with Julie's blood.

"How's Julie?" Josephine asked.

"She lost a lot of blood, but Mr. Williams here happened to be her type. She's resting in the infirmary right now," Richards said.

"For all the good it'll do her," Williams added. "They know right where to find us, probably tracking us so they could find Heath and all the rest of you, wipe us out in one shot. That's probably why the aerial surveillance dried up after that storm. They *wanted* us to move. I knew I should've checked that redneck's work. I might have been able to see the tracker before we ever got on the horses. Somebody please fucking shoot me in the head, I'm too damn stupid to live."

"It's not your fault. How could you have known?" Josephine asked.

"'Cause it's exactly what I would've done," Williams said.

"I'm going to find Heath. He needs to know about this," Josephine said as she started for the door.

"Jo', wait… there's still something else he needs to know, and I don't know if I'm the one to tell him," Phillip said.

Capt. Cartwright sat looking over a map of northern West Virginia and southern Pennsylvania. Black circles had been drawn around both the Pittsburgh Air National Guard field adjacent to the commercial airport and Northgate. A red circle surrounded the coordinates where the message said they would find the survivors and their rescuers. Sommers' plan was risky; more than risky - practically suicidal, really. "This is never going to work," Cartwright said as he took up his mug of cold, black coffee.

"Of course it will," Sommers said. Morgan had long since faded from the planning session and was asleep with his head on the table. The rest of the men were either preparing the weapons Sommers had secured, or were planning their smaller parts for the coming mission. Cartwright stabbed a finger at the circled airbase.

"You think we can just stroll onto an airbase, grab a couple of choppers then fly into the Area?" Cartwright asked.

"I've already made arrangements for the helicopters," Sommers said.

"You've made *arrangements* to enter Area 187 air space? If you've got that kind of juice, why are we even talking about this?" Cartwright asked.

"I didn't say anything about *lawfully* entering the Area; I said I've arranged to get the helicopters. You and your men will be participating in Reservist training exercises," Sommers said.

"I guess it doesn't matter that we're not Reservists, huh?" Cartwright asked.

"As of yesterday, you're all reactivated," Sommers said.

"You reactivated us?" Cartwright asked. To a man, Cartwright's entire unit was ex-military. Most had already made it past their compulsory reservist stage. "No fucking way…"

"Yes," Sommers said. "There is a little-known provision in the Area 187 Act that allows for reactivation of certain retired military in the event the Area suffers a significant breach. It also allows for compulsory annual refresher training of such personnel. You and your team have been slated to attend such a training exercise along the Ohio River. You'll pick up the helicopters this morning with Mason and me along as observers."

"So we've been compulsed?" Cartwright asked. "You're some piece of work, Senator. Remind me why I don't just put a bullet in your head right now?"

"We will refuel at the training site then slip over the river and head straight for the shelter," Sommers said, ignoring Cartwright's question.

"You know, you were more than happy to let everybody in there rot, even made a career of it before your daughter ended up as one of them," Cartwright said.

Sommers smiled at him. "I still am. If I could extract my daughter without all this, I would,do so in a heartbeat. But to ensure her safety in *this* world, that wall has to come down. If you were me, wouldn't you do the same for your little Monica? Is this any different than what you would do if some playground pedophile had abducted your daughter?" he asked.

"This is a hell of a sight different than that. There's no comparison..." Cartwright trailed off, instantly realizing one important fact. *Sommers knew his daughter's name.* The Senator wasn't playing.

"No, Captain Cartwright... it's *exactly* the same. My daughter is in danger, and I'll do anything it takes to see her home safely... the same thing you would do if your daughter were in danger. The only difference between my example and yours is in the scope and scale," Sommers said.

Heath sat under the open window. He'd used the constant moaning of a swarm on more than one occasion, letting it fill his ears with meaningless sound while his mind churned. In the past, it had churned over where to look next, what rock to turn over, what hospital or government building Eileen may have taken refuge in. Wherever she was, was she alive? Was she safe? Heath had been ready for anything. Anything except what he'd found. "Two fucking weeks," he mumbled to himself as he tipped the bottle to drain the last dregs of Williams' cheap whiskey from it. He tossed the empty bottle out the window to land on some unfortunate zombie's head below.

Before this, everyone else was to blame; the military for creating the virus, the government for covering up, Homeland for making prisoners of the people it was sworn to protect. For one brief moment, it'd been Jasper. Had the old man told him about finding Eileen as soon as he'd come back instead of playing games Eileen could very well be alive right now. But Eileen had sworn Jasper to an oath only because she didn't want Heath to come back and risk his life. Even with her own life in peril, she was still trying to protect her husband. No, Jasper wasn't to blame, either. He could easily blame Craig, couldn't he? Yes, he'd found he could. But fate had given John Heath the old high hard one there too, hadn't it? The only man he could clearly hold responsible for her death couldn't pay for it. He could even blame himself, and did to some degree. He'd been the best of the best at getting good people out of bad places. But when it'd come time for him to save Eileen, he'd failed.

Heath had sat for almost two hours now and still no tears would come. Even his rage had left him as soon as he'd climbed up from the shelter. By the time he'd planted himself under the second floor window he felt nothing; nothing good, nothing bad. The only thing he'd lived for, the only thing he'd been ready to die for had been taken away and still he had nothing to show for it. He'd once told Josephine she had two choices; live or die. Now, with Eileen gone, he found he really didn't care which path he chose for himself. He'd spent the last half hour readying his weapons and letting his practiced hands load his magazines in the dark. He was leaving the shelter with the first light of dawn. They didn't need him now. Williams would know ways to get the survivors out. Josephine had been right; he'd never really left the Area. Fate had gone through a lot to get him back here again. It was meant to be. Alive or dead, John Heath belonged in the Area just as much as the undead clawing at the building a few feet below him did. Tomorrow morning he would give fate its chance to make him one with the Area. Whether he made it or not, he knew one thing; he was going to take as many of them with him as he could. Heath pulled a cheroot from his pocket and lit it just as he heard light footsteps on the stairs. He closed the lighter and laid his pistol on the floor beside him. If it was zombies, he would have heard the door crash open. If it was Craig coming to carry out his revenge, the world would have to wait awhile longer for their vaccine. It was neither.

A small child, a girl, came up the stairs. She turned towards the window and took a few steps before the sight of the glowing end of the cigar in the dark room stopped her. "Hello?" her small voice whispered.

"It's okay," Heath said.

"Are you one of the new people?" the girl asked.

"Yeah, I guess I am," Heath said. He took a long drag from the cigar then let the smoke escape slowly from his lips. The girl was obviously young enough to have been born and raised in the Area. What kind of people would allow themselves to bring a child into this world? "You shouldn't be up here alone. Do your parents know where you are?" Heath asked.

"You're here, so I'm not alone. Besides, I come up here to play all the time," she answered. The fact she didn't really answer the question didn't escape Heath.

"It's too dangerous to play here," Heath said.

"No. I can get back down real easy, and I have a light," she said. Her voice was quiet, her words well past her years. It was hard for an adult to survive in the Area, let alone a child. She would've had to grow up quickly or not at all, Heath reasoned.

"You still shouldn't be up here," Heath said, his tone far rougher than he had intended. The girl shirked back a step and took a quick breath, the rabbit-like instincts a small child needed to survive in a place like this preparing her to run. Heath slumped even more and sighed. She already had a hard enough life to deal with and enough to be afraid of without adding him to the list. "I'm sorry. I didn't mean to bark at you."

"So you just thinkin'?" she asked as she moved closer.

"Yeah, honey, guess I'm doing that." Heath felt suddenly tired and blamed it on the cheap whiskey.

"I do that too, sometimes," she said. "You want to play a game?" she asked, her voice a bit brighter though no higher in volume. "Library voice" meant something completely different to a child in Area 187.

"I'm no fun. Ask anybody," Heath said as he shook his head.

"Please? You just came inside so you'll be real good at this

_____

game." Heath cocked his head to the side, a meaningless gesture in the dark room. "I'm Ellen. What's your name?" she asked as she extended her small hand.

"John," Heath said, taking her hand and shaking it gently.

"This game's called 'Whatcha Got?'. It's real easy. You show me five things you're carrying, and I show you five things I'm carrying. It's real fun. You probably have some neat stuff. I used to play it with Mommy all the time when she came back from shopping."

"Shopping?" Heath asked as she opened the flap on her small knapsack.

"That's what Mommy called it when she went out to look for stuff." Ellen stopped for a moment and hung her head. "Mommy's dead now. But Daddy and me and a few others play it, too!" she said, her voice brightening again. "They always try to bring back a couple of neat things. And if you really _really_ like something the other person has, you can offer to trade for it."

Heath smiled despite his mood. The inevitability of life and death in the Area was like life and death on a farm. You didn't last very long in either if you couldn't accept one with the same ease you accepted the other.

"I don't think I'll have anything you'll like," Heath said.

"Sure you will. You probably have some neat stuff. There's a window thingy right there. If you close it I can turn on my light," she said. Heath reached up to his right, found the rod that controlled the heavy blinds and used it to lower them over the window. The zombies already knew they were there but there was no sense in broadcasting to anyone else the building was occupied. Ellen fumbled in the dark for a moment until a dim light from an adjustable lantern much like the one Heath carried rose up slowly from the floor. Ellen placed it a little to the side to leave room between them for their treasures. "Okay, the first type of thing is 'Tool'. I'll go first." She pulled out a heavy combination pocket knife and opened it to reveal pliers and a host of other miniature tools housed in the split handles. "It's my every-tool." Ellen looked up at him and stared for several moments. "Have you been here before?"

she asked suddenly.

"No," Heath said. Her stare gave him the opportunity to study her as well. Aside from the slightly hollowed cheeks and sunken eyes brought on by a life of malnutrition and fear she seemed a bright, normal child. But there was something else about her, something as familiar to him as he seemed to her. Heath shook his head a few times. He cleared his throat softly and turned his attention to the pliers. "Those look very handy."

"They sure are. Daddy gave them to me. Now you show me a tool," she said.

"What do you mean?"

"It's part of the game. Mommy always told me I had to carry at least five things with me all the time; a tool, a book, food, a toy and a weapon. She said if the Singers ever got in, I'd need that stuff," Ellen said, explaining it to Heath as patiently as if he were the child.

"Singers?" Heath asked then felt stupid for it. How did you explain the dead getting up, walking around and wanting to eat you to a child? Obviously, Ellen's parents had given the zombies a name more appropriate for use by their daughter. She would learn in enough time what the zombies really were. For now, she would identify them by their moaning.

"Daddy says they're just really sick people, and they can make other people sick, and that sometimes they can't help themselves and they try to hurt us. He says we shouldn't try to hurt them unless they're trying to hurt us."

"You're daddy's a pretty smart guy," Heath said.

"Yeah, he is. Now it's your turn! Show me a tool!" Ellen said. Heath shrugged then pulled his steel pry bar from his side and laid it on the floor beside hers. "What's that?" Ellen asked as she bent to inspect it.

"It's just a pry bar. I use it to open doors and move things," Heath said.

"It's got blood on it," Ellen noted.

"Yeah... I cut my hand," Heath said. Ellen was smart beyond her years in ways no child should ever be, but there was no sense in giving her gory details.

"Oh, okay," Ellen said. She reached into her pack and pulled out a small, battered pocket Bible. "Here's my book. It's really hard to read but Daddy has one, too, and he's been helping me with it a little every night before bed. So where's your book?"

"I'm sorry, but I don't have one," Heath said.

Ellen frowned. "You should always have a book. I really like new books. Daddy, Esther and Bill always try to find a book for me when they go out. Everybody should have a book. Reading is very important," Ellen said in her best grown-up's voice. "Well, how about food?" she asked. She pulled a chocolate bar from her bag and put it on the floor. The wrapper was faded in spots and some of the chocolate had leaked out from the tin foil coating. "Daddy doesn't like me eating candy, but he said these were okay to have."

Heath reached into his pack and pulled out an MRE pouch. He checked the label then laid it down. "Chicken soup."

"Wow... that looks different than the ones we have," Ellen said as she picked up the foil bag.

The rations the survivors would've found here would've likely been old even before the virus. He pulled his canteen, snapped a scalding packet over his knee then dropped it in. "Have you had dinner yet?"

"No. Daddy said dinner was going to be a little late tonight since the pretty lady that came in with you was on the table," Heath smirked at her honesty as he opened the MRE and poured the hot water into it.

"Would you like some soup?" Heath asked. He dribbled a drop on his finger to test its temperature. "Be careful, it's hot."

Ellen took the bag in her small hands and held it up to her lips. "It smells really good!" she said as she took a sip. "Ooh! Hot!" she said as she blew down into the bag. She took another, cautious sip. "It tastes really good!"

"I've already eaten. Can you finish it?" he asked.

"Sure!" Ellen nursed the soup for a few moments until it cooled a bit then emptied the bag in three big gulps. She wiped the broth from her lips with the back of her hand then licked that clean. Nothing went to waste here. "Is all of the food this good Out

There?" Ellen asked.

"What do you mean?" Heath asked.

"Out There. You're from Out There, aren't you? Everybody talks about the place Out There. Daddy told me that we're all here because everybody Out There thinks we may be sick, like the Singers. Sometimes I hear everybody talking about what it's like."

"And what do they say?" Heath asked around the lump that was developing in his throat.

Ellen's tiny features lit up even brighter than the lantern. "Mommy told me there's no Singers Out There. All the cars work and people aren't afraid of anything. She showed me pictures in a book of cities with more people than you could count, and at night they're all lit up. They look so pretty in the books. And candy stores and toy stores and all the food you could ever want!" Ellen said, her smile growing the lump to the point of constriction. Then just as quickly as it had come the wave of enthusiasm ebbed. "Mommy told me we were going to leave here someday soon to go live Out There. Her and Daddy used to fight about it when they thought I was asleep. Mommy always wanted to go but Daddy would always say it was too dangerous to try." She folded the empty bag in quarters then continued rolling and folding it until it was smaller than a sticky-note. Heath could only stare as she finished and slid the tiny parcel into her pocket. Then she picked up the chocolate bar and broke it in half.

"No, Ellen... that's your candy."

"You shared with me, so I'll share with you."

Heath looked at it for a moment then crushed out his cigar on the floor beside him. It was obvious the chocolate had melted and reformed at some time from the white lines of fat that had separated from the rest of the ingredients. It tasted flat, like baker's chocolate, but he ate it to keep from offending her.

Ellen finished her chocolate and repeated the wrapper ritual with Heath doing the same with his half. After they were done she reached into her pack and pulled out a small, five-round .22 revolver. The original stocks had been replaced with a single wrapping of duct tape around the butt's steel frame to serve as a grip for Ellen's small hands. With her fingers far from the trigger, she laid it down carefully on the floor. "That's my weapon. Mommy and Daddy told me it should only be used if one of the Singers was going to hurt me."

Heath wasn't surprised with her having a gun. It only made sense and spoke volumes about her parents and their practical nature. "That's very good advice," he said. He put his own, massive auto pistol on the floor beside hers. Seeing the large-bore pistol beside the tiny revolver was like looking at Heath and Ellen sitting beside each other.

"Craig has a gun just like that," Ellen said. "I don't like him very much. Mommy and Daddy tell me all the time, if I don't have something nice to say about someone, I shouldn't say anything at all, so..." Ellen held her thumb and forefinger up to her lips and pantomimed zipping them. Heath smiled and shook his head. Ellen laughed out loud then suddenly clamped a hand over her mouth. The Area was bad enough, but to be a kid that could never laugh out loud was worse still. She looked up at him and though her mouth was covered her eyes were smiling. Heath's breath stopped. He knew those eyes and that laugh. Ellen finally dropped her hand then reached into her bag and pulled out another item. "Here's my favorite toy." Ellen placed a plastic dragon complete with a knight in shining armor mounted in a saddle across the beast's back. "That's Sir John the Brave. Hey, your name's John, too! Mommy used to tell me stories about Sir John all the time, especially when I was scared, or when she was scared. Daddy never tells me Sir John stories, though. I don't think he liked them very much, he'd always leave the room when Mommy told them."

"What kind of stories?" Heath asked. His mind was buzzing now, an uncomfortable, screeching sound. This wasn't happening. He was wrong. He had to be.

"Oh, all kinds of stories. Sir John has this magical dragon that can fly really fast and breathe fire and all sorts of stuff. His dragon's name is Blackhawk," Ellen said. She picked up the figurine and swooped it up and down over the items on the floor. "He's really good at saving princesses and all kinds of people. He flies in on Blackhawk and rescues people in trouble then flies them away to the castle where they live happily ever after." She put the toy down and looked at Heath. "John? Are you okay?"

Heath sat there, the blood thrumming hard against the front of his skull. He reached out a trembling hand and gently cupped Ellen's chin. "Ellen... what was your Mommy's name?" Every word stung his tongue like an angry hornet as they left his mouth. Just then more soft footsteps sounded from the first floor heading towards the stairs. Heath didn't bother to look up, didn't care who was coming. Josephine appeared at the top of the steps followed closely by Phillip.

"Ellen, honey, it's time for bed," Phillip said. The man wouldn't leave the top of the stairs and didn't dare take a step into the loft, even when he saw Heath holding his daughter's face and turning it slowly this way and that in the lantern light.

"Aww, Dad! I was playin' Whatcha'_Got with John!" Ellen protested as she pulled her face away from Heath to give her father a pleading look.

"You shouldn't be up here, Ellen. It's too dangerous now. Come on, it's time for dinner and then bed," Phillip said, his voice shaking as badly as his hands were in the dark.

"But I already ate. John and me had soup and everything! Please, Daddy, just five more minutes?" Ellen asked.

"Ellen, honey... you shouldn't argue with your Daddy," Heath said, his own voice threatening to crack at the last word.

"Can we play more tomorrow?" Ellen asked.

Heath nodded then bent his head to help her gather her things and put them back in her bag. He looked away when she was done, angling his face from the lantern's light. "Sure. Go on now, listen to your Dad," Heath said.

"Okay," Ellen said, her voice deflated. She walked halfway to the stairs then turned and waved to his dark silhouette. "G'night, John," she said then followed her father down the stairs, leaving Josephine in the loft alone with Heath.

"Heath... I..." Josephine said. She paused then sat down cross-legged where Ellen had been. "Homeland knows where we are. The bullet they shot Julie with had a tracker in it. And that wound... on your back, it's identical to Craig's. What..."

"She's Eileen's daughter," Heath said softly, the mix of emotions his tone conveyed making it almost unrecognizable as his voice. "Eileen and Phillip's, isn't she?"

"Yes, Heath, she is," Josephine said softly then continued, "but we have bigger problems..."

"Bigger problems? My wife had a child... with another man... you have 'bigger problems'. Fuck you and fuck everybody here." This time his voice was back, strong and enraged.

"Homeland knows where we are! They could be on their way to bomb the hell out of this place! That makes it your problem, too. And why the hell didn't you tell me you were immune-"

The sudden, unexpected flare from Heath's lighter blinded and silenced her as he touched it to his stubbed cigar. Josephine couldn't tell if she saw tears in the man's eyes or if it was just a trick of the light. He snapped the lid shut before she could confirm either theory and watched the angry red ember flare as he inhaled.

"I'm pulling out at dawn. If you're stupid enough to be here past that you deserve to go up in a big fucking fireball."

"You can't be serious. Even if you were going to do that, how are you going to get past the swarm?"

"I won't be going past them, I'll be going *through* them."

"You wouldn't make it two feet from the door."

"Well, at least you've finally figured out the difference between *my* problems and *your* problems."

"You promised you'd get me here and get me back, and if you're immune we have to get you out of here, too..." Josephine stopped. She was losing him. He was stepping over the brink. Jasper was dead, Eileen was dead just days before he got to her and now, Ellen. She had to find some way to reel him back.

"You must've mistaken me for Jasper Connelly. He's dead now. See what happened when he kept *his* fucking promise?" Heath asked. Josephine sat there for a long moment, staring at the ember of his cigar in the void, the moaning outside in her ears.

"I can't say I know what you're feeling right now, Heath..."

"Are you still talking?" Heath asked.

Josephine sighed then took a deep, cleansing breath. "Heath, please... there's a lot more to this than we thought before. Craig..." Josephine started to say. The glowing red ember suddenly shot toward her. Heath's hand wrapped around the back of her neck and drew her close enough that she could smell the curious mixture of cigar smoke, whiskey and chocolate on his breath.

"She fucking told Ellen stories about *Sir John* and his dragon, Blackhawk... a fucking *Blackhawk*... to another man's child!" Heath said. "How Sir John would just swoop in on his fire-breathing dragon, his fucking Blackhawk, and save the day... *Jesus Christ*, Josephine! While I was bustin' my hump all over this fucking place looking for her she was fucking another guy and having his *child*!" Heath said.

Josephine felt her tears rolling but she didn't try to pull away. Phillip had told Josephine about the stories of Sir John that Eileen used to tell their daughter, had recognized the significance just as quickly as Phillip had when Eileen had told Ellen that first tale. Josephine knew this would be her only chance. If she didn't do something now, John Heath would cease to be.

"It wasn't like that, John. You know what it's like here better than I do. She was only human... she didn't know if you were alive or dead... she didn't know if *she* was alive or dead... it was a mistake they made, but it had beautiful consequences. Yes, John, she had another man's child... but even though that child isn't yours she goes to sleep every night dreaming of another man; not her father, but a brave knight in shining armor, a man that stands for something. Phillip may be her father, John... but Eileen made you her fucking *hero*! She's all that's left of Eileen... are you going to just let her die here?" Josephine asked.

Heath let go of her neck and slumped back against the wall. "You never learn, do you? There ain't no Superman, there ain't no Santa Claus... and there sure as hell ain't a Sir John the fucking Brave," Heath said.

Josephine got up from the floor and headed for the stairs. "Eileen's dead. You have no idea how sorry I am for that. There's nothing you or I or anyone else can do to change that. But Ellen and the rest are still alive. We came here to help them… all of them. You told me I needed to cowboy up, to use it," Josephine said as she reached the top of the stairs. She paused there a moment regarding the bobbing red ember across the room. "Feel sorry for yourself later. People need you right now. I need you right now. And no matter who Ellen's father is, *she* needs you most of all."

"I came here for Eileen. I made that clear from the start. You came here for your story. If Homeland does know where we are, this whole place is getting vaporized in short order. I suggest you get your story and be ready to move at dawn. I won't wait for you."

Chapter XX
Acceptance

Julie awoke to find Williams dabbing at her forehead with a damp rag. Her shoulder felt numb until she tried to move it and a dull, pulsing throb traveled down her arm. "Don't try to move. How do you feel?" Williams asked.

"You just love those stupid questions, don't you, Howie? Where are we?" Julie asked. Her voice was rough and her throat was parched.

"We're underground." Williams poured a small glass of water and held it up to her lips. "Sip some of this." Julie leaned her head forward and sipped the water, letting it trickle down her throat then lay her head back on the pillow and winced as a wave of nausea rolled through her.

"Did... did everyone make it inside?" Julie asked.

"Yeah, everybody's okay. You know, that was a pretty stupid thing you and Josephine did," Williams said.

"It worked, didn't it?" she said. Williams shook his head and held the water for her again. "How long have I been out?"

"Most of the night," Williams said as he checked his watch. "It's going on three."

"Did I miss anything?"

Williams sighed and sat back in his chair. "Where to begin..." Williams said. "First, that wasn't a bullet in your shoulder. It was a transmitter. Delmas just patched you up, he didn't go in looking for the bullet."

"What do you mean?" Julie asked.

"They shot you with a tracking device. They weren't trying to kill you; they were tagging you like you were a gazelle in a nature preserve."

Julie closed her eyes and lay still. "So, since they shot me they've been tracking us? They know where we are?" she asked.

"More or less, yes," Williams said.

"I led them right to the survivors." Julie said softly. "I should've listened to you..."

"Wait! I've never heard a woman say that. Let me get a recorder and you can repeat that," Williams said.

Julie opened her eyes and stared at him. "Being a dick doesn't help."

"There's more." Williams told her about Eileen Heath being dead, that both the way they'd come and the secondary door were similarly swarmed, and about Craig's immunity to the virus and his role in Eileen's death.

"I can't believe the man's still alive," Julie said, referring to Craig.

"What's Heath supposed to do? Kill a guy that may be able to provide a vaccine against becoming a zombie? He did try to kill him though, before we knew. I'm not sure if the tables were turned that I'd have that kind of restraint, especially when you add the kid into it," Williams said.

"Uh... *what* kid?" Julie asked.

"Oh, yeah...right. It seems that Heath's wife and a guy here, Phillip, had a bit of a drunken fling a few years ago and they have a little girl about five years old," Williams said.

"Oh my God..." Julie breathed. "I can't imagine that... how the hell could a woman be pregnant out here?"

"Well, see, when a mommy bird and a daddy bird really love each other, the daddy bird fucks the hell out of the mommy bird and nine months later..."

Julie shot him a look that told him he would've been slapped if she'd had the energy. "I meant how could a woman survive with a pregnancy? They haven't been in this shelter that long, have they?" Julie asked.

"I don't know, I came into the conversation a little late. But Phillip and Heath's wife were both doctors. I guess if they found the right safe place and drugs and all, they could've taken care of it. There are a lot of small regional hospitals in the Area. The kind of stuff they would've needed for a baby would've been fairly easy to find. Not too many people out there scavenging stirrup tables and baby formula, you know?" Williams said.

Julie sat for a minute, processing all that had transpired. "What about Josephine?" she finally asked.

"She's been talking to the survivors, interviewing them on camera and stuff. There's not much else to do right now. Either we try to get out of here or we wait for Homeland to come along and take care of us. None of us were counting on finding the place under siege," Williams said. Julie struggled in her bed and managed to prop herself up on her good arm. "What the hell are you doing?"

"If we're going to die, I'm sure not going to do it in this bed," Julie said as she pushed herself into a sitting position. She swayed there for a moment, breathing heavily and letting another wave of nausea subside. "Don't just sit there… help me." Williams stood and helped Julie turn her body so her legs hung over the edge of the bed and her feet touched the floor. "I'm hungry. Is there anything to eat?" Julie asked as she stood, wobbling like a newborn colt.

"Yeah, they have some stew, rabbit or possum or something like that," Williams said as he supported her until she could stand on her own.

"I'll eat anything that won't eat me right now. Hand me my shirt."

"I kinda liked you like this," Williams said, nodding appreciatively at her blood-stained lingerie.

"Underground, surrounded by zombies and with Homeland just a bomb away and men are still horn-dogs," Julie said as he handed her the shirt then helped her pass her damaged shoulder into it then button it. She could move the fingers of her left hand, a good sign after such an injury, but their manual dexterity would take more time to return.

Williams took her by her good arm and guided her to the

common room. She spotted Josephine in a corner, talking to Esther, the camera poised oddly on her shoulder while she tried to take notes. Julie pointed her feet towards them and Williams helped her along. Josephine looked up at them when they came near and reached up to turn the camera off, nearly knocking it to the floor in the process.

"Good, you're alive. I won't feel so bad about killing you later," Josephine said.

"Howie? Can you get me some of that stew?" Julie asked. Williams eyed first her for a moment, then Josephine, before he nodded and walked away. "I deserve that." Julie said to Josephine. Josephine stared at Julie's eyes as if she could see what game they concealed. "Probably worse than that..." Julie continued, "...but I'm no good to anyone here if I'm dead." She dragged a steel folding chair closer to them and sat down, turning the chair so she could face both Esther and Josephine.

"What the hell do you think you're doing?" Josephine asked.

"Helping... if you'll let me," Julie said, nodding at the camera. Josephine looked at her camera and then at Julie.

"You think you know how to work this?" Josephine asked.

"Photojournalism was my minor for a year and a half before my father made me change it to business," Julie said. Josephine kept staring at her. "Jo', look... I know I've done a lot of really shitty things. I can admit that, and I know that nothing I'll ever do will make them all better. But we're both here now, and we both have everything and nothing to lose. I need to do *something*... let me help. Please." Josephine eyed her for another long moment then handed over the camera. Julie examined the controls and made a few changes before holding the camera up in her right hand and adjusting the focus.

"Now... we were talking about how you came to join this group," Josephine said to Esther.

"Ah, Jo... can you two switch places?" Julie asked.

Josephine turned and eyed her darkly. "Why?"

"Well...I've noticed your right side really isn't your best side..."

Williams walked into the shelter's kitchen and saw the large stew pot sitting on an antiquated propane-powered stove. He took two plastic bowls from a stack on the large worktable in the center of the room, ladled some stew into each and turned to find he wasn't alone. A short, thin man sat in the corner in a high-backed wooden chair, staring at him. It wasn't the man's drawn, sinewy appearance or even his shock of hair and beard that stuck out at wild angles from his head that unsettled Williams, it was his eyes; as dull and lifeless as the zombies outside yet still able to focus laser-like on him from across the room.

"Uh... hi," Williams said for lack of anything else. The eyes stayed focused on him. Just then, Phillip walked into the kitchen. Williams looked at him and smiled, happy to see a pair of eyes that blinked. "Everyone calming down?" he asked Phillip.

"As calm as they can be, at any rate." Phillip said. Both men looked to the one in the corner. Phillip cleared his throat and joined Williams. "That's Cook. He, well... cooks for us," he said in a whisper. "He can be a little... unsettling at times, but he's a master at making our supplies eke out and making sure everyone gets fed."

"Good to know," Williams said. Cook's head suddenly turned to his right and he was out of his chair and opening a narrow steel pantry door on the other side of the stove from them. "What's the problem?" Williams asked. Soft squeaking and scratching noises came to them from Cook's cabinet. Phillip angled his head for Williams to follow.

"Cook raises livestock that we use through the winter to supplement the dry foods," Phillip said. Williams looked over Cook's shoulder and saw the deep cabinet was lined with small cages inhabited by rats of various sizes. Williams was no Area prude. When your supplies ran out before your job did you ate what was available, though he'd never seen an actual, intentional rodent farm. "He can make rat stew taste like beef."

"Impressive," Williams said with an honest nod. Necessity was truly a mother. He stared into the cabinet and absently counted. There had to be twenty rats in the pantry, some as long as his forearm without counting their tails. Sudden inspiration came to Williams. "I need one of those rats," he whispered to Phillip. Cook spun and locked his eyes on Williams.

"What do you want with my rats?" Cook asked. His voice was soft and hissed through his teeth. Williams thought that if his rats could speak they would sound like that.

Phillip slipped into the space between the two of them. "What are you talking about?" Phillip asked. His face knitted with concern as he regarded Williams. "He's... not *well*, Howard. He doesn't handle *excitement* well."

"Look...we need to get this tracer the hell away from us. The bombs could already be on their way. We're not going to be able to make it through the swarm out there..." No sooner had the word 'swarm' come from his mouth than Cook was flying across the kitchen to another cabinet on the opposite wall.

"Damn it to hell!" Phillip said as he ran behind Cook and threw his body against the steel doors to keep him from opening them. Cook grabbed the thin doctor by the shoulders and threw him bodily against the table then whipped open the cabinet. Williams was there in time to catch Cook's wrists as his hands came out of the cabinet bearing well-worn twin machetes.

"Swarm?" Cook hissed, this time loud enough to cause Williams to cringe. Williams kept his grip on Cook's wrists as he pushed his body against the flat of the blades, pinning the hands and weapons between them. Cook's eyes were feverish now and a sliver of drool decorated his chin.

"I told you he wasn't stable!" Phillip said as he leaned against the corner of the table and tried to recover his wind.

"No, you said he was unsettling... you didn't say a damn thing about him being *unstable*," Williams said as he struggled to keep Cook's weapons where they were. The deranged man was far stronger than he looked. It was all Williams could do to keep him pinned against the cabinet. Phillip pulled a steel syringe from his pocket, the kind carried long before disposable ones had become the fashion and drew a dosage of a clear liquid from a small vial from another pocket.

"No! Give them to me! Give the dead to me!" Cook screamed. A burst of strength ran through the smaller man's limbs and he managed to push against Williams hard enough to bring the two of them to the floor. Williams grunted as he felt one of the blades bite into his thigh as they struggled. Phillip stepped over the pair and sank the hypodermic deep into Cook's shoulder. Cook's struggles slowed, then stopped several seconds later with him slumped, unconscious, over Williams. Phillip leaned down and helped Williams to stand.

"Jesus!" Williams said as he stood and leaned against the table. The blade hadn't bitten deeply, just enough to break the skin. Williams bent down and took the machetes away from Cook's hands and examined them closely. The blades were clean save for a tiny spot of his fresh blood. He sighed in relief and dropped the weapons on the table.

"Better let me have a look at that," Phillip said, motioning to Williams' leg.

"It's nothin'. I'll clean it up later. You got any other diggers around here I should know about?" Williams asked.

"I should have warned you. We're all so used to sidestepping the issue I never thought to tell you." Phillip looked down at Cook and sighed. "He joined up with us right after we found this shelter. Cook goes manic when he sees zombies. He's a ferocious fighter. We'll have to tie him up. He'll calm down a few hours after he wakes up," Phillip said. He opened a drawer and took out several lengths of thin rope, handed some to Williams then the two bound Cook to his chair. "Now... you said you had an idea?"

Craig Brooks paced the small room he and Scott Cromwell shared, rubbing his throat and chewing on his own bile. Before he'd been bitten, the two had slept in one of the larger rooms with a few of the others. Now that the accident of his immunology had come to light he'd been able to demand separate quarters for him and Scott. There were a few of these smaller rooms that had gone unused since their band of survivors found the shelter. Except for private quarters for Dr. Richards and Phillip and Eileen and their brat, most of these smaller rooms were used as storage with the underground dwellers staying together in several of the larger rooms to conserve resources. In Craig's mind, the additional resources used in heating and lighting another small chamber paled in comparison to the relative comfort of the world's savior from the zombie plague.

"I'm gonna kill that fucking bastard!" Craig spat. One hand was on his throat while the other fingered the hammer on the big automatic at his hip. Scott walked in, gauged the mood of the room and gave his friend a wide berth on his way to his bed. He sat down and watched Craig pace for a few moments when he suddenly spun on him. "Who the fuck does he think he is? Does he know who the fuck he's messin' with?" Craig said as his finger jabbed towards the room's door.

"Guess not," Scott said, choosing his words carefully. Craig had a temper to match his ego. The discovery of his immunity had swelled both his id and his ire to even greater proportions. Scott opened the flap on the bag he'd carried in with him and started rummaging through its contents.

"I can't believe those idiots didn't tell Homeland. Christ, if they only knew I was in here they'd be sending choppers in here right now to pick us up!" Craig said as he sank onto his own bunk. "Man, do you have any idea what I'm worth? Shit... once we get back to the world I can name my price, and I'm takin' you with me. We're gonna have all the money, all the women and all the cars!" Craig said. He pulled a battered pack of cigarettes from his shirt pocket and lit one. Tobacco was a rare commodity in the Area, and even when he was able to find some it was always stale.

"You got that right," Scott said in his best lackey tone. He and Craig had been running the Area together for a few years now, throwing in their lot with their current group about a year before they'd found this shelter. Craig had been full of bluster even then but now he'd become almost unbearable. Scott had stuck with Craig this long though, and if they ever did manage to make it back he'd rather be counted as Craig's friend than his enemy. Craig exhaled and focused on the bag on Scott's lap.

"What you got there?" Craig asked.

"The reporter chick's bag. She's interviewing the others and left it sitting around. Finder's keepers, right?" Scott said.

"Oh, shit yes!" Craig said as he grabbed the bag by the bottom and upended its contents on Scott's lap. Scott stifled his scowl but managed to roll his eyes without Craig noticing. "Let's see what we have here." Craig snatched a few of the MRE's, tossed them on his bed then opened the small canvas bag full of .357 shells Josephine and Heath had taken from the Hanovers. "Oh, hell yes!" Craig said. He rolled the top of the bag down and crammed it into his back pocket.

"Hey, save something for me, huh?" Scott said.

"Buddy, you'll have everything you'll ever want as soon as we get the hell out of here," Craig assured him as he kept rifling. He stopped suddenly and plucked a folded cell phone from Scott's lap. "Hello! What do we have here?" Craig said as he flipped it open. "We've been away for awhile, man... look at this thing, how small they've gotten," he said, displaying the phone to Scott.

"Fat lot of good it'll do," Scott said.

"Yeah, well... still nice to see they've kept the world going for us though." Craig examined the buttons, then turned it on. To his surprise the screen lit up. "Damn, the thing's got juice." Craig said. Scott shook his head then pulled the rest of the MRE's off his lap and piled them behind his back.

"Without a signal it's just a calculator," Scott said.

"It ain't gonna' have a signal underground," Craig said. He sat down on his bed and stared at the phone until a smile spread across his face. "I heard that blonde cunt had a tracer in her, not a bullet. I'll bet you anything Homeland knows where she is. That means they know where *we* are."

"Yeah, they know right where to drop the bombs."

"Not with the hope of the free world sitting here they won't."

"They don't even know about you," Scott said.

Craig smiled even wider as he held up the cell phone. "I

think I can take care of that little problem."

Josephine rubbed her eyes and sipped at the coffee Esther had brought her. It was instant but was still good, especially since they had powdered creamer. Craig may have been right when he said the shelter survivors had saved her and the rest and not the other way around. The survivors were as motley a crew as had ever been assembled. There was Esther and Bill, of course. Esther had been a guard at the women's prison in Alderson, the facility made famous by domestic diva Martha Stewart's short stay there. She'd tried to escape the Area once, shortly after Homeland started ignoring or killing survivors that came too close to the buffer zone. After that she'd returned to Alderson and found the guards and prisoners in an uneasy alliance, turning the former minimum security prison into a respectable safe house. Alderson lasted for almost a year after that before it made the list of artillery practice targets. After that she drifted for a time until she met Bill.

Bill had been a lineman for Monongahela Power near Morgantown. He'd survived in the old family farm's root cellar for "a long time" before finally being driven into the wild. Bill turned out to be a nervous, quiet interview subject and was glad when Esther took over the storytelling about them stumbling onto Dr. Richards and his party. That was three years ago, and they'd followed Richards's lead ever since.

Jeff Goble had been a carnival worker, a heavily-tattooed ne'er-do-well that had the misfortune of hitching his way through West Virginia on his way to Myrtle Beach when the virus was released. He'd survived the first year by moving from rural house to house, eating what food remained and clothing and arming himself as he went. Eventually he fell in with a group of reapers. He'd come across Richards' group in the form of a woman named Betty. It'd been love at first sight and she'd easily convinced him to join the group. He'd stayed with the gang of reapers just long enough to make sure they were off the survivors' trail before coming into the fold. He'd lost Betty a year later and, having nowhere else to go, came here.

It'd taken the better part of a half hour to get Rebecca, the only woman besides Esther left in the group, to open up. Rebecca couldn't remember her last name or much about her life before Area 187. As best she could tell she'd been left behind in a hospital or mental institution, she wasn't sure which. She managed to eke out an existence for several months on the top floor of the hospital, barricading the stairwell doors and living off of vending machine food. She'd made the mistake of leaving a light burning too close to a window one night and a band of reapers found her.

Rebecca refused to talk about that dark period, only to say she wasn't sure how long they'd kept her. Her liberation came when she fell down a sheer 30-foot drop, breaking her leg in several places. The reapers must have thought her a lost cause and the drop not worth the meat they would've gleaned from her and left her for dead. Rebecca's next memory was waking up with Eileen Heath sitting watch over her, dabbing at her head with a cloth. That was right after the group came to this shelter. Rebecca had taken Eileen's death just as hard as Phillip and had become even more withdrawn than she'd been before. Since that day Rebecca had slept little and ate less, leaving her positively emaciated. Josephine had Julie cut the camera before Rebecca got up from her seat to save her pride from having her pronounced limp on camera.

They'd finished the initial interviews more than an hour ago, and though Josephine had no desire to interview Craig and his friend for the sake of the story she knew she eventually needed to. Dr. Richards and Phillip had agreed to sit down with her when there was more time and less over their heads, and Cook was a lost cause, she'd been told. After that, the coffee helped her make it through the next hour and Julie's telling of how she came to be in the Area.

Josephine had remained virtually silent through Julie's entire monologue, sipping her coffee so quietly and intensely that she had to pause several times to make sure Josephine was still listening. It was almost five in the morning by the time Julie finished and now she was staring at Josephine expectantly, the young newswoman having a hard time reading her elder's hard expression. Josephine let most of it roll off her. She didn't have the time or the patience to soothe Julie's injured conscience, nor could she afford to waste energy on the venom she felt. It would be dawn soon and she needed to find Heath before he went off and did something stupid. After a long pause she finally set her empty cup on the bench beside her.

"What do you want me to say? Do you have any idea what your little game caused? What, just because you're stuck in here too I'm supposed to forgive and forget? You could end up getting us all killed, not to mention that Jasper's dead now and if Bill isn't already dead I'd bet he wishes he was. I hold you 100% responsible. If you would've just kept your fucking mouth shut, none of it would've happened to you, Howie, to Jasper. Jesus, Julie... you have no idea how good a man you got killed back there." Josephine said. She leaned in to just inches from Julie. "You made your bed, so whore in it."

Julie bowed her head and sighed through her nose. "Jo'... I don't know how many times I can apologize. 'Sorry' starts to lose its meaning after the 50th or so time. I know I fucked everything up. I'm not asking you to forgive me, not now or ever."

"Then just what the hell *are* you asking from me?"

"I just want to help. All I'm asking is to give me that chance. I want everyone to get out of here, not just me. I've seen a lot in here. No one should have to live like this. When we get back, I'll talk to my father. He can help-"

"People like your father are why we're all here in the first place! And just what the hell do you care for any of these people, huh? Hell, for that matter anybody *anywhere*?" Josephine asked. She looked down into her empty cup then back to Julie. "Know what I think? I think you're stuck in this and now you're trying to grab some of that glory you're always after, so if you do manage to make it back it'll be that much less time on your knees to get to that big chair." Josephine stood up too quickly and felt her thighs tense from the hours spent sitting on uncomfortable wooden benches and makeshift seats.

"It's not like that, Jo'. *I'm* not like that. Not anymore."

"You might be able to fool Howard with that line of bullshit, but not me. Stay out the way and do what you're told... and if I think for even one second your bullshit comes anywhere near putting anyone in danger I'll shoot you myself, and it sure as hell won't be with a tracer." Julie kept her eyes locked with Josephine's even in the face of her threat, a threat Julie felt Josephine was more than capable of making a promise.

"If I do anything like that, I'd want you to," Julie said. She was surprised not only that she'd said the words but also in that she believed them herself. Josephine stared at her for a moment longer then turned and walked away. "Where are you going?"

"I need to find Heath. Go fix your hair or something. The big kids have work to do," Josephine said. She stopped at the end of the bench and looked down, expecting to find her backpack. "Did you see anyone with my stuff?"

"No. Why?" Julie asked. Josephine shook her head then took a quick scan of the room. Phillip must have moved it to the room he'd set up for them. Without another thought she turned to the corridor leading to the upstairs.

Josephine climbed the ladder and was greeted by the song of the undead as soon as she lifted the hatch. She went up the stairs to the loft and called out to Heath as she neared the top; no answer. When she reached the empty loft she went to the window and pulled down one of the slats. Pre-dawn light was already coming from the east, just enough to illuminate the massive swarm as it pulsed against the building in a wash of gray. The window in the room with the trapdoor was made of opaque glass blocks. If Heath had escaped through it she would've noticed. This window was still closed, and as far as she knew it and the first floor door were the only ways outside, meaning he must have slipped past her in the common room while she was conducting interviews.

Josephine returned underground and went from room to room, bumping into Phillip as he was coming out of his quarters. "Looking for something?" Phillip asked.

"Heath; have you seen him?" she asked.

"No, I haven't." Phillip closed the door to the room he and Ellen shared so as not to disturb her. "Does he know? About Ellen, I mean?"

"Yes, Phillip. He knew it when he saw her upstairs." Phillip looked expectantly at her. "You have to understand just what all of this is doing to him…"

"What did he say? Is he angry?"

"Let's just say he's still dealing with everything. He's been through a lot."

"*He's* been through a lot?" Phillip repeated, suddenly alarmed. "He almost killed Craig with his bare hands. Now that he can't kill Craig… I had a child with his *wife*, Jo'. I need to know he's not going to take his anger out on me or my daughter. Can you guarantee that?"

Josephine stared at Phillip for a moment. "He'd never hurt Ellen."

"What about me? How do I know he won't come after me for sleeping with his wife, for having Ellen?"

"I don't think he will…"

"You don't *think* he will?" Phillip asked, his arms flying up at his sides. Josephine took a step back from him, the act calming him somewhat.

"Phillip, get hold of yourself. Right now we need to concentrate on getting out of here. Heath knows that, and he wouldn't do anything to jeopardize it." Phillip eyed her critically.

"I'll feel better when he tells me that himself. I have a feeling I'll never hear those words, though," Phillip said then walked off down the hall.

Josephine watched him go for a moment before continuing her search for Heath. Phillip could have good reason to worry about Heath. Had she had this same conversation with Phillip immediately after seeing Heath upstairs last night, she may have agreed with his apprehension. She only hoped that Heath had had time enough to assimilate everything, to look at the complete situation, to see what their priorities should be.

Josephine stopped outside the closed door of the communal

restroom and listened to the soft sound of running water for a moment before knocking. She waited a moment more then tried the knob; it turned easily, admitting her into what looked like a down-scale locker room. Heath was there, wrapped in a towel around his waist and standing in front of one of the room's sinks. Josephine stepped a few feet into the room, closed the door behind her and waited for him to acknowledge her. When he didn't, she walked across the steam-slick tile floor to sit behind him on one of the benches placed between the sinks and toilet stalls, her eyes lingering on his blackened shoulder wound.

"Hi," she said, not knowing what else to say. Her voice echoed back at her softly off the discolored tile walls. Heath didn't turn around or acknowledge her presence. He opened a slim straight razor and started making long, slow passes over his stubbly head. "I didn't want to say anything, but you were starting to look a little shaggy." It wasn't her best material but she'd expected at least some kind of reaction. Heath continued shaving his head, each pass leaving his skin smooth and clean. He rinsed the razor in the sink then paused with his hands behind his head, trying to find the right angle to shave the back without slicing himself open. Josephine watched his face in the mirror for a moment before she stood and reached for the razor. "Let me get that." Heath gripped the razor for a moment before his fingers relented. "Getting all pretty for the zombies?" Josephine asked, working the razor gently against the back of his head. "I'm sure they'll appreciate the effort."

She finished with the back of his head and neck, careful to avoid touching his old wound then dropped the razor into the sink and moved beside him, leaning her backside against the next sink. There was something comfortable in the position that mirrored how they'd spent many of their few breaks in the field; he watching one direction and she the other.

Heath leaned down, his hands braced against the sink with his face just inches from the mirror. "I got bit about five years ago... probably the same year Ellen was born," Heath said softly. "Long story short, I lived. My old C.O., Lightner, made sure Homeland didn't get their claws into me, swapped some of the blood and tissue tests they took from me when we all escaped at Northgate with one of the guys that got bit on our way in."

"So you've been hiding your immunity all this time?"

"No. Part of the deal with Lightner was that I would make myself available for research. I go to a privately-funded clinic in Minnesota a few times a year so they can run tests and get fresh samples. If Homeland or the military knew, I'd be the one on my way to a blood farm, not Craig. There's really not much else to say about it."

"Are you... contagious?" Josephine asked carefully.

Heath smirked at himself in the mirror. "Yeah... a regular Typhoid Mary. Blood, saliva, tissue... the only difference between me and those guys outside is that my head hasn't figured out that the rest of me is dead yet. I'm stubborn that way."

"I don't think that's the only difference," Josephine said.

"It's the only one that counts, that and the docs say I won't turn when I die. If it can't affect me now, it can't affect me then." He turned to look at her. "I'm being an arrogant, pitiful, self-loathing asshole, huh?"

"That thought had crossed my mind, though my version added 'selfish' and 'suicidal' to the list," Josephine said. Heath sat down on the bench behind him, now facing her. "You've had a lot to process, and Phillip's scared to death of you. You want to talk about it?"

Heath looked up at her. His eyes weren't so intense now that the storm clouds had cleared. He didn't look like the John Heath people thought they knew. He didn't even look like the John Heath she thought she knew. The bright blue eyes she was staring into were the eyes of a living, breathing man that had accepted his pain, his grief and had made it out the other side. The pain was still there; she could see it as if it were scrawled there in blood. His toes may be hanging off the edge, but his soul was still intact. In that moment, Josephine was convinced what sat before her now was the *real* John Heath. She imagined he'd looked like this before Area 187 had consumed his body and soul, his wife and his life. This was the man Eileen Heath had known, had married. This was the man she'd told fairy tales of to her daughter, the man that willingly put his life on the line countless times to save good people from bad places. In that moment Heath grew somehow smaller in stature, but in that same moment he became fully human in her eyes.

"I spent a lot of nights lying awake and afraid out there. Not of zombies, or Homeland, or any of the other thousand things that can kill you here. The fear that I'd never find her, or that when I did she'd be dead gave me a lot of bad dreams. But even that didn't keep me from sleeping. The fear that kept me awake, the fear that kept me going more than anything else was the fear that she'd *forget* me. The Area had already taken her from me. After all this time, my biggest fear was that it would take me away from her, too. Considering her life in here, that's pretty goddamn petty of me, huh?" Josephine wanted to move, to sit beside him, even offer her shoulder but she didn't, afraid that even that small gesture would somehow destroy his moment of clarity.

"She didn't forget you, Sir John," Josephine finally said.

Heath smiled softly. "Christ, she looks just like Eileen. Her smile, even the way she laughs." Heath shook his head then stood and walked a few benches down to his pack. He dressed quickly then grabbed his pack and headed past Josephine to the door.

"Where are you going?" she asked as she came after him. He stopped with his hand on the doorknob and looked back at her, a crooked smile on his face.

"I go to breathe fire on mine enemies and pluck fair maidens from the jaws of death itself," Heath said. "No one deserves to be here. I couldn't help Eileen and I've made my peace with that. But if I walked out of here and left that little girl behind..." Heath paused for a moment. In the space of that pause his smile faded and his eyes hooded themselves again in their storm clouds. "You in?"

Josephine struggled to keep the change in his features from affecting her own. Whatever they decided to do wouldn't be easy, and although she'd appreciated seeing a glimpse of the man he really was, it wasn't the man that would be needed today. She nodded.

"Somebody has to watch your ass when you get sloppy."

Chapter XXI
Snakes in the Garden

"It won't get us out of here, but it may buy us some time without worrying that Homeland is breathing down our necks," Williams said as he braided several thin strips of leather together to serve as a harness for the rat that sat in its cage on the table.

"It's worth trying," Richards acknowledged. Julie mumbled in her half-sleep from a chair in the corner of the small meeting room. Richards watched his patient for a moment then turned his attentions back to the table. "Really, I don't see what other choice we have."

"I'm not so sure about this. If something happens to the rat too close to our door then Homeland will definitely come to investigate," Phillip said. "I'm just not sure if getting rid of the transmitter is worth risking everyone's life."

"Phil, Homeland knows about every swarm anywhere in the Area. They already know there's one here, and where there's a swarm there's food. It's how they managed to wipe out a lot of the survivors in the first few years. They just looked for a swarm then carpet bombed. They don't do that anymore, not enough bang for the multi-million dollar price tag of the munitions. If the signal disappears completely, like it has to be right now, I can guarantee they'll investigate. If the transmitter moves away from here, that's great. If it doesn't they'll see the swarm and maybe think Julie and I are a part of it now. Either way, we need to get the damn thing back on their grid," Williams said.

Phillip shook his head slowly then finally shrugged his

shoulders. "I can see your point, but that won't fool them forever. If the rat makes it away from the swarm it's not going to run away in a straight line."

"So you're saying we should just throw the transmitter from the upstairs window into the swarm and hope they think Howard and Julie were killed?" Richards asked Phillip.

"I don't know," Phillip admitted after a long pause. "Whatever we do we still face the larger problem. Howard's right in that no matter what we decide Homeland will eventually figure out that we're here and probably sooner rather than later. With the swarm outside we're helpless to escape on our own. And since they never saw the message we have to assume Homeland doesn't know about Craig's immunity. We can bargain with Homeland, but we can't bargain with a bomb."

"If Homeland knew about Craig, I can tell you exactly what would happen; they'd send a whole bunch of special ops in here, sort through everybody then slaughter us and leave us in this big honkin' tomb," Williams said. He finished twining the cords and held his work up for close inspection. The transmitter was wrapped tightly between the straps so that its metallic surface couldn't be seen. "So are we going to do this or what?" he asked the table. The two doctors exchanged looks until finally Richards answered.

"I don't see we have another option," Richards said. "Now, what about John?"

"What do you mean?" Williams asked.

"What Dr. Richards means is; can we count on him?" Phillip asked.

"Is that what you meant, Doc, or did you mean can we keep him from chopping Craig and/or Phillip here into bite-sized pieces?" Williams asked. Richards looked at him and cleared his throat.

"Perhaps both questions should be answered," Richards said.

Williams pulled the cage in front of him. The rat was docile and plump, probably one that Cook had raised from birth. "The only person that can answer that question is the man himself. Let me know which one of you is going to ask him so I can watch."

"And just what is that supposed to mean?" Phillip asked. Both Williams and Richards stared at Phillip then. The tone of the younger doctor's voice had become higher and louder. Williams turned his attention back to the rat as he positioned the harness on its back.

"I don't know much more about Heath than the rest of you do, except for the stories my uncle told me. But I do know enough to tell you he might take personal offense at questions like that," Williams said as he carefully cinched the harness in place. "And I can tell you if he *does* decide to kill somebody, that's exactly what he'll do."

"Then he needs to be stopped!" Phillip said suddenly. "We can't take that chance. The world can't take that chance. Craig's far too valuable to get killed just because John Heath wants him to die."

"Phillip... what's gotten into you?" Dr. Richards asked. "I agree that Craig's value to science could be beyond measure, but you're talking about murder."

"So we're supposed to let him kill Craig then?" Phillip asked.

"Who's going to do the deed, Phil? You? You really think you've got a shot in hell of taking Heath down? I mean, it'd be fun to watch you try, but you have a little girl to consider," Williams said.

Phillip jumped up from his seat with a hand on the butt of his revolver. "Are you threatening my daughter?" Phillip asked.

Williams looked at Phillip and shook his head slowly. "No, I'm just saying I'd feel bad for the kid if the last time she saw you, your balls were hanging out of your mouth from Heath reaching down your throat and pulling them up there. Obviously you and Heath have some therapy-type shit to work out. That's a problem better left to the outside. Right now we need every gun we can get and John Heath's one of the best. You're a doctor and Craig has that whole immunity thing going for him. We can't afford to lose any of you to a bunch of petty bullshit. Maybe we should focus more on getting our asses topside and stateside and less on drama, huh?"

"Howard's right, Phillip. Sit down. Please." Richards said.

Phillip kept his eyes locked on Williams and remained

standing. "All right then. But if I see Heath making a move on Craig-"

"All I can tell you is... don't miss," Williams interrupted.

Phillip eyed him darkly then stormed from the room, slamming the steel door behind him. He turned down the hall and almost ran into Craig where he'd been standing just outside the door.

"How long have you been standing here?" Phillip asked.

"Long enough to know we're both gonna have to keep looking over our shoulders as long as Heath's alive," Craig said.

"I don't know what you're talking about," Phillip said.

Craig smiled at him and walked a short way down the hall to one of the storage rooms. He paused in the doorway and waved Phillip to join him. Once inside Craig closed the door. "Heath wants to kill me 'cause he wants to blame me for Eileen. Maybe you blame me for that, too. But it ain't a perfect world and shit happens. Her number came up, and that's not my fault. I know it wasn't easy on you all these years the way Eileen went on about that big fucker, even telling all those damn stories about the great Sir John to your kid... *your* kid. We all knew who she was talking about. Eileen didn't want you because she was always hoping that she'd get back to him. I've been watching you a long time, Phil, and even I could see you wanted her. Now nobody gives two shits that you're hurtin, now that *he's* here. They don't care that you're the one that kept her alive all this time and they sure don't care that she had a kid with you. I'll bet he knows that the kid's yours and Eileen's, doesn't he? You think he's happy about that? You think he's just gonna let it go that you fucked his wife and she had your kid? He doesn't look like the forgiving type to me."

"I don't see what any of this-"

"I ain't a smart doctor like you, Phil, but I'm not stupid either. You know a guy like Heath ain't gonna be *alright* with you fucking his wife and her having your kid. You and me, we're in the same fucking boat, Phil. I'm tellin' you right now, that asshole is just waiting for the chance to put a bullet in both our skulls." Craig said. "You know I'm right, don't you?"

Phillip swallowed hard, felt his face grow red and hot. "I...I don't know," he finally said, shaking just enough for Craig to know he was having the desired effect.

"Bullshit you don't know, Phil," Craig said. "And on top of all that him and his idiot friends are gonna end up talking the rest of them into trying to get out of here without any help from outside. They're gonna get us all killed. But I can guarantee you if he gets half a chance, Heath will kill both of us before then. He knows you fucked his woman and he thinks I killed her. Are you willing to wait for him to come after us? I know I'm not."

Phillip's eyes were darting back and forth now and his breathing was quickening. Had it not been for Richards, John Heath would have choked the life bare-handed from Craig's body. That wasn't the act of a rational man, it was the act of a homicidal, unstable one; the kind of man that walked in on his wife and her lover and killed them both. The only difference in this situation was that Phillip was left alone holding the bag, just like Eileen had left him alone to raise Ellen. Since the swarm that killed Eileen had developed outside their door, Phillip had secretly believed that none but Homeland could save them. He'd been under siege by swarms before. Any survivor in the Area had. But this time they were trapped underground with their only exits sealed by the dead. It would take a lot of firepower from the outside to clear a path for their escape. Anything else would end horribly for them. Even if Heath didn't want to kill anyone here, his and Josephine's egos would get them killed at the head of any harebrained scheme they concocted.

"So what do you propose we do?" Phillip finally asked.

Craig smiled at him. "I say we get the hell out of here." He pulled out Josephine's cell phone and showed it to Phillip.

"What good will that do? You know Homeland monitors for any communications and electronics."

"You're still thinking of Homeland as the enemy. They're the only ones that can get us out of this. I took this from the news-cunt's stuff. If I'm right they'll be monitoring this area real close since this would be the last place they saw the tracer. All we gotta do is go up top and make a call. We'll be able to tell them about me and my immunity to the virus, and to sweeten the deal we can give them Heath and his people," Craig said.

Phillip turned away from him, leaning against the wall and thinking. "It's too risky. Heath will try to stop us and I'm not sure we could rely on the others to help. They don't like you, you know?" Phillip said without turning around.

"We won't need the others. You, me and Scott can handle this. All we have to do is make sure the others can't stop us," Craig said. Phillip remained silent for several moments before Craig delivered the coup de grace. "Don't you want Ellen to get out of here?"

Phillip half-turned at that and regarded Craig. "What do you mean?"

"If we don't get Homeland involved that crazy bastard is gonna get us all killed. Let's face it, Phil... Ellen's just a little girl. You know there's no way in hell she'd survive an escape attempt through those things out there. Hell, she'd probably be the first one to get it. You owe it to her to get her out of here in one piece. And you know that ain't gonna happen without some heavy help from the outside." Phillip turned around fully and sighed with his whole body. Craig smiled. He had him.

"How do we do this?" Phillip asked.

"I don't want to tip our hand too soon. We have to get everybody under wraps before I call Homeland. You still have Cook tied up?"

"Yes."

"Well, somebody has to make breakfast, right? I just came from the infirmary and I know you still have lots of painkillers in there. You think you have enough to add a little something special to the morning stew that'll knock everybody out?" Craig asked.

"I... I don't know... you mean *poison* the food?" Phillip asked.

"Don't think of it as 'poison'... think of it as saving their lives. If we try to subdue everybody we're going to make a lot of noise and there's no guarantee that we'll get everybody before Heath gets wise to what we're doing. We might even get lucky enough to get Heath and his people along with everybody else. It's for their own good. They'll thank us later when they wake up on the other side of the wall."

"So what happens if we don't get Heath and the rest with breakfast?"

"Simple. That little blonde bitch is awfully weak and slow right now. Stay close to her when the shit starts going down. You put a gun to her head and her little boyfriend will make sure Heath stays in line."

"I can't kill her, Craig. I'm a doctor. What about Scott…"

"Save that shit for the outside, Phil. You need to make a choice; which life is more important… hers or Ellen's? Scott will be busy as a back-up in case the drugs don't work, keeping the others under the gun while I go make the call."

"You've got this all thought out, huh?" Phillip asked.

"Like I said, I ain't a doctor. But I ain't stupid, either. And once we get on the outside, it can't hurt to be my friend, you know? Especially for a research doctor like you. I could put in a good word for you. Maybe they'd even let you work on the stuff they get from me. It'd be nice for you and Ellen if you had a high-level job just waitin' for you wouldn't it?" Craig asked. Phillip nodded slowly.

"So when do we start this?"

"Right now. Go get your drugs and hit the kitchen. I'm gonna go see where all the players are. You might want to take Ellen in there with you, too. I don't think you want her eating this morning," Craig said. He stared at Phillip for a moment then cocked an eyebrow at him. "We're together in this, right?"

"Yes," Phillip said. Craig added a smile to his eyebrow, clapped the doctor's shoulder in solidarity then opened the door. With a cautious look down the hall he slipped off to set their plan in motion. Phillip remained in the room for a moment, thinking. There was no worse person to be allied with than Craig. But, he made sense. He hoped everyone would be able to forgive him. Perhaps once they were rescued they would. Regardless, it was his duty to make sure Ellen had every chance. If they remained, he couldn't guarantee even her life. Eileen was gone, and Heath's arrival had spoiled some of his memory and brought buried ones to the fore;

memories such as the name Eileen called out in her passion in that rum-soaked basement those years ago. She'd been too drunk to remember that, but he did. He'd never told her that every time she said that name he didn't hear it the way she said it but the way he heard it that night, making the tales of Sir John the Brave practically unbearable. He shook his head quickly, trying to clear it. He wasn't in league with Craig against John Heath; he was in league with Ellen to get her out.

Phillip walked out of the room and headed for the infirmary, his hand resting on his gun. He stopped at the room he shared with Ellen and peeked in on her. She was still sleeping, the damnable plastic dragon and knight beside her pillow. Phillip crept into the room, picked up Sir John the Brave and his faithful dragon Blackhawk and continued on his way to the infirmary. Once inside the small room he locked the door, turned the toy over in his hands several times then gripped the dragon's body as if to crush it until the hard plastic ridges dug into his palm. Suddenly he launched Sir John and Blackhawk across the room. The pair hit the floor and bounced into a corner. That the rider remained on his mount through their crash-landing disgusted Phillip even more.

He fished in his pocket, pulled out a small key and unlocked the drug cabinet. Most of the drugs they had were gained over time by raiding drugstores, home medicine cabinets and, even more dangerous, hospital pharmacies. Phillip rifled through the cabinet and pulled out a large plastic bottle of a type chain pharmacies used to ship large quantities of pills. He poured the contents of the bottle into a large bowl then took up a heavy ceramic compounding pestle, crushing the three-hundred or so small, white tablets into powder. It was a lot, but he reasoned that the medication was old and nerve-affecting agents weren't known for their long shelf lives. Phillip had picked up the bottle of Clonazepam from a pharmacy in Bailor a few years ago. One of their numbers at the time, Tom, had been prone to seizures and the benzodiazepine derivative would have been just what he'd needed. Unfortunately, Tom had been killed just a few days after that raid. Phillip tried to remember Tom's face as he crushed the pills but the man's features refused to surface, mixing with the memories of other faces he'd found and lost over the years. Finished with his task he checked his watch. Most of the group would be getting up soon, their body clocks set with the rising and setting of the sun from their days spent in less-secure confines. And, they would be hungry.

"What do you have for me?" Fremont asked, sitting down.

"The tracer's been off line since last night," Warner said.

Fremont stopped in the middle of lighting a cigarette and glared at his subordinate. "What? Why didn't you wake me?"

"I didn't see the point. They're under some kind of hard cover right about where that swarm is."

"Or they got torn apart!" Fremont growled as he finished lighting his cigarette.

"Boss, if that had happened the tracer would still be reading," Warner said. "Looks to me like we have 'em where we want 'em. It's just daylight now. If they haven't moved yet it's probably because the swarm has them pinned down. There was no sense in waking you in the middle of the night, nothing we could really do, anyway. Besides, they might just be right where they were trying to go. If it's hardened cover, hard enough that the satellites can't track through, it's a safe bet there's other survivors there. The swarm bears that out, right? I mean, why else would they be there?" Warner was speaking quickly now and wishing that he'd awakened the Secretary.

Fremont stared at him while he processed Warner's logic then exhaled a lungful of smoke. "You say the tracer is still off-line?" Warner nodded even as he turned to Cline on the other side of the table for the agent's silent, confirming nod. The younger agent got up and turned on a flat computer monitor hanging from the wall.

"This is a live feed to the monitors back in the situation room," Cline said, studying the screen for a moment. "The swarm is here, centered on a small building in a clearing," he said, pointing to a red dot on a topographical map of central West Virginia. Cline pulled a small pocket computer linked to the system from his shirt pocket and tapped a few keys. A heavily-magnified satellite image replaced the map showing the swarm and the roof of the underground shelter's entrance building.

"Holy shit…" Warner breathed as he studied the size of the swarm.

"And only one reason why," Fremont concluded. "What do we know about the area? That building's too small to support a large group of survivors."

"A lot of government agencies and even private citizens went bomb-shelter crazy during the Cold War. We can't find anything on file, but that's not unusual. A lot of important people didn't want other important people to know what kind of preparations they had. West Virginia and Pennsylvania are dotted with old fallout and disaster shelters. Many were kept stocked and maintained through slush funds, pork projects and corporate bonus accounts. If our targets managed to find one of those it would explain a lot. They'd be underground in a blast-hardened shelter and would have access to supplies and facilities," Cline said.

"We destroyed all of those," Fremont said.

"We destroyed the ones we *knew* about, Secretary," Cline corrected him. "Some were never recorded. It's entirely possible that everyone who knew about a shelter in this location died off or moved on. Some of those shelters were pretty exotic constructions, sir. The best ones were designed with renewable water sources and buried fuel tanks for generators to run light, heat and communications equipment."

"And you think that's what we're looking at here?" Fremont asked Cline.

"I can say it would be possible given the circumstances and current evidence," Cline said. Fremont sat back in his chair and took a long drag from his cigarette.

"You want me to get a bird in the air for a closer look?" Warner asked.

Fremont regarded him for a moment, finished his cigarette then crushed it out in the crystal ashtray on the table.

"I don't want to spook them. If they're only resting or are just pinned down at that site I don't want to tip our hand that we know where they are. Agent Cline, continue monitoring the situation, and Warner... get my breakfast," Fremont said.

Williams rubbed his eyes and checked his watch. He'd been up for almost 24 hours now and he was starting to feel it. Dr. Richards had wanted to wait until full daylight to release the rat, the better to see how it fared. Until then, he and Julie were supposed to be resting in the small room set aside for them with the promise that someone would come along to wake them for breakfast. Instead of sleeping, Williams sat on a straight-backed wooden chair beside Julie's cot. He was tired, but he knew sleep wouldn't come. He pulled his chair up to a small table and started laying out his weapons for cleaning and reloading. He didn't know what Heath had in mind, but he was pretty sure he wouldn't get much warning when the time came.

Heath was a matter all to himself, of course. Williams had run into Josephine on their way to the room. She'd told him that Heath was 'okay', though under the circumstances that particular word was even more ambiguous than usual. He'd thought about going to Heath and discussing their situation but he didn't want to leave Julie alone. She was still weak from their mad dash to the shelter the night before, and from Dr. Richard's ministrations. He looked over his shoulder at Julie for a moment, shook his head then finished loading his magazines. He stood, holstered his pistol, slung the machine gun over his shoulder and went to the door. He was letting his concern for Julie interfere with keeping his mind on the task at hand, something that would get him killed faster than zombies or crazed diggers. She was sleeping comfortably now, and he knew she could move if she needed to. He paused at the door, turned and went to her bedside. He took her pistol from the table, chambered a round and put it beside her on the bed.

"They got big bedbugs here?" Julie asked sleepily.

Williams looked down and saw her eyes were open to slits. "You can never be too careful. I need to find Heath and see what he has in mind. Stay here, you need to rest. I'll bring you some breakfast."

Julie opened her eyes fully and stretched slowly in the cot, stopping her arms when her shoulder started to ache. "I'm fine. If their cook's down whoever's handling breakfast may need help," Julie said as she started to get up. Williams put a hand on her shoulder and pushed her back down.

"Julie, no offense... but what the hell would you know about cooking?" Williams asked with a grin.

Julie eyed him with mock insult then allowed herself to be pushed onto the cot. "Okay, you've got me there. Besides, after seeing your rat I probably don't need to know what's cooking," she said. Williams smiled at her again then left the room. Julie picked up the pistol and stared at it. Until the bombs fell, they were in possibly the safest place in Area 187. Why had Howie felt compelled to leave her locked and loaded? She knew he didn't trust Craig or his friend but she doubted even those men would be stupid enough to try something, especially with Heath and Williams around.

Phillip had also been a bit of a surprise to her. Like Josephine, she was trained to read people's faces, tones of voice, and body language. Though they thought she was asleep during their meeting about the tracking device she'd just been dozing. Phillip was not only worried about their plans failing but about Heath, too. She didn't know much about Heath, but she knew enough to know the good doctor's thoughts and feelings on the matter might not be completely without grounds. As for Josephine, she had every right to be upset with her. Down-right pissed, really. Julie truly didn't know what she wanted from Josephine. She'd said she wasn't looking for forgiveness, but wasn't that really what she wanted?

She got up and dressed slowly, depositing the automatic in her waistband at the small of her back. She felt the lump that was the switchblade she'd taken from Delmas in her back pocket and remembered the face of the woman in the box. It didn't matter if Josephine forgave her. It didn't matter that even if she did manage to make it out of the Area alive, that her father would likely disown her. Even though she was in a zombie-infested world, trapped underground with a hodge-podge collection of hardened survivors and enough drama to fill a Friday night television line-up, for the first time Julie Sommers felt like she had some sort of control over her life. She pulled on her boots and left for the kitchen. She may not be a cook, but she could chop vegetables and measure ingredients with the best of them.

Phillip jumped as Julie walked into the kitchen, almost spilling the small vat of powdered eggs he was mixing. "Good morning, Phil. Anything I can do to help?" Julie asked. He turned his back to her and kept stirring, folding the white clonazepam dust into the mixture. There had been almost half the amount of the pulverized drug as there was the dry egg powder. He was ready to send Julie away then realized her being here worked perfectly into Craig's plan. Having her in the kitchen would keep her close enough to keep under control without raising suspicions.

"Sure. Can you get the plates and forks?" Phillip asked as he nodded towards a cupboard. Julie smiled and started pulling down the plates with her good arm and picking forks from a drawer. "How are you feeling this morning?"

"A little tired, a lot sore, but still alive thanks to you and Dr. Richards," Julie said. She watched Phillip pour the mixture onto the ancient stove's large griddle surface and adjust the propane control. "Smells good."

"It smells terrible," Phillip said and smiled at her over his shoulder. "But it's hot and somewhat egg-like." Julie looked in the corner and saw Cook still bound to his chair. He was watching them both with his half-dead eyes.

"So that's Cook?" Julie asked. Williams had told her about their altercation in the kitchen, but his description of the digger's hollow stare was nothing compared to seeing the real thing. "Is he...okay?"

"Yes. He always gets morose after an episode. He'll be fine in a day or two," Phillip replied without looking into the corner. "So where are your friends?"

"I'm not sure. I saw Josephine earlier, and Howie just went to find Heath," Julie said. Phillip frowned at the eggs. He hoped Craig and Scott were keeping tabs on the others. Just then the door opened and little Ellen walked into the kitchen.

"Daddy? Have you seen Sir John?" Ellen asked as she rubbed bits of sleep from her eyes. "I had him on my bed last night." Phillip turned around and smiled at his daughter. Julie happened to look at the doctor just then and immediately recognized his fake smile, so like the one she used on camera.

"No, dear, I haven't. I'm sure it'll turn up," Phillip said. He reached behind him and grabbed a plate, filled it with eggs and motioned to Julie. "Can you two start taking these out and putting them on the table?"

"Sure, Daddy," Ellen answered for both of them. They picked up a plate in each hand and held them out to Phillip to fill then took the first four plates of the poisoned meal out to the common room and put them on the table, repeating the process until there was a plate for everyone. In the time Julie had been in the kitchen the rest of the group was up and heading for the breakfast table. "Ellen, honey...don't eat the eggs. I'm going to make something very special just for you," Phillip said.

Ellen smiled and rushed to the stove. "What are you going to make me?" Ellen asked.

"How about a pancake?" Phillip asked. Ellen smiled at her Daddy as he poured a small bit of batter from a coffee cup onto an unused part of the griddle. He'd put a huge amount of the drug in the eggs and he didn't know how such a dose would effect a system as young and small as Ellen's.

"Yay!" Ellen exclaimed.

"Julie, make sure you eat. You need to build your strength," Phillip said.

"I will. I'm just waiting for Howie and the others," Julie said. She turned and walked into the common room with Phillip behind her.

Esther and Bill had already sat down and Jeff and Rebecca were on their way to the table. Phillip nodded to himself, pleased to see that even Rebecca was taking a place at the table. When used in large quantities, clonazepan acted as a slow-acting yet heavy-duty tranquilizer. Most of the group was gathered around the table except for Craig, Scott and Dr. Richards, eating the spiked breakfast Phillip had prepared. He saw Scott sitting across the room watching them eat, then saw Heath come into the room and sit down on a bench against the wall. Phillip picked up one of the plates and handed it to Ellen.

"Ellen, please take this over to John," Phillip said. Ellen beamed and took the plate, nearly tripping over her feet as she took off with it. Just then the smell of burning pancake wafted out of the kitchen. "Julie, can you help me?" Phillip asked. With a quick look at Heath, Phillip bolted back into the kitchen to try and save his daughter's breakfast with Julie just a few steps behind.

"Here, John! Daddy made breakfast," Ellen said as she thrust the plate at Heath. He smiled at her and took the plate then looked down at its contents and shook his head slowly.

"Thank you, Ellen, but I already ate. You take it," Heath said. The little girl made a face and took the plate back.

"Daddy's making me a special breakfast," Ellen said.

Heath sniffed the air and caught the scent of burnt pancakes. "Smells like that didn't go so well. You'll probably want to eat those eggs before they get cold." Ellen sniffed for herself and looked back towards the kitchen. She shrugged and sat down cross-legged on the floor in front of their bench.

"Mommy always said we shouldn't waste food. Just don't tell Daddy. I'll still eat the pancake, too. I don't want him to feel bad," Ellen said as she picked up her fork. Just then Josephine and Williams came into the room from the hall leading to the surface building. Williams nodded to Josephine and split off from her, heading for the table to get their breakfast.

"Ah. Powdered egg surprise. I thought I was done with this stuff when I got out of the service," Williams said with a sigh as he came back with two plates and handed Josephine hers. "Still, any protein in a storm." He leaned against the wall beside the bench and held his plate in one hand and his fork in the other.

Josephine put her plate on her lap and poked at its contents. Craig came into the room and joined his friend, as far from both the table and Heath and company as they could get. Heath sat and watched Ellen as she divided the eggs on her plate so that the mass resembled a smiley face. Ellen looked up just then and caught Heath's gaze then turned her plate so the rough image would be right-side up for him to see. He smiled at her until she looked back down at her plate then looked up to see Craig coming towards them. He gave the group a wide berth and disappeared down the hall towards the ladder. Heath kept him in his peripheral vision until he was gone, and then looked back at Craig's cohort. Scott was still sitting where he'd been and stared at them until he locked eyes with Heath. Scott blinked first and when he opened his eyes again they were staring at the table. The rest of the company were already well into their meals. Even inside their impregnable shelter, the Area habit of eating quickly and quietly was still well in practice.

"Craig and Scott don't eat breakfast?" Heath asked Ellen as she scooped a bit of egg onto her fork.

"Sure they do. Craig can eat a lot," Ellen said.

Just then Phillip came out of the kitchen with a plate in his hand. He scanned the table then looked worriedly around the room until he saw Ellen sitting in front of Heath with a forkful of the tainted eggs heading for her mouth. "Ellen! No!" Phillip cried out.

In that moment the world dropped into slow-motion. Williams shoved eggs into his own mouth then dropped his fork on the plate and his now-free hand to his sidearm. Scott jumped in his seat and half-rose, his own hand moving towards the sawed-off shotgun on the seat beside him. Heath's foot shot out, knocking both the plate and Ellen's laden fork into the air. The survivors at the table started moving as well though several of them only managed to fall from their chairs onto the floor.

"It's a set-up!" Heath said as he got to his feet and stepped over the startled Ellen, keeping her behind him.

"Shit..." Williams said. He turned his head to the side and jammed his fingers down his throat, bringing up the bite of egg he'd just swallowed. Josephine fell off the bench into a crouch and aimed at Scott while Williams retched twice then pulled his pistol and aimed it at Scott as well just as Scott got fully to his feet and racked the pump on the shotgun.

"What the fuck..." was all Esther could manage before she slid down the bench and onto the floor under the table. The entire breakfast table was now either on the floor or struggling to stand, the effects of the clonazepam coursing through them, shorting out their nervous systems. Bill was able to draw his gun but toppled to the floor before he could level it at Phillip. Julie stepped out of the kitchen and stopped dead at the scene before her, giving Phillip the opportunity to drop the burnt pancake and grab Julie's neck, pulling her close with the muzzle of his revolver against her temple.

"Don't do anything stupid, Heath," Phillip said, his face half-hidden by Julie's hair.

"What the hell...?" Julie struggled weakly against Phillip's body.

"Shut up!" Phillip screamed in her ear, tapping her on the side of the head with the barrel to get his point across.

"Daddy?" Ellen said as she peeked around Heath's leg.

"It'll be all right, honey," Phillip said. "Just come over here and stay with Daddy."

"Not fucking likely. Jo', if that asshole over there even breathes, shoot him in the dick," Williams said, nodding at Scott. Josephine tightened her bead on Scott while Williams pointed his pistol at Ellen's head. "She dies and the girl dies," he said.

Heath had already made it several steps from the bench, placing him in the middle of the room and vulnerable to practically everyone's field of fire. He looked over his shoulder at Williams.

"Leave her out of this," Heath said.

"Again, not fucking likely. He lets Julie go and I point this at someone else," Williams said.

"It's not going down like that," Heath said.

"Area rules, Heath. I didn't make 'em, but if he doesn't let Julie go I'll sure as hell play by them."

"Stop pointing that thing at my daughter!" Phillip yelled as he tightened his hold around Julie's neck.

"What's all this about?" Heath asked.

"We're all getting out of here... we're all going home," Phillip said. "Craig has a phone... he's trying to reach Homeland now. I'm sorry Josephine... John... but with that swarm outside we need Homeland's help to get out. I appreciate you... all of you... for risking your lives in coming here, but I can't risk my daughter's life when we have the chance to get *real* help. If everyone can just remain calm, we'll be out of here in just a few hours."

"Daddy?" Ellen asked from behind Heath. She stood up but stayed behind him to peek out at her father from behind Heath's thigh.

"Come over here, Ellen," Phillip said.

Williams took a step forward and braced his pistol in both hands. "Don't move, Ellen. Stay right where you are," he warned.

"Howard... you can't do that," Josephine said. She still had Scott in her sights but she kept Williams in her peripheral vision.

"Watch me," Williams said. Heath looked from Scott to Phillip and his captive then glanced back at Ellen. She looked up at him with Eileen's eyes.

"What is Daddy doing to Julie? He's not supposed to point a gun at *real* people..." Ellen said in a whisper.

"It'll be okay, honey," Heath said to her, then to Phillip, "What did you do to the food?"

"It's just a sedative. Everyone will be okay in a few hours."

"Howie, stop pointing that at her," Julie said suddenly. Her voice was tight and weak from the pressure Phillip's arm exerted on her throat, but her eyes were clear and her words concise. "I want you to point that thing at Phillip's head, and I want you to put a hole in it."

"No shot, Julie," Williams said, his weapon still pointing at Ellen. Phillip moved his head even more behind Julie's.

"I've seen you in action, Howie. You've always got a shot," Julie said.

Phillip tightened his grip even further. "Ellen, no one's going to shoot you. Just come over here to Daddy and everything will be all right." Phillip's voice and the hand holding the gun to Julie's head were quivering dangerously now.

"Howie, take the shot," Julie said. Phillip had only one eye and just the barest glimpse of the right side of his face visible behind Julie's blonde hair.

"Looks like we have a real Mexican stand-off here, huh?" Scott said. "Look, Phillip's right. Craig's upstairs right now trying to raise Homeland. They won't come in here with guns blazing; they'll want Craig for his immunity. We don't want to kill anybody, but we will if you guys do something to fuck that up. I mean, we could've just busted into the sleeping rooms and killed everybody last night so nobody'd get in the way, but we didn't. We don't want to hurt anybody, we just want to go home."

"You idiots!" Josephine said. "They won't give a shit about anybody here *but* Craig. They're going to know who he is now. That bargaining chip won't work now that they'll know which of you is immune. The rest of us are just liabilities."

Just then, Dr. Richards walked into the room with Ellen's toys in his hand. "I found these in the infirmary..." Richards said as he walked into the common room then stopped short. "Phillip... what's going on here?" Both dragon and knight fell from his hands as he started for the survivors lying about the floor around the table.

"James, stop! Please!" Phillip said. Richards stopped in mid-stride and stared wide-eyed first at his colleague and then at the rest of the room.

"What the hell is going on?" he repeated.

"Craig found a cell phone and worked up this little plan so he could go upstairs and call in Homeland," Williams said. "Phillip did something to the food to try and keep everybody nice and quiet. and Scott's over there playing Craig's bullet shield while Phillip holds a gun to Julie's head. Welcome to the party, Doc."

"Phillip! Stop this at once!" Richards said. He made another step towards the table and Phillip thumbed the hammer back on his revolver, putting the weapon on a hair trigger under his shaking hand while his other hand grabbed a handful of Julie's thick hair. He yanked her head back violently and put the muzzle of his gun where her jaw met her right ear. Julie gasped as the act stretched the damaged muscles in her shoulder. Williams reacted to her vocalization and took another step closer to Ellen, leaving the muzzle of his automatic less than a foot from Ellen's head. The little girl looked up into the barrel and froze as if it were a cobra's gaze.

"James! Don't move! They're just unconscious...I wouldn't hurt any of them," Phillip said.

"Hey, Phil? The Doc's the least of your worries right now," Williams said. Phillip focused on his daughter and the weapon hovering over her. "Let Julie go. Now!" Ellen jumped but kept her eyes glued to his gun.

"Stop that!" Phillip said. His gun barrel came away from Julie's skin for just a moment as if he were going to point the weapon elsewhere but stopped just shy of it. All at once the room erupted in a jumble of shouted words and threats and fingers tightening on triggers. Heath looked at the chaos around him then slowly turned and picked Ellen up, holding her against his chest. That move silenced the room as Williams adjusted his aim till no one but him and Heath were sure who he was aiming at.

"Find something else to point that at," Heath said to Williams. Williams' weapon didn't move.

"Tell that to Phil," Williams said.

Heath turned his back on Williams and Josephine to face Scott. "Craig's playing you for a fool," Heath said to Scott then turned his head to Phillip. "You, too. He doesn't care about any of you. He's had long enough to activate the phone and whether he's actually been able to talk to anyone or not, it's too late now. They know exactly where we are. Craig knew this is how this little scheme was going to go down, knew that we'd all just end up pointing guns at each other. If we kill ourselves that just makes it easier on him." Heath put Ellen down on her feet. "Go to Dr. Richards, honey. No one's going to hurt you." Ellen stood there and stared at him for a moment then ran off to hug Richards's leg. Williams started to swing his weapon to track her but stopped when he caught Heath's hand dropping to the pistol at his side. Heath didn't draw the weapon but rather left his hand sitting on the butt.

"I hope you know what you're doing," Williams said to Heath as he adjusted his aim to the sliver of Phillip's face that was visible behind Julie's.

Heath turned back where he could see both Scott and Phillip. "Everyone - and I do mean everyone - put your guns away and get your shit together."

"And what if we don't?" Scott said. Heath flipped the safety loop off his holster but left the automatic in its place.

"You'll be dead before the echo stops. If it makes you feel better, you might even get a shot off, but that's only if Josephine misses, too. You won't miss, will you, Jo'?" Heath asked Josephine without looking down at her in her crouched stance behind and just to his left. Josephine actually smiled a little at Heath's rare use of her name in the familiar. As seen behind the barrel of her heavy revolver, that smile made Scott swallow hard and added to the nervous perspiration over his lip.

"Not fucking likely," Josephine said, echoing Williams' words.

"At that same time, Howie here is going to put a round into Phillip's face. If he does it right, puts the bullet right through the eye, Phillip may not even be able to pull the trigger and save Julie's head from getting blown off. Better think about it, Phil. From what Jasper told me, his nephew is one hell of a shot. But even if he doesn't hit the mark exactly and Julie's brains paint the wall, you'll still be dead and right in front of your daughter, no less. *You're* supposed to be your daughter's hero, not some plastic toy. You think that's how she sees you now? You think that's how *Eileen* sees you now? I've made my peace with all of that, Phillip; with her and with you. This is your chance to do the same. Your daughter's been through enough. She's already lost her mother because of Craig. Don't let one of the last things she sees be her Daddy dying like a coward, hiding behind a woman."

"How do I know you're not just going to kill me anyway?" Scott asked.

"You don't. Sure-things are boring and fear of the unknown is what makes life interesting. You know if I get to 'three' and you're still armed, your death is a sure thing, right?" Heath asked. He waited just a moment, allowing an answer from Scott that wouldn't come. "I suggest you go with the long odds. The sure-thing ain't always the best thing."

"What about Ellen? What about me?" Phillip asked. He'd let go of Julie's hair and moved his hand to her waist; a good sign. That hadn't stopped Williams from drawing even tighter on Phillip's right eye and focusing every ounce of his concentration into his sight picture.

"Ellen? Nothing's going to happen to her so long as I'm alive. *You* have the same odds as Scotty over there, though," Heath said. He lowered his head then and closed his eyes. "One..." Heath said, his voice soft, monotone. Scott tried to catch Phillip's eye but his attention was firmly fixed on Heath. He looked down Josephine's barrel again as Heath's mouth moved. "Two..." Phillip sighed, closed his eyes, then thumbed the hammer back onto the revolver's frame.

"Phil! What are you doing?" Scott said. His face went into a snarl just as Heath lifted his head and opened his eyes.

"Three..." Heath said. His pistol was out and trained even before the word's echo died in the room. Scott flew backwards as a .357 slug dotted each of his eyes; one bullet from Heath and the other from Josephine. Ellen screamed and fell to her knees to hide her face behind Richards as the back of Scott's head blew open from the tandem slugs. Phillip gasped and let go of Julie. Without another word, Heath turned on his heel and headed for the hatch to the surface. "Jo', keep an eye on this hallway. If anyone other than me comes out of it, drop them." Josephine nodded and turned to the hall, watching after Heath as he sprinted down it and out of sight. Richards detached Ellen from his leg and hurried to see to the survivors that littered the area around the table.

As soon as Julie felt Phillip's hand come away from her waist she spun on him. Delmas' switchblade came out in a flash and she rested the tip just below Phillip's left eye.

Williams was already moving towards them with his pistol still trained on Phillip. "Julie! Back away!" Williams said as he covered the distance to the table.

"I've got this one, Howie," Julie said. She leaned in close to Phillip, so close that the back end of the blade almost touched her own face and her words could only be heard by him. "Just so we understand each other... your ass is mine. The only reason I'm giving you a pass now is for Ellen's sake. From here on out, give me a reason - *any* reason - and I'll personally cut you down." Williams got to them and relieved Phillip of his gun. Phillip shivered at the look in Julie's eyes, so like Heath's when he was ready to crush the life from Craig's throat.

"Julie, go find me something to tie him up with," Williams said as he pulled her away from him.

"We need every hand we can get now. Dr. Phil's going to cooperate from here on out, aren't you?" Julie said with a pointed look towards Phillip. Phillip nodded just as his knees went out from under him and he slid to the floor with his back to the wall.

"Daddy!" Ellen screamed as she ran to him. "Don't hurt my Daddy! Please!" Ellen collapsed onto Phillip's splayed legs and threw her arms around his neck.

"That's up to your Daddy," Williams said.

The telephone on the table chimed at them as they poured over the newest satellite images and reports. Warner jumped at the sudden, shrill ringing that broke the room's heavy silence. He gave his boss a questioning look and waited for his nod of approval before answering it.

"Warner," he said into the phone. After a few moments of listening his eyes narrowed. He smiled as he cupped the end of the phone with his hand. "Jackpot, boss. It's the communications room. They've got a call from a cell phone, guy claims he's in the Area. They've already tracked the call and the location matches up."

Fremont sat up in his chair, his hand subconsciously driven to pull another cigarette from the pack in his pocket. "Is he still on the line?" Warner put the phone to his ear and repeated the Secretary's question. After only a moment's pause Warner nodded to Fremont. "Have the control room secure this line and put it through here." Fremont lit his cigarette and stared at the base of the phone. "Cline, go out in the hall and make sure there are no ears within 20 yards of the door." Cline nodded and left the room, his silhouette visible through the smoked glass of the door as he took up his guard position.

Warner sat motionless with the phone to his ear to wait through the odd sounds and electronic beeps as the phone line was tested and encoded against eavesdropping. He finally nodded to Fremont and took the phone away from his ear. "We've got the line," he said. Fremont nodded to the phone. Warner punched one of the buttons on the phone's base and hung up the receiver, putting the call on the speaker.

"This is Secretary Fremont of the Office of Homeland Security. Identify yourself."

"No shit? *The* Secretary? Well how 'bout you put me on with your boss, little lady?" Craig said, laughing at his own joke.

"You are in violation of several communications provisions of the Area 187 Act of 2009, any one of which earns you incarceration without benefit of legal counsel or constitutional protection. Identify yourself *now*," Fremont said.

"Well holy shit, Secretary. Sorry 'bout that, but my books stop at 2007. My name's Craig Brooks, and I'm one of the people that don't exist anymore. You'll want to change that, though."

"And why would I want to do that, Mr. Brooks?"

"It's Craig. Just Craig. And I have a whole lot of shit you want." Just then Cline cracked open the door wide enough to hand Warner a piece of paper. Warner glanced at it then gave it to Fremont. Fremont smiled slightly as he read it.

"How did you come by Miss Terrell's cell phone?" Fremont asked with a wave of the phone trace in his hand.

"I've got her and her little fuck-buddies all nice and tied up for you, Fremont."

"Whom do you have? *Exactly* whom?"

"I've got two reporter chicks, some asshole and big, bad John-fuckin'-Heath himself. But that ain't all I got."

"Go on," Fremont said. He was scribbling notes onto a legal pad and looked only slightly annoyed at dealing with Craig.

"I'm immune," Craig said. Fremont looked at Warner for a moment and put his pen down.

"What are you talking about?" Fremont asked.

"I got bit a few weeks ago, got so sick I almost died. But I didn't. We have two doctors here with us and both of them think I was infected. Well, guess what, Mr. Secretary? I'm still upright and breathin'. What do you suppose something like that's worth to you and everybody else on the planet?" Craig asked, his smugness coming through the phone as easily as his voice.

Warner leaned in to Fremont's ear. "He's lying, Boss. Nobody's immune to that shit. If he did get bit, it was probably from a dried-up one and just a scratch to boot," Warner said.

Fremont eyed Warner for a moment before he spoke again. "Why should I believe you?" he asked Craig.

"Tell you what, Fremont. You got the number of this phone, and it's got a camera. You text-message me an address or a number and I'll send you the proof." Fremont touched the phone's mute button and nodded at the cell phone on Warner's belt.

"Boss, he's just blowing smoke. You're not buying this shit, are you?" Warner asked, though it didn't stop him from pulling the phone from its sheath. Fremont handed the paper to Warner as Warner put on his glasses and looked down his nose through the bifocals to find Josephine's cell number on the page. "I hate this text message crap," Warner said as he punched the number into his phone and sent the blank text message.

"There've been two other known survivors that had a demonstrated immunity to the virus," Fremont informed Warner.

Warner looked up from the phone with his jaw hanging open. "How come I've never heard about that?" Warner asked.

"You didn't need to know," Fremont said. Warner snapped his mouth shut and set the phone down on the table. "One of them, a woman, was found early, in the first few weeks. She died a few months in during a particularly severe battery of tests. The other one was a man that came out with Heath the last time."

"What happened to him? Is he still around?" Warner asked.

"He died within hours of coming out. He'd been injured during their escape and had lost too much blood, dead on his feet by the time they made the wall. He'd been recently infected so there wasn't much for the labs to work with." Fremont reopened the line with Craig. "Do you have the number now, Mr. Brooks?"

"Yeah, I got it. I'm going to have to hang up to send you the pic'."

"Stay where you have a signal until we call you back."

"Where the hell else am I going to go? Fuckin' pusbags are twenty-deep outside."

"We're aware of your location and your situation, Mr. Brooks. In the meantime, make sure that you keep Mr. Heath and his friends under control. I want them alive when we get there; *all* of them."

"Hey, that's up to them. Heath had it in for me even before I called you, and I don't plan on giving the prick the chance to take me out. You wouldn't want anything to happen to me, now would you?"

"That would be...unfortunate. How many are there with you?"

"Sixteen or so, if you count everybody."

"Keep them under control until you receive further instructions, Mr. Brooks."

"Hey, before you go you need to know something. I'm not gonna be some fuckin' lab rat. If you want what I've got, you're gonna pay for it. I haven't made it this far just to end up locked away, getting poked and prodded. You understand, Mr. Secretary?"

Fremont and Warner exchanged glances as Fremont crushed out his cigarette. "You will be amply rewarded, Mr. Brooks, I'll see to it personally. You have my word," Fremont said as he hit the disconnect button.

"So what do you want to do, Boss?" Warner asked just as his phone chirped with Craig's message. Fremont picked up the phone and opened the message to see a close-up image of the bite wound on Craig's leg. He handed the phone back to Warner and stood up.

"You're going to take that downstairs to Dr. Sullivan. I want his professional opinion. If he's telling the truth, Mr. Brooks will become the high-value target and worth dropping a team inside to collect him and Heath and mop up the rest of the survivors."

"Geez, I hate going down there. Way too fucking creepy... all those eyes looking at you. So what's the plan if this Brooks is trying to scam us?"

"Put two extraction teams together, a primary and a reserve. Use Blackhawks with a gunship escort for the teams. Put a bomber with a few bunker-busters on standby from the southern command, spread things around a little. If Mr. Brooks is lying to us we'll simply close the grave they've dug for themselves. But if he isn't, I want him extracted at all costs. Tell Dr. Sullivan to see me after he's examined the picture," Fremont ordered as he turned and left the room.

Warner looked down at the image of Craig's blackened, vicious wound and suppressed a shudder. He thought about giving the phone to Cline and having him take it to Sullivan but dropped the idea just as quickly. Cline didn't have the clearance for the lowest level of Northgate. Besides that, when Fremont told you to do something, he meant *you*. He left the room and started mentally preparing himself for the task ahead as he walked down the hall to the elevator that would take him to the deepest level; research and development. Warner had seen more than his share of the undead since he'd joined Homeland, but none of those sights had prepared him for the antiseptic charnel house that was the basement. He sighed heavily as he swiped his ID badge across the elevator's red eye and punched the button that would send the car deep into the earth.

Chapter XXII
Desperate Times

Cartwright walked away from the blue-shirted Air Force officer and joined Sommers, Morgan and the rest where they stood outside their helicopters. Sommers had been right; they hadn't hit a single snag in securing the choppers from the Pittsburgh air wing. The whole plan had worked smoothly - until now.

"Everbody's grounded until further notice, the exercise has been suspended," Cartwright said.

Sommers looked at the young, clipboard-toting officer that had sent Cartwright away then back to the mercenary. "Reason?"

"Nothing he'd tell me officially, anyway. Buzz around the tarmac is air operations for 50 miles outside the wall from Charleston to all points north are grounded. That usually only happens when there's some sort of special op' going up," Cartwright said.

Sommers pulled out his cell phone, punched a number into it, then turned his back to the group and walked a few feet away. He returned a few minutes later and nodded for Cartwright to join him away from the rest of the men.

"Consider your buzz confirmed. All training and regular surveillance operations have been grounded. A bomber has been placed on standby in Virginia, and I have it on good authority that the Deadheads have been given orders to prepare for an unscheduled 'training exercise'."

"Well, looks like we were a little too late," said Cartwright.

"We're still going, Captain."

"Look, Sommers - this whole plan was crazy enough before,

but now you're just talking suicide. Even if we could get off the ground we'd be blown out of the sky before we got 20 miles inside the Area. I can't ask my men to die for this."

"You're not asking them, Captain; I'm telling *you*. It's your job to get them on board," Sommers said as he turned and headed for the command chopper.

"It's not going to happen, Senator. We had a slim chance before and we have zero chance now," Cartwright said.

Sommers turned to face him. "The only thing more dangerous than having Area 187 is if people found out what's *really* been happening there. Prepare your men, Captain. We're proceeding as planned."

Cartwright walked up to the Senator and folded his arms across his chest. "No, Senator, we're *not* going in, and there ain't a damn thing you can do to change that. Your threats don't mean squat if we're going to die anyway."

"Come with me, Captain," Sommers said, resuming his course to the helicopter. Josh Mason sat waiting for them, smoking a cigarette in the Blackhawk's open doorway.

"It was an interesting gambit, Senator, but it looks like it was all for nothing," Mason said as the two men came near.

"Is your equipment capable of keeping a satellite link from the air?" Sommers asked Mason. Mason looked up at him, confused, then glanced at Cartwright. Cartwright shrugged his shoulders at the reporter.

"Of course, as long as I can keep bouncing the signal off a satellite that is. I don't see what good that'll do us now though," Mason said.

"On the contrary; it will make all the difference."

"The Senator says we're still going," Cartwright said to Mason.

"They've shut everything down. We'll show up like fireworks," Mason said as he stood up and flicked away his cigarette. "I understand your position, Senator. No one wants to see your daughter get killed, and I certainly don't want anything to happen to Josephine. But we're not going to be good for anything if we just fly off and get shot down. Senators can get killed in helicopter 'accidents' the same as soldiers and mercenaries can," Mason said.

"They won't fire on us, not if you do exactly what I tell you to do," Sommers said. "Captain, get everyone loaded. We're going to head north and cross into Area air space as planned."

"You're going to get all of us killed," Cartwright said.

"No, Captain, we're going to give Mr. Mason the story of a lifetime; a live broadcast of a search and rescue mission into Area 187," Sommers said.

Craig whistled a tune as he took the steps two at a time, stopping at the building's only door for a moment to pound on it in imitation of the dead outside before heading for the trapdoor. Had he not blinked as he crossed into the room he may have seen Heath waiting for him. As it was, he opened his eyes just in time to see the heavy slide of a pistol identical to his as it cracked against his forehead.

"I should've killed you last night," Heath growled.

Craig opened his eyes, and immediately closed them as blood from the scrape on his forehead blinded him. He reached for his holster but was stopped short as Heath's boot stomped down on his wrist, pinning his hand to the floor. He screamed and tried to bring his other hand around to hit Heath's leg but missed with the clumsy swipe. Heath kneeled beside him, putting even more of his weight onto Craig's wrist.

"Get the fuck off me!" Craig spat. Heath shoved the barrel of his pistol against Craig's sternum and used his other hand to deliver a powerful, open-handed blow across Craig's face. Craig's head snapped to the side and he grunted, blinking away the blood until he could finally make out Heath's dim silhouette in the faint light from the opaque glass-block window to Heath's right. "You're too late, you fuck! They're coming for me. I'm gonna have all the money, all the women and all the fucking cars and you're gonna get a fucking bullet in the brain."

"Where's the phone?" Heath asked as he relieved Craig of

his pistol and shoved it in his belt.

"Fuck you. You ain't gonna kill me, you know how important I am. I'm the hope of the world, baby!" Heath balled his fist and cracked Craig's jaw with it. Craig screamed and struggled anew until Heath leaned on his pistol against Craig's chest then patted his pockets until he found Josephine's cell phone.

"Get up."

"I'm staying right here," Craig said.

Heath reached down with his free hand and hauled Craig to his feet. "Homeland needs you alive, but I'm sure they won't miss a few pieces," he said as he holstered his pistol and threw Craig against the wall. The breath left Craig's lungs in a whoosh as his knees buckled but the wall kept him from falling. "You can put a man in a lot of pain without killing him. You can cripple him and his body can still make blood and antibodies," Heath said as he stepped towards the wall and unleashed a vicious upwards kick. The toe of his boot connected with Craig's jaw and sent the back of his head against the cinderblock wall. This time even the wall wasn't enough to stop Craig from hitting the floor. He lay there, alternating between moaning and swearing as he held his jaw in both hands and pulled his legs into the fetal position. Heath pulled out the phone and hit the call button. The dates, times and numbers for the last ten calls came on the screen and confirmed that Craig had already made his call. By the rest of the calls listed, Heath could tell the phone was Josephine's. A rush of anger swept over him but he let it go. "Who did you call?"

Craig turned his head to look up at Heath. "Who the hell do you think I called? Homeland got us into this and they're the only ones that can get us out."

"Who did you talk to?"

"The man himself, asshole. The head of the whole shebang," Craig boasted.

Heath knew exactly who Craig was talking about. He had met Fremont the day after the PBS Survivors had escaped, while they were still in debriefing at Northgate. He hadn't liked Fremont then and he had no reason to change his opinion of the Secretary now. "When are they coming?"

"They'll be here before you know it. You ready to die, asshole?"

Heath reached down and picked Craig up again, this time holding the man out in front of him. "Yeah. Are you?" Heath asked.

"You ain't gonna' kill me. I might be the only guy they ever find that's immune. I've been out of circulation for awhile, but if the world still makes terrorists and goofballs you know it's only a matter of time before somebody gets a zombie out or figures out how to make the virus. The Area's only the beginning of this thing and what I got is the best shot they're gonna have of curing it before that happens. With me, hell, you could be the Pope and I'd still cut off your fucking head and shit down your neck. But that ain't you, is it *Sir John*? You didn't do it last night and you're sure as hell not going to do it now," Craig said.

Heath responded by spinning and throwing Craig across the room. He hit the floor again and slid across the cement, his momentum carrying him to just a few inches from the open hatch. "I don't owe the world anything. You get out of line - just once - just the slightest bit, and I'll come down on you so hard you'll think Jesus Christ Himself leaned down from His heaven and kissed you on your little forehead."

Josephine's head popped up from the hatch in the floor just then. She took in Craig's body beside the hole for a moment before she climbed into the room with Williams just behind her.

"Are you boys playing nice up here?" Williams asked as he looked down at Craig.

"He made the call," Heath said, shooting a dark look at Josephine, "with your phone."

Josephine's face paled. "Oh shit..." she said softly. She'd forgotten about having the phone in her missing pack. "Heath, I-"

"If it hadn't been the phone they still would've figured something wasn't right when their tracer didn't move again," Heath said.

"Kinda shoots the rat idea into moot territory, huh? So what do we do now?" Williams asked.

"We're about to have company," Heath said. He grabbed Craig's shoulders, unceremoniously dropped him down the hole, then followed after.

"I wish you'd tell me when you invite people over so I can put out the good towels," Williams yelled down the hatch. Heath let Craig get to his feet then herded him as he stumbled ahead into the common room.

"Good fuckin' job, Phil. Christ, you could fuck up a wet dream," Craig said as he collapsed onto a bench. He spared a glance at Scott's body and smiled at the pool of blood around it. "Thought you guys were here to save us," he said to Josephine.

"Shut the fuck up," Josephine said as she walked past him towards the table where Julie was helping Richards with the rest of the survivors.

"It's not too late for you, ya know? Put that dirty fuckin' mouth of yours to better use and I just may save *your* ass," Craig said through his bloody smile.

Josephine spun on him with her revolver drawn and took several long, rapid strides until the end of her silencer was almost touching his forehead. She paused there a moment, her hand shaking slightly in her rage and her finger tightening on the trigger. Craig had just doomed them all and the fact he'd used her phone to do it, the phone Heath had warned her against taking, had settled deep into the pit of her stomach.

"He's not worth it, Jo'," Julie said as she came up beside her. Josephine kept her gun on Craig for a long moment before she bent her elbow up to point the barrel at the ceiling and thumbed the hammer down. Josephine turned and stared at Julie for a moment before she shook her head dejectedly and sighed.

"No, the problem is he's worth more alive than dead," Josephine said.

"Now you're getting it. So what's say you, me and her make three? If you're good girls I bet I can make it so you can go back to the world. If you're bad girls, I'll guarantee it."

Josephine's arm started to swing down but Heath grabbed her wrist. "Jo', go see if you can help the Doc. Julie, get me something to tie this prick up with...and a gag," Heath said.

Josephine looked up at Heath and he let go of her wrist. "I'm sorry..." Josephine said to him.

Heath cut her off with a look. "We have bigger issues." Josephine nodded and she and Julie went off on their appointed tasks.

"What do you think they'll do? Homeland, I mean?" Williams asked after the women were gone.

"That depends on how good a salesman Craig is," Heath said. He looked down into Craig's crimson-stained grin. "I'm going to ask what you told them one more time. If you don't answer, I'm going to start cutting off extraneous parts," Heath said to Craig as he opened his folding knife. "Hold him, Howie." Williams put on a pair of gloves and grabbed Craig's head with a hand on either side and pushed down to keep the man in his seat while Heath grabbed Craig's right ear and brought the blade close.

"Fuck you!" Craig screamed as he brought his hands up around Williams' and tried to peel them away. "You're all dead! They're comin' for you, assholes!"

"They're coming for you, too," Williams reminded him.

"Big difference between you idiots and me...they'll blast you," Craig said through a sudden burst of maniacal laughter. "Me? I'm getting it all! I got what they need, what everybody needs! You jackasses don't get it, do you? You ain't gonna kill me. You ain't got what it takes to damn the world without a cure for this shit. None of you would be here if you did. Face it, you're fucking *weak*. You talk a real tough game but when it comes down to it there ain't one of you that wouldn't take a bullet for what I got to give."

Williams looked at Heath but his gaze went unmet. Heath leaned down face-to-face with Craig and smiled. "There's not a soul here that didn't make peace with death a long time ago. But let me give you a little preview of what Homeland's got for you." Without breaking his stare, Heath pulled back his knife hand and sank the first inch of the blade into Craig's left shoulder. Craig screamed and bucked against Williams' grip as Heath pulled the knife away. "They're gonna bleed you, Craig," Heath said as he jabbed again, this time producing a shallow puncture wound on the other shoulder. Craig howled anew as Josephine came back to them at a run.

"What the hell are you doing?" Josephine asked. Heath ignored her and flicked his blade across Craig's face, letting his blood roll down his cheeks as he screamed and struggled.

Williams kept his grip, shoving Craig even harder against his seat to keep him in place even as he shot Heath a confused look. "Heath, ease up a little, huh? I don't want to have to carry this guy," Williams said.

"If he needs carrying, I'll be the one to carry him," Heath said as he whipped the blade out again to mark Craig's chin.

"Heath! Stop!" Josephine said. "You're going to kill him!"

"Why not? He'd kill you, me, anyone, if he thought it would save his own ass. Ain't that right, Craig?" Heath asked as he slashed again. This time the blade traced a thin line of blood where the collar of his t-shirt met his neck. Craig gasped at this injury and his eyes went wide as he moved his hands from Williams' to make sure the gash hadn't severed a major artery in his neck. Josephine laid a hand over Heath's knife-wielding one and tugged on him till he turned to face her.

"But *you* wouldn't," Josephine said.

"Keep thinking that," Heath said. He turned back to Craig and was met with a glob of bloody spittle. It smacked against his cheek just a few hairs away from the corner of his mouth.

"Shit," Craig wheezed, "another half-inch and you'd be one of them."

Heath pulled his hand free from Josephine's, wiped his finger down the bloody blade then ran that same finger across his tongue. "You've got something you think's worth living for. I've got something I think's worth dying for. You've got to try a lot harder to keep living than I have to do to die," Heath said. Craig's eyes went wide as Heath smiled, his teeth stained with Craig's tainted blood before wiping the knife on Craig's shirt. "You're still alive Craig, and you'll *stay* alive. They're going to hold you down, Craig. They're going to strap you down and they're going to bleed you. You'll live in a little lab, drugged out, living your life in a haze, forgetting where you are, who you are. You'll be a blood farm, Craig, 'cause that's the only thing you have that's worth anything...to anyone. You won't see a dime, a cunt hair, or daylight ever again. The rest of us may die here, but by the time they're done with you you'll be so far gone you won't even be able to wish you were dead." Heath straightened and turned away from the stunned, bleeding man, passing Julie with her handful of rope as he walked towards the table and Dr. Richards.

"What do you want me to do with him?" Williams asked as he took the rope from Julie and she moved back towards the kitchen.

"Strap him down and let him think about his new life," Heath said.

"Yeah...what about the bleeding thing?" Williams asked to his back. Heath kept walking, forcing Josephine to run a few steps to catch up with him as he reached the table. Phillip was still slumped against the wall, crying and holding Ellen.

"How are they?" Josephine asked as Richards literally fell onto one of the table's benches as far from where Phillip sat as he could. His face was blank as he sighed and closed his eyes.

"Dead," Richards said without opening his eyes. Josephine's were drawn to the sheet-covered lumps on the floor. "All these years...malnutrition, without proper medical care...their bodies couldn't take it. Phillip used an entire shipping bottle of clonazepam. If everyone would've been in better overall health, they may have just had their nervous systems slowed. But with such massive amounts..." Richards trailed off as Julie came out of the kitchen with a jug of water and a stack of plastic tumblers and set them on the table. Richards opened his eyes and looked at Phillip for a long moment before his voice started anew, this time ragged and choked with tears. "In one moment, you've managed to do what years of the dead, the army, disease, floods, fires and famines couldn't do to these people. You've killed them all, Phillip," Richards said. Suddenly, he exploded off the bench and headed for him.

"Stand down, Doc," Heath said as he caught Richards and

held him in place.

Richards' eyes were glassy and wide and his face had contorted to a snarl. "You're a doctor, Phillip. First, do no harm!" Richards screamed. All Phillip could do was cry and continue holding Ellen tightly against his chest. "Do no harm! These people were our friends! Our *family!*"

"Doc, I'm sorry but there's nothing else we can do for them now. Homeland's coming," Heath said as he turned Richards to face him and not Phillip. "Craig called Homeland. I don't know what he told them, but I can guarantee he told them at least about his immunity and about me and the rest being here."

Richards stared at him for a moment before his eyes dropped to the floor and his shoulders sagged, defeated. "What do you think they'll do?" Richards asked in a hollow voice.

"Best case scenario? They'll drop a team of commandos in here to pick up Craig and wipe the rest of us out," Heath said.

"Then what the hell is the worst case scenario?" Josephine asked.

"They don't believe Craig, cave this place in and forget the whole thing. The more time that passes that we don't get missiles shoved up our asses makes it more likely that we'll have dinner guests. Here," Heath said, handing the cellular phone to Josephine. "You should be able to see who he called and what he did."

Josephine shot him a mixed look of bile and embarrassment then flipped through the message log. "He called 911," Josephine said. "Probably as good as anything. Any call would be routed to Homeland regardless of the number."

"So what are we going to do?" Julie said as she poured water in the tumblers.

"Where would we run? We're the proverbial rats in the sinking ship. We're underground with the dead surrounding our only ways out," Richards said.

Heath opened his mouth but Josephine cut him off. "He sent a picture to someone," Josephine said as she showed the image of the zombie bite on Craig's leg he'd taken with the phone's camera. "Looks like he was trying to prove he was telling the truth about his immunity," Richards said.

Julie looked over his shoulder at the picture. "It just looks like a nasty wound. How would that prove anything?"

"It would be enough for them to tell the bite was caused by a human-sized mouth and teeth. An experienced doctor could also make a few extremely educated guesses based on the coloring of the skin around the wound and that the wound is full of dead yet uninfected or inflamed tissue. The site of Craig's wound is nothing but a lump of dead flesh. The nerve endings are completely dead, just like a zombie's complete nervous system. I'm sure Homeland has such skilled and experienced people that know at least as much as that and likely volumes more," Richards said.

"And that's why he's so valuable; because his body was able to create antibodies that stopped the virus from progressing past the wound," Julie said.

"Exactly," Richards said. "His value to science and research is without equal, provided that Homeland hasn't stumbled upon others that share his immunity."

"Right now his only value is as a human shield," Heath said. "And what that means is that Homeland is about to get up-close and personal with us."

"Hey, Heath!" Williams called out from the other side of the room. "Craig's passing out over here from being a few quarts low. Better have somebody do something. I'm not touching his bloody ass."

"What a wuss," Julie said as she grabbed a few rags from a cupboard beside the table. "Afraid of a little blood, Howie?"

"He has reason to be," Richards said.

Julie stopped and looked between Williams and Heath until Heath walked away. "What's that supposed to mean?" she asked.

"He means that along with being immune, he's also a carrier," Phillip said. All heads turned to look at the doctor as he detached Ellen's arms from around his neck and slowly got to his feet then pulled a pair of rubber gloves from his front pocket. "I'll see to him, if you'll let me." Josephine and Richards exchanged looks then the old doctor nodded to his younger counterpart. No resource, especially one so highly prized as a doctor, was wasted in Area 187, regardless of emotion. Phillip nodded back and looked down at his daughter. "Ellen, honey, can you get the white box with the red cross on it from under the sink in the kitchen?" Phillip asked her. She nodded and moved off slowly on unsteady legs through the kitchen door and out of sight as Phillip turned and started for Craig. The sight of the bodies under their sheets stopped him in his tracks. Richards nodded solemnly then looked away. Phillip scanned the faces assembled around the table and found no solace waiting for him there, either.

"Oh God," Phillip said as his shoulders slumped and he leaned against the wall. "What have I done? They..."

"What did you think was going to happen from Craig's little plan, huh?" Josephine said. "You killed them, Phillip."

"Hey!" Williams barked from across the room where he stood over the bound Craig. "I understand the whole 'human drama unfolding' vibe you guys have going on but this asshole's gonna' bleed out if you don't get it together." That was enough to halt Josephine and bolt Phillip into standing up straight, though his eyes were still locked on the draped figures on the floor.

"Right," he said as Ellen came back out of the kitchen with the first aid kit held out in both her tiny arms.

"This is heavy, Daddy," Ellen said. Phillip looked down at his daughter, staring at her big eyes over the dented tin box. After a moment Julie came over to them, took the box from Ellen and shoved it against Phillip's chest, jarring him back to the here and now.

"Go on, Dr. Phil, you've got shit to do," Julie said. Phillip walked away from them towards Williams and Craig. Ellen started to follow but Julie put a hand on her shoulder.

"Ellen, your Daddy's going to be busy. Why don't you help me in the kitchen?" Julie asked. Ellen looked up at her.

"We're going to die, aren't we?" Ellen asked. Julie's mouth opened and closed a few times as she looked around helplessly at the others.

"No, Ellen...of course not," Julie finally said when no help would come, "we're going to be just fine." Ellen gave Julie a look of profound disbelief but dutifully walked towards the kitchen just as Heath came back to meet her at the door.

"Here," Heath said. He'd retrieved Sir John and his trusted plastic dragon from where Richards had dropped them and held them out to her. Ellen took the toys with shaking hands, held them for a moment then put them down on the table before going into the kitchen. Heath watched after her then looked down at the discarded hero. "Looks like she's given up on Sir John."

"I haven't," Josephine said. Heath stared at her for just a moment, his expression unreadable.

"Then you're more naïve than she is. We're going to need a hell of a lot more than a knight in shining armor to get out of this."

"The dragon would be a big help though," Williams said as he joined them. Heath looked over his shoulder to where Phillip was leaning over Craig.

"He still alive?" Heath asked.

"Yeah, unconscious right now. You bled him out a bit there. Good way to keep him quiet though," Williams said as he picked up one of the tumblers of water Julie had poured. "So what's new?"

"Homeland knows where we are and about his immunity. They're coming for him, and for us," Josephine said.

"Oh, right...the usual," Williams said then chugged the tumbler empty. "So what's the plan?"

"I'm open to suggestions. But whatever we do we need to do it fast. I don't know how long we have but it'll be before nightfall. Nobody's stupid enough to try getting in here with that swarm outside in the dark," Heath said.

"Don't forget Cook. He's still in the kitchen," Williams said.

"Alright then, first things first," Heath said, looking at Williams. "Gather all the weapons and ammo you can find. We need to see what we have to work with."

"We've been using the room at the end of that hall over there as the armory but you'll probably find just as many weapons in the sleeping rooms," Dr. Richards said. Williams nodded then left on his appointed task.

"Jo', keep an eye on Julie, Ellen and Cook. Julie's got a lot of heart, but she's still weak and if Cook snaps again I need to know you're there. The last thing we need is for a digger coming at us from the rear while Homeland hits us from the front," Heath said.

"Babysitting duty...yes sir!" Josephine said with sarcasm topped off by a mock salute.

"Doc, keep an eye on Phillip, make sure he doesn't do anything stupid," Heath said.

"I don't think he'll do anything else against us," Richards said.

"Neither do I, but there are a lot of other stupid things a man can do. You two should work up a couple of trauma bags," Heath said.

"You're planning on leaving?" Richards asked.

"If we stay they'll have us pinned down, and if they can't get us without risking us killing Craig on purpose or them killing him on accident they may just go ahead and nuke the place just to be on the safe side. The only chance we have is to get outside."

"What about the swarms? The secondary hatch is a quarter mile away by surface measure and is just as thick with them as the upstairs door is. We'd be running right into their arms," Richards said.

"I didn't say I had all the answers, Doc," Heath said.

"What do we do with Craig if we do manage to get away?" Richards asked.

"We'll have to play that by ear. He's the only ace we've got. Besides, getting out of here's just the start. We'll have a long way to go to get back to the world. He may not make it that far," Heath said.

"I know you two have...issues, and even without what happened this morning Craig has never been what I would call a worthwhile individual. But John, you have to understand his value to science. If he can be saved, he *must* be. He may be the last best chance at studying immunity and developing a vaccine," Richards said.

"No he's not, Dr. Richards," Josephine said to him though

her eyes rested on Heath. "It's just as important for John to get out of here as it is Craig."

Mason folded the screen on his hand-held digital video camera, his eyes still on the Senator. He'd waited more than seven years for this; the moment where the American government admitted, on camera, to the atrocities and scandals surrounding the creation of Area 187. He held in his hands a video deposition more akin to a confession made by Senator Alan Sommers, Chairman of the Senate Committee on Area 187 Affairs. Here in the belly of a stolen Air National Guard Blackhawk sitting on a tarmac just outside Westgate Control south of Marietta, Ohio, Sommers had admitted to those standard reasons given by the government and grudgingly accepted by most of the American people as to the necessity for Area 187. But he'd also given the real reasons; simple economics and political and global condemnation.

Sommers' confession detailed a series of meetings held just hours after the President had declared marshal law throughout the state of West Virginia and just weeks before parts of its neighboring states would also sacrifice pieces of themselves to the cordon effort that would become the walled necropolis of Area 187. Members of the Supreme Court, trusted legal advisors and even the heads of several massive, globe-spanning insurance and finance companies were brought together.

The results of these clandestine meetings had painted a bleak picture. If the government took any direct responsibility for the creation of the virus and didn't take steps to enact severe hold-from-harm legislation, the nation's judicial system would come to a screeching halt as hundreds of thousands of lawsuits tossed their logs into the river. Insurance companies wouldn't be able to escape their liabilities under their various act-of-God clauses, and by placing control of the containment operation under the Department of Homeland Security those insurers wouldn't even be able to countersue the government to reclaim those damages due to the protection from civil litigation that had been woven into the creation of the department's charter shortly after September 11, 2001. These mega-corporations would suffer huge losses, crippling them and ultimately bankrupting them in the space of a year, and businesses as well as private individuals would bankrupt the FDIC as hundreds of thousands of account holders came back on them for their savings. This didn't even take into account the suits that could be brought against the various state governments. Mason was still reeling from it all when Sommers snapped his fingers just inches from his nose.

"All right, Mason, tell me again what you're going to do with that," Sommers said.

Mason sat up in his seat and leaned forward with his elbows on his knees. "I'm going to transmit this to the CBC with instructions to sit on it and not air it unless you or I don't call by midnight. I'm also to tell them to transmit to Homeland at exactly eleven this morning, the moment we plan to cross into the Area with the same disclaimer; if we're not heard from, the CBC will broadcast it. If we make it, you've agreed to give the CBC your exclusive on-camera interview without censorship." Sommers nodded. Cartwright sat in the open side doorway of the helicopter, as much to keep the others out of earshot as he was to hear what Sommers had told the camera.

"Do you think they'll agree?" Sommers asked.

"Are you kidding? They win either way. They either air this or they get you in the hot seat. You've got your audience, Senator, and your insurance," Mason said.

"You're a grade-A asshole, Senator," Cartwright said. The look on his face told the Senator he'd rather slip a bayonet between those Congressional ribs than follow the man into battle. "You and all the rest."

"Curse me when it's over, Captain. Right now I need you and your men to focus," Sommers said.

"Do you really think Fremont is going to just let us waltz in there, even with the threat of going public?" Cartwright asked.

"Like anything else, Captain, we'll have to try it and see. Fremont won't be able to call my bluff, because I'm not bluffing. That the video will come from the CBC and not from some anonymous source will show just how serious I am," Sommers said.

"What if he puts pressure on the CBC and the Canadian government to bury the video? What then?" Cartwright asked.

"He could try," Mason said as he worked to connect to the internet through his laptop and a satellite phone connection. "But Canada never signed onto the censorship. There aren't many Canadians that feel very safe with the U.S. having zombies running around. If the virus gets loose again, it's going to be like every U.S. apocalypse movie you ever saw. Everyone would be running to Canada to escape. We don't like you people well enough to house all your refugees, and we sure as hell don't want your damn virus coming north along with them. Besides, how often does the Canadian government get to put one over on the U.S.? Those 'took' jokes and 'eh' cracks seem somehow less funny now, don't they?" Mason asked.

"So we're depending on *Canada* to save *us*?" Cartwright asked, shaking his head. "There are so many things wrong I don't know who to shoot first."

"Save your bullets, you may need them. I don't know what we'll find when we get there," Sommers said. He checked his watch. It was nearing nine-thirty. "Captain, get the men together and tell them to be ready to move out at ten. I'll secure clearance for us to take off and head back to Pittsburgh. We can cross the river a few miles upstream. That should buy us enough time to make sure Fremont sees the video."

"You're pretty damn sure when you're playing with our lives, Senator," Cartwright said.

"I'm also playing with my life, Captain, and my daughter's. I place her life far above mine and even farther above yours," Sommers said.

Warner led Dr. Sullivan into the conference room. Sullivan was a reed-thin man with a full head of silver hair and eyes that had sunken over the years into the deep hollows of his skull. His emaciated features and well-known propensity for staying in the lowest level of Northgate for weeks without seeing the sun had led many to comment he resembled the zombies he studied more than the living man he proclaimed to be. Sullivan wasted no time in charging across the room to Fremont, violating the boardroom etiquette of staying to one's proper side of the table. The doctor sat next to Fremont and opened a file.

"Good of you to come up for air, Dr. Sullivan," Fremont commented. Sullivan responded by pulling two 8x10 pictures from the folder.

"One of these photos is of the infection wound on a subject I've had in holding for the last three years. The other is taken from the digital photo Agent Warner brought me," Sullivan said. Fremont gave the doctor an annoyed sidelong glance then looked at the pictures. Both displayed a rough bite wound that had sunk through the skin and deep into the meat below. Aside from minor differences in lighting and positioning, the only difference Fremont could really see was in the skin tone between the living example and the undead one.

"I don't have time for games, doctor. Get to your point."

"Look at the wounds, Secretary; they're practically identical. The tissue is obviously dead judging from the discoloration. Both of these are what we call primary transference wounds. You can tell by the discolored flesh that rims each wound," Sullivan said while looking at Fremont as if that was all the explanation needed. After a few moments of Fremont's perturbed glare, he realized it wasn't. Sullivan cleared his throat and sighed. "My subject has been clinically dead for at least three years. The photo you gave me is obviously a living subject that has managed to survive past infection. The rest of the leg is living, healthy tissue," Sullivan explained in his best third-grade teacher voice.

"You feel this is a photo of someone that has survived an actual infection?" Fremont asked.

"Yes, Secretary. I have a technician going over the image to make sure that it wasn't somehow doctored, but barring someone who is very, very good at such things this is the genuine article.

It's obvious it's not a recent attack and the picture taken before the subject would expire. When the infection is first introduced to the body it has the localized effect of expanding the blood vessels starting at the wound sight and ending at the heart, the better to have itself carried throughout the body and eventually into the brain. If this were a recent wound, you would be able to see the veins and arteries as if the subject suffered from a varicose condition. There's no evidence of enlarged blood vessels."

"You need to be sure about this, Doctor. I'll be committing a large amount of time and resources based on your observations."

"You actually spoke to the subject? He is ambulatory... intelligent? He's still inside the Area?"

"I can't speak for his intelligence, but he was able to string a few words together and use a cell phone, and yes, he's currently in the Area."

"Secretary, you need to bring this man to me - *now*." Fremont could tell from the near feverish look in the doctor's small, sunken pupils that he was deadly serious.

"You'll have him by tonight, Dr. Sullivan. In the meantime, I want you to pick your two best field doctors from your staff to accompany the teams."

"I'll send Wilder and McDonald. They have the most combat experience," Sullivan said. With that he gathered his photos and left the room without bothering to wait for dismissal. That was the way of the medical establishment when mixed with the military; medicine could go on without war, but war would be short without medicine.

"Warner, call Brooks. Tell him to be waiting on the roof and make sure he still has Heath and the rest under wraps. If I can get them all, so be it. If not, we will extract Mr. Brooks then send the bombers to fill the bunker," Fremont said.

"Right, Boss," Warner pulled out his phone, scrolled down to the number for Josephine's phone and called it. He waited a few seconds then hung up. "It's just going to voicemail. Maybe he went back inside."

"Keep trying him every five minutes. If you don't get a

response by the time the team lifts off we'll have to go in blind. This may be our only chance to gain both an immunity subject and Heath. I don't want to lose either," Fremont said as he lit a cigarette.

"Hey, Boss, what are you gonna' do with Heath and his buddies, anyway?"

"The rest I'll debrief and have shot. As for Mr. Heath I will have the ultimate pleasure of shooting the man myself, something I should've done when he came back the first time. I would have, too, had it not been for General Lightner."

"Lightner, the Air Force puke? What did he have to do with it?"

"Colonel Lightner was the commander of all Air Force search and rescue groups, including Heath's, when the outbreak occurred. As soon as he caught wind that Heath had surfaced at Northgate five years later, now-General Lightner showed up on executive privilege from the SecDef himself," Fremont said as he exhaled, almost spitting the common military moniker for the Secretary of Defense. "Lightner mother-henned Heath throughout the entire debriefing process. He'd never *officially* accepted Heath's resignation. Since Heath was technically still in the military and in a command grade the General had first dibs on his debriefing and only had to supply me with a report. It didn't hurt that Lightner and Heath had been friendly before he'd gone AWOL."

"So Heath was the one that got away, huh?" Warner asked then almost immediately regretted using such a flip tone and word choice.

Fremont eyed him through the cigarette haze then turned his eyes back to the satellite image. He couldn't see the presence of a roof hatch or fire escape on top of the building and the moat of zombies surrounding the structure would make an approach from the ground impossible. "Call for Mr. Brooks again. And keep your glib observations to yourself."

Josephine sat in the kitchen and stared at Cook while Julie

directed Ellen in gathering supplies. She should've been helping them, really, but she needed downtime; time to process the last few days, the last few hours even. Josephine now understood why Heath hadn't wanted her to treat his wounds back in Derry's Corner, why he'd made her wear gloves when she'd insisted on helping him. He carried the same immunity that Craig enjoyed, and with it, the same burden. Her earlier, off-the-cuff comment to Richards had practically forced Heath into a rapid explanation. The immunity did little to help him except to ensure he wouldn't rise again if he were killed. One-on-one situations with a zombie would often result in the undead simply ignoring Heath so long as he made no sudden moves or sounds such as a living animal would make. He was infected, yes, but still a living man that breathed and produced bodily odors. In such close encounters with lone zombies or small groups, he could often pass himself off as one of their kind by avoiding those motions and relying on whatever signature one zombie used to identify another that ran in his blood. All bets were off in a swarm situation, though. The more Heath exerted himself, the more indicators his body produced that told the dead he was not one of them. And, just because he couldn't rise again as a zombie didn't mean he was immune to their grabbing hands, gnashing teeth and the press of hundreds of bodies dragging him under in their wake.

Richards had been ready to damn him for the callous, careless ass Josephine had believed him to be when she'd first met him until Heath told the doctor about his trips to the Minnesota clinic, and only now was Josephine fully grasping what that immunity really meant. To the world, it was an unmistakable boon. It was hope for a vaccine, for a cure. What it meant to Heath was a lifetime of being alone. He was a carrier of the worst, most communicable virus the world had ever known. He carried it in his blood and who knew what other bodily fluids. He would never be able to have sex in good conscience since doing so would subject his partner to infection. He would never be able to father children for the same reason, and any violent injury would mean his death as medical technicians and doctors would refuse to treat him for fear of contracting the virus.

"Penny for your thoughts?" Julie asked. Josephine snapped her head up as if she'd been dozing and looked around the now-clean kitchen and the stacks of MRE's and bottles of water Julie and Ellen had put on the table. Ellen was at the other end of the room, feeding Cook's rats.

"They're not worth that much," Josephine replied. She exhaled roughly then hoisted herself onto the countertop. "I really fucked up, bringing that phone. I guess nobody's immune to momentary bouts with sheer, utter stupidity. Not you and certainly not me." She paused for a moment then looked at Julie. "I wanted to tell you that I really respected the way you handled yourself this morning. It took a lot of guts to tell Howard not to aim at Ellen. That may have been the only thing that would've kept Phillip from shooting you."

"She's just a kid. None of this is her fault. No sense in her being punished for it. Besides, I knew Phillip wouldn't do it. He was shaking like a leaf. I'm pretty sure if it wasn't for him leaning on me he would've fallen over."

"It's not just that...outside with the horses, too. It took a lot of guts to do that."

"You were there, too. We did what we had to do. I mean, somebody had to save the men." They both smiled at that and fell silent for a moment before Josephine continued.

"I don't want this to be a whole *Ya Ya Sisterhood* moment or anything, but when all this is over, I'd like it if you joined me for a cup of coffee. Do you think you'll have time between manicures and banging the news director?" Josephine asked. Julie looked at her for a moment then smiled. No one was more surprised than Josephine by her expression.

"I'll have to check my calendar. I'm going to have to do a lot of fucking to get out of this one. So what are all of our macho men up to?" Julie asked.

"The doctors are gathering supplies, Howard is rounding up weapons and Heath is doing Heath-stuff," Josephine said. Julie walked a few feet down the counter and poured two cups of coffee from an institutional-sized urn and handed one to Josephine.

"It's the real stuff. I found a big can of it in the back of the cupboard," Julie said.

Josephine accepted the cup, held it in both hands under her nose and inhaled deeply. "You don't know how good that smells."

"So what's the deal with Heath?" That earned Julie a wide-eyed look from Josephine.

"What are you talking about?" Josephine asked.

"I don't know. I just sensed some, you know...*tension*," Julie said with a raised eyebrow. Josephine shook her head slowly.

"With everything going on, you're talking about *tension*?" Josephine asked, mimicking her eyebrow gesture.

"Until someone tells me what we're doing, what else do we have to talk about?" Julie asked.

Josephine thought for a moment then shrugged her shoulders. "No, there's no tension. Not like you're thinking, at least."

"Hmm. Funny, I'm usually pretty good at picking up on stuff like that. I guess this whole helicopter-crash-getting-shot-zombie thing has thrown off my radar," Julie said. "I'm not into the bald look myself, but I guess he's not bad if you're into older guys."

"Julie?"

"Yes?"

"You should probably shut up now."

By the time Heath had finished with his tour of the facility Williams was back at the communal table, now filled with all manner of firearms, blades and blunt improvised weapons. Heath sat down and started examining the impromptu armory. "So what do you think?" Heath asked.

"Well, we've got a good selection. This crew was pretty good at scavenging. There's some military, too. Most of it looks like it dates back to the first teams but it's been pretty well maintained," Williams said.

Heath picked up a Beretta pistol and pulled back the slide to open the breach and found the ramp and throat somewhat worn though still serviceable. "I'm more worried about the ammo."

"We won't know that till we pull the trigger. Still, we've got a pretty good assortment. Take your pick."

"I'll stick with what I've got. Enlighten me, Beret; how are they going to take us?" Heath asked. Williams stopped inspecting a sawed-off shotgun and placed it across his lap.

"If I was in charge? They'll repel onto the roof. They won't take the chance that the roof will support an actual landing. They could get in through the window but they'll be coming in with a fire team at least, and having to swing down and enter opens them to falling into the swarm and will make the entry slow-going. I look for them to pop a hole in the roof and drop gas in case anybody's waiting for them inside," Williams said.

"So they'll be masked. That could work in our favor. I take it you didn't find any gas masks for us?"

"One. It's in unused issued condition but the filter went out of date years ago so I'm not sure it'll work. They'll secure the surface building and leave a team spread out between the first and second floor so their way topside won't get cut off. The rest will eventually find a way downstairs. I can tell you I'd drop so much tear gas in here you couldn't see straight then button it up and wait ten minutes before coming down, like fumigating for roaches. Then it's a clean-and-sweep. They'll look for Craig and shoot the rest of us while we're still choking on snot."

"We don't know that they know what Craig looks like."

"They won't have to. They'll check every leg. Anybody that doesn't have it will get a bullet here or get hauled out and get one later. I guess that would depend on just how badly we've pissed them off."

"How many men do you think they'll use down here?" Heath asked.

"I don't know. If they have the floor plans for this place they'd probably run with four to six topside, a couple on the roof and probably twelve to fifteen down here. The numbers will be a crapshoot though. That's all going to depend on how many people they think are down here," Williams said.

"I'm operating under the assumption Craig told them how many, but that they don't have the shelter plans. If they did, they probably would've reduced it to a crater long before now."

"If we go with that I'd send at least twenty down in three teams with a support team on standby at the closest high ground that could support a landing without attracting its own swarm."

"You're not helping my sense of security, you know?" Heath said as he picked up a grenade from the table and turned it over in his hands.

"Hey, it is what it is. The real question becomes; what are we going to do about it? I mean, I'm all for going out in a blaze of glory if that's the only option. But I was kinda hoping you might have an idea or two running around in that chrome-dome of yours."

"I do. But it's real fucking dangerous," Heath said, still holding the grenade.

"Is it any better odds than sitting here and waiting for the gas and bullets?"

"Just slightly."

"Just slightly is better than zero," Williams said. "What do you have in mind?"

"We're going to let them in."

"Well, yeah. We're not going to be able to stop them from blasting their way in here. They'll have superior numbers and firepower-"

"Not Homeland," Heath interrupted, "the dead."

Morgan closed his phone just as the chopper's engines whined to life. The CBC hadn't believed the scoop he'd sent them and had called to make sure it wasn't one of the practical-joke reports he'd been known to produce. He'd even gone so far as to put Sommers himself on the phone to convince them of the video's validity. After that, they were tripping over themselves to comply with the Senator's stipulations and demands. If a group of men in three-piece suits and dour lives could ever be called *giddy*, it would have been at the end of that call. Mason had even managed to get them to commit to letting him do the full interview with the Senator should they make it back, as well as guaranteeing a live feed now from the satellite uplink. That uplink would either be the last resort if Homeland thought they were bluffing, his sure-fire ticket to a Pulitzer, or both. He already had Sommers' blessing to record anything at any time during the operation and had already set up a camera inside the chopper that would record every moment for posterity. The PBS Survivor file footage would have nothing on him. As long as Homeland didn't decide to shove a missile up their tail rotor, of course.

The two choppers lifted off from Westgate and veered north by northeast to follow the western border of the buffer zone, the Ohio River. The river had proven itself both deep and wide enough to serve as Area 187's western boundary. Special steel mesh gates and locks had been installed over the years to keep both undead that managed to fall into the river away from Ohio and Kentucky as well as help keep grave robbers away from West Virginia and Virginia. But even with these precautions, many grave robbers found it far easier to approach the Area from the western side since there was no way Homeland could patch every hole and mind every inch of waterfront. The two pilots kept their ships at least a mile from the invisible line that marked the start of Area 187's restricted airspace as they sped north. Even with their pseudo-military credentials there was no point in running so close that they attracted notice. Morgan checked his watch; ten minutes to eleven.

At precisely eleven, the two helicopters would veer suddenly east and break Area 187 airspace through a small pocket manned only by electronic surveillance between two monitoring substations separated by more than ten miles of uneven riverbank. With any luck it would buy them several seconds before their intrusion could be detected. In that time, Fremont would receive the video. With any luck he would finish the three-minute length with enough time left over to call off whatever measures had been launched the moment they breached the Area. Cartwright had told them it would take less than thirty minutes for a fighter jet to get within missile range, and that figure didn't take into account the automated surface-to-air missile batteries at strategic locations around the buffer zone. If missiles from one of those were launched, they would have less than three minutes from launch to fireball.

"Nothing like being just minutes from death to get the blood pumping, eh?" Morgan said to Cartwright through his headset, his nervousness letting his normally carefully-concealed Canadian accent roll out.

Cartwright looked across the belly of the chopper at him and frowned. "It loses its appeal after the first few hundred times," he said. He checked his watch then looked at the Senator. "This is your last chance to scrub. Once we break the bubble there's no going back," Cartwright said to Sommers, though his words were available through the helicopter's communications system to anyone wearing a headset.

"Fremont won't risk that video being broadcast. There won't be an American news outlet that'll be afraid to run it after that. And, if they do take action against us, Mr. Mason will go live so the American people can see Homeland firing on a United States Senator involved in a rescue mission on U.S. soil," Sommers said.

"Yeah, and I bet if we make it through this I'll be seeing that footage on election ads, too," Cartwright said.

"Every cloud has a silver lining, Captain. Yours will be wealth and the knowledge you've done your country a great service," Sommers said.

"And yours will be one hell of a feather in your cap in a race for the big chair, huh?" Cartwright asked.

Sommers focused his attention on his own watch for a moment. "Let's all concentrate on the present for now, Captain. The future holds its own rewards."

Eric R. Lowther

Chapter XXIII
Desperate Measures

"You're absolutely insane," Josephine said. There was no excitement in her voice. It was a simple statement of fact. Heath had gathered them together at the communal table to formulate an escape plan, and he could tell Josephine wasn't the only one to receive it with less than enthusiasm.

"I don't see how that enters into it." Heath said. Josephine shook her head slowly and didn't bother to look at the rest of the assemblage for support.

"You want to open the door and let the swarm just roll in so that when Homeland bursts in they'll get a face-full of zombie? Then we all just stroll out through the back door? I think sanity is a relevant consideration," Josephine said.

"Well, when you say it like that..." Williams said.

"We wouldn't be doing this *just* so Homeland will be facing them, although that's a convenient. The swarm won't move away from the door. Letting them inside is the only way to break the siege," Heath explained.

"So, exactly where are we going to be when we throw the doors open for this human buffet?" Julie asked.

Heath sighed and pulled a black marker out of his pocket. He drew a rough representation of the underground on the table and jabbed a finger at the far end of what appeared to be a long passage.

"This is the corridor that runs to the secondary hatch. There's a small utility room here," Heath said, marking the spot with a small circle, "about ten yards from that hatch. It'll be a tight squeeze, but we can bar the door and stay in there until the dead file past us and into the shelter. Once they're past us, we beat feet out the back. We may run into some remnants of the swarm on the outside but nothing like what's there now. The key will be in the timing."

"The key will be in hoping the swarm outside that door isn't so large by now that they don't end up just jamming the hall leaving us trapped in the utility room," Josephine said.

Heath spread his hands and looked around the room. "I'm open to suggestions," he said to the group.

"Pardon me, but regardless of how we plan to escape what are we going to do about Ellen? She can't possibly keep up. I'm not even sure *I'll* be able to keep up. Besides, what are we going to do with them?" Richards said. Almost as one the group looked around at the bodies on the floor.

"They're fresh. They'll serve as bait to make sure the zombies keep coming and not just stand around jamming up the hallway," Heath said. Richards sat aghast.

"I can't allow that! These were real people. I've known some of them for years. I won't have them disrespected in such a manner!" Richards said.

"If they really were friends, Doc, don't you think they'd want you to survive? We can't take them with us and we don't have the time or the places to try and hide them so they can rot in peace," Heath said.

"That... that's ghoulish," Phillip said.

"You should've thought about that before you killed them. If it hadn't been for Heath, you would've killed your own daughter, too," Josephine said. Phillip looked at her for a moment then hung his head.

"I can't do as you ask," Richards said. "These people are family..."

"I'm not asking you to do a damn thing, Doc!" Heath suddenly exploded. "I didn't knock them down, and I sure as hell didn't give Homeland the advantage of picking the timetable. You know the situation, you know what we're up against, and you know you stay down here and you fucking die. We need to get the hell out of here and we're wasting time talking about fucking meat!" Heath said.

"What about you?" Phillip asked, raising his head to look at Heath. "What if Dr. Richards and I decide not to leave, to take our chances with Homeland. Are you going ahead with your plan to let the zombies inside so you can escape?"

"Jesus but you've got balls," Williams said. "This whole deal is in whopping parts *your* fucking fault."

"I'm not risking my daughter's life on some suicide pact! Craig said you people would come up with some crazy scheme..."

Heath silenced him with a look. "No plan will work without everyone's cooperation. If Richards decides he wants to stay down here and let Homeland kill all of you then that's his prerogative. You, I could care less about. You've used up what good will I may have had," Heath said, then turned to Richards. "This is still your dog-and-pony show if you decide to stay down here, Doc. I need to know what you're going to do."

Richards looked at the faces around the table, pausing briefly on Phillip before coming back to Heath. "Even if we do manage to get outside, what good will it do? If what you say is true they'll just hunt us from the air and kill us before we get anywhere near the wall."

"Outside, we have a chance. Down here, nothing," Heath said. The doctor sighed, rubbed his eyes roughly then nodded. The act seemed to age him another ten years right before their eyes.

"So we're all committed to getting out of here?" Heath asked the table though he kept looking at Richards.

"God help us, yes," Richards finally said after a long pause.

"Good. Jo', you and Julie get the supplies ready. Take Ellen with you," Heath said.

Phillip suddenly increased his grip on his daughter and pulled her even closer to him. "Ellen stays with me," Phillip said.

Heath stood and looked down at him from his full height. "I could care less about what you want, Phillip. Do what I say, when I say it, and you might just be able to ride out of here on her coattails. When you're out of my sight I want her with people I trust, and right now that number doesn't include you," Heath said.

"You can't..." Phillip stammered.

Heath was down the table and on him in the blink of an eye. He pulled Ellen away with one hand and grabbed Phillip's face with the other, forcing him to look into his daughter's eyes. "Everything I do from here on is for her. I would expect at the very least her father to understand that. Look at your daughter, Phillip. Look at her. Do you want her to die? Do you want her to know that her Daddy had a chance to get her out of here and he didn't take it because he was afraid...not for her but for himself? She deserves a chance, Phillip, even if you, me or the rest of us don't." Ellen looked up at him then back to her father. Phillip stared at his daughter for a long moment until a tear started in the corner of his eye. Heath put her down and then kneeled beside her.

"What's happening?" Ellen asked.

"Honey, I want you to go get your bag, the one with all your stuff in it, and I want you to come back to the kitchen and stay with Josephine and Julie, okay? We may need to move really, really fast and I need to know that you're safe," Heath said.

She looked back once at her father and then at Heath. "Are we leaving?"

"Yeah...yeah, honey...we're leaving," Heath said.

"Where are we going?"

"Out There...the cities and all the places and the people? That's where we're going," Heath said.

"Is Daddy coming, too?"

"You'll have to ask Daddy that," Heath said. Both he and the little girl looked at Phillip.

Phillip swallowed hard then got up from his seat. "Yes, Ellen, of course I'm coming. I'm not going to leave you."

Ellen smiled then wrapped her arms around her father's legs. "We're going Out There!" Ellen practically screamed through her huge smile. "Can we go to a candy store, and a zoo?"

"We'll go wherever you want to go," Phillip said. The tears

were rolling freely now and he wiped at them with both hands before Ellen's beaming face turned up to him. "Now go do what Heath said. Daddy and Dr. Richards have a lot of work to do."

"Okay!" Ellen chimed. She bounded away a few steps then suddenly stopped, turned and came back to the table. She picked up Sir John the plastic knight and Blackhawk the plastic dragon from beside the huge pile of weapons and ammunition then ran off.

"I hope you know what you're doing," Phillip said to Heath. "I don't want to get her hopes up just to have them crushed," he added bitterly.

"Hope is all any of us have right now," Josephine said as she joined Julie.

Phillip looked at the two women for a moment then took a step closer to Heath. "I want you to know something," Phillip said to Heath in a low hiss. "I *did* love Eileen, John, just as much and as truly as you did. Everything I've done, good or bad in anyone's eyes, has been for her and for Ellen. I couldn't keep Eileen safe. My daughter is all I have left, for me and for Eileen. We both want the same thing, John; to keep Ellen safe. We just have different ideas about it. But you must respect that she's *my* daughter, not yours... and I *demand* that you give me that respect, especially in front of her. You could kill me but doing so won't change the fact that *I'm* her father, not you."

Julie and Josephine exchanged looks then nodded slightly to each other as Julie reached out and took Williams' arm and started leading him towards the kitchen.

"What the hell are you doing? We're going to miss Heath knocking Phil's dick in the dirt," Williams said to them as Julie dragged him away.

After the three were gone Heath took a step himself to close the gap between them to mere inches. Richards got up and went across the room to check on Craig, leaving the two men alone.

"Well, Phil, I *still* love *my* wife, and Ellen is all that's left of her regardless of how she came to be. I can promise you if there's a chance any of us make it back she'll be the first one on the other side. But we're bugging out and that makes this *my* cluster-fucked dog-and-pony show now, and I won't hesitate to mow you down if you get in my way. Once you two are *Out There*, you can be daddy again. Until then, you're sperm donor. You can tell her that only through her father's heroic, singular efforts did the two of you get out alive. But before that can happen, we have to get out. *You* must understand one thing, Phil. I'm not going to risk Ellen's life by giving a shit if I hurt your little feelings or somehow make you less of a man in her eyes."

"Ahem," Richards cleared his throat loudly from behind them. "Phillip and I still have work to do in the infirmary."

Heath stepped aside and let Phillip join Richards. He watched them go then turned to the kitchen. "Howie!" Heath called. Williams appeared almost instantly. "Come on. We've got to figure this thing out."

"Just one question; what the hell are we going to do with Cook? He's still tied up back there, you know?" Williams said as he fell into step beside Heath.

"What? Do I have to think of everything?" Heath asked.

Heath and Williams walked down the corridor, each memorizing minute details with practiced military efficiency. By the time they reached the end not a niche, crack or overhead utility pipe or conduit had gone unnoticed. The upward-sloping ramp that led to the outside of the shelter lay behind a thick steel door at the end of the hallway just as Heath had sketched on the table for the group. Heath left Williams to examine the utility room while he went to inspect the exit door.

"I don't think everyone will fit in here," Williams said as he slid the door into its wall pocket and checked the room's interior. "Besides, you didn't tell me it had a sliding door. There isn't even a way to lock it from the inside." Williams ran his hand down the interior door jamb while his other hand idly flipped the steel hasp mounted on the outside face of the door. The hasp was designed to be used with a padlock and secured from the outside, not from within.

"It'll have to do," Heath said simply as he ran his hands over his own door then put his ear against it. It had been weeks since anyone had been out the door, and it was entirely plausible that the dead could have made it through the surface door and were now crowding the escape ramp to the surface. After several moments of silence he stepped back and scanned every inch of the wall around the door.

"This door's pretty thin to boot, Heath. I could probably punch a hole right through it," Williams added as he rapped his knuckles in several places to sound its hollow nature as Heath joined him.

"It doesn't have to be strong," Heath said as he slid the door closed and stepped back from it. "Zombies aren't big on detail, especially when they have somewhere to go. With any luck they'll just walk right past and into the shelter."

Williams slid the door open and closed several times then stepped back beside Heath. "If even one of them just bumps this door or if they hear or smell something, we'll all be dead. You know that, right? They'll be packed against the walls as they file through the hall. It'd be real easy with as many of them as there will be for them to end up sliding it open completely by accident."

"Yeah, I know," Heath said without taking his eyes off the door before them.

Williams stepped inside the doorway and faced Heath where he stood in the hall. "This wall starts almost exactly with the door. With the angle so close there isn't even a way to rig a hasp or a bar," Williams said. He flicked on the small room's single, dangling light bulb and stared at the top of the door for a moment. "The door's track is mounted to the ceiling, not to the floor. We won't even be able to shove a broom handle into the track." He shook his head slowly. "I don't know if you're going to get the others to go along with this, especially when the only thing standing between us and the zombies will be an unlocked door."

"Instead of figuring out why it *won't* work let's try to focus on how it *can* work, huh?"

"Look, Heath, far be it from me to piss on your parade,

but if we can't secure this door we might as well take our chances with Homeland. At least they'll just shoot us. If even one of those pusbags figures out this door ain't a wall we'll be screwed."

Heath grabbed the lock hasp mounted on the outside of the door and gave it a hard tug to test its strength. "Then we'll have to secure the door from outside," Heath said. Williams chuckled to himself and leaned against the door.

"That means someone has to stay *outside* to lock us in, then live long enough to let us out."

"Yes, it does," Heath said to the ceiling as he inspected the power conduits that ran down the corridor.

"Oh, no. No you don't you little prick. You're not going to get killed out here and leave me stuck in there with a bunch of pissed-off, armed people."

"You volunteering for the job?" Heath asked. He walked down the hall towards the exit door, marking off the distance between it and the utility room.

"No, but there won't be anywhere for you to hide out here. And if something does happen to you we're all screwed."

"Somebody was going to have to be outside the utility room to open the door and let them in anyway," Heath said.

"Yeah, but I understood that to mean you open the door then run hell-bent for leather back here and get into the utility room, one with a door that locks from the inside, before they caught up."

"The dead's in the details," Heath said as he turned and walked down the hall with his eyes still glued to the lines of conduit above their heads.

Williams looked up along with him. "You think those things will support your weight?" Williams asked. Heath answered by jumping and catching a conduit in each hand then hauled himself up, twisting his body until he lay looking down at Williams. The narrow metal tubes had creaked a bit when the big man first hauled himself up and into the ceiling but quieted once Heath's body weight was spread over the half-dozen of them that ran together down the hall. "Oh, great, stop encouraging him, will ya?" Williams said to the pipes. "This is just super. We get the one fucking government-contracted project that was actually built to code," he added under his breath.

Heath swung to the floor and looked back and forth between the two doors. "We can do this."

"Let's put the power of positive thinking aside for a sec. What the hell are we going to do once we do get outside, huh? I mean, I'm with you in getting the hell out of Dodge and all, but we're not home free."

"Once we get away from the swarm we're going to lead everybody east and reverse the route Josephine and I used to get here. Your uncle got us in here with his best way under the wall and there's a safe house near enough that we can hole everybody up there and get Jo's story out. Once it hits the air there won't be any way Homeland or anyone else will be able to stop it."

"There's a whole lot of ground to cover between here and home. You know they're going to be looking for us with everything they've got. They may even send out ground teams."

"If we get to the point where we have to worry about that, it means we were able to get out of *here*. One problem at a time, huh? Let's see if everybody's ready. I don't know how much time we have, but I'm sure it's not enough," Heath said as they started back towards the shelter's rooms.

Fremont walked into the monitoring station. Where there'd been only Cline and another agent working the boards the night before, the room now practically buzzed with activity. "Both teams are en route, Boss," Warner said as he met Fremont behind one of the communications consoles.

"ETA?" Fremont asked.

"52 minutes to the site. There's a group of bald hills with steep approaches about six miles from the site for the choppers to set down once the primary team hits the surface building," Cline said from his terminal. "The secondary team will secure the landing site and wait for further instructions."

"Good. I trust we've sent the appropriate men?" Fremont asked Warner. His accident numbers were already three times higher than normal this month. The President could overlook a lot of things concerning Area 187, but if too many more agents, soldiers and equipment were eliminated he'd have some hefty explaining to do.

"Company men and zombie vets, every one of them," Warner assured him. "Even the pilots." The sudden peal of shrill electronic alarms split the room.

"What the hell is that?" Fremont asked.

"Comm 1, report!" Cline said into the room. An agent at the console in front of Cline half-turned in his chair.

"West Gate reports two bogies breaking the bubble about 30 miles north of them," the agent said.

"Westgate Command, acknowledge," Cline said into his headset microphone. Fremont and Warner both picked up headsets and slipped them on.

"Westgate here," a woman's voice replied.

"Westgate, confirm bogies breaching restricted Area space." Cline said.

"Confirmed, Northgate. Also, be advised we have positively identified the aircraft and have changed their status from 'bogie' to 'rouge'. Unable to contact rouge units designated as Alpha 346 and Tango 218 from today's cancelled maneuvers. We have surface missile lock on both targets," the woman's voice said. Fremont covered his boom mike with his hand and looked at Warner.

"I want to know who's in those rouges, Warner – *now*," Fremont barked. Warner nodded once, threw off his headset, and ran to the phone in the conference area.

Fremont looked up to the far wall and saw several of the monitors had changed to a tracking image much like the one Julie's tracer had used showing the real-time advance of the two rouge choppers. The two red dots were moving with deceptive slowness, but by watching their advance relative to the stationary map on which they rode he could tell they were moving as fast as the ships could go. "Cline, can you show our teams on the same screen with the rouges?"

"Yes sir," Cline's fingers flew across a keyboard and seconds later the choppers carrying Fremont's extraction teams appeared as blue dots with a trailing blue line connecting them to Northgate.

"Now, add the mission site," Fremont said. A small red bull's eye appeared on the screen. It didn't take a genius to see both sets of helicopters were heading for the same place. "Sommers..." Fremont said under his breath. "Blast those rouges out of the sky!"

"Yes sir!" Cline answered. He switched his communications from internal to external and started going through the codes that would launch the missiles from the surface-to-air batteries.

"Harry! You may want to put a hold on that!" Warner called out from the conference table. The phone's receiver was still in his hand. The use of his first name in mixed company jolted Fremont. Cline was already looking up at him expectantly.

"Tell them to standby," Fremont said to Cline. Cline bobbed his head and went back to his work as Fremont stalked to the table. "What is it?"

"The rouges are a specially-activated reserve unit. They were supposed to participate in the war games this morning," Warner said.

"What reserve unit? I didn't authorize any call-up, training or otherwise."

"No, but Sommers pulled some strings. The exercises were being run by the military, not us. The operation wasn't breaking the bubble. That's how he was able to do it without bringing up a red flag. To top it off-"

"Issue an order in my name to find and detain Senator Alan Sommers in connection with the breach of Area 187 security protocols this instant!" Fremont said, interrupting Warner.

"Harry, if you want him, you'll have to go inside to get him. He's aboard one of the rouges," Warner said.

"What?" Fremont practically exploded with the word.

"The main communications room received a video from the CBC. I'm having them pipe it to the private monitor here." Warner then put the phone back to his ear, said a few words and hung up. He went behind Fremont and closed the door to keep the excited chatter of the command center out and, as he'd been told he'd want to do, keep the message in. Fremont lit a cigarette as Warner crossed the room, flicked on the monitor, then punched a button on the display's control mounted to the table. The two men watched the recording that Josh Mason had made less than two hours before. It was barely three minutes long, but that three minutes could easily destroy seven years of calm, plausible denial bought with billions of dollars and hundreds of thousands of lives.

"I'll push the button myself to blow that traitor from the sky!" Fremont said as a computer printer in a corner of the room came to life. Warner turned off the monitor and plucked the paper from the printer's tray. He scanned it quickly then again more slowly accompanied by what could only be called a growl.

"You'll want to think about that, Boss," Warner said as he handed the document to Fremont. Fremont read the e-mail from head of the CBC news division that had accompanied the video clip twice before he dropped his cigarette to the plush carpet, grinding the embers into the shag with his heel as he spun, threw open the door and charged into the command center.

"Cline! At present speed, who will get to the mission site first?" Fremont asked as he took up a position behind the agent's chair.

"Our teams will, sir, by about fifteen minutes," Cline answered.

Fremont turned to find Warner by his side. "Warner, call the SecDef. Explain the situation and tell him he needs to get cooperation from the Canadians to shut down the CBC's report. If Sommers could transmit that video, he may be able to transmit more while they're in flight. When you're done with that find out what operators in the communications room viewed it and have them secured for debriefing," Fremont said.

"Why don't we fire up the static?" Warner asked, referring to the Area's extensive communications jamming technology.

"Because we can't pick and choose; if we black out their communications we'll cut off our own teams as well. You have your orders, now follow them!" Fremont said, adding a hard shove to Warner's chest for emphasis. The fat man's brow knitted together at the unexpected attack but he regained his composure and quickly trotted off. "Order Westgate to scramble a flight of Apaches and Southgate to launch the bomber." Fremont ordered to Cline. "Get the Apaches in front of the rouges and see if they can slow them down, but under no circumstances are they to engage without my consent. I want the bomber to get in place, hold position over the mission site and await further instructions."

"Yes sir. What about the missiles?" Cline asked.

"Keep the lock and await further instructions," Fremont said. "And when you're done with that, I want you to work on getting the rouges to answer their radio. Use my name. Let me know the minute you establish communications."

"Yes sir," Cline said.

Fremont lit another cigarette and started pacing behind Cline's station. Not only did Sommers have him by the balls, he'd dragged them right along with him into Area 187. If the Canadians could be convinced to cooperate, Fremont could take Sommers and his ill-conceived rescue attempt out of the air with virtually no backlash. Even a Senator couldn't violate Area 187, and by tightly controlling their communications Fremont could deny he had knowledge that the Senator was aboard when everything came out in the wash. But if the Canadians decided now would be a good time to express their independence from their overbearing southerly neighbor, he would have a lot more to explain than a few accidents.

By the time Heath and Williams made it back to the common room the rest were busy with their individual preparations. Phillip was making sure Ellen's tiny leather coat was securely fastened and that nothing loose hung from her except her backpack. Julie had scavenged the shelter and had come up with leather jackets and even a few Kevlar pieces for her and Williams. Richards had changed into a pair of jeans and mid-calf military jump boots topped off by a thick denim shirt and his own worn, stained leather jacket.

He carried no weapons. "Arm up, Doc," Heath said as he started checking his own gear. He would have to leave his rifle and pack in the utility room with the others in the interest of speed, leaving only his sidearm and trusted steel bar for his weapons.

"I'm a doctor," Richards said. Heath stopped his own preparations long enough to snag a small .380 automatic pistol from the pile. He checked to make sure the magazine was loaded then handed the gun to the doctor.

"They aren't people anymore. Don't tell me you haven't had to kill one," Heath said.

"I haven't used a gun in years. I'd only be wasting bullets. Phillip is adept, though. I'll see to Ellen. That should be enough to keep me busy," Richards said, avoiding Heath's question as he picked up a crowbar from the table and slid it into one of his belt loops. Heath shrugged and slid the small pistol into his back pocket.

"You sure you want to trust Phillip with a gun?" Julie asked Heath as Phillip loaded spare bullets into the slots on his belt. Phillip looked up at them but didn't stop loading his belt.

"We'll need every bullet we can get," Heath said as he checked his own rifle and pistol magazines then tapped them against his palm to make sure the feed springs weren't bound up. "Phillip's just as prone to death as the rest of us. Doing something stupid only means he dies, too." Heath slid his pistol into his holster and tightened the lash across the bar on his hip. "And you don't want to die, do you, Phil?" Phillip stopped for a moment, opened his mouth and then shut it with a shake of his head.

"So we're going with this plan of yours?" Josephine asked as she finished loading her speed loaders.

"More or less," Heath said.

"More or less; anything else I should know about?" Josephine asked.

"If something happens to me you'll have to lead everybody back the way we came."

"If something happens to you, it's going to happen to us all..."

"They're going to need your story. You and Ellen have to

make it back. The rest of us are expendable at this point. Now, do you know the way back?" Heath asked. Josephine sighed and rubbed a hand down her face. Her lack of sleep was starting to show in her eyes.

"Yes," Josephine said. Heath pulled the map and GPS device from his pack and handed them to her. She thought about refusing them but eventually shoved them in her own pack. Julie came out of the kitchen with the last of the provision packs and gave one to Williams then tried to slip the other onto her own shoulders until a lance of pain stopped her.

"You're not going to be able to carry that," Williams said.

"I have to do something, Howie. I'll be useless in a running fight and now I can't even carry my own stuff. What the hell am I supposed to do?" Julie asked.

"Hey, every horror movie needs the pretty little blonde to scream a lot and burst out of her blouse at the appropriate dramatic moments," Williams said, letting his words trail off through his smirk.

"Laugh it up, funny boy," Julie said.

"Stay close and watch my back. You keep them off our backsides and I'll keep them off our front, okay?" Williams said. Josephine overheard them and grinned softly, their arrangement so like hers and Heath's. Julie nodded at him then checked her own arms. "What about Craig, and Cook for that matter?" Williams asked Heath.

"He's going with us."

"Well, Craig, yeah... but what are we doing with Cook?" Williams asked. Heath went to the bench where Craig was tied and slapped him a few times to wake him.

"We're leaving," Heath told Craig as he removed the restraints that had fastened him to the bench. Craig sat up slowly and mumbled something against his gag. Heath pulled the gag away and Craig promptly spat at him, aiming for his unprotected eyes and missing them.

"What about my hands?" Craig asked, holding up his bound wrists. "You have to untie me and give me a gun."

"No." Heath said as he pushed Craig into a stumbling walk towards the table.

"How am I supposed to defend myself?" Craig asked as he staggered to a stop in front of Julie, Williams and Josephine.

"We'll take care of that. Julie, I need you to keep Craig under your barrel until I come back for all of you. I'll take him from there. Under no circumstances are you to touch him anywhere that he's bled. If he gives you any trouble, you have my express consent to blow his head off," Heath said. Craig opened his mouth to protest but Heath replaced the gag before Craig could say a word.

"Wait a minute...what do you mean, 'come back'?" Josephine asked.

Heath ignored her and turned Craig around to face the wall while he coiled a piece of rope around Craig's waist and worked at attaching the bonds around his wrist to it to keep Craig from being able to raise his hands above his waist.

"The door to the utility room can't be locked from the inside. We'll have to be locked in and sit tight until the dead clear the hallway. Then Heath will let us out and we can scoot on out the back door," Williams said as he adjusted the straps on his pack. Everyone in the room except for Craig turned to stare first at Williams and then at Heath.

"Wait a minute... that wasn't in the plan," Josephine protested.

"I told you; more or less," Heath said as he cinched the knots in Craig's rope.

"You're an idiot! How do you intend to hide from them? What if something happens to you and we're stuck in there?" Josephine asked. Heath held up a hand and looked around the room at everyone.

"Just keep listening at the door. You'll know when the zombies move past. If I don't come back for you within five minutes from the time you can't hear them anymore, use a shotgun up against the door and blow the lock off from the inside. You'll make a hell of a racket but at least you should be able to get everyone through the door and topside before they could turn around and follow," Heath said as easily as if he were giving them a recipe for chocolate cake.

"There has to be another way," Josephine said.

"There isn't and we don't have time to talk about it. Is everyone ready?" Heath asked. He looked at each of them until they nodded in turn. Then he looked down at Ellen. She'd sat quietly at the table throughout the proceedings, content to play with her dragon and let the grown-ups go through their motions. "Ellen? I want you to stay real close to Dr. Richards, okay?"

"What about Daddy?" Ellen asked.

"We may need Daddy to help us in case the Singers get too close. We're all going to be sticking real close together so don't worry, you'll be able to see Daddy the whole time, okay?" Heath said. Ellen didn't answer but nodded once then hopped off the bench and went to stand with Richards. "Okay, let's do this. Howie, get everybody down to the room. I still have something to take care of here."

"Cook?" Williams asked.

"Yeah," Heath said.

"What are you going to do?" Richards asked, suddenly concerned. "He's mentally ill, John. He doesn't deserve to die here like a dog."

"I'm going to give Cook exactly what he wants. Now go on, we're wasting daylight," Heath said. Richards glared at Heath for a moment then turned and walked away with the rest. Just as they reached the mouth of the hall leading to the utility corridor Ellen broke away from the group and ran back to Heath.

"Here," Ellen said, holding up Sir John to him. "He's good luck." Heath looked at the toy then pushed her hand back.

"No, Ellen. You hold onto him. I might lose him. What would Blackhawk do then?" Heath said. Ellen smiled and forced her small hand around Heath's and shoved the knight into his stomach.

"You won't lose him, I know you won't. You can give him back to me when we get Out There," Ellen said. She let go of the toy and Heath caught it out of reflex. Before he could protest further Ellen turned and ran back to the group. Heath watched them go until only Josephine remained where the hall met the common room.

"Heath…" Josephine started.

"Go," Heath ordered gently but commandingly. With a last look at him she disappeared down the hall. Heath looked around the room, empty save for the battered furniture and the bodies of the survivors that had made it through so much only to be brought down by one of their own. He grabbed a small nylon bag from the table then made his way into the kitchen. Cook was awake and sitting quietly, still bound to his chair and looking at his rats in their cages.

"Cook, right?" Heath asked as he leaned against the island counter. Cook didn't answer, just continued to stare and smile at his rats. "We're going away from the dead." Cook's head swiveled at the mention of the word 'dead'. He now had the digger's undivided attention.

"I can't leave the dead. They need me, need me to free their souls to join God in His house. He commands me to send them," Cook said in a voice that couldn't help but remind Heath of Renfield. It was obvious from his wild, glistening eyes that Cook was too far around the bend for reality to faze him now.

"I can respect that, doing God's work. What about your friends?"

"They are my flock. I nourish their souls and their bodies… the body is a temple unto the Lord… the dead are perversions of His temples… they must be cleansed and their souls freed."

"Do you know what's happened?" Heath asked.

"I know most of them are dead now. I saw Phillip this morning. He didn't know I was watching him. Oh, yes, I was watching him. I know everything that happens in my kitchen. It's where I make the food that nourishes our temples to the Lord-"

Heath held up a hand to interrupt him. "Then why didn't you say something to someone?" Heath asked.

"Everything that happens is God's will; *everything*," Cook said.

Heath cleared his throat. "We're all in danger. We're leaving and not coming back. Do you want to go with us?" Heath said.

A deep frown split Cook's face. "I can't leave. God has work for me to do. I must save their souls. I must stay," Cook said. Heath nodded then leaned down and loosened the straps around Cook's chest until they fell away. Cook looked up at him, flexing his hands and moving his arms to return their circulation.

"Your friends...they're not like you. They have to serve Him in their own callings, and they've been called back to the world, to tell everyone about your service to God. I'm going to lead them back. In a little while, the dead are going to come in; a lot of them. You won't survive. If you stay you're going to die," Heath said.

"There is no greater reward than dying for what you believe in," Cook said. From Williams' description of Cook's episode, Heath had expected Cook to leap from his seat and rave and rant at the mention of the dead that would soon be crammed into the shelter. Instead, the digger was calm, poised and possessed of a quiet dignity.

"You can still do one more thing for your flock. We need time. We need to move as many of the dead into the shelter and away from the back door as we can. That means we have to let them come all the way into the common room so I can lead your flock away. Can you wait in the common room for them to come to you? Will you be able to have Job's patience and let as many into the common room as you can before freeing their souls?" Heath asked.

"This will help my flock?"

"Yes. You have to let them into the common room, not bottled up in the hall. Can you do that?" Cook stood up slowly and smiled at Heath.

"You are a just and righteous man. I will do as you ask; the last act for my flock before they become yours. Swear to me you will lead them unto the light and I will swear to you that my blades won't fall before I can see nothing above, below or behind but those souls trapped in decaying flesh."

"You have my word," Heath said and dropped the nylon bag on the counter. Cook nodded and opened the cabinet beside his chair to retrieve his machetes. He strapped them on then went to the cages. One by one he opened the doors and released the rats until they were all scampering about the kitchen.

"Be free, my friends," Cook said then turned to Heath. "*Vade in pace, et Dominus sit tecum.*"

"*Et cum spiritu tuo*," Heath said, the Latin rolling oddly yet cleanly from his tongue. He made a mental apology to Sister Mary Agnes, wherever she may be, for when he'd told her studying Latin was a waste of time. Cook smiled at Heath's response then drew his machetes and laid them on the table. He poured water into a small pitcher, placed it on the table between the blades then laid hands on it while whispering a blessing. Heath turned and walked out of the kitchen, leaving the holy man to his holy preparations.

Heath went to the table, still heavy with the weaponry they couldn't take with them, and picked up several grenades. He hung them from his belt then dug into the pile of hand weapons and tools, made a few selections then headed towards the surface building. Heath had his own preparations to complete, and not one of them holy.

"They're trying to raise us," the pilot said in their earphones. "What do you want me to do?"

"Let Fremont stew a little," Sommers replied.

"Do you think that's wise?" Morgan asked. "If they don't hear from us they may just shoot us down."

"We're better than 50 miles inside. If they were going to they would've already. Fremont has received the video by now, and he knows his only chance is to try and keep the Canadians from airing it. If we suddenly explode, you'll know your government caved to the pressure," Sommers said.

"Rodman, ETA to the site?" Cartwright asked the pilot.

"About 25 minutes... hey, Captain... we have company." the pilot said.

"What is it?" Cartwright asked.

"Two Apaches coming in fast. Those ships are way faster

than us and their wings are full," Rodman said, referring to the small stabilizing wings that also served as weapons pylons on the sides of the attack helicopters. "We won't outrun them and we sure won't outgun them. Orders?"

"Maintain course and speed," Sommers said before Cartwright could respond. "Those helicopters aren't here to bring us down, at least not yet. If they'd wanted to do that they would have sent the jets or a surface missile."

"Don't let them in front of you. They're going to try to slow us down or force us to land. Stay high, don't let them get on top of you and force us to the ground," Cartwright ordered. The pilot nodded, using hand signals through his side window to relay that order to the second chopper speeding along beside them.

"What if they open fire?" Rodman asked.

"If those birds fire, we're gone. Those things are made for killing, and except for a doorgun we've got dick in this grocery-getter," Cartwright said. Then he switched off his mike, motioned for Sommers to do the same, and leaned close so he could hear him over the engine. "They might not blast us en route, but I'm willing to bet they'll keep us from pulling off the extraction. If we hover, they'll box us in and force us to ground. If we land, they'll sit on top of us to make sure we can't take off again. They already know where we're going. If it were me I'd have my own team going in there to beat us to the punch. Without evidence, you're gonna go from Senator to kook right-fucking-quick. You still want to do this? We might be able to work something out with Homeland if we beg off now."

Sommers thought for a moment then motioned for Mason to come close. "Mr. Mason, let's get to that live report now," he said. Mason stared at him blankly until a long smile creased his face.

"What are you up to, Senator?" Cartwright shouted over the whirring of the rotors.

"Just a little more insurance, Captain," Sommers said.

Eric R. Lowther

It was nearly noon under a clear, sunlit sky by the time Homeland's primary extraction team found themselves hovering over the massive swarm surrounding the tiny building. The chopper hung in the air less than five feet above the building's roof just long enough to disgorge its fifteen-man fire team before roaring off to wait out the operation with the secondary team. The zombies, lacking the intelligence required for true depth perception, reached up into the air in an attempt to grab hold of the aircraft. The dead renewed their efforts and enthusiasm against the building, excited by the masked, armored and very much living men that lined the roof's edges looking down into their midst.

"Pop the top," Lieutenant Vargas ordered. Two men went to work on the center of the roof. Moments later both moved away from the large steel dome they'd bolted there to join their comrades around the edges of the roof. The soldiers turned their backs and kneeled low as the charge detonated, the explosion's roar deadened by the dome that forced the power of the blast down and into the much more yielding roof to produce a rough, five-foot diameter hole. Three canisters of tear gas dropped through the hole and into the top floor of the entrance building. Their noxious fumes mixed with the smoke and dust from the explosion to fill the small building with a yellowish haze as the first team slid on their gasmasks and started dropping through the hole and into the building until only two men remained to secure the roof.

Vargas crouched at the top of the stairs and trained his submachine gun into the stairwell before signaling the rest to secure the two rooms that made up the first floor below. He signaled one man to remain at the building's only door, the moaning and pounding of the dead reverberating through it like a primal drum while the rest took up positions in the corners of both rooms.

The Lieutenant had warned his men in the mission briefing that not only would they be facing hardened, deeply-entrenched and quite possibly well-armed survivors, they'd be facing the likes of the storied John Heath as well as Howard Williams, one of the best combat marksmen and urban assault specialists the Army had ever produced. That Fremont wanted both Heath and another

548

subject named Brooks alive made the work even more dangerous, especially when they'd have to search the legs of every man they found for an identifying wound before killing them. Every minute the team took to find the way in was another minute the survivors had to prepare.

Satellite photos had shown another swarm a short distance away, the object of their attention a three-by-five brick shed listed as a water department pump monitoring station. Vargas had agreed this site may be a disguised, secondary entrance. With any luck, the swarms at both ends of the hole had buttoned it up tight, leaving his targets with no other choice but to stay underground and get their lungs full of tear gas and bullets. If all went according to plan, it would be like shooting fish in a barrel.

"Captain! Listen," Rodman said from the pilot's chair. His co-pilot, Denver, flipped a few switches and piped the audio through the ship's communications headsets. Sommers, Cartwright and Mason listened, each watching the others for their reactions to the repeated calls in the name of the Secretary himself.

"Fremont wants to talk, does he?" Sommers said to no one in particular. "It looks like our Canadian friends came through."

"That or he's just trying to get us to break off because he doesn't want to explain to the President why he had to blow a U.S. Senator out of the sky over Area 187." Cartwright said. The world tilted back suddenly, pinning them to their seats for a moment under the pained whine of the rotor over their heads.

"Damn it, Rodman! What the hell are you doing up there?" Cartwright yelled into his mike.

"Evasive maneuvers! The Apaches are playing chicken with us!" Rodman said as he and Denver fought to keep the helicopter under control. A look out the side window showed the other unit was being harassed in the same manner.

"They're trying to slow us down," Cartwright said. The helicopter slowly leveled, then whipped first right then left as Rodman picked his way through a hole between the two war birds outside.

"These old buckets can't take this kind of stress, Captain. We could end up shearing pieces off," Rodman said.

"How much longer?" Mason asked.

"At least another 20 minutes, but that's going to be up to these guys. Every time they make a pass at us, add another minute or two," Denver responded.

"Everyone else, leave your microphones off," Sommers ordered as he flipped his microphone down from his headset. Rodman craned his head back over his shoulder to look at Cartwright. Only when the Captain gave the nod did his pilot flip another switch and return his attentions to the skies.

"This is Senator Allan Sommers. Put the Secretary on the line," Sommers said. There was a long, static-filled pause before Fremont's voice came into their speakers like a snake slithering through mud.

"You've caused quite a commotion, Senator. The only reason I haven't ordered your aircraft destroyed is my respect for your office. However, that respect can only be pushed so far. I order you to divert to Northgate immediately. If you don't comply, I'll be forced to uphold the Area 187 Act and declare you a danger to national security-" Fremont said.

"Have you seen any good news programs lately, Secretary?" Sommers interrupted. The line went silent again until Sommers continued. "I see you have. Have you had the opportunity to view the most recent broadcast from our good northerly neighbors? Believe me when I say to you, Secretary Fremont, we're recording a live feed that is being transmitted directly to the CBC. The Canadians won't bow to your threats. In the face of real, irrefutable evidence and testimony you no longer have the luxury of fear to hide your conspiracies. Your house of cards is going to crumble, Secretary, and in front of another nation's cameras to boot. If your ships make even one more attempt to harry our progress I'll make certain that both my earlier interview and the last piece that Mr. Mason recorded hits the airwaves immediately."

"Damn it, Sommers!" Fremont's voice growled at him.

"You're throwing away years of work and billions of dollars! You're jeopardizing the security and power of our entire nation! No one is worth that! You are a public servant, Senator; this is serving *yourself*."

"I'll let history be the judge of who I'm in service to today, Mr. Secretary. I'm certain it'll be your judge, as well. I've said all I need to say. I'll speak to you again when both my daughter and I are safely on the other side of the wall."

"Sommers, wait..." Fremont said. There was another long pause while Fremont tried to figure out if Sommers was still on the line without caving and asking for him. Eventually, Fremont went on. "I have an extraction team at the site, Senator. It's over. But I can promise you, if you divert to Northgate I'll see to it my men bring your daughter back safely provided you end your cooperation with Mr. Mason and the CBC immediately."

"What about the others?" Sommers asked.

"What about them? The rest are grave robbers and fortune hunters. It's obvious your daughter was a pawn. I saw for myself that she was kidnapped into the Area in the first place," Fremont said. Sommers switched off the external radio and switched to the helicopter's intercom system.

"So what are you going to do?" Mason asked.

"If there's an extraction team already engaged we won't stand a chance," Cartwright interrupted. "They'll have additional air support and teams available. We've got Apaches breathing down our necks and I'll bet the surface missiles have been tracking us since we broke the bubble. Face it, Senator, take the deal. You'll get your daughter back and maybe, just maybe, you can use some of your pull to keep the rest of us from going to jail or worse."

"Captain Cartwright, the Secretary has no intentions of letting my daughter or anyone else live. If she and I both make it back our respective positions and careers would ensure Fremont would lose everything. He *needs* both of us to die inside the Area. The only thing stopping him from doing that now is the fear that Mr. Mason's recordings will make the air," Sommers said.

"Senator? I need an answer," Fremont's voice came back at

them.

Sommers switched back to external communications. "I'll continue to the site and will pick up my daughter myself, Secretary. Our previous dealings have left me with a rather strong distrust of you. You can do whatever you like with whatever and whomever else you may find there. Once I have my daughter safely beside me, on the ground and outside the wall I'll make certain the CBC loses interest in the whole affair."

"I can't condone civilian operations in Area 187, not even for a Senator."

"We'll talk again once I have my daughter safely in my possession."

"Senator, do you have any idea what you're going to find when you get there?" Fremont asked.

"Unlike your earlier report, I'm certain I'll find my daughter alive. That's all that really matters, Secretary, her safety and that of any survivors that may be with her," Sommers said, adding the bit about other survivors as an afterthought.

"Senator, I can't in good conscience allow you to land," Fremont said.

"Mr. Secretary, I doubt there's little you *can* do in good conscience."

"There are two large swarms of reanimates in the immediate vicinity. If your daughter's still alive, if she's even there in the first place, she'll be trapped somewhere in the middle of those swarms. I already have a team actively engaged. If you get in the way, the results could prove disastrous for all involved. I can't let you jeopardize the extraction, Senator, if for nothing else than by the additional element of difficulty your presence will mean. I'll see to it that should your daughter be there we'll bring her back. But I can't allow you to interfere-"

"I suggest you prepare your team for our arrival," Sommers said. He flicked off the exterior communications completely and went to the intercom system again.

"You didn't say anything about swarms, Sommers!" Cartwright said.

"I paid for you, your men and your guns. Why do you think I brought you, Captain? I'm sure you'll be able to handle them."

"Have you ever seen a swarm? And not on TV either, but have you ever been staring down a few hundred - hell, a few *thousand* of those things? You don't just go bang and they all fall down!"

"Let's save the theatrics until we see for ourselves. For all we know Fremont is lying, trying to scare us from getting too close." Small yellow lights started to wink on and off around the cabin as both helicopters started a slow, un-harried and even descent. While the two attack helicopters drifted further behind and away from their ships, the mercenaries in the bellies of both choppers became suddenly active. Some checked their equipment and charged their weapons while others snapped S-hooks from their riggings into steel eyes around the helicopters' doorframes.

"What's going on?" Mason asked Cartwright.

"That's the ten minute warning. That's how long we have before we have a visual," Cartwright answered as one of the men slid open the large side door of the chopper to let the .50 caliber door gun swing free into the rushing air.

"Is it wise to open the doors like that with those other helicopters still out there?" Mason asked over the wind noise.

"With the kind of firepower those birds have it wouldn't matter if the door was open or closed. Those things are designed to take on tanks with a foot of steel plating." Cartwright said. He reached into an ammo box on the floor beside his seat and handed a bundle of nylon and steel to the reporter.

"What's this?" Mason asked.

"Some people call it a gun," Cartwright said.

"I don't know the first thing about guns," Mason said as he tried to hand it back to Cartwright.

"The bullets come out the long, skinny end," Cartwright said. Mason looked at him dubiously but wrapped the belt around his waist and adjusted it until the pistol's unaccustomed weight rode on his left hip.

"I shoot with a camera," Mason said as he pulled the pistol and looked down at it as if it were an alien technology.

"Zombies don't die when you point a camera at them." Cartwright took the pistol, jacked the slide to chamber a round then handed the charged weapon back to him. "I want every man on this mission armed. All you have to do is pull the trigger. You might not shoot a zombie, but if you get bit you may need to take care of yourself. The rest of us may not be around to do it for you."

"They've secured the surface building, Secretary Fremont," Cline said. Warner walked up to Fremont and stood at his elbow, waiting for the Secretary to acknowledge him. Fremont spent a moment longer looking at Cline's screens then turned to Warner.

"What did the SecDef say?" Fremont asked. Warner frowned at him and took a deep breath before he answered.

"The Canadians won't budge, Boss. As I understand it, the Prime Minister told the SecDef if we wanted to stomp on our own to go ahead but they weren't going to help us do it," Fremont stared at him as if Warner had said the words himself and not just relayed them. Fremont walked away from Cline's station and back to the conference room. Warner didn't need to be told to accompany him.

"And what else did my military counterpart have to say? It's the military. They never know when to keep their noses out of things," Fremont said.

Warner sighed again, this time with his whole body. "He called the President. We're to continue the extraction mission but are to do nothing else until we get new orders."

"Orders? This isn't a military operation!" Fremont exploded. He paused took a deep breath to regain his composure. "Do they know about Sommers?"

"If they do, they didn't hear it from me," Warner said. Fremont lit a cigarette then crumpled the empty pack and dropped it on the floor.

"Senator Sommers and his mercenaries are a hindrance to this operation. As such, they are still my purview. The Canadians are going to air those pieces regardless of the outcome," Fremont said as he sat down at the conference table. Warner's boss was growing smaller and smaller by the minute. But it wasn't a diminishment in size, more like the coiling of a snake making ready to strike. "Tell Cline to order the Apaches to engage the Senator's mission and do whatever they have to do short of destroying them to get them to set down. After they're grounded I want the Apaches to sit on them so they can't take off."

"Boss, the whole region's hot now. We've got surveillance from the satellites and the bomber's got a camera rig. All the noise and activity's got every pusbag for three square miles moving around. If we force them down we'll be dropping them right into the middle of-" Warner said.

"That's the second time you've questioned my directives. Don't let there be a third," Fremont said without looking up. He paused for a moment to let his words sink through then continued, "As soon as you give the order, I want you to advise all teams and aircraft that we are going to radio silence, and then I want you to turn on the static."

Warner nodded at the back of Fremont's head then left the room. If Sommers set down anywhere near the shelter his helicopters would very likely become the objects of a swarm of their own. With all radio communications buried by static, not only would Mason's reports fall on deaf ears but the Apache pilots would only know they were to keep the choppers on the ground. If Sommers and his team did get swarmed, the Apaches wouldn't even be able to receive new orders to assist them. They would simply hover there, watching while the grounded birds disappeared in a sea of corpses. Of course, Warner knew that was precisely what Fremont was hoping would happen. By using the static, Fremont could claim he didn't know the Senator was in trouble and would eliminate the threat from Mason and the CBC at the same time. Warner had served under Fremont for a long time, but as he walked out of the conference room and approached Cline's station he was already formulating the language he would use in his resignation letter.

Fremont looked out the conference room's glass wall and watched as Warner stopped at Cline's console and leaned down to speak to the agent. The concern in the younger agent's eyes lasted only a moment before they returned to their normal appearance and he started speaking into his headset. Fremont flicked spent ashes idly onto the polished tabletop and closed his eyes for a moment. Until the team left the shelter he had no intention of leaving this room. It was soundproofed against the noise from the operations center, and it would be his word against Warner's when the inevitable inquiries came into ordering Sommers' mission grounded in the center of an undead maelstrom. No matter what, Area 187 would have its dirty laundry aired before the masses. The only question that remained was in how much would have to be leaked to satisfy public curiosity.

Though no one would have ever guessed it, Fremont was in actuality an optimist. The American people didn't truly want to know everything about the Area. Deep down, they knew in their collective subconscious that they couldn't handle it. The Senator's death would add a creative element to the tale, certainly. But if Fremont played the media correctly, he could easily demonize the Senator by his daughter's involvement with the whole affair. He also had the hole card that was Brooks' immunity to play as well, and was already putting his mind to the proper usage of the man as the best hope for a cure to the virus. Certainly a few lives, even if one of those lives was a U.S. Senator, would be worth that boon to humanity.

By the time he finished his cigarette, Fremont was smiling.

Heath looked inside the closet at the rest of his party. No one looked afraid. He hadn't expected them to. Except for the two women, everyone there had been through many of the same experiences he had. But even Julie and Josephine didn't seem afraid. Both women wore resolute, grim expressions that counterbalanced the two doctors' looks of resignation to the task ahead; just another day in Area 187. Williams wore his typical half-smirk, the expression of a mercenary that knows he may only be a hair away from death yet also somehow knows he'll live to spend his pay. Only Ellen seemed completely unaffected by the utter lunacy of their scheme. Visions of zoos and theme parks and candy stores clouded her mind. All she knew was that they would have to get through a lot of Singers. She'd been doing that her whole life, though now the destination was somewhere she truly wanted to go.

"Everyone ready?" Heath asked.

"Would it matter if we weren't?" Josephine countered.

"No." Heath scanned the group one more time and leaned into the room. "Listen up. When I open this door, you don't look down the hall and you don't stop moving. Get through the door and get to the surface. You're might run into a few in the tunnel and probably more on the surface but most of the faster or stronger ones should already be inside. Watch where you're putting your feet, there may be some that get trampled. Get clear of the room as fast as you can so I can come in, grab Craig and follow you topside. Howie, you take the point; I'll take rear."

"How are you going to carry him *and* watch our asses?" Williams asked, jerking his thumb over his shoulder at Craig where he stood at the back of the room under Julie's watchful muzzle.

"I won't have to carry him. Once the bulls are running, Craig here is in the same boat as us and he knows it," Heath said with a pointed look at Craig. Craig looked back, his eyes sunken deep into his swollen face over his cloth gag. "If you're a good boy, I may even pull your gag."

"We still have time to come up with something else," Phillip said, his voice trembling. Just then the group felt more than heard a distant, short tremble as the reverberation from the extraction team's entry carried through the building's foundation.

"All or nothing." He kneeled down to Ellen. "Are you scared?" Heath asked.

"Maybe a little," Ellen said, though she still looked hopeful.

"It's good to be a little scared sometimes. But I need you to do something for me, okay? I need you to keep an eye on Dr. Richards. Stay with him and keep him out of trouble. Can you do that?" Heath asked. Ellen looked up at Richards and he gave her a tired smile in response.

"Yes," Ellen answered.

Heath started to reach a hand out to her but his fingers stopped just inches from her cheek. He flexed them once then pulled his hand back and stood quickly. There was more of Eileen in her than Phillip. He could see Eileen reflected in her daughter's eyes. The hope and fear and excitement his wife seemed to carry in every glance and stare had found their way into Ellen's eyes.

"You're going to be a beautiful woman someday," Heath said softly. He closed the door on them then slipped the padlock through the hasp, locking them away to wait out the stampede of the dead.

Heath went to the end of the hall and paused a moment with his ear against the steel skin. Satisfied, he turned the key Richards had provided and swung the door inward. A row of naked bulbs suspended by a single electrical cord ran down the length of the tunnel and out of sight as the way took a steep upward turn. He counted his steps, measuring the distance of the tunnel. It came out to forty yards from the inner entry door of the shelter to the outer door and wide enough for three abreast to pass with a ceiling high enough that Heath could stand without hitting his head. He didn't have to put his ear to the outer door to hear the zombies. The moaning and pounding of the dead that had stood sentry outside for weeks carried clearly to him, amplified and echoed by the acoustics of the escape tunnel. He put a palm flat against the door, felt the fists crash and the fingernails scrape as they added their tenor and soprano to the deep bass of the collective moan of the swarm of undead on the other side of the door.

The area immediately outside the door had to have some sort of natural or constructed feature to act as a funnel of sorts or else the constant onslaught of the dead would have surely broken down the door given the amount of time they'd had to work on it. That same feature would make their progression from outside to inside even slower, serving as a bottleneck to impede the swarm's progress. Either way, it didn't matter. Fremont's goons were here. If they managed to find this door before the zombies filled the shelter they had a good chance of securing the door, leaving Heath trapped between it and the swarm as it shambled down the tunnel.

Heath grasped the thick steel bulb that served as a locking lever and threw it back, jumping out of the heavy door's path as the irresistible force of the swarm on the other side lost its immovable object. The first few through crashed to the ground, victims of the rest behind as they pushed, clawed and clamored. Heath backed slowly down the tunnel, staying in the light from the bulbs overhead. Once he was sure the first few had cleared the tangle of bodies in front of the door and were in pursuit he turned and ran at full speed down the tunnel. The dirge turned to a deafening, echoing roar in the confines of the tunnel as more and more of them poured down the sloping passage. Heath cleared the tunnel and back into the comparative brightness of the service hallway. The slope of the tunnel and his advantage of speed guaranteed the dead were far enough behind that they couldn't see him grab the conduit overhead, his momentum throwing his legs out and up to swing him into the ceiling.

Heath turned his body so that he lay facing the floor. Zombies tended not to look up unless they had a reason. If he was right, the blind-herd mentality of the swarm would be pushing from the rear to the front, keeping those in the lead moving until they found what they sought. If he was wrong and they spotted him there'd have be some tall enough to reach him, and the thin pipes were already straining under his weight. It wouldn't take many hands pulling from below to drop him into their midst.

He focused on the door a few feet up the hall as the slow-motion tsunami of broken bodies and dead flesh washed into the shelter. The hallway was slightly wider than the tunnel, causing the swarm to thin slightly just past the door and allowing the head of the snake to move faster and more freely down its length. Heath had suspected the first ones in would be whatever current generation this part of the Area had to offer, their greater strength and drive enough to allow them to work their way from the back of the horde to the exterior door past their older, weaker brethren. He wasn't disappointed.

He watched the tops of their heads as the dead shambled down the hall. A few looked comparatively fresh; survivors that had lasted years in the Area before being consumed by it. Some were still armed and dressed in ragged leather and denim and a few still carried handguns or pipes as evidence they didn't die quietly. Of course, the weapons weren't much more than decoration now, the intelligence to use them lost to the ravages of the virus. But that didn't mean a zombie unconsciously wielding a crowbar couldn't deal a lucky, blind swing.

The utility room door shuddered and pulled against its hasp as the zombies filing down that side of the hall brushed against it. If the flow of bodies managed to pull open the door as they passed everyone inside would be dead and there wouldn't be a damn thing Heath could do about it. He clutched the key to the room's lock in his fist subconsciously until he could feel the individual teeth biting into his palm as the solid mass of them stretched from the door to the bend in the hallway leading to Cook and the common room beyond. He'd tried to keep a rough headcount as the dead passed beneath him but had given up after 100. Counting past that would be nothing more than an academic exercise.

Chapter XXIV
Hell Above, Hell Below

The shelter's survivors had long ago subconsciously blocked out the stale smells generated by so many bodies cohabitating in the comparatively small and poorly-ventilated lair; layered, compounded smells that no amount of hygiene could ever fully defeat. To the dead, the smells of body odors and meals long past meant only that prey was near. Even the smell of teargas and its accompanying yellowish haze couldn't cover the prey-smell. The powerful scent of fresh blood drove them unerringly down the long corridor, made them ignore doors both open and closed as they passed and pulled them deeper and deeper into the heart of the shelter. A few of them fell away to the sides of the compacted swarm once they reached the large, open space of the common room to lap at the streaks and pools of fresh blood and viscera that marked the cement floor. The procession advanced into the room like a slow-motion mushroom cloud with those on the sides straying further and further from the group as their senses sought out the chunks of meat, blood and bones strewn about. There were dozens of them in the room now with still more pouring in. Some fell to the floor to gnaw on a morsel of meat or to wet their tongues on wide, thin slicks of blood while those more towards the center of the stream remained mobile, their attentions clearly set on the huge pile of fresh meat at the far end of the room.

Step by shuffled step the billowing snake of the dead filled the room, each step bringing those in the lead closer to the unmoving prey. The first to reach the bloody pile, a creature that in life had worn the garb of a priest, fell to his knees and reached out with gray-skinned fingers, closing them around a disembodied hand whose fingers had been hacked away. He lifted the meat to his mouth as he kneeled at the last altar he would ever worship before and sank his broken, jagged teeth into flesh. So great was his rapture that he just barely registered movement within the pile of wrecked and ravaged bodies. Severed arms, legs and chunks of meat fell away from the top of the pile as a living piece of the mound emerged from its depths. Its body was caked with blood and meat from its hiding place and its eyes were wide behind the clear plastic shield of a black mask. Only when the moving-meat's arms swung down towards him did he realize this one's hands were made of the hard, cold not-meat.

"Be free, brother!" Cook cackled, his voice muffled and diffused by the gas mask as he brought a sanctified machete down on the once-priest. The keen blade sliced deep into his temple, the weight of the heavy blade combined with the ferocity of the attack driving it horizontally through the head with no more resistance than if it had been a rotten melon. The undead chewed his mouthful, once, twice before the top of his head slid away to the floor, his gnawing hunger falling away with it. "All of you! I am here to send you to the house of the Lord!" Cook said. The presence of so much exposed meat and blood mixed with the sudden appearance of loud, live prey caused as much of a stampede as the dead limbs of the horde could muster, bringing them stumbling, unheeding into the path of Cook's whirring machetes. The man of God had no fear, no worry for his sake or safety. Cook was doing his Lord's bidding, his Master guiding his weapons to free His children from their earthly remains. Cook had no doubt this was the day he was to take his place in His house as well, but when he arrived at His doorstep he would not be alone. Cook would be leading as many of His children as he could free of their rotting carcasses as testament before God from this His most humble servant that His will be done.

Time seemed to stretch for Heath as the undead legion flowed beneath him, but he knew that no matter how slow time had shifted for him it would be even more so for those trapped behind the thin sliding door of the utility room. At least Heath could see what was happening, could tell when the stream slowed to a trickle as it was doing just now. For the rest, every passing second was another chance they would be discovered with no escape from the dead. The swarm had thinned to groups of twos and threes, their desiccated limbs and muscles deteriorated by time and the hunger of their own infections making their progress agonizingly slow but at least, thankfully, far quieter. Heath realized there wouldn't be a point he could say the swarm ended anytime soon. It would take an hour or more at least for the entirety of the horde to drag themselves inside the shelter, and Homeland was already there. They'd have to take their chances and make their way through what remained.

Heath pushed himself up slightly against the straining conduit, enough to look down his body and towards the escape door. He counted to fifteen, enough time for the largest group in the hall to have made the bend and with only a few stragglers coming through before he rolled off the conduit and dropped to the floor. He loosed his club and lashed out, quickly dispatching three of zombies that had had the misfortune to be standing between him and the utility room. Another farther down the hall turned slowly at the commotion and started back. Heath drew his silenced automatic and punched a hole in the skeletal male zombie's skull before he could open his mouth to moan then holstered the gun and unlocked the door. He could hear soft shuffling and moaning sounds coming down the tunnel as he slid the door open and stepped back.

Even before the door had finished opening the room's occupants were slipping past him towards the tunnel. Williams led the way, the picture of the urban assault professional. Josephine followed with eyes wide and constantly scanning while the doctors, Ellen, and Julie brought up the rear. As soon as Julie cleared the doorway, Heath stepped into the room and took a moment to sling his pack over his shoulders before grabbing Craig and shoving him into the hall.

Sergeant Adam Parker had been Vargas's point man in almost every one of the Lieutenant's missions for the last three years and for every mission that had involved Area 187. Going on a real, live extraction inside the Area would've been more than enough to slake his thrill-seeking ways. But when he'd learned they would be going up against the likes of Heath and Williams he'd been practically orgasmic. He'd attended an enclosed-space combat seminar taught by Williams while he was still in the Army and knew that Vargas was running this mission almost chapter and verse to what Williams had instructed. The fact their adversaries knew the playbook just as well as they only added to Parker's thrill. He hoped that Williams had found some sort of protection from the gas. Parker wanted the thrill of killing Williams where he stood, not where he lay in a pool of his own mucus and vomit.

He slowly led the team down the narrow service way. The thick cloud would almost guarantee unprotected survivors would be on the floor, gasping for breath. But seven years was a long time, and given West Virginia's mining and agricultural background and the survivalist nature of the shelter itself, it wasn't outside the realm of possibility that those they sought were masked against the fumes and lying in ambush for them. Parker cursed the gas as it reduced his visibility to mere inches and put his right shoulder to the wall to use it as a guide. It was bad enough that Vargas had ordered an earplug be used in each man's non-radio ear to keep them from getting shell-shocked in the confined space, but the added hindrances of their masks and goggles only meant the soldiers' three main senses were practically shut off.

He could see the overhead lights of the common room burning just a few yards ahead, their light diffusing through the fog to create a soft, yellow glow around them. The original plan had been to get to the throat of the passage and lob more tear gas into the next zone, but the Sergeant was loathe to do so until he could get a mental snapshot of the area beyond the shelter's entrance hallway. The first men down the hole had rolled a few more canisters of gas towards the common room before they'd started in and he'd yet to come across them. That, added to the thinning of the smoke overhead told him they were about to enter an area much larger and with a higher ceiling than the hall. Given the nature of the shelter he didn't expect much air to be moving, either, meaning that the gas wouldn't have the same dispersing effect and would instead hang in clouds in the still air.

When his right foot met no resistance from the wall, Parker stopped and waited for his men so they could identify him and his commands. Once he was sure all eyes were on him he gave a sweeping motion with his arm then stepped out of the hallway to crouch to the right of the opening, allowing free passage for those behind him while establishing his field of fire. The canisters that had made it into the room had been just enough to lend a misty shroud to the air but not enough to completely obscure the horror into which Parker had just led his men.

He flicked on his radio, the act signaling each of his team members' radios to life like links in a chain. The network instantly came alive with muttered curses and Vargas' requests for a situation report. Parker slowly lifted his hand to his ear and pulled the earplug away, allowing him to hear the moans of the zombies mixing with the wet, slurping sounds of their feasting and the gutturally-voiced, muffled scriptures being intoned from somewhere near the back of the shrouded room.

The zombies had all but ignored his men, silent and concealed as they were in the thicker pocket of gas they'd drafted into the room with them in their passing. Parker let his hand fall to the color-coded buttons on his radio. His fingers tapped the various buttons while his eyes scanned the room, waiting for their inevitable discovery. The first code he blasted out was for "contact". That terrible, high-pitched keening stopped all verbal traffic over the radios. The second, a combination of tones, told his men to hold their positions and await instructions. The third was a low, bleating combination tone, the sound that told a mission commander they needed to initiate a pull-back.

"Don't speak, just listen," Lieutenant Vargas' voice whispered in their ears from his position of relative safety back in the surface building. "Parker, how many?" Vargas asked. Parker started tapping on a separate button on the radio, one that sounded a simple, short beep each time it was pressed. Vargas lost count after thirty or so beeps. "There can't be that many survivors down there," Vargas said. Parker pushed and held a button, repeating the tone for "contact" and letting it drone in his commander's ears for several moments before releasing it. Vargas came back on, speaking quickly and issuing orders to his men both inside the shelter and the surface building. "Parker, I'm coming down there with cover fire. When signaled I want your team to fall back in reverse order. We'll make sure the hallway stays open, you men just get topside, understood?" Vargas asked. Parker touched a button to give the affirmative then brought his hand up to the slim stock of his submachine gun. The fog was clearing even more now as it dissipated into the large room, taking away some of their cover but giving them a better view.

They were everywhere. Zombies in varying stages of decay from mummified to perhaps only a few months' dead shambled around the room. Large knots of them lay tangled in piles on the floor, feasting on fresh, bloody meat while others simply sat alone or in small groups to lick blood and viscera from the concrete floor. A hoarse, triumphant scream turned his eyes to a large group of them at the far end of the room. Parker could just make out the upper body of a shirtless and bloodied, screaming man as he lashed out with a pair of machetes over the heads of the horde.

Vargas gathered the remainder of his force into a line before the open trapdoor. "I'll secure the ladder. I want three to a side down the hall. We'll have Parker and his team running back towards us and I don't want to have to send condolence letters over friendly fire. Get down there and back quick. When the last of the team hits the ladder, pull back and do the same," Vargas said as he stepped into the hole and climbed the ladder to the floor below. A few minutes before he'd heard Parker's contact warning, Vargas had received word that all external radio communications were being suspended until further notice. At that time his situation report had been according to plan. And three minutes later, here he was, leading reinforcements deep into the shelter on reports of contact with the undead, reports he couldn't relay to Northgate. The stand-by team was only a few miles away, but nothing short of a flare would let them know they were needed. Of all the men, only Vargas as mission commander and his communications officer waiting on the roof had radios capable of communication outside the Area. They were alone now, but there was no sense in telling the rest they'd been cut off. Vargas had a feeling they'd need their concentration until they were all on the roof again.

Parker's team had climbed down into the shelter slowly, carefully, mindful of their limited visibility and the unknown structural soundness of the ladder they were descending. But now, with their comrades in danger, the reinforcements were nowhere near as careful. The men dropped through the floor rapidly, their boots ringing against the tubular steel ladder rungs. What no one from either the first team or the reinforcements had been able to see in the thick cover of teargas and adrenalin was the short crowbar leaning on a strut that secured the ladder to the wall. By the time the sixth man bounded down the ladder the crowbar could take no more, the vibrations finally dislodging it from its place and suddenly tightening the thin, clear fishing line that had been tied around its shepherd's-crook end.

Vargas caught the motion of the tool as it fell from its perch, but what he couldn't see that his men still stationed above could was the sudden appearance of the clear, nearly invisible fishing line that had been expertly concealed against the inner ledge of the trapdoor to run across the dark room's floor. One of the guards at the trap door reached out of reflex for the string but missed. The line pulled taut as a bowstring for less than a breath before the sudden pull along its length dislodged the moorings at its other end; the pins from the grenades that had been concealed under the room's window sill. The two soldiers in the room barely had time to call out "grenade" as the string pulled away the pins, flinging the devices' spring-loaded trigger handles into the room.

The men nearest the doorway into the front room flung themselves back towards the stairs as the grenades exploded, showering the room and the men inside with shrapnel and bits of concrete, dust and thick opaque glass. Two soldiers died along with the echo of the blast, the shrapnel tearing through their flack jackets at such close range and confines, their blood and bits spraying the room like the grenade's deadly slivers had done. Two others had dived for far corners of the room to huddle their faces and vital organs in the places where the walls met. Another had simply stepped off into the hole to plummet straight to the concrete floor below to escape the blast.

"What the hell is going on up there?" Vargas hissed into his mike even as he realized whispering would no longer be necessary. The blast had echoed down the rabbit hole and into the shelter, the sound more than enough to turn the dead towards him and his men.

"IED, sir! It must have been wired to a trigger down there," the rapid though strong voice of Sergeant Peroni in the building above answered in Vargas's ear. "We've got two dead and two wounded. Alvarez dropped down the hole. Do you have him?" Peroni asked.

Vargas looked towards the bottom of the ladder. Alvarez was there, sitting on the floor while another of his men inspected his leg. It was more than a twelve-foot drop into the shelter and it appeared that Alvarez hadn't fared well.

"They know we're here, sir!" Vargas heard one of his men say. Vargas turned his attentions back down the still-foggy hallway then started in that direction between the rows of his men hugging the wall to either side of him.

"Fire team, pull back! Pull back! Do not engage unless necessary. Defense team, form a barrier across the hall as soon as the last of the fire team gets past my position and fire at will. Once we get the fire team clear of the ladder we'll pull back and regroup upstairs and-"

Vargas's words were cut off by sudden, rapid gunshots coming from the common room accompanied by a throaty scream. "What the hell is going on in there?" Vargas screamed into his mike, the spotty visibility from the teargas that remained in the hall nearly blinding him to anything farther out than a few feet.

"Contact! Contact! We're engaged, Lieutenant!" another voice came over his radio.

"Defense team, push forward and lay down cover fire! Fire team, get behind their line and back them up! Get your asses back to the ladder now!" Vargas said. The first of the fire team to come into his sight through the fog was jogging slowly, his steps heavy under the weight of his equipment and body armor. The first thing Vargas noticed was the absence of the soldier's primary weapon. The second was the blood pouring from under the ripped glove of his left hand. Vargas had to scan his memory then finally looked at the man's name tag to identify him. "Sergeant Dell, report!" Vargas barked at him.

Dell stopped then looked to his bloody hand and then at his commander. "They... I..." Dell stammered.

"Let me see your hand, soldier," Vargas said as he grabbed Dell's wrist and held it up to his face shield. A chunk of meat had been ripped from the soldier's hand. The bleeding had fallen off to a trickle, flowing far too slowly for the viciousness of the injury and the fibers of the exposed muscle tissue were already starting to turn a dull, black-gray.

"Please, Lieutenant...I don't want to die. I don't want to be one of them..." Dell pleaded, his voice odd and alien through his gas mask.

"You won't, soldier. Now get up the ladder," Vargas said. Dell nodded and started towards the ladder. When he was a few feet past Vargas, the lieutenant drew his sidearm and put a bullet through the back of the sergeant's head. Bits of blood and brain blew out from Dell's forehead as his body crumpled to the floor just a few feet from the ladder. None of the men reacted to the mercy killing. Every man on this mission had seen infection first-hand, and every one of them knew the only cure. More screams sounded from the common room as several men in the fire team came running down the hall, their heads craning back over their shoulders as if watching for pursuit.

"They're in the hallway!" one of the fire team said as they ran past Vargas to the ladder. Rapid gunshots filled the hall now, the echo of each shot drowning out the last until the reports blended into a sound much like - but much louder than - the droning of the swarm. The team hadn't been issued laser sights or silencers for this mission. Vargas's commanders had wanted the shock-and-awe of weapons fire to unnerve the survivors and laser lights would've bounced off the teargas, rendering them useless. Now that the hall was full of gunfire, he wished he would have insisted on the silencers. Vargas switched his radio back on and was greeted with shouted orders and panicked screaming.

"Contact! Contact!" Vargas heard again.

"Damn it, I know! Get to the ladder!" Vargas ordered again.

"Negative, sir! This is Peroni - we have contact upstairs! The sonofabitch knew what he was doing. The grenades blew out the window and a chunk of the wall... they're coming inside the building!" Peroni said.

Vargas looked back and could make out the line of his soldiers as they fired into the mist ahead. They had, at best, ten yards from the line of their retreat to the ladder and the dead-end behind it. "Peroni, secure that room! We have to get topside!" Vargas screamed into his mike as he joined his men. He could see them now, or rather, he could see the beast the swarm had become. It was virtually impossible to pick individual targets from the tangled, clawing mass that moaned and reached for them. He could see the bullet hits from his men starting to go wild from panic shooting, impacting with shoulders and arms and doing nothing to stem the wave that was stumbling towards them. Vargas spared a look back towards the ladder and saw Alvarez had been left on the floor and the soldier that had been tending him was rushing up the ladder. "Get Alvarez up that ladder or I'll shoot you myself!" Vargas said through the radio as the deserter's head disappeared through the hole in the ceiling. But he didn't come down, nor did he climb further. The soldier's body stiffened as his scream was lost in the din. A moment later he was being dragged upwards into the entrance building, his feet kicking and twitching against the ladder, his life's blood suddenly rolling down his abdomen and legs to paint the ladder and the floor beneath it red.

"Peroni! Report!" Vargas said. The column of the dead was slowly pushing what remained of the men inside the shelter against the hall's terminus. They were too close now to ensure that everyone would have time to get up the ladder. Any rear guard left to defend the ladder while the rest climbed to the surface would have to be sacrificed to the zombies' hunger. "Fuck! Peroni, we're coming up! Clear that room!" Vargas ordered. He fired a few rounds from his pistol over the heads of his men with one hand while the other reached out blindly for a rung of the ladder.

"Negative, Lieutenant! The entry room is compromised!" Peroni said.

"We're going to die down here, Peroni! Cut us a path from the hole to the stairs!" Vargas said.

"Negative, sir! The entire first floor is full of the damn things! We're pulling back upstairs!" Peroni said.

"Get us out of here, Peroni!" Vargas screamed. The Lieutenant and what remained of his force underground had been shoved back to the ladder. Alvarez had started shooting as well, though from his position on the floor he was having little effect. As Vargas watched, Alvarez stopped firing into the advancing hoard, put the muzzle of his weapon into his mouth and made certain that while he may feed them, he would never be them. "Fuck! Peroni!" Vargas said as he started up the ladder.

"I'm sorry, sir. It's been an honor serving under you, but I can't risk anyone else becoming infected. We're heading for the roof. May God keep *you*, and forgive *me*," Peroni said, the two beeps following his words telling Vargas that Peroni had turned off his radio.

"Peroni! I'll rip your head off!" Vargas said, starting up the ladder as a jumble of dried, gray faces and dull, lifeless eyes looked down at him through the trapdoor. The gunfire of his men just a few feet below him had suddenly ceased. He looked down and watched in horror as the zombies started devouring his men, the press of the swarm so dense it wouldn't even allow the soldiers' bodies to fall to the floor, leaving them to be devoured on their feet in the slow-motion stampede as the zombies finally reached the end of the hall and the bottom of the ladder.

The dead didn't have the dexterity to climb ladders, but in this case they wouldn't need it. Vargas's feet were only inches above them, and the dead would remain there as long as he did. The same could be said for those clamoring for his flesh through the trapdoor above as well. He'd half-expected those to start falling through the hole but they were so entangled with one another they could no longer break free of the group to fall through. Vargas closed his eyes and rested his forehead against the cold steel of the blood-stained ladder while the moans from above and below melted together into so much static. Hell waited for him below and above. He maneuvered his legs through a gap to a sitting position on a rung and leaned against the ladder, freeing his hands to remove his belt. Vargas wrapped the belt around the ladder and his own body, cinched the strap tight then poked his head through the space between the next set of rungs.

"Come and get me!" Vargas screamed as he brought his pistol around to his temple. "You want some of this, you'll have to work for it!" The single gunshot was barely audible over the echoing moans. The twisting of his body through the ladder's rungs and his belt made certain his lifeless body wouldn't fall to the floor. The spattering of Vargas's blood and gray matter was just enough to send both swarms into a new frenzy as each clawed from above and below, his warm body just inches out of reach from either circle of hell.

Chapter XXV
General's Principles

"They're coming around again!" the pilot shouted. Tracer rounds, bright even in the sunlight, zipped past both Blackhawks' windscreens as the wake from their rapid, hair's-breadth passing rocked them. The Apaches performed a tight turn and headed for them again, their chain guns blazing and spraying bullets all around the pair of transport choppers. By the sounds, a few of the bullets managed to graze the hulls of both ships this time.

"They're trying to kill us!" Mason said as he grabbed for a handhold.

"If they wanted us dead, we'd be dead. A bottle rocket from one of those things and we're debris," Cartwright said. On their next pass, the Apaches pulled up at level speed and altitude with the Blackhawks, keeping them fenced between them. Each Apache pilot made a thumbs-down motion to his respective Blackhawk counterpart.

"They want us to land," the pilot said.

"Get me Fremont. Mason, start your broadcast, this time, live," Sommers said. After a moment, the pilot came over the intercom.

"Sorry, Senator, but they've hit the static," the pilot said as he fiddled with the knobs and switches on the radio console.

"He's right, Senator. I can't get a signal either." Mason said.

"Looks like Fremont called your bluff, Sommers," Cartwright said.

Sommers stared hard at the Captain for a moment, then at

Mason. "There's nothing you can do to get a signal out?" he asked. Mason shook his head.

"I don't mean to rush anyone, but there's a guy riding a fucking flying tank at our starboard that's pointing at us and running a finger across his neck," the pilot said.

"He may lift the static once he knows we're on the ground, wanting to talk to me. Take us down but keep monitoring the radio, let me know when we can send and receive. The same goes for you, Mr. Mason. However, the minute you get signal I want you to get word to the CBC to start airing what they have, and I want you going live. Unlike Fremont, I never bluff," Sommers said. Their pilot waved to his cohort in the second Blackhawk and mimicked the Apache pilot's thumb gesture. All four aircraft started sinking through the sky until a suitable, open space appeared below them. When the Blackhawks sat down though, the Apaches didn't join them.

"They're going to sit on us," Cartwright said.

"Won't they run out of fuel at some point?" Mason asked over his laptop screen.

"If they have an extraction operation going, they have back-up teams and choppers. I'm sure they worked all this out before they kicked on the static. No matter how it goes, settle in and cut the engine. We may need the fuel later," Cartwright said as he charged his rifle.

"I doubt they'll give us the opportunity for you to use that, Captain," Sommers said, frowning at what he perceived to be the mercenary's posturing.

"It's not for them," Cartwright said as he moved from his seat to the man sitting at the large door-gun. "Keep your eyes open along the tree line." He didn't have to go next door to the other chopper to know his second-in-command, Riley, would already be preparing in the same way.

"Then who is it for?" Sommers asked.

Cartwright turned where he could see both the Senator inside the helicopter and the wide swath of land visible out the Blackhawk's open side. "We made a whole lot of noise setting down and the birds up there are making even more. We're real close to the site, less than two miles to the east by my reckoning. We could be getting some visitors coming by to see what all the fuss is about." He looked deeper into the chopper's belly at the four mercenaries and made a few hand motions. The men moved past Sommers and out the door to take positions around the parked helicopter. Riley was ordering the same thing.

"We won't be here long, Captain. Fremont won't be able to resist gloating. As soon as he does, the whole world will know what he's done," Sommers assured.

"You mean what *all* of you have been doing, don't you? It's not just Fremont, it's all you pricks. You don't think you're going to walk away from this without getting dirty, do you, Senator?" Cartwright asked.

"I appreciate your concern, Captain. Now, you and your men are supposed to be the best money can buy. If they do come around, you'll have your chance to prove it," Sommers said.

Heath and the rest heard the rumblings of the booby trap just as they started up the slope to the sunlight streaming through the open door ahead. Williams was setting their pace as they climbed, a sort of slow jog that moved them along steadily yet would still let them react to danger without running headlong into it. Williams' skill with his weapons was such that Heath didn't bother to draw his own just yet, allowing him to concentrate on keeping Craig moving at speed. About halfway up the tunnel Craig suddenly stopped in his tracks. Heath stopped with him and jerked his arm violently, spinning Craig around to face him.

"Move your ass or I'll kick it all the way to Pittsburgh!" Heath said. Craig grumbled under his gag and tossed his head back and forth. Heath frowned at the growing distance between them and the rest of the party then pulled the gag from Craig's mouth.

"Untie me! I can't run with my hands tied. You've already fucked us, and you're right, I'm in it right along with you. So if I'm gonna get killed anyway the least you could do is get this shit off me!" Craig said.

Heath opened his knife and slit the bonds at Craig's wrists. "Just because I took the gag off doesn't mean I want to hear your mouth. Keep it shut and your legs moving."

"How about a gun?" Craig asked as he and Heath started after the others.

"I can put the gag back in," Heath said by way of an answer.

"You know, you're going to be one sorry asshole when they get through with you. I'm gonna love watching you burn," Craig said as they rejoined the group just as they slowed at the door to the outside.

"The only thing you're going to be seeing is a lab. If you're a good boy, they may even let you look out a window between blood draws."

"Be ready, here we go!" Williams said as he slipped out the door, clearing it just enough before taking to a knee and sweeping the area around the opening for movement. He fired three times before nodding his head to the right to signal the rest to emerge into the daylight. The rest filed out and lined up to his right, taking over that flank to allow him to concentrate on a smaller piece of the open field they'd come out into. Heath shoved Craig out the door then came into the sunlight himself, only casually noticing that the small brick structure that had hid the shelter's emergency entrance had a retaining wall coming off its side, proving his bottleneck theory. Their plan had been only partially successful, though enough of the dead had stormed the shelter that they now faced several scattered pockets instead of the massive, tightly-compacted mob. With any luck, they'd be able to weave their way between them before they could join up in another swarm.

"Take us north, keep this bus moving until we get a few miles between here and there," Heath said to Williams as he pulled his rifle from the side of his pack and flicked off the safety.

"Got it. Stay with me people. It could get a little bumpy until we get into the woods," Williams said. Just then they heard a soft sound overhead, like the rush of air through a tube. When they looked up they spotted a red flare streaking into the sky. "That came from the building," he said, looking back at Heath.

"Guess they didn't like what they found, huh?" Heath said. He looked around at the groups of the dead that had finally noticed them and were starting to move towards them. "We're drawing a crowd."

"Right," Williams said. "Doc, you and Ellen okay to travel? We're not going to be able to stop for awhile."

"We have little choice in the matter," Richards said.

"I'll help him," Ellen said, her confidence like so much of herself well beyond her years. With that, Williams started the group moving north and away from the shelter.

They skirted two groups of zombies without a shot fired, though in doing so they picked them up like the tail of a comet. The rest would do the same, necessitating a drastic course change once the group got under the cover of the nearby woods to throw off the slowly-building mob behind them. The plan seemed to be working. The flatness of the meadow gave them excellent visibility all the way to the tree line and made for fairly easy foot travel. The nearest pursuer was at least 50 yards behind them and falling steadily more behind with each minute, their dead legs no match for their living prey's longer strides and faster steps. Even Richards seemed to be keeping the pace fairly easily with only a thin sheen of sweat on his forehead to show his exertion.

"You know, if I'm going to be stuck in the back with you as the first line of snacks, I really need a gun," Craig said to Heath as they both looked over their shoulders to check the progress of their pursuers.

"If we do this right none of us will have to fire a shot all the way to the woods," Heath said.

"Well, ain't you just Mr. Fuckin' Optimism?" Craig snorted. "I can't believe a pussy-ass like you made it out of the Area in the first place. The fact you're stupid enough to come back... that ain't saying a lot for you, either. I mean, this one time after Eileen sucked me off, she told me she was almost glad that the whole zombie thing happened... gave her a chance to find a *real* man."

Without breaking stride, Heath turned at the waist and connected the barrel of his rifle with the back of Craig's head. "You can be a guinea pig just as easy without your fucking tongue," he warned.

Craig rubbed the back of his head but, like Heath, kept moving. "What's the matter, Johnny? She had a fuckin' kid with Phil. You don't think she was lookin' for dick? You thought she'd just be pining away in here, just waiting for you to come and save her?" Craig said. This time Heath did stop, and this time when he turned Craig's nose was just inches from the end of his barrel.

"The world may need you, but I don't," Heath said.

Craig stopped as well and smiled down Heath's barrel. "You don't have the guts. You're a soft little prick... at least that's what Eileen told me. At least, I think that's what she said. I couldn't understand her real well with my cock in her mouth like that," Craig said.

Heath moved suddenly, his arms twisting, trading places so that the butt of his rifle clocked Craig in the jaw. Craig went down face-first into the field then wheezed as Heath's knee came down on his back. "You fucking-" Craig started.

"Shut up!" Heath growled softly. Craig managed to turn his head where he could see Heath looming over him out of the corner of his eye. But instead of looking down at Craig he was looking into the sky, scanning it with slow movements of his head.

"Heath!" Williams half-whispered down the line.

"I know... chopper. Everyone, run - get into the woods," Heath said without taking his eyes off the sky.

"'Bout goddamn time my ride got here," Craig said as Heath stood and pulled him to his feet. The group started moving faster towards the tree line even as a large helicopter bristling with weapons suddenly appeared in the sky. It came straight for them, lowering itself to a hover just a few feet off the ground between the group and the woods beyond.

Fremont opened a fresh pack of cigarettes and leaned back in his chair. He'd remained true to his plan and had stayed in the conference room, the better to construct his plausible deniability in the aftermath. And while it was true this was shaping up to be the worst political situation of his career there'd be plenty of people to scatter the blame. If there was any one man that knew where all the bodies, so to speak, of Area 187 were buried, it was him. If he went down, there were more than a few very powerful public and private people that would accompany him. Like Nero before him he was more than prepared to sit and fiddle while Rome burned. He intended to do just that until the conference room door swung open.

Fremont jumped and turned his chair to find a very large, very bald black man with four stars apiece on the shoulders of his black BDU garb, the standard tactical uniform for the Air Force's elite combat Search and Rescue teams. "General Lightner, always a pleasure of course, but I'll have to ask you to leave. We're conducting a delicate operation here, one which doesn't involve the military and which you carry no security clearance to observe. Set an appointment and we can discuss whatever it is you have on your mind." Fremont said. Lightner came completely into the room followed by two military police officers and Warner.

"Boss, I tried to stop him..." Warner said then trailed off with a wince. His jaw was turning three shades of blue under his nursing hand. "He's got orders, and a hell of a right hook." Warner handed a large sheaf of folded, heavy-weight paper to Fremont. He started to unfold them but a flurry of motion outside the room caught his eye. Men in those same black fatigues filled it now. Some had their weapons trained on the Homeland agents at their consoles and were ordering them against the wall while others slipped into their seats. Fremont opened the first fold of the papers to see the embossed Presidential seal.

"Let me save you some time, Fremont," Lightner said, his deep bass bouncing off the room's glass walls. "As of 1200 hours all Area 187 operations have been placed under the emergency control of the United States military. All agents assigned to Area 187 will be treated as non-commissioned military officers until further notice and will be subject to the UCMJ in following all orders given them. Until this situation is under control, anyone violating my orders will be removed and held under a charge of treason. You, Secretary Fremont, are hereby relieved of your duties and have been placed under my authority. You will give me your full cooperation, and any attempt to mislead or otherwise conceal information from me regarding this or any other operation past or present in Area 187 will result in my foot being shoved firmly up your ass."

Fremont scanned the papers then started for the phone. "This is preposterous..." Without warning he found his feet lifting off the ground as he was dumped back into his chair. Lightner still had hold of the back of his neck and leaned down so they were face to face.

"You *will* sit your ass down and you *will* answer my questions or I will personally put a bullet between your beady little eyes!" Lightner said. He gave Fremont's neck a hard, sudden squeeze to emphasize his point then placed his too-large frame into the chair beside Fremont. Fremont rubbed at the back of his neck with one hand and put a cigarette between his lips with the other. Lightner grabbed the cigarette in his huge hand and crushed it to bits on Fremont's lips. "This is now a military installation, and this ain't a designated area," Lightner said. Fremont rocked his head back and sputtered against the shredded tobacco and paper stuck to his dry lips. "First question; where's *Captain* John Heath?"

"Contact," a voice buzzed in Cartwright's ear. The interference Homeland used to blanket the Area in silence didn't eliminate such short-range use of radios but it did have the effect of making voices metallic and alien. "...multiple targets to the south and southwest."

"Three targets from the east," another voice reported. Cartwright walked between Sommers and Mason then went to the cockpit.

"You stay right here and be ready to get this thing moving," Cartwright said.

"If we try to lift off those birds will put us back down," the pilot said.

"I'd rather die in a fireball than in their mouths," Cartwright said, pointing out the chopper's windscreen to a line of bodies shambling into the field.

"Copy that, Captain," the pilot said. Cartwright jumped out the helicopter's side door and nodded at Mason.

"You want some footage? Bring your camera out here. There hasn't been a reporter in seven years that's been able to film zombies in the wild," Cartwright said.

"Mr. Mason has a job to do, Captain. Keep monitoring, Mason. The moment we get the chance, I want you transmitting. How many are out there, Captain?" Sommers asked.

"Maybe a dozen, but there'll be more. Those birds are as good as highway billboards for *Denny's* at three a.m." Cartwright said.

"There's nothing we can do about them?" Sommers asked.

"Not unless your ass can shoot hellfire rockets. Those things are too heavily armored for anything we've got to throw at them, except maybe for the .50's," Cartwright said, motioning to the large machine gun in the chopper's door. "We armed up to shoot zombies, not attack choppers. Even if we tried, they've got 20mm Vulcan chain guns up there. They'd cut us to ribbons." Sommers nodded at Cartwright as the Captain moved away from the door to inspect their situation.

"How close do we let them get, Captain?" one of the mercenaries asked. Cartwright looked out over the field. A few of the dead had managed to get within 70 yards of them, shuffling slowly but steadily over the field's rough terrain.

"As close as they need to be to guarantee a head shot for every bullet. We need to conserve ammo. I don't know how many we're going to be up against, single-taps only," Cartwright said.

"Sir, contact to the west," another man called out. Cartwright looked in his direction to see a few more of them stumbling drunkenly from the woods. The dead already knew they were there. There was no point in his men keeping silent. Cartwright turned on his heel and headed back to the chopper's open pilot's window. The Apaches hadn't reacted to the growing numbers of the dead.

It was becoming clear that Homeland did intend to kill them, but their weapons of choice weren't Hellfire missiles and Vulcan mini-guns. They would use the native weapons of Area 187; teeth and nails.

Lightner strode into the tactical room and found his aide, Colonel Phelps, standing over Cline. Phelps had done a quick analysis of the situation, and while the soldiers were more than adequate to man the consoles it was clear that Cline knew more about the entire operation than even Fremont or Warner. While the rest of the agents and technicians had been removed from the room for debriefing, Cline had been forced to remain under Phelps's watchful eyes.

"It's not good," Phelps said, not waiting for his CO's question. Lightner wasn't accustomed to wasting time and those under his command knew it. "Team Alpha gained entrance to the bunker, full of hostiles. Four members of Team Alpha are on the roof of the entrance building now, waiting for evac'."

"Get them on the horn," Lightner said.

"Can't, General. They have the static on. We only know about the team on the roof from satellite imaging," Phelps said.

"What about Beta team? There's always a Beta." Lightner said.

"The men on the roof popped a flare, but until we figure out how to disengage the communications countermeasures we can't get reports or send orders," Phelps said with a pointed look at the back of Cline's head. Lightner followed Phelps's glance and turned so he could lean against Cline's terminal and look down at him.

"What's your name, Agent?" Lightner asked.

"Cline," he said without looking up from his terminal.

"Agent Cline, do you know how to turn off the static?" Lightner asked. After a long pause, Cline answered.

"The static is always operational in one form or another as per procedure. Only the Secretary can order a change in the intensity of the countermeasures." He looked up at Lightner. The smaller man didn't display real fear in the face of the massive officer, but it was obvious there was at least a healthy respect for the bear-sized man who had to have his uniforms custom-made.

"You're loyal. I like that, Cline. Tell you the truth I admire the hell out of it. To stay loyal to the end, against all odds, even when you know the battle's over and you've lost... that takes a lot of guts, son. Don't confuse loyalty to a man and loyalty to a position, though. Fremont's as good as dead where Homeland is concerned. He's not the Secretary anymore. You've been placed under my authority, by The Man himself. Now, because I respect your loyalty I'm gonna' give you an option; turn off the static or I'm gonna' show you what all those guts you have look like," Lightner said. Cline kept looking at the General's eyes. While there was a smile on Lightner's face, his eyes held nothing but the truth of his words.

"Sir, I can't just turn off the static. There are situations going on that could compromise national security. I'm not as loyal to Fremont as I am to national security." Sweat had broken out across the agent's face in the cool room, but his voice was strong and his eyes were locked onto Lightner's. Lightner looked from Phelps then to Fremont where he stood between the two MP's.

"What's going on out there, Fremont?" Lightner asked. Fremont stood as tall as he was able and smiled.

"It's like Agent Cline said, there are certain national security concerns that have complicated this operation. I doubt you have the proper clearance. If you'd be so good as to get me a secure line to the President, I'm sure he'll clear all this up," Fremont said.

Lightner looked back at Cline. "Agent Cline, you will tell me exactly what you're referring to - *now*." .

"With all due respect, General, Secretary Fremont is correct-" Cline said.

Lightner held up a hand with his index finger extended, stopping Cline in mid-sentence. With the other he waved to a soldier standing guard just inside the tactical room's door.

"Sergeant, give me your sidearm," Lightner ordered. The soldier immediately complied, drawing the weapon and turning it in the same motion so that the butt was offered. Lightner took it, racked the slide and pointed it at Cline. "Agent Cline, Area 187 has been placed under military control... *my* control. I have not only the authority but the duty to clean up this mess. Agent Cline, you *will* tell me what's going on or I will execute you for treason."

Cline's focus turned to the end of the barrel. "The President-" Cline was cut off as the muzzle of the 9mm dipped towards the floor. The echo of the gun going off raced around the room, chased by Cline's scream as the bullet tore through the top of his foot.

"The President isn't the one with the gun," Lightner said. Cline stifled his scream and leaned over his legs, his hands on the sides of his wounded foot.

"General Lightner! I will report you to-" Fremont tried before being cut off.

"If he opens his mouth again without me asking him a question, do the same thing to him," Lightner ordered the MP's to Fremont's sides. They chorused "Sir" without even looking at Fremont. Fremont's mouth shut tight, his lips turning white.

"Now, son, you've got an awful lot of parts I can shoot that will still let you talk, and I don't have a lot of time. I'm not going to ask you again," Lightner said, turning back to Cline. After a moment, Lightner nodded to Colonel Phelps. Phelps stepped behind Cline's chair, grabbed the injured man's shoulders and pulled him violently into a sitting position. While not as physically powerful in comparison to his General, Phelps was more than enough to keep Cline vertical. Cline gritted his teeth as Lightner pointed the weapon towards his right knee. "If you make me do this, you'll never walk right again. You better square yourself with that," Lightner said. This time he rested the muzzle directly on Cline's kneecap.

"General, I can't, please...it's bigger than you know," Cline said, his patriotic veneer finally cracking. Lightner's only reaction was to pull the trigger again. Cline bucked in his chair and shrieked to the ceiling. Phelps managed to keep Cline in his chair, finally leaning down to grab the agent around the neck in a light choke hold so he would be forced to continue looking up at Lightner.

"So enlighten me," Lightner said as he swung the barrel to point at Cline's crotch. Cline's eyes went wild, the pain from his current injuries mixing with the thought of new pain to come.

"Please..." Cline begged. Spittle hung from his bottom lip in a long trail as his eyes pleaded with Lightner. The general straightened his arm, leaving no guess as to where this next bullet would go. "Sommers!" Cline screamed, his spittle launching through the air to paste the pistol's slide just as Lightner's finger tightened on the trigger.

"Cline! No!" Fremont yelled from behind the drama. A moment later another gunshot sounded. Phelps and Lightner both turned to see Fremont on the ground holding his left foot while one of the MP's stood over him with a smoking pistol.

"My men follow their orders, Fremont," Lightner said then turned back to Cline. "Sommers? *Senator* Sommers?" Lightner asked. Cline nodded. His breathing was labored and his skin had taken on an alabaster tone. Saying the Senator's name had opened Cline's floodgates, allowing everything to flow into the room uncensored. Fremont would have a lot to answer for. But first, Lightner had an old friend to see to.

Eric R. Lowther

Chapter XXVI
Karma, Redux

"We're sitting ducks out here," Williams said as the group compacted into a loose knot behind him.

"I knew this was going to happen!" Phillip said. "Damn it all, Heath! I told you this wasn't going to work! Ellen, come here!"

"You stay right where you are, honey," Julie said as she moved beside Ellen and Richards. Phillip stared at her with burning eyes. Heath kept his to their rear, monitoring the slow yet steady progress of what had become a small swarm some 70 yards behind them. Ahead, the side door of the chopper slid open, disgorging seven heavily armed soldiers and allowing the large-caliber machine gun in the door to swing their way. Another soldier, this one with bars on his collar, left the helicopter and started walking towards the group. Williams set his sights on the captain's forehead as the officer came just close enough to be heard over the helicopter's rotor.

"I'm Captain Gordon, Homeland Security. I am ordering you to throw down your weapons and surrender. You'll be taken back to Northgate Command where you'll be processed and charged with the violation of-" Gordon's words were cut off by a single, silenced round from Williams' weapon. Gordon reacted as if shot, causing his men to tense and take aim behind him. After a staggered step, Gordon looked down at his lapel to see a portion of it had been sheared off by Williams' bullet, taking one of his captain's bars with it. Gordon smiled down at his disfigured uniform and shook his head. "You must be Williams. Nice shot, but if you try that again you're going to find yourself target practice for the door gunner." Gordon said, hiking a thumb over his shoulder to indicate the machine gun overlooking the scene.

"Hope you like being zombie chow, then, 'cause you'll be going right along with me," Williams called over the noise. Heath slung his rifle then dragged Craig to the front of the group, tapping Josephine along the way to have her turn and cover their backsides.

"We're about to have a situation, Gordon. You see that little party behind us? They don't give a shit about your bars. Get in your chopper and get the hell out of our way," Heath said.

"Negative. We're *all* going to get in the chopper and we're *all* going back to the world. Which one of you is Brooks?" Gordon asked.

"Me! I am!" Craig spoke up, waving his hand over his head. "Get me the fuck out of here!" Craig took a step towards Gordon but was stopped by Heath's arm wrapping around his neck, burying Brooks' Adam's apple in the crook of his elbow.

"Do you know why they want this asshole, Gordon?" Heath asked.

"It's not my need-to-know. All I know is that all of you are coming with me. By the looks of your fan club back there, you don't have too many other choices," Gordon replied with a nod to the swarm behind them.

"Let me fill in the blanks on your mission briefing, Gordon. Craig Brooks is immune to the virus, that's why they want him alive," Heath said as he pulled his pistol and put the muzzle against Craig's head. "And that's why I'm about to blow his brains out unless you get the fuck out of our way. You'll get him, but it'll be on my terms," Heath said. Gordon looked stunned for just a moment before his composure came back.

"Well, that so? I can see why he's so valuable. You've got a little flaw in your logic, Heath. See, I don't have to do a thing. In about 30 seconds, that swarm back there is going to catch up to you. You're going to have a choice to make then, aren't you? If that man is immune to the virus, it won't matter if he gets a couple of bites along the way, now will it? If you kill him, I won't have a reason not to mow you all down and feed you to them. Whether you do or not, that swarm is just going to roll right into all of you. You're going to have to turn your back to me real soon, Heath. At that point, all I have to do is get him and get in the chopper," Gordon said with a smug smile. He looked away from Heath to the rest, scanning the group to find the weak links. "I don't want to see anyone get hurt here, so I'm giving the rest of you a chance. Throw down your weapons and get in the chopper. You might do some time, but at least you'll be alive. Once I order my men to start shooting, they'll shoot everyone, including the little girl there. It'd be a shame, but it'd happen just the same."

Phillip looked around the group in a panic then suddenly threw down his revolver and made to snatch Ellen. Julie stepped between Phillip and his daughter and leveled her pistol with his chin. "Don't do it, Phil," Julie said. "You step away from the group and they'll shoot you both."

"Give me my fucking daughter!" Phillip screamed as he lunged for Ellen. Julie took a page from Heath's book and brought the butt of her weapon across Phillip's face, sending him reeling backwards. Phillip landed on his back, still screaming for Ellen then scrambled to his feet almost immediately.

"Phillip! Calm down! We can work all of this out," Richards said.

"Daddy!" Ellen cried though she didn't move towards her father. Phillip was snarling now, a wild dog surrounded by predators. He whipped his head around at the group then stepped away from them into the space between Williams and Gordon.

"We're not with them, my daughter and me! We'll come quietly, just shoot that blonde bitch in front of my daughter and we'll leave with you right now!" Phillip said, pointing at Julie. Gordon's smile broadened as the chinks in the group's armor started to show. He pulled his pistol, aimed and put a bullet through Phillip's forehead.

Ellen screamed and tried to run to her father but Julie dropped to her knees and wrapped an arm around the little girl's waist to keep her within the knot of survivors. "Daddy!" Ellen screamed again. Phillip's body lay on its back, his face locked in a snarling death mask as blood rolled from the neat, round hole in his forehead.

"That's your warning shot, everybody gets their asses on the chopper *now* or I will open fire!" Gordon said.

Heath thumbed the hammer back on his pistol in response. "Well, looks like you won't be needing him then," Heath said as his finger tightened on the trigger.

"Heath! Whatever we're gonna do, do it quick, I'm making out eye colors back here!" Josephine said from behind them.

"If you can see their eyes, dot them," Heath said without looking back. Measured hisses sounded behind them as Josephine took cool, quick aim. The leading edge of the horde was within twenty yards now but its tail was still growing. Josephine realized the noise from the helicopter was drawing more of them from the surface building swarm. What they faced now was just the tip of the iceberg.

"I can't wait all day, Heath, but I can wait longer than you," Gordon said. Ellen stood whimpering with Julie's arm still protectively wrapped around her. She'd grown up surrounded by death and hardship enough to know that the dead, not the Singers but the really, *really* dead must be mourned later. Heath put her just-audible whimpering out of his mind.

"You've fucking lost, Heath!" Craig gasped under his arm. "You want to get all these people killed, too? Huh? Like you did your fucking wife? You left her here, man, killed her just as good as if you'd pulled the fucking trigger yourself. You gonna let them eat the girl, too?"

"Heath!" Josephine said behind him. Her shooting had quickened now. Julie looked back to her.

"They're getting awfully thick back here!" Julie said.

"What's your call, big man?" Gordon called out, his voice competing not only with the rotor noise but with the growing moans of the dead. Heath started to open his mouth but closed it when he saw Gordon's fingers come up to his ear piece. Gordon turned his head away from the group so they couldn't see his lips moving. By the way his head bobbed and moved it was obvious he was in an animated conversation.

"Protect her," Julie told Richards as she pocketed her pistol and reached out to slip Heath's silenced rifle off his pack. She pointed it into the swarm behind them. "How do I work this thing?" Julie asked Josephine.

"Point it at their heads and pull the trigger. Anything's better than nothing at this point!" Josephine said between rounds. The dead were close now. Too close. With only two rifles, there would be no way the two women would be able to fire fast enough and accurately enough to keep the dead from overrunning them. They'd have a chance with Heath and Williams' additional firepower, but to turn and face the enemy behind would leave them vulnerable to the enemy at the fore. Josephine only hoped that Sir John still had something up his tin-plated sleeve.

"I've got signal!" Mason said as his fingers flew over his laptop. He and Sommers had been listening to the suppressed gunfire outside the chopper for the last fifteen minutes as the dead got too close for Cartwright's comfort. The firing had become steady, almost rhythmic now, like rain falling on a tin roof.

"I've got radio back," the pilot said then stopped and looked up through the observation window in the cockpit's roof. "Hey, the Apaches are bugging out!" the pilot said. His thoughts of the radio were abandoned as his fingers matched Mason's for speed as he brought the helicopter's engine to life. Cartwright and the rest of his men started piling into their respective choppers. Now that the mercenaries were out of the way the door gunners opened up on the multi-front offensive slouching towards the awakening birds. Though they were nowhere near as accurate, their sheer rate of fire and thumb-sized bullets tore through the undead line like a scythe, tearing off limbs and in some cases cutting bodies completely in half and buying the pilots the time they needed to warm up their birds.

"Why'd they leave?" Mason asked, pointing to the ceiling to

indicate the Apaches.

"Who cares? Get us up!" Cartwright said to the pilot as he put on his headset and settled into his seat. Sommers pulled his headgear on and spared a glance out the door at the now truly dead bodies no more than 20 yards from the helicopter's door.

"A little close for comfort out there, Captain?" Sommers asked through the helicopter intercom.

"Not like you'd know anything about that, Senator! We're getting the hell out of the Area, now!" Cartwright said.

"Captain! You will proceed to the site," Sommers started. He was cut off by the pilot breaking in over the intercom.

"Captain, Senator, somebody calling themselves General Lightner is trying to raise us. Specifically you, Captain," the pilot said. Cartwright and Sommers exchanged looks as the pair of helicopters lifted off.

"It could be a trick," Sommers said.

"Why would Fremont waste time? He's got us dead-bang. Put him through," Cartwright said.

"What the hell is a general doing involved in this?" Mason asked, privy to the conversation through his own headset. "I thought Homeland and the military were separate."

"They are," Cartwright said as he adjusted the volume on his headset. "This is Cartwright."

"*Captain* Cartwright?" Lightner asked.

"Not in your world, General Lightner, just in Sommers'," Cartwright responded.

"Negative, Captain. You and your team got reactivated just yesterday," Lightner said. Cartwright shot Sommers a dark look as Lightner continued. "I still have a shitload of missiles and birds. Don't make me think you're going AWOL on me." Lightner paused a moment to see if he faced an argument. When he didn't, he continued. "Captain Cartwright, you and your men are under my direct authority, and *only* my authority. Since I'm sure you're listening, that includes you, too, Senator Sommers."

"I'm here, General Lightner, though you have no authority over me or-"

"Since I can have you shot down it seems to me that I do, Senator. Secretary Fremont has been removed. Area 187 is now under my direct control. That means everything in the Area, including all of you, answer to me. I already know the story, I know why you're there," Lightner said.

"General, we're gladly turning it all over to you. We'll get out of your way and head to Northgate," Cartwright said.

"General, Captain, you seem to forget that Mr. Mason here is about to send out a live broadcast if we aren't allowed to continue with our mission. Begin your broadcast. Mr. Mason," Sommers said with a nod to the journalist.

"The President has already spoken to the CBC and the Prime Minister. Allowing for some editorial control for national security concerns, Mason can record whatever he likes. It won't go out live, but I've been assured it'll go out. The lid's coming off this can of worms, the way it should've been from the start," Lightner said.

"Great, General, glad to hear it. I'll even give the guy a personal interview once we get back to the Gate," Cartwright said.

"Negative, Captain. Lock and load. And Senator, from here on out you're just along for the ride," Lightner said.

"Eaten from the back or shot from the front! Which is it going to be, Heath?" Josephine screamed. With a last look at Gordon's back, Heath cracked Craig's temple with the side of his automatic. Craig went down with a grunt as Heath turned, drawing Craig's identical pistol in his off hand with his foot firmly on the back of Craig's neck to keep him in place.

"Howie!" Heath called out as he started picking off zombies, the bark of Craig's un-silenced weapon in his left hand harsh in the group's ears. Williams didn't need further explanation. He spun and started firing into the mass behind them while fully expecting a bullet in the back from Gordon and his men. "Richards! Get Phillip's gun, cover Craig and make sure Gordon can see you doing it!" Heath said as shell casings fell like rain at their feet.

"I can't point a gun at a living man!" Richards said.

"Thanks for screaming that out for everybody, Doc!" Williams said as he fired. "For Christ's sake, you ever hear of a little game called *pretend*?"

"Then sit on his back and don't let him up!" Heath said. There was no time to argue with the Hippocratic Oath. Death was on both fronts now. Like Heath, at least Richards would also die as he had lived. Ellen moved before Richards did. She picked up her father's revolver, its grip so wide she could barely hold it with both hands and sat down on Craig's back, crossing her legs one over the other.

"I'll do it," she said. Heath spared a moment to look down at her, his foot still keeping Craig's face buried in the meadow.

"You're too small," Heath started to say. That's when he saw the huge gun in her tiny hands. She put the muzzle at the base of Craig's skull where it met his neck and, using both thumbs and a grunt, locked the hammer back.

"Craig, please don't move. Mommy and Daddy said I shouldn't do this, but they're really, really dead now," Ellen said into his ear. Craig turned his head and found Ellen's deadly-serious eyes. The sight of her tiny face devoid of all emotion staring down at him mixed with the too-solid feel of the barrel on his neck put fear in him greater than Heath's sadism had ever done. He didn't have the faculties to reason with a child. There were no skeletons in her closet to rattle, no scars to reopen. Adults in Area 187 had known a life before this, lives filled with values and the rule of law. Regardless of whether the individual followed them in civilized times, they knew enough to know what had been *right* and what had been *wrong*. Ellen had been raised lock, stock and smoking barrels in the Area. The only values she had were her parents', and the only laws they could respect and still survive were Area Rules. In that moment, Craig had no doubt that Ellen wouldn't hesitate to shoot.

Two small dots appeared on the horizon, coming in fast over the growing crowd of zombies and heading straight for them. "Don't worry about the choppers, just keep shooting!" Heath said. Heath didn't follow his own advice though and took turns placing his shots and flicking his eyes to the newcomers. These weren't Homeland helicopters. Each carried Air Force markings showing them to be from his old command. He could only wonder as he put a gun sight on another scarred, gray forehead if that would be a boon or bust for them.

The two helicopters dropped quickly from the sky, touching down to either side of the survivors. If they had been only metaphorically surrounded before, they were truly surrounded now. Helicopters loaded with armed and unfriendly living sat at their backs and sides and a wall of the dead filled their vision. Heath had only two magazines left for his pistols, and he doubted anyone else in the party was faring much better with their own ammo supplies. He risked a glance behind at Gordon and his men. The Captain was half-running towards one of the newcomers with a hand on his head to keep the competing downdrafts from blowing away his black beret. Gordon didn't get far. Heath could see Gordon's lips moving, but a man in black fatigues leading a small tactical force from the belly of the Blackhawk didn't seem in the mood for talk. A burst of fire from his weapon traced a line in the meadow just in front of Captain Gordon's feet, stopping him instantly.

Heath had expected these new soldiers to join ranks with Gordon's men, completing the circle to wait for the zombies to finally overpower the survivors so they could collect Craig and be on their way. Instead, the black-garbed men took up flanking positions to either side of their rag-tag group. Half started firing into the swarm while the other half kneeled and trained their weapons on Gordon's men. Corpses started falling into themselves, the added fire from another half-dozen guns in hands that knew how to use them giving the survivors the chance to reload and take a breath. That was when the two flanks of men parted and the sweet song of .50 caliber bullets being thrown from the two choppers' door guns rang out around them. Not every shot was a kill, but with the volume of lead tearing into the swarm it didn't need to be. Body parts and bits of dried flesh and viscera filled the air and littered the ground as the big machine guns did their work while the men at their flanks side-stepped across the field to surround Heath and the rest. But instead of turning their guns inward towards the group, they remained facing outward; the ones in front continuing to fire into the swarm while the ones behind made sure that Gordon and his men boarded their helicopter and lifted off towards the vicinity of the shelter's entrance building.

The actions of the newcomers had bought them nearly a thirty yard advantage by the time the man Heath had seen shoot at Gordon's feet walked into their midst. Beside him, Heath heard Julie's breath catch in the now-quieter meadow.

"No way," Julie said softly, just loud enough for Heath to hear her. Josephine looked up as well, and though her mouth opened no words came out at seeing her Canadian counterpart standing beside the Senator. Heath followed their eyes back to the helicopter to their left, instantly recognizing the two men.

"Sommers?" Williams said as he, too, caught Julie's line of sight. "Well, we can still take our chances with the zombies." He resisted the impulse to raise his weapon towards the Senator.

"Captain John Heath?" Cartwright asked. The two men were almost equal in stature and build and they eyed each other warily. "Captain Cartwright. I've been authorized to inform you that your commission has been reinstated by General Lightner, U.S. Air Force and Acting Commandant of Area 187. My orders are to take all of you to Northgate for debriefing by the General himself," Cartwright said. He stuck out his left hand to display the ragged bit of fabric he'd picked up from the field, the one with one of Gordon's captain's bars pinned to it, while his right snapped to a formal salute. Heath glanced back at the meadow to see the swarm, though smaller, was starting to pick their way through the scores of their fallen brethren towards them.

"Bullshit. I'm not falling for that. The Area is Homeland's deal, not the Army's and certainly not the Air Force. You can tell Fremont-" Heath said.

"General Lightner told me to tell you that he'll have you out of debriefing in time to make your appointment at the clinic," Cartwright said, interrupting Heath.

No one save for Josephine, Dr. Richards, Lightner and two

doctors at the clinic where he offered up his blood and bits for testing knew about Heath's immunity or that he'd been making regular donations to the research. Heath was certain of few things in this world, but one he could count on was that Lightner would never divulge his secret. Heath returned the salute quickly and took the insignia.

"No time for pomp and circumstance. Get these people aboard," Heath said. He reached down and plucked Ellen from Craig's back then handed her off to Josephine. "Get her aboard, I'll take care of Craig."

"What the hell is Mason doing here?" Josephine asked as her voice came back to her.

"Mason's been documenting the mission at the Senator's request. Thanks to all of you, the total information blackout of Area 187 has been lifted. Mason's already filed a few reports for the CBC. I can guarantee you they'll make the news at eleven," Cartwright said.

"My God..." Josephine mumbled. Despite the growing moans of the zombies inching nearer, Josephine looked up at Heath with tears in her eyes and a broad smile on her face. "Heath... we did it..." Josephine said.

"Heath, that's fuckin' Senator *Sommers* over there! He's going to make really sure we have a really bad fucking day if we get into those choppers," Williams said, interrupting Josephine's revelry.

"I'll talk to him, Howie. It'll be all right. He's really just a big softy," Julie said as she pulled Williams along.

"You think he's gotten over the whole kidnapping thing yet?" Williams asked as they left Heath's range of hearing.

"Jo, get Ellen and the Doc out of here," Heath said. Josephine nodded quickly and, holding Ellen tightly to her chest, walked off with Richards in tow towards the chopper.

"That Brooks?" Cartwright asked of the man still lying on the ground. Cartwright's men had started shooting again, picking off those zombies that had staggered too close for their comfort. The swarm was recharging now as new waves that had once surrounded the surface building joined them.

"Yeah. Give me a hand with him," Heath said. The two men each grabbed one of Craig's arms and hauled him to his feet.

"He doesn't look so special," Cartwright said as he and Heath carried Craig between them.

"It's what's on the inside that counts," Heath said. Craig let them carry him completely for a few steps before letting his feet get under him.

"I can walk, assholes," Craig said. His voice had an odd inflection as he tried to talk around the swelling in his lips and jaw. "So the military is taking over the Area, huh? With the hubbub you guys won't be able to keep the lid on this thing. Looks like I win in the end, huh, Heath? There's no way they'll be able to keep me a secret now. No lab rat life for me you bald-headed little prick. Nope! Nothin' but a few blood draws at a couple million a pop," Craig said. Heath and Cartwright exchanged looks over Craig's head as the three neared the helicopter, each knowing Craig was right. "Maybe if Jo' and Julie blow me, I'll give them the exclusive interview of the guy that's going to make sure the world stays safe from walking death. Or maybe the other guy there, you said he was Canadian? I bet he could come up with a few million for the most important interview of his career." Craig was smiling back and forth between them, his teeth stained red from the blood evoked from Heath's punishments.

The other helicopter had already collected its mercenaries and had started lifting off to make sure that Gordon or the gunships weren't still in the area before the command chopper with all its precious cargo finished loading its passengers and did the same. The helicopters made the short hop to the same hilltop Fremont's teams had used and landed to better divide the passengers between the two birds for their ride out of Area 187. It wouldn't do for only one chopper to make it back because the other's already-taxed fuel gave out before they could make the Northgate. Once they were on the ground and guard positions were established, everyone disembarked while the pilots took everyone's weights and measures to compare against their fuel.

Julie, her father and Williams stood near the rear of the command chopper. Their conversation was hushed, but it was obvious from the Senator's face he didn't like what he was hearing. Cartwright was walking around the hilltop, positioning his men and watching for any sign of movement. Josephine and Mason sat on the ground outside the helicopter's door with Ellen at her side, exchanging notes on the last few days of their lives. Richards and Craig sat with their legs dangling over the helicopter's open door while Richards tended his superficial facial wounds. Except for the mercenaries' watchful eyes, the mood of the entire mission had made a complete turn. For some it had been years, for others only days, but they were finally safe. They were finally going home.

Heath walked away from the two helicopters towards the edge of the hill. He tapped the mercenary stationed there on the shoulder, relieving him of his post and taking his place. The hillside stretched for perhaps 200 yards almost straight down to the flatter ground below. Small pockets of the dead were there at the base of the hill, their lack of coordination and strength making sure they only made purchase of a few feet uphill before sliding back to the base to try again. Heath knew they would keep trying. So long as they thought there was food to be had they would keep throwing themselves at the hillside, their limited faculties not registering their multiple failures and driving them to continue. Not for the first time, he could empathize with them. He heard the soft footsteps coming up from behind him, breaking him from his self-possessive thoughts.

"We're taking off in a minute," Josephine said. Heath didn't answer, just kept looking down at the dead-infested ground below. Jasper's comment about the edge came back to her, but she quieted it and moved to just a step behind him, the position she'd occupied for much of their time together. "I just want you to know that I'm sorry-"

"Save it," Heath said, interrupting her. His tone wasn't rough or angry. If she hadn't known better, she would've thought it had the undertone of pleading. "The mission was a success. You've got the story and everybody gets out. You, Julie, Mason, hell, even Craig will be instant celebrities. And, for the most part, you'll deserve it. You did a good thing here, whatever your original motives. That beats the hell out of sorry any day."

"What about you? None of this would've been possible without you. I know what stories about you were true now, and which ones weren't," Josephine said.

"You think so, huh? Is that woman's intuition bullshit or the keen intellect of an investigative reporter talking?" Heath asked.

"A little of both. The important thing is that they can't hide this anymore, they can't cover this up. The people still left alive in here have a real chance at coming home now. It's over, Heath. It's really over. Like it or not, you're a big part of that and you know it, whether your macho bullshit banter will let you say it or not."

"Apparently we have differing definitions of the word *over*," Heath said. Cartwright called for his men to return to the chopper just then, stopping Josephine's response as the pilots made ready for the last leg of their journey back to the land of the living. Heath turned on his heel and started back at a brisk walk, forcing Josephine to jog to keep up with him. There was a purpose in his stride that Josephine doubted had anything to do with leaving the Area. By the time the pair reached the chopper almost everyone had taken their seats, saving two for Josephine and Heath. Heath stopped a few feet from the helicopter's runner and motioned for Josephine to board the chopper ahead of him. Once she was inside, Heath leaned into the open door and looked at Craig. "I need to talk to you," Heath said.

"I'm not going anywhere with you, asshole!" Craig said. Richards had used several small adhesive bandages on the worst cuts Heath had inflicted on his face. The rest had quick butterfly stitches to keep the flesh together. Heath leaned into the chopper, grabbed Craig by his shirtfront and pulled him out.

"Should've buckled up," Heath said as he slammed Craig's back against the helicopter's fuselage. The air left Craig's lungs in a whoosh as he slumped against the aircraft and tried to regain his breath. "You took Eileen's life," Heath said as he pulled the steel bar from his side. Craig opened his mouth to speak but lacked the wind to do so as Heath grabbed his right shoulder with his free hand and spun him around so Craig's back was to him.

"Heath!" Josephine screamed as she dove out of the helicopter after him. Cartwright was out the door just behind her while the rest inside started scrambling to see what was going on. "You can't kill him!" Josephine said. She reached out her hand, but it was already too late. The scene before her slowed like a marshal arts movie as Heath's steel spun once, twice in his hand, building its force and power until it collided with Craig's back. Craig didn't even scream as he lost control of his limbs and fell to the ground at Heath's feet. "No!" Josephine sputtered as she wrapped her body around his right arm to keep it from rising again. Heath offered no resistance as he stood there looking down at Craig. Cartwright dropped to one knee and checked Craig's pulse as Dr. Richards struggled free of the helicopter.

"He's alive," Cartwright said as he helped Richards roll Craig onto his back.

Craig's face had turned white and his eyes rolled around wildly. "I can't feel my legs... can't move my legs..." Craig muttered, then, "...my fucking arms! Jesus Christ *I can't feel my body!*" he screamed. Heath leaned over Craig's still body, taking Josephine to the ground in the act as she clung to his arm.

"You'll still enjoy all that money, all that fame," Heath said through a grim smile, "and now you'll be able to park in all the best spots. You can buy sports cars to sit in and the finest pussy in the world to smell. You're still alive. You deserve a hell of a lot worse, but at least this way you'll still be of some use. All I took was your body. You took her life, just as much as if you'd put a gun to her head and pulled the trigger. You took Ellen's mother, and you took my wife. We'll never be even, but it'll have to do." Craig's eyes continued to roll and squint as he tried to make his muscles and nerves move his limbs.

"Heath... my God..." Josephine said as she let go of his arm and stood up. Heath joined her as Cartwright and Richards continued examining Craig.

"Still think you know which stories were true?" Heath asked.

He turned and looked at Ellen where she stood in the open door. He pulled Sir John from behind his belt where the toy had been jabbing his guts since before they left the shelter. The plastic figure's helmet had broken off at some point during their exodus, showing that the manufacturer hadn't thought to give the knight hair under his helm. "I'm sorry, Ellen... he got a little broke," Heath said as he handed the toy to her. She took it in her tiny hands and held it up in front of her.

"That's okay. I like him better this way," Ellen said. She wasn't looking at the knight's bald head though, rather Heath's own scraped, dirty pate. She leaned forward and kissed Heath lightly on the cheek then wrapped her arms around his neck. "I think Mommy believed in Sir John, too," she whispered in his ear. After a moment, Heath separated her from his neck, took a step back then looked down at Josephine. Her eyes were wet and her face was etched with confusion.

"Take care of her, Jo'," Heath said as he reached inside the door, grabbed his pack and rifle then stepped away to allow Cartwright and Richards to haul Craig's limp body into the belly of the chopper. Richards gave Heath a dark look as he passed but wisely kept silent while they secured Craig to the floor of the helicopter.

Williams looked down at Craig then leaned close to Julie. "Remember when I said I didn't believe in karma?" Williams asked. Julie nodded back to him. "Scratch that."

Outside the chopper, Josephine grabbed Heath's arm, turning him towards her. "You're... you're staying, aren't you?"

"Yeah. You're all going home. I'm already here," Heath said, then, "Cartwright, I need your radio." Cartwright finished tightening the strap across Craig's chest then turned and looked at Heath. After a moment he nodded then pulled his radio from his belt, unhooked the microphone from his ear and handed it out the door. "Tell Lightner he can find me on channel five. I'll have it on for two minutes a day at the standard tactical check-in times," Heath said.

"I'll do that, *Captain* Heath," Cartwright said. He turned from Heath without another word and gave the pilot the thumbs-up. A moment later, the chopper's blade started to turn above their heads.

"Please... don't do this..." Josephine said. Tears were streaming down her face now as she laid a hand on his cheek.

"I can't go back, Jo'. Not yet. Take care of Ellen... please." Heath gently removed her hand from his face, holding it for just a moment before releasing it. The engine noise was rising steadily now as the rotor picked up speed. "Your dragon awaits, m'lady." Josephine climbed aboard the chopper slowly, leaving her eyes locked onto Heath for as long as she could in a silent plea for him to follow her. He responded only with a slow shake of his head then shouldered his pack and walked away from the helicopters towards the edge of the hilltop.

Jasper Connelly had been right about one thing; everyone had to make a leap of faith. Jasper's had been in Josephine, in trusting the reporter would bring the plight of the living of Area 187 to light and still somehow manage to bring John Heath to his wife without breaking his promise. Josephine's had been in placing her life in Heath's hands. What neither of them had expected was that Heath's leap, the only one he could take and still keep his soul intact, would take him back to the land of the dead. The last thing Josephine saw in Area 187 was the personification of Heath's leap, watched as he stepped off the edge of the hill without breaking his stride to disappear as the helicopters rose and turned their noses to the northeast. Josephine wiped her eyes with the backs of her hands then wrapped her arms around Ellen and held her close. Sometimes faith led you away from the fire, and sometimes it led you into it. But as long as you kept it, the one thing it would always do was lead you home.

Epilogue

A lot has happened in the weeks since I last wrote. The Congressional hearings are in full sway now. Believe it or not, they're running 18 hours a day. It would almost be funny watching every politician with more than a few years under their belts running for cover as all the dirty secrets come out if it wasn't for the fact that so many people had to die before it happened.

Julie and I have been working about the same hours as Congress, if not on our own stories, then doing interviews and spreading as much of the truth as we can. I've been in contact with several of the former residents of Derry's Corner since I've been back and the network's agreed to let me do a special report about Bobby and Derry's Corner. I think Bobby Miller is going to have celebrity status rivaling yours once the reclamation hits town. There are a lot of people asking about you and I'm not comfortable speaking for you. I've been telling them if they want to talk to you, they need to take a little trip to the other side of the wall and find you themselves.

I have to say, though, that you're adding to your own legend quite nicely, and you're developing a bit of a cult following back here. Everybody knows there's a half-dozen of you running around in there now, playing cowboy ahead of the surge to retake the state. The survivors you guys find get pounced on as soon as they hit the Northgate but if they were rescued by you their stock in the interview and talk-show circuit goes through the roof. It's not everyone that can say they were pulled from the jaws of the undead by the great John Heath, you know? But it's not just you guys. Everybody's jumping on the bandwagon this time with the same enthusiasm that they ignored it before. Corporations are pledging money to Area charities and scholarship funds for each survivor that comes out ahead of the full military operations, and every Friday the President has all the survivors that have been brought out in the past week over to the White House for a photo-op dinner. It's amazing to everyone, even me, just how many you guys are finding in there. There has to be at least thirty of them between you since this all started.

Anyway, Howie accepted his re-commission. Did I tell you about that last time? Hell, you probably already know that, too. Well, if you didn't, General Lightner offered him Colonel if he would come back and oversee the tactical teams they're training for the clean-and-sweep operations and search and rescue teams. He and Julie have been inseparable since we got back. Her father still hates his guts, but with the Presidential pardons we all received (that includes you, you know?) and the fact that Howie's a full-bird colonel now there's not much he can do.

Of course, the honorable Senator Sommers is coming out of all the shit like a rose in bloom. People talked about Reagan being Teflon, but Sommers has got the Gipper beat cold. The right is making him out to be this action-movie hero, leading a team of mercenaries into the Area for truth, justice and the American way. But don't worry, I'll get to him eventually. There's a lot of blood on Sommers' hands. Julie knows I intend to go after him even though she's already told me he's going to throw his hat in the ring for the big chair next year. With any luck you'll be back on this side of the wall in time to see the fireworks.

Ellen is still adjusting. I moved her out into the suburbs. Did I tell you that last time, too? I don't know, the days are just kind of running together for me. We tried to go for a walk around my apartment building but we didn't make it very far. I ended up having to carry her back inside. All the activity, the noise, the people, the smells just sort of short-circuited her head I guess. It's going to take a long time for her to adjust to it all, so we've had to put the zoo and the candy store on hold for awhile. I have her seeing a slew of grief counselors and psychiatrists now. Maybe with the right therapy and time, she'll be okay. School wasn't going to work of course, so she has a tutor that she really likes that comes a few times a week. He can't believe how smart she is. He says that she's practically right in line with her age group's education level. She's a great kid. You need to get out here soon so you don't miss all the growing up she's going to be doing. She asks about you every day, and she never lets Sir John and Blackhawk out of her sight. She's also becoming a rather talented artist. She drew the picture on the back of this letter especially for you.

I'll sign off now. Please, John... be safe and don't take stupid risks, especially since I'm not there to watch your ass. I'd tell you not to be a hero, but we both know those are just like Santa, Superman

*and knights in shining armor astride fire breathing
dragons, don't we?*

With love,
Jo

Heath finished the many-times-read letter then turned
it over. On the back was a masterpiece in crayon; a portrait of a
dragon with lopsided wings, a head too big for its body and a plume
of orange and red smoke coming from its mouth. It was ridden by a
stick-figure knight with no helm or hair and brandished not a lance
but a simple, short, unadorned rectangle in his hand. Heath smiled
and traced one of the dragon's waxy wings with the tip of his finger.
A soft moan near his feet pulled his attention away from Ellen's
art. One of them was still moving, trying to pull itself across the
cement to reach his feet where they dangled down from the hood
of the rusty Chevy. Heath lifted his bar and let it fall on the zombie's
skull, the dry bone beneath the stretched skin cracking audibly in
the stillness of the mega-store parking lot.

More than 20 corpses littered the ground around the car,
the remnants of a swarm he'd been tracking and slowly whittling
away over the last two days. The survivors they'd been following
had holed up in a small metal shed on the side of the building an
hour or so before Heath had arrived. He'd almost caught a hatchet
to the face last week during a similar situation when he'd managed
to lead away what zombies he couldn't kill from a safe house. When
he doubled back and tried to open the door to their refuge one of
the survivors had thought he was a zombie, swung first and asked
questions later. Full spring had come on in central West Virginia
now and it was just past noon. The heat that would build up in the
unvented, windowless metal shed would bring the rabbits out of
their hole in their own time.

Ten minutes later, he saw one of the shed's double-doors
open a crack. As the seconds passed, the door squeaked open on
its rusty hinges wide enough for a shaggy-bearded head to ease out
and scan the area. Heath lit a cheroot, making sure the first large
puff of smoke hit the air and not his lungs so the survivor could see

it and recognize Heath as one of the living before he pulled a fat metal canister from his bag. The man stared at Heath wide-eyed as Heath popped the top on the cylinder and put it on the car's roof behind him. He saw another hand, a woman's, holding the door from opening further to keep him from seeing into the shed while a thick column of blue smoke spewed from the canister and into the air above them. Heath sat and smoked, waiting for the survivor to initiate contact.

He was dressed in torn jeans and t-shirt under a thick, ragged leather jacket. He had a pistol in his hand but kept it down against his thigh while he scanned the parking lot before focusing on Heath. "Who are you?" he asked.

"Who are you?" Heath repeated. The man looked around nervously again then back at Heath. It was obvious Heath wasn't the usual survivor. His smooth black leather coat and chaps were only dirty, not torn or frayed, and it was obvious by his size and appearance that he ate better than any survivor this man had seen in years.

"Tom... my name's Tom," he said finally, as if by giving his name he was giving away an advantage to the strange man sitting amid a pile of corpses that had only moments ago chased Tom and his family into the shed.

"How many are with you, Tom?" Heath asked. Again, Tom hesitated to answer. Heath slid off the car's hood to keep out of the path of the smoke as it billowed behind him.

"What's that for?" Tom asked. Heath smiled, flicked the ashes from his cigar then looked up into the sky over the huge building as a dark speck materialized into a large helicopter. "I'm not letting them kill my family!" Tom screamed over the approaching noise. The woman behind Tom opened the shed door and came out with a cut-down double barrel shotgun pointed in Heath's direction. Another woman, this one younger and even scrawnier than the first, came out after with a tire iron clutched in her dirty hands.

"If I'd wanted you dead I'd have killed you yesterday," Heath answered. "It's a new world outside the wall, Tom. I leave it up to you if you want to join it." Heath walked away from the car, stepping over the finally-dead corpses as the helicopter set down in the empty parking lot beyond and shut down the rotor. It would take several seconds for the bird to take off again like this, but their earliest experiences had taught them that survivors were more likely to approach when the rotors were stopped.

Heath and a few select others lived in the Area full-time now; scouting for survivors and setting up extractions wherever they could ahead of the massive force now being trained by men like Lightner and Howie to wade into Area 187 and retake it, inch by painstaking inch. Every other extraction he made included a care package from Lightner and Uncle Sam. Fresh ammo, clean underwear and a steady supply of the best MRE's the U.S. government could get from the lowest bidder competed for the limited space in the bag with updated maps, fresh batteries and whatever other special surprises Lightner had for him. And, of course, there were the letters from Josephine and Ellen. He pulled two small envelopes from his jacket and handed them to the door gunner while Tom and his family raced across the parking lot to the waiting chopper.

"Post those for me, Dave," Heath said to the gunner.

"You've got it!" Dave said as he exchanged a small nylon bag containing the supplies for Heath's letters. Tom and the two women stopped just short of the helicopter's open door and stared inside. No team of surly-looking Homeland agents or men dressed in MOP gear and gasmasks waited to drag them inside. Only the pilot and the door gunner were aboard.

"Is this for real?" Tom asked Heath.

"If you're tired of this shit, it is," Heath said, waving his hand to encompass all of Area 187. Tom looked around at his family and waited for their nods before having them clamor aboard ahead of him. When Tom got in, he turned back to Heath.

"Ain't you coming?" Tom asked.

"My shift's not over yet," Heath said. Tom cocked his head for a moment then finally shrugged his shoulders and moved deeper into the helicopter. "Thanks, Dave," Heath said as he put the care package over his shoulder. "Any news?"

"There's a swarm about twelve miles due north of here in an RV park. The way they have everything parked, it looks like somebody circled the wagons and flattened the tires so nothing could crawl under. We buzzed it earlier today and saw some campfires still smoldering. I guess word hasn't got out yet 'cause they wouldn't respond to the leaflets or the bullhorns," Dave said, indicating a pile of bright yellow papers beside him that proclaimed the new way of Area 187. "It'll get a lot easier when we can get the full teams on the ground. They might believe it more."

"Yeah, keep thinking that. See ya, Dave," Heath said.

"Oh! Hey, wait a minute!" the gunner said as the chopper's rotors started up. "A promise is a promise!" Dave held a long, white paper bag out the door. Heath took it, opened the bag and took a deep breath. "Straight from Primanti's," Dave said. Heath smelled the fresh bread and beef again and smiled.

"From the downtown one, right?" Heath asked with mock wariness.

"The one and only," the gunner smiled.

"You're a good man, Dave. Don't ever change," Heath said.

"You keep doing what you're doing and I'll keep you in sandwiches! If you find me a pretty young thing out here, I might even throw in some fries," Dave said.

"Dave, haven't these people been through enough?" Heath asked with a smile then pounded twice on the side of the ship. Seconds later it was lifting off and moving northward. Heath watched the helicopter disappear then set his feet in the same direction. He could've had the chopper drop him near the RV park, but what he would've made in time he would've lost in surprise from the noise of his delivery. Besides, he would leave the derring-do of dramatic helicopter rescues to the teams that Williams was putting together. Let Howie have the shock-and-awe. Heath had had enough of helicopters and noise, enough of hiding from the living and the dead. Now that Lightner was in command, Area 187 as Heath knew it wouldn't last more than a few years at best.

He unwrapped his sandwich and started on it, the animal part of his brain constantly scanning for movement while he walked and enjoyed the rare treat. The first thing he'd done when Josephine and the others had escaped almost a month ago was to go back to Derry's Corner. The young man there, Robert Miller, had been happy to see Heath but he'd refused extraction all the same. He'd left Bobby with a smoke canister and told him if he ever changed his mind, just wait till he saw a helicopter and activate the signal. Heath doubted Bobby would ever use it, though. Like Heath, Robert Miller was a caretaker. Somebody had to keep the place going, keep the memories alive and safe. It had only taken the young man the first few days of the outbreak to realize what was worth fighting and even dying for, something it had taken Heath seven years to figure out. The Area was their home, and neither of them would leave it.

14263946R00351

Made in the USA
Lexington, KY
18 March 2012